W9-AYV-416

Little Women

~

Little Women

or
Meg, Jo, Beth, and Amy

~

Louisa May Alcott

Illustrated by
Clara M. Burd

SMITHMARK

This edition published in 1995
by SMITHMARK Publishers Inc.
16 East 32nd Street
New York
NY 10016
USA

SMITHMARK books are available for bulk
purchase for sales and promotion and premium
use. For details write or call the
manager of special sales,
SMITHMARK Publishers Inc.
16 East 32nd Street
New York
NY 10016
(212) 532-6600

Produced by
Anness Publishing Limited
Boundary Row Studios
1 Boundary Row
London SE1 8HP

ISBN 0 8317 1212 0

Editorial Director Joanna Lorenz
Project Editor Belinda Wilkinson

CONTENTS

PREFACE

Go then, my little Book, and show to all
  That entertain, and bid thee welcome shall,
What thou dost keep close shut up in thy breast;
  And wish what thou dost show them may be blest
To them for good, may make them choose to be
  Pilgrims better, by far, then thee or me.
Tell them of Mercy; she is one
  Who early hath her pilgrimage begun.
Yea, let young damsels learn of her to prize
  The world which is to come, and so be wise;
For little tripping maids may follow God
  Along the ways which saintly feet have trod.
                    Adapted from John Bunyan

ILLUSTRATIONS

Jo laid down her head and cried. (Half-title)

Amy told Marmee all her trials. (Frontispiece)

The old gentleman turned up her face. (Chapter 5)

The sisters sat together in the shady nook. (Chapter 6)

Jo leaned over her sister. (Chapter 8)

Jo threw open the door of the closet and displayed Laurie.
(Chapter 10)

Jo assumed an indifferent air as she rumpled up the brown
bush. (Chapter 15)

Aunt March came hobbling in at this interesting minute.
(Chapter 23)

Jo appeared, proudly bearing a small flannel bundle.
(Chapter 28)

The Professor caught Tina up with a laugh. (Chapter 33)

Beth lay on the warm rocks with her head in Jo's lap.
(Chapter 36)

Jo laid her head down and cried. (Chapter 42)

There stood a stout, bearded gentleman. (Chapter 43)

CHAPTER ONE

PLAYING PILGRIMS

~

"Christmas won't be Christmas without any presents," grumbled Jo, lying on the rug.

"It's so dreadful to be poor!" sighed Meg, looking down at her old dress.

"I don't think it's fair for some girls to have plenty of pretty things, and other girls nothing at all," added little Amy, with an injured sniff.

"We've got father and mother and each other," said Beth, contentedly, from her corner.

The four young faces on which the firelight shone brightened at the cheerful words, but darkened again as Jo said sadly, —

"We haven't got father, and shall not have him for a long time." She didn't say "perhaps never," but each silently added it, thinking of father far away, where the fighting was.

Nobody spoke for a minute; then Meg said in an altered tone, —

"You know the reason mother proposed not having any presents this Christmas, was because it's going to be a hard winter for every one; and she

9

thinks we ought not to spend money for pleasure, when our men are suffering so in the army. We can't do much, but we can make our little sacrifices, and ought to do it gladly. But I am afraid I don't;" and Meg shook her head, as she thought regretfully of all the pretty things she wanted.

"But I don't think the little we should spend would do any good. We've each got a dollar, and the army wouldn't be much helped by our giving that. I agree not to expect anything from mother or you, but I do want to buy 'Undine and Sintram' for myself; I've wanted it *so* long," said Jo, who was a bookworm.

"I planned to spend mine on new music," said Beth, with a little sigh, which no one heard but the hearth brush and the kettle-holder.

"I shall get a nice box of Faber's drawing pencils; I really need them," said Amy, decidedly.

"Mother didn't say anything about our money, and she won't wish us to give up everything. Let's each buy what we want, and have a little fun; I'm sure we grub hard enough to earn it," cried Jo, examining the heels of her shoes in a gentlemanly manner.

"I know *I* do, – teaching those dreadful children nearly all day, when I am longing to enjoy myself at home," began Meg, in the complaining tone again.

"You don't have half such a hard time as I do," said Jo. "How would you like to be shut up for hours with a nervous, fussy old lady, who keeps you trotting, is never satisfied, and worries you till you're ready to fly out of the window or box her ears?"

"It's naughty to fret, – but I do think washing dishes and keeping things tidy is the worst work in the world. It makes me cross; and my hands get so stiff, I can't practise good a bit." And Beth looked at her rough hands with a sigh that any one could hear that time.

"I don't believe any of you suffer as I do," cried Amy; "for you don't have to go to school with impertinent girls, who plague you if you don't know your lessons, and laugh at your dresses, and label your father if he isn't rich, and insult you when your nose isn't nice."

"If you mean *libel* I'd say so, and not talk about *labels*, as if pa was a pickle-bottle," advised Jo, laughing.

"I know what I mean, and you needn't be '*statirical*' about it. It's proper to use good words, and improve your *vocabilary*," returned Amy, with dignity.

"Don't peck at one another, children. Don't you wish we had the money papa lost when we were little, Jo? Dear me, how happy and good we'd be, if we had no worries," said Meg, who could remember better times.

"You said the other day you thought we were a deal happier than the King children, for they were fighting and fretting all the time, in spite of their money."

"So I did, Beth. Well, I guess we are; for though we do have to work, we make fun for ourselves, and are a pretty jolly set, as Jo would say."

"Jo does use such slang words," observed Amy, with a reproving look at the long figure stretched on the rug. Jo immediately sat up, put her hands in her apron pockets, and began to whistle.

"Don't, Jo; it's so boyish."

"That's why I do it."

"I detest rude, unladylike girls."

"I hate affected, niminy piminy chits."

"Birds in their little nests agree," sang Beth, the peacemaker, with such a funny face that both sharp voices softened to a laugh, and the "pecking" ended for that time.

"Really, girls, you are both to be blamed," said Meg, beginning to lecture in her elder sisterly fashion. "You are old enough to leave off boyish tricks, and behave better, Josephine. It didn't matter so much when you were a little girl; but now you are so tall, and turn up your hair, you should remember that you are a young lady."

"I ain't! and if turning up my hair makes me one, I'll wear it in two tails till I'm twenty," cried Jo, pulling off her net, and shaking down a chestnut mane. "I hate to think I've got to grow up and be Miss March, and wear long gowns, and look as prim as a China-aster. It's bad enough to be a girl, any way, when I like boy's games, and work, and manners. I can't get over my disappointment in not being a boy, and it's worse than ever now, for I'm dying to go and fight with papa, and I can only stay at home and knit like a poky old woman;" and Jo shook the blue army-sock till the needles rattled like castanets, and her ball bounded across the room.

"Poor Jo; it's too bad! But it can't be helped, so you must try to be contented with making your name boyish, and playing brother to us girls," said Beth, stroking the rough head at her knee with a hand that all the dish washing and dusting in the world could not make ungentle in its touch.

"As for you, Amy," continued Meg, "you are altogether too particular and prim. Your airs are funny now, but you'll grow up an affected little goose if you don't take care. I like your nice manners, and refined ways of speaking, when you don't try to be elegant; but your absurd words are as bad as Jo's slang."

"If Jo is a tom boy, and Amy a goose, what am I, please?" asked Beth, ready to share the lecture.

"You're a dear, and nothing else," answered Meg, warmly; and no one contradicted her, for the "Mouse" was the pet of the family.

As young readers like to know "how people look," we will take this moment to give them a little sketch of the four sisters, who sat knitting away in the twilight, while the December snow fell quietly without, and the fire crackled cheerfully within. It was a comfortable old room, though the carpet was faded and the furniture very plain, for a good picture or two hung on the walls, books filled the recesses, chrysanthemums and Christmas roses bloomed in the windows, and a pleasant atmosphere of home peace pervaded it.

Margaret, the eldest of the four, was sixteen, and very pretty, being plump and fair, with large eyes, plenty of soft brown hair, a sweet mouth, and white hands, of which she was rather vain. Fifteen-year-old Jo was very tall, thin and brown, and reminded one of a colt; for she never seemed to know what to do with her long limbs, which were very much in her way. She had a decided mouth, a comical nose, and sharp gray eyes, which appeared to see everything, and were by turns fierce, funny, or thoughtful. Her long, thick hair was her one beauty; but it was usually bundled into a net, to be out of her way. Round shoulders had Jo, big hands and feet, a fly-away look to her clothes, and the uncomfortable appearance of a girl who was rapidly shooting up into a woman, and didn't like it. Elizabeth – or Beth, as every one called her – was a rosy, smooth-haired, bright-eyed girl of thirteen, with a shy manner, a timid voice, and a peaceful expression, which was seldom disturbed. Her father called her "Little Tranquillity," and the name suited her excellently; for she seemed to live in a happy world of her own, only venturing out to meet the few whom she trusted and loved. Amy, though the youngest, was a most important person, in her own opinion at least. A regular snow maiden, with blue eyes, and yellow hair curling on her shoulders; pale and slender, and always carrying herself like a young lady mindful of her manners. What the characters of the four sisters were, we will leave to be found out.

The clock struck six; and, having swept up the hearth, Beth put a pair of slippers down to warm. Somehow the sight of the old shoes had a good effect upon the girls, for mother was coming, and every one brightened to welcome her. Meg stopped lecturing, and lit the lamp, Amy got out of the easy chair without being asked, and Jo forgot how tired she was as she sat up to hold the slippers nearer to the blaze.

"They are quite worn out; Marmee must have a new pair."

"I thought I'd get her some with my dollar," said Beth.

"No, I shall!" cried Amy.

"I'm the oldest," began Meg, but Jo cut in with a decided –

"I'm the man of the family, now papa is away, and *I* shall provide the slippers, for he told me to take special care of mother while he was gone."

"I'll tell you what we'll do," said Beth; "let's each get her something for Christmas, and not get anything for ourselves."

"That's like you, dear! What will we get?" exclaimed Jo.

Every one thought soberly for a minute; then Meg announced, as if the idea was suggested by the sight of her own pretty hands, "I shall give her a nice pair of gloves."

"Army shoes, best to be had," cried Jo.

"Some handkerchiefs, all hemmed," said Beth.

"I'll get a little bottle of Cologne; she likes it, and it won't cost much, so I'll have some left to buy something for me," added Amy.

"How will we give the things?" asked Meg.

"Put 'em on the table, and bring her in and see her open the bundles. Don't you remember how we used to do on our birthdays?" answered Jo.

"I used to be *so* frightened when it was my turn to sit in the big chair with the crown on, and see you all come marching round to give the presents, with a kiss. I liked the things and the kisses, but it was dreadful to have you sit looking at me while I opened the bundles," said Beth, who was toasting her face and the bread for tea, at the same time.

"Let Marmee think we are getting things for ourselves, and then surprise her. We must go shopping to-morrow afternoon, Meg; there is lots to do about the play for Christmas night," said Jo, marching up and down with her hands behind her back, and her nose in the air.

"I don't mean to act any more after this time; I'm getting too old for such things," observed Meg, who was as much a child as ever about "dressing up" frolics.

"You won't stop, I know, as long as you can trail round in a white gown with your hair down, and wear gold-paper jewelry. You are the best actress we've got, and there'll be an end of everything if you quit the boards," said Jo. "We ought to rehearse to-night; come here, Amy, and do the fainting scene, for you are as stiff as a poker in that."

"I can't help it; I never saw any one faint, and I don't choose to make myself all black and blue, tumbling flat as you do. If I can go down easily, I'll drop; if I can't, I shall fall into a chair and be graceful; I don't care if Hugo does come at me with a pistol," returned Amy, who was not gifted with dramatic power, but was chosen because she was small enough to be borne out shrieking by the hero of the piece.

"Do it this way; clasp your hands so, and stagger across the room, crying frantically, 'Roderigo! save me! save me!'" and away went Jo, with a melodramatic scream which was truly thrilling.

Amy followed, but she poked her hands out stiffly before her, and jerked herself along as if she went by machinery; and her "Ow!" was more suggestive of pins being run into her than of fear and anguish. Jo gave a despairing groan, and Meg laughed outright, while Beth let her bread burn as she watched the fun, with interest.

"It's no use! do the best you can when the time comes, and if the audience shout, don't blame me. Come on, Meg."

Then things went smoothly, for Don Pedro defied the world in a speech of two pages without a single break; Hagar, the witch, chanted an awful incantation over her kettleful of simmering toads, with weird effect; Roderigo rent his chains asunder manfully, and Hugo died in agonies of remorse and arsenic, with a wild "Ha! ha!"

"It's the best we've had yet," said Meg, as the dead villain sat up and rubbed his elbows.

"I don't see how you can write and act such splendid things, Jo. You're a regular Shakespeare!" exclaimed Beth, who firmly believed that her sisters were gifted with wonderful genius in all things.

"Not quite," replied Jo, modestly. "I do think 'The Witch's Curse, an Operatic Tragedy,' is rather a nice thing; but I'd like to try Macbeth, if we only had a trap-door for Banquo. I always wanted to do the killing part. 'Is that a dagger I see before me?'" muttered Jo, rolling her eyes and clutching at the air, as she had seen a famous tragedian do.

"No, it's the toasting fork, with ma's shoe on it instead of the bread. Beth's stage-struck!" cried Meg, and the rehearsal ended in a general burst of laughter.

"Glad to find you so merry, my girls," said a cheery voice at the door, and actors and audience turned to welcome a stout, motherly lady, with a "can-I-help-you" look about her which was truly delightful. She wasn't a particularly handsome person, but mothers are always lovely to their children, and the girls thought the gray cloak and unfashionable bonnet covered the most splendid woman in the world.

"Well, dearies, how have you got on to-day? There was so much to do, getting the boxes ready to go to-morrow, that I didn't come home to dinner. Has anyone called, Beth? How is your cold, Meg? Jo, you look tired to death. Come and kiss me, baby."

While making these maternal inquiries, Mrs. March got her wet things off, her hot slippers on, and sitting down in the easy chair, drew Amy to her lap, preparing to enjoy the happiest hour of her busy day. The girls flew about, trying to make things comfortable, each in her own way. Meg arranged the tea table; Jo brought wood and set chairs, dropping, overturning, and clattering everything she touched; Beth trotted to and fro between parlor and kitchen, quiet and busy; while Amy gave directions to every one, as she sat with her hands folded.

As they gathered about the table, Mrs. March said, with a particularly happy face, "I've got a treat for you after supper."

A quick, bright smile went round like a streak of sunshine. Beth clapped her hands, regardless of the hot biscuit she held, and Jo tossed up her napkin, crying, "A letter! a letter! Three cheers for father!"

"Yes, a nice long letter. He is well, and thinks he shall get through the cold season better than we feared. He sends all sorts of loving wishes for Christmas, and an especial message to you girls," said Mrs. March, patting her pocket as if she had got a treasure there.

"Hurry up, and get done. Don't stop to quirk your little finger, and prink over your plate, Amy," cried Jo, choking in her tea, and dropping her bread, butter side down, on the carpet, in her haste to get at the treat.

Beth ate no more, but crept away, to sit in her shadowy corner and brood over the delight to come, till the others were ready.

"I think it was so splendid in father to go as chaplain when he was too old to be drafted, and not strong enough for a soldier," said Meg, warmly.

"Don't I wish I could go as a drummer, a *vivan* — what's its name? or a nurse, so I could be near him and help him," exclaimed Jo, with a groan.

"It must be very disagreeable to sleep in a tent, and eat all sorts of bad-tasting things, and drink out of a tin mug," sighed Amy.

"When will he come home, Marmee?" asked Beth, with a little quiver in her voice.

"Not for many months, dear, unless he is sick. He will stay and do his work faithfully as long as he can, and we won't ask for him back a minute sooner than he can be spared. Now come and hear the letter."

They all drew to the fire, mother in the big chair with Beth at her feet, Meg and Amy perched on either arm of the chair, and Jo leaning on the back, where no one would see any sign of emotion if the letter should happen to be touching.

Very few letters were written in those hard times that were not touching, especially those which fathers sent home. In this one little was said of the hardships endured, the dangers faced, or the home-sickness conquered; it was a cheerful, hopeful letter, full of lively descriptions of camp life, marches, and military news; and only at the end did the writer's heart overflow with fatherly love and longing for the little girls at home.

"Give them all my dear love and a kiss. Tell them I think of them by day, pray for them by night, and find my best comfort in their affection at all times. A year seems very long to wait before I see them, but remind them that while we wait we may all work, so that these hard days need not be wasted. I know they will remember all I said to them, that they will be loving children to you, will do their duty faithfully, fight their bosom enemies bravely, and conquer themselves so beautifully, that when I come back to them I may be fonder and prouder than ever of my little women."

Everybody sniffed when they came to that part; Jo wasn't ashamed of the great tear that dropped off the end of her nose, and Amy never minded the rumpling of her curls as she hid her face on her mother's shoulder and sobbed out, "I *am* a selfish pig! but I'll truly try to be better, so he mayn't be disappointed in me by and by."

"We all will!" cried Meg. "I think too much of my looks, and hate to work, but won't any more, if I can help it."

"I'll try and be what he loves to call me, 'a little woman,' and not be rough and wild; but do my duty here instead of wanting to be somewhere else," said Jo, thinking that keeping her temper at home was a much harder task than facing a rebel or two down South.

Beth said nothing, but wiped away her tears with the blue army-sock, and began to knit with all her might, losing no time in doing the duty that lay nearest her, while she resolved in her quiet little soul to be all that father hoped to find her when the year brought round the happy coming home.

Mrs. March broke the silence that followed Jo's words, by saying in her cheery voice, "Do you remember how you used to play Pilgrim's Progress when you were little things? Nothing delighted you more than to have me tie my piece-bags on your backs for burdens, give you hats and sticks, and rolls of paper, and let you travel through the house from the cellar, which was the City of Destruction, up, up, to the house-top, where you had all the lovely things you could collect to make a Celestial City."

"What fun it was, especially going by the lions, fighting Apollyon, and passing through the Valley where the hobgoblins were," said Jo.

"I liked the place where the bundles fell off and tumbled down stairs," said Meg.

"My favorite part was when we came out on the flat roof where our flowers and arbors, and pretty things were, and all stood and sung for joy up there in the sunshine," said Beth, smiling, as if that pleasant moment had come back to her.

"I don't remember much about it, except that I was afraid of the cellar and the dark entry, and always liked the cake and milk we had up at the top. If I wasn't too old for such things, I'd rather like to play it over again," said Amy, who began to talk of renouncing childish things at the mature age of twelve.

"We never are too old for this, my dear, because it is a play we are playing all the time in one way or another. Our burdens are here, our road is before us, and the longing for goodness and happiness is the guide that leads us through many troubles and mistakes to the peace which is a true Celestial City. Now, my little pilgrims, suppose you begin again, not in play, but in earnest, and see how far on you can get before father comes home."

"Really, mother? where are our bundles?" asked Amy, who was a very literal young lady.

"Each of you told what your burden was just now, except Beth; I rather think she hasn't got any," said her mother.

"Yes, I have; mine is dishes and dusters, and envying girls with nice pianos, and being afraid of people."

Beth's bundle was such a funny one that everybody wanted to laugh; but nobody did, for it would have hurt her feelings very much.

"Let us do it," said Meg, thoughtfully. "It is only another name for trying to be good, and the story may help us; for though we do want to be good, it's hard work, and we forget, and don't do our best."

"We were in the Slough of Despond to-night, and mother came and pulled us out as Help did in the book. We ought to have our roll of directions, like Christian. What shall we do about that?" asked Jo, delighted with the fancy which lent a little romance to the very dull task of doing her duty.

"Look under your pillows, Christmas morning, and you will find your guide-book," replied Mrs. March.

They talked over the new plan while old Hannah cleared the table; then out came the four little work-baskets, and the needles flew as the girls made sheets for Aunt March. It was uninteresting sewing, but to-night no one grumbled. They adopted Jo's plan of dividing the long seams into four parts, and calling the quarters, Europe, Asia, Africa and America, and in that way got on capitally, especially when they talked about the different countries as they stitched their way through them.

At nine they stopped work, and sung, as usual, before they went to bed. No one but Beth could get much music out of the old piano; but she had a way of softly touching the yellow keys, and making a pleasant accompaniment to the simple songs they sung. Meg had a voice like a flute, and she and her mother led the little choir. Amy chirped like a cricket, and Jo wandered through the airs at her own sweet will, always coming out at the wrong place with a croak or a quaver that spoilt the most pensive tune. They had always done this from the time they could lisp

Crinkle, crinkle, 'ittle 'tar.

and it had become a household custom, for the mother was a born singer. The first sound in the morning was her voice, as she went about the house singing like a lark; and the last sound at night was the same cheery sound, for the girls never grew too old for that familiar lullaby.

CHAPTER TWO

A MERRY CHRISTMAS

~

Jo was the first to wake in the gray dawn of Christmas morning. No stockings hung at the fireplace, and for a moment she felt as much disappointed as she did long ago, when her little sock fell down because it was so crammed with goodies. Then she remembered her mother's promise, and slipping her hand under her pillow, drew out a little crimson-covered book. She knew it very well, for it was that beautiful old story of the best life ever lived, and Jo felt that it was a true guide-book for any pilgrim going the long journey. She woke Meg with a "Merry Christmas," and bade her see what was under her pillow. A green-covered book appeared, with the same picture inside, and a few words written by their mother, which made their one present very precious in their eyes. Presently Beth and Amy woke, to rummage and find their little books also, – one dove-colored, the other blue; and all sat looking at and talking about them, while the East grew rosy with the coming day.

In spite of her small vanities, Margaret had a sweet and pious nature, which unconsciously influenced her sisters, especially Jo, who loved her very tenderly, and obeyed her because her advice was so gently given.

"Girls," said Meg seriously, looking from the tumbled head beside her to the two little night-capped ones in the room beyond, "mother wants us to read and love and mind these books, and we must begin at once. We used to be faithful about it; but since father went away, and all this war trouble unsettled us, we have neglected many things. You can do as you please; but I shall keep my book on the table here, and read a little every morning as soon as I wake, for I know it will do me good, and help me through the day."

Then she opened her new book and began to read. Jo put her arm round her, and, leaning cheek to cheek, read also, with the quiet expression so seldom seen on her restless face.

"How good Meg is! Come, Amy, let's do as they do. I'll help you with the hard words, and they'll explain things if we don't understand," whispered Beth, very much impressed by the pretty books and her sister's example.

"I'm glad mine is blue," said Amy; and then the rooms were very still while the pages were softly turned, and the winter sunshine crept in to touch the bright heads and serious faces with a Christmas greeting.

"Where is mother?" asked Meg, as she and Jo ran down to thank her for their gifts, half an hour later.

"Goodness only knows. Some poor creeter come a-beggin', and your ma went straight off to see what was needed. There never *was* such a woman for givin' away vittles and drink, clothes and firin'," replied Hannah, who had lived with the family since Meg was born, and was considered by them all more as a friend than a servant.

"She will be back soon, I guess; so do your cakes, and have everything ready," said Meg, looking over the presents which were collected in a basket and kept under the sofa, ready to be produced at the proper time. "Why, where is Amy's bottle of Cologne?" she added, as the little flask did not appear.

"She took it out a minute ago, and went off with it to put a ribbon on it, or some such notion," replied Jo, dancing about the room to take the first stiffness off the new army-slippers.

"How nice my handkerchiefs look, don't they! Hannah washed and ironed them for me, and I marked them all myself," said Beth, looking proudly at the somewhat uneven letters which had cost her such labor.

"Bless the child! she's gone and put 'Mother' on them instead of 'M. March;' how funny!" cried Jo, taking up one.

"Isn't it right? I thought it was better to do it so, because Meg's initials are 'M. M.,' and I don't want any one to use these but Marmee," said Beth, looking troubled.

"It's all right, dear, and a very pretty idea; quite sensible, too, for no one can ever mistake now. It will please her very much, I know," said Meg, with a frown for Jo and a smile for Beth.

"There's mother; hide the basket, quick!" cried Jo, as a door slammed, and steps sounded in the hall.

Amy came in hastily, and looked rather abashed when she saw her sisters all waiting for her.

"Where have you been, and what are you hiding behind you?" asked Meg, surprised to see, by her hood and cloak, that lazy Amy had been out so early.

"Don't laugh at me, Jo, I didn't mean any one should know till the time came. I only meant to change the little bottle for a big one, and I gave *all* my money to get it, and I'm truly trying not to be selfish any more."

As she spoke, Amy showed the handsome flask which replaced the cheap one; and looked so earnest and humble in her little effort to forget herself, that Meg hugged her on the spot, and Jo pronounced her "a trump," while Beth ran to the window, and picked her finest rose to ornament the stately bottle.

"You see, I felt ashamed of my present, after reading and talking about being good this morning, so I ran round the corner and changed it the minute I was up; and I'm *so* glad, for mine is the handsomest now."

Another bang of the street-door sent the basket under the sofa, and the girls to the table eager for breakfast.

"Merry Christmas, Marmee! Lots of them! Thank you for our books; we read some, and mean to every day," they cried, in chorus.

"Merry Christmas, little daughters! I'm glad you began at once, and hope you will keep on. But I want to say one word before we sit down. Not far away from here lies a poor woman with a little new-born baby. Six children are huddled into one bed to keep from freezing, for they have no fire. There is nothing to eat over there; and the oldest boy came to tell me they were suffering hunger and cold. My girls, will you give them your breakfast as a Christmas present?"

They were all unusually hungry, having waited nearly an hour, and for a minute no one spoke; only a minute, for Jo exclaimed impetuously, –

"I'm so glad you came before we began!"

"May I go and help carry the things to the poor little children?" said Beth, eagerly.

"*I* shall take the cream and the muffins," added Amy heroically, giving up the articles she most liked.

Meg was already covering the buckwheats, and piling the bread into one big plate.

"I thought you'd do it," said Mrs. March, smiling as if satisfied. "You shall all go and help me, and when we come back we will have bread and milk for breakfast, and make it up at dinner-time."

They were soon ready, and the procession set out. Fortunately it was early, and they went through back streets, so few people saw them, and no one laughed at the funny party.

A poor, bare, miserable room it was, with broken windows, no fire, ragged bed-clothes, a sick mother, wailing baby, and a group of pale, hungry children cuddled under one old quilt, trying to keep warm. How the big eyes stared, and blue lips smiled, as the girls went in!

"Ach, mein Gott! it is good angels come to us!" cried the poor woman, crying for joy.

"Funny angels in hoods and mittens," said Jo, and set them laughing.

In a few minutes it really did seem as if kind spirits had been at work here. Hannah, who had carried wood, made a fire, and stopped up the broken panes with old hats, and her own shawl. Mrs. March gave the mother tea and gruel, and comforted her with promises of help, while she dressed the little baby as tenderly as if it had been her own. The girls, meantime, spread the table, set the children round the fire, and fed them like so many hungry birds; laughing, talking, and trying to understand the funny broken English.

"Das ist gute!" "Die angel-kinder!" cried the poor things, as they ate, and warmed their purple hands at the comfortable blaze. The girls had never been called angel children before, and thought it very agreeable, especially Jo, who had been considered "a Sancho" ever since she was born. That was a very happy breakfast, though they didn't get any of it; and when they went away, leaving comfort behind, I think there were not in all the city four merrier people than the hungry little girls who gave away their breakfasts, and contented themselves with bread and milk on Christmas morning.

"That's loving our neighbor better than ourselves, and I like it," said Meg, as they set out their presents, while their mother was up stairs collecting clothes for the poor Hummels.

Not a very splendid show, but there was a great deal of love done up in the few little bundles; and the tall vase of red roses, white chrysanthemums, and trailing vines, which stood in the middle, gave quite an elegant air to the table.

"She's coming! strike up, Beth, open the door, Amy! Three cheers for Marmee!" cried Jo, prancing about, while Meg went to conduct mother to the seat of honor.

Beth played her gayest march, Amy threw open the door, and Meg enacted escort with great dignity. Mrs. March was both surprised and touched; and smiled with her eyes full as she examined her presents, and read the little notes which accompanied them. The slippers went on at once, a new handkerchief was slipped into her pocket, well scented with Amy's Cologne, the rose was fastened in her bosom, and the nice gloves were pronounced a "perfect fit."

There was a good deal of laughing, and kissing, and explaining, in the simple, loving fashion which makes these home-festivals so pleasant at the time, so sweet to remember long afterward, and then all fell to work.

The morning charities and ceremonies took so much time, that the rest of the day was devoted to preparations for the evening festivities. Being still to young to go often to the theatre, and not rich enough to afford any great outlay for private performances, the girls put their wits to work, and, necessity being the mother of invention, made whatever they needed. Very clever were some of their productions; paste-board guitars, antique lamps made of old-fashioned butter-boats, covered with silver paper, gorgeous robes of old cotton, glittering with tin spangles from the pickle factory, and armor covered with the same useful diamond-shaped bits, left in the sheets when the lids of tin preserve-pots were cut out. The furniture was used to being turned topsy-turvy, and the big chamber was the scene of many innocent revels.

No gentlemen were admitted; so Jo played male parts to her heart's content, and took immense satisfaction in a pair of russet-leather boots given her by a friend, who knew a lady who knew an actor. These boots, an old foil, and a slashed doublet once used by an artist for some picture, were Jo's chief treasures, and appeared on all occasions. The smallness of the company made it necessary for the two principal actors to take several parts apiece; and they certainly deserved some credit for the hard work they did in learning three or four different parts, whisking in and out of various costumes, and managing the stage besides. It was excellent drill for their memories, a harmless amusement, and employed many hours which otherwise would have been idle, lonely, or spent in less profitable society.

On Christmas night, a dozen girls piled on to the bed, which was the dress-circle, and sat before the blue and yellow chintz curtains, in a most flattering state of expectancy. There was a good deal of rustling and whispering behind the curtain, a trifle of lamp-smoke, and an occasional giggle from Amy, who was apt to get hysterical in the excitement of the moment. Presently a bell sounded, the curtains flew apart, and the Operatic Tragedy began.

"A gloomy wood," according to the one play-bill, was represented by a few shrubs in pots, a green baize on the floor, and a cave in the distance. This cave was made with a clothes-horse for a roof, bureaus for walls; and in it was a small furnace in full blast, with a black pot on it, and an old witch bending over it. The stage was dark, and the glow of the furnace had a fine effect, especially as real steam issued from the kettle when the witch took off the cover. A moment was allowed for the first thrill to subside; then Hugo, the villain, stalked in with a clanking sword at his side, a slouched hat, black beard, mysterious cloak, and the boots. After pacing to and fro in much agitation, he struck his forehead and burst out in a wild strain, singing of his hatred to Roderigo, his love for Zara, and his pleasing resolution to kill the one and win the other. The gruff tones of Hugo's voice, with an occasional shout when his feelings overcame him, were very impressive, and the audience applauded the moment he paused for breath. Bowing with the air of one accustomed to public praise, he stole to the cavern and ordered Hagar to come forth with a commanding "What ho! minion! I need thee!"

Out came Meg, with gray horse-hair hanging about her face, a red and black robe, a staff, and cabalistic signs upon her cloak. Hugo demanded a potion to make Zara adore him, and one to destroy Roderigo. Hagar, in a fine dramatic melody, promised both, and proceeded to call up the spirit who would bring the love philter:

> *Hither, hither, from my home,*
> *Airy sprite, I bid thee come.*
> *Born of roses, fed on dew,*
> *Charms and potions canst thou brew?*
> *Bring me here, with elfin speed,*
> *The fragrant philter which I need;*
> *Make it sweet, and swift and strong;*
> *Spirit, answer now my song!*

A soft strain of music sounded, and then at the back of the cave appeared a little figure in cloudy white, with glittering wings, golden hair, and a garland of roses on its head. Waving a wand, it sung:

> *Hither I come,*
> *From my airy home,*
> *Afar in the silver moon;*
> *Take the magic spell,*
> *Oh, use it well!*
> *Or its power will vanish soon!*

and dropping a small gilded bottle at the witch's feet, the spirit vanished. Another chant from Hagar produced another apparition, – not a lovely one, for, with a bang, an ugly, black imp appeared, and having croaked a reply, tossed a dark bottle at Hugo, and disappeared with a mocking laugh. Having warbled his thanks, and put the potions in his boots, Hugo departed; and Hagar informed the audience that, as he had killed a few of her friends in times past, she has cursed him, and intends to thwart his plans, and be revenged on him. Then the curtain fell, and the audience reposed and ate candy while discussing the merits of the play.

A good deal of hammering went on before the curtain rose again; but when it became evident what a masterpiece of stage carpentering had been got up, no one murmured at the delay. It was truly superb! A tower rose to the ceiling; half-way up appeared a window with a lamp burning at it, and behind the white curtain appeared Zara in a lovely blue and silver dress, waiting for Roderigo. He came in gorgeous array, with plumed cap, red cloak, chestnut love-locks, a guitar, and the boots, of course. Kneeling at the foot of the tower, he sung a serenade in melting tones. Zara replied, and after a musical dialogue, consented to fly. Then came the grand effect of the play. Roderigo produced a rope-ladder with five steps to it, threw up one end, and invited Zara to descend. Timidly she crept from her lattice, put her hand on Roderigo's shoulder, and was about to leap gracefully down, when, "alas! alas for Zara!" she forgot her train, – it caught in the window; the tower tottered, leaned forward, fell with a crash and buried the unhappy lovers in the ruins!

A universal shriek arose as the russet boots waved wildly from the wreck, and a golden head emerged, exclaiming, "I told you so! I told you so!" With wonderful presence of mind Don Pedro, the cruel sire, rushed in, dragged out his daughter with a hasty aside, –

"Don't laugh, act as if it was all right!" and ordering Roderigo up, banished him from the kingdom with wrath and scorn. Though decidedly shaken by the fall of the tower upon him, Roderigo defied the old gentleman, and refused to stir. This dauntless example fired Zara; she also defied her sire, and he ordered them both to the deepest dungeons of the castle. A stout little retainer came in with chains, and led them away, looking very much frightened, and evidently forgetting the speech he ought to have made.

Act third was the castle hall; and here Hagar appeared, having come to free the lovers and finish Hugo. She hears him coming, and hides; sees him put the potions into two cups of wine, and bid the timid little servant "Bear them to the captives in their cells, and tell them I shall come anon." The servant takes Hugo aside to tell him something, and Hagar changes the cups for two others which are harmless. Ferdinando, the "minion," carries them away, and Hagar puts back the cup which holds the poison meant for Roderigo. Hugo, getting thirsty after a long warble, drinks it, loses his wits, and after a good deal of clutching and stamping, falls flat and dies; while Hagar informs him what she has done in a song of exquisite power and melody.

This was a truly thrilling scene; though some persons might have thought that the sudden tumbling down of a quantity of long hair rather marred the effect of the villain's death. He was called before the curtain, and with great propriety appeared leading Hagar, whose singing was considered more wonderful than all the rest of the performance put together.

Act fourth displayed the despairing Roderigo on the point of stabbing himself, because he has been told that Zara has deserted him. Just as the dagger is at his heart, a lovely song is sung under his window, informing him that Zara is true, but in danger, and he can save her if he will. A key is thrown in, which unlocks the door, and in a spasm of rapture he tears off his chains, and rushes away to find and rescue his lady-love.

Act fifth opened with a stormy scene between Zara and Don Pedro. He wishes her to go into a convent, but she won't hear of it; and, after a touching appeal, is about to faint, when Roderigo dashes in and demands her hand. Don Pedro refuses, because he is not rich. They shout and gesticulate tremendously, but cannot agree, and Roderigo is about to bear away the exhausted Zara, when the timid servant enters with a letter and a bag from Hagar, who has mysteriously disappeared. The latter informs the party that she bequeaths untold wealth to the young pair, and an awful doom to Don Pedro if he doesn't make them happy. The bag is opened, and several quarts of tin money shower down upon the stage, till it is quite glorified with the glitter. This entirely softens the "stern sire;" he consents without a murmur, all join in a joyful chorus, and the curtains falls upon the lovers kneeling to receive Don Pedro's blessing, in attitudes of the most romantic grace.

Tumultuous applause followed, but received an unexpected check; for the cot-bed, on which the "dress-circle" was built, suddenly shut up, and extinguished the enthusiastic audience. Roderigo and Don Pedro flew to the rescue, and all were taken out unhurt, though many were speechless with laughter. The excitement had hardly subsided when Hannah appeared, with "Mrs. March's compliments, and would the ladies walk down to supper."

This was a surprise, even to the actors; and when they saw the table they looked at one another in rapturous amazement. It was like "Marmee" to get up a little treat for them, but anything so fine as this was unheard of since the departed days of plenty. There was ice cream, — actually two dishes of it, — pink and white, — and cake, and fruit, and distracting French bonbons, and in the middle of the table, four great bouquets of hot-house flowers!

It quite took their breath away; and they stared first at the table and then at their mother, who looked as if she enjoyed it immensely.

"Is it fairies?" asked Amy.

"It's Santa Claus," said Beth.

"Mother did it;" and Meg smiled her sweetest, in spite of her gray beard and white eyebrows.

"Aunt March had a good fit, and sent the supper," cried Jo, with a sudden inspiration.

"All wrong; old Mr. Laurence sent it," replied Mrs. March.

"The Laurence boy's grandfather! What in the world put such a thing into his head? We don't know him," exclaimed Meg.

"Hannah told one of his servants about your breakfast party; he is an odd old gentleman, but that pleased him. He knew my father, years ago, and he sent me a polite note this afternoon, saying he hoped I would allow him to express his friendly feeling toward my children by sending them a few trifles in honor of the day. I could not refuse, and so you have a little feast at night to make up for the bread and milk breakfast."

"That boy put it into his head, I know he did! He's a capital fellow, and I wish we could get acquainted. He looks as if he'd like to know us; but he's bashful, and Meg is so prim she won't let me speak to him when we pass," said Jo, as the plates went round, and the ice began to melt out of sight, with ohs! and ahs! of satisfaction.

"You mean the people who live in the big house next door, don't you?" asked one of the girls. "My mother knows old Mr. Laurence, but says he's very proud, and don't like to mix with his neighbors. He keeps his grandson shut up when he isn't riding or walking with his tutor, and makes him study dreadful hard. We invited him to our party, but he didn't come. Mother says he's very nice, though he never speaks to us girls."

"Our cat ran away once, and he brought her back, and we talked over the fence, and were getting on capitally, all about cricket, and so on, when he saw Meg coming, and walked off. I mean to know him some day, for he needs fun, I'm sure he does," said Jo, decidedly.

"I like his manners, and he looks like a little gentleman, so I've no objection to your knowing him if a proper opportunity comes. He brought the flowers himself, and I should have asked him in if I had been sure what was going on upstairs. He looked so wistful as he went away, hearing the frolic, and evidently having none of his own."

"It's a mercy you didn't, mother!," laughed Jo, looking at her boots. "But we'll have another play some time, that he *can* see. Maybe he'll help act; wouldn't that be jolly?"

"I never had a bouquet before; how pretty it is," and Meg examined her flowers with great interest.

"They *are* lovely, but Beth's roses are sweeter to me," said Mrs. March, sniffing at the half-dead posy in her belt.

Beth nestled up to her, and whispered, softly, "I wish I could send my bunch to father. I'm afraid he isn't having such a merry Christmas as we are."

CHAPTER THREE

THE LAURENCE BOY

~

"Jo! Jo! where are you?" cried Meg, at the foot of the garret stairs.

"Here," answered a husky voice from above; and running up, Meg found her sister eating apples and crying over the "Heir of Redclyffe," wrapped up in a comforter on an old three-legged sofa by the sunny window. This was Jo's favorite refuge; and here she loved to retire with half a dozen russets and a nice book, to enjoy the quiet and the society of a pet rat who lived near by, and didn't mind her a particle. As Meg appeared, Scrabble whisked into his hole. Jo shook the tears off her cheeks, and waited to hear the news.

"Such fun! only see! a regular note of invitation from Mrs. Gardiner for to-morrow night!" cried Meg, waving the precious paper, and then proceeding to read it, with girlish delight.

"'Mrs. Gardiner would be happy to see Miss March and Miss Josephine at a little dance on New Year's Eve.'" Marmee is willing we should go; now what *shall* we wear?"

"What's the use of asking that, when you know we shall wear our poplins, because we haven't got anything else," answered Jo, with her mouth full.

"If I only had a silk!" sighed Meg; "mother says I may when I'm eighteen, perhaps; but two years is an everlasting time to wait."

"I'm sure our pops look like silk, and they are nice enough for us. Yours is as good as new, but I forgot the burn and the tear in mine; whatever shall I do? the burn shows horridly and I can't take any out."

"You must sit still all you can, and keep your back out of sight; the front is all right. I shall have a new ribbon for my hair, and Marmee will lend me her little pearl pin, and my new slippers are lovely, and my gloves will do, though they aren't as nice as I'd like."

"Mine are spoilt with lemonade, and I can't get any new ones, so I shall have to go without," said Jo, who never troubled herself much about dress.

"You *must* have gloves, or I won't go," cried Meg, decidedly. "Gloves are more important than anything else; you can't dance without them, and if you don't I should be *so* mortified."

"Then I'll stay still; I don't care much for company dancing; it's no fun to go sailing round, I like to fly about and cut capers."

"You can't ask mother for new ones, they are so expensive, and you are so careless. She said, when you spoilt the others, that she shouldn't get you any more this winter. Can't you fix them any way?" asked Meg, anxiously.

"I can hold them crunched up in my hand, so no one will know how stained they are; that's all I can do. No! I'll tell you how we can manage — each wear one good one and carry a bad one; don't you see?"

"Your hands are bigger than mine, and you will stretch my glove dreadfully," began Meg, whose gloves were a tender point with her.

"Then I'll go without. I don't care what people say," cried Jo, taking up her book.

"You may have it, you may! only don't stain it, and do behave nicely; don't put your hands behind you, or stare, or say 'Christopher Columbus!' will you?"

"Don't worry about me; I'll be as prim as a dish, and not get into any scrapes, if I can help it. Now go and answer your note, and let me finish this splendid story."

So Meg went away to "accept with thanks," look over her dress, and sing blithely as she did up her one real lace frill; while Jo finished her story, her four apples, and had a game of romps with Scrabble.

On New Year's Eve the parlor was deserted, for the two younger girls played dressing maids, and the two older were absorbed in the all-important business of "getting ready for the party." Simple as the toilets were, there was a great deal of running up and down, laughing and talking, and at one time a strong smell of burnt hair pervaded the house. Meg wanted a few curls about her face, and Jo undertook to pinch the papered locks with a pair of hot tongs.

"Ought they to smoke like that?" asked Beth, from her perch on the bed.

"It's the dampness drying," replied Jo.

"What a queer smell! it's like burnt feathers," observed Amy, smoothing her own pretty curls with a superior air.

"There, now I'll take off the papers and you'll see a cloud of little ringlets," said Jo, putting down the tongs.

She did take off the papers, but no cloud of ringlets appeared, for the hair came with the papers, and the horrified hair dresser laid a row of little scorched bundles on the bureau before her victim.

"Oh, oh, oh! what *have* you done? I'm spoilt! I can't go! my hair, oh, my hair!" wailed Meg, looking with despair at the uneven frizzle on her forehead.

"Just my luck! you shouldn't have asked me to do it; I always spoil everything. I'm no end sorry, but the tongs were too hot, and so I've made a mess," groaned poor Jo, regarding the black pancakes with tears of regret.

"It isn't spoilt; just frizzle it, and tie your ribbon so the ends come on your forehead a bit, and it will look like the last fashion. I've seen many girls do it so," said Amy, consolingly.

"Serves me right for trying to be fine. I wish I'd let my hair alone," cried Meg, petulantly.

"So do I, it was so smooth and pretty. But it will soon grow out again," said Beth, coming to kiss and comfort the shorn sheep.

After various lesser mishaps, Meg was finished at last, and by the united exertions of the family, Jo's hair was got up, and her dress on. They looked very well in their simple suits, Meg in silvery drab, with a blue velvet snood, lace frills, and the pearl pin; Jo in maroon, with a stiff, gentlemanly linen collar, and a white chrysanthemum or two for her only ornament. Each put on the one nice light glove, and carried one soiled one, and all pronounced the effect "quite easy and nice." Meg's high-heeled slippers were dreadfully tight, and hurt her, though she would not own it, and Jo's nineteen hairpins all seemed stuck straight into her head, which was not exactly comfortable; but, dear me, let us be elegant or die.

"Have a good time, dearies," said Mrs. March, as the sisters went daintily down the walk. "Don't eat much supper, and come away at eleven, when I send Hannah for you." As the gate clashed behind them, a voice cried from a window, –

"Girls, girls! *have* you both got nice pocket-handkerchiefs?"

"Yes, yes, spandy nice, and Meg has Cologne on hers," cried Jo, adding, with a laugh, as they went on, "I do believe Marmee would ask that if we were all running away from an earthquake."

"It is one of her aristocratic tastes, and quite proper, for a real lady is always known by neat boots, gloves, and handkerchief," replied Meg, who had a good many little "aristocratic tastes" of her own.

"Now don't forget to keep the bad breadth out of sight, Jo. Is my sash right; and does my hair look *very* bad?" said Meg, as she turned from the glass in Mrs. Gardiner's dressing-room, after a prolonged prink.

"I know I shall forget. If you see me doing anything wrong, just remind me by a wink, will you?" returned Jo, giving her collar a twitch and her hair a hasty brush.

"No, winking isn't ladylike; I'll lift my eyebrows if anything is wrong, and nod if you are all right. Now hold your shoulders straight, and take short steps, and don't shake hands if you are introduced to any one, it isn't the thing."

"How *do* you learn all the proper quirks? I never can. Isn't that music gay?"

Down they went, feeling a trifle timid, for they seldom went to parties, and, informal as this little gathering was, it was an event to them. Mrs. Gardiner, a stately old lady, greeted them kindly, and handed them over to the eldest of her six daughters. Meg knew Sallie, and was at her ease very soon; but Jo, who didn't care much for girls or girlish gossip, stood about with her back carefully against the wall, and felt as much out of place as a colt in a flower-garden. Half a dozen jovial lads were talking about skates in another part of the room, and she longed to go and join them, for skating was one of the joys of her life. She telegraphed her wish to Meg, but the eyebrows went up so alarmingly that she dared not stir. No one came to talk to her, and one by one the group near her dwindled away, till she was left alone. She could not roam about and amuse herself, for the burnt breadth would show, so she stared at people rather forlornly till the dancing began. Meg was asked at once, and the tight slippers tripped about so briskly that none would have guessed the pain their wearer suffered smilingly. Jo saw a big red-headed youth approaching her corner, and fearing he meant to engage her, she slipped into a curtained recess, intending to peep and enjoy herself in peace. Unfortunately, another bashful person had chosen the same refuge, for, as the curtain fell behind her, she found herself face to face with the "Laurence boy."

"Dear me, I didn't know any one was here!" stammered Jo, preparing to back out as speedily as she had bounced in.

But the boy laughed, and said, pleasantly, though he looked a little startled, —

"Don't mind me; stay, if you like."

"Shan't I disturb you?"

"Not a bit; I only came here because I don't know many people, and felt rather strange at first, you know."

"So did I. Don't go away, please, unless you'd rather."

The boy sat down again and looked at his boots, till Jo said, trying to be polite and easy, —

"I think I've had the pleasure of seeing you before; you live near us, don't you?"

"Next door;" and he looked up and laughed outright, for Jo's prim manner was rather funny when he remembered how they had chatted about cricket when he brought the cat home.

That put Jo at her ease; and she laughed too, as she said, in her heartiest way, —

"We did have such a good time over your nice Christmas present."

"Grandpa sent it."

"But you put it into his head, didn't you, now?"

"How is your cat, Miss March?" asked the boy, trying to look sober, while his black eyes shone with fun.

"Nicely, thank you, Mr. Laurence; but I ain't Miss March, I'm only Jo," returned the young lady.

"I'm not Mr. Laurence, I'm only Laurie."

"Laurie Laurence; what an odd name."

"My first name is Theodore, but I don't like it, for the fellows called me Dora, so I made them say Laurie instead."

"I hate my name, too — so sentimental! I wish every one would say Jo, instead of Josephine. How did you make the boys stop calling you Dora?"

"I thrashed 'em."

"I can't thrash Aunt March, so I suppose I shall have to bear it;" and Jo resigned herself with a sigh.

"Don't you like to dance, Miss Jo?" asked Laurie, looking as if he thought the name suited her.

"I like it well enough if there is plenty of room, and every one is lively. In a place like this I'm sure to upset something, tread on people's toes, or do something dreadful, so I keep out of mischief, and let Meg do the pretty. Don't you dance?"

"Sometimes; you see I've been abroad a good many years, and haven't been about enough yet to know how you do things here."

"Abroad!" cried Jo; "oh, tell me about it! I love dearly to hear people describe their travels."

Laurie didn't seem to know where to begin; but Jo's eager questions soon set him going, and he told her how he had been at school in Vevey, where the boys never wore hats, and had a fleet of boats on the lake, and for holiday fun went walking trips about Switzerland with their teachers.

"Don't I wish I'd been there!" cried Jo. "Did you go to Paris?"

"We spent last winter there."

"Can you talk French?"

"We were not allowed to speak anything else at Vevey."

"Do say some. I can read it, but can't pronounce."

"Quel nom à cette jeune demoiselle en les pantoufles jolis?" said Laurie, good-naturedly.

"How nicely you do it! Let me see — you said, 'Who is the young lady in the pretty slippers,' didn't you?"

"Oui, mademoiselle."

"It's my sister Margaret, and you knew it was! Do you think she is pretty?"

"Yes; she makes me think of the German girls, she looks so fresh and quiet, and dances like a lady."

Jo quite glowed with pleasure at this boyish praise of her sister, and stored it up to repeat to Meg. Both peeped, and criticised, and chatted, till they felt like old acquaintances. Laurie's bashfulness soon wore off, for Jo's gentlemanly demeanor amused and set him at his ease, and Jo was her merry self again, because her dress was forgotten, and nobody lifted their eyebrows at her. She liked the "Laurence boy" better than ever, and took several good looks at him, so that she might describe him to the girls; for they had no brothers, very few male cousins, and boys were almost unknown creatures to them.

"Curly black hair, brown skin, big, black eyes, long nose, nice teeth, little hands and feet, tall as I am; very polite for a boy, and altogether jolly. Wonder how old he is?"

It was on the tip of Jo's tongue to ask; but she checked herself in time, and, with unusual tact, tried to find out in a roundabout way.

"I suppose you are going to college soon? I see you pegging away at your books – no, I mean studying hard;" and Jo blushed at the dreadful "pegging" which had escaped her.

Laurie smiled, but didn't seem shocked, and answered, with a shrug,

"Not for two or three years yet; I won't go before seventeen, any way."

"Aren't you but fifteen?" asked Jo, looking at the tall lad, whom she had imagined seventeen already.

"Sixteen, next month."

"How I wish I was going to college; you don't look as if you liked it."

"I hate it! nothing but grinding or skylarking; and I don't like the way fellows do either, in this country."

"What do you like?"

"To live in Italy, and to enjoy myself in my own way."

Jo wanted very much to ask what his own way was; but his black brows looked rather threatening as he knit them, so she changed the subject by saying, as her foot kept time, "That's a splendid polka; why don't you go and try it?"

"If you will come too," he answered, with a queer little French bow.

"I can't; for I told Meg I wouldn't, because – " there Jo stopped, and looked undecided whether to tell or to laugh.

"Because what?" asked Laurie, curiously.

"You won't tell?"

"Never!"

"Well, I have a bad trick of standing before the fire, and so I burn my frocks, and I scorched this one; and, though it's nicely mended, it shows, and Meg told me to keep still, so no one would see it. You may laugh if you want to; it is funny, I know."

But Laurie didn't laugh; he only looked down a minute, and the expression of his face puzzled Jo, when he said very gently, –

"Never mind that; I'll tell you how we can manage: there's a long hall out there, and we can dance grandly, and no one will see us. Please come."

Jo thanked him, and gladly went, wishing she had two neat gloves, when she saw the nice, pearl-colored ones her partner put on. The hall was empty, and they had a grand polka, for Laurie danced well, and taught her the German step, which delighted Jo, being full of swing and spring. When the music stopped they sat down on the stairs to get their breath; and Laurie was in the midst of an account of a student's festival at Heidelberg, when Meg appeared in search of her sister. She beckoned, and Jo reluctantly followed her into a side room, where she found her on a sofa holding her foot, and looking pale.

"I've sprained my ankle. That stupid high heel turned, and gave me a horrid wrench. It aches so, I can hardly stand, and I don't know how I'm ever going to get home," she said, rocking to and fro in pain.

"I knew you'd hurt your feet with those silly things. I'm sorry; but I don't see what you can do, except get a carriage, or stay here all night," answered Jo, softly rubbing the poor ankle, as she spoke.

"I can't have a carriage without its costing ever so much; I daresay I can't get one at all, for most people come in their own, and it's a long way to the stable, and no one to send."

"I'll go."

"No, indeed; it's past ten, and dark as Egypt. I can't stop here, for the house is full; Sallie has some girls staying with her. I'll rest till Hannah comes, and then do the best I can."

"I'll ask Laurie; he will go," said Jo, looking relieved as the idea occurred to her.

"Mercy, no! don't ask or tell any one. Get me my rubbers, and put these slippers with our things. I can't dance any more; but as soon as supper is over, watch for Hannah, and tell me the minute she comes."

"They are going out to supper now. I'll stay with you; I'd rather."

"No, dear; run along, and bring me some coffee. I'm so tired, I can't stir!"

So Meg reclined, with rubbers well hidden, and Jo went blundering away to the dining-room, which she found after going into a china-closet and opening the door of a room where old Mr. Gardiner was taking a little private refreshment. Making a dive at the table, she secured the coffee, which she immediately spilt, thereby making the front of her dress as bad as the back.

"Oh, dear! what a blunderbuss I am!" exclaimed Jo, finishing Meg's glove by scrubbing her gown with it.

"Can I help you?" said a friendly voice; and there was Laurie, with a full cup in one hand and a plate of ice in the other.

"I was trying to get something for Meg, who is very tired, and some one shook me, and here I am, in a nice state," answered Jo, glancing dismally, from the stained skirt to the coffee-colored glove.

"To bad! I was looking for some one to give this to; may I take it to your sister?"

"Oh, thank you; I'll show you where she is. I don't offer to take it myself, for I should only get into another scrape if I did."

Jo led the way; and, as if used to waiting on ladies, Laurie drew up a little table, brought a second instalment of coffee and ice for Jo, and was so obliging that even particular Meg pronounced him a "nice boy." They had a merry time over the bonbons and mottos, and were in the midst of a quiet game of "buzz" with two or three other young people who had strayed in, when Hannah appeared. Meg forgot her foot, and rose so quickly that she was forced to catch hold of Jo, with an exclamation of pain.

"Hush! don't say anything," she whispered; adding aloud, "It's nothing; I turned my foot a little, – that's all," and limped up stairs to put her things on.

Hannah scolded, Meg cried, and Jo was at her wits' end, till she decided to take things into her own hands. Slipping out, she ran down, and finding a servant, asked if he could get her a carriage. It happened to be a hired waiter, who knew nothing about the neighborhood; and Jo was looking round for help, when Laurie, who had heard what she said, came up and offered his grandfather's carriage, which had just come for him, he said.

"It's so early, – You can't mean to go yet," began Jo, looking relieved, but hesitating to accept the offer.

"I always go early, – I do, truly! Please let me take you home; it's all on my way, you know, and it rains, they say."

That settled it; and telling him of Meg's mishap, Jo gratefully accepted, and rushed up to bring down the rest of the party. Hannah hated rain as much as a cat does; so she made no trouble, and they rolled away in the luxurious close carriage, feeling very festive and elegant. Laurie went on the box, so Meg could keep her foot up, and the girls talked over their party in freedom.

"I had a capital time; did you?" asked Jo, rumpling up her hair, and making herself comfortable.

"Yes, till I hurt myself. Sallie's friend, Annie Moffat, took a fancy to me, and asked me to come and spend a week with her when Sallie does. She is going in the spring, when the opera comes, and it will be perfectly splendid if mother only lets me go," answered Meg, cheering up at the thought.

"I saw you with the red-headed man I ran away from; was he nice?"

"Oh, very! His hair is auburn, not red; and he is very polite, and I had a delicious redowa with him!"

"He looked like a grasshopper in a fit, when he did the new step. Laurie and I couldn't help laughing; did you hear us?"

"No, but it was very rude. What *were* you about all that time, hidden away there?"

Jo told her adventures, and by the time she had finished they were at home. With many thanks, they said "Good-night," and crept in, hoping to disturb no one; but the instant their door creaked, two little night-caps bobbed up, and two sleepy but eager voices cried out, –

"Tell about the party! tell about the party!"

With what Meg called "a great want of manners," Jo had saved some bonbons for the little girls, and they soon subsided, after hearing the most thrilling events of the evening.

"I declare, it really seems like being a fine young lady, to come home from my party in my carriage, and sit in my dressing-gown with a maid to wait on me," said Meg, as Jo bound up her foot with arnica, and brushed her hair.

"I don't believe fine young ladies enjoy themselves a bit more than we do, in spite of our burnt hair, old gowns, one glove apiece, and tight slippers, that sprain our ankles when we are silly enough to wear them." And I think Jo was quite right.

CHAPTER FOUR

BURDENS

~

"Oh, dear, how hard it does seem to take up our packs and go on," sighed Meg, the morning after the party; for now the holidays were over, the week of merry-making did not fit her for going on easily with the task she never liked.

"I wish it was Christmas or New Year all the time; wouldn't it be fun?" answered Jo, yawning dismally.

"We shouldn't enjoy ourselves half so much as we do now. But it does seem so nice to have little suppers and bouquets, and go to parties, and drive home in a carriage, and read and rest, and not grub. It's like other people, you know, and I always envy girls who do such things; I'm so fond of luxury," said Meg, trying to decide which of two shabby gowns was the least shabby.

"Well, we can't have it, so don't let us grumble, but shoulder our bundles and trudge along as cheerfully as Marmee does. I'm sure Aunt March is a regular Old Man of the Sea to me, but I suppose when I've learned to carry her without complaining, she will tumble off, or get so light that I shan't mind her."

This idea tickled Jo's fancy, and put her in good spirits; but Meg didn't brighten, for her burden, consisting of four spoilt children, seemed heavier than ever. She hadn't heart enough even to make herself pretty, as usual, by putting on a blue neck-ribbon, and dressing her hair in the most becoming way.

"Where's the use of looking nice, when no one sees me but those cross midgets, and no one cares whether I'm pretty or not?" she muttered, shutting her drawer with a jerk. "I shall have to toil and moil all my days, with only little bits of fun now and then, and get old and ugly and sour, because I'm poor, and can't enjoy my life as other girls do. It's a shame!"

So Meg went down, wearing an injured look, and wasn't at all agreeable at breakfast-time. Everyone seemed rather out of sorts, and inclined to croak. Beth had a headache, and lay on the sofa trying to comfort herself with the cat and three kittens; Amy was fretting because her lessons were not learned, and she couldn't find her rubbers; Jo *would* whistle, and make a great racket getting ready; Mrs. March was very busy trying to finish a letter, which must go at once; and Hannah had the grumps, for being up late didn't suit her.

"There never *was* such a cross family!" cried Jo, losing her temper when she had upset an inkstand, broken both boot-lacings, and sat down upon her hat.

"You're the crossest person in it!" returned Amy, washing out the sum, that was all wrong, with the tears that had fallen on her slate.

"Beth, if you don't keep these horrid cats down cellar I'll have them drowned," exclaimed Meg, angrily, as she tried to get rid of the kitten, which had swarmed up her back, and stuck like a burr just out of reach.

Jo laughed, Meg scolded, Beth implored, and Amy wailed, because she couldn't remember how much nine times twelve was.

"Girls! girls! do be quiet one minute. I *must* get this off by the early mail, and you drive me distracted with your worry," cried Mrs. March, crossing out the third spoilt sentence in her letter.

There was a momentary lull, broken by Hannah, who bounced in, laid two hot turn-overs on the table, and bounced out again. These turn-overs were an institution; and the girls called them "muffs," for they had no others, and found the hot pies very comforting to their hands on cold mornings. Hannah never forgot to make them, no matter how busy or grumpy she might be, for the walk was long and bleak; the poor things got no other lunch, and were seldom home before three.

"Cuddle your cats, and get over your headache, Bethy. Good-by, Marmee; we are a set of rascals this morning, but we'll come home regular angels. Now then, Meg," and Jo tramped away, feeling that the pilgrims were not setting out as they ought to do.

They always looked back before turning the corner, for their mother was always at the window, to nod, and smile, and wave her hand to them. Somehow it seemed as if they couldn't have got through the day without that, for whatever their mood might be, the last glimpse of that motherly face was sure to affect them like sunshine.

"If Marmee shook her fist instead of kissing her hand to us, it would serve us right, for more ungrateful minxes than we are were never seen," cried Jo, taking a remorseful satisfaction in the slushy road and bitter wind.

"Don't use such dreadful expressions," said Meg, from the depths of the veil in which she had shrouded herself like a nun sick of the world.

"I like good, strong, words, that mean something," replied Jo, catching her hat as it took a leap off her head, preparatory to flying away altogether.

"Call yourself any names you like; but *I* am neither a rascal nor a minx, and I don't choose to be called so."

"You're a blighted being, and decidedly cross to-day, because you can't sit in the lap of luxury all the time. Poor dear! just wait till I make my fortune, and you shall revel in carriages, and ice cream and high-heeled slippers, and posies, and red-headed boys to dance with."

"How ridiculous you are, Jo!" but Meg laughed at the nonsense, and felt better in spite of herself.

"Lucky for you I am; for if I put on crushed airs, and tried to be dismal, as you do, we should be in a nice state. Thank goodness, I can always find something funny to keep me up. Don't croak any more, but come home jolly, there's a dear."

Jo gave her sister an encouraging pat on the shoulder as they parted for the day, each going a different way, each hugging her little warm turn-over, and each trying to be cheerful in spite of wintry weather, hard work, and the unsatisfied desires of pleasure-loving youth.

When Mr. March lost his property in trying to help an unfortunate friend, the two oldest girls begged to be allowed to do something towards their own support, at least. Believing that they could not begin too early to cultivate energy, industry, and independence, their parents consented, and both fell to work with the hearty good-will which, in spite of all obstacles, is sure to succeed at last. Margaret found a place as nursery governess, and felt rich with her small salary. As she said, she *was* "fond of luxury," and her chief trouble was poverty. She found it harder to bear than the others, because she could remember a time when home was beautiful, life full of ease and pleasure, and want of any kind unknown. She tried not to be envious or discontented, but it was very natural that the young girl should long for pretty things, gay friends, accomplishments, and a happy life. At the Kings' she daily saw all she wanted, for the children's older sisters were just out, and Meg caught frequent glimpses of dainty ball-dresses and bouquets, heard lively gossip about theatres, concerts, sleighing parties and merry-making of all kinds, and saw money lavished on trifles which would have been so precious to her. Poor Meg seldom complained, but a sense of injustice made her feel bitter toward every one sometimes, for she had not yet learned to know how rich she was in the blessings which alone can make life happy.

Jo happened to suit Aunt March, who was lame, and needed an active person to wait upon her. The childless old lady had offered to adopt one of the girls when the troubles came, and was much offended because her offer was declined. Other friends told the Marches that they had lost all chance of being remembered in the rich old lady's will; but the unworldly Marches only said, –

"We can't give up our girls for a dozen fortunes. Rich or poor, we will keep together and be happy in one another."

The old lady wouldn't speak to them for a time, but, happening to meet Jo at a friend's, something in her comical face and blunt manners struck the old lady's fancy, and she proposed to take her for a companion. This did not suit Jo at all; but she accepted the place, since nothing better appeared, and, to every one's surprise, got on remarkably well with her irascible relative. There was an occasional tempest, and once Jo had marched home, declaring she couldn't bear it any longer; but Aunt March always cleared up quickly and sent for her back again with such urgency that she could not refuse, for in her heart she rather liked the peppery old lady.

I suspect that the real attraction was a large library of fine books, which was left to dust and spiders since Uncle March died. Jo remembered the kind old gentleman who used to let her build railroads and bridges with his big dictionaries, tell her stories about the queer pictures in his Latin books, and buy her cards of gingerbread whenever he met her in the street. The dim, dusty room, with the busts staring down from the tall book-cases, the cosy chairs, the globes, and, best of all, the wilderness of books, in which she could wander where she liked, made the library a region of bliss to her. The moment Aunt March took her nap, or was busy with company, Jo hurried to this quiet place, and, curling herself up in the big chair, devoured poetry, romance, history, travels, and pictures, like a regular bookworm. But, like all happiness, it did not last long; for as sure as she had just reached the heart of the story, the sweetest verse of the song, or the most perilous adventure of her traveller, a shrill voice called, "Josy-phine! Josy-phine!" and she had to leave her paradise to wind yarn, wash the poodle, or read Belsham's Essays, by the hour together.

Jo's ambition was to do something very splendid; what it was she had no idea, but left it for time to tell her; and, meanwhile, found her greatest affliction in the fact that she couldn't read, run, and ride as much as she liked. A quick temper, sharp tongue, and restless spirit were always getting her into scrapes, and her life was a series of ups and downs, which were both comic and pathetic. But the training she received at Aunt March's was just what she needed; and the thought that she was doing something to support herself made her happy, in spite of the perpetual "Josy-phine!"

Beth was too bashful to go to school; it had been tried, but she suffered so much that it was given up, and she did her lessons at home with her father. Even when he went away, and her mother was called to devote her skill and energy to Soldiers' Aid Societies, Beth went faithfully on by herself, and did the best she could. She was a housewifely little creature, and helped Hannah keep home neat and comfortable for the workers, never thinking of any reward but to be loved. Long, quiet days she spent, not lonely nor idle, for her little world was peopled with imaginary friends, and she was by nature a busy bee. There were six dolls to be taken up and dressed every morning, for Beth was a child still, and loved her pets as well as ever; not one whole or handsome one among them; all were outcasts till Beth took them in; for, when her sisters outgrew these idols, they passed to her, because Amy would have nothing old or ugly. Beth cherished them all the more tenderly for that very reason, and set up a hospital for infirm dolls. No pins were ever stuck into their cotton vitals; no harsh words or blows were ever given them; no neglect ever saddened the heart of the most repulsive, but all were fed and clothed, nursed and caressed, with an affection which never failed. One forlorn fragment of *dollanity* had belonged to Jo; and, having led a tempestuous life, was left a wreck in the rag-bag, from which dreary poor-house it was rescued by Beth, and taken to her refuge. Having no top to its head, she tied on a neat little cap, and, as both arms and legs were gone, she hid these deficiencies by folding it in a blanket, and devoting her best bed to this chronic invalid. If any one had known the care lavished on that dolly, I think it would have touched their hearts, even while they laughed. She brought it bits of bouquets; she read to it, took it out to breathe the air, hidden under her coat; she sung it lullabies, and never went to bed without kissing its dirty face, and whispering tenderly, "I hope you'll have a good night, my poor dear."

Beth had her troubles as well as the others; and not being an angel, but a very human little girl, she often "wept a little weep," as Jo said, because she couldn't take music lessons and have a fine piano. She loved music so dearly, tried so hard to learn, and practised away so patiently at the jingling old instrument, that it did seem as if some one (not to hint Aunt March) ought to help her. Nobody did, however, and nobody saw Beth wipe the tears off the yellow keys, that wouldn't keep in tune when she was all alone. She sung like a little lark about her work, never was too tired to play for Marmee and the girls, and day after day said hopefully to herself, "I know I'll get my music some time, if I'm good."

There are many Beths in the world, shy and quiet, sitting in corners till needed, and living for others so cheerfully, that no one sees the sacrifices till the little cricket on the hearth stops chirping, and the sweet, sunshiny presence vanishes, leaving silence and shadow behind.

If anybody had asked Amy what the greatest trial of her life was, she would have answered at once, "My nose." When she was a baby, Jo had accidentally dropped her into the coal-hod, and Amy insisted that the fall had ruined her nose forever. It was not big, nor red, like poor "Petrea's;" it was only rather, flat and all the pinching in the world could not give it an aristocratic point. No one minded it but herself, and it was doing its best to grow, but Amy felt deeply the want of a Grecian nose, and drew whole sheets of handsome ones to console herself.

"Little Raphael," as her sisters called her, had a decided talent for drawing, and was never so happy as when copying flowers, designing fairies, or illustrating stories with queer specimens of art. Her teachers complained that instead of doing her sums, she covered her slate with animals; the blank pages of her atlas were used to copy maps on, and caricatures of the most ludicrous description came fluttering out of all her books at unlucky moments. She got through her lessons as well as she could, and managed to escape reprimands by being a model of deportment. She was a great favorite with her mates, being good-tempered, and possessing the happy art of pleasing without effort. Her little airs and graces were much admired, so were her accomplishments; for beside her drawing, she could play twelve tunes, crochet, and read French without mispronouncing more than two-thirds of the words. She had a plaintive way of saying, "When papa was rich we did so-and-so," which was very touching; and her long words were considered "perfectly elegant" by the girls.

Amy was in a fair way to be spoilt; for every one petted her, and her small vanities and selfishness were growing nicely. One thing, however, rather quenched the vanities; she had to wear her cousin's clothes. Now Florence's mamma hadn't a particle of taste, and Amy suffered deeply at having to wear a red instead of a blue bonnet, unbecoming gowns, and fussy aprons that did not fit. Everything was good, well made, and little worn; but Amy's artistic eyes were much afflicted, especially this winter, when her school dress was a dull purple, with yellow dots, and no trimming.

"My only comfort," she said to Meg, with tears in her eyes, "is that mother don't take tucks in my dresses whenever I'm naughty, as Maria Parks' mother does. My dear, it's really dreadful; for sometimes she is so bad, her frock is up to her knees, and she can't come to school. When I think of this *deggerredation*, I feel that I can bear even my flat nose and purple gown, with yellow sky-rockets on it."

Meg was Amy's confidante and monitor, and, by some strange attraction of opposites, Jo was gentle Beth's. To Jo alone did the shy child tell her thoughts; and over her big, harum-scarum sister, Beth unconsciously exercised more influence than any one in the family. The two elder girls were a great deal to each other, but each took one of the younger into their keeping, and watched over them in their own way; "playing mother" they called it, and put their sisters in the places of discarded dolls, with the maternal instincts of little women.

"Has anybody got anything to tell? It's been such a dismal day I'm really dying for some amusement," said Meg, as they sat sewing together that evening.

"I had a queer time with aunt to-day, and, as I got the best of it, I'll tell you about it," began Jo, who dearly loved to tell stories. "I was reading that everlasting Belsham, and droning away as I always do, for aunt soon drops off, and then I take out some nice book, and read like fury, till she wakes up. I actually made myself sleepy; and, before she began to nod, I gave such a gape that she asked me what I meant by opening my mouth wide enough to take the whole book in at once.

"'I wish I could, and be done with it,' said I, trying not to be saucy.

"Then she gave me a long lecture on my sins, and told me to sit and think them over while she just 'lost' herself for a moment. She never finds herself very soon; so the minute her cap began to bob, like a top-heavy dahlia, I whipped the 'Vicar of Wakefield' out of my pocket, and read away, with one eye on him, and one on aunt. I'd just got to where they all tumbled into the water, when I forgot, and laughed out loud. Aunt woke up; and, being more good-natured after her nap, told me to read a bit, and show what frivolous work I preferred to the worthy and instructive Belsham. I did my very best, and she liked it, though she only said, –

'I don't understand what it's all about; go back and begin it, child.'

"Back I went, and made the Primroses as interesting as ever I could. Once I was wicked enough to stop in a thrilling place, and say meekly, 'I'm afraid it tires you, ma'am; shan't I stop now?'

"She caught up her knitting which had dropped out of her hands, gave me a sharp look through her specs, and said, in her short way, –

"'Finish the chapter, and don't be impertinent, miss.'"

"Did she own she liked it?" asked Meg.

"Oh, bless you, no! but she let old Belsham rest; and, when I ran back after my gloves this afternoon, there she was, so hard at the Vicar, that she didn't hear me laugh as I danced a jig in the hall, because of the good time coming. What a pleasant life she might have, if she only chose. I don't envy her much, in spite of her money, for after all rich people have about as many worries as poor ones, I guess," added Jo.

"That reminds me," said Meg, "that I've got something to tell. It isn't funny, like Jo's story, but I thought about it a good deal as I came home. At the Kings' to-day I found everybody in a flurry, and one of the children said that her oldest brother had done something dreadful, and papa had sent him away. I heard Mrs. King crying, and Mr. King talking very loud, and Grace and Ellen turned away their faces when they passed me, so I shouldn't see how red their eyes were. I didn't ask any questions, of course; but I felt so sorry for them, and was rather glad I hadn't any wild brothers to do wicked things, and disgrace the family."

"I think being disgraced in school is a great deal try*inger* than anything bad boys can do," said Amy, shaking her head, as if her experience of life had been a deep one. "Susie Perkins came to school to-day with a lovely red carnelian ring; I wanted it dreadfully, and wished I was her with all my might. Well, she drew a picture of Mr. Davis, with a monstrous nose and a hump, and the words, 'Young ladies, my eye is upon you!' coming out of his mouth in a balloon thing. We were laughing over it, when all of a sudden his eye *was* on us, and he ordered Susie to bring up her slate. She was *parry*lized with fright, but she went, and oh, what *do* you think he did? He took her by the ear, the ear! just fancy how horrid! and led her to the recitation platform, and made her stand there half an hour, holding that slate so everyone could see."

"Didn't the girls laugh at the picture?" asked Jo, who relished the scrape.

"Laugh! Not a one; they sat as still as mice, and Susie cried quarts, I know she did. I didn't envy her then, for I felt that millions of carnelian rings wouldn't have made me happy after that. I never, never should have got over such an agonizing mortification;" and Amy went on with her work, in the proud consciousness of virtue, and the successful utterance of two long words in a breath.

"I saw something that I liked this morning, and I meant to tell it at dinner, but I forgot," said Beth, putting Jo's topsy-turvy basket in order as she talked. "When I went to get some oysters for Hannah, Mr. Laurence was in the fish shop, but he didn't see me, for I kept behind a barrel, and he was busy with Mr. Cutter, the fish-man. A poor woman came in with a pail and a mop, and asked Mr. Cutter if he would let her do some scrubbing for a bit of fish, because she hadn't any dinner for her children, and had been disappointed of a day's work. Mr. Cutter was in a hurry, and said, 'No,' rather crossly; so she was going away, looking hungry and sorry, when Mr. Laurence hooked up a big fish with the crooked end of his cane, and held it out to her. She was so glad and surprised she took it right in her arms, and thanked him over and over. He told her to 'go along and cook it,' and she hurried off, so happy! wasn't it nice of him? Oh, she did look so funny, hugging the big, slippery fish, and hoping Mr. Laurence's bed in heaven would be 'aisy.'"

When they had laughed at Beth's story, they asked their mother for one; and, after a moment's thought, she said soberly, –

"As I sat cutting out blue flannel jackets to-day, at the rooms, I felt very anxious about father, and thought how lonely and helpless we should be if anything happened to him. It was not a wise thing to do, but I kept on worrying, till an old man came in with an order for some things. He sat down near me, and I began to talk to him, for he looked poor, and tired, and anxious.

"'Have you sons in the army?' I asked, for the note he brought was not to me.

"'Yes, ma'am, I had four; but two were killed; one is a prisoner, and I'm going to the other, who is very sick in a Washington hospital,' he answered, quietly.

"'You have done a great deal for your country, sir,' I said, feeling respect now, instead of pity.

"'Not a mite more than I ought, ma'am. I'd go myself, if I was any use; as I ain't, I give my boys, and give 'em free.'

"He spoke so cheerfully, looked so sincere, and seemed so glad to give his all, that I was ashamed of myself. I'd given one man, and thought it too much, while he gave four, without grudging them; I had all my girls to comfort me at home, and his last son was waiting, miles away, to say 'good-by' to him, perhaps. I felt so rich, so happy, thinking of my blessings, that I made him a nice bundle, gave him some money, and thanked him heartily for the lesson he had taught me."

"Tell me another story, mother; one with a moral to it, like this. I like to think about them afterwards, if they are real, and not too preachy," said Jo, after a minute's silence.

Mrs. March smiled, and began at once; for she had told stories to this audience for many years, and knew how to please them.

"Once upon a time, there were four girls, who had enough to eat, and drink, and wear; a good many comforts and pleasures, kind friends and parents, who loved them dearly, and yet they were not contented." (Here the listeners stole sly looks at one another, and began to sew diligently.) "These girls were anxious to be good, and made many excellent resolutions, but somehow they did not keep them very well, and were constantly saying, 'If we only had this,' or 'If we could only do that,' quite forgetting how much they already had, and how many pleasant things they actually could do; so they asked an old woman what spell they could use to make them happy, and she said, 'When you feel discontented, think over your blessings, and be grateful.'" (Here Jo looked up quickly, as if about to speak, but changed her mind, seeing that the story was not done yet.)

"Being sensible girls, they decided to try her advice, and soon were surprised to see how well off they were. One discovered that money couldn't keep shame and sorrow out of rich people's houses; another that though she was poor, she was a great deal happier with her youth, health, and good spirits, than a certain fretful, feeble old lady, who couldn't enjoy her comforts; a third, that, disagreeable as it was to help get dinner, it was harder still to have to go begging for it; and the fourth, that even carnelian rings were not so valuable as good behaviour. So they agreed to stop complaining, to enjoy the blessings already possessed, and try to deserve them, lest they should be taken away entirely, instead of increased; and I believe they were never disappointed, or sorry that they took the old woman's advice."

"Now, Marmee, that is very cunning of you to turn our own stories against us, and give us a sermon instead of a 'spin,'" cried Meg.

"I like that kind of sermon; it's the sort father used to tell us," said Beth, thoughtfully, putting the needles straight on Jo's cushion.

"I don't complain near as much as the others do, and I shall be more careful than ever now, for I've had warning from Susie's downfall," said Amy, morally.

"We needed that lesson, and we won't forget it. If we do, you just say to us as old Chloe did in Uncle Tom, – 'Tink ob yer marcies, chillen, tink ob yer marcies,'" added Jo, who could not for the life of her help getting a morsel of fun out of the little sermon, though she took it to heart as much as any of them.

CHAPTER FIVE

BEING NEIGHBORLY

~

"What in the world are you going to do now, Jo?" asked Meg, one snowy afternoon, as her sister came clumping through the hall, in rubber boots, old sack and hood, with a broom in one hand and a shovel in the other.

"Going out for exercise," answered Jo, with a mischievous twinkle in her eyes.

"I should think two long walks, this morning, would have been enough. It's cold and dull out, and I advise you to stay, warm and dry, by the fire, as I do," said Meg, with a shiver.

"Never take advice; can't keep still all day, and not being a pussy-cat, I don't like to doze by the fire. I like adventures, and I'm going to find some."

Meg went back to toast her feet, and read "Ivanhoe," and Jo began to dig paths with great energy. The snow was light; and with her broom she soon swept a path all round the garden, for Beth to walk in when the sun came out; and the invalid dolls needed air. Now the garden separated the Marches' house from that of Mr. Laurence; both stood in a suburb of the city, which was still country-like, with groves and lawns, large gardens, and quiet streets. A low hedge parted the two estates. On one side was an old brown house, looking rather bare and shabby, robbed of the vines that in summer covered its walls, and the flowers which then surrounded it. On the other side was a stately mansion, plainly betokening every sort of comfort and luxury, from the big coach-house and well-kept grounds to the conservatory, and the glimpses of lovely things one caught between the rich curtains. Yet it seemed a lonely, lifeless sort of house; for no children frolicked on the lawn, no motherly face ever smiled at the windows, and few people went in and out, except the old gentleman and his grandson.

To Jo's lively fancy this fine house seemed a kind of enchanted palace, full of splendors and delights, which no one enjoyed. She had long wanted to behold these hidden glories, and to know the "Laurence boy," who looked as if he would like to be known, if he only knew how to begin. Since the party she had been more eager than ever, and had planned many ways of making friends with him; but he had not been seen lately, and Jo began to think he had gone away, when she one day spied a brown face at an upper window, looking wistfully down into their garden, where Beth and Amy were snow-balling one another.

"That boy is suffering for society and fun," she said to herself. "His grandpa don't know what's good for him, and keeps him shut up all alone. He needs a lot of jolly boys to play with, or somebody young and lively. I've a great mind to go over and tell the old gentleman so."

The idea amused Jo, who liked to do daring things, and was always scandalizing Meg by her queer performances. The plan of "going over" was not forgotten; and, when the snowy afternoon came, Jo resolved to try what could be done. She saw Mr. Laurence drive off, and then sallied out to dig her way down to the hedge, where she paused, and took a survey. All quiet; curtains down at the lower windows; servants out of sight, and nothing human visible but a curly black head leaning on a thin hand, at the upper window.

"There he is," thought Jo, "poor boy! all alone, and sick, this dismal day! It's a shame! I'll toss up a snow-ball, and make him look out, and then say a kind word to him."

Up went a handful of soft snow, and the head turned at once, showing a face which lost its listless look in a minute, as the big eyes brightened, and the mouth began to smile. Jo nodded, and laughed, and flourished her broom as she called out, –

"How do you do? Are you sick?"

Laurie opened the window and croaked out as hoarsely as a raven, –

"Better, thank you. I've had a horrid cold, and been shut up a week."

"I'm sorry. What do you amuse yourself with?"

"Nothing; it's as dull as tombs up here."

"Don't you read?"

"Not much; they won't let me."

"Can't somebody read to you?"

"Grandpa does, sometimes; but my books don't interest him and I hate to ask Brooke all the time."

"Have someone come and see you, then."

"There isn't any one I'd like to see. Boys make such a row, and my head is weak."

"Isn't there some nice girl who'd read and amuse you? Girls are quiet, and like to play nurse."

"Don't know any."

"You know me," began Jo, then laughed, and stopped.

"So I do! Will you come, please?" cried Laurie.

"I'm not quiet and nice; but I'll come, if mother will let me. I'll go ask her. Shut that window, like a good boy, and wait till I come."

With that, Jo shouldered her broom and marched into the house, wondering what they would all say to her. Laurie was in a little flutter of excitement at the idea of having company, and flew about to get ready; for, as Mrs. March said, he was "a little gentleman," and did honor to the coming guest by brushing his curly pate, putting on a fresh collar, and trying to tidy up the room, which, in spite of half a dozen servants, was anything but neat. Presently, there came a loud ring, then a decided voice, asking for "Mr. Laurie," and a surprised-looking servant came running up to announce a young lady.

"All right, show her up, it's Miss Jo," said Laurie, going to the door of his little parlor to meet Jo, who appeared, looking rosy and kind, and quite at her ease, with a covered dish in one hand, and Beth's three kittens in the other.

"Here I am, bag and baggage," she said, briskly. "Mother sent her love, and was glad if I could do anything for you. Meg wanted me to bring some of her blanc-mange; she makes it very nice, and Beth thought her cats would be comforting. I knew you'd shout at them, but I couldn't refuse, she was so anxious to do something."

It so happened that Beth's funny loan was just the thing; for, in laughing over the kits, Laurie forgot his bashfulness, and grew sociable at once.

"That looks too pretty to eat," he said, smiling with pleasure, as Jo uncovered the dish, and showed the blanc-mange, surrounded by a garland of green leaves, and the scarlet flowers of Amy's pet geranium.

"It isn't anything, only they all felt kindly, and wanted to show it. Tell the girl to put it away for your tea; it's so simple, you can eat it; and, being soft, it will slip down without hurting your sore throat. What a cosy room this is."

"It might be, if it was kept nice; but the maids are lazy, and I don't know how to make them mind. It worries me, though."

"I'll right it up in two minutes; for it only needs to have the hearth brushed, so, – and the things stood straight on the mantelpiece, so, – and the books put here, and the bottles there, and your sofa turned from the light, and the pillows plumped up a bit. Now, then, you're fixed."

And so he was; for, as she laughed and talked, Jo had whisked things into place, and given quite a different air to the room. Laurie watched her in respectful silence; and, when she beckoned him to his sofa, he sat down with a sigh of satisfaction, saying, gratefully, –

"How kind you are! Yes, that's what it wanted. Now please take the big chair, and let me do something to amuse my company."

"No; I came to amuse you. Shall I read aloud?" and Jo looked affectionately toward some inviting books near by.

"Thank you; I've read all those, and if you don't mind, I'd rather talk," answered Laurie.

"Not a bit; I'll talk all day if you'll only set me going. Beth says I never know when to stop."

"Is Beth the rosy one, who stays at home a good deal, and sometimes goes out with a little basket?" asked Laurie, with interest.

"Yes, that's Beth; she's my girl, and a regular good one she is, too."

"The pretty one is Meg, and the curly-haired one is Amy, I believe?"

"How did you find that out?"

Laurie colored up, but answered, frankly, "Why, you see, I often hear you calling to one another, and when I'm alone up here, I can't help looking over at your house, you always seem to be having such good times. I beg your pardon for being so rude, but sometimes you forget to put down the curtains at the window where the flowers are; and, when the lamps are lighted, it's like looking at a picture to see the fire, and you all round the table with your mother; her face is right opposite, and it looks so sweet behind the flowers, I can't help watching it. I haven't got any mother, you know;" and Laurie poked the fire to hide a little twitching of the lips that he could not control.

The solitary, hungry look in his eyes went straight to Jo's warm heart. She had been so simply taught that there was no nonsense in her head, and at fifteen she was as innocent and frank as any child. Laurie was sick and lonely; and, feeling how rich she was in home-love and happiness, she gladly tried to share it with him. Her brown face was friendly, and her sharp voice unusually gentle, as she said, —

"We'll never draw that curtain any more, and I give you leave to look as much as you like. I just wish, though, instead of peeping, you'd come over and see us. Mother is so splendid, she'd do you heaps of good, and Beth would sing to you if *I* begged her to, and Amy would dance; Meg and I would make you laugh over our funny stage properties, and we'd have jolly times. Wouldn't your grandpa let you?"

"I think he would, if your mother asked him. He's very kind, though he don't look it; and he lets me do what I like, pretty much, only he's afraid I might be a bother to strangers," began Laurie, brightening more and more.

"We are not strangers, we are neighbors, and you needn't think you'd be a bother. We *want* to know you, and I've been trying to do it this ever so long. We haven't been here a great while, you know, but we have got acquainted with all our neighbors but you."

"You see, grandpa lives among his books, and doesn't mind much what happens outside. Mr. Brooke, my tutor, don't stay here, you know, and I have no one to go round with me, so I just stop at home and get on as I can."

"That's bad; you ought to make a dive, and go visiting everywhere you are asked; then you'll have lots of friends, and pleasant places to go to. Never mind being bashful, it won't last long if you keep going."

Laurie turned red again, but wasn't offended at being accused of bashfulness; for there was so much good-will in Jo, it was impossible not to take her blunt speeches as kindly as they were meant.

"Do you like your school?" asked the boy, changing the subject, after a little pause, during which he stared at the fire, and Jo looked about her well pleased.

"Don't go to school; I'm a business man – girl, I mean. I go to wait on my aunt, and a dear, cross old soul she is, too," answered Jo.

Laurie opened his mouth to ask another question; but remembering just in time that it wasn't manners to make too many inquiries into people's affairs, he shut it again, and looked uncomfortable. Jo liked his good breeding, and didn't mind having a laugh at Aunt March, so she gave him a lively description of the fidgety old lady, her fat poodle, the parrot that talked Spanish, and the library where she revelled. Laurie enjoyed that immensely; and when she told about the prim old gentleman who came once to woo Aunt March, and, in the middle of a fine speech, how Poll had tweaked his wig off to his great dismay, the boy lay back and laughed till the tears ran down his cheeks, and a maid popped her head in to see what was the matter.

"Oh! that does me no end of good; tell on, please," he said, taking his face out of the sofa-cushion, red and shining with merriment.

Much elated with her success, Jo did "tell on," all about their plays and plans, their hopes and fears for father, and the most interesting events of the little world in which the sisters lived. Then they got to talking about books; and to Jo's delight she found that Laurie loved them as well as she did, and had read even more than herself.

"If you like them so much, come down and see ours. Grandpa is out, so you needn't be afraid,' said Laurie, getting up.

"I'm not afraid of anything," returned Jo, with a toss of the head.

"I don't believe you are!" exclaimed the boy, looking at her with much admiration, though he privately thought she would have good reason to be a trifle afraid of the old gentleman, if she met him in some of his moods.

The atmosphere of the whole house being summer-like, Laurie led the way from room to room, letting Jo stop to examine whatever struck her fancy; and so at last they came to the library, where she clapped her hands, and pranced, as she always did when especially delighted. It was lined with books, and there were pictures and statues, and distracting little cabinets full of coins and curiosities, and Sleepy-Hollow chairs, and queer tables, and bronzes; and, best of all, a great, open fireplace, with quaint tiles all round it.

"What richness!" sighed Jo, sinking into the depths of a velvet chair, and gazing about her with an air of intense satisfaction. "Theodore Laurence, you ought to be the happiest boy in the world," she added, impressively.

"A fellow can't live on books," said Laurie, shaking his head, as he perched on a table opposite.

Before he could say more, a bell rung, and Jo flew up, exclaiming with alarm, "Mercy me! it's your grandpa!"

"Well, what if it is? You are not afraid of anything, you know," returned the boy, looking wicked.

"I think I am a little bit afraid of him, but I don't know why I should be. Marmee said I might come, and I don't think you're any the worse for it," said Jo, composing herself, though she kept her eyes on the door.

"I'm a great deal better for it, and ever so much obliged. I'm only afraid you are very tired talking to me; it was *so* pleasant, I couldn't bear to stop," said Laurie, gratefully.

"The doctor to see you, sir," and the maid beckoned as she spoke.

"Would you mind if I left you for a minute? I suppose I must see him," said Laurie.

"Don't mind me. I'm as happy as a cricket here," answered Jo.

Laurie went away, and his guest amused herself in her own way. She was standing before a fine portrait of the old gentleman, when the door opened again, and, without turning, she said decidedly, "I'm sure now that I shouldn't be afraid of him, for he's got kind eyes, though his mouth is grim, and he looks as if he had a tremendous will of his own. He isn't as handsome as *my* grandfather, but I like him."

"Thank you, ma'am," said a gruff voice behind her; and there, to her great dismay, stood old Mr. Laurence.

Poor Jo blushed till she couldn't blush any redder, and her heart began to beat uncomfortably fast as she thought what she had said. For a minute a wild desire to run away possessed her; but that was cowardly, and the girls would laugh at her; so she resolved to stay, and get out of the scrape as she could. A second look showed her that the living eyes, under the bushy gray eyebrows, were kinder even than the painted ones; and there was a sly twinkle in them, which lessened her fear a good deal. The gruff voice was gruffer than ever, as the old gentleman said abruptly, after that dreadful pause, "So, you're not afraid of me, hey?"

"Not much, sir."

"And you don't think me as handsome as your grandfather?"

"Not quite, sir."

"And I've got a tremendous will, have I?"

"I only said I thought so."

"But you like me, in spite of it?"

"Yes, I do, sir."

That answer pleased the old gentleman; he gave a short laugh, shook hands with her, and putting his fingers under her chin, turned up her face, examined it gravely, and let it go, saying, with a nod, "You've got your grandfather's spirit, if you haven't his face. He *was* a fine man, my dear; but, what is better, he was a brave and an honest one, and I was proud to be his friend."

"Thank you, sir;" and Jo was quite comfortable after that, for it suited her exactly.

"What have you been doing to this boy of mine, hey?" was the next question, sharply put.

"Only trying to be neighborly, sir;" and Jo told how her visit came about.

"You think he needs cheering up a bit, do you?"

"Yes, sir; he seems a little lonely, and young folks would do him good, perhaps. We are only girls, but we should be glad to help if we could, for we don't forget the splendid Christmas present you sent us," said Jo, eagerly.

"Tut, tut, tut; that was the boy's affair. How is the poor woman?"

"Doing nicely, sir;" and off went Jo, talking very fast, as she told all about the Hummels, in whom her mother had interested richer friends

The old gentleman turned up her face. (Chapter 5)

The sisters sat together in the shady nook.
(Chapter 6)

than they were.

"Just her father's way of doing good. I shall come and see your mother some fine day. Tell her so. There's the tea-bell; we have it early, on the boy's account. Come down, and go on being neighborly."

"If you'd like to have me, sir."

"Shouldn't ask you, if I didn't;" and Mr. Laurence offered her his arm with old-fashioned courtesy.

"What *would* Meg say to this?" thought Jo, as she was marched away, while her eyes danced with fun as she imagined herself telling the story at home.

"Hey! why what the dickens has come to the fellow?" said the old gentleman, as Laurie came running down stairs, and brought up with a start of surprise at the astonishing sight of Jo arm in arm with his redoubtable grandfather.

"I didn't know you'd come, sir," he began, as Jo gave him a triumphant little glance.

"That's evident, by the way you racket down stairs. Come to your tea, sir, and behave like a gentleman;" and having pulled the boy's hair by way of a caress, Mr. Laurence walked on, while Laurie went through a series of comic evolutions behind their backs, which nearly produced an explosion of laughter from Jo.

The old gentleman did not say much as he drank his four cups of tea, but he watched the young people, who soon chatted away like old friends, and the change in his grandson did not escape him. There was color, light and life in the boy's face now, vivacity in his manner, and genuine merriment in his laugh.

"She's right; the lad *is* lonely. I'll see what these little girls can do for him," thought Mr. Laurence, as he looked and listened. He liked Jo, for her odd, blunt ways suited him; and she seemed to understand the boy almost as well as if she had been one herself.

If the Laurences had been what Jo called "prim and poky," she would not have got on at all, for such people always made her shy and awkward; but finding them free and easy, she was so herself, and made a good impression. When they rose, she proposed to go, but Laurie said he had something more to show her, and took her away to the conservatory, which had been lighted for her benefit. It seemed quite fairy-like to Jo, as she went up and down the walks, enjoying the blooming walls on either side, – the soft light, the damp, sweet air, and the wonderful vines and trees that hung above her, – while her new friend cut the finest flowers till his hands were full; then he tied them up, saying, with the happy look Jo liked to see, "Please give these to your mother, and tell her I like the medicine she sent me very much."

They found Mr. Laurence standing before the fire in the great drawing-room, but Jo's attention was entirely absorbed by a grand piano which stood open.

"Do you play?" she asked, turning to Laurie with a respectful expression.

"Sometimes," he answered, modestly.

"Please do now; I want to hear it, so I can tell Beth."

"Won't you first?"

"Don't know how; too stupid to learn, but I love music dearly."

So Laurie played, and Jo listened, with her nose luxuriously buried in heliotrope and tea roses. Her respect and regard for the "Laurence boy" increased very much, for he played remarkably well, and didn't put on any airs. She wished Beth could hear him, but she did not say so; only praised him till he was quite abashed and his grandfather came to the rescue. "That will do, that will do, young lady; too many sugar-plums are not good for him. His music isn't bad, but I hope he will do as well in more important things. Going? Well, I'm much obliged to you, and I hope you'll come again. My respects to your mother; good night, Doctor Jo."

He shook hands kindly, but looked as if something did not please him. When they got into the hall, Jo asked Laurie if she had said anything amiss; he shook his head.

"No, it was me; he don't like to hear me play."

"Why not?"

"I'll tell you some day. John is going home with you, as I can't."

"No need of that; I ain't a young lady, and it's only a step. Take care of yourself, won't you?"

"Yes, but you will come again, I hope?"

"If you promise to come and see us after you are well."

"I will."

"Good-night, Laurie!"

"Good-night, Jo, good-night!"

When all the afternoon's adventures had been told, the family felt inclined to visiting in a body, for each found something very attractive in the big house on the other side of the hedge. Mrs. March wanted to talk of her father with the old man who had not forgotten him; Meg longed to walk in the conservatory; Beth sighed for the grand piano; and Amy was eager to see the fine pictures and statues.

"Mother, why didn't Mr. Laurence like to have Laurie play?" asked Jo, who was of an inquiring disposition.

"I am not sure, but I think it was because his son, Laurie's father, married an Italian lady, a musician, which displeased the old man, who is very proud. The lady was good and lovely and accomplished, but he did not like her, and never saw his son after he married. They both died when Laurie was a little child, and then his grandfather took him home. I fancy the boy, who was born in Italy, is not very strong, and the old man is afraid of losing him, which makes him so careful. Laurie comes naturally by his love of music, for he is like his mother, and I dare say his grandfather fears that he may want to be a musician; at any rate, his skill reminds him of the woman he did not like, and so he 'glowered,' as Jo said."

"Dear me, how romantic!" exclaimed Meg.

"How silly," said Jo; "let him be a musician, if he wants to, and not plague his life out sending him to college, when he hates to go."

"That's why he has such handsome black eyes and pretty manners, I suppose; Italians are always nice," said Meg, who was a little sentimental.

"What do you know about his eyes and his manners? You never spoke to him, hardly," cried Jo, who was *not* sentimental.

"I saw him at the party, and what you tell shows that he knows how to behave. That was a nice little speech about the medicine Mother sent him."

"He meant the blanc-mange, I suppose."

"How stupid you are, child; he meant you, of course."

"Did he?" and Jo opened her eyes as if it had never occurred to her before.

"I never saw such a girl! You don't know a compliment when you get it," said Meg, with the air of a young lady who knew all about the matter.

"I think they are a great nonsense, and I'll thank you not to be silly, and spoil my fun. Laurie's a nice boy, and I like him, and I won't have any sentimental stuff about compliments and such rubbish. We'll all be good to him, because he hasn't got any mother, and he *may* come over and see us, mayn't he, Marmee?"

"Yes, Jo, your little friend is very welcome, and I hope Meg will remember that children should be children as long as they can."

"I don't call myself a child, and I'm not in my teens yet," observed Amy. "What do you say, Beth?"

"I was thinking about our 'Pilgrim's Progress,'" answered Beth, who had not heard a word. "How we got out of the Slough and through the Wicket Gate by resolving to be good, and up the steep hill, by trying; and that maybe the house over there, full of splendid things, is going to be our Palace Beautiful."

"We have got to get by the lions, first," said Jo, as if she rather liked the prospect.

BETH FINDS THE PALACE BEAUTIFUL

~

The big house did prove a Palace Beautiful, though it took some time for all to get in, and Beth found it very hard to pass the lions. Old Mr. Laurence was the biggest one; but. after he had called, said something funny or kind to each one of the girls, and talked over old times with their mother, nobody felt much afraid of him, except timid Beth. The other lion was the fact that they were poor and Laurie rich; for this made them shy of accepting favors which they could not return. But after a while they found that he considered them the benefactors, and could not do enough to show how grateful he was for Mrs. March's motherly welcome, their cheerful society, and the comfort he took in that humble home of theirs; so they soon forgot their pride, and interchanged kindnesses without stopping to think which was the greater.

All sorts of pleasant things happened about that time, for the new friendship flourished like grass in spring. Every one liked Laurie, and he privately informed his tutor that "the Marches were regular splendid girls."

With the delightful enthusiasm of youth, they took the solitary boy into their midst, and made much of him, and he found something very charming in the innocent companionship of these simple-hearted girls. Never having known mother or sisters, he was quick to feel the influences they brought about him; and their busy, lively ways made him ashamed of the indolent life he led. He was tired of books, and found people so interesting now, that Mr. Brooke was obliged to make very unsatisfactory reports; for Laurie was always playing truant, and running over to the Marches.

"Never mind, let him take a holiday, and make it up afterward," said the old gentleman. "The good lady next door says he is studying too hard, and needs young society, amusement, and exercise. I suspect she is right, and that I've been coddling the fellow as if I'd been his grandmother. Let him do what he likes, as long as he is happy; he can't get into mischief in that little nunnery over there, and Mrs. March is doing more for him than we can."

What good times they had, to be sure! Such plays and tableaux; such sleigh-rides and skating frolics; such pleasant evenings in the old parlor, and now and then such gay little parties at the great house. Meg could walk in the conservatory whenever she liked, and revel in bouquets; Jo browsed over the new library voraciously, and convulsed the old gentleman with her criticisms; Amy copied pictures and enjoyed beauty to her heart's content, and Laurie played lord of the manor in the most delightful style.

But Beth, though yearning for the grand piano, could not pluck up courage to go to the "mansion of bliss," as Meg called it. She went once with Jo, but the old gentleman, not being aware of her infirmity, stared at her so hard from under his heavy eyebrows, and said "hey!" so loud, that he frightened her so much her "feet chattered on the floor," she told her mother; and she ran away, declaring she would never go there any more, not even for the dear piano. No persuasions or enticements could overcome her fears, till the fact coming to Mr. Laurence's ear in some mysterious way, he set about mending matters. During one of the brief calls he made, he artfully led the conversation to music, and talked away about great singers whom he had seen, fine organs he had heard, and told such charming anecdotes, that Beth found it impossible to stay in her distant corner, but crept nearer and nearer, as if fascinated. At the back of his chair she stopped, and stood listening with her great eyes wide open, and her cheeks red with the excitement of this unusual performance. Taking no more notice of her than if she had been a fly, Mr. Laurence talked on about Laurie's lessons and teachers; and presently, as if the idea had just occurred to him, he said to Mrs. March, –

"The boy neglects his music now, and I'm glad of it, for he was getting too fond of it. But the piano suffers for want of use; wouldn't some of your girls like to run over, and practise on it now and then, just to keep it in tune, you know, ma'am?"

Beth took a step forward, and pressed her hands tightly together, to keep from clapping them, for this was an irresistible temptation; and the thought of practising on that splendid instrument quite took her breath away. Before Mrs. March could reply, Mr. Laurence went on with an odd little nod and smile, –

"They needn't see or speak to any one, but run in at any time, for I'm shut up in my study at the other end of the house. Laurie is out a great deal, and the servants are never near the drawing-room after nine o'clock." Here he rose, as if going, and Beth made up her mind to speak, for that last arrangement left nothing to be desired. "Please tell the young ladies what I say, and if they don't care to come, why, never mind;" here a little hand slipped into his, and Beth looked up at him with a face full of gratitude, as she said, in her earnest, yet timid way, –

"Oh sir, they do care, very, very much!"

"Are you the musical girl?" he asked, without any startling "hey!" as he looked down at her very kindly.

"I'm Beth; I love it dearly, and I'll come if you are quite sure nobody will hear me – and be disturbed," she added, fearing to be rude, and trembling at her own boldness as she spoke.

"Not a soul, my dear; the house is empty half the day, so come and drum away as much as you like, and I shall be obliged to you."

"How kind you are, sir."

Beth blushed like a rose under the friendly look he wore, but she was not frightened now, and gave the big hand a grateful squeeze, because she had no words to thank him for the precious gift he had given her. The old gentleman softly stroked the hair off her forehead, and, stooping down, he kissed her, saying, in a tone few people ever heard, –

"I had a little girl once with eyes like these; God bless you, my dear; good-day, madam," and away he went, in a great hurry.

Beth had a rapture with her mother, and then rushed up to impart the glorious news to her family of invalids, as the girls were not at home. How blithely she sung that evening, and how they all laughed at her, because she woke Amy in the night by playing the piano on her face in her sleep. Next day, having seen both the old and the young gentleman out of the house, Beth, after two or three retreats, fairly got in at the side-door, and made her way, as noiselessly as any mouse to the drawing-room, where her idol stood. Quite by accident, of course, some pretty, easy music lay on the piano; and, with trembling fingers, and frequent stops to listen and look about, Beth at last touched the great instrument, and straightway forgot her fear, herself, and everything else but the unspeakable delight which the music gave her, for it was like the voice of a beloved friend.

She stayed till Hannah came to take her home to dinner; but she had no appetite, and could only sit and smile upon every one in a general state of beatitude.

After that, the little brown hood slipped through the hedge nearly every day, and the great drawing-room was haunted by a tuneful spirit that came and went unseen. She never knew that Mr. Laurence often opened his study door to hear the old-fashioned airs he liked; she never saw Laurie mount guard in the hall, to warn the servants away; she never suspected that the exercise-books and new songs which she found in the rack were put there for her especial benefit; and when he talked to her about music at home, she only thought how kind he was to tell things that helped her so much. So she enjoyed herself heartily, and found, what isn't always the case, that her granted wish was all she had hoped. Perhaps it was because she was so grateful for this blessing that a greater was given her; at any rate, she deserved both.

"Mother, I'm going to work Mr. Laurence a pair of slippers. He is so kind to me I must thank him, and I don't know any other way. Can I do it?" asked Beth, a few weeks after that eventful call of his.

"Yes, dear; it will please him very much, and be a nice way of thanking him. The girls will help you about them, and I will pay for the making up," replied Mrs. March, who took peculiar pleasure in granting Beth's requests, because she so seldom asked anything for herself.

After many serious discussions with Meg and Jo, the pattern was chosen, the materials bought, and the slippers begun. A cluster of grave yet cheerful pansies on a deeper purple ground, was pronounced very appropriate and pretty, and Beth worked away early and late, with occasional lifts over hard parts. She was a nimble little needle-woman, and they were finished before anyone got tired of them. Then she wrote a very short, simple note, and, with Laurie's help, got them smuggled on to the study-table one morning before the old gentleman was up.

When this excitement was over, Beth waited to see what would happen. All that day passed, and a part of the next, before any acknowledgement arrived, and she was beginning to fear she had offended her crotchety friend. On the afternoon of the second day she went out to do an errand, and give poor Joanna, the invalid doll, her daily exercise. As she came up the street on her return she saw three — yes, four heads popping in and out of the parlor windows; and the moment they saw her several hands were waved, and several joyful voices screamed, —

"Here's a letter from the old gentleman; come quick, and read it!"

"Oh, Beth! he's sent you — " began Amy, gesticulating with unseemly energy; but she got no further, for Jo quenched her by slamming down the window.

Beth hurried on in a twitter of suspense; at the door her sisters seized and bore her to the parlor in a triumphal procession, all pointing, and all saying at once, "Look there! look there!" Beth did look, and turned pale with delight and surprise; for there stood a little cabinet piano, with a letter lying on the glossy lid, directed like a sign-board, to "Miss Elizabeth March."

"For me?" gasped Beth, holding on to Jo, and feeling as if she should tumble down, it was such an overwhelming thing altogether.

"Yes; all for you, my precious! Isn't it splendid of him? Don't you think he's the dearest old man in the world? Here's the key in the letter; we didn't open it, but we are dying to know what he says," cried Jo, hugging her sister, and offering the note.

"You read it; I can't, I feel so queer. Oh, it is too lovely!" and Beth hid her face in Jo's apron, quite upset by her present.

Jo opened the paper, and began to laugh, for the first words she saw were:—

MISS MARCH:

Dear Madam —

"How nice it sounds! I wish some one would write to me so!" said Amy, who thought the old-fashioned address very elegant.

I have had many pairs of slippers in my life, but I never had any that suited me so well as yours, [continued Jo]. Heart's-ease is my favorite flower, and these will always remind me of the gentle giver. I like to pay my debts, so I know you will allow "the old gentleman" to send you something which once belonged to the little granddaughter he lost. With hearty thanks, and best wishes, I remain,

Your grateful friend and humble servant,

JAMES LAURENCE.

"There, Beth, that's an honor to be proud of, I'm sure! Laurie told me how fond Mr. Laurence used to be of the child who died, and how he kept all her little things carefully. Just think; he's given you her piano! That comes of having big blue eyes, and loving music," said Jo, trying to soothe Beth, who trembled, and looked more excited than she had ever been before.

"See the cunning brackets to hold candles, and the nice green silk, puckered up with a gold rose in the middle, and the pretty rack and stool, all complete," added Meg, opening the instrument, and displaying its beauties.

"'Your humble servant, James Laurence;'" only think of his writing that to you. I'll tell the girls; they'll think it's killing," said Amy, much impressed by the note.

"Try it, honey; let's hear the sound of the baby pianny," said Hannah, who always took a share in the family joys and sorrows.

So Beth tried it, and every one pronounced it the most remarkable piano ever heard. It had evidently been newly tuned, and put in apple-pie order; but, perfect as it was, I think the real charm of it lay in the happiest of all happy faces which leaned over it, as Beth lovingly touched the beautiful black and white keys, and pressed the bright pedals.

"You'll have to go and thank him," said Jo, by way of a joke; for the idea of the child's really going, never entered her head.

"Yes, I mean to; I guess I'll go now, before I get frightened thinking about it;" and, to the utter amazement of the assembled family, Beth walked deliberately down the garden, through the hedge, and in at the Laurences' door.

"Well, I wish I may die, if it ain't the queerest thing I ever see! The pianny has turned her head; she'd never have gone, in her right mind," cried Hannah, staring after her, while the girls were rendered quite speechless by the miracle.

They would have been still more amazed, if they had seen what Beth did afterward. If you will believe me, she went and knocked at the study door, before she gave herself time to think; and when a gruff voice called out, "Come in!" she did go in, right up to Mr. Laurence, who looked quite taken aback, and held out her hand, saying, with only a small quaver in her voice, "I came to thank you, sir, for – " but she didn't finish, for he looked so friendly that she forgot her speech; and, only remembering that he had lost the little girl he loved, she put both her arms round his neck, and kissed him.

If the roof of the house had suddenly flown off, the old gentleman wouldn't have been more astonished; but he liked it – oh, dear, yes! he liked it amazingly; and was so touched and pleased by that confiding little kiss, that all his crustiness vanished; and he just set her on his knee, and laid his wrinkled cheek against her rosy one, feeling as if he had got his own little granddaughter back again. Beth ceased to fear him from that moment, and sat there talking to him as cosily as if she had known him all her life; for love casts out fear, and gratitude can conquer pride. When she went home, he walked with her to her own gate, shook hands cordially, and touched his hat as he marched back again, looking very stately and erect, like a handsome, soldierly old gentleman, as he was.

When the girls saw that performance, Jo began to dance a jig, by way of expressing her satisfaction; Amy nearly fell out of the window in her surprise, and Meg exclaimed, with uplifted hands, "Well, I do believe the world is coming to an end!"

CHAPTER SEVEN

AMY'S VALLEY
OF HUMILIATION
~

"That boy is a perfect Cyclops, isn't he?" said Amy, one day, as Laurie clattered by on horse-back, with a flourish of his whip as he passed.

"How dare you say so, when he's got both his eyes? and very handsome ones they are, too," cried Jo, who resented any slighting remarks about her friend.

"I didn't mean anything about his eyes, and I don't see why you need fire up when I admire his riding."

"Oh, my goodness! that little goose means a centaur, and she called him a Cyclops," exclaimed Jo, with a burst of laughter.

"You needn't be so rude, it's only a 'lapse of lingy,' as Mr. Davis says," retorted Amy, finishing Jo with her Latin. "I just wish I had a little of the money Laurie spends on that horse," she added, as if to herself, yet hoping her sisters would hear.

"Why?" asked Meg, kindly, for Jo had gone off in another laugh at

Amy's second blunder.

"I need it so much; I'm dreadfully in debt, and it won't be my turn to have the rag-money for a month."

"In debt, Amy; what do you mean?" and Meg looked sober.

"Why, I owe at least a dozen pickled limes, and I can't pay them, you know, till I have money, for Marmee forbid my having anything charged at the shop."

"Tell me all about it. Are limes the fashion now? It used to be pricking bits of rubber to make balls;" and Meg tried to keep her countenance, Amy looked so grave and important.

"Why, you see, the girls are always buying them, and unless you want to be thought mean, you must do it, too. It's nothing but limes now, for everyone is sucking them in their desks in school time, and trading them off for pencils, bead-rings, paper dolls, or something else, at recess. If one girl likes another, she gives her a lime; if she's mad with her, she eats one before her face, and don't offer even a suck. They treat by turns; and I've had ever so many, but haven't returned them, and I ought, for they are debts of honor, you know."

"How much will pay them off, and restore your credit?" asked Meg, taking out her purse.

" A quarter would more than do it, and leave a few cents over for a treat for you. Don't you like limes?"

"Not much; you may have my share. Here's the money; make it last as long as you can, for it isn't very plenty, you know."

"Oh, thank you! it must be so nice to have pocket-money. I'll have a grand feast, for I haven't tasted a lime this week. I felt delicate about taking any, as I couldn't return them, and I'm actually suffering for one."

Next day Amy was rather late at school; but could not resist the temptation of displaying, with pardonable pride, a moist brown paper parcel, before she consigned it to the inmost recesses of her desk. During the next few minutes the rumor that Amy March had got twenty-four delicious limes (she ate one on the way), and was going to treat, circulated through her "set," and the attentions of her friends became quite overwhelming. Katy Brown invited her to her next party on the spot; Mary Kingsley insisted on lending her her watch till recess; and Jenny Snow, a satirical young lady who had basely twitted Amy upon her limeless state, promptly buried the hatchet, and offered to furnish answers to certain appalling sums. But Amy had not forgotten Miss Snow's cutting remarks about "some persons whose noses were not too flat to smell other people's limes, and stuck-up people, who were not too proud to ask for them;" and she instantly crushed "that Snow girl's" hopes by the withering telegram, "You needn't be so polite all of a sudden, for you won't get any."

A distinguished personage happened to visit the school that morning, and Amy's beautifully drawn maps received praise, which honor to her foe rankled in the soul of Miss Snow, and caused Miss March to assume the airs of a studious young peacock. But, alas, alas! pride goes before a fall, and the revengeful Snow turned the tables with disastrous success. No sooner had the guest paid the usual stale compliments, and bowed himself out, than Jenny, under pretence of asking an important question, informed Mr. Davis, the teacher, that Amy March had pickled limes in her desk.

Now Mr. Davis had declared limes a contraband article, and solemnly vowed to ferule publicly the first person who was found breaking the law. This much-enduring man had succeeded in banishing gum after a long and stormy war, had made a bonfire of the confiscated novels and newspapers, had suppressed a private post-office, had forbidden distortions of the face, nicknames, and caricatures, and done all that one man could do to keep half a hundred rebellious girls in order. Boys are trying enough to human patience, goodness knows! but girls are infinitely more so, especially to nervous gentlemen with tyrannical tempers, and no more talent for teaching than "Dr. Blimber". Mr. Davis knew any quantity of Greek, Latin, Algebra, and ologies of all sorts, so he was called a fine teacher; and manners, morals, feelings, and examples were not considered of any particular importance. It was a most unfortunate moment for denouncing Amy, and Jenny knew it. Mr. Davis had evidently taken his coffee too strong that morning; there was an east wind, which always affected his neuralgia, and his pupils had not done him the credit which he felt he deserved; therefore, to use the expressive, if not elegant, language of a school-girl, "he was as nervous as a witch and as cross as a bear." The word "limes" was like fire to powder; his yellow face flushed, and he rapped on his desk with an energy which made Jenny skip to her seat with unusual rapidity.

"Young ladies, attention, if you please!"

At the stern order the buzz ceased, and fifty pairs of blue, black, gray and brown eyes were obediently fixed upon his awful countenance.

"Miss March, come to the desk."

Amy rose to comply, with outward composure, but a secret fear oppressed her, for the limes weighed upon her conscience.

"Bring with you the limes you have in your desk," was the unexpected command which arrested her before she got out of her seat.

"Don't take all," whispered her neighbor, a young lady of great presence of mind.

Amy hastily shook out half a dozen, and laid the rest down before Mr. Davis, feeling that any man possessing a human heart would relent when that delicious perfume met his nose. Unfortunately, Mr. Davis particularly detested the odor of the fashionable pickle, and disgust added to his wrath.

"Is that all?"

"Not quite," stammered Amy.

"Bring the rest, immediately."

With a despairing glance at her set she obeyed.

"You are sure there are no more?"

"I never lie, sir."

"So I see. Now take these disgusting things two by two, and throw them out of the window."

There was a simultaneous sigh, which created quite a little gust as the last hope fled, and the treat was ravished from their longing lips. Scarlet with shame and anger, Amy went to and fro twelve mortal times; and as each doomed couple, looking, oh, so plump and juicy! fell from her reluctant hands, a shout from the street completed the anguish of the girls, for it told them that their feast was being exulted over by the little Irish children, who were their sworn foes. This — this was too much; all flashed indignant or appealing glances at the inexorable Davis, and one passionate lime-lover burst into tears.

As Amy returned from her last trip, Mr. Davis gave a portentous "hem," and said, in his most impressive manner, —

"Young ladies, you remember what I said to you a week ago. I am sorry this has happened; but I never allow my rules to be infringed, and I *never* break my word. Miss March, hold out your hand."

Amy started, and put both her hands behind her, turning on him an imploring look, which pleaded for her better than the words she could not utter. She was rather a favorite with "old Davis," as, of course, he was called, and it's my private belief that he *would* have broken his word if the indignation of one irrepressible young lady had not found vent in a hiss. That hiss, faint as it was, irritated the irascible gentleman, and sealed the culprit's fate.

"Your hand, Miss March!" was the only answer her mute appeal received; and, too proud to cry or beseech, Amy set her teeth, threw back her head defiantly, and bore without flinching several tingling blows on her little palm. They were neither many nor heavy, but that made no difference to her. For the first time in her life she had been struck; and the disgrace, in her eyes, was as deep as if he had knocked her down.

"You will now stand on the platform till recess," said Mr. Davis, resolved to do the thing thoroughly, since he had begun.

That was dreadful; it would have been bad enough to go to her seat and see the pitying faces of her friends, or the satisfied ones of her few enemies; but to face the whole school, with that shame fresh upon her, seemed impossible, and for a second she felt as if she could only drop down where she stood, and break her heart with crying. A bitter sense of wrong, and the thought of Jenny Snow, helped her to bear it; and, taking the ignominious place, she fixed her eyes on the stove-funnel above what now seemed a sea of faces, and stood there so motionless and white, that the girls found it very hard to study, with that pathetic little figure before them.

During the fifteen minutes that followed, the proud and sensitive little girl suffered a shame and pain which she never forgot. To others it might seem a ludicrous or trivial affair, but to her it was a hard experience; for during the twelve years of her life she had been governed by love alone, and a blow of that sort had never touched her before. The smart of her hand, the ache of her heart, were forgotten in the sting of the thought, –

"I shall have to tell at home, and they will be so disappointed in me!"

The fifteen minutes seemed an hour; but they came to an end at last, and the word "recess!" had never seemed so welcome to her before.

"You can go, Miss March," said Mr. Davis, looking, as he felt, uncomfortable.

He did not soon forget the reproachful look Amy gave him, as she went, without a word to any one, straight into the anteroom, snatched her things, and left the place "forever," as she passionately declared to herself. She was in a sad state when she got home; and when the older girls arrived, some time later, an indignation meeting was held at once. Mrs. March did not say much, but look disturbed, and comforted her afflicted little daughter in her tenderest manner. Meg bathed the insulted hand with glycerine and tears; Beth felt that even her beloved kittens would fail as a balm for griefs like this, and Jo wrathfully proposed that Mr. Davis be arrested without delay, while Hannah shook her fist at the "villain," and pounded potatoes for dinner as if she had him under her pestle.

No notice was taken of Amy's flight, except by her mates; but the sharp-eyed demoiselles discovered that Mr. Davis was quite benignant in the afternoon, also unusually nervous. Just before school closed, Jo appeared, wearing a grim expression, as she stalked up to the desk, and delivered a letter from her mother; then collected Amy's property, and departed, carefully scraping the mud from her boots on the door-mat, as if she shook the dust of the place off her feet.

"Yes, you can have a vacation from school, but I want you to study a little every day, with Beth," said Mrs. March, that evening. "I don't approve of corporal punishment, especially for girls. I dislike Mr. Davis' manner of teaching, and don't think the girls you associate with are doing you any good, so I shall ask your father's advice before I send you anywhere else."

"That's good! I wish all the girls would leave, and spoil his old school. It's perfectly maddening to think of those lovely limes," sighed Amy, with the air of a martyr.

"I am not sorry you lost them, for you broke the rules, and deserved some punishment for disobedience," was the severe reply which rather disappointed the young lady, who expected nothing but sympathy.

"Do you mean you are glad I was disgraced before the whole school?" cried Amy.

"I should not have chosen that way of mending a fault," replied her mother; "but I'm not sure that it won't do you more good than a milder method. You are getting to be altogether too conceited and important, my dear, and it is quite time you set about correcting it. You have a good many little gifts and virtues, but there is no need of parading them, for conceit spoils the finest genius. There is not much danger that real talent or goodness will be overlooked long; even if it is, the consciousness of possessing and using it well should satisfy one, and the great charm of all power is modesty."

"So it is," cried Laurie, who was playing chess in a corner with Jo. "I knew a girl, once, who had a really remarkable talent for music, and she didn't know it; never guessed what sweet little things she composed when she was alone, and wouldn't have believed it if any one had told her."

"I wish I'd known that nice girl, maybe she would have helped me, I'm so stupid," said Beth, who stood beside him, listening eagerly.

"You do know her, and she helps you better than any one else could," answered Laurie, looking at her with such mischievous meaning in his merry black eyes, that Beth suddenly turned very red, and hid her face in the sofa-cushion, quite overcome by such an unexpected discovery.

Jo let Laurie win the game, to pay for that praise of her Beth, who could not be prevailed upon to play for them after her compliment. So Laurie did his best, and sang delightfully, being in a particularly lively humor, for to the Marches he seldom showed the moody side of his character. When he was gone, Amy, who had been pensive all evening, said, suddenly, as if busy over some new idea, —

"Is Laurie an accomplished boy?"

"Yes; he has had an excellent education, and has much talent; he will make a fine man, if not spoilt by petting," replied her mother.

"And he isn't conceited, is he?" asked Amy.

"Not in the least; that is why he is so charming, and we all like him so much."

"I see; it's nice to have accomplishments, and be elegant; but not to show off, or get perked up," said Amy, thoughtfully.

"These things are always seen and felt in a person's manner and conversation, if modestly used; but it is not necessary to display them," said Mrs. March.

"Any more than it's proper to wear all your bonnets, and gowns, and ribbons, at once, that folks may know you've got 'em," added Jo; and the lecture ended in a laugh.

CHAPTER EIGHT

JO MEETS APOLLYON

~

"Girls, where are you going?" asked Amy, coming into their room one Saturday afternoon, and finding them getting ready to go out, with an air of secrecy which excited her curiosity. "Never mind; little girls shouldn't ask questions," returned Jo, sharply.

Now if there *is* anything mortifying to our feelings, when we are young, it is to be told that; and to be bidden to "run away, dear," is still more trying to us. Amy bridled up at this insult, and determined to find out the secret, if she teased for an hour. Turning to Meg, who never refused her anything very long, she said, coaxingly, "Do tell me! I should think you might let me go, too; for Beth is fussing over her dolls, and I haven't got anything to do, and am *so* lonely."

"I can't, dear, because you aren't invited," began Meg; but Jo broke in impatiently, "Now, Meg, be quiet, or you will spoil it all. You can't go, Amy; so don't be a baby, and whine about it."

"You are going somewhere with Laurie, I know you are, you were whispering and laughing together, on the sofa, last night, and you stopped when I came in. Aren't you going with him?"

"Yes, we are; now do be still, and stop bothering."

Amy held her tongue, but used her eyes, and saw Meg slip a fan into her pocket.

"I know! I know! you're going to the hall to see the 'Seven Castles!'" she cried; adding, resolutely, "and I *shall* go, for mother said I might see it; and I've got my rag-money, and it was mean not to tell me in time."

"Just listen to me a minute, and be a good child," said Meg, soothingly. "Mother doesn't wish you to go this week, because your eyes are not well enough yet to bear the light of this fairy piece. Next week you can go with Beth and Hannah, and have a nice time."

"I don't like that half as well as going with you and Laurie. Please let me; I've been sick with this cold so long, and shut up, I'm dying for some fun. Do, Meg! I'll be ever so good," pleaded Amy, looking as pathetic as she could.

"Suppose we take her. I don't believe mother would mind, if we bundle her up well," began Meg.

"If *she* goes I shan't; and if I don't, Laurie won't like it; and it will be very rude, after he invited only us, to go and drag in Amy. I should think she'd hate to poke herself where she isn't wanted," said Jo, crossly, for she disliked the trouble of overseeing a fidgety child, when she wanted to enjoy herself.

Her tone and manner angered Amy, who began to put her boots on, saying, in her most aggravating way, "I *shall* go; Meg says I may; and if I pay for myself, Laurie hasn't anything to do with it."

"You can't sit with us, for our seats are reserved, and you mustn't sit alone; so Laurie will give you his place, and that will spoil our pleasure; or he'll get another seat for you, and that isn't proper, when you weren't asked. You shan't stir a step; so you may just stay where you are," scolded Jo, crosser than ever, having just pricked her finger in her hurry.

Sitting on the floor, with one boot on, Amy began to cry, and Meg to reason with her, when Laurie called from below, and the two girls hurried down, leaving their sister wailing; for now and then she forgot her grown-up ways, and acted like a spoilt child. Just as the party was setting out, Amy called over the banisters, in a threatening voice, "You'll be sorry for this, Jo March! see if you ain't."

"Fiddlesticks!" returned Jo, slamming the door.

They had a charming time, for "The Seven Castles of the Diamond Lake" was as brilliant and wonderful as heart could wish. But, in spite of the comical red imps, sparkling elves, and gorgeous princes and princesses, Jo's pleasure had a drop of bitterness in it; the fairy queen's yellow curls reminded her of Amy; and between the acts she amused herself with wondering what her sister would do to make her "sorry for it." She and Amy had had many lively skirmishes in the course of their lives, for both had quick tempers, and were apt to be violent when fairly roused. Amy teased Jo, and Jo irritated Amy, and semi-occasional explosions occurred, of which both were much ashamed afterward. Although the oldest, Jo had the least self-control, and had hard times trying to curb the fiery spirit which was continually getting her into trouble; her anger never lasted long, and, having humbly confessed her fault, she sincerely repented, and tried to do better. Her sisters used to say, that they rather liked to get Jo into a fury, because she was such an angel afterward. Poor Jo tried desperately to be good, but her bosom enemy was always ready to flame up and defeat her; and it took years of patient effort to subdue it.

When they got home, they found Amy reading in the parlor. She assumed an injured air as they came in; never lifted her eyes from her book, or asked a single question. Perhaps curiosity might have conquered resentment, if Beth had not been there to inquire, and receive a glowing description of the play. On going up to put away her best hat, Jo's first look was toward the bureau; for, in their last quarrel, Amy had soothed her feelings by turning Jo's top drawer upside down, on the floor. Everything was in its place, however; and after a hasty glance into her various closets, bags and boxes, Jo decided that Amy had forgiven and forgotten her wrongs.

There Jo was mistaken; for next day she made a discovery which produced a tempest. Meg, Beth, and Amy were sitting together, late in the afternoon, when Jo burst into the room, looking excited, and demanding, breathlessly, "Has any one taken my story?"

Meg and Beth said "No," at once, and looked surprised; Amy poked the fire, and said nothing. Jo saw her color rise, and was down upon her in a minute.

"Amy, you've got it!"

"No, I haven't."

"You know where it is, then!"

"No, I don't."

"That's a fib!" cried Jo, taking her by the shoulders, and looking fierce enough to frighten a much braver child than Amy.

"It isn't. I haven't got it, don't know where it is now, and don't care."

"You know something about it, and you'd better tell at once, or I'll make you," and Jo gave her a slight shake.

"Scold as much as you like, you'll never see your silly old story again," cried Amy, getting excited in her turn.

"Why not?"

"I burnt it up."

"What! my little book I was so fond of, and worked over, and meant to finish before father got home! Have you really burnt it?" said Jo, turning very pale, while her eyes kindled and her hands clutched Amy nervously.

"Yes, I did! I told you I'd make you pay for being so cross yesterday, and I have, so – "

Amy got no further, for Jo's hot temper mastered her, and she shook Amy till her teeth chattered in her head; crying in a passion of grief and anger, –

"You wicked, wicked girl! I never can write it again, and I'll never forgive you as long as I live."

Meg flew to rescue Amy, and Beth to pacify Jo, but Jo was quite beside herself, and, with a parting box on her sister's ear, she rushed out of the room up to the old sofa in the garret, and finished her fight alone.

The storm cleared up below, for Mrs. March came home, and, having heard the story, soon brought Amy to a sense of the wrong she had done her sister. Jo's book was the pride of her heart, and was regarded by her family as a literary sprout of great promise. It was only half a dozen little fairy tales, but Jo had worked over them patiently, putting her whole heart into her work, hoping to make something good enough to print. She had just copied them with great care, and had destroyed the old manuscript, so that Amy's bonfire had consumed the loving work of several years. It seemed a small loss to others, but to Jo it was a dreadful calamity, and she felt that it never could be made up to her. Beth mourned as for a departed kitten, and

Meg refused to defend her pet; Mrs. March looked grave and grieved, and Amy felt that no one would love her till she had asked pardon for the act which she now regretted more than any of them.

When the tea-bell rung, Jo appeared, looking so grim and unapproachable, that it took all Amy's courage to say, meekly, –

"Please forgive me, Jo; I'm very, very sorry."

"I never shall forgive you," was Jo's stern answer, and, from that moment, she ignored Amy entirely.

No one spoke of the great trouble, – not even Mrs. March, – for all had learned by experience that when Jo was in that mood words were wasted; and the wisest course was to wait till some little accident, or her own generous nature, softened Jo's resentment, and healed the breach. It was not a happy evening; for, though they sewed as usual, while their mother read aloud from Bremer, Scott, or Edgeworth, something was wanting, and the sweet home-peace was disturbed. They felt this most when singing time came; for Beth could only play, Jo stood dumb as a stone, and Amy broke down, so Meg and mother sung alone. But in spite of their efforts to be as cheery as larks, the flute-like voices did not seem to chord as well as usual, and all felt out of tune.

As Jo received her good-night kiss, Mrs. March whispered gently, –

"My dear, don't let the sun go down upon your anger; forgive each other, help each other, and begin again to-morrow."

Jo wanted to lay her head down on that motherly bosom, and cry her grief and anger all away; but tears were an unmanly weakness, and she felt so deeply injured that she really *couldn't* quite forgive yet. So she winked hard, shook her head, and said, gruffly, because Amy was listening, –

"It was an abominable thing, and she don't deserve to be forgiven."

With that she marched off to bed, and there was no merry or confidential gossip that night.

Amy was much offended that her overtures of peace had been repulsed, and began to wish she had not humbled herself, to feel more injured than ever, and to plume herself on her superior virtue in a way which was particularly exasperating. Jo still looked like a thunder-cloud, and nothing went well all day. It was bitter cold in the morning; she dropped her precious turn-over in the gutter, Aunt March had an attack of fidgets, Meg was pensive, Beth *would* look grieved and wistful when she got home, and Amy kept making remarks about people who were always talking about being good, and yet wouldn't try, when other people set them a virtuous example.

"Everybody is so hateful, I'll ask Laurie to go skating. He is always kind and jolly, and will put me to rights, I know," said Jo to herself, and off she went.

Amy heard the clash of skates, and looked out with an impatient exclamation, —

"There! she promised I should go next time, for this is the last ice we shall have. But it's no use to ask such a cross patch to take me."

"Don't say that; you *were* very naughty, and it *is* hard to forgive the loss of her precious little book; but I think she might do it now, and I guess she will, if you try her at the right minute," said Meg. "Go after them; don't say anything till Jo has got good-natured with Laurie, then take a quiet minute, and just kiss her, or do some kind thing, and I'm sure she'll be friends again, with all her heart."

"I'll try," said Amy, for the advice suited her; and, after a flurry to get ready, she ran after the friends, who were just disappearing over the hill.

It was not far to the river, but both were ready before Amy reached them. Jo saw her coming, and turned her back; Laurie did not see, for he was carefully skating along the shore, sounding the ice, for a warm spell had preceded the cold snap.

"I'll go on to the first bend, and see if it's all right, before we begin to race," Amy heard him say, as he shot away, looking like a young Russian, in his fur-trimmed coat and cap.

Jo heard Amy panting after her run, stamping her feet, and blowing her fingers, as she tried to put her skates on; but Jo never turned, and went slowly zigzagging down the river, taking a bitter, unhappy sort of satisfaction in her sister's troubles. She had cherished her anger till it grew strong, and took possession of her, as evil thoughts and feelings always do, unless cast out at once. As Laurie turned the bend, he shouted back, —

"Keep near the shore; it isn't safe in the middle."

Jo heard, but Amy was just struggling to her feet, and did not catch a word. Jo glanced over her shoulder, and the little demon she was harboring said in her ear, —

"No matter whether she heard or not, let her take care of herself."

Laurie had vanished round the bend; Jo was just at the turn, and Amy, far behind, striking out toward the smoother ice in the middle of the river. For a minute Jo stood still, with a strange feeling at her heart; then she resolved to go on, but something held and turned her round, just in time to see Amy throw up her hands and go down, with a sudden crash of rotten ice, the splash of water, and a cry that made Jo's heart stand still with fear. She tried to call Laurie, but her voice was gone; she tried to rush forward, but her feet seemed to have no strength in them; and, for a second, she could only stand motionless, staring, with a terror-stricken face, at the little blue hood above the black water. Something rushed swiftly by her, and Laurie's voice cried out, —

"Bring a rail; quick, quick!"

How she did it, she never knew; but for the next few minutes she worked as if possessed, blindly obeying Laurie, who was quite self-possessed; and, lying flat, held Amy up by his arm and hockey, till Jo dragged a rail from the fence, and together they got the child out, more frightened than hurt.

"Now then, we must walk her home as fast as we can; pile our things on her, while I get off these confounded skates," cried Laurie, wrapping his coat round Amy, and tugging away at the straps, which never seemed so intricate before.

Shivering, dripping, and crying, they got Amy home; and, after an exciting time of it, she fell asleep, rolled in blankets, before a hot fire. During the bustle Jo had scarcely spoken; but flown about, looking pale and wild, with her things half off, her dress torn, and her hands cut and bruised by ice and rails, and refractory buckles. When Amy was comfortably asleep, the house quiet, and Mrs. March sitting by the bed, she called Jo to her, and began to bind up the hurt hands.

"Are you sure she is safe?" whispered Jo, looking remorsefully at the golden head, which might have been swept away from her sight forever under the treacherous ice.

"Quite safe, dear; she is not hurt, and won't even take cold, I think, you were so sensible in covering and getting her home quickly," replied her mother, cheerfully.

"Laurie did it all; I only let her go. Mother, if she *should* die, it would be my fault;" and Jo dropped down beside the bed, in a passion of penitent tears, telling all that had happened, bitterly condemning her hardness of heart, and sobbing out her gratitude for being spared the heavy punishment which might have come upon her.

"It's my dreadful temper! I try to cure it; I think I have, and then it breaks out worse than ever. Oh, mother! what shall I do! what shall I do?" cried poor Jo, in despair.

"Watch and pray, dear; never get tired of trying; and never think it is impossible to conquer your fault," said Mrs. March, drawing the blowzy head to her shoulder, and kissing the wet cheek so tenderly, that Jo cried harder than ever.

"You don't know; and you can't guess how bad it is! It seems as if I could do anything when I'm in a passion; I get so savage, I could hurt any one, and enjoy it. I'm afraid I *shall* do something dreadful some day, and spoil my life, and make everybody hate me. Oh, mother! help me, do help me!"

"I will, my child; I will. Don't cry so bitterly, but remember this day, and resolve, with all your soul, that you will never know another like it. Jo, dear, we all have our temptations, some far greater than yours, and it often takes us all our lives to conquer them. You think your temper is the worst in the world; but mine used to be just like it."

"Yours, mother? Why, you are never angry!" and, for the moment, Jo forgot remorse in surprise.

"I've been trying to cure it for forty years, and have only succeeded in controlling it. I am angry nearly every day of my life, Jo; but I have learned not to show it; and I still hope to learn not to feel it, though it may take me another forty years to do so."

The patience and the humility of the face she loved so well, was a better lesson to Jo than the wisest lecture, the sharpest reproof. She felt comforted at once by the sympathy and confidence given her; the knowledge that her mother had a fault like hers, and tried to mend it, made her own easier to bear, and strengthened her resolution to cure it; though forty years seemed a rather long time to watch and pray, to a girl of fifteen.

"Mother, are you angry when you fold your lips tight together, and go out of the room sometimes, when Aunt March scolds, or people worry you?" asked Jo, feeling nearer and dearer to her mother than ever before.

"Yes, I've learned to check the hasty words that rise to my lips; and when I feel that they mean to break out against my will, I just go away a minute, and give myself a little shake, for being so weak and wicked," answered Mrs. March, with a sigh and a smile, as she smoothed and fastened up Jo's dishevelled hair.

"How did you learn to keep still? That is what troubles me – for the sharp words fly out before I know what I'm about; and the more I say the worse I get, till it's a pleasure to hurt people's feelings, and say dreadful things. Tell me how you do it, Marmee dear."

"My good mother used to help me – "

"As you do us – " interrupted Jo, with a grateful kiss.

"But I lost her when I was a little older than you are, and for years had to struggle on alone, for I was too proud to confess my weakness to anyone else. I had a hard time, Jo, and shed a good many bitter tears over my failures; for, in spite of my efforts, I never seemed to get on. Then your father came, and I was so happy that I found it easy to be good. But by and by, when I had four little daughters round me, and we were poor, then the old trouble began again; for I am not patient by nature, and it tried me very much to see my children wanting anything."

"Poor mother! What helped you then?"

"Your father, Jo. He never loses patience, – never doubts or complains, – but always hopes, and works, and waits so cheerfully, that one is ashamed to do otherwise before him. He helped and comforted me, and showed me that I must try to practise all the virtues I would have my little girls possess, for I was their example. It was easier to try for your sakes than for my own; a startled or surprised look from one of you, when I spoke sharply, rebuked me more than any words could have done; and the love, respect, and confidence of my children was the sweetest reward I could receive for my efforts to be the woman I would have them copy."

"Oh, mother! if I'm ever half as good as you, I shall be satisfied," cried Jo, much touched.

"I hope you will be a great deal better, dear; but you must keep watch over your 'bosom enemy,' as father calls it, or it may sadden, if not spoil your life. You have had a warning; remember it, and try with heart and soul to master this quick temper, before it brings you greater sorrow and regret than you have known to-day."

"I will try, mother; I surely will. But you must help me, remind me, and keep me from flying out. I used to see father sometimes put his finger on his lips, and look at you with a very kind, but sober face; and you always folded your lips tight, or went away; was he reminding you then?" asked Jo, softly.

"Yes; I asked him to help me so, and he never forgot it, but saved me from many a sharp word by that little gesture and kind look."

Jo saw that her mother's eyes filled, and her lips trembled, as she spoke; and, fearing that she had said too much, she whispered anxiously, "Was it wrong to watch you, and to speak of it? I didn't mean to be rude, but it's so comfortable to say all I think of you, and feel so safe and happy here."

"My Jo, you may say anything to your mother, for it is my greatest happiness and pride to feel that my girls confide in me, and know how much I love them."

"I thought I'd grieve you."

"No, dear; but speaking of father reminded me how much I miss him, how much I owe him, and how faithfully I should watch and work to keep his little daughters safe and good for him."

"Yet you told him to go, mother, and didn't cry when he went, and never complain now, or seem as if you needed any help," said Jo, wondering.

"I gave my best to the country I love, and kept my tears till he was gone. Why should I complain, when we both have merely done our duty, and will surely be the happier for it in the end? If I don't seem to need help, it is because I have a better friend, even than father, to comfort and sustain me. My child, the troubles and temptations of your life are beginning, and may be many; but you can overcome and outlive them all, if you learn to feel the strength and tenderness of your Heavenly Father as you do that of your earthly one. The more you love and trust Him, the nearer you will feel to Him, and the less you will depend on human power and wisdom. His love and care never tire or change, can never be taken from you, but may become the source of life-long peace, happiness, and strength. Believe this heartily, and go to God with all your little cares, and hopes, and sins, and sorrows, as freely and confidingly as you come to your mother."

Jo's only answer was to hold her mother close, and, in the silence which followed, the sincerest prayer she had ever prayed left her heart, without words; for in that sad, yet happy hour, she had learned not only the bitterness of remorse and despair, but the sweetness of self-denial and self-control; and, led by her mother's hand, she had drawn nearer to the Friend who welcomes every child with a love stronger than that of any father, tenderer than that of any mother.

Amy stirred, and sighed in her sleep; and, as if eager to begin at once to mend her fault, Jo looked up with an expression on her face which it had never worn before.

"I let the sun go down on my anger; I wouldn't forgive her, and to-day, if it hadn't been for Laurie, it might have been too late! How could I be so wicked?" said Jo, half aloud, as she leaned over her sister, softly stroking the wet hair scattered on the pillow.

As if she heard, Amy opened her eyes, and held out her arms, with a smile that went straight to Jo's heart. Neither said a word, but they hugged one another close, in spite of the blankets, and everything was forgiven and forgotten in one hearty kiss.

CHAPTER NINE

MEG GOES TO VANITY FAIR

~

"I do think it was the most fortunate thing in the world, that those children should have the measles just now," said Meg, one April day, as she stood packing the "go abroady" trunk in her room, surrounded by her sisters.

"And so nice of Annie Moffat, not to forget her promise. A whole fortnight of fun will be regularly splendid," replied Jo, looking like a windmill, as she folded skirts with her long arms.

"And such lovely weather; I'm so glad of that," added Beth, tidily sorting neck and hair ribbons in her best box, lent for the great occasion.

"I wish I was going to have a fine time, and wear all these nice things," said Amy, with her mouth full of pins, as she artistically replenished her sister's cushion.

"I wish you were all going; but, as you can't, I shall keep my adventures to tell you when I come back. I'm sure it's the least I can do, when you have been so kind, lending me things, and helping me get ready," said Meg, glancing round the room at the very simple outfit, which seemed nearly perfect in their eyes.

"What did mother give you out of the treasure-box?" asked Amy, who had not been present at the opening of a certain cedar chest, in which Mrs. March kept a few relics of past splendor, as gifts for her girls when the proper time came.

"A pair of silk stockings, that pretty carved fan, and a lovely blue sash. I wanted the violet silk; but there isn't time to make it over, so I must be contented with my old tarlatan."

"It will look nicely over my new muslin skirt, and the sash will set it off beautifully. I wish I hadn't smashed my coral bracelet, for you might have had it," said Jo, who loved to give and lend, but whose possessions were usually too dilapidated to be of much use.

"There is a lovely old-fashioned pearl set in the treasure-box; but mother said real flowers were the prettiest ornament for a young girl, and Laurie promised to send me all I want," replied Meg. "Now, let me see; there's my new gray walking-suit, – just curl up the feather in my hat, Beth, – then my poplin, for Sunday, and the small party, – it looks heavy for spring, don't it? the violet silk would be so nice; oh dear!"

"Never mind; you've got the tarlatan for the big party, and you always look like an angel in white," said Amy, brooding over the little store of finery in which her soul delighted.

"It isn't low-necked, and it doesn't sweep enough, but it will have to do. My blue house-dress looks so well, turned and freshly trimmed, that I feel as if I'd got a new one. My silk sacque isn't a bit the fashion, and my bonnet don't look like Sallie's; I didn't like to say anything, but I was dreadfully disappointed in my umbrella. I told mother black, with a white handle, but she forgot, and bought a green one, with an ugly yellowish handle. It's strong and neat, so I ought not to complain, but I know I shall feel ashamed of it beside Annie's silk one, with a gold top,' sighed Meg, surveying the little umbrella with great disfavor.

"Change it," advised Jo.

"I won't be so silly, or hurt Marmee's feelings, when she took so much pains to get my things. It's a nonsensical notion of mine, and I'm not going to give up to it. My silk stockings and two pairs of spandy gloves are my comfort. You are a dear, to lend me yours, Jo; I feel so rich, and sort of elegant, with two new pairs, and the old ones cleaned up for common;" and Meg took a refreshing peep at her glove-box.

"Annie Moffat has blue and pink bows on her night-caps; would you put some on mine?" she asked, as Beth brought up a pile of snowy muslins, fresh from Hannah's hands.

"No, I wouldn't; for the smart caps won't match the plain gowns, without any trimming on them. Poor folks shouldn't rig," said Jo, decidedly.

"I wonder if I shall *ever* be happy enough to have real lace on my clothes, and bows on my caps?" said Meg, impatiently.

"You said the other day that you'd be perfectly happy if you could only go to Annie Moffat's," observed Beth, in her quiet way.

"So I did! Well, I *am* happy and I *won't* fret; but it does seem as if the more one gets the more one wants, don't it? There, now, the trays are ready, and everything in but my ball-dress, which I shall leave for mother," said Meg, cheering up, as she glanced from the half-filled trunk to the many-times pressed and mended white tarlatan, which she called her "ball-dress", with an important air.

The next day was fine, and Meg departed, in style, for a fortnight of novelty and pleasure. Mrs. March had consented to the visit rather reluctantly, fearing that Margaret would come back more discontented than she went. But she had begged so hard, and Sallie had promised to take good care of her, and a little pleasure seemed so delightful after a winter of hard work, that the mother yielded, and the daughter went to take her first taste of fashionable life.

The Moffats *were* very fashionable, and simple Meg was rather daunted, at first, by the splendor of the house, and the elegance of its occupants. But they were kindly people, in spite of the frivolous life they led, and soon put their guest at her ease. Perhaps Meg felt, without understanding why, that they were not particularly cultivated or intelligent people, and that all their gilding could not quite conceal the ordinary material of which they were made. It certainly was agreeable to fare sumptuously, drive in a fine carriage, wear her best frock every day, and do nothing but enjoy herself. It suited her exactly; and soon she began to imitate the manners and conversation of those about her; to put on little airs and graces, use French phrases, crimp her hair, take in her dresses, and talk about the fashions, as well as she could. The more she saw of Annie Moffat's pretty things, the more she envied her, and sighed to be rich. Home now looked bare and dismal as she thought of it, work grew harder than ever, and she felt that she was a very destitute and much injured girl, in spite of the new gloves and silk stockings.

She had not much time for repining, however, for the three young girls were busily employed in "having a good time." They shopped, walked, rode, and called all day; went to theatres and operas, and frolicked at home in the evening; for Annie had many friends, and knew how to entertain them. Her older sisters were very fine young ladies, and one was engaged, which was extremely interesting and romantic, Meg thought. Mr. Moffat was a fat, jolly old gentleman, who knew her father; and Mrs. Moffat a fat, jolly old lady, who took as great a fancy to Meg as her daughter had done. Every one petted her; and "Daisy," as they called her, was in a fair way to have her head turned.

When the evening for the "small party" came, she found that the poplin wouldn't do at all, for the other girls were putting on thin dresses, and making themselves very fine indeed; so out came the tarlatan, looking older, limper, and shabbier than ever, beside Sallie's crisp new one. Meg saw the girls glance at it, and then at one another, and her cheeks began to burn; for, with all her gentleness, she was very proud. No one said a word about it, but Sallie offered to dress her hair, and Annie to tie her sash, and Belle, the engaged sister, praised her white arms; but, in their kindness, Meg saw only pity for her poverty, and her heart felt very heavy as she stood by herself, while the others laughed and, chattered, prinked, and flew about like gauzy butterflies. The hard, bitter feeling was getting pretty bad, when the maid brought in a box of flowers. Before she could speak, Annie had the cover off, and all were exclaiming at the lovely roses, heath, and ferns within.

"It's for Belle, of course; George always sends her some, but these are altogether ravishing," cried Annie, with a great sniff.

"They are for Miss March, the man said. And here's a note," put in the maid, holding it to Meg.

"What fun! Who are they from? Didn't know you had a lover," cried the girls, fluttering about Meg in a high state of curiosity and surprise.

"The note is from mother, and the flowers from Laurie," said Meg, simply, yet much gratified that he had not forgotten her.

"Oh, indeed!" said Annie, with a funny look, as Meg slipped the note in her pocket, as a sort of talisman against envy, vanity, and false pride; for the few loving words had done her good, and the flowers cheered her up by their beauty.

Feeling almost happy again, she laid by a few ferns and roses for herself, and quickly made the rest up in dainty bouquets for the breasts, hair, or skirts of her friends, offering them so prettily, that Clara, the elder sister, told her she was "the sweetest little thing she ever saw;" and they looked quite charmed with her small attention. Somehow the kind act finished her despondency; and, when all the rest went to show themselves to Mrs. Moffat, she saw a happy, bright-eyed face in the mirror, as she laid her ferns against her rippling hair, and fastened the roses in the dress that didn't strike her as so *very* shabby now.

She enjoyed herself very much that evening, for she danced to her heart's content; every one was very kind, and she had three compliments. Annie made her sing, and some one said she had a remarkably fine voice; Major Lincoln asked who "the fresh little girl, with the beautiful eyes, was;" and Mr. Moffat insisted on dancing with her, because she "didn't dawdle, but had some spring in her," as he gracefully expressed it. So, altogether, she had a very nice time, till she overheard a bit of conversation, which disturbed her extremely. She was sitting just inside the conservatory, waiting for her partner to bring her an ice, when she heard a voice ask, on the other side of the flowery wall, —

"How old is she?"

"Sixteen or seventeen, I should say," replied another voice.

"It would be a grand thing for one of those girls, wouldn't it? Sallie says they are very intimate now, and the old man quite dotes on them."

"Mrs. M. has made her plans, I dare say, and will play her cards well, early as it is. The girl evidently doesn't think of it yet," said Mrs. Moffat.

"She told that fib about her mamma, as if she did know, and colored up when the flowers came, quite prettily. Poor thing! she'd be so nice if she was only got up in style. Do you think she'd be offended if we offered to lend her a dress for Thursday?" asked another voice.

"She's proud, but I don't believe she'd mind, for that dowdy tarlatan is all she has got. She may tear it to-night, and that will be a good excuse for offering a decent one."

"We'll see, I shall ask that Laurence, as a compliment to her, and we'll have fun about it afterwards."

Here Meg's partner appeared, to find her looking much flushed, and rather agitated. She was proud, and her pride was useful just then, for it helped her hide her mortification, anger, and disgust, at what she had just heard; for, innocent and unsuspicious as she was, she could not help understanding the gossip of her friends. She tried to forget it, but could not, and kept repeating to herself, "Mrs. M. has made her plans," "that fib about her mamma," and "dowdy tarlatan," till she was ready to cry, and rush home to tell her troubles, and ask for advice. As that was impossible, she did her best to seem gay; and, being rather excited, she succeeded so well that no one dreamed what an effort she was making. She was very glad when it was all over, and she was quiet in her bed, where she could think and wonder and fume till her head ached, and her hot cheeks were cooled by a few natural tears. Those foolish, yet well-meant words, had opened a new world to Meg, and much disturbed the peace of the old one, in which, till now, she had lived as happily as a child. Her innocent friendship with Laurie was spoilt by the silly speeches she had overheard; her faith in her mother was a little shaken by the worldly plans attributed to her by Mrs. Moffat, who judged others by herself; and the sensible resolution to be contented with the simple wardrobe which suited a poor man's daughter was weakened by the unnecessary pity of girls, who thought a shabby dress one of the greatest calamities under heaven.

Poor Meg had a restless night, and got up heavy-eyed, unhappy, half resentful toward her friends, and half ashamed of herself for not speaking out frankly, and setting everything right. Everybody dawdled that morning, and it was noon before the girls found energy enough even to take up their worsted work. Something in the manner of her friends struck Meg at once; they treated her with more respect, she thought; took quite a tender interest in what she said, and looked at her with eyes that plainly betrayed curiosity. All this surprised and flattered her, though she did not understand it till Miss Belle looked up from her writing, and said, with a sentimental air, –

"Daisy, dear, I've sent an invitation to your friend, Mr. Laurence, for Thursday. We should like to know him, and it's only a proper compliment to you."

Meg colored, but a mischievous fancy to tease the girls made her reply, demurely, –

"You are very kind, but I'm afraid he won't come."

"Why not, cherie?" asked Miss Belle.

"He's too old."

"My child, what do you mean? What is his age, I beg to know!" cried Miss Clara.

"Nearly seventy, I believe," answered Meg, counting stitches to hide the merriment in her eyes.

"You sly creature! of course we meant the young man," exclaimed Miss Belle, laughing.

"There isn't any; Laurie is only a little boy," and Meg laughed also at the queer look which the sisters exchanged, as she thus described her supposed lover.

"About your age," Nan said.

"Nearer my sister Jo's; *I* am seventeen in August," returned Meg, tossing her head.

"It's very nice of him to send you flowers, isn't it?" said Annie, looking wise about nothing.

"Yes, he often does to all of us; for their house is full, and we are so fond of them. My mother and old Mr. Laurence are friends, you know, so it is quite natural that we children should play together;" and Meg hoped they would say no more.

"It's evident Daisy isn't out yet," said Miss Clara to Belle, with a nod.

"Quite a pastoral state of innocence all round," returned Miss Belle, with a shrug.

"I'm going out to get some little matters for my girls; can I do anything for you, young ladies?" asked Mrs. Moffat, lumbering in, like an elephant, in silk and lace.

"No, thank you, ma'am," replied Sallie. "I've got my new pink silk for Thursday, and don't want a thing."

"Nor I – " began Meg, but stopped, because it occurred to her that she *did* want several things, and could not have them.

"What shall you wear?" asked Sallie.

"My old white one again, if I can mend it fit to be seen; it got sadly torn last night," said Meg, trying to speak quite easily, but feeling very uncomfortable.

"Why don't you send home for another?" said Sallie, who was not an observing young lady.

"I haven't got any other." It cost Meg an effort to say that, but Sallie did not see it, and exclaimed, in amiable surprise, –

"Only that? how funny – ," She did not finish her speech, for Belle shook her head at her, and broke in, saying, kindly, –

"Not at all; where is the use of having a lot of dresses when she isn't out? There's no need of sending home, Daisy, even if you had a dozen, for I've got a sweet blue silk laid away, which I've outgrown, and you shall wear it to please me; won't you, dear?"

"You are very kind, but I don't mind my old dress, if you don't; it does well enough for a little girl like me," said Meg.

"Now do let me please myself by dressing you up in style. I admire to do it, and you'd be a regular little beauty, with a touch here and there. I shan't let any one see you till you are done, and then we'll burst upon them like Cinderella and her godmother, going to the ball," said Belle, in her persuasive tone.

Meg couldn't refuse the offer so kindly made, for a desire to see if she would be "a little beauty" after touching up caused her to accept, and forget all her former uncomfortable feelings towards the Moffats.

On the Thursday evening, Belle shut herself up with her maid; and, between them, they turned Meg into a fine lady. They crimped and curled her hair, they polished her neck and arms with some fragrant powder, touched her lips with coralline salve, to make them redder, and Hortense would have added "a *soupçon* of rouge," if Meg had not rebelled. They laced her into a sky-blue dress, which was so tight she could hardly breathe, and so low in the neck that modest Meg blushed at herself in the mirror. A set of silver filigree was added, bracelets, necklace, brooch, and even earrings, for Hortense tied them on with a bit of pink silk which did not show. A cluster of tea rose-buds at the bosom, and a *ruche,* reconciled Meg to the display of her pretty white shoulders, and a pair of high-heeled blue silk boots satisfied the last wish of her heart. A laced handkerchief, a plumy fan, and a bouquet in a silver holder, finished her off; and Miss Belle surveyed her with the satisfaction of a little girl with a newly dressed doll.

"Mademoiselle is charmante, tres jolie, is she not?" cried Hortense, clasping her hands in an affected rapture.

"Come and show yourself," said Miss Belle, leading the way to the room where the others were waiting.

As Meg went rustling after, with her long skirts trailing, her earrings tinkling, her curls waving, and her heart beating, she felt as if her "fun" had really begun at last, for the mirror had plainly told her that she *was* "a little beauty." Her friends repeated the pleasing phrase enthusiastically; and, for several minutes she stood, like a jackdaw in the fable, enjoying her borrowed plumes, while the rest chattered like a party of magpies.

"While I dress, do you drill her, Nan, in the management of her skirt, and those French heels, or she will trip herself up. Put your silver butterfly in the middle of that white barbe, and catch up that long curl on the left side of her head, Clara, and don't any of you disturb the charming work of my hands," said Belle, as she hurried away, looking well pleased with her success.

I'm afraid to go down, I feel so queer and stiff, and half dressed," said Meg to Sallie, as the bell rang, and Mrs. Moffat sent to ask the young ladies to appear at once.

"You don't look a bit like yourself, but you are very nice. I'm nowhere beside you, for Belle has heaps of taste, and you're quite French, I assure you. Let your flowers hang; don't be so careful of them, and be sure you don't trip,"returned Sallie, trying not to care that Meg was prettier than herself.

Keeping that warning carefully in mind, Margaret got safely down stairs, and sailed into the drawing-rooms, where the Moffats and a few early guests were assembled. She very soon discovered that there is a charm about fine clothes which attracts a certain class of people, and secures their respect. Several young ladies who had taken no notice of her before, were very affectionate all of a sudden; several young gentlemen, who had only stared at her at the other party, now not only stared, but asked to be introduced, and said all manner of foolish, but agreeable things to her; and several old ladies, who sat on sofas, and criticised the rest of the party, inquired who she was, with an air of interest. She heard Mrs. Moffat reply to one of them, –

"Daisy March — father a colonel in the army — one of our first families, but reverses of fortune, you know; intimate friends of the Laurences; sweet creature, I assure you; my Ned is quite wild about her."

"Dear me!" said the old lady, putting up her glass for another observation of Meg, who tried to look as if she had not heard, and been rather shocked at Mrs. Moffat's fibs.

The "queer feeling" did not pass away, but she imagined herself acting the new part of a fine lady, and so got on pretty well, though the tight dress gave her a side-ache, the train kept getting under her feet, and she was in constant fear lest her earrings should fly off, and get lost or broken. She was flirting her fan, and laughing at the feeble jokes of a young gentleman who tried to be witty, when she suddenly stopped laughing, and looking confused; for, just opposite, she saw Laurie. He was staring at her with undisguised surprise, and disapproval also, she thought; for, though he bowed and smiled, yet something in his honest eyes made her blush, and wish she had her old dress on. To complete her confusion, she saw Belle nudge Annie, and both glance from her to Laurie, who, she was happy to see, looked unusually boyish and shy.

"Silly creatures, to put such thoughts into my head! I won't care for it, or let it change me a bit," thought Meg, and rustled across the room to shake hands with her friend.

"I'm glad you've come, I was afraid you wouldn't," she said, with her most grown-up air.

"Jo wanted me to come, and tell her how you looked, so I did," answered Laurie, without turning his eyes upon her, though he half smiled at her maternal tone.

"What shall you tell her?" asked Meg, full of curiosity to know his opinion of her, yet feeling ill at ease with him, for the first time.

"I shall say I didn't know you; for you look so grown-up, and unlike yourself, I'm quite afraid of you," he said, fumbling at his glove-button.

"How absurd of you! the girls dressed me up for fun, and I rather like it. Wouldn't Jo stare if she saw me?" said Meg, bent on making him say whether he thought her improved or not.

"Yes, I think she would," returned Laurie, gravely.

"Don't you like me so?" asked Meg.

"No, I don't," was the blunt reply.

"Why not?" in an anxious tone.

He glanced at her frizzled head, bare shoulders, and fantastically trimmed dress, with an expression that abashed her more than his answer, which had not a particle of his usual politeness about it.

"I don't like fuss and feathers."

That was altogether too much from a lad younger than herself; and Meg walked away, saying petulantly, –

"You are the rudest boy I ever saw."

Feeling very much ruffled, she went and stood at a quiet window, to cool her cheeks, for the tight dress gave her an uncomfortably brilliant color. As she stood there, Major Lincoln passed by; and, a minute after, she heard him saying to his mother, –

"They are making a fool of that little girl; I wanted you to see her, but they have spoilt her entirely; she's nothing but a doll, to-night."

"Oh dear!" sighed Meg; "I wish I'd been sensible, and worn my own things; then I should not have disgusted other people, or felt so uncomfortable and ashamed of myself."

She leaned her forehead on the cool pane, and stood half hidden by the curtains, never minding that her favorite waltz had begun, till some one touched her; and, turning, she saw Laurie looking penitent, as he said, with his very best bow, and his hand out, –

"Please forgive my rudeness, and come and dance with me."

"I'm afraid it will be too disagreeable to you," said Meg, trying to look offended, and failing entirely.

"Not a bit of it; I'm dying to do it. Come, I'll be good, I don't like your gown, but I do think you are – just splendid;" and he waved his hands, as if words failed to express his admiration.

Meg smiled, and relented, and whispered, as they stood waiting to catch the time, –

"Take care my skirt don't trip you up; it's the plague of my life, and I was a goose to wear it."

"Pin it round your neck, and then it will be useful," said Laurie, looking down at the little blue boots, which he evidently approved of.

Away they went, fleetly and gracefully; for, having practised at home, they were well-matched, and the blithe young couple were a pleasant sight to see, as they twirled merrily round and round, feeling more friendly than ever after their small tiff.

"Laurie, I want you to do me a favor; will you?" said Meg, as he stood fanning her, when her breath gave out, which it did, very soon, though she would not own why.

"Won't I!" said Laurie, with alacrity.

"Please don't tell them at home about my dress to-night. They won't understand the joke, and it will worry mother."

"Then why did you do it?" said Laurie's eyes, so plainly, that Meg hastily added, –

"I shall tell them, myself, all about it, and ''fess' to mother how silly I've been. But I'd rather do it myself; so you'll not tell, will you?"

"I give you my word I won't; only what shall I say when they ask me?"

"Just say I looked nice, and was having a good time."

"I'll say the first, with all my heart; but how about the other? You don't look as if you were having a good time; are you?" and Laurie looked at her with an expression which made her answer, in a whisper, –

"No; not just now. Don't think I'm horrid; I only wanted a little fun, but this sort don't pay, I find, and I'm getting tired of it."

"Here comes Ned Moffat; what does he want?" said Laurie, knitting his black brows, as if he did not regard his young host in the light of a pleasant addition to the party.

"He put his name down for three dances, and I suppose he's coming for them; what a bore!" said Meg, assuming a languid air, which amused Laurie immensely.

He did not speak to her again till supper-time, when he saw her drinking champagne with Ned, and his friend Fisher, who were behaving "like a pair of fools," as Laurie said to himself, for he felt a brotherly sort of right to watch over the Marches, and fight their battles, whenever a defender was needed.

"You'll have a splitting headache to-morrow, if you drink much of that. I wouldn't, Meg; your mother don't like it, you know," he whispered, leaning over her chair, as Ned turned to refill her glass, and Fisher stooped to pick up her fan.

"I'm not Meg to-night; I'm a 'doll,' who does all sorts of crazy things. To-morrow I shall put away my 'fuss and feathers,' and be desperately good again," she answered, with an affected little laugh.

"Wish to-morrow was here, then," muttered Laurie, walking off, ill-pleased at the change he saw in her.

Meg danced and flirted, chattered and giggled, as the other girls did; after supper she undertook the German, and blundered through it, nearly upsetting her partner with her long skirt, and romping in a way that scandalized Laurie, who looked on and meditated a lecture. But he got no chance to deliver it, for Meg kept away from him till he came to say good-night.

"Remember!" she said, trying to smile, for the splitting headache had already begun.

"Silence à la mort," replied Laurie, with a melodramatic flourish, as he went away.

This little bit of by-play excited Annie's curiosity; but Meg was too tired for gossip, and went to bed, feeling as if she had been to a masquerade, and hadn't enjoyed herself as much as she expected. She was sick all the next day, and on Saturday went home, quite used up with her fortnight's fun, and feeling that she had sat in the lap of luxury long enough.

"It does seem pleasant to be quiet, and not have company manners on all the time. Home *is* a nice place, though it isn't splendid," said Meg, looking about her with a restful expression, as she sat with her mother and Jo on the Sunday evening.

"I'm glad to hear you say so, dear, for I was afraid home would seem dull and poor to you, after your fine quarters," replied her mother, who had given her many anxious looks that day; for motherly eyes are quick to see any change in children's faces.

Meg had told her adventures gayly, and said over and over what a charming time she had had; but something still seemed to weigh upon her spirits, and, when the younger girls were gone to bed, she sat thoughtfully staring at the fire, saying little, and looking worried. As the clock struck nine, and Jo proposed bed, Meg suddenly left her chair, and, taking Beth's stool, leaned her elbows on her mother's knee, saying, bravely, —

"Marmee, I want to ''fess.'"

"I thought so; what is it, dear?"

"Shall I go away?" asked Jo, discreetly.

"Of course not; don't I always tell you everything? I was ashamed to speak of it before the children, but I want you to know all the dreadful things I did at the Moffats."

"We are prepared," said Mrs. March, smiling, but looking a little anxious.

"I told you they rigged me up, but I didn't tell you that they powdered, and squeezed, and frizzled, and made me look like a fashion-plate. Laurie thought I wasn't proper; I know he did, though he didn't say so, and one man called me a 'doll.' I knew it was silly, but they flattered me, and said I was a beauty, and quantities of nonsense, so I let them make a fool of me."

"Is that all?" asked Jo, as Mrs. March looked silently at the downcast face of her pretty daughter, and could not find it in her heart to blame her little follies.

"No; I drank champagne, and romped, and tried to flirt, and was, altogether, abominable," said Meg, self-reproachfully.

"There is something more, I think," and Mrs. March smoothed the soft cheek, which suddenly grew rosy, as Meg answered, slowly, –

"Yes; it's very silly, but I want to tell it, because I hate to have people say and think such things about us and Laurie."

Then she told the various bits of gossip she had heard at the Moffats; and, as she spoke, Jo saw her mother fold her lips tightly, as if ill pleased that such ideas should be put into Meg's innocent mind.

"Well, if that isn't the greatest rubbish I ever heard," cried Jo, indignantly. "Why didn't you pop out and tell them so, on the spot?"

"I couldn't, it was so embarrassing for me. I couldn't help hearing, at first, and then I was so angry and ashamed, I didn't remember that I ought to go away."

"Just wait till *I* see Annie Moffat, and I'll show you how to settle such ridiculous stuff. The idea of having 'plans,' and being kind to Laurie, because he's rich, and may marry us by and by! Won't he shout, when I tell him what those silly things say about us poor children?" and Jo laughed, as if, on second thoughts, the thing struck her as a good joke.

"If you tell Laurie, I'll never forgive you! She mustn't, must she, mother?" said Meg, looking distressed.

"No; never repeat that foolish gossip, and forget it as soon as you can," said Mrs. March, gravely. "I was very unwise to let you go among people of whom I know so little, kind, I dare say, but worldly, ill-bred, and full of these vulgar ideas about young people. I am more sorry than I can express, for the mischief this visit may have done you, Meg."

"Don't be sorry, I won't let it hurt me; I'll forget all the bad, and remember only the good; for I did enjoy a great deal, and thank you very much for letting me go. I'll not be sentimental or dissatisfied, mother; I know I'm a silly little girl, and I'll stay with you till I'm fit to take care of myself. But it *is* nice to be praised and admired, and I can't help saying I like it," said Meg, looking half ashamed of the confession.

"That is perfectly natural, and quite harmless, if the liking does not become a passion, and lead one to do foolish or unmaidenly things. Learn to know and value the praise which is worth having, and to excite the admiration of excellent people, by being modest as well as pretty, Meg."

Margaret sat thinking a moment, while Jo stood with her hands behind her, looking both interested and a little perplexed; for it was a new thing to see Meg blushing and talking about admiration, lovers, and things of that sort, and Jo felt as if during that fortnight, her sister had grown up amazingly, and was drifting away from her into a world where she could not follow.

"Mother, do you have 'plans,' as Mrs. Moffat said?" asked Meg, bashfully.

"Yes, my dear, I have a great many; all mothers do, but mine differ somewhat from Mrs. Moffat's, I suspect. I will tell you some of them, for the time has come when a word may set this romantic little head and heart of yours right, on a very serious subject. You are young, Meg; but not too young to understand me, and mothers' lips are the fittest to speak of such things to girls like you. Jo, your turn will come in time, perhaps, so listen to my 'plans,' and help me carry them out, if they are good."

Jo went and sat on one arm of the chair, looking as if she thought they were about to join in some very solemn affair. Holding a hand of each, and watching the two young faces wistfully, Mrs. March said, in her serious yet cheery way, —

"I want my daughters to be beautiful, accomplished, and good; to be admired, loved, and respected, to have a happy youth, to be well and wisely married, and to lead useful, pleasant lives, with as little care and sorrow to try them as God sees fit to send. To be loved and chosen by a good man is the best and sweetest thing which can happen to a woman; and I sincerely hope my girls may know this beautiful experience. It is natural to think of it, Meg; right to hope and wait for it, and wise to prepare for it; so that, when the happy time comes, you may feel ready for the duties, and worthy of the joy. My dear girls, I *am* ambitious for you, but not to have you make a dash in the world, — marry rich men merely because they are rich, or have splendid houses, which are not homes, because love is wanting. Money is a needful and precious thing, — and, when well used, a noble thing, — but I never want you to think it is the first or only prize to strive for. I'd rather see you poor men's wives, if you were happy, beloved, contented, than queens on thrones, without self-respect and peace."

"Poor girls don't stand any chance, Belle says, unless they put themselves forward," sighed Meg.

"Then we'll be old maids," said Jo, stoutly.

"Right, Jo; better be happy old maids than unhappy wives, or unmaidenly girls, running about to find husbands," said Mrs. March, decidedly. "Don't be troubled, Meg; poverty seldom daunts a sincere lover. Some of the best and most honored women I know were poor girls, but so love-worthy that they were not allowed to be old maids. Leave these things to time; make this home happy, so that you may be fit for homes of your own, if they are offered you, and contented here if they are not. One thing remember, my girls, mother is always ready to be your confidant, father to be your friend; and both of us trust and hope that our daughters, whether married or single, will be the pride and comfort of our lives."

"We will, Marmee, we will!" cried both, with all their hearts, as she bade them good-night.

CHAPTER TEN

THE P.C. AND P.O.

~

As spring came on, a new set of amusements became the fashion, and the lengthening days gave long afternoons for work and play of all sorts. The garden had to be put in order, and each sister had a quarter of the little plot to do what she liked with. Hannah used to say, "I'd know which each of them gardings belonged to, ef I see 'em in Chiny;" and so she might, for the girls' tastes differed as much as their characters. Meg's had roses and heliotrope, myrtle, and a little orange tree in it. Jo's bed was never alike two seasons, for she was always trying experiments; this year it was to be a plantation of sunflowers, the seeds of which cheerful and aspiring plant were to feed "Aunt Cockle-top" and her family of chicks. Beth had old-fashioned, fragrant flowers in her garden; sweet peas and mignonette, larkspur, pinks, pansies, and southernwood, with chickweed for the bird, and catnip for the pussies. Amy had a bower in hers, — rather small and earwiggy, but very pretty to look at, — with honeysuckles and morning-glories hanging their colored horns and bells in graceful wreaths all over it; tall white lilies, delicate ferns, and as many brilliant, picturesque plants as would consent to blossom there.

Gardening, walks, rows on the river, and flower-hunts employed the fine days; and for rainy ones, they had house diversions, – some old, some new, – all more or less original. One of these was the "P.C."; for, as secret societies were the fashion, it was thought proper to have one; and, as all of the girls admired Dickens, they called themselves the Pickwick Club. With a few interruptions, they had kept this up for a year, and met every Saturday evening in the big garret, on which occasions the ceremonies were as follows: Three chairs were arranged in a row before a table, on which was a lamp, also four white badges, with a big "P.C." in different colors on each, and the weekly newspaper, called "The Pickwick Portfolio," to which all contributed something; while Jo, who revelled in pens and ink, was the editor. At seven o'clock, the four members ascended to the club-room, tied their badges round their heads, and took their seats with great solemnity. Meg, as the eldest, was Samuel Pickwick; Jo, being of a literary turn, Augustus Snodgrass; Beth, because she was round and rosy, Tracy Tupman; and Amy, who was always trying to do what she couldn't, was Nathaniel Winkle. Pickwick, the President, read the paper, which was filled with original tales, poetry, local news, funny advertisements, and hints, in which they good-naturedly reminded each other of their faults and short-comings. On one occasion Mr. Pickwick put on a pair of spectacles without any glasses, rapped upon the table, hemmed, and, having stared hard at Mr. Snodgrass, who was tilting back in his chair, till he arranged himself properly, began to read, –

"The Pickwick Portfolio"

MAY 20, 18–

Poet's Corner

ANNIVERSARY ODE

Again we meet to celebrate
  With badge and solemn rite,
Our fifty-second anniversary,
  In Pickwick Hall, to-night.

We are all here in perfect health,
  None gone from our small band;
Again we see each well-known face,
  And press each friendly hand.

Our Pickwick, always at his post,
  With reverence we greet,
As, spectacles on nose, he reads
  Our well-filled weekly sheet.

Although he suffers from a cold,
  We joy to hear him speak,
For words of wisdom from him fall,
  In spite of croak or squeak.

Old six-foot Snodgrass looms on
  high,
With elephantine grace,
And beams upon the company,
  With brown and jovial face.

Poetic fire lights up his eye,
  He struggles 'gainst his lot;
Behold ambition on his brow,
  And on his nose a blot!

Next our peaceful Tupman comes,
  So rosy, plump and sweet,
Who chokes with laughter at the
  puns,
  And tumbles off his seat.

Prim little Winkle too is here,
  With every hair in place,
A model of propriety,
  Though he hates to wash his
  face.

The year is gone, we still unite
  To joke and laugh and read,
And tread the path of literature
  That doth to glory lead.

Long may our paper prosper well,
  Our club unbroken be,
And coming years their blessings
  pour
  On the useful, gay "P.C."
                    A. SNODGRASS.

THE MASKED MARRIAGE
A TALE OF VENICE

Gondola after gondola swept up to the marble steps, and left its lovely load to swell the brilliant throng that filled the stately halls of Count de Adelon. Knights and ladies, elves and pages, monks and flower-girls, all mingled gaily in the dance. Sweet voices and rich melody filled the air; and so with mirth and music the masquerade went on.

"Has your Highness seen the Lady Viola to-night?" asked a gallant troubadour of the fairy queen who floated down the hall upon his arm.

"Yes; is she not lovely, though so sad? Her dress is well chosen, too, for in a week she weds Count Antonio, whom she passionately hates."

"By my faith, I envy him. Yonder he comes, arrayed like a bridegroom, except the black mask. When that is off we shall see how he regards the fair maid whose heart he cannot win, though her stern father bestows her hand," returned the troubadour.

"'Tis whispered that she loves the young English artist who haunts her steps, and is spurned by the old count," said the lady, as they joined the dance.

The revel was at its height when a priest appeared, and, withdrawing the young pair to an alcove hung with purple velvet, he motioned them to kneel. Instant silence fell upon the gay throng; and not a sound, but the dash of fountains or the rustle of orange groves sleeping in the moonlight, broke the hush, as Count de Adelon spoke thus: —

"My lords and ladies; pardon the ruse by which I have gathered you here to witness the marriage of my daughter. Father, we wait your services."

All eyes turned toward the bridal party, and a low murmur of amazement went through the throng, for neither bride nor groom removed their masks. Curiosity and wonder possessed all hearts, but respect restrained all tongues till the holy rite was over. Then the eager spectators gathered round the count, demanding an explanation.

"Gladly would I give it if I could; but I only know that it was the whim of my timid Viola, and I yielded to it. Now, my children, let the play end. Unmask, and receive my blessing."

But neither bent the knee; for the young bridegroom replied, in a tone that startled all listeners, as the mask fell, disclosing the noble face of Ferdinand Devereux, the artist lover; and, leaning on the breast where now flashed the star of an English earl, was the lovely Viola, radiant with joy and beauty.

"My Lord, you scornfully bade me claim your daughter when I could boast as high a name and vast a fortune as the Count Antonio. I can do more; for even your ambitious soul cannot refuse the Earl of Devereux and De Vere, when he gives his ancient name and boundless wealth in return for the beloved hand of this fair lady, now my wife."

The count stood like one changed to stone; and, turning to the bewildered crowd, Ferdinand added, with a gay smile of triumph, "To you, my gallant friends, I can only wish that your wooing may prosper as mine has done; and that you may all win as fair a bride as I have, by this masked marriage."

S. PICKWICK.

Why is the P.C. like the Tower of Babel? It is full of unruly members.

THE HISTORY OF A SQUASH

One upon a time a farmer planted a little seed in his garden, and after a while it sprouted and became a vine, and bore many squashes. One day in October, when they were ripe, he picked one and took it to market. A grocer man bought and put it in his shop. That same morning, a little girl, in a brown hat and blue dress, with a round face and snubby nose, went and bought it for her mother. She lugged it home, cut it up, and boiled it in the big pot; mashed some of it, with salt and butter, for dinner; and to the rest she added a pint of milk, two eggs, four spoons of sugar, nutmeg, and some crackers; put it in a deep dish, and baked it till it was brown and nice; and next day it was eaten by a family named March.

T. TUPMAN.

MR. PICKWICK, *Sir:–*

I address you upon the subject of sin the sinner I mean is a man named Winkle who makes trouble in his club by laughing and sometimes won't write his piece in this fine paper I hope you will pardon his badness and let him send a French fable because he can't write out of his head as he has so many lessons to do and no brains in future I will try to take time by the fetlock and prepare some work which will be all *commy la fo* that means all right I am in haste as it is nearly school time.

Yours respectably, N. WINKLE.

[The above is a manly and handsome acknowledgement of past misdemeanors. If our young friend studied punctuation, it would be well.]

A SAD ACCIDENT

On Friday last, we were startled by a violent shock in our basement, followed by cries of distress. On rushing, in a body, to the cellar, we discovered our beloved President prostrate upon the floor, having tripped and fallen while getting wood for domestic purposes. A perfect scene of ruin met our eyes; for in his fall Mr. Pickwick had plunged his head and shoulders into a tub of water, upset a keg of soft soap upon his manly form, and torn his garments badly. On being removed from this perilous situation, it was discovered that he had suffered no injury but several bruises; and, we are happy to add, is now doing well.

ED.

THE PUBLIC BEREAVEMENT

It is our painful duty to record the sudden and mysterious disappearance of our cherished friend, Mrs. Snowball Pat Paw. This lovely and beloved cat was the pet of a large circle of warm and admiring friends; for her beauty attracted all eyes, her grace and virtues endeared her to all hearts, and her loss is deeply felt by the whole community.

When last seen, she was sitting at the gate, watching the butcher's cart; and it is feared that some villain, tempted by her charms, basely stole her. Weeks have passed, but no trace of her has been discovered; and we relinquish all hope, tie a black ribbon to her basket, set aside her dish, and weep for her as one lost to us forever.

A sympathizing friend sends the following gem:—

A LAMENT
FOR S. B. PAT PAW

We mourn the loss of our little pet,
  And sigh o'er her hapless fate,
For never more by the fire she'll sit
  Nor play by the old green gate.

The little grave where her infant
  sleeps,
Is 'neath the chestnut tree;
  But o'er *her* grave we may not
  weep,
  We know not where it may be.

Her empty bed, her idle ball,
  Will never see her more;
No gentle tap, no loving purr
  Is heard at the parlor door.

Another cat comes after her mice,
A cat with a dirty face;
But she does not hunt as our darling
did,
Nor play with her airy grace.

Her stealthy paws tread the very
hall
Where Snowball used to play,
But she only spits at the dogs our pet
So gallantly drove away.

She is useful and mild, and does
her best,
But she is not fair to see;
And we cannot give her your place,
dear,
Nor worship her as we worship
thee.

A.S.

ADVERTISEMENTS

MISS ORANTHY BLUGGAGE, the accomplished Strong-Minded Lecturer, will deliver her famous Lecture on "WOMAN AND HER POSITION," at Pickwick Hall, next Saturday Evening, after the usual performances.

A WEEKLY MEETING will be held at Kitchen Place, to teach young ladies how to cook. Hannah Brown will preside; and all are invited to attend.

THE DUSTPAN SOCIETY will meet on Wednesday next, and parade in the upper story of the Club House. All members to appear in uniform and shoulder their brooms at nine precisely.

MRS. BETH BOUNCER will open her new assortment of Doll's Millinery next week. The latest Paris Fashions have arrived, and orders are respectfully solicited.

A NEW PLAY will appear at the Barnville Theatre, in the course of a few weeks, which will surpass anything ever seen on the American stage. "THE GREEK SLAVE, or Constantine the Avenger," is the name of this thrilling drama!!!

HINTS

If S. P. didn't use so much soap on his hands, he wouldn't always be late at breakfast. A. S. is requested not to whistle in the street. T. T. please don't forget Amy's napkin. N. W. must not fret because his dress has not nine tucks.

WEEKLY REPORT.
Meg – Good.
Jo – Bad.
Beth – Very good.
Amy – Middling.

As the President finished reading the paper (which I beg leave to assure my readers is a *bona fide* copy of one written by *bona fide* girls once upon a time), a round of applause followed, and then Mr. Snodgrass rose to make a proposition.

"Mr. President and gentlemen," he began, assuming a parliamentary attitude and tone, "I wish to propose the admission of a new member; one who highly deserves the honor, would be deeply grateful for it, and would add immensely to the spirit of the club, the literary value of the paper, and be no end jolly and nice. I propose Mr. Theodore Laurence as an honorary member of the P.C. Come now, do have him."

Jo's sudden change of tone made the girls laugh; but all looked rather anxious, and no one said a word, as Snodgrass took his seat.

"We'll put it to the vote," said the President. "All in favour of this motion please to manifest it by saying 'Aye.'"

A loud response from Snodgrass, followed, to everybody's surprise, by a timid one from Beth.

"Contrary minded say 'No.'"

Meg and Amy were contrary minded; and Mr. Winkle rose to say, with great elegance, "We don't wish any boys; they only joke and bounce about. This is a ladies' club, and we wish it to be private and proper."

"I'm afraid he'll laugh at our paper, and make fun of us afterwards," observed Pickwick, pulling the little curl on her forehead, as she always did when doubtful.

Up rose Snodgrass, very much in earnest. "Sir! I give you my word as a gentleman, Laurie won't do anything of the sort. He likes to write, and he'll give a tone to our contributions, and keep us from being sentimental, don't you see? We can do so little for him, and he does so much for us, I think the least we can do is to offer him a place here, and make him welcome, if he comes."

This artful allusion to benefits conferred, brought Tupman to his feet, looking as if he had quite made up his mind.

"Yes; we ought to do it, even if we *are* afraid. I say he *may* come, and his grandpa too, if he likes."

This spirited burst from Beth electrified the club, and Jo left her seat to shake hands approvingly. "Now then, vote again. Everybody remember it's our Laurie, and say 'Aye!'" cried Snodgrass, excitedly.

"Aye! aye! aye!" replied three voices at once.

"Good! bless you! now, as there's nothing like 'taking time by the *fetlock*,' as Winkle characteristically observes, allow me to present the new member;" and, to the dismay of the rest of the club, Jo threw open the door of the closet, and displayed Laurie sitting on a rag-bag, flushed and twinkling with suppressed laughter.

"You rogue! you traitor! Jo, how could you?" cried the three girls, as Snodgrass led her friend triumphantly forth; and, producing both a chair and a badge, installed him in a jiffy.

"The coolness of you two rascals is amazing," began Mr. Pickwick, trying to get up an awful frown, and only succeeding in producing an amiable smile. But the new member was equal to the occasion; and, rising with a grateful salutation to the Chair, said, in the most engaging manner, —

"Mr. President and ladies, — I beg pardon, gentlemen, — allow me to introduce myself as Sam Weller, the very humble servant of the club."

"Good! good!" cried Jo, pounding with the handle of the old warming-pan, on which she leaned.

"My faithful friend and noble patron," continued Laurie, with a wave of the hand, "who has so flatteringly presented me, is not to be blamed for the base stratagem of to-night. I planned it, and she only gave in after lots of teasing."

"Come now, don't lay it all on yourself; you know I proposed the cupboard," broke in Snodgrass, who was enjoying the joke amazingly.

"Never mind what she says. I'm the wretch that did it, sir," said the new member, with a Welleresque nod to Mr. Pickwick. "But on my honor, I never will do so again, and henceforth *dewote* myself to the interest of this immortal club."

"Hear! hear!" cried Jo, clashing the lid of the warming-pan like a cymbal.

"Go on, go on!" added Winkle and Tupman, while the President bowed benignly.

"I merely wish to say, that as a slight token of my gratitude for the honor done me, and as a means of promoting friendly relations between adjoining nations, I have set up a post-office in the hedge in the lower corner of the garden; a fine, spacious building, with padlocks on the doors, and every convenience for the mails, — also the females, if I may be allowed the expression. It's the old martin-house; but I've stopped up the door, and made the roof open, so it will hold all sorts of things, and save our valuable time. Letters, manuscripts, books and bundles can be passed in there; and, as each nation has a key, it will be uncommonly nice, I fancy. Allow me to present the club key; and, with many thanks for your favor, take my seat."

Great applause as Mr. Weller deposited a little key on the table, and subsided; the warming-pan clashed and waved wildly, and it was some time before order could be restored. A long discussion followed, and every one came out surprising, for every one did her best; so it was an unusually lively meeting, and did not adjourn till a late hour, when it broke up with three shrill cheers for the new member.

No one ever regretted the admittance of Sam Weller, for a more devoted, well-behaved, and jovial member no club could have. He certainly did add "spirit" to the meetings, and "a tone" to the paper; for his orations convulsed his hearers, and his contributions were excellent, being patriotic, classical, comical, or dramatic, but never sentimental. Jo regarded them as worthy of Bacon, Milton, or Shakespeare; and remodelled her own works with good effect, she thought.

The P.O. was a capital little institution, and flourished wonderfully, for nearly as many queer things passed through it as through the real office. Tragedies and cravats, poetry and pickles, garden seeds and long letters, music and gingerbread, rubbers, invitations, scoldings, and puppies. The old gentleman liked the fun, and amused himself by sending odd bundles, mysterious messages, and funny telegrams; and his gardener, who was smitten with Hannah's charms, actually sent a love-letter to Jo's care. How they laughed when the secret came out, never dreaming how many love-letters that little post-office would hold in the years to come!

CHAPTER ELEVEN

EXPERIMENTS

~

"The first of June; the Kings are off to the seashore to-morrow, and I'm free! Three months' vacation! how I shall enjoy it!" exclaimed Meg, coming home one warm day to find Jo laid upon the sofa in an unusual state of exhaustion, while Beth took off her dusty boots, and Amy made lemonade for the refreshment of the whole party.

"Aunt March went to-day, for which, oh, be joyful!" said Jo. "I was mortally afraid she'd ask me to go with her; if she had, I should have felt as if I ought to do it; but Plumfield is about as festive as a churchyard, you know, and I'd rather be excused. We had a flurry getting the old lady off, and I had a scare every time she spoke to me, for I was in such a hurry to be through that I was uncommonly helpful and sweet, and feared she'd find it impossible to part from me. I quaked till she was fairly in the carriage, and had a final fright, for, as it drove off, she popped out her head, saying, "Josyphine, won't you – ?" I didn't hear any more, for I basely turned and fled; I did actually run, and whisked round the corner, where I felt safe."

"Poor old Jo! she came in looking as if bears were after her," said Beth, as she cuddled her sister's feet with a motherly air.

"Aunt March is a regular samphire, is she not?" observed Amy, tasting her mixture critically.

"She means *vampire*, not sea-weed; but it don't matter; it's too warm to be particular about one's parts of speech," murmured Jo.

"What shall you do all your vacation?" asked Amy, changing the subject, with tact.

"I shall lie abed, and do nothing," replied Meg, from the depths of the rocking-chair. "I've been routed up early all winter, and had to spend my days working for other people; so now I'm going to rest and revel to my heart's content."

"Hum!" said Jo; "that dozy way wouldn't suit me. I've laid in a heap of books, and I'm going to improve my shining hours reading on my perch in the old apple tree, when I'm not having l—"

"Don't say 'larks!'" implored Amy, as a return snub for the "samphire" correction.

"I'll say 'nightingales,' then, with Laurie; that's proper and appropriate, since he's a warbler."

"Don't let us do any lessons, Beth, for a while, but play all the time, and rest, as the girls mean to," proposed Amy.

"Well, I will, if mother don't mind. I want to learn some new songs, and my children need fixing up for the summer; they are dreadfully out of order, and really suffering for clothes."

"May we, mother?" asked Meg, turning to Mrs. March, who sat sewing, in what they called "Marmee's corner."

"You may try your experiment for a week, and see how you like it. I think by Saturday night you will find that all play, and no work, is as bad as all work, and no play."

"Oh, dear, no! it will be delicious, I'm sure," said Meg, complacently.

"I now propose a toast, as my 'friend and pardner, Sairy Gamp,' says. Fun forever, and no grubbage," cried Jo, rising, glass in hand, as the lemonade went round.

They all drank it merrily, and began the experiment by lounging for the rest of the day. Next morning, Meg did not appear till ten o'clock; her solitary breakfast did not taste good, and the room seemed lonely and untidy, for Jo had not filled the vases, Beth had not dusted, and Amy's books lay scattered about. Nothing was neat and pleasant but "Marmee's corner," which looked as usual; and there she sat, to "rest and read," which meant yawn, and imagine what pretty summer dresses she would get with her salary. Jo spent the morning on the river, with Laurie, and the afternoon reading and crying over "The Wide, Wide World," up in the apple tree. Beth began by rummaging everything out of the big closet, where her family resided; but, getting tired before half done, she left her establishment topsy-turvy, and went to her music, rejoicing that she had no dishes to wash. Amy arranged her bower, put on her best white frock, smoothed her curls, and sat down to draw, under the honeysuckles, hoping some one would see and inquire who the young artist was. As no one appeared but an inquisitive daddy-long-legs, who examined her work with interest, she went to walk, got caught in a shower, and came home dripping.

At tea-time they compared notes, and all agreed that it had been a delightful, though unusually long day. Meg, who went shopping in the afternoon, and got a "sweet blue muslin," had discovered, after she had cut the breadths off, that it wouldn't wash, which mishap made her slightly cross. Jo had burnt the skin off her nose boating, and got a raging headache by reading too long. Beth was worried by the confusion of her closet, and the difficulty of learning three or four songs at once; and Amy deeply regretted the damage done her frock, for Katy Brown's party was to be the next day; and now, like Flora McFlimsy, she had "nothing to wear." But these were mere trifles; and they assured their mother that the experiment was working finely. She smiled, said nothing, and, with Hannah's help, did their neglected work, keeping home pleasant, and the domestic machinery running smoothly. It was astonishing what a peculiar and uncomfortable state of things was produced by the "resting and revelling" process. The days kept getting longer and longer; the weather was unusually variable, and so were tempers; an unsettled feeling possessed every one, and Satan found plenty of mischief for the idle hands to do. As the height of luxury, Meg put out some of her sewing, and then found time hang so heavily, that she fell to snipping and spoiling her clothes, in her attempts to furbish them up, à la Moffat. Jo read till her eyes gave out, and she was sick of books; got so fidgety that even good-natured Laurie had a quarrel with her, and so reduced in spirits that she desperately wished she had gone with Aunt March. Beth got on pretty well, for she was constantly forgetting that it was to be *all play, and no work*, and fell back into her old ways, now and then; but something in the air affected her, and, more than once, her tranquillity was much disturbed; so much so, that, on one occasion, she actually shook poor dear Joanna, and told her she was a "fright." Amy fared worst of all, for her resources were small; and, when her sisters left her to amuse and care for herself, she soon found that accomplished and important little self a great burden. She didn't like dolls; fairy tales were childish, and one couldn't draw all the time. Tea parties didn't amount to much, neither did picnics, unless very well conducted. "If one could have a fine house, full of nice girls, or go travelling, the summer would be delightful; but to stay at home with three selfish sisters, and a grown-up boy, was enough to try the patience of a Boaz," complained Miss Malaprop, after several days devoted to pleasure, fretting, and *ennui*.

No one would own that they were tired of the experiment; but, by Friday night, each acknowledged to herself that they were glad the week was nearly done. Hoping to impress the lesson more deeply, Mrs. March, who had a good deal of humor, resolved to finish off the trial in an appropriate manner; so she gave Hannah a holiday, and let the girls enjoy the full effect of the play system.

When they got up on Saturday morning, there was no fire in the kitchen, no breakfast in the dining-room, and no mother anywhere to be seen.

"Mercy on us! what *has* happened?" cried Jo, staring about her in dismay.

Meg ran upstairs, and soon came back again, looking relieved, but rather bewildered, and a little ashamed.

"Mother isn't sick, only very tired, and she says she is going to stay quietly in her room all day, and let us do the best we can. It's a very queer thing for her to do, she don't act a bit like herself; but she says it *has* been a hard week for her, so we mustn't grumble, but take care of ourselves."

"That's easy enough, and I like the idea; I'm aching for something to do – that is, some new amusement, you know," added Jo, quickly.

In fact it *was* an immense relief to them all to have a little work, and they took hold with a will, but soon realized the truth of Hannah's saying,

"Housekeeping ain't no joke." There was plenty of food in the larder, and, while Beth and Amy set the table, Meg and Jo got breakfast; wondering, as they did so, why servants ever talked about hard work.

"I shall take some up to mother, though she said we were not to think of her, for she'd take care of herself," said Meg, who presided, and felt quite matronly behind the teapot.

So a tray was fitted out before any one began, and taken up, with the cook's compliments. The boiled tea was very bitter, the omelette scorched, and the biscuits speckled with saleratus; but Mrs. March received her repast with thanks, and laughed heartily over it after Jo was gone.

"Poor little souls, they will have a hard time, I'm afraid; but they won't suffer, and it will do them good," she said, producing the more palatable viands with which she had provided herself, and disposing of the bad breakfast, so that their feelings might not be hurt; — a motherly little deception, for which they were grateful.

Many were the complaints below, and great the chagrin of the head cook, at her failures. "Never mind, I'll get the dinner, and be servant; you be missis, keep your hands nice, see company, and give orders," said Jo, who knew still less than Meg about culinary affairs.

This obliging offer was gladly accepted; and Margaret retired to the parlor, which she hastily put in order by whisking the litter under the sofa, and shutting the blinds, to save the trouble of dusting. Jo, with perfect faith in her own powers, and a friendly desire to make up the quarrel, immediately put a note in the office, inviting Laurie to dinner.

"You'd better see what you have got before you think of having company," said Meg, when informed of the hospitable, but rash act.

"Oh, there's corned beef, and plenty of potatoes; and I shall get some asparagus, and a lobster, 'for a relish,' as Hannah says. We'll have lettuce, and make a salad; I don't know how, but the book tells. I'll have blanc-mange and strawberries for dessert; and coffee, too, if you want to be elegant."

"Don't try too many messes, Jo, for you can't make anything but gingerbread and molasses candy, fit to eat. I wash my hands of the dinner-party; and, since you have asked Laurie on your own responsibility, you may just take care of him."

"I don't want you to do anything but be clever to him, and help to the pudding. You'll give me your advice if I get stuck, won't you?" asked Jo, rather hurt.

"Yes; but I don't know much, except about bread, and a few trifles. You had better ask mother's leave before you order anything," returned Meg, prudently.

"Of course I shall; I ain't a fool," and Jo went off in a huff at the doubts expressed of her powers.

"Get what you like, and don't disturb me; I'm going out to dinner, and can't worry about things at home," said Mrs. March, when Jo spoke to her. "I never enjoyed housekeeping, and I'm going to take a vacation to-day, and read, write, go visiting, and amuse myself."

The unusual spectacle of her busy mother rocking comfortably, and reading early in the morning, made Jo feel as if some natural phenomenon had occurred; for an eclipse, an earthquake, or a volcanic eruption would hardly have seemed stranger.

"Everything is out of sorts, somehow," she said to herself, going down stairs. "There's Beth crying; that's a sure sign that something is wrong with this family. If Amy is bothering, I'll shake her."

Feeling very much out of sorts herself, Jo hurried into the parlor to find Beth sobbing over Pip, the canary, who lay dead in the cage, with his little claws pathetically extended, as if imploring for food, for want of which he had died.

"It's all my fault — I forgot him — there isn't a seed or a drop left — oh, Pip! oh, Pip! how could I be so cruel to you?" cried Beth, taking the poor thing in her hands, and trying to restore him.

Jo peeped into his half-open eye, felt his little heart, and finding him stiff and cold, shook her head, and offered her domino box for a coffin.

"Put him in the oven, and maybe he will get warm, and revive," said Amy, hopefully.

"He's been starved, and he shan't be baked, now he's dead. I'll make him a shroud, and he shall be buried in the grave; and I'll never have another bird, never, my Pip! for I'm too bad to own one," murmured Beth, sitting on the floor with her pet folded in her hands.

"The funeral shall be this afternoon, and we will all go. Now, don't cry, Bethy; it's a pity, but nothing goes right this week, and Pip has had the worst of the experiment. Make the shroud, and lay him in my box; and,

Jo leaned over her sister. (Chapter 8)

Jo threw open the door of the closet and displayed
Laurie. (Chapter 10)

after the dinner-party, we'll have a nice little funeral," said Jo, beginning to feel as if she had undertaken a good deal.

Leaving the others to console Beth, she departed to the kitchen, which was in a most discouraging state of confusion. Putting on a big apron, she fell to work, and got the dishes piled up ready for washing, when she discovered that the fire was out.

"Here's a sweet prospect!" muttered Jo, slamming the stove door open, and poking vigorously among the cinders.

Having rekindled it, she thought she would go to market while the water heated. The walk revived her spirits; and, flattering herself that she had made good bargains, she trudged home again, after buying a very young lobster, some very old asparagus, and two boxes of acid strawberries. By the time she got cleared up, the dinner arrived, and the stove was red-hot. Hannah had left a pan of bread to rise, Meg had worked it up early, set it on the hearth for a second rising, and forgotten it. Meg was entertaining Sallie Gardiner, in the parlor, when the door flew open, and a floury, crocky, flushed, and dishevelled figure appeared, demanding, tartly, –

"I say, isn't bread 'riz' enough when it runs over the pans?"

Sallie began to laugh; but Meg nodded, and lifted her eyebrows as high as they would go, which caused the apparition to vanish, and put the sour bread into the oven without further delay. Mrs. March went out, after peeping here and there to see how matters went, also saying a word of comfort to Beth, who sat making a winding-sheet, while the dear departed lay in a state in the domino box. A strange sense of helplessness fell upon the girls as the gray bonnet vanished round the corner; and despair seized them, when, a few minutes later, Miss Crocker appeared, and said she'd come to dinner. Now, this lady was a thin, yellow spinster, with a sharp nose, and inquisitive eyes, who saw everything, and gossiped about all she saw. They disliked her, but had been taught to be kind to her, simply because she was old and poor, and had few friends. So Meg gave her the easy-chair, and tried to entertain her, while she asked questions, criticised everything, and told stories of the people whom she knew.

Language cannot describe the anxieties, experiences, and exertions which Jo underwent that morning; and the dinner she served up became a standing joke. Fearing to ask any more advice, she did her best alone, and discovered that something more than energy and good-will is necessary to make a cook. She boiled the asparagus hard for an hour, and was grieved to find the heads cooked off, and the stalks harder than ever. The bread burnt black; for the salad dressing so aggravated her, that she let everything else go, till she had convinced herself that she could not make it fit to eat. The lobster was a scarlet mystery to her, but she hammered and poked till it was unshelled, and its meagre proportions concealed in a grove of lettuce leaves. The potatoes had to be hurried, not to keep the asparagus waiting, and were not done at last. The blanc-mange was lumpy, and the strawberries not as ripe as they looked, having been skilfully "deaconed."

"Well, they can eat beef, and bread and butter, if they are hungry; only it's mortifying to have to spend your whole morning for nothing," thought Jo, as she rang the bell half an hour later than usual, and stood hot, tired, and dispirited, surveying the feast spread for Laurie, accustomed to all sorts of elegance, and Miss Crocker, whose curious eyes would mark all failures, and whose tattling tongue would report them far and wide.

Poor Jo would gladly have gone under the table, as one thing after another was tasted and left; while Amy giggled, Meg looked distressed, Miss Crocker pursed up her lips, and Laurie talked and laughed with all his might, to give a cheerful tone to the festive scene. Jo's one strong point was the fruit, for she had sugared it well, and had a pitcher of rich cream to eat with it. Her hot cheeks cooled a trifle, and she drew a long breath, as the pretty glass plates went round, and every one looked graciously at the little rosy islands floating in a sea of cream. Miss Crocker tasted first, made a wry face, and drank some water hastily. Jo, who had refused, thinking there might not be enough, for they dwindled sadly after the picking over, glanced at Laurie, but he was eating away manfully, though there was a slight pucker about his mouth, and he kept his eye fixed on his plate. Amy, who was fond of delicate fare, took a heaping spoonful, choked, hid her face in her napkin, and left the table precipitately.

"Oh, what is it?" exclaimed Jo, trembling.

"Salt instead of sugar, and the cream is sour," replied Meg, with a tragic gesture.

Jo uttered a groan, and fell back in her chair; remembering that she had given a last hasty powdering to the berries out of one of the two boxes on the kitchen table, and had neglected to put the milk in the refrigerator. She turned scarlet, and was on the verge of crying, when she met Laurie's eyes, which *would* look merry in spite of his heroic efforts; the comical side of the affair suddenly struck her, and she laughed till the tears ran down her cheeks. So did everyone else, even "Croaker," as the girls called the old lady; and the unfortunate dinner ended gaily, with bread and butter, olives and fun.

"I haven't strength of mind enough to clear up now, so we will sober ourselves with a funeral," said Jo, as they rose; and Miss Crocker made ready to go, being eager to tell the new story at another friend's dinner-table.

They did sober themselves, for Beth's sake; Laurie dug a grave under the ferns in the grove, little Pip was laid in, with many tears, by his tender-hearted mistress, and covered with moss, while a wreath of violets and chickweed was hung on the stone which bore this epitaph, composed by Jo, while she struggled with the dinner, –

> *Here lies Pip March,*
> *Who died the 7th of June;*
> *Loved and lamented sore,*
> *And not forgotten soon.*

At the conclusion of the ceremonies, Beth retired to her room, overcome with emotion and lobster; but there was no place for repose, for the beds were not made, and she found her grief much assuaged by beating up the pillows and putting things in order. Meg helped Jo clear away the remains of the feast, which took half the afternoon, and left them so tired that they agreed to be contented with tea and toast for supper. Laurie took Amy for a drive, which was a deed of charity, for the sour cream seemed to have had a bad effect upon her temper. Mrs. March came home to find the three older girls hard at work in the middle of the afternoon; and a glance at the closet gave her an idea of the success of one part of the experiment.

Before the housewives could rest, several people called, and there was a scramble to get ready to see them; then tea must be got, errands done; and one or two were bits of sewing necessary, but neglected till the last minute. As twilight fell, dewy and still, one by one they gathered in the porch where the June roses were budding beautifully, and each groaned or sighed as she sat down, as if tired or troubled.

"What a dreadful day this has been!" began Jo, usually the first to speak.

"It has been shorter than usual, but *so* uncomfortable," said Meg.

"Not a bit like home," added Amy.

"It can't seem so without Marmee and little Pip," sighed Beth, glancing, with full eyes, at the empty cage above her head.

"Here's mother, dear, and you shall have another bird to-morrow, if you want it."

As she spoke, Mrs. March came and took her place among them, looking as if her holiday had not been much pleasanter than theirs.

"Are you satisfied with your experiment, girls, or do you want another week of it?" she asked, as Beth nestled up to her, and the rest turned toward her with brightening faces, as flowers turn toward the sun.

"I don't!" cried Jo, decidedly.

"Nor I," echoed the others.

"You think, then, that it is better to have a few duties, and live a little for others, do you?"

"Lounging and larking don't pay," observed Jo, shaking her head. "I'm tired of it, and mean to go to work at something right off."

"Suppose you learn plain cooking; that's a useful accomplishment, which no woman should be without," said Mrs. March, laughing audibly at the recollection of Jo's dinner-party; for she had met Miss Crocker, and heard her account of it.

"Mother! did you go away and let everything be, just to see how we'd get on?" cried Meg, who had had suspicions all day.

"Yes; I wanted you to see how the comfort of all depends on each doing her share faithfully. While Hannah and I did your work, you got on pretty well, though I don't think you were very happy or amiable; so I thought, as a little lesson, I would show you what happens when every one thinks only of herself. Don't you feel that it is pleasanter to help one another, to have daily duties which make leisure sweet when it comes, and to bear and forbear, that home may be comfortable and lovely to us all?"

"We do, mother, we do!" cried the girls.

"Then let me advise you to take up your little burdens again; for though they seem heavy sometimes, they are good for us, and lighten as we learn to carry them. Work is wholesome, and there is plenty for every one; it keeps us from *ennui* and mischief; is good for health and spirits, and gives us a sense of power and independence better than money or fashion."

"We'll work like bees, and love it too; see if we don't!" said Jo. "I'll learn plain cooking for my holiday task; and the next dinner-party I have shall be a success."

"I'll make the set of shirts for father, instead of letting you do it, Marmee. I can and I will, though I'm not fond of sewing; that will be better than fussing over my own things, which are plenty nice enough as they are," said Meg.

"I'll do my lessons every day, and not spend so much time with my music and dolls. I am a stupid thing, and ought to be studying, not playing," was Beth's resolution; while Amy followed their example by heroically declaring, "I shall learn to make buttonholes, and attend to my parts of speech."

"Very good! then I am quite satisfied with the experiment, and fancy that we shall not have to repeat it; only don't go to the other extreme, and delve like slaves. Have regular hours for work and play; make each day both useful and pleasant, and prove that you understand the worth of time by employing it well. Then youth will be delightful, old age will bring few regrets, and life become a beautiful success, in spite of poverty."

"We'll remember, mother!" and they did.

CHAPTER TWELVE

CAMP LAURENCE

~

Beth was post-mistress, for, being most at home, she could attend to it regularly, and dearly like the daily task of unlocking the little door and distributing the mail. One July day she came in with her hands full, and went about the house leaving letters and parcels, like the penny post.

"Here's your posy, mother! Laurie never forgets that," she said, putting the fresh nosegay in the vase that stood in "Marmee's corner," and was kept supplied by the affectionate boy.

"Miss Meg March, one letter and a glove," continued Beth, delivering the article to her sister, who sat near her mother, stitching wristbands.

"Why, I left a pair over there, and here is only one," said Meg, looking at the gray cotton glove.

"Didn't you drop the other in the garden?"

"No, I'm sure I didn't; for there was only one in the office."

"I hate to have odd gloves! Never mind, the other may be found. My letter is only a translation of the German song I wanted; I guess Mr. Brooke did it, for this isn't Laurie's writing."

Mrs. March glanced at Meg, who was looking very pretty in her gingham morning-gown, with the little curls blowing about her forehead, and very womanly, as she sat sewing at her little work-table, full of tidy white rolls; so, unconscious of the thought in her mother's mind, she sewed and sung while her fingers flew, and her mind was busied with girlish fancies as innocent and fresh as the pansies in her belt, that Mrs. March smiled, and was satisfied.

"Two letters for Doctor Jo, a book, and a funny old hat, which covered the whole post-office, stuck outside," said Beth, laughing, as she went into the study, where Jo sat writing.

"What a sly fellow Laurie is! I said I wished bigger hats were the fashion, because I burn my face every hot day. He said, 'Why mind the fashion? Wear a big hat, and be comfortable!' I said I would, if I had one, and he has sent me this, to try me; I'll wear it, for fun, and show him I *don't* care for the fashion;" and, hanging the antique broad-brim on a bust of Plato, Jo read her letters.

One from her mother made her cheeks glow, and her eyes fill, for it said to her, —

MY DEAR:
I write a little word to tell you with how much satisfaction I watch your efforts to control your temper. You say nothing about your trials, failures, or successes, and think, perhaps, that no one sees them but the Friend whose help you daily ask, if I may trust the well-worn cover of your guide-book. *I*, too, have seen them all, and heartily believe in the sincerity of your resolution, since it begins to bear fruit. Go on, dear, patiently and bravely, and always believe that no one sympathizes more tenderly with you than your loving

MOTHER.

"That does me good! that's worth millions of money, and pecks of praise. Oh, Marmee, I do try! I will keep on trying, and not get tired, since I have you to help me."

Laying her head on her arms, Jo wet her little romance with a few happy tears, for she *had* thought no one saw and appreciated her efforts to do good, and this assurance was doubly precious, doubly encouraging, because unexpected, and from the person whose commendation she most valued. Feeling stronger than ever to meet and subdue her Apollyon, she pinned the note inside her frock, as a shield and a reminder, lest she be taken unaware, and proceeded to open her other letter, quite ready for either good or bad news. In a big, dashing hand, Laurie wrote, –

Dear Jo,
What ho!
Some English girls and boys are coming to see me to-morrow, and I want to have a jolly time. If it's fine, I'm going to pitch my tent in Longmeadow, and row up the whole crew to lunch and croquet; – have a fire, make messes, gypsy fashion, and all sorts of larks. They are nice people, and like such things. Brooke will go, to keep us boys steady, and Kate Vaughn will play propriety for the girls. I want you all to come; can't let Beth off, at any price, and nobody shall worry her. Don't bother about rations, – I'll see to that, and everything else, – only do come, there's a good fellow!

In a tearing hurry,
Yours ever, LAURIE.

"Here's richness!" cried Jo, flying in to tell the news to Meg. "Of course we can go, mother! it will be such a help to Laurie, for I can row, and Meg see to the lunch, and the children be useful in some way."

"I hope the Vaughns are not fine, grown-up people. Do you know anything about them, Jo?" asked Meg.

"Only that there are four of them. Kate is older than you, Fred and Frank (twins) about my age, and a little girl (Grace), who is nine or ten. Laurie knew them abroad, and liked the boys; I fancied, from the way he primmed up his mouth in speaking of her, that he didn't admire Kate much."

"I'm so glad my French print is clean, it's just the thing, and so becoming!" observed Meg, complacently. "Have you anything decent, Jo?"

"Scarlet and gray boating suit, good enough for me. I shall row and tramp about, so I don't want any starch to think of. You'll come, Betty?"

"If you won't let any of the boys talk to me."

"Not a boy!"

"I like to please Laurie; and I'm not afraid of Mr. Brooke, he is so kind; but I don't want to play, or sing, or say anything. I'll work hard, and not trouble any one; and you'll take care of me, Jo, so I'll go."

"That's my good girl; you do try to fight off your shyness, and I love you for it; fighting faults isn't easy, as I know; and a cheery word kind of gives a lift. Thank you, mother," and Jo gave the thin cheek a grateful kiss, more precious to Mrs. March than if it had given back the rosy roundness of her youth.

"I had a box of chocolate drops, and the picture I wanted to copy," said Amy, showing her mail.

"And I got a note from Mr. Laurence, asking me to come over and play to him to-night before the lamps are lighted, and I shall go," added Beth, whose friendship with the old gentleman prospered finely.

"Now let's fly round, and do double duty to-day, so that we can play to-morrow with free minds," said Jo, preparing to replace her pen with a broom.

When the sun peeped into the girls' room early next morning, to promise them a fine day, he saw a comical sight. Each had made such preparation for the fête as seemed necessary and proper. Meg had an extra row of little curl papers across her forehead, Jo had copiously anointed her afflicted face with cold cream, Beth had taken Joanna to bed with her to atone for the approaching separation, and Amy had capped the climax by putting a clothes-pin on her nose, to uplift the offending feature. It was one of the kind artists used to hold the paper on their drawing-boards; therefore, quite appropriate and effective for the purpose to which it was now put. This funny spectacle appeared to amuse the sun, for he burst out with such radiance that Jo woke up, and roused all her sisters by a hearty laugh at Amy's ornament.

Sunshine and laughter were good omens for a pleasure party, and soon a lively bustle began in both houses. Beth, who was ready first, kept reporting what went on next door, and enlivened her sisters' toilets by frequent telegrams from the window.

"There goes the man with the tent! I see Mrs. Barker doing up the lunch, in a hamper, and a great basket. Now Mr. Laurence is looking up at the sky, and the weathercock; I wish he would go, too! There's Laurie looking like a sailor, – nice boy! Oh, mercy me! here's a carriage full of people – a tall lady, a little girl, and two dreadful boys. One is lame; poor thing, he's got a crutch! Laurie didn't tell us that. Be quick, girls! it's getting late. Why, there is Ned Moffat, I do declare. Look, Meg! isn't that the man who bowed to you one day, when we were shopping?"

"So it is; how queer that he should come! I thought he was at the Mountains. There is Sallie; I'm glad she got back in time. Am I all right, Jo?" cried Meg, in a flutter.

"A regular daisy; hold up your dress, and put your hat straight; it looks sentimental tipped that way, and will fly off at the first puff. Now, then, come on!"

"Oh, oh! Jo! you ain't going to wear that awful hat? It's too absurd! You shall *not* make a guy of yourself," remonstrated Meg, as Jo tied down, with a red ribbon, the broad-brimmed, old-fashioned Leghorn Laurie had sent for a joke.

"I just will, though! it's capital; so shady, light, and big. It will make fun; and I don't mind being a guy, if I'm comfortable." With that Jo marched straight away, and the rest followed; a bright little band of sisters, all looking their best, in summer suits, with happy faces, under the jaunty hat-brims.

Laurie ran to meet, and present to his friends, in the most cordial manner. The lawn was the reception room, and for several minutes a lively scene was enacted there. Meg was grateful to see that Miss Kate, though twenty, was dressed with a simplicity which American girls would do well to imitate; and she was much flattered by Mr. Ned's assurances that he came especially to see her. Jo understood why Laurie "primmed up his mouth" when speaking of Kate, for that young lady had a stand-off-don't touch-me air, which contrasted strongly with the free and easy demeanor of the other girls. Beth took an observation of the new boys, and decided that the lame one was not "dreadful," but gentle and feeble, and she would be kind to him, on that account. Amy found Grace a well-mannered, merry little person; and, after staring dumbly at one another for a few minutes, they suddenly became very good friends.

Tents, lunch, and croquet utensils had been sent on beforehand, the party was soon embarked, and the two boats pushed off together, leaving Mr. Laurence waving his hat on the shore. Laurie and Jo rowed one boat; Mr. Brooke and Ned the other; while Fred Vaughn, the riotous twin, did his best to upset both, by paddling about in a wherry, like a disturbed water-bug. Jo's funny hat deserved a vote of thanks, for it was of general utility; it broke the ice in the beginning, by producing a laugh; it created quite a refreshing breeze, flapping to and fro, as she rowed, and would make an excellent umbrella for the whole party, if a shower came up, she said. Kate looked rather amazed at Jo's proceedings, especially as she exclaimed "Christopher Columbus!" when she lost her oar; and Laurie said, "My dear fellow, did I hurt you?" when he tripped over her feet in taking his place. But after putting up her glass to examine the queer girl several times, Miss Kate decided that she was "odd, but rather clever", and smiled upon her from afar.

Meg, in the other boat, was delightfully situated, face to face with the rowers, who both admired the prospect, and feathered their oars with uncommon "skill and dexterity". Mr. Brooke was a grave, silent young man, with handsome brown eyes, and a pleasant voice. Meg liked his quiet manners, and considered him a walking encyclopædia of useful knowledge. He never talked to her much; but he looked at her a good deal, and she felt sure that he did not regard her with aversion. Ned being in college, of course put on all the airs which Freshmen think it their bounden duty to assume; he was not very wise, but very good-natured and merry, and, altogether, an excellent person to carry on a picnic. Sallie Gardiner was absorbed in keeping her white piqué dress clean, and chattering with the ubiquitous Fred, who kept Beth in constant terror by his pranks.

It was not far to Longmeadow; but the tent was pitched, and the wickets down, by the time they arrived. A pleasant green field, with three wide-spreading oaks in the middle, and a smooth strip of turf for croquet.

"Welcome to Camp Laurence!" said the young host, as they landed, with exclamations of delight. "Brooke is commander-in-chief; I am commissary general; the other fellows are staff-officers; and you, ladies, are company. The tent is for your especial benefit, and that oak is your drawing-room; this is the mess-room, and the third is the camp kitchen. Now let's have a game before it gets hot, and then we'll see about dinner."

Frank, Beth, Amy, and Grace sat down to watch the game played by the other eight. Mr. Brooke chose Meg, Kate, and Fred; Laurie took Sallie, Jo, and Ned. The Englishers played well; but the Americans played better, and contested every inch of the ground as strongly as if the spirit of '76 inspired them. Jo and Fred had several skirmishes, and once narrowly escaped high words. Jo was through the last wicket, and had missed the stroke, which failure ruffled her a good deal. Fred was close behind her, and his turn came before hers; he gave a stroke, his ball hit the wicket, and stopped an inch on the wrong side. No one was very near; and, running up to examine, he gave it a sly nudge with his toe, which put it just an inch on the right side.

"I'm through! Now, Miss Jo, I'll settle you, and get in first," cried the young gentleman, swinging his mallet for another blow.

"You pushed it; I saw you; it's my turn now," said Jo, sharply.

"Upon my word, I didn't move it! it rolled a bit, perhaps, but that is allowed; so stand off, please, and let me have a go at the stake."

"We don't cheat in America; but *you* can, if you choose," said Jo, angrily.

"Yankees are a deal the most tricky, everybody knows. There you go," returned Fred, croqueting her ball far away.

Jo opened her lips to say something rude; but checked herself in time, colored up to her forehead, and stood a minute, hammering down a wicket with all her might, while Fred hit the stake, and declared himself out, with much exultation. She went off to get her ball, and was a long time finding it, among the bushes; but she came back, looking cool and quiet, and waited her turn patiently. It took several strokes to regain the place she had lost; and, when she got there, the other side had nearly won, for Kate's ball was the last but one, and lay near the stake.

"By George, it's all up with us! Good-by, Kate; Miss Jo owes me one, so you are finished," cried Fred, excitedly, as they all drew near to see the finish.

"Yankees have a trick of being generous to their enemies," said Jo, with a look that made the lad redden, "especially when they beat them," she added, as, leaving Kate's ball untouched, she won the game by a clever stroke.

Laurie threw up his hat; then remembered that it wouldn't do to exult over the defeat of his guests, and stopped in the middle of a cheer to whisper to his friend, —

"Good for you, Jo! he did cheat, I saw him; we can't tell him so, but he won't do it again, take my word for it."

Meg drew her aside, under pretence of pinning up a loose braid, and said, approvingly, –

"It was dreadfully provoking; but you kept your temper, and I'm so glad, Jo."

"Don't praise me, Meg, for I could box his ears this minute. I should certainly have boiled over if I hadn't stayed among the nettles till I got my rage under enough to hold my tongue. It's simmering now, so I hope he'll keep out of my way," returned Jo, biting her lips, as she glowered at Fred from under her big hat.

"Time for lunch," said Mr. Brooke, looking at his watch. "Commissary general, will you make the fire, and get water, while Miss March, Miss Sallie, and I spread the table? Who can make good coffee?"

"Jo can," said Meg, glad to recommend her sister. So Jo, feeling that her late lessons in cookery were to do her honor, went to preside over the coffee-pot, while the children collected dry sticks, and the boys made a fire, and got water from a spring near by. Miss Kate sketched, and Frank talked to Beth, who was making little mats of braided rushes, to serve as plates.

The commander-in-chief and his aides soon spread the tablecloth with an inviting array of eatables and drinkables, prettily decorated with green leaves. Jo announced that the coffee was ready, and every one settled themselves to a hearty meal; for youth is seldom dyspeptic, and exercise develops wholesome appetites. A very merry lunch it was; for everything seemed fresh and funny, and frequent peals of laughter startled a venerable horse, who fed near by. There was a pleasant inequality in the table, which produced many mishaps to cups and plates; acorns dropped into the milk, little black ants partook of the refreshments without being invited, and fuzzy caterpillars swung down from the tree, to see what was going on. Three white-headed children peeped over the fence, and an objectionable dog barked at them from the other side of the river, with all his might and main.

"There's salt, here, if you prefer it," said Laurie, as he handed Jo a saucer of berries.

"Thank you; I prefer spiders," she replied, fishing up two unwary little ones, who had gone to a creamy death. "How dare you remind me of that horrid dinner-party, when yours is so nice in every way?" added Jo, as they both laughed, and ate out of one plate, the china having run short.

"I had an uncommonly good time that day, and haven't got over it yet. This is no credit to me, you know; I don't do anything; it's you, and Meg, and Brooke, who make it go, and I'm no end obliged to you. What shall you do when we can't eat any more?" asked Laurie, feeling that his trump card had been played when lunch was over.

"Have games, till it's cooler. I brought 'Authors,' and I dare say Miss Kate knows something new and nice. Go and ask her; she's company, and you ought to stay with her more."

"Aren't you company, too? I thought she'd suit Brooke; but he keeps talking to Meg, and Kate just stares at them through that ridiculous glass of hers. I'm going, so you needn't try to preach propriety, for you can't do it, Jo."

Miss Kate did know several new games; and as the girls would not, and the boys could not, eat any more, they all adjourned to the drawing-room to play "Rigmarole."

"One person begins a story, any nonsense you like, and tells as long as they please, only taking care to stop short at some exciting point, when the next takes it up, and does the same. It's very funny, when well done, and makes a perfect jumble of tragical comical stuff to laugh over. Please start it, Mr. Brooke," said Kate, with a commanding gesture, which surprised Meg, who treated the tutor with as much respect as any other gentleman.

Lying on the grass, at the feet of the two young ladies, Mr. Brooke obediently began the story, with the handsome brown eyes steadily fixed upon the sunshiny river.

"Once upon a time, a knight went out into the world to seek his fortune, for he had nothing but his sword and his shield. He travelled a long while, nearly eight-and-twenty years, and had a hard time of it, till he came to the palace of a good old king, who had offered a reward to any one who would tame and train a fine, but unbroken colt, of which he was very fond. The knight agreed to try, and got on slowly, but surely; for the colt was a gallant fellow, and soon learned to love his new master, though he was freakish and wild. Every day, when he gave his lessons to this pet of the king's, the knight rode him through the city; and, as he rode, he looked everywhere for a certain beautiful face, which he had seen many times in his dreams, but never found. One day, as he went prancing down a quiet street, he saw at the window of a ruinous castle the lovely face. He was delighted, inquired who lived in this old castle, and was told that several captive princesses were kept there by a spell, and spun all day to lay up money to buy their liberty. The knight wished intensely that he could free them; but he was poor, and could only go by each day, watching for the sweet face, and longing to see it out in the sunshine. At last he resolved to get into the castle, and ask how he could help them. He went and knocked; the great door flew open, and he beheld – "

"A ravishingly lovely lady, who exclaimed, with a cry of rapture, 'At last! at last'" continued Kate, who had read French novels, and admired the style. "''Tis she!' cried Count Gustave, and fell at her feet in an ecstasy of joy. 'Oh, rise!' she said, extending a hand of marble fairness. 'Never! till you tell me how I may rescue you,' swore the knight, still kneeling. 'Alas, my cruel fate condemns me to remain here till my tyrant is destroyed,' 'Where is the villain?' 'In the mauve salon; go, brave heart, and save me from despair.' 'I obey, and return victorious or dead!' With these thrilling words he rushed away, and, flinging open the door of the mauve salon, was about to enter, when he received – "

"A stunning blow from the big Greek lexicon, which an old fellow in a black gown fired at him," said Ned. "Instantly Sir What's-his-name recovered himself, pitched the tyrant out of the window, and turned to join the lady, victorious, but with a bump on his brow; found the door locked, tore up the curtains, made a rope ladder, got half-way down when the ladder broke, and he went head first into the moat, sixty feet below. Could swim like a duck, paddled round the castle till he came to a little door guarded by two stout fellows; knocked their heads together till they cracked like a couple of nuts, then, by a trifling exertion of his prodigious strength, he smashed in the door, went up a pair of stone steps covered with dust a foot thick, toads as big as your fist, and spiders that would frighten you into hysterics, Miss March. At the top of these steps he came plump upon a sight that took his breath away and chilled his blood – "

"A tall figure, all in white, with a veil over its face, and a lamp in its wasted hand," went on Meg. "It beckoned, gliding noiselessly before him down a corridor as dark and cold as any tomb. Shadowy effigies in armor stood on either side, a dead silence reigned, the lamp burned blue, and the ghostly figure ever and anon turned its face toward him, showing the glitter of awful eyes through its white veil. They reached a curtained door, behind which sounded lovely music; he sprang forward to enter, but the spectre plucked him back, and waved, threateningly, before him a – "

"Snuff-box," said Jo, in a sepulchral tone, which convulsed the audience. " 'Thankee,' said the knight, politely, as he took a pinch, and sneezed seven times so violently that his head fell off. 'Ha! ha!' laughed the ghost; and, having peeped through the keyhole at the princesses spinning away for dear life, the evil spirit picked up her victim and put him in a large tin box, where there were eleven other knights packed together without their heads, like sardines, who all rose and began to – "

"Dance a hornpipe," cut in Fred, as Jo paused for breath; "and, as they danced, the rubbishy old castle turned to a man-of-war in full sail. 'Up with the jib, reef the tops'l halliards, helm hard a lee, and man the guns,' roared the captain, as a Portuguese pirate hove in sight, with a flag black as ink flying from her foremast. 'Go in and win, my hearties!' says the captain; and a tremendous fight begun. Of course the British beat – they always do; and, having taken the pirate captain prisoner, sailed slap over the schooner, whose decks were piled with dead, and whose lee-scuppers ran blood, for the order had been 'Cutlasses, and die hard.' 'Bosun's mate, take a bight of the flying jib sheet, and start this villain if he don't confess his sins double quick,' said the British captain. The Portuguese held his tongue like a brick, and walked the plank, while the jolly tars cheered like mad. But the sly dog dived, came up under the man-of-war, scuttled her, and down she went, with all sail set, 'To the bottom of the sea, sea, sea,' where – "

"Oh, gracious! what *shall* I say?" cried Sallie, as Fred ended his rigmarole, in which he had jumbled together, pell-mell, nautical phrases and facts, out of one of his favorite books. "Well, they went to the bottom, and a nice mermaid welcomed them, but was much grieved on finding the box of headless knights, and kindly pickled them in brine, hoping to discover the mystery about them; for, being a woman, she was curious. By and by a diver came down, and the mermaid said, 'I'll give you this box of pearls if you can take it up;' for she wanted to restore the poor things to life, and couldn't raise the heavy load herself. So the diver hoisted it up, and was much disappointed, on opening it, to find no pearls. He left it in a great lonely field, where it was found by a – "

"Little goose-girl, who kept a hundred fat geese in the field," said Amy, when Sallie's invention gave out. "The little girl was sorry for them, and asked an old woman what she should do to help them. 'Your geese will tell you, they know everything,' said the old woman. So she asked what she should use for new heads, since the old ones were lost, and all the geese opened their hundred mouths, and screamed – "

"'Cabbages!'" continued Laurie, promptly. "'Just the thing,' said the girl, and ran to get twelve fine ones from her garden. She put them on, the knights revived at once, thanked her, and went on their way rejoicing, never knowing the difference, for there were so many other heads like them in the world, that no one thought anything of it. The knight in whom I'm interested went back to find the pretty face, and learned that the princesses had spun themselves free, and all gone to be married, but one. He was in a great state of mind at that; and, mounting the colt, which stood by him through thick and thin, rushed to the castle to see which was left. Peeping over the hedge, he saw the queen of his affections picking flowers in her garden. 'Will you give me a rose?' said he. 'You must come and get it; I can't come to you; it isn't proper,' she said, as sweet as honey. He tried to climb over the hedge, but it seemed to grow higher and higher; then he tried to push through, but it grew thicker and thicker, and he was in despair. So he patiently broke twig after twig till he had made a little hole, through which he peeped, saying, imploringly, 'Let me in! let me in!' But the pretty princess did not seem to understand, for she picked her roses quietly, and left him to fight his way in. Whether he did or not, Frank will tell you."

"I can't; I'm not playing, I never do," said Frank, dismayed at the sentimental predicament out of which he was to rescue the absurd couple. Beth had disappeared behind Jo, and Grace was asleep.

"So the poor knight is to be left sticking in the hedge, is he?" asked Mr. Brooke, still watching the river, and playing with the wild rose in his button-hole.

"I guess the princess gave him a posy, and opened the gate, after a while," said Laurie, smiling to himself, as he threw acorns at his tutor.

"What a piece of nonsense we have made! With practice we might do something quite clever. Do you know 'Truth'?" asked Sallie, after they had laughed over their story.

"I hope so," said Meg, soberly.

"The game, I mean?"

"What is it?" said Fred.

"Why, you pile up your hands, choose a number, and draw out in turn, and the person who draws at the number has to answer truly any questions put by the rest. It's great fun."

"Let's try it," said Jo, who liked new experiments.

Miss Kate and Mr. Brooke, Meg, and Ned, declined; but Fred, Sallie, Jo and Laurie piled and drew; and the lot fell to Laurie.

"Who are your heroes?" asked Jo.

"Grandfather and Napoleon."

"Which lady here do you think prettiest?" said Sallie.

"Margaret."

"Which do you like best?" from Fred.

"Jo, of course."

"What silly questions you ask!" and Jo gave a disdainful shrug as the rest laughed at Laurie's matter-of-fact tone.

"Try again; Truth isn't a bad game," said Fred.

"It's a very good one for you," retorted Jo, in a low voice.

Her turn came next.

"What is your greatest fault?" asked Fred, by way of testing in her the virtue he lacked himself.

"A quick temper."

"What do you most wish for?" said Laurie.

"A pair of boot-lacings," returned Jo, guessing and defeating his purpose.

"Not a true answer; you must say what you really do want most."

"Genius; don't you wish you could give it to me, Laurie?" and she slyly smiled in his disappointed face.

"What virtues do you most admire in a man?" asked Sallie.

"Courage and honesty."

"Now my turn," said Fred, as his hand came last.

"Let's give it to him," whispered Laurie to Jo, who nodded, and asked at once, –

"Didn't you cheat at croquet?"

"Well, yes, a little bit."

"Good! Didn't you take your story out of 'The Sea Lion?'" said Laurie.

"Rather."

"Don't you think the English nation perfect in every respect?" asked Sallie.

"I should be ashamed of myself if I didn't."

"He's a true John Bull. Now, Miss Sallie, you shall have a chance without waiting to draw. I'll harrow up your feelings first by asking if you don't think you are something of a flirt," said Laurie, as Jo nodded to Fred, as a sign that peace was declared.

"You impertinent boy! of course I'm not," exclaimed Sallie, with an air that proved the contrary.

"What do you hate most?" asked Fred.

"Spiders and rice pudding."

"What do you like best?" asked Jo.

"Dancing and French gloves."

"Well, *I* think Truth is a very silly play; let's have a sensible game of Authors, to refresh our minds," proposed Jo.

Ned, Frank, and the little girls joined in this, and, while it went on the three elders sat apart, talking. Miss Kate took out her sketch again, and Margaret watched her, while Mr. Brooke lay on the grass, with a book, which he did not read.

"How beautifully you do it; I wish I could draw," said Meg, with mingled admiration and regret in her voice.

"Why don't you learn? I should think you had taste and talent for it," replied Miss Kate, graciously.

"I haven't time."

"Your mamma prefers other accomplishments, I fancy. So did mine; but I proved to her that I had talent by taking a few lessons privately, and then she was quite willing I should go on. Can't you do the same with your governess?"

"I have none."

"I forgot; young ladies in America go to school more than with us. Very fine schools they are, too, papa says. You go to a private one, I suppose?"

"I don't go at all; I am a governess myself."

"Oh, indeed!" said Miss Kate; but she might as well have said, "Dear me, how dreadful!" for her tone implied it, and something in her face made Meg color, and wish she had not been so frank.

Mr. Brooke looked up, and said, quickly, "Young ladies in America love independence as much as their ancestors did, and are admired and respected for supporting themselves."

"Oh, yes; of course! it's very nice and proper in them to do so. We have many most respectable and worthy young women, who do the same; and are employed by the nobility, because, being the daughters of gentlemen, they are both well-bred and accomplished, you know," said Miss Kate, in a patronizing tone, that hurt Meg's pride, and made her work seem not only more distasteful, but degrading.

"Did the German song suit, Miss March?" inquired Mr. Brooke, breaking an awkward pause.

"Oh, yes! it was very sweet, and I'm obliged to whoever translated it for me," and Meg's downcast face brightened as she spoke.

"Don't you read German?" asked Miss Kate, with a look of surprise.

"Not very well. My father, who taught me, is away, and I don't get on very fast alone, for I've no one to correct my pronunciation."

"Try a little now; here is Schiller's 'Mary Stuart', and a tutor who loves to teach," and Mr. Brooke laid his book on her lap, with an inviting smile.

"It's so hard, I'm afraid to try," said Meg, grateful, but bashful in the presence of the accomplished young lady beside her.

"I'll read a bit to encourage you;" and Miss Kate read one of the most beautiful passages in a perfectly correct, but perfectly expressionless, manner.

Mr. Brooke made no comment, so she returned the book to Meg, who said innocently, —

"I thought it was poetry."

"Some of it is; try this passage."

There was a queer smile about Mr. Brooke's mouth, as he opened at poor Mary's lament.

Meg, obediently following the long grass-blade which her new tutor used to point with, read, slowly and timidly, unconsciously making poetry of the hard words, by the soft intonation of her musical voice. Down the page went the green guide, and presently, forgetting her listener in the beauty of the sad scene, Meg read as if alone, giving a little touch of tragedy to the words of the unhappy queen. If she had seen the brown eyes then, she would have stopped short: but she never looked up, and the lesson was not spoilt for her.

"Very well, indeed!" said Mr. Brooke, as she paused, quite ignoring her many mistakes, and looking as if he did, indeed, "love to teach."

Miss Kate put up her glass, and, having taken a survey of the little tableau before her, shut her sketch book, saying, with condescension:

"You've a nice accent, and, in time will be a clever reader. I advise you to learn, for German is a valuable accomplishment to teachers. I must look after Grace, she is romping;" and Miss Kate strolled away adding to herself, with a shrug, "I didn't come here to chaperone a governess, though she *is* young and pretty. What odd people these Yankees are! I'm afraid Laurie will be quite spoilt among them."

"I forgot that English people rather turn up their noses at governesses, and don't treat them as we do," said Meg, looking after the retreating figure with an annoyed expression.

"Tutors, also, have rather a hard time of it there, as I know to my sorrow. There's no place like America for us workers, Miss Margaret," and Mr. Brooke looked so contented and cheerful, that Meg was ashamed to lament her hard lot.

"I'm glad I live in it, then. I don't like my work, but I get a good deal of satisfaction out of it, after all, so I won't complain; I only wish I liked teaching as you do."

"I think you would, if you had Laurie for a pupil. I shall be very sorry to lose him next year," said Mr. Brooke, busily punching holes in the turf.

"Going to college, I suppose?" Meg's lips asked that question, but her eyes added, "And what becomes of you?"

"Yes; it's high time he went, for he is ready, and as soon as he is off I shall turn soldier."

"I am glad of that!" exclaimed Meg; "I should think every young man would want to go; though it is hard for the mothers and sisters, who stay at home," she added, sorrowfully.

"I have neither, and very few friends, to care whether I live or die," said Mr. Brooke, rather bitterly, as he absently put the dead rose in the hole he had made, and covered it up, like a little grave.

"Laurie and his grandfather would care a great deal, and we should all be very sorry to have any harm happen to you," said Meg, heartily.

"Thank you; that sounds pleasant," began Mr. Brooke, looking cheerful again; but, before he could finish his speech, Ned, mounted on the old horse, came lumbering up, to display his equestrian skill before the young ladies, and there was no more quiet that day.

"Don't you love to ride?" asked Grace of Amy, as they stood resting, after a race round the field with the others, led by Ned.

"I dote upon it; my sister Meg used to ride, when papa was rich, but we don't keep any horses now, – except Ellen Tree," added Amy, laughing.

"Tell me about Ellen Tree; is it a donkey?" asked Grace, curiously.

"Why, you see, Jo is crazy about horses, and so am I, but we've only got an old side-saddle, and no horse. But in our garden is an apple tree, that has a nice low branch; so I put the saddle on it, fixed some reins on the part that turns up, and we bounce away on Ellen Tree whenever we like."

"How funny!" laughed Grace. "I have a pony at home, and ride nearly every day in the park, with Fred and Kate; it's very nice, for my friends go too, and the Row is full of ladies and gentlemen."

"Dear, how charming! I hope I shall go abroad, some day; but I'd rather go to Rome than the Row," said Amy, who had not the remotest idea what the Row was, and wouldn't have asked for the world.

Frank, sitting just behind the little girls, heard what they were saying, and pushed his crutch away from him with an impatient gesture, as he watched the active lads going through all sorts of comical gymnastics. Beth, who was collecting the scattered Author-cards, looked up, and said, in her shy yet friendly way, –

"I'm afraid you are tired; can I do anything for you?"

"Talk to me, please; it's dull, sitting by myself," answered Frank, who had evidently been used to being made much of at home.

If he had asked her to deliver a Latin oration, it would not have seemed a more impossible task to bashful Beth; but there was no place to run to, no Jo to hide behind now, and the poor boy looked so wistfully at her, that she bravely resolved to try.

"What do you like to talk about?" she asked, fumbling over the cards, and dropping half as she tried to tie them up.

"Well, I like to hear about cricket, and boating, and hunting," said Frank, who had not yet learned to suit his amusements to his strength.

"My heart! whatever shall I do? I don't know anything about them," thought Beth; and , forgetting the boy's misfortune in her flurry, she said, hoping to make him talk, "I never saw any hunting, but I suppose you know all about it."

"I did once; but I can never hunt again, for I got hurt leaping a confounded five-barred gate; so there's no more horses and hounds for me," said Frank, with a sigh that made Beth hate herself for her innocent blunder.

"Your deer are much prettier than our ugly buffaloes," she said, turning to the prairies for help, and feeling glad that she had read one of the boy's books in which Jo delighted.

Buffaloes proved soothing and satisfactory; and, in her eagerness to amuse another, Beth forgot herself, and was quite unconscious of her sister's surprise and delight at the unusual spectacle of Beth talking away to one of the dreadful boys, against whom she had begged protection.

"Bless her heart! She pities him, so she is good to him," said Jo, beaming at her from the croquet ground.

"I always said she was a little saint," added Meg, as if there could be no further doubt about it.

"I haven't heard Frank laugh so much for ever so long," said Grace to Amy, as they sat discussing dolls, and making tea-sets out of acorn-cups.

"My sister Beth is a very fastidious girl when she likes to be," said Amy, well pleased at Beth's success. She meant "fascinating," but as Grace didn't know the exact meaning of either word, "fastidious" sounded well, and made a good impression.

An impromptu circus, fox and geese, and an amicable game of croquet, finished the afternoon. At sunset the tent was struck, hampers packed, wickets pulled up, boats loaded, and the whole party floated down the river, singing at the tops of their voices. Ned, getting sentimental, warbled a serenade with the pensive refrain, –

Alone, alone, ah! woe, alone,

and at the lines—

> *We each are young, we each have a heart,*
> *Oh, why should we stand thus coldly apart?*

he looked at Meg with such a lackadaisical expression, that she laughed outright, and spoilt his song.

"How can you be so cruel to me?" he whispered, under cover of a lively chorus; "you've kept close to that starched-up English woman all day, and now you snub me."

"I didn't mean to; but you looked so funny I really couldn't help it," replied Meg, passing over the first part of his reproach; for it was quite true that she *had* shunned him, remembering the Moffat party and the talk after it.

Ned was offended, and turned to Sallie for consolation, saying to her, rather pettishly, "There isn't a bit of flirt in that girl, is there?"

"Not a particle; but she's a dear," returned Sallie, defending her friend even while confessing her short-comings.

"She's not a stricken deer, anyway," said Ned, trying to be witty, and succeeding as well as very young gentlemen usually do.

On the lawn where it had gathered, the little party separated with cordial good-nights and good-byes, for the Vaughns were going to Canada. As the four sisters went home through the garden, Miss Kate looked after them, saying, without the patronizing tone in her voice, "In spite of their demonstrative manners, American girls are very nice when one knows them."

"I quite agree with you," said Mr. Brooke.

CHAPTER THIRTEEN

CASTLES IN THE AIR

~

Laurie lay luxuriously swinging to and fro in his hammock, one warm September afternoon, wondering what his neighbors were about, but too lazy to go and find out. He was in one of his moods; for the day had been both unprofitable and unsatisfactory, and he was wishing he could live it over again. The hot weather made him indolent; and he had shirked his studies, tried Mr. Brooke's patience to the utmost, displeased his grandfather by practising half the afternoon, frightened the maid-servants half out of their wits, by mischievously hinting that one of his dogs was going mad, and, after high words with the stableman about some fancied neglect of his horse, he had flung himself into his hammock, to fume over the stupidity of the world in general, till the peace of the lovely day quieted him in spite of himself. Staring up into the green gloom of the horse-chestnut trees above him, he dreamed dreams of all sorts, and was just imagining himself tossing on the ocean, in a voyage round the world, when the sound of voices brought him ashore in a flash. Peeping through the meshes of his hammock, he saw the Marches coming out, as if bound on some expedition.

"What in the world are those girls about now?" thought Laurie, opening his sleepy eyes to take a good look, for there was something rather peculiar in the appearance of his neighbors. Each wore a large, flapping hat, a brown linen pouch slung over one shoulder, and carried a long staff; Meg had a cushion, Jo a book, Beth a dipper, and Amy a portfolio. All walked quietly through the garden, out at the little back gate, and began to climb the hill that lay between the house and the river.

"Well, that's cool!" said Laurie to himself, "to have a picnic and never ask me. They can't be going in the boat, for they haven't got the key. Perhaps they forgot it; I'll take it to them, and see what's going on."

Though possessed of half a dozen hats, it took him some time to find one; then there was a hunt for the key, which was at last discovered in his pocket; so that the girls were quite out of sight when he leaped the fence and ran after them. Taking the shortest way to the boat-house, he waited for them to appear; but no one came, and he went up the hill to take an observation. A grove of pines covered one part of it, and from the heart of his green spot came a clearer sound than the soft sigh of the pines, or the drowsy chirp of the crickets.

"Here's a landscape!" thought Laurie, peeping through the bushes, and looking wide awake and good-natured already.

It *was* rather a pretty little picture; for the sisters sat together in the shady nook, with sun and shadow flickering over them, — the aromatic wind lifting their hair and cooling their hot cheeks, — and all the little wood-people going on with their affairs as if these were no strangers, but old friends. Meg sat upon her cushion, sewing daintily with her white hands, and looking as fresh and as sweet as a rose, in her pink dress, among the green. Beth was sorting the cones that lay thick under the hemlock near by, for she made pretty things of them. Amy was sketching a group of ferns, and Jo was knitting as she read aloud. A shadow passed over the boy's face as he watched them, feeling that he ought to go, because uninvited; yet lingering, because home seemed very lonely, and this quiet party in the woods most attractive to his restless spirit. He stood so still, that a squirrel, busy with its harvesting, ran down a pine close beside him, saw him suddenly, and skipped back, scolding so shrilly that Beth looked up, espied the wistful face behind the birches, and beckoned with a reassuring smile.

"May I come in, please? or shall I be a bother?" he asked, advancing slowly.

Meg lifted her eyebrows, but Jo scowled at her defiantly, and said at once, "Of course you may. We should have asked you before, only we thought you wouldn't care for such a girl's game as this."

"I always like your games; but if Meg don't want me, I'll go away."

"I've no objection, if you do something; it's against the rule to be idle here," replied Meg, gravely, but graciously.

"Much obliged; I'll do anything if you'll let me stop a bit, for it's as dull as the desert of Sahara down there. Shall I sew, read, cone, draw, or do all at once? Bring on your bears; I'm ready," and Laurie sat down with a submissive expression delightful to behold.

"Finish this story while I set my heel," said Jo, handing him the book.

"Yes'm," was the meek answer, as he began, doing his best to prove his gratitude for the favor of an admission into the "Busy Bee Society."

The story was not a long one, and, when it was finished, he ventured to ask a few questions as a reward of merit.

"Please, mum, could I inquire if this highly instructive and charming institution is a new one?"

"Would you tell him?" asked Meg of her sisters.

"He'll laugh," said Amy, warningly.

"Who cares?" said Jo.

"I guess he'll like it," added Beth.

"Of course I shall! I give you my word I won't laugh. Tell away, Jo, and don't be afraid."

"The idea of being afraid of you! Well, you see we used to play 'Pilgrim's Progress,' and we have been going on with it in earnest, all winter and summer."

"Yes, I know," said Laurie, nodding wisely.

"Who told you?" demanded Jo.

"Spirits."

"No, it was me; I wanted to amuse him one night when you were all away, and he was rather dismal. He did like it, so don't scold, Jo," said Beth, meekly.

"You can't keep a secret. Never mind; it saves trouble now."

"Go on, please," said Laurie, as Jo became absorbed in her work, looking a trifle displeased.

"Oh, didn't she tell you about this new plan of ours? Well, we have tried not to waste our holiday but each has had a task, and worked at it with a will. The vacation is nearly over, the stints are all done, and we are ever so glad that we didn't dawdle."

"Yes, I should think so;" and Laurie thought regretfully of his own idle days.

"Mother likes to have us out of doors as much as possible; so we bring our work here, and have nice times. For the fun of it we bring our things in these bags, wear the old hats, use poles to climb the hill, and play pilgrims, as we used to do years ago. We call this hill the 'Delectable Mountain,' for we can look far away and see the country where we hope to live some time."

Jo pointed, and Laurie sat up to examine; for through an opening in the wood one could look across the wide, blue river, – the meadows on the other side – far over the outskirts of the great city, to the green hills that rose to meet the sky. The sun was low, and the heavens glowed with the splendor of an autumn sunset. Gold and purple clouds lay on the hill-tops; and rising high into the ruddy light were silvery white peaks, that shone like the airy spires of some Celestial City.

"How beautiful that is!" said Laurie, softly, for he was quick to see and feel beauty of any kind.

"It's often so; and we like to watch it, for it is never the same, but always splendid," replied Amy, wishing she could paint it.

"Jo talks about the country where we hope to live some time; the real country, she means, with pigs and chickens, and hay-making. It would be nice, but I wish the beautiful country up there was real, and we could ever go to it," said Beth, musingly.

"There is a lovelier country even than that, where we *shall* go, by and by, when we are good enough," answered Meg, with her sweet voice.

"It seems so long to wait, so hard to do; I want to fly away at once, as those swallows fly, and go in at that splendid gate."

"You'll get there, Beth, sooner or later; no fear of that," said Jo; "I'm the one that will have to fight and work and climb and wait, and maybe never get in after all."

"You'll have me for company, if that's any comfort. I shall have to do a deal of travelling before I come in sight of your Celestial City. If I arrive late, you'll say a good word for me, won't you, Beth?"

Something in the boy's face troubled his little friend; but she said cheerfully, with her quiet eyes on the changing clouds, "If people really want to go, and really try all their lives, I think they will get in; for I don't believe there are any locks on that door, or any guards at the gate. I always imagine it is as it is in the picture, where the shining ones stretch out their hands to welcome poor Christian as he comes up from the river."

"Wouldn't it be fun if all the castles in the air which we make could come true, and we could live in them?" said Jo, after a little pause.

"I've made such quantities it would be hard to choose which I'd have," said Laurie, lying flat, and throwing cones at the squirrel who had betrayed him.

"You'd have to take your favorite one. What is it?" asked Meg.

"If I tell mine, will you tell yours?"

"Yes, if the girls will too."

"We will. Now, Laurie!"

"After I'd seen as much of the world as I want to, I'd like to settle in Germany, and have just as much music as I choose. I'm to be a famous musician myself, and all creation is to rush to hear me; and I'm never to be bothered about money or business, but just enjoy myself, and live for what I like. That's my favorite castle. What's yours, Meg?"

Margaret seemed to find it a little hard to tell hers, and moved a brake before her face, as if to disperse imaginary gnats, while she said, slowly, "I should like a lovely house, full of all sorts of luxurious things; nice food, pretty clothes, handsome furniture, pleasant people, and heaps of money. I am to be mistress of it, and imagine it as I like, with plenty of servants, so I never need work a bit. How I should enjoy it! for I wouldn't be idle, but do good, and make every one love me dearly."

"Wouldn't you have a master for your castle in the air?" asked Laurie, slyly.

"I said 'pleasant people,' you know;" and Meg carefully tied up her shoe as she spoke, so that no one saw her face.

"Why don't you say you'd have a splendid, wise, good husband, and some angelic little children? You know your castle wouldn't be perfect without," said blunt Jo, who had no tender fancies yet, and rather scorned romance, except in books.

"You'd have nothing but horses, inkstands, and novels in yours," answered Meg, petulantly.

"Wouldn't I, though! I'd have a stable full of Arabian steeds, rooms piled with books, and I'd write out of a magic inkstand, so that my works should be as famous as Laurie's music. I want to do something splendid before I go into my castle, — something heroic or wonderful, — that won't be forgotten after I'm dead. I don't know what, but I'm on the watch for it, and mean to astonish you all, some day. I think I shall write books, and get rich and famous; that would suit me, so that is *my* favorite dream."

"Mine is to stay at home safe with father and mother, and help take care of the family," said Beth, contentedly.

"Don't you wish for anything else?" asked Laurie.

"Since I had my little piano I am perfectly satisfied. I only wish we may all keep well, and be together; nothing else."

"I have so many wishes; but the pet one is to be an artist, and go to Rome, and do fine pictures, and be the best artist in the whole world," was Amy's modest desire.

"We're an ambitious set, aren't we? Every one of us, but Beth, wants to be rich and famous, and gorgeous in every respect. I do wonder if any of us will ever get our wishes," said Laurie, chewing grass, like a meditative calf.

"I've got the key to my castle in the air; but whether I can unlock the door, remains to be seen," observed Jo, mysteriously.

"I've got the key to mine, but I'm not allowed to try it. Hang college!" muttered Laurie, with an impatient sigh.

"Here's mine!" and Amy waved her pencil.

"I haven't got any," said Meg, forlornly.

"Yes, you have," said Laurie, at once.

"Where?"

"In your face."

"Nonsense; that's of no use."

"Wait and see if it doesn't bring you something worth having," replied the boy, laughing at the thought of a charming little secret which he fancied he knew.

Meg colored behind the brake, but asked no questions, and looked across the river with the same expectant expression which Mr. Brooke had worn when he told the story of the knight.

"If we are all alive ten years hence, let's meet, and see how many of us have got our wishes, or how much nearer we are then than now," said Jo, always ready with a plan.

"Bless me! how old shall I be, – twenty-seven!" exclaimed Meg, who felt grown up already, having just reached seventeen.

"You and I shall be twenty-six, Teddy; Beth twenty-four, and Amy twenty-two; what a venerable party!" said Jo.

"I hope I shall have done something to be proud of by that time; but I'm such a lazy dog, I'm afraid I shall 'dawdle,' Jo."

"You need a motive, mother says; and when you get it, she is sure you'll work splendidly."

"Is she? By Jupiter, I will, if I only get the chance!" cried Laurie, sitting up with sudden energy. "I ought to be satisfied to please grandfather, and I do try, but it's working against the grain, you see, and comes hard. He wants me to be an India merchant, as he was, and I'd rather be shot. I hate tea, and silk, and spices, and every sort of rubbish his old ships bring, and I don't care how soon they go to the bottom when I own them. Going to college ought to satisfy him, for if I give him four years he ought to let me off from business; but he's set, and I've got to do just as he did, unless I break away and please myself, as my father did. If there was any one left to stay with the old gentleman, I'd do it to-morrow."

Laurie spoke excitedly, and looked ready to carry his threat into execution on the slightest provocation; for he was growing up very fast, and, in spite of his indolent ways, had a young man's hatred of subjection, – a young man's restless longing to try the world for himself.

"I advise you to sail away in one of your ships, and never come home again till you have tried your own way," said Jo, whose imagination was fired by the thought of such a daring exploit, and whose sympathy was excited by what she called "Teddy's wrongs."

"That's not right, Jo; you mustn't talk in that way, and Laurie mustn't take your bad advice. You should do just what your grandfather wishes, my dear boy," said Meg, in her most maternal tone. "Do your best at college, and, when he sees that you try to please him, I'm sure he won't be hard or unjust to you. As you say, there is no one else to stay with and love him, and you'd never forgive yourself if you left him without his permission. Don't be dismal, or fret, but do your duty; and you'll get your reward, as good Mr. Brooke has, by being respected and loved."

"What do you know about him?" asked Laurie, grateful for the good advice, but objecting to the lecture, and glad to turn the conversation from himself, after his unusual outbreak.

"Only what your grandpa told mother about him; how he took good care of his own mother till she died, and wouldn't go abroad as tutor to some nice person, because he wouldn't leave her; and how he provides now for an old woman who nursed his mother; and never tells any one, but is just as generous and patient, and good as he can be."

"So he is, dear old fellow!" said Laurie, heartily, as Meg paused, looking flushed and earnest, with her story. "It's like grandpa to find out all about him, without letting him know, and to tell all his goodness to others, so that they might like him. Brooke couldn't understand why your mother was so kind to him, asking him over with me, and treating him in her beautiful, friendly way. He thought she was just perfect, and talked about it for days and days, and went on about you all, in flaming style. If ever I get my wish, you see what I'll do for Brooke."

"Begin to do something now, by not plaguing his life out," said Meg, sharply.

"How do you know I do, miss?"

"I can always tell by his face, when he goes away. If you have been good, he looks satisfied, and walks briskly; if you have plagued him, he's sober, and walks slowly, as if he wanted to go back and do his work better."

"Well, I like that! So you keep an account of my good and bad marks in Brooke's face, do you? I see him bow and smile as he passes your window, but I didn't know you'd got up a telegraph."

"We haven't; don't be angry, and oh, don't tell him I said anything! It was only to show that I cared how you get on, and what is said here is said in confidence, you know," cried Meg, much alarmed at the thought of what might follow from her careless speech.

"*I* don't tell tales," replied Laurie, with his "high and mighty" air, as Jo called a certain expression which he occasionally wore. "Only if Brooke is going to be a barometer, I must mind and have fair weather for him to report."

"Please don't be offended; I didn't mean to preach or tell tales, or be silly; I only thought Jo was encouraging you in a feeling which you'd be sorry for, by and by. You are so kind to us, we feel as if you were our brother, and say just what we think; forgive me, I meant it kindly." And Meg offered her hand with a gesture both affectionate and timid.

Ashamed of his momentary pique, Laurie squeezed the kind little hand, and said, frankly, "I'm the one to be forgiven; I'm cross, and have been out of sorts all day, I like to have you tell me my faults, and be sisterly; so don't mind if I am grumpy sometimes; I thank you all the same."

Bent on showing that he was not offended, he made himself as agreeable as possible; wound cotton for Meg, recited poetry to please Jo, shook down cones for Beth, and helped Amy with her ferns, – proving himself a fit person to belong to the "Busy Bee Society." In the midst of an animated discussion on the domestic habits of turtles (one of those amiable creatures having strolled up from the river), the faint sound of a bell warned them that Hannah had put the tea "to draw," and they would just have time to get home to supper.

"May I come again?" asked Laurie.

"Yes, if you are good, and love your book, as the boys in the primer are told to do," said Meg, smiling.

"I'll try."

"Then you may come, and I'll teach you to knit as the Scotchmen do; there's a demand for socks just now," added Jo, waving hers, like a big, blue worsted banner, as they parted at the gate.

That night, when Beth played to Mr. Laurence in the twilight, Laurie, standing in the shadow of the curtain, listened to the little David, whose simple music always quieted his moody spirit, and watched the old man, who sat with his gray head on his hand, thinking tender thoughts of the dead child he had loved so much. Remembering the conversation of the afternoon, the boy said to himself, with the resolve to make the sacrifice cheerfully, "I'll let my castles go, and stay with the dear old gentleman while he needs me, for I am all he has."

CHAPTER FOURTEEN

SECRETS

~

Jo was very busy in the garret, for the October days began to grow chilly, and the afternoons were short. For two or three hours the sun lay warmly in the high window, showing Jo seated on the old sofa writing busily, with her papers spread out upon a trunk before her, while Scrabble, the pet rat, promenaded the beams overhead, accompanied by his oldest son, a fine young fellow, who was evidently very proud of his whiskers. Quite absorbed in her work, Jo scribbled away till the last page was filled, when she signed her name with a flourish, and threw down her pen, exclaiming, –

"There, I've done my best! If this don't suit, I shall have to wait till I can do better."

Lying back on the sofa, she read the manuscript carefully through, making dashes here and there, and putting in many exclamation points, which looked like little balloons; then she tied it up with a smart red ribbon, and sat a minute looking at it with a sober, wistful expression, which plainly showed how earnest her work had been. Jo's desk up here was an old tin kitchen, which hung against the wall. In it she kept her papers and a few books, safely shut away from Scrabble, who, being likewise of a literary turn, was fond of making a circulating library of such books as were left in his way, by eating the leaves. From this tin receptable Jo produced another manuscript; and, putting both in her pocket, crept quietly down stairs, leaving her friends to nibble her pens and taste her ink.

She put on her hat and jacket as noiselessly as possible, and, going to the back entry window, got out upon the roof of a low porch, swung herself down to the grassy bank, and took a roundabout way to the road. Once there, she composed herself, hailed a passing omnibus, and rolled away to town, looking very merry and mysterious.

If any one had been watching her, he would have thought her movements decidedly peculiar; for, on alighting, she went off at a great pace till she reached a certain number in a certain busy street; having found the place with some difficulty, she went into the doorway, looked up the dirty stairs, and, after standing stock still a minute, suddenly dived into the street, and walked away as rapidly as she came. This manœuvre she repeated several times, to the great amusement of a black-eyed young gentleman lounging in the window of the building opposite. On returning for the third time, Jo gave herself a shake, pulled her hat over her eyes, and walked up the stairs, looking as if she was going to have all her teeth out.

There was a dentist's sign, among others, which adorned the entrance, and, after staring a minute at the pair of artificial jaws which slowly opened and shut to draw attention to a fine set of teeth, the young gentleman put on his coat, took his hat, and went down to post himself in the opposite doorway, saying, with a smile and shiver, –

"It's like her to come alone, but if she has a bad time she'll need some one to help her home."

In ten minutes Jo came running down stairs with a very red face, and the general appearance of a person who had just passed through a trying ordeal of some sort. When she saw the young gentleman she looked anything but pleased, and passed him with a nod; but he followed, asking with an air of sympathy, –

"Did you have a bad time?"

"Not very."

"You got through quickly."

"Yes, thank goodness!"

"Why did you go alone?"

"Didn't want any one to know."

"You're the oddest fellow I ever saw. How many did you have out?"

Jo looked at her friend as if she did not understand him; then began to laugh, as if mightily amused at something.

"There are two which I want to have come out, but I must wait a week."

"What are you laughing at? You are up to some mischief, Jo," said Laurie, looking mystified.

"So are you. What were you doing, sir, up in that billiard saloon?"

"Begging your pardon, ma'am, it wasn't a billiard saloon, but a gymnasium, and I was taking a lesson in fencing."

"I'm glad of that."

"Why?"

"You can teach me, and then, when we play Hamlet, you can be Laertes, and we'll make a fine thing of the fencing scene."

Laurie burst out with a hearty boy's laugh, which made several passers-by smile in spite of themselves.

"I'll teach you, whether we play Hamlet or not; it's grand fun, and will straighten you up capitally. But I don't believe that was your reason for saying 'I'm glad,' in that decided way; was it, now?"

"No, I was glad that you were not in the saloon, because I hope you never go to such places. Do you?"

"Not often."

"I wish you wouldn't."

"It's no harm, Jo. I have billiards at home, but it's no fun unless you have good players, so, as I'm fond of it, I come in sometimes and have a game with Ned Moffat or some of the other fellows."

"Oh dear, I'm so sorry, for you'll get to liking it better and better, and will waste time and money, and grow like those dreadful boys. I did hope you'd stay respectable, and be a satisfaction to your friends," said Jo, shaking her head.

"Can't a fellow take a little innocent amusement now and then without losing his respectability?" asked Laurie, looking nettled.

"That depends upon how and where he takes it. I don't like Ned and his set, and wish you'd keep out of it. Mother won't let us have him at our house, though he wants to come, and if you grow like him she won't be willing to have us frolic together as we do now."

"Won't she?" asked Laurie, anxiously.

"No, she can't bear fashionable young men, and she'd shut us all up in bandboxes rather than have us associate with them."

"Well, she needn't get out her bandboxes yet; I'm not a fashionable party, and don't mean to be; but I do like harmless larks now and then, don't you?"

"Yes, nobody minds them, so lark away, but don't get wild, will you? or there will be an end of all our good times."

"I'll be a double distilled saint."

"I can't bear saints; just be a simple, honest, respectable boy, and we'll never desert you. I don't know what I *should* do if you acted like Mr. King's son; he had plenty of money, but didn't know how to spend it, and got tipsy, and gambled, and ran away, and forged his father's name, I believe, and was altogether horrid."

"You think I'm likely to do the same? Much obliged."

"No, I don't – oh, *dear*, no! – but I hear people talking about money being such a temptation, and I sometimes wish you were poor; I shouldn't worry then."

"Do you worry about me, Jo?"

"A little, when you look moody or discontented, as you sometimes do, for you've got such a strong will, if you once get started wrong, I'm afraid it would be hard to stop you."

Laurie walked in silence for a few minutes, and Jo watched him, wishing she had held her tongue, for his eyes looked angry, though his lips still smiled as if at her warnings.

"Are you going to deliver lectures all the way home?" he asked presently.

"Of course not; why?"

"Because if you are, I'll take a 'bus; if you are not, I'd like to walk with you, and tell you something very interesting."

"I won't preach any more, and I'd like to hear the news immensely."

"Very well, then; come on. It's a secret, and if I tell you, you must tell me yours."

"I haven't got any," began Jo, but stopped suddenly, remembering that she had.

"You know you have; you can't hide anything, so up and 'fess, or I won't tell," cried Laurie.

"Is your secret a nice one?"

"Oh, isn't it! all about people you know, and such fun! You ought to hear it, and I've been aching to tell it this long time. Come! you begin."

"You'll not say anything about it at home, will you?"

"Not a word."

"And you won't tease me in private?"

"I never tease."

"Yes, you do; you get everything you want out of people. I don't know how you do it, but you are a born wheedler."

"Thank you; fire away!"

"Well, I've left two stories with a newspaper man, and he's to give his answer next week," whispered Jo, in her confidant's ear.

"Hurrah for Miss March, the celebrated American authoress!" cried Laurie, throwing up his hat and catching it again, to the great delight of two ducks, four cats, five hens, and half a dozen Irish children; for they were out of the city now.

"Hush! it won't come to anything, I dare say; but I couldn't rest till I had tried, and I said nothing about it, because I didn't want any one else to be disappointed."

"It won't fail. Why, Jo, your stories are works of Shakespeare compared to half the rubbish that's published every day. Won't it be fun to see them in print; and shan't we feel proud of our authoress?"

Jo's eyes sparkled, for it's always pleasant to be believed in; and a friend's praise is always sweeter than a dozen newspaper puffs.

"Where's *your* secret? Play fair, Teddy, or I'll never believe you again," she said, trying to extinguish the brilliant hopes that blazed up at a word of encouragement.

"I may get into a scrape for telling; but I didn't promise not to, so I will, for I never feel easy in my mind till I've told you any plummy bit of news I get. I know where Meg's glove is."

"Is that all?" said Jo, looking disappointed, as Laurie nodded and twinkled, with a face full of mysterious intelligence.

"It's quite enough for the present, as you'll agree when I tell you where it is."

"Tell then."

Laurie bent and whispered three words in Jo's ear, which produced a comical change. She stood and stared at him for a minute, looking both surprised and displeased, then walked on, saying sharply, "How do you know?"

"Saw it."

"Where?"

"Pocket."

"All this time?"

"Yes; isn't that romantic?"

"No, it's horrid."

"Don't you like it?"

"Of course I don't; it's ridiculous; it won't be allowed. My patience! what would Meg say?"

"You are not to tell any one; mind that."

"I didn't promise."

"That was understood, and I trusted you."

"Well, I won't for the present, any way; but I'm disgusted, and wish you hadn't told me."

"I thought you'd be pleased."

"At the idea of anybody coming to take Meg away? No, thank you."

"You'll feel better about it when somebody comes to take you away."

"I'd like to see any one try it," cried Jo, fiercely.

"So should I!" and Laurie chuckled at the idea.

"I don't think secrets agree with me; I feel rumpled up in my mind since you told me that," said Jo, rather ungratefully.

"Race down this hill with me, and you'll be all right," suggested Laurie.

No one was in sight; the smooth road sloped invitingly before her, and, finding the temptation irresistible, Jo darted away, soon leaving hat and comb behind her, and scattering hairpins as she ran. Laurie reached the goal first, and was quite satisfied with the success of his treatment; for his Atalanta came panting up with flying hair, bright eyes, ruddy cheeks, and no signs of dissatisfaction in her face.

"I wish I was a horse; then I could run for miles in this splendid air, and not lose my breath. It was capital; but see what a guy it's made me. Go, pick up my things, like a cherub as you are," said Jo, dropping down under a maple tree, which was carpeting the bank with crimson leaves.

Laurie leisurely departed to recover the lost property, and Jo bundled up her braids, hoping no one would pass by till she was tidy again. But some one did pass, and who should it be but Meg, looking particularly lady-like in her state and festival suit, for she had been making calls.

"What in the world are you doing here?" she asked, regarding her dishevelled sister with well-bred surprise.

"Getting leaves," meekly answered Jo, sorting the rosy handful she had just swept up.

"And hairpins," added Laurie, throwing half a dozen into Jo's lap. "They grow on this road, Meg; so do combs and brown straw hats."

"You have been running, Jo; how could you? When *will* you stop such romping ways?" said Meg, reprovingly, as she settled her cuffs and smoothed her hair, with which the wind had taken liberties.

"Never till I'm stiff and old, and have to use a crutch. Don't try to make me grow up before my time, Meg; it's hard enough to have you change all of a sudden; let me be a little girl as long as I can."

As she spoke, Jo bent over her work to hide the trembling of her lips; for lately she had felt that Margaret was fast getting to be a woman, and Laurie's secret made her dread the separation which must surely come some time, and now seemed very near. He saw the trouble in her face, and drew Meg's attention from it by asking quickly, "Where have you been calling, all so fine?"

"At the Gardiners; and Sallie has been telling me all about Belle Moffat's wedding. It was very splendid, and they have gone to spend the winter in Paris; just think how delightful that must be!"

"Do you envy her, Meg?" Laurie asked.

"I'm afraid I do."

"I'm glad of it!" muttered Jo, tying on her hat with a jerk.

"Why?" asked Meg, looking surprised.

"Because, if you care so much about riches, you will never go and marry a poor man," said Jo, frowning at Laurie, who was mutely warning her to mind what she said.

"I shall never 'go and marry' any one," observed Meg, walking on with great dignity, while the others followed, laughing, whispering, skipping stones, and "behaving like children," as Meg said to herself, though she might have been tempted to join them if she had not had her best dress on.

For a week or two Jo behaved so queerly, that her sisters got quite bewildered. She rushed to the door when the postman rang; was rude to Mr. Brooke whenever they met; would sit looking at Meg with a woe-begone face, occasionally jumping up to shake, and then to kiss her, in a very mysterious manner; Laurie and she were always making signs to one another, and talking about "Spread Eagles," till the girls declared they had both lost their wits. On the second Saturday after Jo got out of the window, Meg, as she sat sewing at her window, was scandalized by the sight of Laurie chasing Jo all over the garden, and finally capturing her in Amy's bower. What went on in there, Meg could not see, but shrieks of laughter were heard, followed by the murmur of voices and a great flapping of newspapers.

"What shall we do with that girl? She never *will* behave like a young lady," sighed Meg, as she watched the race with a disapproving face.

"I hope she won't; she is so funny and dear as she is," said Beth, who had never betrayed that she was a little hurt at Jo's having secrets with any one but her.

"It's very trying, but we can never make her *comme la fo*," added Amy, who sat making some new frills for herself, with her curls tied up in a very becoming way, — two agreeable things, which made her feel unusually elegant and lady-like.

In a few minutes Jo bounced in, laid herself on the sofa, and affected to read.

"Have you anything interesting there?" asked Meg, with condescension.

"Nothing but a story; don't amount to much, I guess," returned Jo, carefully keeping the name of the paper out of sight.

"You'd better read it aloud; that will amuse us, and keep you out of mischief," said Amy, in her most grown-up tone.

"What's the name?" asked Beth, wondering why Jo kept her face behind the sheet.

"The Rival Painters.*"

"That sounds well; read it," said Meg.

With a loud "hem!" and a long breath, Jo began to read very fast. The girls listened with interest, for the tale was romantic, and somewhat pathetic, as most of the characters died in the end.

"I like that about the splendid picture," was Amy's approving remark, as Jo paused.

"I prefer the lovering part. Viola and Angelo are two of our favorite names; isn't that queer?" said Meg, wiping her eyes, for the "lovering part" was tragical.

"Who wrote it?" asked Beth, who had caught a glimpse of Jo's face.

The reader suddenly sat up, cast away the paper, displaying a flushed countenance, and, with a funny mixture of solemnity and excitement, replied in a loud voice, "Your sister!"

"You?" cried Meg, dropping her work.

"It's very good," said Amy, critically.

"I knew it! I knew it! oh, my Jo, I *am* so proud!" and Beth began to hug her sister and exult over this splendid success.

Dear me, how delighted they all were, to be sure; how Meg wouldn't believe it till she saw the words, "Miss Josephine March," actually printed in the paper; how graciously Amy criticised the artistic parts of the story, and offered hints for a sequel, which unfortunately couldn't be carried out, as the hero and heroine were dead; how Beth got excited, and skipped and sung with joy; how Hannah came in to exclaim, "Sakes alive; well, I never!" in great astonishment at "that Jo's doins;" how proud Mrs. March was when she knew it; how Jo laughed, with tears in her eyes, as she declared she might as well be a peacock and done with it; and how the "Spread Eagle" might be said to flap his wings triumphantly over the house of March, as the paper passed from hand to hand.

"Tell us all about it." "When did it come?" "How much did you get for it?" "What *will* father say?" "Won't Laurie laugh?" cried the family, all in one breath, as they clustered about Jo; for these foolish affectionate people made a jubilee of every little household joy.

"Stop jabbering, girls, and I'll tell you everything," said Jo, wondering if Miss Burney felt any grander over her "Evelina" than she did over her "Rival Painters." Having told how she disposed of her tales, Jo added, – "And when I went to get my answer the man said he liked them both, but didn't pay beginners, only let them print in his paper, and noticed the stories. It was good practice, he said; and, when the beginners improved, any one would pay. So I let him have the two stories, and to-day this was sent to me, and Laurie caught me with it, and insisted on seeing it, so I let him; and he said it was good, and I shall write more, and he's going to get the next paid for, and oh I *am* so happy, for in time I may be able to support myself and help the girls."

Jo's breath gave out here; and, wrapping her head in the paper, she bedewed her little story with a few natural tears; for to be independent, and earn the praise of those she loved, were the dearest wishes of her heart, and this seemed to be the first step toward that happy end.

CHAPTER FIFTEEN

A TELEGRAM

~

"Ovember is the most disagreeable month in the whole year," said Margaret, standing at the window one dull afternoon, looking out at the frost-bitten garden.

"That's the reason I was born in it," observed Jo, pensively, quite unconscious of the blot on her nose.

"If something very pleasant should happen now, we should think it a delightful month," said Beth, who took a hopeful view of everything, even November.

"I dare say; but nothing pleasant ever *does* happen in this family," said Meg, who was out of sorts. "We go grubbing along day after day, without a bit of change, and very little fun. We might as well be in a tread-mill."

"My patience, how blue we are!" cried Jo. "I don't much wonder, poor dear, for you see other girls having splendid times, while you grind, grind, year in and year out. Oh, don't I wish I could fix things for you as I

do for my heroines! you're pretty enough and good enough already, so I'd
have some rich relation leave you a fortune unexpectedly; then you'd dash
out as an heiress, scorn every one who has slighted you, go abroad, and
come home my Lady Something, in a blaze of splendor and elegance."

"People don't have fortunes left them in that style nowadays; men
had to work, and women to marry for money. It's a dreadfully unjust
world," said Meg, bitterly.

"Jo and I are going to make fortunes for you all, just wait ten years,
and see if we don't," said Amy, who sat in a corner, making "mud pies," as
Hannah called her little clay models of birds, fruit and faces.

"Can't wait, and I'm afraid I haven't much faith in ink and dirt,
though I'm grateful for your good intentions."

Meg sighed, and turned to the frost-bitten garden again; Jo groaned,
and leaned both elbows on the table in a despondent attitude, but Amy
spatted away energetically; and Beth, who sat at the other window, said,
smiling, "Two pleasant things are going to happen right away; Marmee is
coming down the street, and Laurie is tramping through the garden as if he
had something nice to tell."

In they both came, Mrs. March with the usual questions, "Any letter
from father, girls?" and Laurie to say, in his persuasive way, "Won't some of
you come for a drive? I've been pegging away at mathematics till my head
is in a muddle, and I'm going to freshen my wits by a brisk turn. It's a dull
day, but the air isn't bad, and I'm going to take Brooke home, so it will be
gay inside, if it isn't out. Come, Jo, you and Beth will go, won't you?"

"Of course we will."

"Much obliged, but I'm busy;" and Meg whisked out her work-
basket, for she had agreed with her mother that it was best, for her at least,
not to drive often with the young gentleman.

"We three will be ready in a minute," cried Amy, running away to
wash her hands.

"Can I do anything for you, Madam Mother?" asked Laurie, leaning
over Mrs. March's chair, with the affectionate look and tone he always gave
her.

"No, thank you, except call at the office, if you'll be so kind, dear.
It's our day for a letter, and the penny postman hasn't been. Father is as
regular as the sun, but there's some delay on the way, perhaps."

A sharp ring interrupted her, and a minute after Hannah came in with a letter.

"It's one of them horrid telegraph things, mum," she said, handling it as if she was afraid it would explode, and do some damage.

At the word "telegraph," Mrs. March snatched it, read the two lines it contained, and dropped back into her chair as white as if the little paper had sent a bullet to her heart. Laurie dashed down stairs for water, while Meg and Hannah supported her, and Jo read aloud, in a frightened voice, —

MRS. MARCH:
> Your husband is very ill. Come at once.
> S. HALE,
> Blank Hospital, Washington.

How still the room was as they listened breathlessly! how strangely the day darkened outside! and how suddenly the whole world seemed to change, as the girls gathered about their mother, feeling as if all the happiness and support of their lives was about to be taken from them. Mrs. March was herself again directly; read the message over, and stretched out her arms to her daughters, saying, in a tone they never forgot, "I shall go at once, but it may be too late; oh, children, children! help me to bear it!"

For several minutes there was nothing but the sound of sobbing in the room, mingled with broken words of comfort, tender assurances of help, and hopeful whispers, that died away in tears. Poor Hannah was the first to recover, and with unconscious wisdom she set all the rest a good example; for, with her, work was the panacea for most afflictions.

"The Lord keep the dear man! I won't waste no time a cryin', but git your things ready right away, mum," she said, heartily, as she wiped her face on her apron, gave her mistress a warm shake of the hand with her own hard one, and went away, to work, like three women in one.

"She's right; there's no time for tears now. Be calm, girls, and let me think."

They tried to be calm, poor things, as their mother sat up, looking pale, but steady, and put away her grief to think and plan for them.

"Where's Laurie?" she asked presently, when she had collected her thoughts, and decided on the first duties to be done.

"Here, ma'am; oh, let me do something!" cried the boy, hurrying from the next room, whither he had withdrawn, feeling that their first sorrow was too sacred for even his friendly eyes to see.

"Send a telegram saying I will come at once. The next train goes early in the morning; I'll take that."

"What else? The horses are ready; I can go anywhere, — do anything," he said, looking ready to fly to the ends of the earth.

"Leave a note at Aunt March's. Jo, give me that pen and paper."

Tearing off the blank side of one of her newly copied pages, Jo drew the table before her mother, well knowing that money for the long, sad journey, must be borrowed, and feeling as if she could do anything to add a little to the sum for her father.

"Now go, dear; but don't kill yourself driving at a desperate pace; there is no need of that."

Mrs. March's warning was evidently thrown away; for five minutes later Laurie tore by the window, on his own fleet horse, riding as if for his life.

"Jo, run to the rooms, and tell Mrs. King that I can't come. On the way get these things. I'll put them down; they'll be needed, and I must go prepared for nursing. Hospital stores are not always good. Beth, go and ask Mr. Laurence for a couple of bottles of old wine; I'm not too proud to beg for father; he shall have the best of everything. Amy, tell Hannah to get down the black trunk; and Meg, come and help me find my things, for I'm half bewildered."

Writing, thinking, and directing all at once, might well bewilder the poor lady, and Meg begged her to sit down quietly in her room for a little while, and let them work. Every one scattered, like leaves before a gust of wind; and the quiet, happy household was broken up as suddenly as if the paper had been an evil spell.

Mr. Laurence came hurrying back with Beth, bringing every comfort the kind old gentleman could think of for the invalid, and friendliest promises of protection for the girls, during their mother's absence, which comforted her very much. There was nothing he didn't offer, from his own dressing-gown to himself as escort. But that last was impossible. Mrs. March would not hear of the old gentleman's undertaking the long journey; yet an expression of relief was visible when he spoke of it, for anxiety ill fits one for travelling. He saw the look, knit his heavy eyebrows, rubbed his hands, and marched abruptly away, saying he'd be back directly. No one had time to think of him again till, as Meg ran through the entry, with a pair of rubbers in one hand and a cup of tea in the other, she came suddenly upon Mr. Brooke.

"I'm very sorry to hear of this, Miss March," he said, in the kind, quiet tone which sounded pleasantly to her perturbed spirit. "I came to offer myself as escort to your mother. Mr. Laurence has commissions for me in Washington, and it will give me real satisfaction to be of service to her there."

Down dropped the rubbers, and the tea was very near following, as Meg put out her hand, with a face so full of gratitude, that Mr. Brooke would have felt repaid for a much greater sacrifice than the trifling one of time and comfort, which he was about to make.

"How kind you are! Mother will accept, I'm sure; and it will be such a relief to know that she has some one to take care of her. Thank you very, very much!"

Meg spoke earnestly, and forgot herself entirely till something in the brown eyes looking down at her made her remember that cooling tea, and lead the way into the parlor, saying she would call her mother.

Everything was arranged by the time Laurie returned with a note from Aunt March, enclosing the desired sum, and a few lines repeating what she had often said before, that she had always told them it was absurd for March to go into the army, always predicted that no good would come of it, and she hoped they would take her advice next time. Mrs. March put the note in the fire, the money in her purse, and went on with her preparations, with her lips folded tightly, in a way which Jo would have understood if she had been there.

The short afternoon wore away; all the other errands were done, and Meg and her mother busy at some necessary needlework, while Beth and Amy got tea, and Hannah finished her ironing with what she called a "slap and a bang," but still Jo did not come. They began to get anxious; and Laurie went off to find her, for no one ever knew what freak Jo might take into her head. He missed her, however, and she came walking in with a very queer expression of countenance, for there was a mixture of fun and fear, satisfaction and regret in it, which puzzled the family as much as did the roll of bills she laid before her mother, saying, with a little choke in her voice, "That's my contribution towards making father comfortable, and bringing him home!"

"My dear, where did you get it! Twenty-five dollars! Jo, I hope you haven't done anything rash?"

"No, it's mine honestly; I didn't beg, borrow, nor steal it. I earned it; and I don't think you'll blame me, for I only sold what was my own."

As she spoke, Jo took off her bonnet, and a general outcry arose, for all her abundant hair was cut short.

"Your hair! Your beautiful hair!" "Oh, Jo, how could you? Your one beauty." "My dear girl, there was no need of this." "She doesn't look like my Jo any more, but I love her dearly for it!"

As every one exclaimed, and Beth hugged the cropped head tenderly, Jo assumed an indifferent air, which did not deceive any one a particle, and said, rumpling up the brown bush, and trying to look as if she liked it, "It doesn't affect the fate of the nation, so don't wail, Beth. It will be good for my vanity; I was getting too proud of my wig. It will do my brains good to have that mop taken off; my head feels deliciously light and cool, and the barber said I could soon have a curly crop, which will be boyish, becoming, and easy to keep in order. I'm satisfied; so please take the money, and let's have supper.'

"Tell me all about it, Jo. I am not quite satisfied, but I can't blame you, for I know how willingly you sacrificed your vanity, as you call it, to your love. But, my dear, it was not necessary, and I'm afraid you will regret it, one of these days," said Mrs. March.

"No, I won't!" returned Jo, stoutly, feeling much relieved that her prank was not entirely condemned.

"What made you do it?" asked Amy, who would as soon have thought of cutting off her head as her pretty hair.

"Well, I was wild to do something for father," replied Jo, as they gathered about the table, for healthy young people can eat even in the midst of trouble. "I hate to borrow as much as mother does, and I knew Aunt March would croak; she always does, if you ask for a ninepence. Meg gave all her quarterly salary toward the rent, and I only got some clothes with mine, so I felt wicked, and was bound to have some money, if I sold the nose off my face to get it."

"You needn't feel wicked, my child, you had no winter things, and

Jo assumed an indifferent air as she rumpled up the brown bush.

got the simplest, with your own hard earnings," said Mrs. March, with a look that warmed Jo's heart.

"I hadn't the least idea of selling my hair at first, but as I went along I kept thinking *what* I could do, and feeling as if I'd like to dive into some of the rich stores and help myself. In a barber's window I saw tails of hair with the prices marked; and one black tail, longer, but not so thick as mine, was forty dollars. It came over me all of a sudden that I had one thing to make money out of, and, without stopping to think, I walked in, asked if they bought hair, and what they would give for mine."

"I don't see how you dared to do it," said Beth, in a tone of awe.

"Oh, he was a little man who looked as if he merely lived to oil his hair. He rather stared, at first, as if he wasn't used to having girls bounce into his shop and ask him to buy their hair. He said he didn't care about mine, it wasn't the fashionable color, and he never paid much for it in the first place; the work put into it made it dear, and so on. It was getting late, and I was afraid, if it wasn't done right away, that I shouldn't have it done at all, and you know, when I start to do a thing, I hate to give it up; so I begged him to take it, and told him why I was in such a hurry. It was silly, I dare say, but it changed his mind, for I got rather excited, and told the story in my topsy turvy way, and his wife heard, and said so kindly, —

"'Take it, Thomas, and oblige the young lady; I'd do as much for our Jimmy any day if I had a spire of hair worth selling.'"

"Who was Jimmy?" asked Amy, who liked to have things explained as they went along.

"Her son, she said, who was in the army. How friendly such things make strangers feel, don't they? She talked away all the time the man clipped, and diverted my mind nicely."

"Didn't you feel dreadfully when the first cut came?" asked Meg, with a shiver.

"I took a last look at my hair while the man got his things, and that was the end of it. I never snivel over trifles like that; I will confess, though, I felt queer when I saw the dear old hair laid out on the table, and felt only the short, rough ends on my head. It almost seemed as if I'd an arm or a leg off. The woman saw me look at it, and picked out a long lock for me to keep. I'll give it to you, Marmee, just to remember past glories by; for a crop is so comfortable I don't think I shall ever have a mane again."

Mrs. March folded the wavy, chestnut lock, and laid it away with a short gray one in her desk. She only said, "Thank you, deary," but something in her face made the girls change the subject, and talk as cheerfully as they could about Mr. Brooke's kindness, the prospect of a fine day to-morrow, and the happy times they would have when father came home to be nursed.

No one wanted to go to bed, when, at ten o'clock, Mrs. March put by the last finished job, and said, "Come, girls." Beth went to the piano and played the father's favorite hymn; all began bravely, but broke down one by one till Beth was left alone, singing with all her heart, for to her music was always a sweet consoler.

"Go to bed and don't talk, for we must be up early, and shall need all the sleep we can get. Good-night, my darlings," said Mrs. March, as the hymn ended, for no one cared to try another.

They kissed her quietly, and went to bed as silently as if the dear invalid lay in the next room. Beth and Amy soon fell asleep in spite of the great trouble, but Meg lay awake thinking the most serious thoughts she had ever known in her short life. Jo lay motionless, and her sister fancied that she was asleep, till a stifled sob made her exclaim, as she touched a wet cheek, –

"Jo, dear, what is it? Are you crying about father?"

"No, not now."

"What then?"

"My – my hair," burst out poor Jo, trying vainly to smother her emotion in the pillow.

It did not sound at all comical to Meg, who kissed and caressed the afflicted heroine in the tenderest manner.

"I'm not sorry," protested Jo, with a choke. "I'd do it again to-morrow, if I could. It's only the vain, selfish part of me that goes and cries in this silly way. Don't tell any one, it's all over now. I thought you were asleep, so I just made a little private moan for my one beauty. How came you to be awake?"

"I can't sleep, I'm so anxious," said Meg.

"Think about something pleasant, and you'll soon drop off."

"I tried it, but felt wider awake than ever."

"What did you think of?"

"Handsome faces; eyes particularly," answered Meg, smilingly, to herself, in the dark.

"What color do you like best?"

"Brown — that is sometimes — blue are lovely."

Jo laughed, and Meg sharply ordered her not to talk, then amiably promised to make her hair curl, and fell asleep to dream of living in her castle in the air.

The clocks were striking midnight, and the rooms were very still, as a figure glided quietly from bed to bed, smoothing a coverlid here, settling a pillow there, and pausing to look long and tenderly at each unconscious face, to kiss each with lips that mutely blessed, and to pray the fervent prayers which only mothers utter. As she lifted the curtain to look out into the dreary night, the moon broke suddenly from behind the clouds, and shone upon her like a bright benignant face, which seemed to whisper in the silence, "Be comforted, dear soul! There is always light behind the clouds."

CHAPTER SIXTEEN

LETTERS

~

In the cold gray dawn the sisters lit their lamp, and read their chapter with an earnestness never felt before, for now the shadow of real trouble had come, showing them how rich in sunshine their lives had been. The little books were full of help and comfort; and, as they dressed, they agreed to say good-by cheerfully, hopefully, and send their mother on her anxious journey unsaddened by tears or complaints from them. Everything seemed very strange when they went down; so dim and still outside, so full of light and bustle within. Breakfast at that early hour seemed odd, and even Hannah's familiar face looked unnatural as she flew about her kitchen with her night cap on. The big trunk stood ready in the hall, mother's cloak and bonnet lay on the sofa, and mother herself sat trying to eat, but looking so pale and worn with sleeplessness and anxiety, that the girls found it very hard to keep their resolution. Meg's eyes kept filling in spite of herself; Jo was obliged to hide her face in the kitchen roller more than once; and the little girls' young faces wore a grave, troubled expression, as if sorrow was a new experience to them.

Nobody talked much, but, as the time drew very near, and they sat waiting for the carriage, Mrs. March said to the girls, who were all busied about her, one folding her shawl, another smoothing out the strings of her bonnet, a third putting on her overshoes, and a fourth fastening up her travelling bag, –

"Children, I leave you in Hannah's care and Mr. Laurence's protection. Hannah is faithfulness itself, and our good neighbor will guard you as if you were his own. I have no fears for you, yet I am anxious that you should take this trouble rightly. Don't grieve and fret when I am gone, or think that you can comfort yourselves by being idle, and trying to forget. Go on with your work as usual, for work is a blessed solace. Hope, and keep busy; and, whatever happens, remember that you never can be fatherless."

"Yes, mother."

"Meg dear, be prudent, watch over your sisters, consult Hannah, and, in any perplexity, go to Mr. Laurence. Be patient, Jo, don't get despondent or do rash things; write to me often, and be my brave girl, ready to help and cheer us all. Beth, comfort yourself with your music, and be faithful to the little home duties; and you, Amy, help all you can, be obedient, and keep happy safe at home."

"We will, mother! we will!"

The rattle of an approaching carriage made them all start and listen. That was the hard minute, but the girls stood it well; no one cried, no one ran away, or uttered a lamentation, though their hearts were very heavy as they sent loving messages to father, remembering, as they spoke, that it might be too late to deliver them. They kissed their mother quietly, clung about her tenderly, and tried to wave their hands cheerfully, when she drove away.

Laurie and his grandfather came over to see her off, and Mr. Brooke looked so strong, and sensible, and kind, that the girls christened him "Mr Greatheart," on the spot.

"Good-by, my darlings! God bless and keep us all," whispered Mrs. March, as she kissed one dear little face after the other, and hurried into the carriage.

As she rolled away, the sun came out, and, looking back, she saw it shining on the group at the gate, like a good omen. They saw it also, and smiled and waved their hands; and the last thing she beheld, as she turned the corner, was the four bright faces, and behind them, like a body-guard, old Mr. Laurence, faithful Hannah, and devoted Laurie.

"How kind everyone is to us," she said, turning to find fresh proof of it in the respectful sympathy of the young man's face.

"I don't see how they can help it," returned Mr. Brooke, laughing so infectiously that Mrs. March could not help smiling; and so the long journey began with the good omens of sunshine, smiles, and cheerful words.

"I feel as if there had been an earthquake," said Jo, as their neighbors went home to breakfast, leaving them to rest and refresh themselves.

"It seems as if half the house was gone," added Meg, forlornly.

Beth opened her lips to say something, but could only point to the pile of nicely mended hose which lay on mother's table, showing that even in her last hurried moments she had thought and worked for them. It was a little thing, but it went straight to their hearts; and, in spite of their brave resolutions, they all broke down, and cried bitterly.

Hannah wisely allowed them to relieve their feelings; and, when the shower showed signs of clearing up, she came to the rescue, armed with a coffee-pot.

"Now, my dear young ladies, remember what your ma said, and don't fret; come and have a cup of coffee all round, and then let's fall to work and be a credit to the family."

Coffee was a treat, and Hannah showed great tact in making it that morning. No one could resist her persuasive nods, or the fragrant invitation issuing from the nose of the coffee-pot. They drew up to the table, exchanged their handkerchiefs for napkins, and, in ten minutes, were all right again.

"'Hope and keep busy;' that's the motto for us, so let's see who will remember it best. I shall go to Aunt March, as usual; oh, won't she lecture, though!" said Jo, as she sipped, with returning spirit.

"I shall go to my Kings, though I'd much rather stay at home and attend to things here," said Meg, wishing she hadn't made her eyes so red.

"No need of that; Beth and I can keep house perfectly well," put in Amy, with an important air.

"Hannah will tell us what to do; and we'll have everything nice when you come home," added Beth, getting out her mop and dish-tub without delay.

"I think anxiety is very interesting," observed Amy, eating sugar, pensively.

The girls couldn't help laughing, and felt better for it, though Meg shook her head at the young lady who could find consolation in a sugar-bowl.

The sight of the turn-overs made Jo sober again; and, when the two went out to their daily tasks, they looked sorrowfully back at the window where they were accustomed to see their mother's face. It was gone; but Beth had remembered the little house-hold ceremony, and there she was, nodding away at them like a rosy-faced mandarin.

"That's so like my Beth!" said Jo, waving her hat, with a grateful face. "Good-by, Meggy; I hope the Kings won't train to-day. Don't fret about father, dear," she added, as they parted.

"And I hope Aunt March won't croak. Your hair *is* becoming, and it looks very boyish and nice," returned Meg, trying not to smile at the curly head, which looked comically small on her sister's shoulders.

"That's my only comfort;" and, touching her hat, à la Laurie, away went Jo, feeling like a shorn sheep on a wintry day.

News from their father comforted the girls very much; for, though dangerously ill, the presence of the best and tenderest of nurses had already done him good. Mr. Brooke sent a bulletin every day, and, as the head of the family, Meg insisted on reading the despatches, which grew more and more cheering as the week passed. At first, everyone was eager to write, and plump envelopes were carefully poked into the letter-box, by one or other of the sisters, who felt rather important with their Washington correspondence. As one of these packets contained characteristic notes from the party, we will rob an imaginary mail, and read them: —

MY DEAREST MOTHER, —

It is impossible to tell you how happy your last letter made us, for the news was so good we couldn't help laughing and crying over it. How very kind Mr. Brooke is, and how fortunate that Mr. Laurence's business detains him near you so long, since he is so useful to you and father. The girls are all as good as gold. Jo helps me with the sewing, and insists on doing all sorts of hard jobs. I should be afraid she might overdo, if I didn't know that her "moral fit" wouldn't last long. Beth is as regular about her tasks as a clock, and never forgets what you told her. She grieves about father, and looks sober, except when she is at her little piano. Amy minds me nicely, and I take great care of her. She does her own hair, and I am teaching her how to make buttonholes, and mend her stockings. She tries very hard, and I know you will be pleased with her improvement when you come. Mr. Laurence watches over us like a motherly old hen, as Jo says; and Laurie is very kind and neighborly. He and Jo keep us merry, for we get pretty blue sometimes, and feel like orphans, with you so far away. Hannah is a perfect saint; she does not scold at all, and always calls me "Miss Margaret," which is quite proper, you know, and treats me with respect. We are all well and busy; but we long, day and night, to have you back. Give my dearest love to father, and believe me, ever your own

MEG.

This note, prettily written on scented paper, was a great contrast to the next, which was scribbled on a big sheet of thin, foreign paper, ornamented with blots, and all manner of flourishes and curly-tailed letters:

MY PRECIOUS MARMEE, —

Three cheers for dear old father! Brooke was a trump to telegraph right off, and let us know the minute he was better. I rushed up garret when the letter came, and tried to thank God for being so good to us; but I could only cry, and say, "I'm glad! I'm glad!" Didn't that do as well as a regular prayer? for I felt a great many in my heart. We have such funny times; and now I can enjoy 'em, for every one is so desperately good, it's like living in a nest of turtle doves. You'd laugh to see Meg head the table, and try to be motherish. She gets prettier every day, and I'm in love with her sometimes. The children are regular archangels, and I — well, I'm Jo, and never shall be anything else. Oh, I must tell you that I came near having a quarrel with Laurie. I freed my mind about a silly little thing, and he was offended. I was right, but didn't speak as I ought, and he marched home, saying he wouldn't come again till I begged pardon. I declared I wouldn't, and got mad. It lasted all day; I felt bad, and wanted you very much. Laurie and I are both so proud, it's hard to beg pardon; but I thought he'd come to it, for I *was* in the right. He didn't come; and just at night I remembered what you said when Amy fell into the river. I read my little book, felt better, resolved not to let the sun set on *my* anger, and ran over to tell Laurie I was sorry. I met him at the gate, coming for the same thing. We both laughed, begged each other's pardon, and felt all good and comfortable again.

I made a "pome" yesterday, when I was helping Hannah wash; and, as father likes my silly little things, I put it in to amuse him. Give him the lovingest hug that ever was, and kiss yourself a dozen times for your

TOPSY-TURVY JO.

A SONG FROM THE SUDS

Queen of my tub, I merrily sing,
*   While the white foam rises high;*
And sturdily wash, and rinse, and wring,
*   And fasten the clothes to dry;*
Then out in the free fresh air they swing,
*   Under the sunny sky.*

I wish we could wash from our hearts and souls
*   The stains of the week away,*
And let water and air by their magic make
*   Ourselves as pure as they;*
Then on the earth there would be indeed
*   A glorious washing-day!*

Along the path of a useful life,
*   Will heart's-ease ever bloom;*
The busy mind has no time to think
*   Of sorrow, or care, or gloom;*
And anxious thoughts may be swept away,
*   As we bravely wield a broom.*

I am glad a task to me is given,
*   To labor at day by day;*
For it brings me health, and strength, and hope,
*   And I cheerfully learn to say, —*
"Head you may think, Heart you may feel,
*   But Hand you shall work alway!"*

DEAR MOTHER:

There is only room for me to send my love, and some pressed pansies from the root I have been keeping safe in the house, for father to see. I read every morning, try to be good all day, and sing myself to sleep with father's tune. I can't sing "Land of the Leal" now; it makes me cry. Every one is very kind, and we are as happy as we can be without you. Amy wants the rest of the page, so I must stop. I didn't forget to cover the holders, and I wind the clock and air the rooms every day.

Kiss dear father on the cheek he calls mine. Oh, do come soon to your loving

LITTLE BETH.

MA CHERE MAMMA:

We are all well I do my lessons always and never corroberate the girls — Meg says I mean contradick so I put in both words and you can take the properest. Meg is a great comfort to me and lets me have jelly every night at tea its so good for me Jo says because it keeps me sweet tempered. Laurie is not as respeckful as he ought to be now I am almost in my teens, he calls me Chick and hurts my feelings by talking French to me very fast when I say Merci or Bon jour as Hattie King does. The sleeves of my blue dress were all worn out and Meg put in new ones but the full front came wrong and they are more blue than the dress. I felt bad but did not fret I bear my troubles well but I do wish Hannah would put more starch in my aprons and have buck wheats every day. Can't she? Didn't I make that interrigation point nice. Meg says my punchtuation and spelling are disgraceful and I am mortyfied but dear me I have so many things to do I can't stop. Adieu, I send heaps of love to Papa.
Your affectionate daughter,

AMY CURTIS MARCH.

DEAR MIS MARCH:

I jes drop a line to say we git on fust rate. The girls is clever and fly round right smart. Miss Meg is goin to make a proper good housekeeper; she hes the liking for it, and gits the hang of things surprisin quick. Jo doos beat all for goin ahead, but she don't stop to calk'late fust, and you never know where she's like to bring up. She done out a tub of clothes on Monday, but she starched em afore they was wrenched, and blued a pink calico dress till I thought I should a died a laughin. Beth is the best of little creeters, and a sight of help to me, being so forehanded and dependable. She tries to learn everything, and really goes to market beyond her years; likewise keeps accounts, with my help, quite wonderful. We have got on very economical so fur; I don't let the girls hev coffee only once a week, accordin to your wish, and keep em on plain wholesome vittles. Amy does well about frettin, wearin her best clothes and eatin sweet stuff. Mr. Laurie is as full of didoes as usual, and turns the house upside down frequent; but he heartens up the girls, and so I let em hev full swing. The old man sends heaps of things, and is rather wearin, but means wal, and it ain't my place to say nothin. My bread is riz, so no more at this time. I send my duty to Mr. March, and hope he's seen the last of his Pewmonia.

Yours Respectful

HANNAH MULLET.

HEAD NURSE OF WARD II:

All serene on the Rappahannock, troops in fine condition, commissary department well conducted, the Home Guard under Colonel Teddy always on duty, Commander-in-Chief General Laurence reviews the army daily, Quartermaster Mullet keeps order in camp, and Major Lion does picket duty at night. A salute of twenty-four guns was fired on receipt of good news from Washington, and a dress parade took place at headquarters. Commander-in-chief sends his best wishes, in which he is heartily joined by

COLONEL TEDDY.

DEAR MADAM: The little girls are all well; Beth and my boy report daily; Hannah is a model servant, and guards pretty Meg like a dragon. Glad the fine weather holds; pray make Brooke useful, and draw on me for funds if expenses exceed your estimate. Don't let your husband want anything. Thank God he is mending.

Your sincere friend and servant,

JAMES LAURENCE.

CHAPTER SEVENTEEN

LITTLE FAITHFUL

~

For a week the amount of virtue in the old house would have supplied the neighborhood. It was really amazing, for every one seemed in a heavenly frame of mind, and self-denial was all the fashion. Relieved of their first anxiety about their father, the girls insensibly relaxed their praise-worthy efforts a little, and began to fall back into the old ways. They did not forget their motto, but hoping and keeping busy seemed to grow easier; and, after such tremendous exertions, they felt that Endeavour deserved a holiday, and gave it a good many.

Jo caught a bad cold through neglecting to cover the shorn head enough, and was ordered to stay at home till she was better, for Aunt March didn't like to hear people read with cold in their heads. Jo liked this, and after an energetic rummage from garret to cellar, subsided on the sofa to nurse her cold with arsenicum and books. Amy found that house-work and art did not go well together, and returned to her mud pies. Meg went daily to her kingdom, and sewed, or thought she did, at home, but much time was spent in writing long letters to her mother, or reading the Washington despatches over and over. Beth kept on with only slight relapses into idleness or grieving. All the little duties were faithfully done each day, and many of her sisters' also, for they were forgetful, and the house seemed like a clock, whose pendulum was gone a-visiting. When her heart got heavy with longings for mother, or fears for father, she went away into a certain closet, hid her face in the folds of a certain dear old gown, and made her little moan, and prayed her little prayer quietly by herself. Nobody knew what cheered her up after a sober fit, but every one felt how sweet and helpful Beth was, and fell into a way of going to her for comfort or advice in their small affairs.

All were unconscious that this experience was a test of character; and, when the first excitement was over, felt that they had done well, and deserved praise. So they did; but their mistake was in ceasing to do well, and they learned this lesson through much anxiety and regret.

"Meg, I wish you would go and see the Hummels; you know mother told us not to forget them," said Beth, ten days after Mrs. March's departure.

"I'm too tired to go this afternoon," replied Meg, rocking comfortably, as she sewed.

"Can't you, Jo?" asked Beth.

"Too stormy for me, with my cold."

"I thought it was most well."

"It's well enough for me to go out with Laurie, but not well enough to go to the Hummels," said Jo, laughing, but looking a little ashamed of her inconsistency.

"Why don't you go yourself?" asked Meg.

"I *have* been every day, but the baby is sick, and I don't know what to do for it. Mrs. Hummel goes away to work, and Lottchen takes care of it; but it gets sicker and sicker, and I think you or Hannah ought to go."

Beth spoke earnestly, and Meg promised she would go to-morrow.

"Ask Hannah for some nice little mess, and take it round, Beth, the air will do you good;" said Jo, adding apologetically, "I'd go, but I want to finish my story.'

"My head aches, and I'm tired, so I thought maybe some of you would go," said Beth.

"Amy will be in presently, and she will run down for us," suggested Meg.

"Well, I'll rest a little, and wait for her."

So Beth lay down on the sofa, and others returned to their work, and the Hummels were forgotten. An hour passed, Amy did not come; Meg went to her room to try on a new dress; Jo was absorbed in her story, and Hannah was sound asleep before the kitchen fire, when Beth quietly put on her hood, filled her basket with odds and ends for the poor children, and went out into the chilly air with a heavy head, and a grieved look in her patient eyes. It was late when she came back, and no one saw her creep up stairs and shut herself into her mother's room. Half an hour after Jo went to "mother's closet" for something, and there found Beth sitting on the medicine chest, looking very grave, with red eyes, and a camphor bottle in her hand.

"Christopher Columbus! what's the matter?" cried Jo, as Beth put out her hand as if to warn her off, and asked quickly, —

"You've had scarlet fever, haven't you?"

"Years ago, when Meg did. Why?"

"Then I'll tell you — oh, Jo, the baby's dead!"

"What baby?"

"Mrs. Hummel's; it died in my lap before she got home," cried Beth, with a sob.

"My poor dear, how dreadful for you! I ought to have gone," said Jo, taking her sister in her lap as she sat down in her mother's big chair, with a remorseful face.

"It wasn't dreadful, Jo, only so sad! I saw in a minute that it was sicker, but Lottchen said her mother had gone for a doctor, so I took the baby and let Lotty rest. It seemed asleep, but all of a sudden it gave a little cry, and trembled, and then lay very still. I tried to warm its feet, and Lotty gave it some milk, but it didn't stir, and I knew it was dead."

"Don't cry, dear! what did you do?"

"I just sat and held it softly till Mrs. Hummel came with the doctor. He said it was dead, and looked at Heinrich and Minna, who have got sore throats. 'Scarlet fever, ma'am; ought to have called me before,' he said, crossly. Mrs. Hummel told him she was poor, and had tried to cure the baby herself, but now it was too late, and she could only ask him to help the others, and trust to charity for his pay. He smiled then, and was kinder, but it was very sad, and I cried with them till he turned round all of a sudden, and told me to go home and take belladonna right away, or I'd have the fever."

"No, you won't!" cried Jo, hugging her close, with a frightened look. "Oh, Beth, if you should be sick I never could forgive myself! What *shall* we do?"

"Don't be frightened, I guess I shan't have it badly; I looked in mother's book, and saw that it begins with headache, sore throat, and queer feelings like mine, so I did take some belladonna, and I feel better," said Beth, laying her cold hands on her hot forehead, and trying to look well.

"If mother was only at home!" exclaimed Jo, seizing the book, and feeling that Washington was an immense way off. She read a page, looked at Beth, felt her head, peeped into her throat, and then said, gravely, "You've been over the baby every day for more than a week, and among the others who are going to have it, so I'm afraid you're going to have it, Beth. I'll call Hannah; she knows all about sickness."

"Don't let Amy come; she never had it, and I should hate to give it to her. Can't you and Meg have it over again?" asked Beth, anxiously.

"I guess not; don't care if I do; serve me right, selfish pig, to let you go, and stay writing rubbish myself!" muttered Jo, as she went to consult Hannah.

The good soul was wide awake in a minute, and took the lead at once, assuring Jo that there was no need to worry; everyone had scarlet fever, and, if rightly treated, nobody died; all of which Jo believed, and felt much relieved as they went up to call Meg.

"Now I'll tell you what we'll do," said Hannah, when she had examined and questioned Beth; "we will have Dr. Bangs, just to take a look at you, dear, and see that we start right; then we'll send Amy off to Aunt March's, for a spell, to keep her out of harm's way, and one of you girls can stay at home and amuse Beth for a day or two."

"I shall stay, of course, I'm oldest;" began Meg, looking anxious and self-reproachful.

"*I* shall, because it's my fault she is sick; I told mother I'd do the errands, and I haven't," said Jo, decidedly.

"Which will you have, Beth? there ain't no need of but one," said Hannah.

"Jo, please;" and Beth leaned her head against her sister, with a contented look, which effectively settled that point.

"I'll go and tell Amy," said Meg, feeling a little hurt, yet rather relieved, on the whole, for she did not like nursing, and Jo did.

Amy rebelled outright, and passionately declared that she had rather have the fever than go to Aunt March. Meg reasoned, pleaded, and commanded, all in vain. Amy protested that she would *not* go; and Meg left her in despair, to ask Hannah what should be done. Before she came back, Laurie walked into the parlor to find Amy sobbing, with her head in the sofa cushions. She told her story, expecting to be consoled; but Laurie only put his hands in his pockets and walked about the room, whistling softly, as he knit his brows in deep thought. Presently he sat down beside her, and said, in his most wheedlesome tone, "Now, be a sensible little woman, and do as they say. No, don't cry, but hear what a jolly plan I've got. You go to Aunt March's, and I'll come and take you out every day, driving or walking, and we'll have capital times. Won't that be better than moping here?"

"I don't wish to be sent off as if I was in the way," began Amy, in an injured voice.

"Bless your heart, child! it's to keep you well. You don't want to be sick, do you?"

"No, I'm sure I don't; but I dare say I shall be, for I've been with Beth all the time."

"That's the very reason you ought to go away at once, so that you may escape it. Change of air and care will keep you well I dare say; or, if it don't entirely, you will have the fever more lightly. I advise you to be off as soon as you can, for scarlet fever is no joke, miss."

"But it's dull at Aunt March's, and she is so cross," said Amy, looking rather frightened.

"It won't be dull with me popping in every day to tell you how Beth is, and take you out gallivanting. The old lady likes me, and I'll be as clever as possible to her, so she won't peck at us, whatever we do."

"Will you take me out in the trotting waggon with Puck?"

"On my honor as a gentleman."

"And come every single day?"

"See if I don't."

"And bring me back the minute Beth is well?"

"The identical minute."

"And go to the theatre, truly?"

"A dozen theatres, if we may."

"Well – I guess – I will," said Amy, slowly.

"Good girl! Sing out for Meg, and tell her you'll give in," said Laurie, with an approving pat, which annoyed Amy more than the "giving in".

Meg and Jo came running down to behold the miracle which had been wrought; and Amy, feeling very precious and self-sacrificing, promised to go, if the doctor said Beth was going to be ill.

"How is the little dear?" asked Laurie; for Beth was his especial pet, and he felt more anxious about her than he liked to show.

"She is lying down on mother's bed, and feels better. The baby's death troubled her, but I dare say she has only got cold. Hannah *says* she thinks so; but she *looks* worried, and that makes me fidgety," answered Meg.

"What a trying world it is!" said Jo, rumpling up her hair in a fretful sort of way. "No sooner do we get out of one trouble than down comes another. There don't seem to be anything to hold on to when mother's gone; so I'm all at sea."

"Well, don't make a porcupine of yourself, it isn't becoming. Settle your wig, Jo, and tell me if I shall telegraph to your mother, or do anything?" asked Laurie, who never had been reconciled to the loss of his friend's one beauty.

"That is what troubles me," said Meg. "I think we ought to tell her if Beth is really ill, but Hannah says we mustn't, for mother can't leave father, and it will only make them anxious. Beth won't be sick long, and Hannah knows just what to do, and mother said we were to mind her, so I suppose we must, but it don't seem quite right to me."

"Hum, well, I can't say; suppose you ask grandfather, after the doctor has been."

"We will. Jo, go and get Dr. Bangs at once," commanded Meg; "we can't decide anything till he has been."

"Stay where you are, Jo; I'm the errand boy to this establishment," said Laurie, taking up his cap.

"I'm afraid you are busy," began Meg.

"No, I've done my lessons for the day."

"Do you study in vacation time?" asked Jo.

"I follow the good example my neighbors set me," was Laurie's answer, as he swung himself out of the room.

"I have great hopes of my boy," observed Jo, watching him fly over the fence with an approving smile.

"He does very well – for a boy," was Meg's somewhat ungracious answer, for the subject did not interest her.

Dr. Bangs came, said Beth had symptoms of the fever, but thought she would have it lightly, though he looked sober over the Hummel story. Amy was ordered off at once, and provided with something to ward off danger; she departed in great state, with Jo and Laurie as escort.

Aunt March received them both with her usual hospitality.

"What do you want now?" she asked, looking sharply over her spectacles, while the parrot, sitting on the back of her chair, called out, –

"Go away; no boys allowed here."

Laurie retired to the window, and Jo told her story.

"No more than I expected, if you are allowed to go poking about among poor folks. Amy can stay and make herself useful if she isn't sick, which I've no doubt she will be, – looks like it now. Don't cry, child, it worries me to hear people sniff."

Amy *was* on the point of crying, but Laurie slyly pulled the parrot's tail, which caused Polly to utter an astonished croak, and call out, –

"Bless my boots!" in such a funny way, that she laughed instead.

"What do you hear from your mother?" asked the old lady, gruffly.

"Father is much better," replied Jo, trying to keep sober.

"Oh, is he? Well, that won't last long, I fancy, March never had any stamina," was the cheerful reply.

"Ha, ha! never say die, take a pinch of snuff, good-by, good-by!" squalled Polly, dancing on her perch, and clawing at the old lady's cap as Laurie tweaked him in the rear.

"Hold your tongue, you disrespectful old bird! and, Jo, you'd better go at once; it isn't proper to be gadding about so late with a rattle-pated boy like – "

"Hold your tongue, you disrespectful old bird!" cried Polly, tumbling off the chair with a bounce and running to peck the "rattle-pated" boy, who was shaking with laughter at the last speech.

"I don't think I *can* bear it, but I'll try," thought Amy, as she was left alone with Aunt March.

"Get along, you're a fright!" screamed Polly, and at that rude speech Amy could not restrain a sniff.

CHAPTER EIGHTEEN

DARK DAYS

~

Beth did have the fever, and was much sicker than anyone but Hannah and the doctor suspected. The girls knew nothing about illness, and Mr. Laurence was not allowed to see her, so Hannah had everything all her own way, and busy Dr. Bangs did his best, but left a good deal to the excellent nurse. Meg stayed at home, lest she should infect the Kings, and kept house, feeling very anxious, and a little guilty, when she wrote letters in which no mention was made of Beth's illness. She could not think it right to deceive her mother, but she had been bidden to mind Hannah, and Hannah wouldn't hear of "Mrs. March bein' told, and worried just for sech a trifle." Jo devoted herself to Beth day and night, not a hard task, for Beth was very patient, and bore her pain uncomplainingly as long as she could control herself. But there came a time when during the fever fits she began to talk in a hoarse, broken voice, to play on the coverlet, as if on her beloved little piano, and try to sing with a throat so swollen, that there was no music left; a time when she did not know the familiar faces round her, but addressed them by wrong names, and called imploringly for her mother. Then Jo grew frightened, Meg begged to be allowed to write the truth, and even Hannah said she "would think of it, though there was no danger *yet*." A letter from Washington added to their trouble, for Mr. March had had a relapse, and could not think of coming home for a long while.

How dark the days seemed now, how sad and lonely the house, and how heavy were the hearts of the sisters as they worked and waited, while the shadow of death hovered over the once happy home! Then it was that Margaret, sitting alone with tears dropping often on her work, felt how rich she had been in things more precious than any luxuries money could buy; in love, protection, peace, and health, the real blessings of life. Then it was that Jo, living in the darkened room with that suffering little sister always before her eyes, and that pathetic voice sounding in her ears, learned to see the beauty and the sweetness of Beth's nature, to feel how deep and tender a place she filled in all hearts, and to acknowledge the worth of Beth's unselfish ambition, to live for others, and make home happy by the exercise of those simple virtues which all may possess, and which all should love and value more than talent, wealth, or beauty. And Amy, in her exile, longed eagerly to be at home, that she might work for Beth, feeling now that no service would be hard or irksome, and remembering, with regretful grief, how many neglected tasks those willing hands had done for her. Laurie haunted the house like a restless ghost, and Mr. Laurence locked the grand piano, because he could not bear to be reminded of the young neighbor who used to make the twilight pleasant for him. Every one missed Beth. The milkman, baker, grocer, and butcher inquired how she did; poor Mrs. Hummel came to beg pardon for her thoughtlessness, and to get a shroud for Minna; the neighbors sent all sorts of comforts and good wishes, and even those who knew her best, were surprised to find how many friends shy little Beth had made.

Meanwhile she lay on her bed with old Joanna at her side, for even in her wanderings she did not forget her forlorn *protégé*. She longed for her cats, but would not have them brought, lest they should get sick; and, in her quiet hours, she was full of anxiety about Jo. She sent loving messages to Amy, bade them tell her mother that she would write soon; and often begged for pencil and paper to try and say a word, that father might not think she had neglected him. But soon even these intervals of consciousness ended, and she lay hour after hour tossing to and fro with incoherent words on her lips, or sank into a heavy sleep which brought her no refreshment. Dr. Bangs came twice a day, Hannah sat up at night, Meg kept a telegram in her desk all ready to send off at any minute, and Jo never stirred from Beth's side.

The first of December was a wintry day indeed to them, for a bitter wind blew, snow fell fast, and the year seemed getting ready for its death. When Dr. Bangs came that morning, he looked long at Beth, held the hot hand in both his own a minute, and laid it gently down, saying, in a low tone, to Hannah, –

"If Mrs March *can* leave her husband she'd better be sent for."

Hannah nodded without speaking, for her lips twitched nervously; Meg dropped down into a chair as the strength seemed to go out of her limbs at the sound of these words, and Jo, after standing with a pale face for a minute, ran to the parlor, snatched up the telegram, and, throwing on her things, rushed out into the storm. She was soon back, and, while noiselessly taking off her cloak, Laurie came in with a letter, saying that Mr. March was mending again. Jo read it thankfully, but the heavy weight did not seem lifted off her heart, and her face was so full of misery that Laurie asked, quickly, –

"What is it? is Beth worse?"

"I've sent for mother," said Jo, tugging at her rubber boots with a tragical expression.

"Good for you, Jo! Did you do it on your own responsibility?" asked Laurie, as he seated her in the hall chair, and took off the rebellious boots, seeing how her hands shook.

"No, the doctor told us to."

"Oh, Jo, it's not as bad as that?" cried Laurie, with a startled face.

"Yes, it is; she don't know us, she don't even talk about the flocks of green doves, as she calls the vine leaves on the wall; she don't look like my Beth, and there's nobody to help us bear it; mother and father both gone, and God seems so far away I can't find Him."

As the tears streamed fast down poor Jo's cheeks, she stretched out her hand in a helpless sort of way, as if groping in the dark and Laurie took it in his, whispering, as well as he could, with a lump in his throat, –

"I'm here, hold on to me, Jo, dear!"

She could not speak, but she did "hold on," and the warm grasp of the friendly human hand comforted her sore heart, and seemed to lead her nearer to the Divine arm which alone could uphold her in her trouble. Laurie longed to say something tender and comfortable, but no fitting words came to him, so he stood silent, gently stroking her bent head as her mother used to do. It was the best thing he could have done; far more soothing that the most eloquent words, for Jo felt the unspoken sympathy, and, in the silence, learned the sweet solace which affection administers to sorrow. Soon she dried the tears which had relieved her, and looked up with a grateful face.

"Thank you, Teddy, I'm better now; I don't feel so forlorn, and will try to bear it if it comes."

"Keep hoping for the best; that will help you lots, Jo. Soon your mother will be here, and then everything will be all right."

"I'm so glad father is better; now she won't feel so bad about leaving him. Oh, me! it does seem as if all the troubles came in a heap, and I got the heaviest part on my shoulders," sighed Jo, spreading her wet handkerchief over her knees to dry.

"Doesn't Meg pull fair?" asked Laurie, looking indignant.

"Oh, yes; she tries to, but she don't love Bethy as I do; and she won't miss her as I shall. Beth is my conscience, and I *can't* give her up; I can't! I can't!"

Down went Jo's face into the wet handkerchief, and she cried despairingly; for she had kept up bravely till now, and never shed a tear. Laurie drew his hand across his eyes, but could not speak till he had subdued the choky feeling in his throat, and steadied his lips. It might be unmanly, but he couldn't help it, and I am glad of it. Presently, as Jo's sobs quieted, he said, hopefully, "I don't think she will die; she's so good, and we all love her so much, I don't believe God will take her away yet."

"The good and dear people always do die," groaned Jo, but she stopped crying, for her friend's words cheered her up, in spite of her own doubts and fears.

"Poor girl! you're worn out. It isn't like you to be forlorn. Stop a bit; I'll hearten you up in a jiffy."

Laurie went off two stairs at a time, and Jo laid her wearied head down on Beth's little brown hood, which no one had thought of moving from the table where she left it. It must have possessed some magic, for the submissive spirit of its gentle owner seemed to enter into Jo; and, when Laurie came running down with a glass of wine, she took it with a smile and said, bravely, "I drink – Health to my Beth! You are a good doctor, Teddy, and *such* a comfortable friend; how can I ever pay you?" she added, as the wine refreshed her body, as the kind words had done her troubled mind.

"I'll send in my bill, by and by; and to-night I'll give you something that will warm the cockles of your heart better than quarts of wine," said Laurie, beaming at her with a face of suppressed satisfaction at something.

"What is it?" cried Jo, forgetting her woes for a minute, in her wonder.

"I telegraphed your mother yesterday, and Brooke answered she'd come at once, and she'll be here to-night, and everything will be all right. Aren't you glad I did it?"

Laurie spoke very fast, and turned red and excited all in a minute, for he had kept his plot a secret, for fear of disappointing the girls or harming Beth. Jo grew quite white, flew out of her chair, and the moment he stopped speaking she electrified him by throwing her arms round his neck, and crying out, with a joyful cry, "Oh, Laurie! Oh, mother! I *am* so glad!" She did not weep again, but laughed hysterically, and trembled and clung to her friend as if she was a little bewildered by the sudden news. Laurie, though decidedly amazed, behaved with great presence of mind; he patted her back soothingly, and, finding that she was recovering, followed it up by a bashful kiss or two, which brought Jo round at once. Holding on to the banisters, she put him gently away, saying, breathlessly, "Oh, don't! I didn't mean to; it was dreadful of me; but you were such a dear to go and do it in spite of Hannah, that I couldn't help flying at you. Tell me all about it, and don't give me wine again; it makes me act so."

"I don't mind!" laughed Laurie, as he settled his tie. "Why, you see I got fidgety, and so did grandpa. We thought Hannah was overdoing the authority business, and your mother ought to know. She'd never forgive us if Beth, – well, if anything happened, you know. So I got grandpa to say it was high time we did something, and off I pelted to the office yesterday, for the doctor looked sober, and Hannah most took my head off when I proposed a telegram. I never *can* bear to be 'marmed' over; so that settled my mind, and I did it. Your mother will come, I know, and the late train is in at two A.M. I shall go for her; and you've only got to bottle up your rapture, and keep Beth quiet, till that blessed lady gets here."

"Laurie, you're an angel! How shall I ever thank you?"

"Fly at me again; I rather like it," said Laurie, looking mischievous – a thing he had not done for a fortnight.

"No, thank you. I'll do it by proxy, when your grandpa comes. Don't tease, but go home and rest, for you'll be up half the night. Bless you, Teddy; bless you!"

Jo had backed into a corner; and, as she finished her speech, she vanished precipitately into the kitchen, where she lay down upon the dresser, and told the assembled cats, that she was "happy, oh, *so* happy!" while Laurie departed, feeling that he had made rather a neat thing of it.

"That's the interferingest chap I ever see; but I forgive him, and do hope Mrs. March is coming on right away," said Hannah, with an air of relief, when Jo told the good news.

Meg had a quiet rapture, and then brooded over the letter, while Jo set the sick-room in order, and Hannah "knocked up a couple of pies in case of company unexpected". A breath of fresh air seemed to blow through the house, and something better than sunshine brightened the quiet rooms;. everything appeared to feel the hopeful change; Beth's bird began to chirp again, and a half-blown rose was discovered on Amy's bush in the window; the fires seemed to burn with unusual cheeriness, and every time the girls met their pale faces broke into smiles as they hugged one another, whispering encouragingly, "Mother's coming, dear! mother's coming!" Every one rejoiced but Beth; she lay in that heavy stupor, alike unconscious of hope and joy, doubt and anger. It was a piteous sight – the once rosy face so changed and vacant, the once busy hands so weak and wasted, the once smiling lips quite dumb, and the once pretty, well-kept hair scattered rough and tangled on the pillow. All day she lay so, only rousing now and then to mutter, "Water!" with lips so parched they could hardly shape the word; all day Jo and Meg hovered over her, watching, waiting, hoping, and trusting in God and mother; and all day the snow fell, the bitter wind raged, and the hours dragged slowly by. But night came at last; and every time the clock struck the sisters, still sitting on either side of the bed, looked at each other with brightening eyes, for each hour brought help nearer. The doctor had been in to say that some change for better or worse would probably take place about midnight, at which time he would return.

Hannah, quite worn out, lay down on the sofa at the bed's foot, and fell fast asleep; Mr. Laurence marched to and fro in the parlor feeling that he would rather face a rebel battery than Mrs. March's anxious countenance as she entered; Laurie lay on the rug, pretending to rest, but staring into the fire with the thoughtful look which made his black eyes beautifully soft and clear.

The girls never forgot that night, for no sleep came to them as they kept their watch. with that dreadful sense of powerlessness which comes to us in hours like those.

"If God spares Beth I never will complain again," whispered Meg, earnestly.

"If God spares Beth I'll try to love and serve Him all my life," answered Jo, with equal fervor.

"I wish I had no heart, it aches so," sighed Meg, after a pause.

"If life is often as hard as this, I don't see how we ever shall get through it," added her sister, despondently.

Here the clock struck twelve, and both forgot themselves in watching Beth, for they fancied a change passed over her wan face. The house still as death, and nothing but the wailing of the wind broke the deep hush. Weary Hannah slept on, and no one but the sisters saw the pale shadow which seemed to fall upon the little bed. An hour went by, and nothing happened except Laurie's quiet departure for the station. Another hour – still no one came; and anxious fears of delay in the storm, or accidents by the way, or worst of all, a great grief at Washington, haunted the poor girls.

It was past two, when Jo, who stood at the window thinking how dreary the world looked in its winding-sheet of snow, heard a movement by the bed, and turning quickly, saw Meg kneeling before her mother's easy-chair, with her face hidden. A dreadful fear passed coldly over Jo, as she thought, "Beth is dead, and Meg is afraid to tell me."

She was back at her post in an instant, and to her excited eyes a great change seemed to have taken place. The fever flush, and the look of pain, were gone, and the beloved little face looked so pale and peaceful in its utter repose, that Jo felt no desire to weep or to lament. Leaning low over this dearest of her sisters, she kissed the damp forehead with her heart on her lips, and softly whispered, "Good-by, my Beth; good-by!"

As if waked by the stir, Hannah started out of her sleep, hurried to the bed, looked at Beth, felt her hands, listened at her lips, and then, throwing her apron over her head, sat down to rock to and fro, exclaiming, under her breath, "The fever's turned; she's sleepin' nat'ral; her skin's damp, and she breathes easy. Praise be given! Oh, my goodness me!"

Before the girls could believe the happy truth, the doctor came in to confirm it. He was a homely man, but they thought his face quite heavenly when he smiled, and said, with a fatherly look at them, "Yes, my dears; I think the little girl will pull through this time. Keep the house quiet; let her sleep, and when she wakes, give her – "

What they were to give, neither heard; for both crept into the dark hall, and, sitting on the stairs, held each other close, rejoicing with hearts too full for words. When they went back to be kissed and cuddled by faithful Hannah, they found Beth lying, as she used to do, with her cheek pillowed on her hand, the dreadful pallor gone, and breathing quietly, as if just fallen asleep.

"If mother would only come now!" said Jo, as the winter night began to wane.

"See," said Meg, coming up with a white, half-opened rose, "I thought this would hardly be ready to lay in Beth's hand tomorrow if she – went away from us. But it has blossomed in the night, and now I mean to put in in my vase here, so that when the darling wakes, the first thing she sees will be the little rose, and mother's face."

Never had the sun risen so beautifully, and never had the world seemed so lovely, as it did to the heavy eyes of Meg and Jo, as they looked out in the early morning, when their long, sad vigil was done.

"It looks like a fairy world," said Meg, smiling to herself, as she stood behind the curtain, watching the dazzling sight.

"Hark!" cried Jo, starting to her feet.

Yes, there was a sound of bells at the door below, a cry from Hannah, and then Laurie's voice, saying in a joyful whisper, "Girls! she's come! she's come!"

CHAPTER NINETEEN

AMY'S WILL

~

While these things were happening at home, Amy was having hard times at Aunt March's. She felt her exile deeply, and, for the first time in her life, realized how much she was beloved and petted at home. Aunt March never petted any one; she did not approve of it; but she meant to be kind, for the well-behaved little girl pleased her very much, and Aunt March had a soft place in her old heart for her nephew's children, though she didn't think proper to confess it. She really did her best to make Amy happy, but, dear me, what mistakes she made! Some old people keep young at heart in spite of wrinkles and gray hairs, can sympathize with children's little cares and joys, make them feel at home, and can hide wise lessons under pleasant plays, giving and receiving friendship in the sweetest way. But Aunt March had not this gift, and she worried Amy most to death with her rules and orders, her prim ways, and long, prosy talks. Finding the child more docile and amiable than her sister, the old lady felt it her duty to try and counteract, as far as possible, the bad effects of home freedom and indulgence. So she took Amy in hand, and taught her as she herself had been taught sixty years ago; a process which carried dismay to Amy's soul, and made her feel like a fly in the web of a very strict spider.

She had to wash the cups every morning, and polish up the old-fashioned spoons, the fat silver teapot, and the glasses, till they shone. Then she must dust the room, and what a trying job that was! Not a speck escaped Aunt March's eye, and all the furniture had claw legs, and much carving, which was never dusted to suit. Then Polly must be fed, the lap-dog combed, and a dozen trips upstairs and down, to get things or deliver orders, for the old lady was very lame, and seldom left her big chair. After these tiresome labors, she must do her lessons, which was a daily trial of every virtue she possessed. Then she was allowed one hour for exercise or play, and didn't she enjoy it? Laurie came every day, and wheedled Aunt March till Amy was allowed to go out with him, when they walked and rode, and had capital times. After dinner she had to read aloud, and sit still while the old lady slept, which she usually did for an hour, as she dropped off over the first page. Then patch-work or towels appeared, and Amy sewed with outward meekness and inward rebellion till dusk, when she was allowed to amuse herself as she liked, till tea-time. The evenings were the worst of all, for Aunt March fell to telling long stories about her youth, which were so unutterably dull, that Amy was always ready to go to bed, intending to cry over her hard fate, but usually going to sleep before she had squeezed out more than a tear or two.

If it had not been for Laurie and old Esther, the maid, she felt that she never could have got through that dreadful time. The parrot alone was enough to drive her distracted, for he soon felt that she did not admire him, and revenged himself by being as mischievous as possible. He pulled her hair whenever she came near him, upset his bread and milk to plague her when she had newly cleaned his cage, made Mop bark by pecking at him while Madame dozed; called her names before company, and behaved in all respects like a reprehensible old bird. Then she could not endure the dog, a fat, cross beast, who snarled and yelped at her when she made his toilet, and who lay on his back with all his legs in the air, and a most idiotic expression of countenance, when he wanted something to eat, which was about a dozen times a day. The cook was bad-tempered, the old coachman deaf, and Esther the only one who ever took any notice of the young lady.

Esther was a French woman, who had lived with "Madame," as she called her mistress, for many years, and who rather tyrannized over the old lady, who could not get along without her. Her real name was Estelle; but Aunt March ordered her to change it, and she obeyed, on condition that she was never asked to change her religion. She took a fancy to Mademoiselle, and amused her very much, with odd stories of her life in France, when Amy sat with her while she got up Madame's laces. She also allowed her to roam about the great house, and examine the curious and pretty things stored away in the big wardrobes and the ancient chests; for Aunt March hoarded like a magpie. Amy's chief delight was an Indian cabinet full of queer drawers, little pigeon-holes, and secret places in which were kept all sorts of ornaments, some precious, some merely curious, all more or less antique. To examine and arrange these things gave Amy great satisfaction, especially the jewel cases; in which, on velvet cushions, reposed the ornaments which had adorned a belle forty years ago. There was the garnet set which Aunt March wore when she came out, the pearls her father gave her on her wedding day, her lover's diamonds, the jet mourning rings and pins, and queer lockets, with portraits of dead friends, and weeping willows made of hair inside, the baby bracelets her one little daughter had worn; Uncle March's big watch, with the red seal so many childish hands had played with, and in a box, all by itself, lay Aunt March's wedding ring, too small now for her fat finger, but put carefully away, like the most precious jewel of them all.

"Which would Mademoiselle choose if she had her will?" asked Esther, who always sat near to watch over and lock up the valuables.

"I like the diamonds best, but there is no necklace among them, and I'm fond of necklaces, they are so becoming. I should choose this if I might," replied Amy, looking with great admiration at a string of gold and ebony beads, from which hung a heavy cross of the same.

"I, too, covet that, but not as a necklace; ah, no! to me it is a rosary, and as such I should use it like a good Catholic," said Esther, eyeing the handsome thing wistfully.

"Is it meant to use as you use the string of good-smelling wooden beads hanging over your glass?" asked Amy.

"Truly, yes, to pray with. It would be pleasing to the saints if one used so fine a rosary as this, instead of wearing it as a vain bijou."

"You seem to take a great deal of comfort in your prayers, Esther, and always come down looking quiet and satisfied. I wish I could."

"If Mademoiselle was a Catholic, she would find true comfort; but, as that is not to be, it would be well if you went apart each day to meditate, and pray, as did the good mistress whom I served before Madame. She has a little chapel, and in it found solacement for much trouble."

"Would it be right for me to do so too?" asked Amy, who, in her loneliness, felt the need of help of some sort, and found that she was apt to forget her little book, now that Beth was not there to remind her of it.

"It would be excellent and charming; and I shall gladly arrange the little dressing-room for you, if you like it. Say nothing to Madame, but when she sleeps go you and sit alone a while to think good thoughts, and pray the dear God to preserve your sister."

Esther was truly pious, and quite sincere in her advice; for she had an affectionate heart, and felt much for the sisters in their anxiety. Amy liked the idea, and gave her leave to arrange the light closet next her room, hoping it would do her good.

"I wish I knew where all these pretty things would go when Aunt March dies," she said, as she slowly replaced the shining rosary, and shut the jewel cases one by one.

"To you and your sisters. I know it; Madame confides in me; I witnessed her will, and it is to be so," whispered Esther, smiling.

"How nice! but I wish she'd let us have them now. Pro-cras-ti-nation is not agreeable," observed Amy, taking a last look at the diamonds.

"It is too soon yet for the young ladies to wear these things. The first one who is affianced will have the pearls — Madame has said it; and I have a fancy that the little turquoise ring will be given to you when you go, for Madame approves your good behavior and charming manners."

"Do you think so? Oh, I'll be a lamb, if I can only have that lovely ring! It's ever so much prettier than Kitty Bryant's. I do like Aunt March, after all;" and Amy tried on the blue ring with a delightful face, and a firm resolve to earn it.

From that day she was a model of obedience, and the old lady complacently admired the success of her training. Esther fitted up the closet with a little table, placed a footstool before it, and over it a picture, taken from one of the shut-up rooms. She thought it was of no great value, but, being appropriate, she borrowed it, well knowing that Madame would never know it, nor care if she did. It was, however, a very valuable copy of one of the famous pictures of the world, and Amy's beauty-loving eyes were never tired of looking up at the sweet face of the divine mother, while tender thoughts of her own were busy at her heart. On the table she laid her little Testament and hymn-book, kept a vase always full of the best flowers Laurie brought her, and came every day to "sit alone, thinking good thoughts, and praying the dear God to preserve her sister." Esther had given her a rosary of black beads, with a silver cross, but Amy hung it up, and did not use it, feeling doubtful as to its fitness for Protestant prayers.

The little girl was very sincere in all this, for, being left alone outside the safe home-nest, she felt the need of some kind hand to hold by so sorely, that she instinctively turned to the strong and tender Friend, whose fatherly love most closely surrounds His little children. She missed her mother's help to understand and rule herself, but having been taught where to look, she did her best to find the way, and walk in it confidently. But Amy was a young pilgrim, and just now her burden seemed very heavy. She tried to forget herself, to keep cheerful, and be satisfied with doing right, though no one saw or praised her for it. In her first effort at being very, very good, she decided to make her will, as Aunt March had done; so that if she *did* fall ill and die, her possessions might be justly and generously divided. It cost her a pang even to think of giving up the little treasures which in her eyes were as precious as the old lady's jewels.

During one of her play hours she wrote out the important document as well as she could, with some help from Esther as to certain legal terms; and, when the good-natured French woman had signed her name, Amy felt relieved, and laid it by to show Laurie, whom she wanted as a second witness. As it was a rainy day, she went up stairs to amuse herself in one of the large chambers, and took Polly with her for company. In this room there was a wardrobe full of old-fashioned costumes, with which Esther allowed her to play, and it was her favorite amusement to array herself in the faded brocades, and parade up and down before the long mirror; making stately courtesies, and sweeping her train about, with a rustle which delighted her ears. So busy was she on this day, that she did not hear Laurie's ring, nor see his face peeping in at her, as she gravely promenaded to and fro, flirting her fan and tossing her head, on which she wore a great pink turban, contrasting oddly with her blue brocade dress and yellow quilted petticoat. She was obliged to walk carefully, for she had on high-heeled shoes, and, as Laurie told Jo afterwards, it was a comical sight to see her mince along in her gay suit, with Polly sidling and bridling just behind her, imitating her as well as he could, and occasionally stopping to laugh, or exclaim, "Ain't we fine? Get along, you fright! Hold your tongue! Kiss me, dear; ha! ha!"

Having with difficulty restrained an explosion of merriment, lest it should offend her majesty, Laurie tapped, and was graciously received.

"Sit down and rest while I put these things away; then I want to consult you about a very serious matter," said Amy, when she had shown her splendor, and driven Polly into a corner. "That bird is the trial of my life," she continued, removing the pink mountain from her head, while Laurie seated himself astride of a chair. "Yesterday, when aunt was asleep, and I was trying to be as still as a mouse, Polly began to squall and flap about in his cage; so I went to let him out, and found a big spider there. I poked it out, and it ran under the book-case; Polly marched straight after it, stooped down and peeped under the book-case, saying, in his funny way, with a cock of his eye, 'Come out and take a walk, my dear.' I *couldn't* help laughing, which made Poll swear, and aunt woke up and scolded us both."

"Did the spider accept the old fellow's invitation? asked Laurie, yawning.

"Yes; out it came, and away ran Polly, frightened to death, and scrambled up on aunt's chair, calling out, 'Catch her! catch her! catch her!' as I chased the spider."

"That's a lie! Oh, lor!" cried the parrot, pecking at Laurie's toes.

"I'd wring your neck if you were mine, you old torment," cried Laurie, shaking his fist at the bird, who put his head on one side, and gravely croaked, "Allyluyer! bless your buttons, dear!"

"Now I'm ready," said Amy, shutting the wardrobe, and taking a paper out of her pocket. "I want you to read that, please, and tell me if it is legal and right. I feel that I ought to do it, for life is uncertain, and I don't want any ill-feeling over my tomb."

Laurie bit his lips, and turning a little from the pensive speaker read the following document, with praiseworthy gravity, considering the spelling: –

My Last Will and Testament

I, Amy Curtis March, being in my sane mind, do give and bequeethe all my earthly property: — viz. to wit: — namely

To my father, my best pictures, sketches, maps, and works of art, including frames. Also my $100, to do what he likes with.

To my mother, all my clothes, except the blue apron with pockets, — also my likeness, and my medal, with much love.

To my dear sister Margaret, I give my turkquoise ring (if I get it), also my green box with the doves on it, also my piece of real lace for her neck, and my sketch of her as a memorial of her "little girl."

To Jo I leave my breast-pin, the one mended with sealing wax, also my bronze inkstand — she lost the cover, — and my most precious plaster rabbit, because I am sorry I burnt up her story.

To Beth (if she lives after me) I give my dolls and the little bureau, my fan, my linen collars and my new slippers if she can wear them being thin when she gets well. And I herewith also leave her my regret that I ever made fun of old Joanna.

To my friend and neighbor Theodore Laurence I bequeethe my paper marshay portfolio, my clay model of a horse, though he did say it hadn't any neck. Also in return for his great kindness in the hour of affliction any one of my artistic works he likes, Noter Dame is the best.

To our venerable benefactor Mr. Laurence I leave my purple box with a looking glass in the cover which will be nice for his pens and remind him of the departed girl who thanks him for his favors to her family, specially Beth.

I wish my favorite playmate Kitty Bryant to have the blue silk apron and my gold-bead ring with a kiss.

To Hannah I give the band-box she wanted and all the patch work I leave hoping she will "remember me, when it you see."

And now having disposed of my most valuable property I hope all will be satisfied and not blame the dead. I forgive every one, and trust we may all meet when the trump shall sound. Amen.

To this will and testament I set my hand and seal on this 20th day of Nov. Anni Domino 1861.

    Amy Curtis March.

Witnesses: Estelle Valnor,

    Theodore Laurence.

The last name was written in pencil, and Amy explained that he was to rewrite it in ink, and seal it up for her properly.

"What put it into your head? Did anyone tell you about Beth's giving away her things?" said Laurie, soberly, as Amy laid a bit of red tape, with sealing-wax, a taper, and a standish before him.

She explained; and then asked, anxiously, "What about Beth?"

"I'm sorry I spoke; but as I did, I'll tell you. She felt so ill one day, that she told Jo she wanted to give her piano to Meg, her bird to you, and the poor old doll to Jo, who would love it for her sake. She was sorry she had so little to give, and left locks of hair to the rest of us, and her best love to grandpa. *She* never thought of a will."

Laurie was signing and sealing as he spoke, and did not look up till a great tear dropped on the paper. Amy's face was full of trouble; but she only said, "Don't people put sort of postscripts to their wills, sometimes."

"Yes; 'codicils,' they call them."

"Put one in mine, then — that I wish *all* my curls cut off, and given round to my friends. I forgot it; but I want it done, though it will spoil my looks."

Laurie added it, smiling at Amy's last and greatest sacrifice. Then he amused her for an hour, and was much interested in all her trials. But when he came to go, Amy held him back to whisper, with trembling lips, "Is there really any danger about Beth?"

"I'm afraid there is; but we must hope for the best, so don't cry, dear;" and Laurie put his arm about her with a brotherly gesture, which was very comforting.

When he had gone, she went to her little chapel, and, sitting in the twilight, prayed for Beth with streaming tears and an aching heart, feeling that a million turquoise rings would not console her for the loss of her gentle little sister.

CONFIDENTIAL

~

I don't think I have any words in which to tell the meeting of the
mother and daughters; such hours are beautiful to live, but very
hard to describe, so I will leave it to the imagination of my readers; merely
saying that the house was full of genuine happiness, and that Meg's tender
hope was realized; for when Beth woke from that long, healing sleep, the
first objects on which her eyes fell *were* the little rose and mother's face. Too
weak to wonder at anything, she only smiled, and nestled close into the
loving arms about her, feeling that the hungry longing was satisfied at last.
Then she slept again, and the girls waited upon their mother, for she would
not unclasp the thin hand which clung to hers, even in sleep. Hannah had
"dished up" an astonishing breakfast for the traveller, finding it impossible
to vent her excitement in any other way; and Meg and Jo fed their mother
like dutiful young storks, while they listened to her whispered account of
father's state, Mr. Brooke's promise to stay and nurse him, the delays which
the storm occasioned on the homeward journey, and the unspeakable

217

comfort Laurie's hopeful face had given her when she arrived, worn out with fatigue, anxiety, and cold.

What a strange, yet pleasant day that was! so brilliant and gay without, for all the world seemed abroad to welcome the first snow; so quiet and reposeful within, for every one slept, spent with watching, and a Sabbath stillness reigned through the house, while nodding Hannah mounted guard at the door. With a blissful sense of burdens lifted off, Meg and Jo closed their weary eyes, and lay at rest like storm-beaten boats, safe at anchor in a quiet harbor. Mrs. March would not leave Beth's side, but rested in the big chair, waking often to look at, touch, and brood over her child, like a miser over some recovered treasure.

Laurie, meanwhile, posted off to comfort Amy, and told his story so well that Aunt March actually "sniffed" herself, and never once said, "I told you so." Amy came out so strong on this occasion, that I think the good thoughts in the little chapel really began to bear fruit. She dried her tears quickly, restrained her impatience to see her mother, and never even thought of the turquoise ring, when the old lady heartily agreed in Laurie's opinion, that she behaved "like a capital little woman." Even Polly seemed impressed, for he called her "good girl," blessed her buttons, and begged her to "come and take a walk, dear," in his most affable tone. She would very gladly have gone out to enjoy the bright wintry weather; but, discovering that Laurie was dropping with sleep in spite of manful efforts to conceal the fact, she persuaded him to rest on the sofa, while she wrote a note to her mother. She was a long time about it; and, when she returned, he was stretched out, with both arms under his head, sound asleep, while Aunt March had pulled down the curtains, and sat doing nothing in an unusual fit of benignity.

After a while, they began to think he was not going to wake till night, and I'm not sure that he would, had he not been effectually roused by Amy's cry of joy at sight of her mother. There probably were a good many happy little girls in and about the city that day, but it is my private opinion that Amy was the happiest of all, when she sat in her mother's lap and told her trials, receiving consolation and compensation in the shape of approving smiles and fond caresses. They were alone together in the chapel, to which her mother did not object when its purpose was explained to her.

"On the contrary, I like it very much, dear," looking from the dusty roasary to the well-worn little book, and the lovely picture with its garland of evergreen. "It is an excellent plan to have some place where we can go to be quiet, when things vex or grieve us. There are a good many hard times in this life of ours, but we can always bear them if we ask help in the right way. I think my little girl is learning this?"

"Yes, mother; and when I go home I mean to have a corner in the big closet to put my books, and the copy of that picture which I've tried to make. The woman's face is not good, it's too beautiful for me to draw, but the baby is done better, and I love it very much. I like to think He was a little child once, for then I don't seem so far away, and that helps me."

As Amy pointed to the smiling Christ-child on his mother's knee, Mrs. March saw something on the lifted hand that made her smile. She said nothing, but Amy understood the look, and, after a minute's pause, she added, gravely, –

"I wanted to speak to you about this, but I forgot it. Aunt gave me the ring to-day; she called me to her and kissed me, and put it on my finger, and said I was a credit to her, and she'd like to keep me always. She gave me that funny guard to keep the turquoise on, as it's too big. I'd like to wear them, mother; can I?"

"They are very pretty, but I think you're rather too young for such ornaments, Amy," said Mrs. March, looking at the plump little hand, with the band of sky-blue stones on the forefinger, and the quaint guard, formed of two tiny, golden hands clasped together.

"I'll try not to be vain," said Amy. "I don't think I like it only because it's so pretty; but I want to wear it as the girl in the story wore her bracelets, to remind me of something."

"Do you mean Aunt March?" asked her mother, laughing.

"No, to remind me not to be selfish." Amy looked so earnest and sincere about it, that her mother stopped laughing, and listened respectfully to the little plan.

"I've thought a great deal lately about my 'bundle of naughties,' and being selfish is the largest one in it; so I'm going to try hard to cure it, if I can. Beth isn't selfish, and that's the reason every one loves her, and feels so bad at the thoughts of losing her. People wouldn't feel half so bad about me if I was sick, and I don't deserve to have them; but I'd like to be loved and missed by a great many friends, so I'm going to try and be like Beth all I can. I'm apt to forget my resolutions; but, if I had something always about me to remind me, I guess I should do better. May I try this way?"

"Yes; but I have more faith in the corner of the big closet. Wear your ring, dear, and do your best; I think you will prosper, for the sincere wish to be good is half the battle. Now, I must go back to Beth. Keep up your heart, little daughter, and we will soon have you home again."

That evening, while Meg was writing to her father, to report the traveller's safe arrival, Jo slipped upstairs into Beth's room, and, finding her mother in her usual place, stood a minute twisting her fingers in her hair, with a worried gesture and an undecided look.

"What is it, deary?" asked Mrs. March, holding out her hand with a face which invited confidence.

"I want to tell you something, mother."

"About Meg?"

"How quick you guessed! Yes, it's about her, and though it's a little thing, it fidgets me."

"Beth is asleep; speak low, and tell me all about it. That Moffat hasn't been here, I hope?" asked Mrs. March, rather sharply.

"No; I should have shut the door in his face if he had," said Jo, settling herself on the floor at her mother's feet. "Last summer Meg left a pair of gloves over at the Laurences, and only one was returned. We forgot all about it, till Teddy told me that Mr. Brooke had it. He kept it in his waistcoat pocket, and once it fell out, and Teddy joked him about it, and Mr. Brooke owned that he liked Meg but didn't dare say so, she was so young and he so poor. Now isn't it a *dreadful* state of things?"

"Do you think Meg cares for him?" asked Mrs. March, with an anxious look.

"Mercy me! I don't know anything about love, and such nonsense!" cried Jo, with a funny mixture of interest and contempt. "In novels, the girls show it by starting and blushing, fainting away, growing thin, and acting like fools. Now Meg don't do anything of the sort; she eats and drinks, and sleeps, like a sensible creature; she looks straight in my face when I talk about that man, and only blushes a little bit when Teddy jokes about lovers. I forbid him to do it, but he don't mind me as he ought."

"Then you fancy that Meg is *not* interested in John?"

"Who?" cried Jo, staring.

"Mr. Brooke; I call him 'John' now; we fell into the way of doing so at the hospital, and he likes it."

"Oh, dear! I know you'll take his part; he's been good to father, and you won't send him away, but let Meg marry him, if she wants to. Mean thing! to go petting pa and truckling to you, just to wheedle you into liking him;" and Jo pulled her hair again with a wrathful tweak.

"My dear, don't get angry about it, and I will tell you how it happened. John went with me at Mr. Laurence's request, and was so devoted to poor father, that we couldn't help getting fond of him. He was perfectly open and honorable about Meg, for he told us he loved her; but would earn a comfortable home before he asked her to marry him. He only wanted our leave to love her and work for her, and the right to make her love him if he could. He is a truly excellent young man, and we could not refuse to listen to him; but I will not consent to Meg engaging herself so young."

"Of course not; it would be idiotic! I knew there was mischief brewing; I felt it; and now it's worse than I imagined. I just wish I could marry Meg myself, and keep her safe in the family."

This odd arrangement made Mrs. March smile; but she said, gravely, "Jo, I confide in you, and don't wish you to say anything to Meg yet. When John comes back, and I see them together, I can judge better of her feelings toward him."

"She'll see his in those handsome eyes that she talks about, and then it will be all up with her. She's got such a soft heart, it will melt like butter in the sun if any one looks sentimentally at her. She read the short reports he sent more than she did your letters, and pinched me when I spoke of it, and likes brown eyes, and doesn't think John an ugly name, and she'll go and fall in love, and there's an end of peace and fun, and cosy times, together. I see it all! they'll go lovering around the house, and we shall have to dodge; Meg will be absorbed, and no good to me any more; Brooke will scratch up a fortune somehow, – carry her off and make a hole in the family; and I shall break my heart, and everything will be abominably uncomfortable. Oh, deary me! why weren't we all boys? then there wouldn't be any bother!"

Jo leaned her chin on her knees, in a disconsolate attitude, and shook her fist at the reprehensible John. Mrs. March sighed, and Jo looked up with an air of relief.

"You don't like it, mother? I'm glad of it; let's send him about his business, and not tell Meg a word of it, but all be jolly together as we always have been."

"I did wrong to sigh, Jo. It is natural and right you should all go to homes of your own, in time; but I do want to keep my girls as long as I can; and I am sorry that this happened so soon, for Meg is only seventeen, and it will be some years before John can make a home for her. Your father and I have agreed that she shall not bind herself in any way, nor be married, before twenty. If she and John love one another, they can wait, and test the love by doing so. She is conscientious, and I have no fear of her treating him unkindly. My pretty, tender-hearted girl! I hope things will go happily with her."

"Hadn't you rather have her marry a rich man?" asked Jo, as her mother's voice faltered a little over the last words.

"Money is a good and useful thing, Jo; and I hope my girls will never feel the need of it too bitterly, nor be tempted by too much. I should like to know that John was firmly established in some good business, which gave him an income large enough to keep free from debt, and make Meg comfortable. I'm not ambitious for a splendid fortune, a fashionable position, or a great name for my girls. If rank and money come with love and virtue, also, I should accept them gratefully, and enjoy your good fortune; but I know, by experience, how much genuine happiness can be had in a plain little house, where the daily bread is earned, and some privations give sweetness to the few pleasures; I am content to see Meg begin humbly, for, if I am not mistaken, she will be rich in the possession of a good man's heart, and that is better than a fortune."

"I understand, mother, and quite agree; but I'm disappointed about Meg, for I'd planned to have her marry Teddy by and by, and sit in the lap of luxury all her days. Wouldn't it be nice?" asked Jo, looking up with a brighter face.

"He is younger than she, you know," began Mrs. March; but Jo broke in, —

"Oh, that don't matter; he's old for his age, and tall; and can be quite grown-up in his manners, if he likes. Then he's rich, and generous, and good, and loves us all; and I say it's a pity my plan is spoilt."

"I'm afraid Laurie is hardly grown-up enough for Meg, and

altogether too much of a weathercock, just now, for any one to depend on. Don't make plans, Jo; but let time and their own hearts mate your friends. We can't meddle safely in such matters, and had better not get 'romantic rubbish,' as you call it, into our heads, lest it spoil our friendship."

"Well, I won't; but I hate to see things going all criss-cross, and getting snarled up, when a pull here, and a snip there, would straighten it out. I wish wearing flat-irons on our heads would keep us from growing up. But buds will be roses, and kittens cats, – more's the pity!"

"What's that about flat-irons and cats?" asked Meg, as she crept into the room, with the finished letter in her hand.

"Only one of my stupid speeches. I'm going to bed; come on, Peggy," said Jo, unfolding herself, like an animated puzzle.

"Quite right, and beautifully written. Please add that I send my love to John," said Mrs. March, as she glanced over the letter, and gave it back.

"Do you call him 'John'?" asked Meg, smiling, with her innocent eyes looking down into her mother's.

"Yes; he has been like a son to us, and we are very fond of him," replied Mrs. March, returning the look with a keen one.

"I'm glad of that; he is so lonely. Good-night, mother dear. It is so inexpressibly comfortable to have you here," was Meg's quiet answer.

The kiss her mother gave her was a very tender one; and, as she went away, Mrs. March said, with a mixture of satisfaction and regret, "She does not love John yet, but will soon learn to."

CHAPTER TWENTY-ONE

LAURIE MAKES MISCHIEF, AND JO MAKES PEACE

~

Jo's face was a study next day, for the secret rather weighed upon her, and she found it hard not to look mysterious and important. Meg observed it, but did not trouble herself to make inquiries, for she had learned that the best way to manage Jo was by the law of contraries, so she felt sure of being told everything if she did not ask. She was rather surprised, therefore, when the silence remained unbroken, and Jo assumed a patronizing air, which decidedly aggravated Meg, who in her turn assumed an air of dignified reserve, and devoted herself to her mother. This left Jo to her own devices; for Mrs. March had taken her place as nurse, and bade her rest, exercise, and amuse herself after her long confinement. Amy being gone, Laurie was her only refuge; and, much as she enjoyed his society, she rather dreaded him just then, for he was an incorrigible tease, and she feared he would coax her secret from her.

She was quite right; for the mischief-loving lad no sooner suspected a mystery, than he set himself to find it out, and led Jo a trying life of it.

He wheedled, bribed, ridiculed, threatened, and scolded; affected indifference, that he might surprise the truth from her; declared he knew, then that he didn't care; and, at last, by dint of perseverance, he satisfied himself that it concerned Meg and Mr. Brooke. Feeling indignant that he was not taken into his tutor's confidence, he set his wits to work to devise some proper retaliation for the slight.

Meg meanwhile had apparently forgotten the matter, and was absorbed in preparations for her father's return; but all of a sudden a change seemed to come over her, and, for a day or two, she was quite unlike herself. She started when spoken to, blushed when looked at, was very quiet, and sat over her sewing with a timid, troubled look on her face. To her mother's inquiries she answered that she was quite well, and Jo's she silenced by begging to be let alone.

"She feels it in the air — love, I mean — and she's going very fast. She's got most of the symptoms, is twittery and cross, don't eat, lies awake, and mopes in corners. I caught her singing that song about 'the silver-voiced brook,' and once she said 'John,' as you do, and then turned as red as a poppy. Whatever shall we do?" said Jo, looking ready for any measures, however violent.

"Nothing but wait. Let her alone, be kind and patient, and father's coming will settle everything," replied her mother.

"Here's a note to you, Meg, all sealed up. How odd! Teddy never seals mine," said Jo, next day, as she distributed the contents of the little post-office.

Mrs. March and Jo were deep in their own affairs, when a sound from Meg made them look up to see her staring at her note, with a frightened face.

"My child, what is it?" cried her mother, running to her, while Jo tried to take the paper which had done the mischief.

"It's all a mistake — he didn't send it — oh, Jo, how could you do it?" and Meg hid her face in her hands, crying as if her heart was quite broken.

"Me! I've done nothing! What's she talking about?" cried Jo, bewildered.

Meg's mild eyes kindled with anger as she pulled a crumpled note from her pocket, and threw it at Jo, saying reproachfully, —

"You wrote it, and that bad boy helped you. How could you be so rude, so mean, and cruel to us both?"

Jo hardly heard her, for she and her mother were reading the note, which was written in a peculiar hand.

MY DEAREST MARGARET, —

I can no longer restrain my passion, and must know my fate before I return. I dare not tell your parents yet, but I think they would consent if they knew that we adored one another. Mr. Laurence will help me to some good place, and then, my sweet girl, you will make me happy. I implore you to say nothing to your family yet, but to send one word of hope through Laurie to

Your devoted
JOHN.

"Oh, the little villain! that's the way he meant to pay me for keeping my word to mother. I'll give him a hearty scolding, and bring him over to beg pardon," cried Jo, burning to execute immediate justice. But her mother held her back, saying, with a look she seldom wore, —

"Stop, Jo, you must clear yourself first. You have played so many pranks, that I am afraid you have had a hand in this."

"On my word, mother, I haven't! I never saw that note before, and I don't know anything about it, as true as I live!" said Jo, so earnestly, that they believed her. "If I *had* taken a part in it I'd have done it better than this, and have written a sensible note. I should think you'd have known Mr. Brooke wouldn't write such stuff as that," she added, scornfully tossing down the paper.

"It's like his writing," faltered Meg, comparing it with the note in her hand.

"Oh, Meg, you didn't answer it?" cried Mrs. March, quickly.

"Yes, I did!" and Meg hid her face again, overcome with shame.

"Here's a scrape! *Do* let me bring that wicked boy over to explain, and be lectured. I can't rest till I get hold of him;" and Jo made for the door again.

"Hush! let me manage this, for it is worse than I thought. Margaret, tell me the whole story," commanded Mrs. March, sitting down by Meg, yet keeping hold of Jo, lest she should fly off.

"I received the first letter from Laurie, who didn't look as if he knew anything about it," began Meg, without looking up. "I was worried at first, and meant to tell you; then I remembered how you like Mr. Brooke, so I thought you wouldn't mind if I kept my little secret for a few days. I'm so silly that I liked to think no one knew; and, while I was deciding what to say, I felt like the girls in books, who have such things to do. Forgive me, mother, I'm paid for my silliness now; I never can look him in the face again."

"What did you say to him?" asked Mrs. March.

"I only said I was too young to do anything about it yet; that I didn't wish to have secrets from you, and he must speak to father. I was very grateful for his kindness, and would be his friend, but nothing more, for a long while."

Mrs. March smiled, as if well pleased, and Jo clapped her hands, exclaiming, with a laugh, —

"You are almost equal to Caroline Percy, who was a pattern of prudence! Tell on, Meg. What did he say to that?"

"He writes in a different way entirely, telling me that he never sent any love-letter at all, and is very sorry that my roguish sister, Jo, should take such liberties with our names. It's very kind and respectful, but think how dreadful for me!"

Meg leaned against her mother, looking the image of despair, and Jo tramped about the room, calling Laurie names. All of a sudden she stopped, caught up the two notes, and, after looking at them closely, said, decidedly, "I don't believe Brooke ever saw either of these letters. Teddy wrote both, and keeps yours to crow over me with, because I wouldn't tell him my secret."

"Don't have any secrets, Jo; tell it to mother, and keep out of trouble, as I should have done," said Meg, warningly.

"Bless you, child! mother told me."

"That will do, Jo. I'll comfort Meg while you go and get Laurie. I shall sift the matter to the bottom, and put a stop to such pranks at once."

Away ran Jo, and Mrs. March gently told Meg Mr. Brooke's real feelings. "Now, dear, what are your own? Do you love him enough to wait till he can make a home for you, or will you keep yourself quite free for the present?"

"I've been so scared and worried, I don't want to have anything to do with lovers for a long while, — perhaps never," answered Meg, petulantly.

"If John *doesn't* know anything about this nonsense, don't tell him, and make Jo and Laurie hold their tongues. I won't be deceived and plagued, and made a fool of, – it's a shame!"

Seeing that Meg's usually gentle temper was roused, and her pride hurt by this mischievous joke, Mrs. March soothed her by promises of entire silence, and great discretion for the future. The instant Laurie's step was heard in the hall, Meg fled into the study, and Mrs. March received the culprit alone. Jo had not told him why he was wanted, fearing he wouldn't come; but he knew the minute he saw Mrs. March's face, and stood twirling his hat with a guilty air, which convicted him at once. Jo was dismissed, but chose to march up and down the hall like a sentinel, having some fear that the prisoner might bolt. The sound of voices in the parlor rose and fell for half an hour; but what happened during that interview the girls never knew.

When they were called in, Laurie was standing by their mother with such a penitent face, that Jo forgave him on the spot, but did not think it wise to betray the fact. Meg received his humble apology, and was much comforted by the assurance that Brooke knew nothing of the joke.

"I'll never tell him to my dying day – wild horses shan't drag it out of me; so you'll forgive me, Meg, and I'll do anything to show how out-and-out sorry I am," he added, looking very much ashamed of himself.

"I'll try; but it was a very ungentlemanly thing to do. I didn't think you would be so sly and malicious, Laurie," replied Meg, trying to hide her maidenly confusion under a gravely reproachful air.

"It was altogether abominable, and I don't deserve to be spoken to for a month; but you will, though, won't you?" and Laurie folded his hands together, with such an imploring gesture, and rolled up his eyes in such a meekly repentant way, as he spoke in his irresistibly persuasive tone, that it was impossible to frown upon him, in spite of his scandalous behavior. Meg pardoned him, and Mrs. March's grave face relaxed, in spite of her efforts to keep sober, when she heard him declare that he would atone for his sins by all sorts of penances, and abase himself like a worm before the injured damsel.

Jo stood aloof, meanwhile, trying to harden her heart against him, and succeeding only in primming up her face into an expression of entire disapprobation. Laurie looked at her once or twice, but, as she showed no sign of relenting, he felt injured, and turned his back on her till the others were done with him, when he made her a low bow, and walked off without a word.

As soon as he had gone, she wished she had been more forgiving, and when Meg and her mother went up stairs she felt lonely, and longed for Teddy. After resisting for some time, she yielded to the impulse, and, armed with a book to return, went over to the big house.

"Is Mr. Laurence in?" asked Jo, of a housemaid, who was coming down stairs.

"Yes, miss; but I don't believe he's seeable just yet."

"Why not; is he ill?"

"La, no, miss! but he's had a scene with Mr. Laurie, who is in one of his tantrums about something, which vexes the old gentleman, so I dursn't go nigh him."

"Where is Laurie?"

"Shut up in his room, and he won't answer, though I've been a-tapping. I don't know what's to become of the dinner, for it's ready, and there's no one to eat it."

"I'll go and see what the matter is. I'm not afraid of either of them."

Up went Jo, and knocked smartly at the door of Laurie's little study.

"Stop that, or I'll open the door and make you!" called out the young gentleman, in a threatening tone.

Jo immediately knocked again; the door flew open, and in she bounced, before Laurie could recover from his surprise. Seeing that he really *was* out of temper, Jo, who knew how to manage him, assumed a contrite expression, and, going artistically down upon her knees, said meekly, "Please forgive me for being so cross. I came to make it up, and can't go away till I have."

"It's all right; get up, and don't be a goose, Jo," was the cavalier reply to her petition.

"Thank you; I will. Gould I ask what's the matter? You don't look exactly easy in your mind."

"I've been shaken, and I won't bear it!" growled Laurie, indignantly.

"Who did it?" demanded Jo.

"Grandfather; if it had been any one else I'd have — " and the injured youth finished his sentence by an energetic gesture of the right arm.

"That's nothing; I often shake you, and you don't mind," said Jo, soothingly.

"Pooh! you're a girl, and it's fun; but I'll allow no man to shake *me*."

"I don't think any one would care to try it, if you looked as much like a thunder-cloud as you do now. Why were you treated so?"

"Just because I wouldn't say what your mother wanted me for. I'd promised not to tell, and of course I wasn't going to break my word."

"Couldn't you satisfy your grandpa in any other way?"

"No; he *would* have the truth, the whole truth, and nothing but the truth. I'd have told my part of the scrape, if I could, without bringing Meg in. As I couldn't, I held my tongue, and bore the scolding till the old gentleman collared me. Then I got angry, and bolted, for fear I should forget myself."

"It wasn't nice, but he's sorry, I know; so go down and make up. I'll help you."

"Hanged if I do! I'm not going to be lectured and pummelled by every one, just for a bit of a frolic. I *was* sorry about Meg, and begged pardon like a man; but I won't do it again, when I wasn't in the wrong."

"He didn't know that."

"He ought to trust me, and not act as if I was a baby. It's no use, Jo; he's got to learn that I'm able to take care of myself, and don't need any one's apron-string to hold on by."

"What pepper-pots you are!" sighed Jo. "How do you mean to settle this affair?"

"Well, he ought to beg pardon, and believe me when I say I can't tell him what the row's about."

"Bless you! he won't do that."

"I won't go down till he does."

"Now, Teddy, be sensible; let it pass, and I'll explain what I can. You can't stay here, so what's the use of being melodramatic?"

"I don't intend to stay here long, any way. I'll slip off and take a journey somewhere, and when grandpa misses me he'll come round fast enough."

"I dare say; but you ought not to go and worry him."

"Don't preach. I'll go to Washington and see Brooke; it's gay there, and I'll enjoy myself after the troubles."

"What fun you'd have! I wish I could run off too!" said Jo, forgetting her part of Mentor in lively visions of martial life at the capital.

"Come on, then! Why not? You go and surprise your father, and I'll stir up old Brooke. It would be a glorious joke; let's do it, Jo! We'll leave a letter saying we are all right, and trot off at once. I've got money enough; it will do you good, and be no harm, as you go to your father."

For a moment Jo looked as if she would agree; for, wild as the plan was, it just suited her. She was tired of care and confinement, longed for change, and thoughts of her father blended temptingly with the novel charms of camps and hospitals, liberty and fun. Her eyes kindled as they turned wistfully toward the window, but they fell on the old house opposite, and she shook her head with sorrowful decision.

"If I was a boy, we'd run away together, and have a capital time; but as I'm a miserable girl, I must be proper, and stop at home. Don't tempt me, Teddy, it's a crazy plan."

"That's the fun of it!" began Laurie, who had got a wilful fit on him, and was possessed to break out of bounds in some way.

"Hold your tongue!" cried Jo, covering her ears. " 'Prunes and prisms' are my doom, and I may as well make up my mind to it. I came here to moralize, not to hear about things that make me skip to think of."

"I know Meg would wet-blanket such a proposal, but I thought you had more spirit," began Laurie, insinuatingly.

"Bad boy, be quiet. Sit down and think of your own sins, don't go making me add to mine. If I get your grandpa to apologize for the shaking, will you give up running away?" asked Jo, seriously.

"Yes, but you won't do it," answered Laurie, who wished to "make up," but felt that his outraged dignity must be appeased first.

"If I can manage the young one I can the old one," muttered Jo, as she walked away, leaving Laurie bent over a railroad map, with his head propped up on both hands.

"Come in!" and Mr. Laurence's gruff voice sounded gruffer than ever, as Jo tapped at his door.

"It's only me, sir, come to return a book," she said, blandly, as she entered.

"Want any more?" asked the old gentleman, looking grim and vexed, but trying not to show it.

"Yes, please, I like old Sam so well, I think I'll try the second volume," returned Jo, hoping to propitiate him by accepting a second dose of "Boswell's Johnson," as he had recommended that lively work.

The shaggy eyebrows unbent a little, as he rolled the steps toward the shelf where the Johnsonian literature was placed. Jo skipped up, and, sitting on the top step, affected to be searching for her book, but was really wondering how best to introduce the dangerous object of her visit. Mr. Laurence seemed to suspect that something was brewing in her mind; for, after taking several brisk turns about the room, he faced round on her, speaking so abruptly that "Rasselas" tumbled face downward on the floor.

"What has that boy been about? Don't try to shield him, now! I know he has been in mischief, by the way he acted when he came home. I can't get a word from him; and, when I threatened to shake the truth out of him, he bolted upstairs, and locked himself into his room."

"He did do wrong, but we forgave him, and all promised not to say a word to any one," began Jo, reluctantly.

"That won't do; he shall not shelter himself behind a promise from you soft-hearted girls. If he's done anything amiss, he shall confess, beg pardon, and be punished. Out with it, Jo! I won't be kept in the dark."

Mr. Laurence looked so alarming, and spoke so sharply, that Jo would have gladly run away, if she could, but she was perched aloft on the steps, and he stood at the foot, a lion in the path, so she had to stay and brave it out.

"Indeed, sir, I cannot tell, mother forbid it. Laurie has confessed, asked pardon, and been punished quite enough. We don't keep silence to shield him, but some one else, and it will make more trouble if you interfere. Please don't; it was partly my fault, but it's all right now; so let's forget it, and talk about the 'Rambler,' or something pleasant."

"Hang the 'Rambler!' come down and give me your word that this harum-scarum boy of mine hasn't done anything ungrateful or impertinent. If he has, after all your kindness to him, I'll thrash him with my own hands."

The threat sounded awful, but did not alarm Jo, for she knew the irascible old man would never lift a finger against his grandson, whatever he might say to the contrary. She obediently descended, and made as light of the prank as she could without betraying Meg, or forgetting the truth.

"Hum! ha! well, if the boy held his tongue because he'd promised, and not for obstinacy, I'll forgive him. He's a stubborn fellow, and hard to manage," said Mr. Laurence, rubbing up his hair till it looked as if he'd been out in a gale, and smoothing the frown from his brow with an air of relief.

"So am I; but a kind word will govern me when all the king's horses and all the king's men couldn't," said Jo, trying to say a kind word for her friend, who seemed to get out of one scrape only to fall into another.

"You think I'm not kind to him, hey?" was the sharp answer.

"Oh, dear, no, sir; you are rather too kind sometimes, and then just a trifle hasty when he tries your patience. Don't you think you are?"

Jo was determined to have it out now, and tried to look quite placid, though she quaked a little after her bold speech. To her great relief and surprise, the old gentleman only threw his spectacles on to the table, with a rattle, and exclaimed frankly, —

"You're right, girl, I am! I love the boy, but he tries my patience past bearing, and I don't know how it will end, if we go on so."

"I'll tell you, — he'll run away." Jo was sorry for that speech the minute it was made; she meant to warn him that Laurie would not bear much restraint, and hoped he would be more forbearing with the lad.

Mr. Laurence's ruddy face changed suddenly, and he sat down with a troubled glance at the picture of a handsome man, which hung over his table. It was Laurie's father, who *had* run away in his youth, and married against the imperious old man's will. Jo fancied he remembered and regretted the past, and she wished she had held her tongue.

"He won't do it unless he is very much worried, and only threatens it sometimes, when he gets tired of studying. I often think I should like to, especially since my hair was cut; so if you ever miss us, you may advertise for two boys, and look among the ships bound for India."

She laughed as she spoke, and Mr. Laurence looked relieved, evidently taking the whole thing as a joke.

"You hussy, how dare you talk in that way? Where's your respect for me, and your proper bringing up? Bless the boys and girls! what torments they are; yet we can't do without them," he said, pinching her cheeks good-humoredly.

"Go and bring that boy down to his dinner, tell him it's all right, and advise him not to put on tragedy airs with his grandfather; I won't bear it."

"He won't come, sir; he feels badly because you didn't believe him when he said he couldn't tell. I think the shaking hurt his feelings very much."

Jo tried to look pathetic, but must have failed, for Mr. Laurence began to laugh, and she knew the day was won.

"I'm sorry for that, and ought to thank him for not shaking *me*, I suppose. What the dickens does the fellow expect?" and the old gentleman looked a trifle ashamed of his own testiness.

"If I were you, I'd write him an apology, sir. He says he won't come down till he has one; and talks about Washington, and goes on in an absurd way. A formal apology will make him see how foolish he is, and bring him down quite amiable. Try it; he likes fun, and this way is better than talking. I'll carry it up, and teach him his duty."

Mr. Laurence gave her a sharp look, and put on his spectacles, saying, slowly, "You're a sly puss! but I don't mind being managed by you and Beth. Here, give me a bit of paper, and let us have done with this nonsense."

The note was written in the terms which one gentleman would use to another after offering some deep insult. Jo dropped a kiss on the top of Mr Laurence's bald head, and ran up to slip the apology under Laurie's door, advising him, through the keyhole, to be submissive, decorous, and a few other agreeable impossibilities. Finding the door locked again, she left the note to do its work, and was going quietly away, when the young gentleman slid down the banisters, and waited for her at the bottom, saying, with his most virtuous expression of countenance, "What a good fellow you are, Jo! Did you get blown up?" he added, laughing.

"No; he was pretty clever, on the whole."

"Ah! I got it all round! even you cast me off over there, and I felt just ready to go to the deuce," he began, apologetically.

"Don't talk in that way; turn over a new leaf and begin again, Teddy, my son."

"I keep turning over new leaves, and spoiling them, as I used to spoil my copy-books; and I make so many beginnings there never will be an end," he said, dolefully.

"Go and eat your dinner; you'll feel better after it. Men always croak when they are hungry," and Jo whisked out at the front door after that.

"That's a 'label' on my 'sect,'" answered Laurie, quoting Amy, as he went to partake of humble-pie dutifully with his grandfather, who was quite saintly in temper, and overwhelmingly respectful in manner, all the rest of the day.

Every one thought the matter ended, and the little cloud blown over; but the mischief was done, for, although others forgot it, Meg remembered. She never alluded to a certain person, but she thought of him a good deal, dreamed dreams more than ever; and, once, Jo, rummaging her sister's desk for stamps, found a bit of paper scribbled over with the words, "Mrs. John Brooke;" whereat she groaned tragically, and cast it into the fire, feeling that Laurie's prank had hastened the evil day for her.

CHAPTER TWENTY-TWO

PLEASANT MEADOWS

~

Like sunshine after storm were the peaceful weeks which followed. The invalids improved rapidly, and Mr. March began to talk of returning early in the new year. Beth was soon able to lie on the study sofa all day, amusing herself with the well-beloved cats, at first, and, in time, the doll's sewing, which had fallen sadly behindhand. Her once active limbs were so stiff and feeble that Jo took her a daily airing about the house in her strong arms. Meg cheerfully blackened and burnt her white hands cooking delicate messes for "the dear;" while Amy, a loyal slave of the ring, celebrated her return by giving away as many of her treasures as she could prevail on her sisters to accept.

As Christmas approached, the usual mysteries began to haunt the house, and Jo frequently convulsed the family by proposing utterly impossible or magnificently absurd ceremonies, in honor of this unusually merry Christmas. Laurie was equally impractical, and would have had bonfires, sky-rockets, and triumphal arches, if he had had his own way.

After many skirmishes and snubbings, the ambitious pair were considered effectually quenched, and went about with forlorn faces, which were rather belied by explosions of laughter when the two got together.

Several days of unusually mild weather fitly ushered in a splendid Christmas day. Hannah "felt in her bones that it was going to be an uncommonly plummy day," and she proved herself a true prophetess, for everybody and everything seemed bound to produce a grand success. To begin with: Mr. March wrote that he should soon be with them; then Beth felt uncommonly well that morning, and, being dressed in her mother's gift, — a soft crimson merino wrapper, — was borne in triumph to the window to behold the offering of Jo and Laurie. The Unquenchables had done their best to be worthy of the name, for, like elves, they had worked by night, and conjured up a comical surprise. Out in the garden stood a stately snow-maiden, crowned with holly, bearing a basket of fruit and flowers in one hand, a great roll of new music in the other, a perfect rainbow of an Afghan round her chilly shoulders, and a Christmas carol issuing from her lips, on a pink paper streamer:

THE JUNGFRAU TO BETH

God bless you, dear Queen Bess!
May nothing you dismay,
But health, and peace, and happiness,
Be yours, this Christmas Day.

Here's fruit to feed our busy bee,
And flowers for her nose;
Here's music for her pianee, —
An Afghan for her toes.

A portrait of Joanna, see,
By Raphael No. 2,
Who labored with great industry,
To make it fair and true.

Accept a ribbon red I beg,
For Madam Purrer's tail;
And ice cream made by lovely Peg, —
A Mont Blanc in a pail.

Their dearest love my makers laid
Within my breast of snow,
Accept it, and the Alpine maid,
From Laurie and from Jo.

How Beth laughed when she saw it! how Laurie ran up and down to bring in the gifts, and what ridiculous speeches Jo made as she presented them!

"I'm so full of happiness, that, if father was only here, I couldn't hold one drop more," said Beth, quite sighing with contentment as Jo carried her off to the study to rest after the excitement, and to refresh herself with some of the delicious grapes the "Jungfrau" had sent her.

"So am I," added Jo, slapping the pocket wherein reposed the long-desired "Undine and Sintram".

"I'm sure I am," echoed Amy, poring over the engraved copy of the Madonna and Child, which her mother had given her, in a pretty frame.

"Of course I am," cried Meg, smoothing the silvery folds of her first silk dress; for Mr. Laurence had insisted on giving it.

"How can *I* be otherwise!" said Mrs. March, gratefully, as her eyes went from her husband's letter to Beth's smiling face, and her hand caressed the brooch made of gray and golden, chestnut and dark brown hair, which the girls had just fastened on her breast.

Now and then, in this work-a-day world, things do happen in the delightful story-book fashion, and what a comfort that is. Half an hour after every one had said they were so happy they could only hold one drop more, the drop came. Laurie opened the parlor door, and popped his head in very quietly. He might just as well have turned a somersault, and uttered an Indian war-whoop; for his face was so full of suppressed excitement, and his voice so treacherously joyful, that every one jumped up, though he only said, in a queer, breathless voice, "Here's another Christmas present for the March family."

Before the words were well out of his mouth, he was whisked away somehow, and in his place appeared a tall man, muffled up to the eyes, leaning on the arm of another tall man, who tried to say something and couldn't. Of course there was a general stampede; and for several minutes everybody seemed to lose their wits, for the strangest things were done, and no one said a word. Mr. March became invisible in the embrace of four pairs of loving arms; Jo disgraced herself by nearly fainting away, and had to be doctored by Laurie in the china closet; Mr. Brooke kissed Meg entirely by mistake, as he somewhat incoherently explained; and Amy, the dignified, tumbled over a stool, and, never stopping to get up, hugged and cried over her father's boots in the most touching manner. Mrs. March was the first to recover herself, and held up her hand with a warning, "Hush! remember Beth!"

But it was too late; the study door flew open, – the little red wrapper appeared on the threshold, – joy put strength into the feeble limbs, – and Beth ran straight into her father's arms. Never mind what happened just after that; for the full hearts overflowed, washing away the bitterness of the past, and leaving only the sweetness of the present.

It was not at all romantic, but a hearty laugh set everybody straight again, – for Hannah was discovered behind the door, sobbing over the fat turkey, which she had forgotten to put down when she rushed up from the kitchen. As the laugh subsided, Mrs. March began to thank Mr. Brooke for his faithful care of her husband, at which Mr. Brooke suddenly remembered that Mr. March needed rest, and, seizing Laurie, he precipitately retired. Then the two invalids were ordered to repose, which they did, by both sitting in one big chair, and talking hard.

Mr. March told how he had longed to surprise them, and how, when the fine weather came, he had been allowed by his doctor to take advantage of it; how devoted Brooke had been, and how he was altogether a most estimable and upright young man. Why Mr. March paused a minute just there, and, after a glance at Meg, who was violently poking the fire, looked at his wife with an inquiring lift of the eyebrows, I leave you to imagine; also why Mrs. March gently nodded her head, and asked, rather abruptly, if he wouldn't have something to eat. Jo saw and understood the look; and she stalked grimly away, to get wine and beef tea, muttering to herself, as she slammed the door, "I hate estimable young men with brown eyes!"

There never *was* such a Christmas dinner as they had that day. The fat turkey was a sight to behold, when Hannah sent him up, stuffed, browned, and decorated. So was the plum-pudding, which quite melted in one's mouth; likewise the jellies, in which Amy revelled like a fly in a honey-pot. Everything turned out well; which was a mercy, Hannah said, "For my mind was that flustered, mum, that it's a merrycle I didn't roast the pudding and stuff the turkey with raisins, let alone bilin' of it in a cloth."

Mr. Laurence and his grandson dined with them, also Mr. Brooke — at whom Jo glowered darkly, to Laurie's infinite amusement. Two easy-chairs stood side by side at the head of the table, in which sat Beth and her father, feasting, modestly, on chicken and a little fruit. They drank healths, told stories, sung songs, "reminisced," as the old folk say, and had a thoroughly good time. A sleigh-ride had been planned, but the girls would not leave their father; so the guests departed early, and, as twilight gathered, the happy family sat together round the fire.

"Just a year ago we were groaning over the dismal Christmas we expected to have. Do you remember?" asked Jo, breaking a short pause which had followed a long conversation about many things.

"Rather a pleasant year on the whole!" said Meg, smiling at the fire, and congratulating herself on having treated Mr. Brooke with dignity.

"I think it's been a pretty hard one," observed Amy, watching the light shine on her ring, with thoughtful eyes.

"I'm glad it's over, because we've got you back," whispered Beth, who sat on her father's knee.

"Rather a rough road for you to travel, my little pilgrims, especially the latter part of it. But you have got on bravely; and I think the burdens are in a fair way to tumble off very soon," said Mr. March, looking with fatherly satisfaction at the four young faces gathered round him.

"How do you know? Did Mother tell you?" asked Jo.

"Not much; straws show which way the wind blows; and I've made several discoveries to-day."

"Oh, tell us what they are!" cried Meg, who sat beside him.

"Here is one!" and, taking up the hand which lay on the arm of his chair, he pointed to the roughened forefinger, a burn on the back, and two or three little hard spots on the palm. "I remember a time when this hand was white and smooth, and your first care was to keep it so. It was very pretty then, but to me it is much prettier now, – for in these seeming blemishes I read a little history. A burnt offering has been made of vanity; this hardened palm has earned something better than blisters, and I'm sure the sewing done by these pricked fingers will last a long time, so much good-will went into the stitches. Meg, my dear, I value the womanly skill which keeps home happy more than white hands or fashionable accomplishments; I'm proud to shake this good, industrious little hand, and hope I shall not soon be asked to give it away."

If Meg had wanted a reward for hours of patient labor, she received it in the hearty pressure of her father's hand, and the approving smile he gave her.

"What about Jo? Please say something nice; for she has tried so hard, and been so very, very good to me," said Beth, in her father's ear.

He laughed, and looked across at the tall girl who sat opposite, with an unusually mild expression in her brown face.

"In spite of the curly crop, I don't see the 'son Jo' whom I left a year ago," said Mr. March. "I see a young lady who pins her collar straight, laces her boots neatly, and neither whistles, talks slang, nor lies on the rug, as she used to do. Her face is rather thin and pale, just now, with watching and anxiety; but I like to look at it, for it has grown gentler, and her voice is lower; she doesn't bounce, but moves quietly, and takes care of a certain little person in a motherly way, which delights me. I rather miss my wild girl; but if I get a strong, helpful, tender-hearted woman in her place, I shall feel quite satisfied. I don't know whether the shearing sobered our black sheep, but I do know that in all Washington I couldn't find anything beautiful enough to be bought with the five-and-twenty dollars which my good girl sent me."

Jo's keen eyes were rather dim for a minute, and her thin face grew rosy in the firelight, as she received her father's praise, feeling that she did deserve a portion of it.

'Now, Beth," said Amy, longing for her turn, but ready to wait.

"There's so little of her I'm afraid to say much, for fear she will slip away altogether, though she is not so shy as she used to be," began their father cheerfully; but, recollecting how nearly he *had* lost her, he held her close, saying, tenderly, with her cheek against his own, "I've got you safe, my Beth, and I'll keep you so, please God."

After a minute's silence, he looked down at Amy, who sat on the cricket at his feet, and said, with a caress of the shining hair, —

"I observed that Amy took drumsticks at dinner, ran errands for her mother all the afternoon, gave Meg her place to-night, and has waited on every one with patience and good-humor. I also observe that she does not fret much, nor prink at the glass, and has not even mentioned a very pretty ring which she wears; so I conclude that she has learned to think of other people more, and of herself less, and has decided to try and mould her character as carefully as she moulds her little clay figures. I am glad of this: for though I should be very proud of a graceful statue made by her, I shall be infinitely prouder of a lovable daughter, with a talent for making life beautiful to herself and others."

"What are you thinking of, Beth?" asked Jo, when Amy had thanked her father, and told about her ring.

"I read in 'Pilgrim's Progress' to-day, how, after many troubles, Christian and Hopeful came to a pleasant green meadow, where lilies bloomed all the year round, and there they rested happily, as we do now, before they went on to their journey's end," answered Beth; adding, as she slipped out of her father's arms, and went slowly to the instrument, "It's singing time now, and I want to be in my old place. I'll try to sing the song of the shepherd-boy which the Pilgrims heard. I made the music for father, because he likes the verses."

So, sitting at the dear little piano, Beth softly touched the keys, and, in the sweet voice they had never thought to hear again, sung, to her own accompaniment, the quaint hymn, which was a singularly fitting song for her:

> *He that is down need fear no fall;*
> *He that is low no pride;*
> *He that is humble ever shall*
> *Have God to be his guide.*

I am content with what I have,
Little be it or much;
And, Lord! contentment still I crave,
Because Thou savest such.

Fulness to them a burden is,
That go on Pilgrimage;
Here little, and hereafter bliss,
Is best from age to age!

CHAPTER TWENTY-THREE

AUNT MARCH SETTLES
THE QUESTION

~

Like bees swarming after their queen, mother and daughters hovered about Mr. March the next day, neglecting everything to look at, wait upon, and listen to, the new invalid, who was in a fair way to be killed by kindness. As he sat propped up in a big chair by Beth's sofa, with the other three close by, and Hannah popping in her head now and then, "to peek at the dear man," nothing seemed needed to complete their happiness. But something *was* needed, and the elder ones felt it, though none confessed the fact. Mr. and Mrs. March looked at one another with an anxious expression, as their eyes followed Meg. Jo had sudden fits of sobriety, and was seen to shake her fist at Mr. Brooke's umbrella, which had been left in the hall; Meg was absent-minded, shy and silent, started when the bell rang, and colored when John's name was mentioned; Amy said "every one seemed waiting for something, and couldn't settle down, which was queer, since father was safe at home," and Beth innocently wondered why their neighbors didn't run over as usual.

Laurie went by in the afternoon, and, seeing Meg at the window, seemed suddenly possessed with a melodramatic fit, for he fell down upon one knee in the snow, beat his breast, tore his hair, and clasped his hands imploringly, as if begging some boon; and when Meg told him to behave himself, and go away, he wrung imaginary tears out of his handkerchief, and staggered round the corner as if in utter despair.

"What does the goose mean?" said Meg, laughing, and trying to look unconscious.

"He's showing you how your John will go on by and by. Touching, isn't it?" answered Jo, scornfully.

"Don't say *my John*, it isn't proper or true;" but Meg's voice lingered over the words as if they sounded pleasant to her. "Please don't plague me, Jo; I've told you I don't care *much* about him, and there isn't to be anything said, but we are all to be friendly, and go on as before."

"We can't, for something *has* been said, and Laurie's mischief has spoilt you for me. I see it, and so does mother; you are not like your old self a bit, and seem ever so far away from me. I don't mean to plague you, and will bear it like a man, but I do wish it was all settled. I hate to wait; so if you mean ever to do it, make haste, and have it over quick," said Jo, pettishly.

"*I* can't say or do anything till he speaks, and he won't, because father said I was too young," began Meg, bending over her work with a queer little smile, which suggested that she did not quite agree with her father on that point.

"If he did speak, you wouldn't know what to say, but would cry or blush, or let him have his own way, instead of giving a good, decided, No."

"I'm not so silly and weak as you think. I know just what I should say, for I've planned it all, so I needn't be taken unawares; there's no knowing what may happen, and I wish to be prepared."

Jo couldn't help smiling at the important air which Meg had unconsciously assumed, and which was as becoming as the pretty color varying in her cheeks.

"Would you mind telling me what you'd say?" asked Jo, more respectfully.

"Not at all; you are sixteen now, quite old enough to be my confidant, and my experience will be useful to you by and by, perhaps, in your own affairs of this sort."

"Don't mean to have any; it's fun to watch other people philander, but I should feel like a fool doing it myself," said Jo, looking alarmed at the thought.

"I guess not, if you liked any one very much, and he liked you." Meg spoke as if to herself, and glanced out at the lane, where she had often seen lovers walking together in the summer twilight.

"I thought you were going to tell your speech to that man," said Jo, rudely shortening her sister's little revery.

"Oh, I should merely say, quite calmly and decidedly, 'Thank you, Mr. Brooke, you are very kind, but I agree with father that I am too young to enter into any engagement at present; so please say no more, but let us be friends as we were.'"

"Hum! that's stiff and cool enough. I don't believe you'll ever say it, and I know he won't be satisfied if you do. If he goes on like the rejected lovers in books, you'll give in, rather than hurt his feelings."

"No, I won't! I shall tell him I've made up my mind, and shall walk out of the room with dignity."

Meg rose as she spoke, and was just going to rehearse the dignified exit, when a step in the hall made her fly into her seat, and begin to sew as if her life depended on finishing that particular seam in a given time. Jo smothered a laugh at the sudden change, and, when someone gave a modest tap, opened the door with a grim aspect, which was anything but hospitable.

"Good afternoon. I came to get my umbrella – that is, to see how your father finds himself to-day," said Mr. Brooke, getting a trifle confused as his eye went from one tell-tale face to the other.

"It's very well, he's in the rack, I'll get him, and tell it you are here," and having jumbled her father and the umbrella well together in her reply, Jo slipped out of the room to give Meg a chance to make her speech, and air her dignity. But the instant she vanished, Meg began to sidle towards the door, murmuring, –

"Mother will like to see you, pray sit down, I'll call her."

"Don't go; are you afraid of me, Margaret?" and Mr. Brooke looked so hurt, that Meg thought she must have done something very rude. She blushed up to the little curls on her forehead, for he had never called her Margaret before, and she was surprised to find how natural and sweet it seemed to hear him say it. Anxious to appear friendly and at her ease, she put out her hand with a confiding gesture, and said, gratefully, –

"How can I be afraid when you have been so kind to father? I only wish I could thank you for it."

"Shall I tell you how?" asked Mr. Brooke, holding the small hand fast in both his big ones, and looking down at Meg with so much love in the brown eyes, that her heart began to flutter, and she both longed to run away and to stop and listen.

"Oh no, please don't – I'd rather not," she said, trying to withdraw her hand, and looking frightened in spite of her denial.

"I won't trouble you, I only want to know if you care for me a little, Meg, I love you so much, dear," added Mr. Brooke, tenderly.

This was the moment for the calm, proper speech, but Meg didn't make it, she forgot every word of it, hung her head, and answered, "I don't know," so softly, that John had to stoop down to catch the foolish little reply.

He seemed to think it was worth the trouble, for he smiled to himself as if quite satisfied, pressed the plump hand gratefully, and said, in his most persuasive tone, "Will you try and find out? I want to know *so* much; for I can't go to work with any heart until I learn whether I am to have my reward in the end or not."

"I'm too young," faltered Meg, wondering why she was so fluttered, yet rather enjoying it.

"I'll wait; and, in the mean time, you could be learning to like me. Would it be a very hard lesson, dear?"

"Not if I chose to learn it, but – "

"Please choose to learn, Meg. I love to teach, and this is easier than German," broke in John, getting possession of the other hand, so that she had no way of hiding her face, as he bent to look into it.

His tone was properly beseeching; but, stealing a shy look at him, Meg saw that his eyes were merry as well as tender, and that he wore the satisfied smile of one who had no doubt of his success. This nettled her; Annie Moffat's foolish lessons in coquetry came into her mind, and the love of power, which sleeps in the bosoms of the best of little women, woke up all of a sudden and took possession of her. She felt excited and strange, and, not knowing what else to do, followed a capricious impulse, and, withdrawing her hands, said, petulantly, "I *don't* choose; please go away and let me be!"

Poor Mr. Brooke looked as if his lovely castle in the air was tumbling about his ears, for he had never seen Meg in such a mood before, and it rather bewildered him.

"Do you really mean that?" he asked, anxiously, following her as she walked away.

"Yes, I do; I don't want to be worried about such things. father says I needn't; it's too soon, and I'd rather not."

"Mayn't I hope you'll change your mind by and by? I'll wait, and say nothing till you have had more time. Don't play with me, Meg. I didn't think that of you."

"Don't think of me at all. I'd rather you wouldn't," said Meg, taking a naughty satisfaction in trying her lover's patience and her own power.

He was grave and pale, now, and looked decidedly more like the novel heroes whom she admired; but he neither slapped his forehead nor tramped about the room, as they did; he just stood looking at her so wistfully, so tenderly, that she found her heart relenting in spite of her. What would have happened next I cannot say, if Aunt March had not come hobbling in at this interesting minute.

The old lady couldn't resist her longing to see her nephew; for she had met Laurie as she took her airing, and, hearing of Mr. March's arrival, drove straight out to see him. The family were all busy in the back part of the house, and she had made her way quietly in, hoping to surprise them. She did surprise two of them so much, that Meg started as if she had seen a ghost, and Mr. Brooke vanished into the study.

"Bless me! what's all this?" cried the old lady, with a rap of her cane, as she glanced from the pale young gentleman to the scarlet young lady.

"It's father's friend. I'm *so* surprised to see you!" stammered Meg, feeling that she was in for a lecture now.

"That's evident," returned Aunt March, sitting down. "But what is father's friend saying, to make you look like a peony? There's mischief going on, and I insist upon knowing what it is!" with another rap.

"We were merely talking. Mr. Brooke came for his umbrella," began Meg, wishing that Mr. Brooke and the umbrella were safely out of the house.

"Brooke? That boy's tutor? Ah! I understand now. I know all about it. Jo blundered into a wrong message in one of your pa's letters, and I made her tell me. You haven't gone and accepted him, child?" cried Aunt March, looking scandalized.

"Hush! he'll hear, Shan't I call mother?" said Meg, much troubled.

"Not yet. I've something to say to you, and I must free my mind at once. Tell me, do you mean to marry this Cook? If you do, not one penny of my money ever goes to you. Remember that, and be a sensible girl," said the old lady, impressively.

Now Aunt March possessed, in perfection, the art of rousing the spirit of opposition in the gentlest people, and enjoyed doing it. The best of us have a spice of perversity in us, especially when we are young, and in love. If Aunt March had begged Meg to accept John Brooke, she would probably have declared she couldn't think of it; but as she was peremptorily ordered *not* to like him, she immediately made up her mind that she would. Inclination as well as perversity made the decision easy, and, being already much excited, Meg opposed the old lady with unusual spirit.

"I shall marry whom I please, Aunt March, and you can leave your money to any one you like," she said, nodding her head with a resolute air.

"Highty tighty! Is that the way to take my advice, miss? You'll be sorry for it, by and by, when you've tried love in a cottage, and found it a failure."

"It can't be a worse one than some people find in big houses," retorted Meg.

Aunt March put on her glasses and took a look at the girl, – for she did not know her in this new mood. Meg hardly knew herself, she felt so brave and independent, – so glad to defend John, and assert her right to love him, if she liked. Aunt March saw that she had begun wrong, and, after a little pause, made a fresh start, saying, as mildly as she could, "Now, Meg, my dear, be reasonable, and take my advice. I mean it kindly, and don't want you to spoil your whole life by making a mistake at the beginning. You ought to marry well, and help your family; it's your duty to make a rich match, and it ought to be impressed upon you."

"Father and mother don't think so; they like John, though he *is* poor."

"Your pa and ma, my dear, have no more worldly wisdom than two babies."

"I'm glad of it," cried Meg, stoutly.

Aunt March took no notice, but went on with her lecture. "This Rook is poor, and hasn't got any rich relations, has he?"

"No; but he has many warm friends."

"You can't live on friends; try it, and see how cool they'll grow. He hasn't any business, has he?"

"Not yet; Mr. Laurence is going to help him."

"That won't last long. James Laurence is a crotchety old fellow, and not to be depended upon. So you intend to marry a man without money, position, or business, and go on working harder than you do now, when you might be comfortable all your days by minding me, and doing better? I thought you had more sense, Meg."

"I couldn't do better if I waited half my life! John is good and wise; he's got heaps of talent; he's willing to work, and sure to get on, he's so energetic and brave. Every one likes and respects him, and I'm proud to think he cares for me, though I'm so poor, and young, and silly," said Meg, looking prettier than ever in her earnestness.

"He knows *you* have got rich relations, child; that's the secret of his liking, I suspect."

"Aunt March, how dare you say such a thing? John is above such meanness, and I won't listen to you a minute if you talk so," cried Meg, indignantly, forgetting everything but the injustice of the old lady's suspicions. "My John wouldn't marry for money, any more than I would. We are willing to work, and we mean to wait. I'm not afraid of being poor, for I've been happy so far, and I know I shall be with him, because he loves me, and I – "

Meg stopped there, remembering, all of a sudden, that she hadn't made up her mind; that she had told "her John" to go away, and that he might be overhearing her inconsistent remarks.

Aunt March was very angry, for she had set her heart on having her pretty niece make a fine match, and something in the girl's happy young face made the lonely old woman feel both sad and sour.

"Well, I wash my hands of the whole affair! You are a wilful child, and you've lost more than you know by this piece of folly. No, I won't stop; I'm disappointed in you, and haven't spirits to see your pa now. Don't expect anything from me when you are married; your Mr. Book's friends must take care of you. I've done with you forever."

And, slamming the door in Meg's face, Aunt March drove off in high dudgeon. She seemed to take all the girl's courage with her; for, when left alone, Meg stood a moment undecided whether to laugh or cry. Before she could make up her mind, she was taken possession of by Mr. Brooke, who said, all in one breath, "I couldn't help hearing, Meg. Thank you for defending me, and Aunt March for proving that you *do* care for me a little bit."

"I didn't know how much, till she abused you," began Meg.

"And I needn't go away, but may stay and be happy, – may I, dear?"

Here was another fine chance to make the crushing speech and the stately exit, but Meg never thought of doing either, and disgraced herself for ever in Jo's eyes, by meekly whispering, "Yes, John," and hiding her face on Mr. Brooke's waistcoat.

Fifteen minutes after Aunt March's departure, Jo came softly down stairs, paused an instant at the parlor door, and, hearing no sound within, nodded and smiled, with a satisfied expression, saying to herself, "She has sent him away as we planned, and that affair is settled. I'll go and hear the fun, and have a good laugh over it."

But poor Jo never got her laugh, for she was transfixed upon the threshold by a spectacle which held her there, staring with her mouth nearly as wide open as her eyes. Going to exult over a fallen enemy, and to praise a strong-minded sister for the banishment of an objectionable lover, it certainly *was* a shock to behold the aforesaid enemy serenely sitting on the sofa, with the strong-minded sister enthroned upon his knee, and wearing an expression of the most abject submission. Jo gave a sort of gasp as if a cold shower-bath had suddenly fallen upon her, – for such an unexpected turning of the tables actually took her breath away. At the odd sound, the lovers turned and saw her. Meg jumped up, looking both proud and shy; but "that man," as Jo called him, actually laughed, and said, coolly, as he kissed the astonished new comer, "Sister Jo, congratulate us!"

That was adding insult to injury! it was altogether too much! and, making some wild demonstration with her hands, Jo vanished without a word. Rushing up stairs, she startled the invalids by exclaiming, tragically, as she burst into the room, – "Oh, *do* somebody go down quick! John Brooke is acting dreadfully, and Meg likes it!"

Mr. and Mrs. March left the room with speed; and, casting herself upon the bed, Jo cried and scolded tempestuously as she told the awful news to Beth and Amy. The little girls, however, considered it a most agreeable and interesting event, and Jo got little comfort from them; so she went up to her refuge in the garret, and confided her troubles to the rats.

Nobody ever knew what went on in the parlor that afternoon, but a great deal of talking was done, and quiet Mr. Brooke astonished his friends by the eloquence and spirit with which he pleaded his suit, told his plans, and persuaded them to arrange everything just as he wanted it.

The tea-bell rang before he had finished describing the paradise which he meant to earn for Meg, and he proudly took her in to supper, both looking so happy, that Jo hadn't the heart to be jealous or dismal. Amy was very much impressed by John's devotion and Meg's dignity. Beth beamed at them from a distance, while Mr. and Mrs. March surveyed the young couple with such tender satisfaction, that it was perfectly evident Aunt March was right in calling them as "unworldly as a pair of babies." No one ate much, but every one looked very happy, and the old room seemed to brighten up amazingly when the first romance of the family began there.

"You can't say 'nothing pleasant every happens now,' can you, Meg?" said Amy, trying to decide how she would group the lovers in the sketch she was planning to take.

"No, I'm sure I can't. How much has happened since I said that! It seems a year ago," answered Meg, who was in a blissful dream, lifted far above such common things as bread and butter.

"The joys come close upon the sorrows this time, and I rather think the changes have begun," said Mrs. March. "In most families there comes, now and then, a year full of events; this has been such a one, but it ends well, after all."

"Hope the next will end better," muttered Jo, who found it very hard to see Meg absorbed in a stranger before her face; for Jo loved a few persons very dearly, and dreaded to have their affection lost or lessened in any way.

"I hope the third year from this *will* end better; I mean it shall, if I live to work out my plans," said Mr. Brooke, smiling at Meg, as if everything had become possible to him now.

"Doesn't it seem very long to wait?" asked Amy, who was in a hurry for the wedding.

"I've got so much to learn before I shall be ready, it seems a short time to me," answered Meg, with a sweet gravity in her face, never seen there before.

"You have only to wait. I have to do the work," said John, beginning his labors by picking up Meg's napkin, with an expression which caused Jo to shake her head, and then say to herself, with an air of relief, as the front door banged, "Here comes Laurie; now we shall have a little sensible conversation."

But Jo was mistaken; for Laurie came prancing in, overflowing with spirits, bearing a great bridal-looking bouquet for "Mrs. John Brooke," and evidently laboring under the delusion that the whole affair had been brought about by his excellent management.

"I knew Brooke would have it all his own way, – he always does; for when he makes up his mind to accomplish anything, it's done, though the sky falls," said Laurie, when he had presented his offering and his congratulations.

"Much obliged for that recommendation. I take it as a good omen for the future, and invite you to my wedding on the spot," answered Mr. Brooke, who felt at peace with all mankind, even his mischievous pupil.

"I'll come if I'm at the ends of the earth; for the sight of Jo's face alone, on that occasion, would be worth a long journey. You don't look festive, ma'am; what's the matter?" asked Laurie, following her into a corner of the parlor, whither all had adjourned to greet Mr. Laurence.

"I don't approve of the match, but I've made up my mind to bear it, and shall not say a word against it," said Jo, solemnly. "You can't know how hard it is for me to give up Meg," she continued, with a little quiver in her voice.

"You don't give her up. You only go halves," said Laurie, consolingly.

"It never can be the same again. I've lost my dearest friend," sighed Jo.

"You've got me, anyhow. I'm not good for much, I know; but I'll stand by you, Jo, all the days of my life; upon my word I will!" and Laurie meant what he said.

"I know you will, and I'm ever so much obliged; you are always a great comfort to me, Teddy," returned Jo, gratefully shaking hands.

"Well, now, don't be dismal, there's a good fellow. It's all right, you see. Meg is happy; Brooke will fly round and get settled immediately; grandpa will attend to him, and it will be very jolly to see Meg in her own little house. We'll have capital times after she is gone, for I shall be through college before long, and then we'll go abroad, or some nice trip or other. Wouldn't that console you?"

"I rather think it would; but there's no knowing what may happen in three years," said Jo, thoughtfully.

"That's true! Don't you wish you could take a look forward, and see where we shall all be then? I do," returned Laurie.

"I think not, for I might see something sad; and every one looks so happy now, I don't believe they could be much improved;" and Jo's eyes went slowly round the room, brightening as they looked, for the prospect was a pleasant one.

Father and mother sat together quietly re-living the first chapter of the romance which for them began some twenty years ago. Amy was drawing the lovers, who sat apart in a beautiful world of their own, the light of which touched their faces with a grace the little artist could not copy. Beth lay on her sofa talking cheerily with her old friend, who held her little hand as if he felt that it possessed the power to lead him along the peaceful ways she walked. Jo lounged in her favorite low seat, with the grave, quiet look which best became her; and Laurie, leaning on the back of her chair, his chin on a level with her curly head, smiled with his friendliest aspect, and nodded at her in the long glass which reflected them both.

So grouped, the curtain falls upon Meg, Jo, Beth, and Amy.

Aunt March came hobbling in at this interesting minute. (Chapter 23)

Beth lay on the warm rocks with her head in
Jo's lap. (Chapter 36)

CHAPTER TWENTY-FOUR

GOSSIP

~

*I*n order that we may start afresh and go to Meg's wedding with free minds, it will be well to begin with a little gossip about the Marches. And here let me premise, that if any of the elders think there is too much "lovering" in the story, as I fear they may (I'm not afraid the young folks will make that objection), I can only say with Mrs. March, "What *can* you expect when I have four gay girls in the house, and a dashing neighbor over the way?"

The three years that have passed have brought but few changes to the quiet family. The war is over, and Mr. March safely at home, busy with his books and the small parish which found in him a minister by nature as by grace. A quiet, studious man, rich in the wisdom that is better than learning, the charity which calls all mankind "brother," the piety that blossoms into character, making it august and lovely.

These attributes, in spite of poverty and the strict integrity which shut him out from the more worldly successes, attracted to him many admirable persons, as naturally as sweet herbs draw bees, and as naturally he gave them the honey into which fifty years of hard experience had distilled no bitter drop. Earnest young men found the gray-headed scholar as earnest and as young at heart as they; thoughtful or troubled women instinctively brought their doubts and sorrows to him, sure of finding the gentlest sympathy, the wisest counsel; sinners told their sins to the pure-hearted old man, and were both rebuked and saved; gifted men found a companion in him; ambitious men caught glimpses of nobler ambitions than their own; and even worldlings confessed that his beliefs were beautiful and true, although "they wouldn't pay."

To outsiders, the five energetic women seemed to rule the house, and so they did in many things; but the quiet man sitting among his books was still the head of the family, the household conscience, anchor, and comforter; for to him the busy, anxious women always turned in troublous times, finding him, in the truest sense of those sacred words, husband and father.

The girls gave their hearts into their mother's keeping — their souls into their father's; and to both parents who lived and labored so faithfully for them, they gave a love that grew with their growth, and bound them tenderly together by the sweetest tie which blesses life and outlives death.

Mrs. March is as brisk and cheery, though rather grayer than when we saw her last, and just now so absorbed in Meg's affairs, that the hospitals and homes, still full of wounded "boys" and soldiers' widows, decidedly miss the motherly missionary's visits.

John Brooke did his duty manfully for a year, got wounded, was sent home, and not allowed to return. He received no stars or bars, but he deserved them, for he cheerfully risked all he had; and life and love are very precious when both are in full bloom. Perfectly resigned to his discharge, he devoted himself to getting well, preparing for business, and earning a home for Meg. With the good sense and sturdy independence that characterized him, he refused Mr. Laurence's more generous offers, and accepted the place of under bookkeeper, feeling better satisfied to begin with an honestly earned salary, than by running any risks with borrowed money.

Meg had spent the time in working as well as waiting, growing womanly in character, wise in housewifery arts, and prettier than ever; for love is a great beautifier. She had her girlish ambitions and hopes, and felt some disappointment at the humble way in which the new life must begin. Ned Moffat had just married Sallie Gardiner, and Meg couldn't help contrasting their fine house and carriage, many gifts, and splendid outfit, with her own, and secretly wishing she could have had the same. But somehow envy and discontent soon vanished when she thought of all the patient love and labor John had put into the little home awaiting her; and when they sat together in the twilight, talking over their small plans, the future always grew so beautiful and bright, that she forgot Sallie's splendor, and felt herself the richest, happiest girl in Christendom.

Jo never went back to Aunt March, for the old lady took such a fancy to Amy, that she bribed her with the offer of drawing lessons from one of the best teachers going; and for the sake of this advantage, Amy would have served a far harder mistress. So she gave her mornings to duty, her afternoons to pleasure, and prospered finely. Jo, meantime, devoted herself to literature and Beth, who remained delicate long after the fever was a thing of the past. Not an invalid exactly, but never again the rosy, healthy creature she had been; yet always hopeful, happy and serene, busy with the quiet duties she loved, every one's friend, and an angel in the house, long before those who loved her most had learned to know it.

As long as "The Spread Eagle" paid her a dollar a column for her "rubbish," as she called it, Jo felt herself a woman of means, and spun her little romances diligently. But great plans fermented in her busy brain and ambitious mind, and the old tin kitchen in the garret held a slowly increasing pile of blotted manuscript, which was one day to place the name of March upon the roll of fame.

Laurie, having dutifully gone to college to please his grandfather, was now getting through it in the easiest possible manner to please himself. A universal favorite, thanks to money, manners, much talent, and the kindest heart that ever got its owner into scrapes by trying to get other people out of them, he stood in great danger of being spoilt, and probably would have been, like many another promising boy, if he had not possessed a talisman against evil in the memory of the kind old man who was bound up in his success, the motherly friend who watched over him as if he were her son, and last, but not least by any means, the knowledge that four innocent girls loved, admired, and believed in him with all their hearts.

Being only "a glorious human boy," of course he frolicked and flirted, grew dandified, aquatic, sentimental or gymnastic, as college fashions ordained; hazed and was hazed, talked slang, and more than once came perilously near suspension and expulsion. But as high spirits and love of fun were the causes of these pranks, he always managed to save himself by frank confession, honorable atonement, or the irresistible power of persuasion which he possessed in perfection. In fact, he rather prided himself on his narrow escapes, and liked to thrill the girls with graphic accounts of his triumphs over wrathful tutors, dignified professors, and vanquished enemies. The "men of my class" were heroes in the eyes of the girls, who never wearied of the exploits of "our fellows," and were frequently allowed to bask in the smiles of these great creatures, when Laurie brought them home with him.

Amy especially enjoyed this high honor, and became quite a belle among them; for her ladyship early felt and learned to use the gift of fascination with which she was endowed. Meg was too much absorbed in her private and particular John to care for any other lords of creation, and Beth too shy to do more than peep at them, and wonder how Amy dared to order them about so; but Jo felt quite in her element, and found it very difficult to refrain from imitating the gentlemanly attitudes, phrases, and feats which seemed more natural to her than the decorums prescribed for young ladies. They all liked Jo immensely, but never fell in love with her, though very few escaped without paying the tribute of a sentimental sigh or two at Amy's shrine. And speaking of sentiment brings us very naturally to the "Dovecote."

That was the name of the little brown house which Mr. Brooke had prepared for Meg's first home. Laurie had christened it, saying it was highly appropriate to the gentle lovers, who "went on together like a pair of turtle-doves, with first a bill and then a coo." It was a tiny house, with a little garden behind, and a lawn about as big as a pocket-handkerchief in front. Here Meg meant to have a fountain, shrubbery, and a profusion of lovely flowers; though just at present the fountain was represented by a weather-beaten urn, very like a dilapidated slop-bowl; the shrubbery consisted of several young larches, who looked undecided whether to live or die, and the profusion of flowers was merely hinted by regiments of sticks, to show where seeds were planted. But inside, it was altogether charming, and the happy bride saw no fault from garret to cellar. To be sure, the hall was so narrow, it was fortunate that they had no piano, for one never could have been got in whole. The dining-room was so small, that six people were a tight fit, and the kitchen stairs seemed built for the express purpose of precipitating both servants and china pell-mell into the coal-bin. But once get used to these slight blemishes, and nothing could be more complete, for good sense and good taste had presided over the furnishing, and the result was highly satisfactory. There were no marble-topped tables, long mirrors, or lace curtains in the little parlor, but simple furniture, plenty of books, a fine picture or two, a stand of flowers in the bay-window, and, scattered all about, the pretty gifts which came from friendly hands, and were the fairer for the loving messages they brought.

I don't think the Parian Psyche Laurie gave, lost any of its beauty because Brooke put up the bracket it stood upon; that any upholsterer could have draped the plain muslin curtains more gracefully than Amy's artistic hand; or that any store-room was ever better provided with good wishes, merry words, and happy hopes, than that in which Jo and her mother put away Meg's few boxes, barrels, and bundles; and I am morally certain that the spandy-new kitchen never *could* have looked so cosy and neat, if Hannah had not arranged every pot and pan a dozen times over, and laid the fire all ready for lighting, the minute "Mis. Brooke came home." I also doubt if any young matron ever began life with so rich a supply of dusters, holders, and piece-bags, – for Beth made enough to last till the silver wedding came round, and invented three different kinds of dishcloths for the express service of the bridal china.

People who hire all these things done for them, never know what they lose; for the homeliest tasks get beautified if loving hands do them, and Meg found so many proofs of this, that everything in her small nest, from the kitchen roller to the silver vase on her parlor table, was eloquent of home love and tender forethought.

What happy times they had planning together; what solemn shopping excursions, what funny mistakes they made, and what shouts of laughter arose over Laurie's ridiculous bargains! In his love of jokes, this young gentleman, though nearly through college, was as much of a boy as ever. His last whim had been to bring with him, on his weekly visits, some new, useful, and ingenious article for the young housekeeper. Now a bag of remarkable clothes-pins; next a wonderful nutmeg grater, which fell to pieces at the first trial, a knife-cleaner that spoilt all the knives; or a sweeper that picked the nap neatly off the carpet, and left the dirt; labor-saving soap that took the skin off one's hands; infallible cements which stuck firmly to nothing but the fingers of the deluded buyer; and every kind of tinware, from a toy savings-bank for odd pennies, to a wonderful boiler which would wash articles in its own steam, with every prospect of exploding in the process.

In vain Meg begged him to stop. John laughed at him, and Jo called him "Mr. Toodles." He was possessed with a mania for patronizing Yankee ingenuity, and seeing his friends fitly furnished forth. So each week beheld some fresh absurdity.

Everything was done at last, even to Amy's arranging different colored soaps to match the different colored rooms, and Beth's setting the table for the first meal.

"Are you satisfied? Does it seem like home, and do you feel as if you should be happy here?" asked Mrs. March, as she and her daughter went through the new kingdom, arm-in-arm — for just then they seemed to cling together more tenderly than ever.

"Yes, mother, perfectly satisfied, thanks to you all, and *so* happy that I can't talk about it," answered Meg, with a look that was better than words.

"If she only had a servant or two it would be all right," said Amy, coming out of the parlor, where she had been trying to decide whether the bronze Mercury looked best on the whatnot or the mantel-piece.

"Mother and I have talked that over, and I have made up my mind to try her way first. There will be so little to do, that, with Lotty to run my errands and help me here and there, I shall only have enough work to keep me from getting lazy or homesick," answered Meg, tranquilly.

"Sallie Moffat has four," began Amy.

"If Meg had four the house wouldn't hold them, and master and missis would have to camp in the garden," broke in Jo, who, enveloped in a big blue pinafore, was giving a last polish to the door-handles.

"Sallie isn't a poor man's wife, and many maids are in keeping with her fine establishment. Meg and John begin humble, but I have a feeling that there will be quite as much happiness in the little house as in the big one. It's a great mistake for young girls like Meg to leave themselves nothing to do but dress, give orders, and gossip. When I was first married I used to long for my new clothes to wear out, or get torn, so that I might have the pleasure of mending them; for I got heartily sick of doing fancy work and tending my pocket handkerchief."

"Why didn't you go into the kitchen and make messes, as Sallie says she does, to amuse herself, though they never turn out well, and the servants laugh at her," said Meg.

"I did, after a while; not to 'mess,' but to learn of Hannah how things should be done, that my servants need *not* laugh at me. It was play then; but there came a time when I was truly grateful that I not only possessed the will, but the power to cook wholesome food for my little girls, and help myself when I could no longer afford to hire help. You begin at the other end, Meg dear, but the lessons you learn now will be of use to you by and by, when John is a richer man, for the mistress of a house, however splendid, should know how work *ought* to be done, if she wishes to be well and honestly served."

"Yes, mother, I'm sure of that," said Meg, listening respectfully to the little lecture; for the best of women will hold forth upon the all-absorbing subject of housekeeping. "Do you know I like this room best of all in my baby-house," added Meg, a minute after, as they went upstairs, and she looked into her well-stored linen closet.

Beth was there, laying the snowy piles smoothly on the shelves, and exulting over the goodly array. All-three laughed as Meg spoke; for that linen closet was a joke. You see, having said that if Meg married "that Brooke" she shouldn't have a cent of her money, Aunt March was rather in a quandary, when time had appeased her wrath, and made her repent her vow. She never broke her word, and was much exercised in her mind how to get round it, and at last devised a plan whereby she could satisfy herself. Mrs. Carrol, Florence's mamma, was ordered to buy, have made and marked a generous supply of house and table linen, and sent it as *her* present. All of which was faithfully done, but the secret leaked out, and was greatly enjoyed by the family; for Aunt March tried to look utterly unconscious, and insisted that she could give nothing but the old-fashioned pearls, long promised to the first bride.

"That's a housewifely taste, which I am glad to see. I had a young friend who set up housekeeping with six sheets, but she had finger bowls for company, and that satisfied her," said Mrs. March, patting the damask table-cloths with a truly feminine appreciation of their fineness.

"I haven't a single finger bowl, but this is a 'set out' that will last me all my days, Hannah says;" and Meg looked quite contented, as well she might.

"Toodles is coming," cried Jo from below, and they all went down to meet Laurie, whose weekly visit was an important event in their quiet lives.

A tall, broad-shouldered young fellow, with a cropped head, a felt-basin of a hat, and a fly-away coat, came tramping down the road at a great pace, walked over the low fence, without stopping to open the gate, straight up to Mrs. March, with both hands out, and a hearty —

"Here I am, mother! Yes, it's all right."

The last words were in answer to the look the elder lady gave him; a kindly, questioning look, which the handsome eyes met so frankly that the little ceremony closed as usual, with a motherly kiss.

"For Mrs. John Brooke, with the maker's congratulations and compliments. Bless you, Beth! What a refreshing spectacle you are, Jo! Amy, you are getting altogether too handsome for a single lady."

As Laurie spoke, he delivered a brown paper parcel to Meg, pulled Beth's hair ribbon, stared at Jo's big pinafore, and fell into an attitude of mock rapture before Amy, then shook hands all round, and every one began to talk.

"Where is John?" asked Meg, anxiously.

"Stopped to get the license for to-morrow, ma'am."

"Which side won the last match, Teddy?" inquired Jo, who persisted in feeling an interest in manly sports, despite her nineteen years.

"Ours, of course. Wish you'd been there to see."

"How is the lovely Miss Randal?" asked Amy, with a significant smile.

"More cruel than ever; don't you see how I'm pining away?" and Laurie gave his broad chest a sounding slap, and heaved a melodramatic sigh.

"What's the last joke? Undo the bundle and see, Meg," said Beth, eyeing the knobby parcel with curiosity.

"It's a useful thing to have in the house in case of fire or thieves," observed Laurie, as a small watchman's rattle appeared amid the laughter of the girls.

"Any time when John is away, and you get frightened, Mrs. Meg, just swing that out of the front window, and it will rouse the neighborhood in a jiffy. Nice thing, isn't it?" and Laurie gave them a sample of its powers that made them cover up their ears.

"There's gratitude for you! and, speaking of gratitude, reminds me to mention that you may thank Hannah for saving your wedding-cake from destruction. I saw it going into your house as I came by, and if she hadn't defended it manfully I'd have had a pick at it, for it looked like a remarkably plummy one."

"I wonder if you will ever grow up, Laurie," said Meg, in a matronly tone.

"I'm doing my best, ma'am, but can't get much higher, I'm afraid, as six feet is about all men can do in these degenerate days," responded the young gentleman, whose head was about level with the little chandelier. "I suppose it would be profanation to eat anything in this bran-new bower, so, as I'm tremendously hungry, I propose an adjournment," he added, presently.

"Mother and I are going to wait for John. There are some last things to settle," said Meg, bustling away.

"Beth and I are going over to Kitty Bryant's to get more flowers for to-morrow," added Amy, tying a picturesque hat over her picturesque curls, and enjoying the effect as much as anybody.

"Come, Jo, don't desert a fellow. I'm in such a state of exhaustion I can't get home without help. Don't take off your apron, whatever you do; it's peculiarly becoming," said Laurie, as Jo bestowed his especial aversion in her capacious pocket, and offered him her arm to support his feeble steps.

"Now, Teddy, I want to talk seriously to you about to-morrow," began Jo, as they strolled away together. "You *must* promise to behave well, and not cut up any pranks, and spoil our plans."

"Not a prank."

"And don't say funny things when we ought to be sober."

"I never do; you are the one for that."

"And I implore you not to look at me during the ceremony; I shall certainly laugh if you do."

"You won't see me; you'll be crying so hard that the thick fog round you will obscure the prospect."

"I never cry unless for some great affliction."

"Such as old fellows going to college, hey?" cut in Laurie, with a suggestive laugh.

"Don't be a peacock. I only moaned a trifle to keep the girls company."

"Exactly. I say, Jo, how is grandpa this week; pretty amiable?"

"Very; why, have you got into a scrape, and want to know how he'll take it?" asked Jo, rather sharply.

"Now, Jo, do you think I'd look your mother in the face, and say 'All right,' if it wasn't?" – and Laurie stopped short, with an injured air.

"No, I don't."

"Then don't go and be suspicious; I only want some money," said Laurie, walking on again, appeased by her hearty tone.

"You spend a great deal, Teddy."

"Bless you, I don't spend it; it spends itself, somehow, and is gone before I know it."

"You are so generous and kind-hearted, that you let people borrow, and can't say 'No' to any one. We heard about Henshaw, and all you did for him. If you always spent money in that way, no one would blame you," said Jo, warmly.

"Oh, he made a mountain out of a mole-hill. You wouldn't have me let that fine fellow work himself to death, just for the want of a little help, when he is worth a dozen of us lazy chaps, would you?"

"Of course not; but I don't see the use of your having seventeen waistcoats, endless neckties, and a new hat every time you come home. I thought you'd got over the dandy period; but every now and then it breaks out in a new spot. Just now it's the fashion to be hideous; to make your head look like a scrubbing brush, wear a strait-jacket, orange gloves, and clumping, square-toed boots. If it was cheap ugliness, I'd say nothing; but it costs as much as the other, and I don't get any satisfaction out of it."

Laurie threw back his head, and laughed so heartily at this attack, that the felt-basin fell off, and Jo trampled on it, which insult only afforded him an opportunity for expatiating on the advantages of a rough-and-ready costume, as he folded up the maltreated hat, and stuffed it into his pocket.

"Don't lecture any more, there's a good soul; I have enough all through the week, and like to enjoy myself when I come home. I'll get myself up regardless of expense, to-morrow, and be a satisfaction to my friends."

"I'll leave you in peace if you'll *only* let your hair grow. I'm not aristocratic, but I do object to being seen with a person who looks like a young prize-fighter," observed Jo, severely.

"This unassuming style promotes study; that's why we adopt it," returned Laurie, who certainly could not be accused of vanity, having voluntarily sacrificed a handsome, curly crop, to the demand for quarter of an inch long stubble.

"By the way, Jo, I think that little Parker is really getting desperate about Amy. He talks of her constantly, writes poetry, and moons about in a most suspicious manner. He'd better nip his little passion in the bud, hadn't he?" added Laurie, in a confidential, elder-brother tone, after a minute's silence.

"Of course he had; we don't want any more marrying in this family for years to come. Mercy on us, what *are* the children thinking of!" and Jo looked as much scandalized as if Amy and little Parker were not yet in their teens.

"It's a fast age, and I don't know what we are coming to, ma'am. You are a mere infant, but you'll go next, Jo, and we'll be left lamenting," said Laurie, shaking his head over the degeneracy of the times.

"Me! don't be alarmed; I'm not one of the agreeable sort. Nobody will want me, and it's a mercy, for there should always be one old maid in a family."

"You won't give any one a chance," said Laurie, with a sidelong glance, and a little more color than before in his sunburnt face. "You won't show the soft side of your character; and if a fellow gets a look at it by accident, and can't help showing that he likes it, you treat him as Mrs. Gummidge did her sweetheart; throw cold water over him, and get so thorny no one dares touch or look at you."

"I don't like that sort of thing; I'm too busy to be worried with nonsense, and I think it's dreadful to break up families so. Now don't say anything more about it; Meg's wedding has turned all our heads, and we talk of nothing but lovers and such absurdities. I don't wish to get raspy, so let's change the subject;" and Jo looked quite ready to fling cold water on the slightest provocation.

Whatever his feelings might have been, Laurie found a vent for them in a long low whistle, and the fearful prediction, as they parted at the gate, —

"Mark my words, Jo, you'll go next."

CHAPTER TWENTY-FIVE

THE FIRST WEDDING

~

The June roses over the porch were awake bright and early on that morning, rejoicing with all their hearts in the cloudless sunshine, like friendly little neighbors, as they were. Quite flushed with excitement were their ruddy faces, as they swung in the wind, whispering to one another what they had seen; for some peeped in at the dining-room windows, where the feast was spread, some climbed up to nod and smile at the sisters, as they dressed the bride, others waved a welcome to those who came and went on various errands in garden, porch and hall, and all, from the rosiest full-blown flower to the palest baby-bud, offered their tribute of beauty and fragrance to the gentle mistress who had loved and tended them so long.

Meg looked very like a rose herself; for all that was best and sweetest in heart and soul, seemed to bloom into her face that day, making it fair and tender, with a charm more beautiful than beauty. Neither silk, lace, nor orange flowers would she have. "I don't want to look strange or fixed up, to-day," she said; "I don't want a fashionable wedding, but only those about me whom I love, and to them I wish to look and be my familiar self."

So she made her wedding gown herself, sewing into it the tender hopes and innocent romances of a girlish heart. Her sisters braided up her pretty hair, and the only ornaments she wore were the lilies of the valley, which "her John" liked best of all the flowers that grew.

"You *do* look just like our own dear Meg, only so very sweet and lovely, that I should hug you if it wouldn't crumple your dress," cried Amy, surveying her with delight, when all was done.

"Then I am satisfied. But please hug and kiss me, every one, and don't mind my dress; I want a great many crumples of this sort put into it to-day;" and Meg opened her arms to her sisters, who clung about her with April faces, for a minute, feeling that the new love had not changed the old.

"Now I'm going to tie John's cravat for him, and then to stay a few minutes with father, quietly in the study;" and Meg ran down to perform these little ceremonies, and then to follow her mother wherever she went, conscious that in spite of the smiles on the motherly face, there was a secret sorrow hidden in the motherly heart, at the flight of the first bird from the nest.

As the younger girls stand together, giving the last touches to their simple toilet, it may be a good time to tell of a few changes which three years have wrought in their appearance; for all are looking their best, just now.

Jo's angles are much softened; she has learned to carry herself with ease, if not grace. The curly crop has been lengthened into a thick coil, more becoming to the small head atop of the tall figure. There is a fresh color in her brown cheeks, a soft shine in her eyes; only gentle words fall from her sharp tongue to-day.

Beth has grown slender, pale, and more quiet than ever; the beautiful, kind eyes, are larger, and in them lies an expression that saddens one, although it is not sad itself. It is the shadow of pain which touches the young face with such pathetic patience; but Beth seldom complains, and always speaks hopefully of "being better soon."

Amy is with truth considered "the flower of the family"; for at sixteen she has the air and bearing of a full-grown woman — not beautiful, but possessed of that indescribable charm called grace. One saw in the lines of her figure, the make and motion of her hands, the flow of her dress, the droop of her hair – unconscious, yet harmonious, and as attractive to many as beauty itself. Amy's nose still afflicted her, for it never *would* grow Grecian; so did her mouth, being too wide, and having a decided underlip. These offending features gave character to her whole face, but she never could see it, and consoled herself with her wonderfully fair complexion, keen blue eyes, and curls, more golden and abundant than ever.

All three wore suits of thin, silvery gray (their best gowns for the summer), with blush roses in hair and bosom; and all three looked just what they were – fresh-faced, happy-hearted girls, pausing a moment in their busy lives to read with wistful eyes the sweetest chapter in the romance of womanhood.

There were to be no ceremonious performances; everything was to be as natural and homelike as possible; so when Aunt March arrived, she was scandalized to see the bride come running to welcome and lead her in, to find the bridegroom fastening up a garland that had fallen down, and to catch a glimpse of the paternal minister up stairs with a grave countenance, and a wine bottle under each arm.

"Upon my word, here's a state of things!" cried the old lady, taking the seat of honor prepared for her, and settling the folds of her lavender *moire* with a great rustle. "You oughtn't to be seen till the last minute, child."

"I'm not a show, aunty, and no one is coming to stare at me, to criticise my dress, or count the cost of my luncheon. I'm too happy to care what any one says or thinks, and I'm going to have my little wedding just as I like it. John, dear, here's your hammer," and away went Meg to help "that man" in his highly improper employment.

Mr. Brooke didn't even say "Thank you," but as he stooped for the unromantic tool, he kissed his little bride behind the folding door, with a look that made Aunt March whisk out her pocket handkerchief, with a sudden dew in her sharp old eyes.

A crash, a cry, and a laugh from Laurie, accompanied by the indecorous exclamation, "Jupiter Ammon! Jo's upset the cake again!" caused a momentary flurry, which was hardly over, when a flock of cousins arrived, and "the party came in," as Beth used to say when a child.

"Don't let that young giant come near me; he worries me worse than mosquitoes," whispered the old lady to Amy, as the rooms filled, and Laurie's black head towered above the rest.

"He has promised to be very good to-day, and he *can* be perfectly elegant if he likes," returned Amy, gliding away to warn Hercules to beware of the dragon, which warning caused him to haunt the old lady with a devotion that nearly distracted her.

There was no bridal procession, but a sudden silence fell upon the room as Mr. March and the young pair took their places under the green arch. Mother and sisters gathered close, as if loath to give Meg up; the fatherly voice broke more than once, which only seemed to make the service more beautiful and solemn: the bridegroom's hand trembled visibly, and no one heard his replies; but Meg looked straight up in her husband's eyes, and said, "I will!" with such tender trust in her own face and voice, that her mother's heart rejoiced, and Aunt March sniffed audibly.

Jo did *not* cry, though she was very near it once, and was only saved from a demonstration by the consciousness that Laurie was staring fixedly at her, with a comical mixture of merriment and emotion in his wicked black eyes. Beth kept her face hidden on her mother's shoulder, but Amy stood like a graceful statue, with a most becoming ray of sunshine touching her white forehead and the flower in her hair.

It wasn't at all the thing, I'm afraid, but the minute she was fairly married, Meg cried, "The first kiss for Marmee!" and, turning, gave it with her heart on her lips. During the next fifteen minutes she looked more like a rose than ever, for every one availed themselves of their privileges to the fullest extent, from Mr. Laurence to old Hannah, who, adorned with a head-dress fearfully and wonderfully made, fell upon her in the hall, crying, with a sob and a chuckle, "Bless you, deary, a hundred times! The cake ain't hurt a mite, and everything looks lovely."

Everybody cleared up after that, and said something brilliant, or tried to, which did just as well, for laughter is ready when hearts are light. There was no display of gifts, for they were already in the little house, nor was there an elaborate breakfast, but a plentiful lunch of cake and fruit, dressed with flowers. Mr. Laurence and Aunt March shrugged and smiled at one another when water, lemonade, and coffee were found to be the only sorts of nectar which the three Hebes carried round. No one said anything, however, till Laurie, who insisted on serving the bride, appeared before her with a loaded salver in his hand, and a puzzled expression on his face.

"Has Jo smashed all the bottles by accident?" he whispered, "or am I merely laboring under a delusion that I saw some lying about loose this morning?"

"No; your grandfather kindly offered us his best, and Aunt March actually sent some, but father put away a little for Beth, and despatched the rest to the Soldiers' Home. You know he thinks that wine should only be used in illness, and mother says that neither she nor her daughters will ever offer it to any young man under her roof."

Meg spoke seriously, and expected to see Laurie frown or laugh; but he did neither, – for after a quick look at her, he said, in his impetuous way, "I like that; for I've seen enough harm done to wish other women would think as you do!"

"You are not made wise by experience, I hope?" and there was an anxious accent in Meg's voice.

"No; I give you my word for it. Don't think too well of me, either; this is not one of my temptations. Being brought up where wine is as common as water, and almost as harmless, I don't care for it; but when a pretty girl offers it, one don't like to refuse, you see."

"But you will, for the sake of others, if not for you own. Come, Laurie, promise, and give me one more reason to call this the happiest day of my life."

A demand so sudden and so serious, made the young man hesitate a moment, for ridicule is often harder to bear than self-denial. Meg knew that if he gave the promise he would keep it at all costs; and, feeling her power, used it as a woman may for her friend's good. She did not speak, but she looked up at him with a face made very eloquent by happiness, and a smile which said, "No one can refuse me anything to-day." Laurie, certainly, could not; and, with an answering smile, he gave her his hand, saying, heartily, "I promise, Mrs. Brooke!"

"I thank you, very, very much."

"And I drink 'Long life to your resolution,' Teddy," cried Jo, baptizing him with a splash of lemonade, as she waved her glass, and beamed approvingly upon him.

So the toast was drunk, the pledge made, and loyally kept, in spite of many temptations; for, with instinctive wisdom, the girls had seized a happy moment to do their friend a service, for which he thanked them all his life.

After lunch, people strolled about, by twos and threes, through house and garden, enjoying the sunshine without and within. Meg and John happened to be standing together in the middle of the grass-plot, when Laurie was seized by an inspiration which put the finishing touch to this unfashionable wedding.

"All the married people take hands and dance round the new-made husband and wife, as the Germans do, while we bachelors and spinsters prance in couples outside!" cried Laurie, galloping down the path with Amy, with such infectious spirit and skill that every one else followed their example without a murmur. Mr. and Mrs. March, Aunt and Uncle Carrol, began it; others rapidly joined in; even Sallie Moffat, after a moment's hesitation, threw her train over her arm, and whisked Ned into the ring. But the crowning joke was Mr. Laurence and Aunt March; for when the stately old gentleman *chasséed* solemnly up to the old lady, she just tucked her cane under her arm, and hopped briskly away to join hands with the rest, and dance about the bridal pair, while the young folks pervaded the garden, like butterflies on a mid-summer day.

Want of breath brought the impromptu ball to a close, and then people began to go.

"I wish you well, my dear; I heartily wish you well; but I think you'll be sorry for it," said Aunt March to Meg, adding to the bridegroom, as he led her to the carriage, "You've got a treasure, young man, – see that you deserve it."

"That is the prettiest wedding I've been to for an age, Ned, and I don't see why, for there wasn't a bit of style about it," observed Mrs. Moffat to her husband, as they drove away.

"Laurie, my lad, if you ever want to indulge in this sort of thing, get one of these girls to help you, and I shall be perfectly satisfied," said Mr. Laurence, settling himself in his easy-chair to rest, after the excitement of the morning.

"I'll do my best to gratify you, sir," was Laurie's unusually dutiful reply, as he carefully unpinned the posy Jo had put in his buttonhole.

The little house was not far away, and the only bridal journey Meg had was the quiet walk with John, from the old home to the new. When she came down, looking like a pretty Quakeress, in her dove-colored suit and straw bonnet tied with white, they all gathered about her to say "good-by," as tenderly as if she had been going to make the grand tour.

"Don't feel that I am separated from you, Marmee dear, or that I love you any the less for loving John so much," she said, clinging to her mother, with full eyes, for a moment. "I shall come every day, father, and expect to keep my old place in all your hearts, though I *am* married. Beth is going to be with me a great deal, and the other girls will drop in now and then to laugh at my housekeeping struggles. Thank you all for my happy wedding day. Good-by, good-by!"

They stood watching her with faces full of love, and hope, and tender pride, as she walked away, leaning on her husband's arm, with her hands full of flowers, and the June sunshine brightening her happy face, — and so Meg's married life began.

CHAPTER TWENTY-SIX

ARTISTIC ATTEMPTS

~

*I*t takes people a long time to learn the difference between talent and genius, especially ambitious young men and women. Amy was learning this distinction through much tribulation; for, mistaking enthusiasm for inspiration, she attempted every branch of art with youthful audacity. For a long time there was a lull in the "mud-pie" business, and she devoted herself to the finest pen-and-ink drawing, in which she showed such taste and skill, that her graceful handiwork proved both pleasant and profitable. But overstrained eyes soon caused pen and ink to be laid aside for a bold attempt at poker-sketching. While this attack lasted, the family lived in constant fear of a conflagration, for the odor of burning wood pervaded the house at all hours; smoke issued from the attic and shed with alarming frequency, red-hot pokers lay about promiscuously, and Hannah never went to bed without a pail of water and the dinner-bell at her door, in case of fire. Raphael's face was found boldly executed on the under side of the moulding board, and Bacchus on the head of a beer barrel; a chanting cherub adorned the cover of the sugar bucket, and attempts to portray "Garrick buying gloves of the grisette," supplied kindlings for some time.

From fire to oil was a natural transition for burnt fingers, and Amy fell to painting with undiminished ardor. An artist friend fitted her out with his cast-off palettes, brushes, and colors, and she daubed away, producing pastoral and marine views, such as were never seen on land or sea. Her monstrosities in the way of cattle would have taken prizes at an agricultural fair; and the perilous pitching of her vessels would have produced sea-sickness in the most nautical observer, if the utter disregard to all known rules of ship building and rigging had not convulsed him with laughter at the first glance. Swarthy boys and dark eyed Madonnas staring at you from one corner of the studio, did *not* suggest Murillo; oily brown shadows of faces, with a lurid streak in the wrong place, meant Rembrandt; buxom ladies and dropsical infants, Rubens; and Turner appeared in tempests of blue thunder, orange lightning, brown rain, and purple clouds, with a tomato-colored splash in the middle, which might be the sun or a buoy, a sailor's shirt or a king's robe, as the spectator pleased.

Charcoal portraits came next; and the entire family hung in a row, looking as wild and crocky as if just evoked from a coal-bin. Softened into crayon sketches, they did better; for the likenesses were good, and Amy's hair, Jo's nose, Meg's mouth, and Laurie's eyes were pronounced "wonderfully fine." A return to clay and plaster followed, and ghostly casts of her acquaintances haunted corners of the house, or tumbled off closet shelves on to people's heads. Children were enticed in as models, till their incoherent accounts of her mysterious doings caused Miss Amy to be regarded in the light of a young ogress. Her efforts in this line, however, were brought to an abrupt close by an untoward accident, which quenched her ardor. Other models failing her for a time, she undertook to cast her own pretty foot, and the family were one day alarmed by an unearthly bumping and screaming; and, running to the rescue, found the young enthusiast hopping wildly about the shed, with her foot held fast in a pan-full of plaster, which had hardened with unexpected rapidity. With much difficulty and some danger, she was dug out; for Jo was so overcome with laughter while she excavated, that her knife went too far, cut the poor foot, and left a lasting memorial of one artistic attempt, at least.

After this Amy subsided, till a mania for sketching from nature set her to haunting river, field, and wood, for picturesque studies, and sighing for ruins to copy. She caught endless colds sitting on damp grass to book "a delicious bit," composed of a stone, a stump, one mushroom, and a broken mullein stalk, or "a heavenly mass of clouds," that looked like a choice display of feather beds when done. She sacrificed her complexion floating on the river in the mid-summer sun, to study light and shade, and got a wrinkle over her nose, trying after "points of sight," or whatever the squint-and-string performance is called.

If "genius is eternal patience," as Michael Angelo affirms, Amy certainly had some claim to the divine attribute, for she persevered in spite of all obstacles, failures, and discouragements, firmly believing that in time she should do something worthy to be called "high art."

She was learning, doing, and enjoying other things, meanwhile, for she had resolved to be an attractive and accomplished woman, even if she never became a great artist. Here she succeeded better; for she was one of those happily created beings who please without effort, make friends everywhere, and take life so gracefully and easily, that less fortunate souls are tempted to believe that such are born under a lucky star. Everybody liked her, for among her good gifts was tact. She had an instinctive sense of what was pleasing and proper, always said the right thing to the right person, did just what suited the time and place, and was so self-possessed that her sisters used to say, "If Amy went to court without any rehearsal beforehand, she'd know exactly what to do."

One of her weaknesses was a desire to move in "our best society," without being quite sure what the *best* really was. Money, position, fashionable accomplishments, and elegant manners, were most desirable things in her eyes, and she liked to associate with those who possessed them; often mistaking the false for the true, and admiring what was not admirable. Never forgetting that by birth she was a gentlewoman, she cultivated her aristocratic tastes and feelings, so that when the opportunity came, she might be ready to take the place from which poverty now excluded her.

"My lady," as her friends called her, sincerely desired to be a genuine lady, and was so, at heart, but had yet to learn that money cannot buy refinement of nature, that rank does not always confer nobility, and that true breeding makes itself felt in spite of external drawbacks.

"I want to ask a favor of you, mamma," Amy said, coming in with an important air, one day.

"Well, little girl, what is it?" replied her mother, in whose eyes the stately young lady still remained "the baby."

"Our drawing class breaks up next week, and before the girls separate for the summer, I want to ask them out here for a day. They are wild to see the river, sketch the broken bridge, and copy some of the things they admire in my book. They have been very kind to me in many ways, and I am grateful; for they are all rich, and know I am poor, yet they never made any difference."

"Why should they!" and Mrs. March put the question with what the girls called her "Maria Theresa air."

"You know as well as I that it *does* make a difference with nearly every one, so don't ruffle up like a dear, motherly hen, when your chickens get pecked by smarter birds; the ugly duckling turned out a swan you know;" and Amy smiled without bitterness, for she possessed a happy temper and hopeful spirit.

Mrs. March laughed, and smoothed down her maternal pride, as she asked, –

"Well, my swan, what is your plan?"

"I should like to ask the girls out to lunch next week, to take them a drive to the places they want to see, – a row on the river, perhaps, – and make a little artistic fête for them."

"That looks feasible. What do you want for lunch? Cake, sandwiches, fruit and coffee, will be all that is necessary, I suppose?"

"Oh, dear, no! we must have cold tongue and chicken, French chocolate and ice cream, besides. The girls are used to such things, and I want my lunch to be proper and elegant, though I *do* work for my living."

"How many young ladies are there?" asked her mother, beginning to look sober.

"Twelve or fourteen in the class, but I dare say they won't all come."

"Bless me, child, you will have to charter an omnibus to carry them about."

"Why, mother, how can you think of such a thing; not more than six or eight will probably come, so I shall hire a beach-wagon and borrow Mr. Laurence's cherry-bounce." (Hannah's pronunciation of char-a-banc.)

"All this will be very expensive, Amy."

"Not very; I've calculated the cost, and I'll pay for it myself."

"Don't you think, dear, that as these girls are used to such things, and the best we can do will be nothing new, that some simpler plan would be pleasanter to them, as a change, if nothing more, and much better for us than buying or borrowing what we don't need, and attempting a style not in keeping with our circumstances?"

"If I can't have it as I like I don't care to have it at all. I know that I can carry it out perfectly well, if you and the girls will help a little; and I don't see why I can't, if I'm willing to pay for it," said Amy, with the decision which opposition was apt to change into obstinacy.

Mrs. March knew that experience was an excellent teacher, and, when it was possible, she left her children to learn alone the lessons which she would gladly have made easier, if they had not objected to taking advice as much as they did salts and senna.

"Very well, Amy; if your heart is set upon it, and you see your way through without too great an outlay of money, time, and temper, I'll say no more. Talk it over with the girls, and whichever way you decide, I'll do my best to help you."

"Thanks, mother; you are always *so* kind," and away went Amy to lay her plans before her sisters.

Meg agreed at once, and promised her aid, — gladly offering anything she possessed, from her little house itself to her very best salt-spoons. But Jo frowned upon the whole project, and would have nothing to do with it at first.

"'Why in the world should you spend your money, worry your family, and turn the house upside down for a parcel of girls who don't care a sixpence for you? I thought you had too much pride and sense to truckle to any mortal woman just because she wears French boots and rides in a *coupé*," said Jo, who, being called from the tragical climax of her novel, was not in the best mood for social enterprises.

"I *don't* truckle, and I hate being patronized as much as you do!" returned Amy, indignantly, for the two still jangled when such questions arose. "The girls do care for me, and I do for them, and there's a great deal of kindness, and sense, and talent among them, in spite of what you call fashionable nonsense. You don't care to make people like you, to go into good society, and cultivate your manners and tastes. I do, and I mean to make the most of every chance that comes. *You* can go through the world with your elbows out and your nose in the air, and call it independence, if you like. That's not my way."

When Amy whetted her tongue and freed her mind she usually got the best of it, for she seldom failed to have common sense on her side, while Jo carried her love of liberty and hate of conventionalities to such an unlimited extent, that she naturally found herself worsted in an argument. Amy's definition of Jo's idea of independence was such a good hit, that both burst out laughing, and the discussion took a more amiable turn. Much against her will, Jo at length consented to sacrifice a day to Mrs. Grundy, and help her sister through what she regarded as "a nonsensical business."

The invitations were sent, most all accepted, and the following Monday was set apart for the grand event. Hannah went out of humor because her week's work was deranged, and prophesied that "ef the washin' and ironin' warn't done reg'lar nothin' would go well anywheres." This hitch in the main-spring of the domestic machinery had a bad effect upon the whole concern; but Amy's motto was "*Nil desperandum*," and having made up her mind what to do, she proceeded to do it in spite of all obstacles. To begin with: Hannah's cooking didn't turn out well; the chicken was tough, the tongue too salt, and the chocolate wouldn't froth properly. Then the cake and ice cost more than Amy expected, so did the wagon; and various other expenses, which seemed trifling at the outset, counted up rather alarmingly afterward. Beth got cold and took to her bed; Meg had an unusual number of callers to keep her at home, and Jo was in such a divided state of mind that her breakages, accidents, and mistakes were uncommonly numerous, serious, and trying.

"If it hadn't been for mother I never should have got through," as Amy declared afterward, and gratefully remembered, when "the best joke of the season" was entirely forgotten by everybody else.

If it was not fair on Monday, the young ladies were to come on Tuesday, an arrangement which aggravated Jo and Hannah to the last degree. On Monday morning the weather was in that undecided state which is more exasperating than a steady pour. It drizzled a little, shone a little, blew a little, and didn't make up its mind till it was too late for any one else to make up theirs. Amy was up at dawn, hustling people out of their beds and through their breakfasts, that the house might be got in order. The parlor struck her as looking uncommonly shabby, but without stopping to sigh for what she had not, she skilfully made the best of what she had, arranging chairs over the worn places in the carpet, covering stains on the wall with pictures framed in ivy, and filling up empty corners with home-made statuary, which gave an artistic air to the room, as did the lovely vases of flowers Jo scattered about.

The lunch looked charmingly; and, as she surveyed it, she sincerely hoped it would taste good, and that the borrowed glass, china, and silver would get safely home again. The carriages were promised, Meg and mother were all ready to do the honors, Beth was able to help Hannah behind the scenes, Jo had engaged to be as lively and amiable as an absent mind, an aching head, and a very decided disapproval of everybody and everything would allow, and, as she wearily dressed, Amy cheered herself with anticipations of the happy moment when, lunch safely over, she should drive away with her friends for an afternoon of artistic delights; for the "cherry-bounce" and the broken bridge were her strong points.

Then came two hours of suspense, during which she vibrated from parlor to porch, while public opinion varied like the weather-cock. A smart shower, at eleven, had evidently quenched the enthusiasm of the young ladies who were to arrive at twelve, for nobody came; and, at two, the exhausted family sat down in a blaze of sunshine to consume the perishable portions of the feast, that nothing might be lost.

"No doubt about the weather to-day; they will certainly come, so we must fly round and be ready for them," said Amy, as the sun woke her next morning. She spoke briskly, but in her secret soul she wished she had said nothing about Tuesday, for her interest, like her cake, was getting a little stale.

"I can't get any lobsters, so you will have to do without salad to-day," said Mr. March, coming in half an hour later, with an expression of placid despair.

"Use the chicken then, the toughness won't matter in a salad," advised his wife.

"Hannah left it on the kitchen table a minute, and the kittens got at it. I've very sorry, Amy," added Beth, who was still a patroness of cats.

"Then, I *must* have a lobster, for tongue alone won't do," said Amy, decidedly.

"Shall I rush into town and demand one?" asked Jo, with the magnanimity of a martyr.

"You'd come bringing it home under your arm, without any paper, just to try me. I'll go myself," answered Amy, whose temper was beginning to fail.

Shrouded in a thick veil, and armed with a genteel travelling-basket, she departed, feeling that a cool drive would soothe her ruffled spirit, and fit her for the labors of the day. After some delay, the object of her desire was procured, likewise a bottle of dressing, to prevent further loss of time at home, and off she drove again, well pleased with her own forethought.

As the omnibus contained only one passenger, a sleepy old lady, Amy pocketed her veil, and beguiled the tedium of the way by trying to find out where all her money had gone to. So busy was she with her card full of refractory figures that she did not observe a new-comer, who entered without stopping the vehicle, till a masculine voice said, "Good morning, Miss March," and looking up she beheld one of Laurie's most elegant college friends. Fervently hoping that he would get out before she did, Amy utterly ignored the basket at her feet, and congratulating herself that she had on her new travelling dress, returned the young man's greeting with her usual suavity and spirit.

They got on excellently; for Amy's chief care was soon set at rest, by learning that the gentleman would leave first, and she was chatting away in a peculiarly lofty strain, when the old lady got out. In stumbling to the door, she upset the basket, and oh, horror! the lobster, in all its vulgar size and brilliancy, was revealed to the high-born eyes of a Tudor!

"By Jove, she's forgot her dinner!" cried the unconscious youth poking the scarlet monster into its place with his cane, and preparing to hand out the basket after the old lady.

"Please don't — it's — it's mine," murmured Amy, with a face nearly as red as the fish.

"Oh, really, I beg pardon; it's an uncommonly fine one, isn't it?" said Tudor, with great presence of mind, and an air of sober interest that did credit to his breeding.

Amy recovered herself in a breath, set her basket boldly on the seat, and said, laughing, —

"Don't you wish you were to have some of the salad he's to make, and to see the charming young ladies who are to eat it?"

Now that was tact, for two of the ruling foibles of the masculine mind were touched; the lobster was instantly surrounded by a halo of pleasing reminiscences, and curiosity about "the charming young ladies" diverted his mind from the comical mishap.

"I suppose he'll laugh and joke over it with Laurie, but I shan't see them; that's a comfort," thought Amy, as Tudor bowed and departed.

She did not mention this meeting at home (though she discovered that, thanks to the upset, her new dress was much damaged by the rivulets of dressing that meandered down the skirt), but went through with the preparations which now seemed more irksome than before; and at twelve o'clock all was ready again. Feeling that the neighbors were interested in her movements, she wished to efface the memory of yesterday's failure by a grand success to-day; so she ordered the "cherry-bounce," and drove away in state to meet and escort her guests to the banquet.

"There's the rumble, they're coming! I'll go into the porch to meet them; it looks hospitable, and I want the poor child to have a good time after all her trouble," said Mrs. March, suiting the action to the word. But after one glance, she retired with an indescribable expression, for, looking quite lost in the big carriage, sat Amy and one young lady.

"Run, Beth, and help Hannah clear half the things off the table; it will be too absurd to put a luncheon for twelve before a single girl," cried Jo, hurrying away to the lower regions, too excited to stop even for a laugh.

In came Amy, quite calm, and delightfully cordial to the one guest who had kept her promise; the rest of the family, being of a dramatic turn, played their parts equally well, and Miss Elliott found them a most hilarious set; for it was impossible to entirely control the merriment which possessed them. The remodelled lunch being gaily partaken of, the studio and garden visited, and art discussed with enthusiasm, Amy ordered a buggy (alas for the elegant cherry-bounce!) and drove her friend quietly about the neighborhood till sunset, when "the party went out."

As she came walking in, looking very tired, but as composed as ever, she observed that every vestige of the unfortunate fête had disappeared, except a suspicious pucker about the corners of Jo's mouth.

"You've have a lovely afternoon for your drive, dear," said her mother, as respectfully as if the whole twelve had come.

"Miss Elliott is a very sweet girl, and seemed to enjoy herself, I thought," observed Beth, with unusual warmth.

"Could you spare me some of your cake? I really need some, I have so much company, and I can't make such delicious stuff as yours," asked Meg, soberly.

"Take it all; I'm the only one here who likes sweet things, and it will mould before I can dispose of it," answered Amy, thinking with a sigh of the generous store she had laid in for such an end as this!

"It's a pity Laurie isn't here to help us," began Jo, as they sat down to ice cream and salad for the fourth time in two days.

A warning look from her mother checked any further remarks, and the whole family ate in heroic silence, till Mr. March mildly observed, "Salad was one of the favorite dishes of the ancients, and Evelyn" – here a general explosion of laughter cut short the "history of sallets," to the great surprise of the learned gentleman.

"Bundle everything into a basket, and send it to the Hummels – Germans like messes. I'm sick of the sight of this; and there's no reason you should all die of a surfeit because I've been a fool," cried Amy, wiping her eyes.

"I thought I *should* have died when I saw you two girls rattling about in the what-you-call-it, like two little kernels in a very big nutshell, and mother waiting in state to receive the throng," sighed Jo, quite spent with laughter.

"I'm very sorry you were disappointed, dear, but we all did our best to satisfy you," said Mrs. March, in a tone full of motherly regret.

"I *am* satisfied; I've done what I undertook, and it's not my fault that it failed; I comfort myself with that," said Amy, with a little quiver in her voice. "I thank you all very much for helping me, and I'll thank you still more, if you won't allude to it for a month, at least."

No one did for several months; but the word "fête" always produced a general smile, and Laurie's birthday gift to Amy was a tiny coral lobster in the shape of a charm for her watch-guard.

LITERARY LESSONS

~

ortune suddenly smiled upon Jo, and dropped a good-luck penny in her path. Not a golden penny, exactly, but I doubt if half a million would have given more real happiness than did the little sum that came to her in this wise.

Every few weeks she would shut herself up in her room, put on her scribbling suit, and "fall into a vortex," as she expressed it, writing away at her novel with all her heart and soul, for till that was finished she could find no peace. Her "scribbling suit" consisted of a black pinafore on which she could wipe her pen at will, and a cap of the same material, adorned with a cheerful red bow, into which she bundled her hair when the decks were cleared for action. This cap was a beacon to the inquiring eyes of her family, who, during these periods, kept their distance, merely popping in their heads semi-occasionally, to ask, with interest, "Does genius burn, Jo?" They did not always venture even to ask this question, but took an observation of the cap, and judged accordingly. If this expressive article of dress was drawn low upon the forehead, it was a sign that hard work was going on; in exciting moments it was pushed rakishly askew, and when despair seized the author it was plucked wholly off, and cast upon the floor. At such times the intruder silently withdrew; and not until the red bow was seen gaily erect upon the gifted brow, did any one dare address Jo.

She did not think herself a genius by any means; but when the writing fit came on, she gave herself up to it with entire abandon, and led a blissful life, unconscious of want, care, or bad weather, while she sat safe and happy in an imaginary world, full of friends almost as real and dear to her as any in the flesh. Sleep forsook her eyes, meals stood untasted, day and night were all too short to enjoy the happiness which blessed her only at such times, and made these hours worth living, even if they bore no other fruit. The divine afflatus usually lasted a week or two, and then she emerged from her "vortex" hungry; sleepy, cross, or despondent.

She was just recovering from one of these attacks when she was prevailed upon to escort Miss Crocker to a lecture, and in return for her virtue was rewarded with a new idea. It was a People's Course, – the lecture on the Pyramids, – and Jo rather wondered at the choice of such a subject for such an audience, but took it for granted that some social evil would be remedied, or some great want supplied by unfolding the glories of the Pharaohs, to an audience whose thoughts were busy with the price of coal and flour, and whose lives were spent in trying to solve harder riddles than that of the Sphinx.

They were early; and while Miss Crocker set the heel of her stocking, Jo amused herself by examining the faces of the people who occupied the seat with them. On her left were two matrons with massive foreheads, and bonnets to match, discussing Woman's Rights and making tatting. Beyond sat a pair of humble lovers artlessly holding each other by the hand, a sombre spinster eating peppermints out of a paper bag, and an old gentleman taking his preparatory nap behind a yellow bandanna. On her right, her only neighbor was a studious-looking lad absorbed in a newspaper.

It was a pictorial sheet, and Jo examined the work of art nearest her, idly wondering what unfortuitous concatenation of circumstances needed the melodramatic illustration of an Indian in full war costume, tumbling over a precipice with a wolf at his throat, while two infuriated young gentlemen, with unnaturally small feet and big eyes, were stabbing each other close by, and a dishevelled female was flying away in the background, with her mouth wide open. Pausing to turn a page, the lad saw her looking, and, with boyish good nature, offered half his paper, saying, bluntly, "Want to read it? That's a first-rate story."

Jo accepted it with a smile, for she had never out-grown her liking for lads, and soon found herself involved in the usual labyrinth of love, mystery, and murder, for the story belonged to that class of light literature in which the passions have a holiday, and when the author's invention fails, a grand catastrophe clears the stage of one-half the *dramatis personæ*, leaving the other half to exult over their downfall.

"Prime, isn't it?" asked the boy, as her eye went down the last paragraph of her portion.

"I guess you and I could do most as well as that if we tried," returned Jo, amused at this admiration of the trash.

"I should think I was a pretty lucky chap if I could. She makes a good living out of such stories, they say;" and he pointed to the name of Mrs. S. L. A. N. G. Northbury, under the title of the tale.

"Do you know her?" asked Jo, with sudden interest.

"No; but I read all her pieces, and I know a fellow that works in the office where this paper is printed."

"Do you say she makes a good living out of stories like this?" and Jo looked more respectfully at the agitated group and thickly-sprinkled exclamation points that adorned the page.

"Guess she does! she knows just what folks like, and gets paid well for writing it."

Here the lecture began, but Jo heard very little of it, for while Professor Sands was prosing away about Belzoni, Cheops, scarabei, and hieroglyphics, she was covertly taking down the address of the paper, and boldly resolved to try for the hundred dollar prize offered in its columns for a sensational story. By the time the lecture ended, and the audience awoke, she had built up a splendid fortune for herself (not the first founded upon paper), and was already deep in the concoction of her story, being unable to decide whether the duel should come before the elopement or after the murder.

She said nothing of her plan at home, but fell to work next day, much to the disquiet of her mother, who always looked a little anxious when "genius took to burning." Jo had never tried this style before, contenting herself with very mild romances for the "Spread Eagle." Her theatrical experience and miscellaneous reading were of service now, for they gave her some idea of dramatic effect, and supplied plot, language, and costumes. Her story was as full of desperation and despair as her limited acquaintance with those uncomfortable emotions enabled her to make it, and, having located it in Lisbon, she wound up with an earthquake, as a striking and appropriate *dénouement*. The manuscript was privately despatched, accompanied by a note, modestly saying that if the tale didn't get the prize, which the writer hardly dared expect, she would be very glad to receive any sum it might be considered worth.

Six weeks is a long time to wait, and a still longer time for a girl to keep a secret; but Jo did both, and was just beginning to give up all hope of ever seeing her manuscript again, when a letter arrived which almost took her breath away; for, on opening it, a check for a hundred dollars fell into her lap. For a minute she stared at it as if it had been a snake, then she read her letter, and began to cry. If the amiable gentleman who wrote that kindly note could have known what intense happiness he was giving a fellow-creature, I think he would devote his leisure hours, if he has any, to that amusement; for Jo valued the letter more than the money, because it was encouraging; and after years of effort it was so pleasant to find that she had learned to do *something*, though it was only to write a sensation story.

A prouder young woman was seldom seen than she, when, having composed herself, she electrified the family by appearing before them with the letter in one hand, the check in the other, announcing that she had won the prize! Of course there was a great jubilee, and when the story came every one read and praised it; though after her father had told her that the language was good, the romance fresh and hearty, and the tragedy quite thrilling, he shook his head, and said in his unworldly way,—

"You can do better than this, Jo. Aim at the highest, and never mind the money."

"*I* think the money is the best part of it. What *will* you do with such a fortune?" asked Amy, regarding the magic slip of paper with a reverential eye.

"Send Beth and mother to the sea-side for a month or two," answered Jo promptly.

"Oh, how splendid! No, I can't do it, deat, it would be so selfish," cried Beth, who had clapped her thin hands, and taken a long breath, as if pining for fresh ocean breezes; then stopped herself, and motioned away the check which her sister waved before her.

"Ah, but you shall go, I've set my heart on it; that's what I tried for, and that's why I succeeded. I never get on when I think of myself alone, so it will help me to work for you, don't you see. Besides, Marmee needs the change, and she won't leave you, so you *must* go. Won't it be fun to see you come home plump and rosy again? Hurrah for Dr. Jo, who always cures her patients!"

To the sea-side they went, after much discussion; and though Beth didn't come home as plump and rosy as could be desired, she was much better, while Mrs. March declared she felt ten years younger; so Jo was satisfied with the investment of her prize-money, and fell to work with a cheery spirit, bent on earning more of those delightful checks. She did earn several that year, and began to feel herself a power in the house; for by the magic of a pen, her "rubbish" turned into comforts for them all. "The Duke's Daughter" paid the butcher's bill, "A Phantom Hand" put down a new carpet, and "The Curse of the Coventrys" proved the blessing of the Marches in the way of groceries and gowns.

Wealth is certainly a most desirable thing, but poverty has its sunny side, and one of the sweet uses of adversity, is the genuine satisfaction which comes from hearty work of head or hand; and to the inspiration of necessity, we owe half the wise, beautiful, and useful blessings of the world. Jo enjoyed a taste of this satisfaction, and ceased to envy richer girls, taking great comfort in the knowledge that she could supply her own wants, and need ask no one for a penny.

Little notice was taken of her stories, but they found a market; and, encouraged by this fact, she resolved to make a bold stroke for fame and fortune. Having copied her novel for the fourth time, read it to all her confidential friends, and submitted it with fear and trembling to three publishers, she at last disposed of it, on condition that she would cut it down one-third, and omit all the parts which she particularly admired.

"Now I must either bundle it back into my tin-kitchen, to mould, pay for printing it myself, or chop it to suit purchasers, and get what I can for it. Fame is a very good thing to have in the house, but cash is more convenient; so I wish to take the sense of the meeting on this important subject," said Jo, calling a family council.

"Don't spoil your book, my girl, for there is more in it than you know, and the idea is well worked out. Let it wait and ripen," was her father's advice; and he practised as he preached, having waited patiently thirty years for fruit of his own to ripen, and being in no haste to gather it, even now, when it was sweet and mellow.

"It seems to me that Jo will profit more by making the trial than by waiting," said Mrs. March. "Criticism is the best taste of such work, for it will show her both unsuspected merits and faults, and help her to do better next time. We are too partial; but the praise and blame of outsiders will prove useful, even if she gets but little money."

"Yes," said Jo, knitting her brows, "that's just it; I've been fussing over the thing too long, I really don't know whether it's good, bad, or indifferent. It will be a great help to have cool, impartial persons take a look at it, and tell me what they think of it."

"I wouldn't leave out a word of it; you'll spoil it if you do, for the interest of the story is more in the minds than in the actions of the people, and it will be all a muddle if you don't explain as you go on," said Meg, who firmly believed that this book was the most remarkable novel ever written.

"But Mr. Allen says, 'Leave out the explanations, make it brief and dramatic, and let the characters tell the story,'" interrupted Jo, turning to the publisher's note.

"Do as he tells you; he knows what will sell, and we don't. Make a good, popular book, and get as much money as you can. By and by, when you've got a name, you can afford to digress, and have philosophical and metaphysical people in your novels," said Amy, who took a strictly practical view of the subject.

"Well," said Jo, laughing, "if my people *are* 'philosophical and metaphysical,' it isn't my fault, for I know nothing about such things, except what I hear father say, sometimes. If I've got some of his wise ideas jumbled up with my romance, so much the better for me. Now, Beth, what do you say?"

"I should so like to see it printed *soon*," was all Beth said, and smiled in saying it; but there was an unconscious emphasis on the last word, and a wistful look in the eyes that never lost their child-like candor, which chilled Jo's heart, for a minute, with a foreboding fear, and decided her to make her little venture "soon."

So, with Spartan firmness, the young authoress laid her first-born on her table, and chopped it up as ruthlessly as any ogre. In the hope of pleasing every one, she took every one's advice; and, like the old man and his donkey in the fable, suited nobody.

Her father liked the metaphysical streak which had unconsciously got into it, so that was allowed to remain, though she had her doubts about it. Her mother thought that there *was* a trifle too much description; out, therefore, it nearly came, and with it many necessary links in the story. Meg admired the tragedy; so Jo piled up the agony to suit her, while Amy objected to the fun, and, with the best intentions in life, Jo quenched the sprightly scenes which relieved the sombre character of the story. Then, to complete the ruin, she cut it down one-third, and confidingly sent the poor little romance, like a picked robin, out into the big, busy world, to try its fate.

Well, it was printed, and she got three hundred dollars for it; likewise plenty of praise and blame, both so much greater than she expected, that she was thrown into a state of bewilderment, from which it took her some time to recover.

"You said, mother, that criticism would help me; but how can it, when it's so contradictory that I don't know whether I have written a promising book, or broken all the ten commandments," cried poor Jo, turning over a heap of notices, the perusal of which filled her with pride and joy one minute — wrath and dire dismay the next. "This man says 'An exquisite book, full of truth, beauty, and earnestness; all is sweet, pure, and healthy,'" continued the perplexed authoress. "The next, 'The theory of the book is bad, — full of morbid fancies, spiritualistic ideas, and unnatural characters.' Now, as I had no theory of any kind, don't believe in spiritualism, and copied my characters from life, I don't see how this critic *can* be right. Another says, 'It's one of the best American novels which has appeared for years'" (I know better than that); "and the next asserts that 'though it is original and written with great force and feeling, it is a dangerous book.' 'Tisn't! Some make fun of it, some over-praise, and nearly all insist that I had a deep theory to expound, when I only wrote it for the pleasure and the money. I wish I'd printed it whole, or not at all, for I do hate to be so horridly misjudged."

Her family and friends administered comfort and commendation liberally; yet it was a hard time for sensitive, high-spirited Jo, who meant so well, and had apparently done so ill. But it did her good, for those whose opinion had real value, gave her the criticism which is an author's best education; and when the first soreness was over, she could laugh at her poor little book, yet believe in it still, and feel herself the wiser and stronger for the buffeting she had received.

"Not being a genius, like Keats, it won't kill me," she said stoutly; "and I've got the joke on my side, after all; for the parts that were taken straight out of real life, are denounced as impossible and absurd, and the scenes that I made up out of my own silly head, are pronounced 'charmingly natural, tender, and true.' So I'll comfort myself with that; and, when I'm ready, I'll up again and take another."

CHAPTER TWENTY-EIGHT

DOMESTIC EXPERIENCES

~

*L*ike most other young matrons, Meg began her married life with the determination to be a model housekeeper. John should find home a paradise; he should always see a smiling face, should fare sumptuously every day, and never know the loss of a button. She brought so much love, energy, and cheerfulness to the work, that she could not but succeed, in spite of some obstacles. Her paradise was not a tranquil one; for the little woman fussed, was over-anxious to please, and bustled about like a true Martha, cumbered with many cares. She was too tired, sometimes, even to smile; John grew dyspeptic after a course of dainty dishes, and ungratefully demanded plain fare. As for buttons, she soon learned to wonder where they went, to shake her head over the carelessness of men, and to threaten to make him sew them on himself, and then see if *his* work would stand impatient tugs and clumsy fingers any better than hers.

They were very happy, even after they discovered that they couldn't live on love alone. John did not find Meg's beauty diminished, though she beamed at him from behind the family coffee-pot; nor did Meg miss any of the romance from the daily parting, when her husband followed up his kiss with the tender inquiry, "Shall I send home veal or mutton for dinner, darling?" The little house ceased to be a glorified bower, but it became a home, and the young couple soon felt that it was a change for the better. At first they played keep-house, and frolicked over it like children; then John took steadily to business, feeling the cares of the head of a family upon his shoulders; and Meg laid by her cambric wrappers, put on a big apron, and fell to work, as before said, with more energy than discretion.

While the cooking mania lasted she went through Mrs. Cornelius's Receipt Book as if it was a mathematical exercise, working out the problems with patience and care. Sometimes her family were invited in to help eat up a too bounteous feast of successes, or Lotty would be privately despatched with a batch of failures which were to be concealed from all eyes, in the convenient stomachs of the little Hummels. An evening with John over the accounts books usually produced a temporary lull in the culinary enthusiasm, and a frugal fit would ensue, during which the poor man was put through a course of bread pudding, hash, and warmed-over coffee, which tried his soul, although he bore it with praiseworthy fortitude. Before the golden mean was found, however, Meg added to her domestic possessions what young couples seldom get on long without, – a family jar.

Fired with a housewifely wish to see her store-room stocked with home-made preserves, she undertook to put up her own currant jelly. John was requested to order home a dozen or so of little pots, and an extra quantity of sugar, for their own currants were ripe, and were to be attended to at once. As John firmly believed that "my wife" was equal to anything, and took a natural pride in her skill, he resolved that she should be gratified, and their only crop of fruit laid by in a most pleasing form for winter use. Home came four dozen delightful little pots, half a barrel of sugar, and a small boy to pick the currants for her. With her pretty hair tucked into a little cap, arms bared to the elbow, and a checked apron which had a coquettish look in spite of the bib, the young housewife fell to work, feeling no doubts about her success; for hadn't she seen Hannah do it hundreds of times? The array of pots rather amazed her at first, but John was so fond of jelly, and the nice little jars would look so well on the top shelf, that Meg resolved to fill them all, and spent a long day picking, boiling, straining, and fussing over her jelly. She did her best; she asked advice of Mrs. Cornelius; she racked her brain to remember what Hannah did that she had left undone; she reboiled, resugared, and restrained, but that dreadful stuff wouldn't "*jell.*"

She longed to run home, bib and all, and ask mother to lend a hand, but John and she had agreed that they would never annoy any one with their private worries, experiments, or quarrels. They had laughed over that last word as if the idea it suggested was a most preposterous one; but they had held to their resolve, and whenever they could get on without help they did so, and no one interfered, – for Mrs. March had advised the plan. So Meg wrestled alone with the refractory sweetmeats all that hot summer day, and at five o'clock sat down in her topsy-turvy kitchen, wrung her bedaubed hands, lifted up her voice, and wept.

Now in the first flush of the new life, she had often said, –

"My husband shall always feel free to bring a friend home whenever he likes. I shall always be prepared; there shall be no flurry, no scolding, no discomfort, but a neat house, a cheerful wife, and a good dinner. John, dear, never stop to ask my leave, invite whom you please, and be sure of a welcome from me."

How charming that was, to be sure! John quite glowed with pride to hear her say it, and felt what a blessed thing it was to have a superior wife. But, although they had company from time to time, it never happened to be unexpected, and Meg had never had an opportunity to distinguish herself, till now. It always happens so in this vale of tears; there is an inevitability about such things which we can only wonder at, deplore, and bear as best we can.

If John had not forgotten all about the jelly, it really would have been unpardonable in him to choose that day, of all the days in the year, to bring a friend home to dinner unexpectedly. Congratulating himself that a handsome repast had been ordered that morning, feeling sure that it would be ready to the minute, and indulging in pleasant anticipations of the charming effect it would produce, when his pretty wife came running out to meet him, he escorted his friend to his mansion, with the irrepressible satisfaction of a young host and husband.

It is a world of disappointments, as John discovered when he reached the Dovecote. The front door usually stood hospitably open; now it was not only shut, but locked, and yesterday's mud still adorned the steps. The parlor windows were closed and curtained, no picture of the pretty wife sewing on the piazza, in white, with a distracting little bow in her hair, or a bright-eyed hostess, smiling a shy welcome as she greeted her guest. Nothing of the sort – for not a soul appeared, but a sanguinary-looking boy asleep under the currant bushes.

"I'm afraid something has happened; step into the garden, Scott, while I look up Mrs. Brooke," said John, alarmed at the silence and solitude.

Round the house he hurried, led by a pungent smell of burnt sugar, and Mr. Scott strolled after him, with a queer look on his face. He paused discreetly at a distance when Brooke disappeared; but he could both see and hear, and, being a bachelor, enjoyed the prospect mightily.

In the kitchen reigned confusion and despair; one edition of jelly was trickled from pot to pot, another lay upon the floor, and a third was burning gaily on the stove. Lotty, with Teutonic phlegm, was calmly eating bread and currant wine, for the jelly was still in a hopelessly liquid state, while Mrs. Brooke, with her apron over her head, sat sobbing dismally.

"My dearest girl, what is the matter?" cried John, rushing in with awful visions of scalded hands, sudden news of affliction, and secret consternation at the thought of the guest in the garden.

"Oh, John, I *am* so tired, and hot, and cross, and worried! I've been at it till I'm all worn out. Do come and help me, or I *shall* die;" and the exhausted housewife cast herself upon his breast, giving him a sweet welcome in every sense of the word, for her pinafore had been baptized at the same time as the floor.

"What worries you, dear? Has anything dreadful happened?" asked the anxious John, tenderly kissing the crown of the little cap, which was all askew.

"Yes," sobbed Meg, despairingly

"Tell me quick, then; don't cry, I can bear anything better than that. Out with it, love."

"The – the jelly won't jell – and I don't know what to do!"

John Brooke laughed then as he never dare to laugh afterward; and the derisive Scott smiled involuntarily as he heard the hearty peal, which put the finishing stroke to poor Meg's woe.

"Is that all? Fling it out of the window, and don't bother any more about it. I'll buy you quarts if you want it; but for heaven's sake don't have hysterics, for I've brought Jack Scott home to dinner, and – "

John got no further, for Meg cast him off, and clasped her hands with a tragic gesture as she fell into a chair, exclaiming in a tone of mingled indignation, reproach, and dismay, –

"A man to dinner, and everything in a mess! John Brooke, how *could* you do such a thing?"

"Hush, he's in the garden; I forgot the confounded jelly, but it can't be helped now," said John, surveying the prospect with an anxious eye.

"You ought to have sent word, or told me this morning, and you ought to have remembered how busy I was," continued Meg, petulantly; for even turtle-doves will peck when ruffled.

"I didn't know it this morning, and there was no time to send word, for I met him on the way out. I never thought of asking leave, when you have always told me to do as I liked. I never tried it before, and hang me if I ever do again!" added John, with an aggrieved air.

"I should hope not! Take him away at once; I can't see him, and there isn't any dinner."

"Well, I like that! Where's the beef and vegetables I sent home, and the pudding you promised?" cried John, rushing to the larder.

"I hadn't time to cook anything; I meant to dine at mother's. I'm sorry, but I was *so* busy," – and Meg's tears began again.

John was a mild man, but he was human; and after a long day's work, to come home tired, hungry and hopeful, to find a chaotic house, an empty table, and a cross wife, was not exactly conducive to repose of mind or manner. He restrained himself, however, and the little squall would have blown over but for one unlucky word.

"It's a scrape, I acknowledge; but if you will lend a hand, we'll pull through, and have a good time yet. Don't cry, dear, but just exert yourself a bit, and knock us up something to eat. We're both hungry as hunters, so we shan't mind what it is. Give us the cold meat, and bread and cheese; we won't ask for jelly."

He meant it for a good-natured joke; but that one word sealed his fate. Meg thought it was *too* cruel to hint about her sad failure, and the last atom of patience vanished as she spoke.

"You must get yourself out of the scrape as you can; I'm too used up to 'exert' myself for any one. It's like a man, to propose a bone and vulgar bread and cheese for company. I won't have anything of the sort in my house. Take that Scott up to mother's, and tell him I'm away – sick, dead, anything. I won't see him, and you two can laugh at me and my jelly as much as you like; you won't have anything else here;" and having delivered her defiance all in one breath, Meg cast away her pinafore, and precipitately left the field to bemoan herself in her own room.

What those two creatures did in her absence, she never knew; but Mr. Scott was not taken "up to mother's," and when Meg descended, after they had strolled away together, she found traces of a promiscuous lunch which filled her with horror. Lotty reported that they had eaten "a much, and greatly laughed; and the master bid her throw away all the sweet stuff, and hide the pots."

Meg longed to go and tell mother; but a sense of shame at her own short-comings, of loyalty to John, "who might be cruel, but nobody should know it," restrained her; and after a summary clearing up, she dressed herself prettily, and sat down to wait for John to come and be forgiven.

Unfortunately, John didn't come, not seeing the matter in that light. He had carried it off as a good joke with Scott, excused his little wife as well as he could, and played the host so hospitably, that his friend enjoyed the impromptu dinner, and promised to come again. But John was angry, though he did not show it; he felt that Meg had got him into a scrape, and then deserted him in his hour of need. "It wasn't fair to tell a man to bring folks home any time, with perfect freedom, and when he took you at your word, to flare up and blame him, and leave him in the lurch, to be laughed at or pitied. No, by George, it wasn't! and Meg must know it." He had fumed inwardly during the feast, but when the flurry was over, and he strolled home, after seeing Scott off, a milder mood came over him. "Poor little thing! it was hard upon her when she tried so heartily to please me. She was wrong, of course, but then she was so young. I must be patient, and teach her." He hoped she had not gone home – he hated gossip and interference. For a minute he was ruffled again at the mere thought of it; and then the fear that Meg would cry herself sick, softened his heart, and sent him on at a quicker pace, resolving to be calm and kind, but firm, quite firm, and show her where she had failed in her duty to her spouse.

Meg likewise resolved to be "calm and kind, but firm," and show *him* his duty. She longed to run to meet him, and beg pardon, and be kissed and comforted, as she was sure of being; but, of course, she did nothing of the sort; and when she saw John coming, began to hum quite naturally, as she rocked and sewed like a lady of leisure in her best parlor.

John was a little disappointed not to find a tender Niobe; but, feeling that his dignity demanded the first apology, he made none: only came leisurely in, and laid himself upon the sofa, with the singularly relevant remark, –

"We are going to have a new moon, my dear."

"I've no objection," was Meg's equally soothing remark.

A few other topics of general interest were introduced by Mr. Brooke, and wet-blanketed by Mrs. Brooke, and conversation languished. John went to one window, unfolded his paper, and wrapt himself in it, figuratively speaking. Meg went to the other window, and sewed as if new rosettes for her slippers were among the necessaries of life. Neither spoke – both looked quite "calm and firm," and both felt desperately uncomfortable.

"Oh, dear," thought Meg, "married life is very trying, and does need infinite patience, as well as love, as mother says." The word "mother" suggested other maternal counsels given long ago, and received with unbelieving protests.

"John is a good man, but he has his faults, and you must learn to see and bear with them, remembering your own. He is very decided, but never will be obstinate, if you reason kindly, not oppose impatiently. He is very accurate, and particular about the truth – a good trait, though you call him 'fussy.' Never deceive him by look or word, Meg, and he will give you the confidence you deserve, the support you need. He has a temper, not like ours, – one flash, and then all over – but the white, still anger that is seldom stirred, but once kindled, is hard to quench. Be careful, very careful, not to wake this anger against yourself, for peace and happiness depend on keeping his respect. Watch yourself, be the first to ask pardon if you both err, and guard against the little piques, misunderstandings, and hasty words that often pave the way for bitter sorrow and regret."

These words came back to Meg, as she sat sewing in the sunset, – especially the last. This was the first serious disagreement; her own hasty speeches sounded both silly and unkind, as she recalled them, her own anger looked childish now, and thoughts of poor John coming home to such a scene quite melted her heart. She glanced at him with tears in her eyes, but he did not see them; she put down her work and got up, thinking, "I *will* be the first to say, 'forgive me,'" but he did not seem to hear her; she went very slowly across the room, for pride was hard to swallow, and stood by him, but he did not turn his head. For a minute, she felt as if she really couldn't do it; then came the thought, "This is the beginning, I'll do my part, and have nothing to reproach myself with," and stooping down she softly kissed her husband on the forehead. Of course that settled it; the penitent kiss was better than a world of words, and John had her on his knee in a minute, saying tenderly, –

"It was too bad to laugh at the poor little jelly-pots; forgive me, dear, I never will again!"

But he did, oh, bless you, yes, hundreds of times, and so did Meg, both declaring that it was the sweetest jelly they ever made; for family peace was preserved in that little family jar.

After this, Meg had Mr. Scott to dinner by special invitation, and served him a pleasant feast without a cooked wife for the first course; on which occasion she was so gay and gracious, and made everything go off so charmingly, that Mr. Scott told John he was a happy fellow, and shook his head over the hardships of bachelorhood all the way home.

In the autumn, new trials and experiences came to Meg. Sallie Moffat renewed her friendship, was always running out for a dish of gossip at the little house, or inviting "that poor dear" to come in and spend the day at the big house. It was pleasant, for in dull weather Meg often felt lonely; – all were busy at home, John absent till night, and nothing to do but sew, or read, or potter about. So it naturally fell out that Meg got into the way of gadding and gossiping with her friend. Seeing Sallie's pretty things made her long for such, and pity herself because she had not got them. Sallie was very kind, and often offered her the coveted trifles; but Meg declined them, knowing that John wouldn't like it; and then this foolish little woman went and did what John disliked infinitely worse.

She knew her husband's income, and she loved to feel that he trusted her, not only with his happiness, but what some men seem to value more, his money. She knew where it was, was free to take what she liked, and all he asked was that she should keep account of every penny, pay bills once a month, and remember that she was a poor man's wife. Till now she had done well, been prudent and exact, kept her little account books neatly, and showed them to him, monthly, without fear. But that autumn the serpent got into Meg's paradise, and tempted her, like many a modern Eve, not with apples, but with dress. Meg didn't like to be pitied and made to feel poor; it irritated her; but she was ashamed to confess it, and now and then she tried to console herself by buying something pretty, so that Sallie needn't think she had to scrimp. She always felt wicked after it, for the pretty things were seldom necessaries; but then they cost so little, it wasn't worth worrying about; so the trifles increased unconsciously, and in the shopping excursions she was no longer a passive looker-on.

But the trifles cost more than one would imagine; and when she cast up her accounts at the end of the month, the sum total rather scared her. John was busy that month, and left the bills to her; the next month he was absent; but the third he had a grand quarterly settling up, and Meg never forgot it. A few days before she had done a dreadful thing, and it weighed upon her conscience. Sallie had been buying silks, and Meg ached for a new one – just a handsome light one for parties – her black silk was so common, and thin things for evening wear were only proper for girls. Aunt March usually gave the sisters a present of twenty-five dollars apiece, at New-Year; that was only a month to wait, and here was a lovely violet silk going at a bargain, and she had the money, if she only dared to take it. John always said what was his was hers; but would he think it right to spend not only the prospective five-and-twenty, but another five-and-twenty out of the house-hold fund? That was the question. Sallie had urged her to do it, had offered to loan the money, and with the best intentions in life, had tempted Meg beyond her strength. In an evil moment the shopman held up the lovely, shimmering folds, and said, "A bargain, I assure you, ma'am." She answered, "I'll take it;" and it was cut off and paid for, and Sallie had exulted, and she had laughed as if it was a thing of no consequence, and driven away feeling as if she had stolen something, and the police were after her.

When she got home, she tried to assuage the pangs of remorse by spreading forth the lovely silk; but it looked less silvery now, didn't become her, after all, and the words "fifty dollars" seemed stamped like a pattern down each breadth. She put it away; but it haunted her, not delightfully, as a new dress should, but dreadfully, like the ghost of a folly that was not easily laid. When John got out his books that night, Meg's heart sank; and, for the first time in her married life, she was afraid of her husband. The kind, brown eyes looked as if they could be stern; and though he was unusually merry, she fancied he had found her out, but didn't mean to let her know it. The house bills were all paid, the books all in order. John had praised her, and was undoing the old pocket-book which they called the "bank," when Meg, knowing that it was quite empty, stopped his hand, saying nervously, '

"You haven't seen my private expense book, yet."

John never asked to see it; but she always insisted on his doing so, and used to enjoy his masculine amazement at the queer things women wanted, and make him guess what "piping" was, demand fiercely the meaning of a "hug-me-tight," or wonder how a little thing composed of three rosebuds, a bit of velvet and a pair of strings, could possibly be a bonnet, and cost five or six dollars. That night he looked as if would like the fun of quizzing her figures, and pretending to be horrified at her extravagance, as he often did, being particularly proud of his prudent wife.

The little book was brought slowly out, and laid down before him. Meg got behind his chair, under pretence of smoothing the wrinkles out of his tired forehead, and standing there, she said, with her panic increasing with every word, –

"John, dear, I'm ashamed to show my book, for I've really been dreadfully extravagant lately. I go about so much I must have things, you know, and Sallie advised my getting it, so I did; and my New-Year's money will partly pay for it; but I was sorry after I'd done it, for I knew you'd think it wrong in me."

John laughed, and drew her round beside him, saying good-humoredly, "Don't go and hide, I won't beat you if you *have* got a pair of killing boots; I'm rather proud of my wife's feet, and don't mind if she does pay eight or nine dollars for her boots, if they are good ones."

That had been one of her last "trifles," and John's eye had fallen on it as she spoke. "Oh, what *will* he say when he comes to that awful fifty dollars!" thought Meg, with a shiver.

"It's worse than boots, it's a silk dress," she said, with the calmness of desperation, for she wanted the worst over.

"Well, dear, what is 'the dem'd total'? as Mr. Mantalini says."

That didn't sound like John, and she knew he was looking at her with the straightforward look that she had always been ready to meet and answer with one as frank, till now. She turned the page and her head at the same time, pointing to the sum which would have been bad enough without the fifty, but which was appalling to her with that added. For a minute the room was very still; then John said, slowly – but she could feel it cost him an effort to express no displeasure, –

"Well, I don't know that fifty is much for a dress, with all the furbelows and quinny-dingles you have to have to finish it off these days."

"It isn't made or trimmed," sighed Meg faintly; for a sudden recollection of the cost still to be incurred quite overwhelmed her.

"Twenty yards of silk seems a good deal to cover one small woman, but I've no doubt my wife will look as fine as Ned Moffat's when she gets it on," said John dryly.

"I know you are angry, John, but I can't help it; I don't mean to waste your money, and I didn't think those little things would count up so. I can't resist them when I see Sallie buying all she wants, and pitying me because I don't; I try to be contented, but it is hard, and I'm tired of being poor."

The last words were spoken so low she thought he did not hear them, but he did, and they wounded him deeply, for he had denied himself many pleasures for Meg's sake. She could have bitten her tongue out the minute she had said it, for John pushed the books away and got up, saying, with a little quiver in his voice, "I was afraid of this; I do my best, Meg." If he had scolded her, or even shaken her, it would not have broken her heart like those few words. She ran to him and held him close, crying, with repentant tears, "Oh, John! my dear, kind, hard-working boy, I didn't mean it! It was so wicked, so untrue and ungrateful, how could I say it! Oh, how could I say it!"

He was very kind, forgave her readily, and did not utter one reproach; but Meg knew that she had done and said a thing which would not be forgotten soon, although he might never allude to it again. She had promised to love him for better or worse; and then she, his wife, had reproached him with his poverty, after spending his earnings recklessly. It

Jo appeared, proudly bearing a small flannel bundle.

was dreadful; and the worst of it was John went on so quietly afterward, just as if nothing had happened, except that he stayed in town later, and worked at night when she had gone to cry herself to sleep. A week of remorse nearly made Meg sick; and the discovery that John had counter-manded the order for his new great-coat, reduced her to a state of despair which was pathetic to behold. He had simply said, in answer to her surprised inquiries as to the change, "I can't afford it, my dear."

Meg said no more, but a few minutes after he found her in the hall with her face buried in the old great-coat, crying as if her heart would break.

They had a long talk that night, and Meg learned to love her husband better for his poverty, because it seemed to have made a man of him – giving him the strength and courage to fight his own way – and taught him a tender patience with which to bear and comfort the natural longings and failures of those he loved.

Next day she put her pride in her pocket, went to Sallie, told the truth, and asked her to buy the silk as a favor. The good-natured Mrs. Moffat willingly did so, and had the delicacy not to make her a present of it immediately afterward. Then Meg ordered home the great-coat, and, when John arrived, she put it on, and asked him how he liked her new silk gown. One can imagine what answer he made, how he received his present, and what a blissful state of things ensued. John came home early, Meg gadded no more; and that great-coat was put on in the morning by a very happy husband, and taken off at night by a most devoted little wife. So the year rolled round, and at midsummer there came to Meg a new experience, – the deepest and tenderest of a woman's life.

Laurie came creeping into the kitchen of the Dovecote one Saturday, with an excited face, and was received with the clash of cymbals; for Hannah clapped her hands with a saucepan in one, and the cover in the other.

"How's the little Ma? Where is everybody? Why didn't you tell me before I came home?" began Laurie, in a loud whisper.

"Happy as a queen, the dear! Every soul of 'em is up stairs a worshipin'; we didn't want no hurrycanes round. Now you go into the parlor, and I'll send 'em down to you," with which somewhat involved reply Hannah vanished, chuckling ecstatically.

Presently Jo appeared, proudly bearing a small flannel bundle laid forth upon a large pillow. Jo's face was very sober, but her eyes twinkled, and there was an odd sound in her voice of repressed emotion of some sort.

"Shut your eyes and hold out your arms," she said invitingly.

Laurie backed precipitately into a corner, and put his hands behind him with an imploring gesture, — "No, thank you; I'd rather not. I shall drop it, or smash it, as sure as fate."

"Then you shan't see your nevvy," said Jo, decidedly, turning as if to go.

"I will, I will! only you must be responsible for damages;" and, obeying orders, Laurie heroically shut his eyes while something was put into his arms. A peal of laughter from Jo, Amy, Mrs. March, Hannah and John, caused him to open them the next minute, to find himself invested with two babies instead of one.

No wonder they laughed, for the expression on his face was droll enough to convulse a Quaker, as he stood and stared wildly from the unconscious innocents to the hilarious spectators, with such dismay that Jo sat down on the floor and screamed.

"Twins, by Jupiter!" was all he said for a minute; then turning to the women with an appealing look that was comically piteous, he added, "Take 'em quick, somebody! I'm going to laugh, and I shall drop 'em."

John rescued his babies, and marched up and down, with one on each arm, as if already initiated into the mysteries of baby-tending, while Laurie laughed till the tears ran down his cheeks.

"It's the best joke of the season, isn't it? I wouldn't have you told, for I set my heart on surprising you, and I flatter myself I've done it," said Jo, when she got her breath.

"I never was more staggered in my life. Isn't it fun? Are they boys? What are you going to name them? Let's have another look. Hold me up, Jo; for upon my life it's one too many for me," returned Laurie, regarding the infants with the air of a big, benevolent Newfoundland looking at a pair of infantile kittens.

"Boy and girl. Aren't they beauties?" said the proud papa, beaming upon the little, red squirmers as if they were unfledged angels.

"Most remarkable children I ever saw. Which is which?" and Laurie bent like a well-sweep to examine the prodigies.

"Amy put a blue ribbon on the boy and a pink on the girl, French fashion, so you can always tell. Besides, one has blue eyes and one brown. Kiss them, Uncle Teddy," said wicked Jo.

"I'm afraid they mightn't like it," began Laurie, with unusual timidity in such matters.

"Of course they will; they are used to it now; do it this minute, sir," commanded Jo, fearing he might propose a proxy.

Laurie screwed up his face, and obeyed with a gingerly peck at each little cheek that produced another laugh, and made the babies squeal.

"There, I knew they didn't like it! That's the boy; see him kick! he hits out with his fists like a good one. Now then, young Brooke, pitch into a man of your own size, will you?" cried Laurie, delighted with a poke in the face from a tiny fist, flapping aimlessly about.

"He's to be named John Laurence, and the girl Margaret, after mother and grandmother. We shall call her Daisy, so as not to have two Megs, and I suppose the mannie will be Jack, unless we find a better name," said Amy, with aunt-like interest.

"Name him Demijohn, and call him 'Demi' for short," said Laurie.

"Daisy and Demi, – just the thing! I *knew* Teddy would do it," cried Jo, clapping her hands.

Teddy certainly had done it that time, for the babies were "Daisy" and "Demi" to the end of the chapter.

CHAPTER TWENTY-NINE

CALLS

~

"Come, Jo, it's time."

"For what?"

"You don't mean to say you have forgotten that you promised to make half a dozen calls with me to-day?"

"I've done a good many rash and foolish things in my life, but I don't think I ever was mad enough to say I'd make six calls in one day, when a single one upsets me for a week."

"Yes you did; it was a bargain between us. I was to finish the crayon of Beth for you, and you were to go properly with me, and return our neighbors' visits."

"If it was fair — that was in the bond; and I stand to the letter of my bond, Shylock. There is a pile of clouds in the east; it's *not* fair, and I don't go."

"Now that's shirking. It's a lovely day, no prospect of rain, and you pride yourself on keeping promises; so be honorable; come and do your duty, and then be at peace for another six months."

At that minute Jo was particularly absorbed in dressmaking; for she was mantua-maker general to the family, and took especial credit to herself because she could use a needle as well as a pen. It was very provoking to be arrested in the act of a first trying-on, and ordered out to make calls in her best array, on a warm July day. She hated calls of the formal sort, and never made any till Amy cornered her with a bargain, bribe, or promise. In the present instance, there was no escape; and having clashed her scissors rebelliously, while protesting that she smelt thunder, she gave in, put away her work, and taking up her hat and gloves with an air of resignation, told Amy the victim was ready.

"Jo March, you are perverse enough to provoke a saint! You don't intend to make calls in that state, I hope," cried Amy, surveying her with amazement.

"Why not? I'm neat and cool, and comfortable; quite proper for a dusty walk on a warm day. If people care more for my clothes than they do for me, I don't wish to see them. You can dress for both, and be as elegant as you please; it pays for you to be fine; it doesn't for me, and furbelows only worry me."

"Oh, dear!" sighed Amy; "now she's in a contrary fit, and will drive me distracted before I can get her properly ready. I'm sure it's no pleasure to me to go to-day, but it's a debt we owe society, and there's no one to pay it but you and me. I'll do anything for you, Jo, if you'll only dress yourself nicely, and come and help me do the civil. You can talk so well, look so aristocratic in your best things, and behave so beautifully, if you try, that I'm proud of you. I'm afraid to go alone; do come and take care of me."

"You're an artful little puss to flatter and wheedle your cross old sister in that way. The idea of my being aristocratic and well-bred, and your being afraid to go anywhere alone! I don't know which is the most absurd. Well, I'll go if I must, and do my best; you shall be commander of the expedition, and I'll obey blindly; will that satisfy you?" said Jo, with a sudden change from perversity to lamb-like submission.

"You're a perfect cherub! Now put on all your best things, and I'll tell you how to behave at each place, so that you will make a good impression. I want people to like you, and they would if you'd only try to be a little more agreeable. Do your hair the pretty way, and put the pink rose in your bonnet; it's becoming, and you look too sober in your plain suit. Take your light kids and the embroidered handkerchief. We'll stop at Meg's, and borrow her white sun-shade, and then you can have my dove-colored one."

While Amy dressed, she issued her orders, and Jo obeyed them; not without entering her protest, however, for she sighed as she rustled into her new organdie, frowned darkly at herself as she tied her bonnet strings in an irreproachable bow, wrestled viciously with pins as she put on her collar, wrinkled up her features generally as she shook out the handkerchief, whose embroidery was as irritating to her nose as the present mission was to her feelings; and when she had squeezed her hands into tight gloves with two buttons and tassel, as the last touch of elegance, she turned to Amy with an imbecile expression of countenance, saying meekly, –

"I'm perfectly miserable; but if you consider me presentable, I die happy."

"You are highly satisfactory; turn slowly round, and let me get a careful view." Jo revolved, and Amy gave a touch here and there, then fell back with her head on one side, observing graciously, "Yes, you'll do, your head is all I could ask, for that white bonnet *with* the rose is quite ravishing. Hold back your shoulders, and carry your hands easily, no matter if your gloves do pinch. There's one thing you can do well, Jo, that is, wear a shawl – I can't; but it's very nice to see you, and I'm so glad Aunt March gave you that lovely one; it's simple, but handsome, and those folds over the arm are really artistic. Is the point of my mantle in the middle, and have I looped my dress evenly? I like to show my boots, for my feet *are* pretty, though my nose isn't."

"You are a thing of beauty, and a joy forever," said Jo, looking through her hand with the air of a connoisseur at the blue feather against the gold hair. "Am I to drag my best dress through the dust, or loop it up, please ma'am?"

"Hold it up when you walk, but drop it in the house; the sweeping style suits you best, and you must learn to trail your skirts gracefully. You haven't half buttoned one cuff; do it at once. You'll never look finished if you are not careful about the little details, for they make up the pleasing whole."

Jo sighed, and proceeded to burst the buttons of her glove, in doing up her cuff; but at last both were ready, and sailed away, looking as "pretty as picters," Hannah said, as she hung out of the upper window to watch them.

"Now, Jo dear, the Chesters are very elegant people, so I want you to put on your best deportment. Don't make any of your abrupt remarks, or do anything odd, will you? Just be calm, cool and quiet, – that's safe and lady-like; and you can easily do it for fifteen minutes," said Amy, as they approached the first place, having borrowed the white parasol and been inspected by Meg, with a baby on each arm.

"Let me see; 'Calm, cool and quiet'! yes, I think I can promise that. I've played the part of a prim young lady on the stage, and I'll try it off. My powers are great, as you shall see; so be easy in your mind, my child."

Amy looked relieved, but naughty Jo took her at her word; for, during the first call, she sat with every limb gracefully composed, every fold correctly draped, calm as a summer sea, cool as a snow-bank, and as silent as a sphinx. In vain Mrs. Chester alluded to her "charming novel," and the Misses Chester introduced parties, picnics, the Opera and the fashions; each and all were answered by a smile, a bow, and a demure "Yes" or "No," with the chill on. In vain Amy telegraphed the word "Talk," tried to draw her out, and administered covert pokes with her foot; Jo sat as if blandly unconscious of it all, with deportment like "Maud's" face, "Icily regular, splendidly null."

"What a haughty uninteresting creature that oldest Miss March is!" was the unfortunate audible remark of one of the ladies, as the door closed upon their guests. Jo laughed noiselessly all through the hall, but Amy looked disgusted at the failure of her instructions, and very naturally laid the blame on Jo.

"How could you mistake me so? I merely meant you to be properly dignified and composed, and you made yourself a perfect stock and stone. Try to be sociable at the Lambs; gossip as other girls do, and be interested in dress, and flirtations, and whatever nonsense comes up. They move in the best society, are valuable persons for us to know, and I wouldn't fail to make a good impression there for anything."

"I'll be agreeable; I'll gossip and giggle, and have horrors and raptures over any trifle you like. I rather enjoy this, and now I'll imitate what is called 'a charming girl'; I can do it, for I have May Chester as a model, and I'll improve upon her. See if the Lambs don't say, 'What a lively, nice creature that Jo March is!'"

Amy felt anxious, as well she might, for when Jo turned freakish there was no knowing where she would stop. Amy's face was a study when she saw her sister skim into the next drawing-room, kiss all the young ladies with effusion, beam graciously upon the young gentlemen, and join in the chat with a spirit which amazed the beholder. Amy was taken possession of by Mrs. Lamb, with whom she was a favorite, and forced to hear a long account of Lucretia's last attack, while three delightful young gentlemen hovered near, waiting for a pause when they might rush in and rescue her. So situated she was powerless to check Jo, who seemed possessed by a spirit of mischief, and talked away as volubly as the old lady. A knot of heads gathered about her, and Amy strained her ears to hear what was going on; for broken sentences filled her with alarm, round eyes and uplifted hands tormented her with curiosity, and frequent peals of laughter made her wild to share the fun. One may imagine her suffering on overhearing fragments of this sort of conversation:–

"She rides splendidly, – who taught her?"

"No one; she used to practise mounting, holding the reins, and sitting straight on an old saddle in a tree. Now she rides anything, for she don't know what fear is, and the stable-man lets her have horses cheap, because she trains them to carry ladies so well. She has such a passion for it, I often tell her if everything else fails she can be a pretty horse-breaker, and get her living so."

At this awful speech Amy contained herself with difficulty, for the impression was being given that she was rather a fast young lady, which was her especial aversion. But what could she do? for the old lady was in the middle of her story, and long before it was done Jo was off again, making more droll revelations, and committing still more fearful blunders.

"Yes, Amy was in despair that day, for all the good beasts were gone, and of three left, one was lame, one blind, and the other so balky that you had to put dirt in his mouth before he would start. Nice animal for a pleasure party, wasn't it?"

"Which did she choose?" asked one of the laughing gentlemen, who enjoyed the subject.

"None of them; she heard of a young horse at the farm-house over the river, and, though a lady had never ridden him, she resolved to try, because he was handsome and spirited. Her struggles were really pathetic; there was no one to bring the horse to the saddle, so she took the saddle to the horse. My dear creature, she actually rowed it over the river, put it on her head, and marched up to the barn, to the utter amazement of the old man!"

"Did she ride the horse?"

"Of course she did, and had a capital time. I expected to see her brought home in fragments, but she managed him perfectly, and was the life of the party."

"Well, I call that plucky!" and young Mr. Lamb turned an approving glance upon Amy, wondering what his mother could be saying to make the girl look so red and uncomfortable.

She was still redder and more uncomfortable a moment after, when a sudden turn in the conversation introduced the subject of dress. One of the young ladies asked Jo where she got the pretty drab hat she wore to the picnic; and stupid Jo, instead of mentioning the place where it was bought two years ago, must needs answer, with unnecessary frankness, "Oh, Amy painted it; you can't buy those soft shades, so we paint ours any color we like. It's a great comfort to have an artistic sister."

"Isn't that an original idea?" cried Miss Lamb, who found Jo great fun.

"That's nothing compared to some of her brilliant performances. There's nothing the child can't do. Why, she wanted a pair of blue boots for Sallie's party, so she just painted her soiled white ones the loveliest shade of sky-blue you ever saw, and they looked exactly like satin," added Jo, with an air of pride in her sister's accomplishments that exasperated Amy till she felt that it would be a relief to throw her card-case at her.

"We read a story of yours the other day, and enjoyed it very much," observed the elder Miss Lamb, wishing to compliment the literary lady, who did not look the character just then, it must be confessed. Any mention of her "works" always had a bad effect upon Jo, who either grew rigid and looked offended, or changed the subject with a *brusque* remark, as now. "Sorry you could find nothing better to read. I write that rubbish because it sells, and ordinary people like it. Are you going to New York this winter?"

As Miss Lamb had "enjoyed" the story, this speech was not exactly grateful or complimentary. The minute it was made Jo saw her mistake; but, fearing to make the matter worse, suddenly remembered that it was for her to make the first move toward departure, and did so with an abruptness that left three people with half-finished sentences in their mouths.

"Amy, we *must* go. *Good*-by, dear; *do* come and see us; we are *pining* for a visit. I don't dare to ask *you*, Mr. Lamb; but if you *should* come, I don't think I shall have the heart to send you away."

Jo said this with such a droll imitation of May Chester's gushing style, that Amy got out of the room as rapidly as possible, feeling a strong desire to laugh and cry at the same time.

"Didn't I do that well?" asked Jo, with a satisfied air, as they walked away.

"Nothing could have been worse," was Amy's crushing reply. "What possessed you to tell those stories about my saddle, and the hats and boots, and all the rest of it?"

"Why, it's funny, and amuses people. They know we are poor, so it's no use pretending that we have grooms, buy three or four hats a season, and have things as easy and fine as they do."

"You needn't go and tell them all our little shifts, and expose our poverty in that perfectly unnecessary way. You haven't a bit of proper pride, and never will learn when to hold your tongue, and when to speak," said Amy despairingly.

Poor Jo looked abashed, and silently chafed the end of her nose with the stiff handkerchief, as if performing a penance for her misdemeanors.

"How shall I behave here?" she asked, as they approached the third mansion.

"Just as you please; I wash my hands of you," was Amy's short answer.

"Then I'll enjoy myself. The boys are at home, and we'll have a comfortable time. Goodness knows I need a little change, for elegance has a bad effect upon my constitution," returned Jo, gruffly, being disturbed by her failures to suit.

An enthusiastic welcome from three big boys and several pretty children, speedily soothed her ruffled feelings; and, leaving Amy to entertain the hostess and Mr. Tudor, who happened to be calling likewise, Jo devoted herself to the young folks, and found the change refreshing. She listened to college stories with deep interest, caressed pointers and poodles without a murmur, agreed heartily that "Tom Brown was a brick," regardless of the improper form of praise; and when one lad proposed a visit to his turtle-tank, she went with an alacrity which caused mamma to smile upon her, as that motherly lady settled the cap, which was left in a ruinous condition by filial hugs, – bear-like but affectionate, – and dearer to her than the most faultless *coiffure* from the hands of an inspired Frenchwoman.

Leaving her sister to her own devices, Amy proceeded to enjoy herself to her heart's content. Mr. Tudor's uncle had married an English lady who was third cousin to a living lord, and Amy regarded the whole family with great respect. For, in spite of her American birth and breeding, she possessed that reverence for titles which haunts the best of us, – that unacknowledged loyalty to the early faith in kings which set the most democratic nation under the sun in a ferment at the coming of a royal yellow-haired laddie, some years ago, and which still has something to do with the love the young country bears the old, – like that of a big son for an imperious little mother, who held him while she could, and let him go with a farewell scolding when he rebelled. But even the satisfaction of talking with a distant connection of the British nobility did not render Amy forgetful of time; and, when the proper number of minutes had passed, she reluctantly tore herself from this aristocratic society, and looked about for Jo, – fervently hoping that her incorrigible sister would not be found in any position which should bring disgrace upon the name of March.

It might have been worse; but Amy considered it bad, for Jo sat on the grass with an encampment of boys about her, and a dirty-footed dog reposing on the skirt of her state and festival dress, as she related one of Laurie's pranks to her admiring audience. One small child was poking turtles with Amy's cherished parasol, a second was eating gingerbread over Jo's best bonnet, and a third playing ball with her gloves. But all were enjoying themselves; and when Jo collected her damaged property to go, her escort accompanied her, begging her to come again, "it was such fun to hear about Laurie's larks."

"Capital boys, aren't they? I feel quite young and brisk again after that," said Jo, strolling along with her hands behind her, partly from habit, partly to conceal the bespattered parasol.

"Why do you always avoid Mr. Tudor?" asked Amy, wisely refraining from any comment upon Jo's dilapidated appearance.

"Don't like him; he puts on airs, snubs his sisters, worries his father, and don't speak respectfully of his mother. Laurie says he is fast, and I don't consider him a desirable acquaintance; so I let him alone."

"You might treat him civilly, at least. You gave him a cool nod; and just now you bowed and smiled in the politest way to Tommy Chamberlain, whose father keeps a grocery store. If you had just reversed the nod and the bow, it would have been right," said Amy, reprovingly.

"No, it wouldn't," returned perverse Jo; "I neither like, respect, nor admire Tudor, though his grandfather's uncle's nephew's niece *was* third cousin to a lord. Tommy is poor, and bashful, and good, and very clever; I think well of him, and like to show that I do, for he *is* a gentleman in spite of the brown paper parcels."

"It's no use trying to argue with you," began Amy.

"Not the least, my dear," cut in Jo; "so let us look amiable and drop a card here, as the Kings are evidently out, for which I'm deeply grateful."

The family card-case having done its duty, the girls walked on, and Jo uttered another thanksgiving on reaching the fifth house, and being told that the young ladies were engaged.

"Now let us go home, and never mind Aunt March to-day. We can run down there any time, and it's really a pity to trail through the dust in our best bibs and tuckers, when we are tired and cross."

"Speak for yourself, if you please; aunt likes to have us pay her the compliment of coming in style, and making a formal call; it's a little thing to do, but it gives her pleasure, and I don't believe it will hurt your things half so much as letting dirty dogs and clumping boys spoil them. Stoop down, and let me take the crumbs off of your bonnet."

"What a good girl you are, Amy," said Jo, with a repentant glance from her own damaged costume to that of her sister, which was fresh and spotless still. "I wish it was as easy for me to do little things to please people, as it is for you. I think of them, but it takes too much time to do them; so I wait for a chance to confer a big favor, and let the small ones slip; but they tell best in the end, I guess."

Amy smiled, and was mollified at once, saying with a maternal air, –

"Women should learn to be agreeable, particularly poor ones; for they have no other way of repaying the kindnesses they receive. If you'd remember that, and practise it, you'd be better liked than I am, because there is more of you."

"I'm a crotchety old thing, and always shall be; but I'm willing to own that you are right; only it's easier for me to risk my life for a person than to be pleasant to them when I don't feel like it. It's a great misfortune to have such strong likes and dislikes, isn't it?"

"It's a greater not to be able to hide them. I don't mind saying that I don't approve of Tudor any more than you do; but I'm not called upon to tell him so; neither are you, and there is no use in making yourself disagreeable because he is."

"But I think girls ought to show when they disapprove of young men; and how can they do it except by their manners? Preaching don't do any good, as I know to my sorrow, since I've had Teddy to manage; but there are many little ways in which I can influence him without a word, and I say we *ought* to do it to others if we can."

"Teddy is a remarkable boy, and can't be taken as a sample of other boys," said Amy, in a tone of solemn conviction, which would have convulsed the "remarkable boy," if he had heard it. "If we were belles, or women of wealth and position, we might do something, perhaps; but for us to frown at one set of young gentlemen, because we don't approve of them, and smile upon another set, because we do, wouldn't have a particle of effect, and we should only be considered odd and Puritanical."

"So we are to countenance things and people which we detest, merely because we are not belles and millionaires, are we? That's a nice sort of morality."

"I can't argue about it, I only know that it's the way of the world; and people who set themselves against it, only get laughed at for their pains. I don't like reformers, and I hope you will never try to be one."

"I do like them, and I shall be one if I can; for in spite of the laughing, the world would never get on without them. We can't agree about that, for you belong to the old set, and I to the new; you will get on the best, but I shall have the liveliest time of it. I should rather enjoy the brickbats and hooting, I think."

"Well, compose yourself now, and don't worry aunt with your new ideas."

"I'll try not to, but I'm always possessed to burst out with some particularly blunt speech or revolutionary sentiment before her; it's my doom, and I can't help it."

They found Aunt Carrol with the old lady, both absorbed in some very interesting subject; but they dropped it as the girls came in, with a conscious look which betrayed that they had been talking about their nieces. Jo was not in a good humor, and the perverse fit returned; but Amy, who had virtuously done her duty, kept her temper, and pleased everybody, was in a most angelic frame of mind. This amiable spirit was felt at once, and both the aunts "my dear'd" her affectionately, looking what they afterwards said emphatically, – "That child improves every day."

"Are you going to help about the fair, dear?" asked Mrs. Carrol, as Amy sat down beside her with the confiding air elderly people like so well in the young.

"Yes, aunt, Mrs. Chester asked me if I would, and I offered to tend a table, as I have nothing but my time to give."

"I'm not," put in Jo, decidedly; "I hate to be patronized, and the Chesters think it's a great favor to allow us to help with their highly connected fair. I wonder you consented, Amy – they only want you to work."

"I am willing to work, – it's for the Freedmen as well as the Chesters, and I think it very kind of them to let me share the labor and the fun. Patronage don't trouble me when it is well meant."

"Quite right and proper; I like your grateful spirit, my dear; it's a pleasure to help people who appreciate our efforts; some don't, and that is trying," observed Aunt March, looking over her spectacles at Jo, who sat apart rocking herself with a somewhat morose expression.

If Jo had only known what a great happiness was wavering in the balance of one of them, she would have turned dove-like in a minute; but, unfortunately, we don't have windows in our breasts, and cannot see what goes on in the minds of our friends; better for us that we cannot as a general thing, but now and then it would be such a comfort – such a saving of time and temper. By her next speech, Jo deprived herself of several years of pleasure, and received a timely lesson in the art of holding her tongue.

"I don't like favors; they oppress and make me feel like a slave; I'd rather do everything for myself, and be perfectly independent."

"Ahem!" coughed Aunt Carrol, softly, with a look at Aunt March.

"I told you so." said Aunt March, with a decided nod to Aunt Carrol.

Mercifully unconscious of what she had done, Jo sat with her nose in the air, and a revolutionary aspect, which was anything but inviting.

"Do you speak French, dear?" asked Mrs. Carrol, laying her hand on Amy's.

"Pretty well, thanks to Aunt March, who lets Esther talk to me as often as I like," replied Amy, with a grateful look, which caused the old lady to smile affably.

"How are you about languages?" asked Mrs. Carrol of Jo.

"Don't know a word; I'm very stupid about studying anything; can't bear French, it's such a slippery, silly sort of language," was the *brusque* reply.

Another look passed between the ladies, and Aunt March said to Amy, "You are quite strong and well, now dear, I believe? Eyes don't trouble you any more, do they?"

"Not at all, thank you, ma'am; I'm very well, and mean to do great things next winter, so that I may be ready for Rome, whenever that joyful time arrives."

"Good girl! you deserve to go, and I'm sure you will some day," said Aunt March, with an approving pat on the head, as Amy picked up her ball for her.

"Cross patch, draw the latch,
Sit by the fire and spin,"

squalled Polly, bending down from his perch on the back of her chair, to peep into Jo's face, with such a comical air of impertinent inquiry, that it was impossible to help laughing.

"Most observing bird," said the old lady.

"Come and take a walk, my dear?" cried Polly, hopping toward the china-closet, with a look suggestive of lump-sugar.

"Thank you, I will – come, Amy," and Jo brought the visit to an end, feeling, more strongly than ever, that calls did have a bad effect upon her constitution. She shook hands in a gentlemanly manner, but Amy kissed both the aunts, and the girls departed, leaving behind them the impression of shadow and sunshine; which impression caused Aunt March to say, as they vanished, —

"You'd better do it, Mary; I'll supply the money," and Aunt Carrol to reply decidedly, "I certainly will, if her father and mother consent."

CHAPTER THIRTY

CONSEQUENCES

~

Mrs. Chester's fair was so very elegant and select, that it was considered a great honor by the young ladies of the neighborhood to be invited to take a table, and every one was much interested in the matter. Amy was asked, but Jo was not, which was fortunate for all parties, as her elbows were decidedly akimbo at this period of her life, and it took a good many hard knocks to teach her how to get on easily. The "haughty, uninteresting creature" was let severely alone; but Amy's talent and taste were duly complimented by the offer of the Art table, and she exerted herself to prepare and secure appropriate and valuable contributions to it.

Everything went on smoothly till the day before the fair opened; then there occurred one of the little skirmishes which it is almost impossible to avoid, when some five-and-twenty women, old and young, with all their private piques and prejudices, try to work together.

May Chester was rather jealous of Amy because the latter was a greater favorite than herself; and, just at this time, several trifling circumstances occurred to increase the feeling. Amy's dainty pen-and-ink work entirely eclipsed May's painted vases; that was one thorn; then the all-conquering Tudor had danced four times with Amy, at a late party, and only once with May; that was thorn number two; but the chief grievance that rankled in her soul, and gave her an excuse for her unfriendly conduct, was a rumor which some obliging gossip had whispered to her, that the March girls had made fun of her at the Lambs. All the blame of this should have fallen upon Jo, for her naughty imitation had been too life-like to escape detection, and the frolicksome Lambs had permitted the joke to escape. No hint of this had reached the culprits, however, and Amy's dismay can be imagined, when, the very evening before the fair, as she was putting her last touches to her pretty table, Mrs. Chester, who, of course, resented the supposed ridicule of her daughter, said in a bland tone, but with a cold look, –

"I find, dear, that there is some feeling among the young ladies about my giving this table to any one but my girls. As this is the most prominent, and some say the most attractive table of all – and they are the chief getters-up of the fair – it is thought best for them to take this place. I'm sorry, but I know you are too sincerely interested in the cause to mind a little personal disappointment, and you shall have another table if you like."

Mrs. Chester had fancied beforehand that it would be easy to deliver this little speech; but when the time came, she found it rather difficult to utter it naturally, with Amy's unsuspicious eyes looking straight at her, full of surprise and trouble.

Amy felt that there was something behind this, but could not guess what, and said quietly – feeling hurt, and showing that she did, –

"Perhaps you had rather I took no table at all?"

"Now, my dear, don't have any ill feeling, I beg; it's merely a matter of expediency, you see; my girls will naturally take the lead, and this table is considered their proper place. *I* think it very appropriate to you, and feel very grateful for your efforts to make it so pretty; but we must give up our private wishes, of course, and I will see that you have a good place elsewhere. Wouldn't you like the flower-table? The little girls undertook it, but they are discouraged. You could make a charming thing of it, and the flower-table is always attractive, you know."

"Especially to gentlemen," added May, with a look which enlightened Amy as to one cause of her sudden fall from favor. She colored angrily, but took no other notice of that girlish sarcasm, and answered with unexpected amiability, –

"It shall be as you please, Mrs. Chester; I'll give up my place here at once, and attend to the flowers, if you like."

"You can put your own things on your own table, if you prefer," began May, feeling a little conscience-stricken, as she looked at the pretty racks, the painted shells, and quaint illuminations Amy had so carefully and so gracefully arranged. She meant it kindly, but Amy mistook her meaning, and said quickly, –

"Oh, certainly, if they are in your way;" and sweeping her contributions into her apron, pell-mell, she walked off, feeling that herself and her works of art had been insulted past forgiveness.

"Now she's mad. Oh dear, I wish I hadn't asked you to speak, mamma," said May, looking disconsolately at the empty spaces on her table.

"Girls' quarrels are soon over," returned her mother, feeling a trifle ashamed of her own part in this one, as well she might.

The little girls hailed Amy and her treasures with delight, which cordial reception somewhat soothed her perturbed spirit, and she fell to work, determined to succeed florally, if she could not artistically. But everything seemed against her; it was late, and she was tired; every one was too busy with their own affairs to help her, and the little girls were only hindrances, for the dears fussed and chattered like so many magpies, making a great deal of confusion in their artless efforts to preserve the most perfect order. The evergreen arch wouldn't stay firm after she got it up, but wiggled and threatened to tumble down on her head when the hanging baskets were filled; her best tile got a splash of water, which left a sepia tear on the cupid's cheek; she bruised her hands with hammering, and got cold working in a draught, which last affliction filled her with apprehensions for the morrow. Any girl-reader who has suffered like afflictions, will sympathize with poor Amy, and wish her well through with her task.

There was great indignation at home when she told her story that evening. Her mother said it was a shame, but told her she had done right.

Beth declared she wouldn't go to the old fair at all, and Jo demanded why she didn't take all her pretty things and leave those mean people to get on without her.

"Because they are mean is no reason why I should be. I hate such things; and though I think I've a right to be hurt, I don't intend to show it. They will feel that more than angry speeches or huffy actions, won't they, Marmee?"

"That's the right spirit, my dear; a kiss for a blow is always best, though it's not very easy to give it, sometimes," said her mother, with the air of one who had learned the difference between preaching and practising.

In spite of various very natural temptations to resent and retaliate, Amy adhered to her resolution all the next day, bent on conquering her enemy by kindness. She began well, thanks to a silent reminder that came to her unexpectedly, but most opportunely. As she arranged her table that morning, while the little girls were in an ante-room filling the baskets, she took up her pet production, a little book, the antique cover of which her father had found among his treasures, and in which, on leaves of vellum, she had beautifully illuminated different texts. As she turned the pages, rich in dainty devices, with very pardonable pride, her eye fell upon one verse that made her stop and think. Framed in a brilliant scroll-work of scarlet, blue and gold, with little spirits of good-will helping one another up and down among the thorns and flowers, were the words, "Thou shalt love thy neighbor as thyself."

"I ought, but I don't," thought Amy, as her eye went from the bright page to May's discontented face behind the big vases, that could not hide the vacancies her pretty work had once filled. Amy stood a minute, turning the leaves in her hand, reading on each some sweet rebuke for all her heart-burnings and uncharitableness of spirit. Many wise and true sermons are preached us every day by unconscious ministers in street, school, office, or home; even a fair-table may become a pulpit, if it can offer the good and helpful words which are never out of season. Amy's conscience preached her a little sermon from that text, then and there; and she did what many of us don't always do — took the sermon to heart, and straightway put it in practice.

A group of girls were standing about May's table, admiring the pretty things, and talking over the change of saleswomen. They dropped their voices, but Amy knew they were speaking of her, hearing one side of the story, and judging accordingly. It was not pleasant, but a better spirit had come over her, and, presently, a chance offered for proving it. She heard May say, sorrowfully, –

"It's too bad, for there is no time to make other things, and I don't want to fill up with odds and ends. The table was just complete then – now it's spoilt."

"I dare say she'd put them back if you asked her," suggested some one.

"How could I, after all the fuss;" began May, but she did not finish, for Amy's voice came across the hall, saying pleasantly, –

"You may have them, and welcome, without asking, if you want them. I was just thinking I'd offer to put them back, for they belong to your table rather than mine. Here they are; please take them, and forgive me if I was hasty in carrying them away last night."

As she spoke, Amy returned her contribution with a nod and a smile, and hurried away again, feeling that it was easier to do a friendly thing than it was to stay and be thanked for it.

"Now I call that lovely of her, don't you?" cried one girl.

May's answer was inaudible; but another young lady, whose temper was evidently a little soured by making lemonade, added, with a disagreeable laugh, "Very lovely; for she knew she wouldn't sell them at her own table."

Now that was hard; when we make little sacrifices we like to have them appreciated, at least; and for a minute Amy was sorry she had done it, feeling that virtue was not always its own reward. But it is, – as she presently discovered; for her spirits began to rise, and her table to blossom under her skilful hands; the girls were very kind, and that one little act seemed to have cleared the atmosphere amazingly.

It was a very long day, and a hard one to Amy, as she sat behind her table often quite alone, for the little girls deserted very soon; few cared to buy flowers in summer, and her bouquets began to droop long before night.

The Art table *was* the most attractive in the room; there was a crowd about it all day long, and the tenders were constantly flying to and fro with important faces and rattling money boxes. Amy often looked wistfully across, longing to be there, where she felt at home and happy, instead of in a corner with nothing to do. It might seem no hardship to some of us; but to a pretty, blithe young girl, it was not only tedious, but very trying; and the thought of being found there in the evening by her family, and Laurie and his friends, made it a real martyrdom.

She did not go home till night, and then she looked so pale and quiet that they knew the day had been a hard one, though she made no complaint, and did not even tell what she had done. Her mother gave her an extra cordial cup of tea, Beth helped her dress, and made a charming little wreath for her hair, while Jo astonished her family by getting herself up with unusual care, and hinting, darkly, that the tables were about to be turned.

"Don't do anything rude, pray, Jo; I won't have any fuss made, so let it all pass, and behave yourself," begged Amy, as she departed early, hoping to find a reinforcement of flowers to refresh her poor little table.

"I merely intend to make myself entrancingly agreeable to every one I know, and to keep them in your corner as long as possible. Teddy and his boys will lend a hand, and we'll have a good time yet," returned Jo, leaning over the gate to watch for Laurie. Presently the familiar tramp was heard in the dusk, and she ran out to meet him.

"Is that my boy?"

"As sure as this is my girl!" and Laurie tucked her hand under his arm with the air of a man whose very wish was gratified.

"Oh, Teddy, such doings!" and Jo told Amy's wrongs with sisterly zeal.

"A flock of our fellows are going to drive over by and by, and I'll be hanged if I don't make them buy every flower she's got, and camp down before her table afterward," said Laurie, espousing her cause with warmth.

"The flowers are not at all nice, Amy says, and the fresh ones may not arrive in time. I don't wish to be unjust or suspicious, but I shouldn't wonder if they never came at all. When people do one thing they are very likely to do another," observed Jo, in a disgusted tone.

"Didn't Hayes give you the best out of our gardens? I told him to."

"I didn't know that; he forgot, I suppose; and, as your grandpa was poorly, I didn't like to worry him by asking, though I did want some."

"Now, Jo, how could you think there was any need of asking! They are just as much yours as mine; don't we always go halves in everything?" began Laurie, in the tone that always made Jo turn thorny.

"Gracious! I hope not! half of some of your things wouldn't suit me at all. But we mustn't stand philandering here; I've got to help Amy, so you go and make yourself splendid; and if you'll be so very kind as to let Hayes take a few nice flowers up to the Hall, I'll bless you forever."

"Couldn't you do it now?" asked Laurie, so suggestively that Jo shut the gate in his face with inhospitable haste, and called through the bars, "Go away, Teddy; I'm busy."

Thanks to the conspirators, the tables *were* turned that night, for Hayes sent a wilderness of flowers, with a lovely basket arranged in his best manner for a center-piece; then the March family turned out *en masse*, and Jo exerted herself to some purpose, for people not only came, but stayed, laughing at her nonsense, admiring Amy's taste, and apparently enjoying themselves very much. Laurie and his friends gallantly threw themselves into the breach, bought up the bouquets, encamped before the table, and made that corner the liveliest spot in the room. Amy was in her element now, and, out of gratitude, if nothing more, was as sprightly and gracious as possible, – coming to the conclusion, about that time, that virtue *was* its own reward, after all.

Jo behaved herself with exemplary propriety; and when Amy was happily surrounded by her guard of honor, Jo circulated about the hall, picking up various bits of gossip, which enlightened her upon the subject of the Chester change of base. She reproached herself for her share of the ill-feeling, and resolved to exonerate Amy as soon as possible; she also discovered what Amy had done about the things that morning, and considered her a model of magnanimity. As she passed the Art table, she glanced over it for her sister's things, but saw no signs of them. "Tucked away out of sight, I dare say," thought Jo, who could forgive her own wrongs, but hotly resented any insult offered to her family.

"Good evening, Miss Jo; how does Amy get on?" asked May, with a conciliatory air, – for she wanted to show that she also could be generous.

"She has sold everything she had that was worth selling, and now she is enjoying herself. The flower-table is always attractive, you know, 'especially to gentlemen.'"

Jo *couldn't* resist giving that little slap, but May took it so meekly she regretted it a minute after, and fell to praising the great vases, which still remained unsold.

"Is Amy's illumination anywhere about? I took a fancy to buy that for father," said Jo, very anxious to learn the fate of her sister's work.

"Everything of Amy's sold long ago; I took care that the right people saw them, and they made a nice little sum of money for us," returned May, who had overcome sundry small temptations as well as Amy that day.

Much gratified, Jo rushed back to tell the good news; and Amy looked both touched and surprised by the report of May's words and manners.

"Now, gentlemen, I want you to go and do your duty by the other tables as generously as you have by mine — especially the Art table," she said, ordering out "Teddy's Own," as the girls called the college friends.

"'Charge, Chester, charge!' is the motto for that table; but do your duty like men, and you'll get your money's worth of *art* in every sense of the word," said the irrepressible Jo, as the devoted phalanx prepared to take the field.

"To hear is to obey, but March is fairer far than May," said little Parker, making a frantic effort to be both witty and tender, and getting promptly quenched by Laurie, who said: "Very well, my son, for a small boy!" and walked him off with a paternal pat on the head.

"Buy the vases," whispered Amy to Laurie, as a final heaping of coals of fire on her enemy's head.

To May's great delight, Mr. Laurence not only bought the vases, but pervaded the hall with one under each arm. The other gentlemen speculated with equal rashness in all sorts of frail trifles, and wandered helplessly about afterward, burdened with wax flowers, painted fans, filigree portfolios, and other useful and appropriate purchases.

Aunt Carrol was there, heard the story, looked pleased, and said something to Mrs. March in a corner, which made the latter lady beam with satisfaction, and watch Amy with a face full of mingled pride and anxiety, though she did not betray the cause of her pleasure till several days later.

The fair was pronounced a success; and when May bid Amy "good-night," she did not "gush," as usual, but gave her an affectionate kiss, and a look which said, "Forgive and forget." That satisfied Amy; and when she got home she found the vases paraded on the parlor chimney-piece, with a great bouquet in each. "The reward of merit for a magnanimous March," as Laurie announced with a flourish.

"You've a deal more principle, and generosity, and nobleness of character than I ever gave you credit for, Amy. You've behaved sweetly, and I respect you with all my heart," said Jo, warmly, as they brushed their hair together late that night.

"Yes, we all do, and love her for being so ready to forgive. It must have been dreadfully hard, after working so long, and setting your heart on selling your own pretty things. I don't believe I could have done it as kindly as you did," added Beth, from her pillow.

"Why, girls, you needn't praise me so; I only did as I'd be done by. You laugh at me when I say I want to be a lady, but I mean a true gentlewoman in mind and manners, and I try to do it as far as I know how. I can't explain exactly, but I want to be above the little meannesses, and follies, and faults that spoil so many women. I'm far from it now, but I do my best, and hope in time to be what mother is."

Amy spoke earnestly, and Jo said, with a cordial hug, –

"I understand now what you mean, and I'll never laugh at you again. You are getting on faster than you think, and I'll take lessons of you in true politeness, for you've learned the secret, I believe. Try away, deary, you'll get your reward some day, and no one will be more delighted than I shall."

A week later Amy did get her reward, and poor Jo found it hard to be delighted. A letter came from Aunt Carrol, and Mrs. March's face was illuminated to such a degree when she read it, that Jo and Beth, who were with her, demanded what the glad tidings were.

"Aunt Carrol is going abroad next month, and wants – "

"Me to go with her!" burst in Jo, flying out of her chair in an uncontrollable rapture.

"No, dear, not you, it's Amy."

"Oh, mother! she's too young; it's my turn first; I've wanted it so long – it would do me so much good, and be so altogether splendid – I *must* go."

"I'm afraid it's impossible, Jo; aunt says Amy, decidedly, and it is not for us to dictate when she offers such a favor."

"It's always so; Amy has all the fun, and I have all the work. It isn't fair, oh, it isn't fair!" cried Jo, passionately.

"I'm afraid it is partly your own fault dear. When aunt spoke to me the other day, she regretted your blunt manners and too independent spirit;

and here she writes as if quoting something you had said, – 'I planned at first to ask Jo; but as "favors burden her," and she "hates French," I think I won't venture to invite her. Amy is more docile, will make a good companion for Flo, and receive gratefully any help the trip may give her.'"

"Oh, my tongue, my abominable tongue! why can't I learn to keep it quiet?" groaned Jo, remembering words which had been her undoing. When she had heard the explanation of the quoted phrases, Mrs. March said, sorrowfully, –

"I wish you could have gone, but there is no hope of it this time; so try to bear it cheerfully, and don't sadden Amy's pleasure by reproaches or regrets."

"I'll try," said Jo, winking hard, as she knelt down to pick up the basket she had joyfully upset. "I'll take a leaf out of her book, and try not only to seem glad, but to be so, and not grudge her one minute of happiness; but it won't be easy, for it is a dreadful disappointment;" and poor Jo bedewed the little fat pincushion she held, with several very bitter tears.

"Jo, dear, I'm very selfish, but I couldn't spare you, and I'm glad you ain't going quite yet," whispered Beth, embracing her, basket and all, with such a clinging touch and loving face, that Jo felt comforted in spite of the sharp regret that made her want to box her own ears, and humbly beg Aunt Carrol to burden her with this favor, and see how gratefully she would bear it.

By the time Amy came in, Jo was able to take her part in the family jubilation; not quite as heartily as usual, perhaps, but without repinings at Amy's good fortune. The young lady herself received the news as tidings of great joy, went about in a solemn sort of rapture, and began to sort her colors and pack her pencils that evening, leaving such trifles as clothes, money, and passports to those less absorbed in visions of art than herself.

"It isn't a mere pleasure trip to me, girls," she said impressively, as she scraped her best palette. "It will decide my career; for if I have any genius, I shall find it out in Rome, and will do something to prove it."

"Suppose you haven't?" said Jo, sewing away, with red eyes, at the new collars which were to be handed over to Amy.

"Then I shall come home and teach drawing for my living," replied the aspirant for fame, with philosophic composure; but she made a wry face at the prospect, and scratched away at her palette as if bent on vigorous measures before she gave up her hopes.

"No, you won't; you hate hard work, and you'll marry some rich man, and come home to sit in the lap of luxury all your days," said Jo.

"Your predictions sometimes come to pass, but I don't believe that one will. I'm sure I wish it would, for if I can't be an artist myself, I should like to be able to help those who are," said Amy, smiling, as if the part of Lady Bountiful would suit her better than that of a poor drawing teacher.

"Hum!" said Jo, with a sigh; "if you wish it you'll have it, for your wishes are always granted – mine never."

"Would you like to go?" asked Amy, thoughtfully flattening her nose with her knife.

"Rather!"

"Well, in a year or two I'll send for you, and we'll dig in the Forum for relics, and carry out all the plans we've made so many times."

"Thank you; I'll remind you of your promise when that joyful day comes, if it ever does," returned Jo, accepting the vague but magnificent offer as gratefully as she could.

There was not much time for preparation, and the house was in a ferment till Amy was off. Jo bore up very well till the last flutter of blue ribbon vanished, when she retired to her refuge, the garret, and cried till she couldn't cry any more. Amy likewise bore up stoutly till the steamer sailed; then, just as the gangway was about to be withdrawn, it suddenly came over her, that a whole ocean was soon to roll between her and those who loved her best, and she clung to Laurie, the last lingerer, saying with a sob, –

"Oh, take care of them for me; and if anything should happen – "

"I will, dear, I will; and if anything happens, I'll come and comfort you," whispered Laurie, little dreaming how soon he would be called upon to keep his word.

So Amy sailed away to find the old world, which is always new and beautiful to young eyes, while her father and friend watched her from the shore, fervently hoping that none but gentle fortunes would befall the happy-hearted girl, who waved her hand to them till they could see nothing but the summer sunshine dazzling on the sea.

CHAPTER THIRTY-ONE

OUR FOREIGN
CORRESPONDENT

~

*D*EAREST PEOPLE:

Here I really sit at a front window of the Bath Hotel, Piccadilly. It's not a fashionable place, but uncle stopped here years ago, and won't go anywhere else; however, we don't mean to stay long, so it's no great matter. Oh, I can't begin to tell you how I enjoy it all; I never can, so I'll only give you bits out of my note-book, for I've done nothing but sketch and scribble since I started.

I sent a line from Halifax when I felt pretty miserable, but after that I got on delightfully, seldom ill, on deck all day, with plenty of pleasant people to amuse me. Every one was very kind to me, especially the officers. Don't laugh, Jo, gentlemen really are very necessary aboard ship, to hold on to, or to wait upon one; and as they have nothing to do, it's a mercy to make them useful, otherwise they would smoke themselves to death, I'm afraid.

Aunt and Flo were poorly all the way, and liked to be let alone, so when I had done what I could for them, I went and enjoyed myself. Such walks on deck, such sunsets, such splendid air and waves! It was almost as exciting as riding a fast horse, when we went rushing on so grandly. I wish Beth could have come, it would have done her so much good; as for Jo, she would have gone up and sat on the main-top jib, or whatever the high thing is called, made friends with the engineers, and tooted on the Captain's speaking trumpet, she'd have been in such a state of rapture.

It was all heavenly, but I was glad to see the Irish coast, and found it very lovely, so green and sunny, with brown cabins here and there, ruins on some of the hills, and gentlemen's country seats in the valleys, with deer feeding in the parks. It was early in the morning, but I didn't regret getting up to see it, for the bay was full of little boats, the shore *so* picturesque, and a rosy sky over head; I never shall forget it.

At Queenstown one of my new acquaintances left us, – Mr. Lennox, – and when I said something about the Lakes of Killarney, he sighed, and sung, with a look at me, –

> *Oh, have you ever heard of Kate Kearney,*
> *She lives on the banks of Killarney;*
> > *From the glance of her eye,*
> > *Shun danger and fly,*
> *For fatal's the glance of Kate Kearney.*

Wasn't that nonsensical?

We only stopped at Liverpool a few hours. It's a dirty, noisy place, and I was glad to leave it. Uncle rushed out and bought a pair of dog-skin gloves, some ugly, thick shoes, and an umbrella, and got shaved *à la* mutton chop, the first thing. Then he flattered himself that he looked like a true Briton; but the first time he had the mud cleaned off his shoes, the little boot-black knew that an American stood in them, and said, with a grin, "There yer har, sir, I've give 'em the latest Yankee shine." It amused uncle immensely. Oh, I *must* tell you what that absurd Lennox did! He got his friend Ward, who came on with us, to order a bouquet for me, and the first thing I saw in my room, was a lovely one, with "Robert Lennox's compliments," on the card. Wasn't that fun, girls? I like travelling.

I never *shall* get to London if I don't hurry. The trip was like riding through a long picture gallery, full of lovely landscapes. The farm-houses were my delight; with thatched roofs, ivy up to the eaves, latticed windows, and stout women with rosy children at the doors. The very cattle looked more tranquil than ours, as they stood knee-deep in clover, and the hens had a contented cluck, as if they never got nervous, like Yankee biddies. Such perfect color I never saw — the grass so green, sky so blue, grain so yellow, woods so dark — I was in a rapture all the way. So was Flo; and we kept bouncing from one side to the other, trying to see everything while we were whisking along at the rate of sixty miles an hour. Aunt was tired, and went to sleep, but uncle read his guide-book, and wouldn't be astonished at anything. This is the way we went on: Amy flying up, — "Oh, that must be Kenilworth, that gray place among the trees!" Flo darting to my window, — "How sweet; we must go there some time, won't we, pa?" Uncle calmly admiring his boots, — "No, my dear, not unless you want beer; that's a brewery."

A pause, — then Flo cried out, "Bless me, there's a gallows and a man going up." "Where, where!" shrieks Amy, staring out at two tall posts with a crossbeam, and some dangling chains. "A colliery," remarks uncle, with a twinkle of the eye. "Here's a lovely flock of lambs all lying down," says Amy. "See, pa, aren't they pretty!" added Flo, sentimentally. "Geese, young ladies," returns uncle, in a tone that keeps us quiet till Flo settles down to enjoy "The Flirtations of Capt. Cavendish," and I have the scenery all to myself.

Of course it rained when we got to London, and there was nothing to be seen but fog and umbrellas. We rested, unpacked, and shopped a little between the showers. Aunt Mary got me some new things, for I came off in such a hurry I wasn't half ready. A sweet white hat and blue feather, a distracting muslin to match, and the loveliest mantle you ever saw. Shopping in Regent Street is perfectly splendid; things seem so cheap — nice ribbons only sixpence a yard. I laid in a stock, but shall get my gloves in Paris. Don't that sound sort of elegant and rich?

Flo and I, for the fun of it, ordered a hansom cab, while aunt and uncle were out, and went for a drive, though we learned afterward that it wasn't the thing for young ladies to ride in them alone. It was so droll! for when we were shut in by the wooden apron the man drove so fast that Flo was frightened, and told me to stop him. But he was up outside behind somewhere, and I couldn't get at him. He didn't hear me call, nor see me flap my parasol in front, and there we were, quite helpless, rattling away, and whirling round corners, at a break-neck pace. At last, in my despair, I saw a little door in the roof, and on poking it open, a red eye appeared, and a beery voice said, –

'Now then, mum?'

I gave my order as soberly as I could, and slamming down the door, with a "Aye, aye, mum," the old thing made his horse walk, as if going to a funeral. I poked again, and said, "A little faster;" then off he went, helter-skelter, as before, and we resigned ourselves to our fate.

To-day was fair, and we went to Hyde Park, close by, for we are more aristocratic than we look. The Duke of Devonshire lives near. I often see his footmen lounging at the back gate; and the Duke of Wellington's house is not far off. Such sights as I saw, my dear! It was as good as Punch, for there were fat dowagers, rolling about in their red and yellow coaches, with gorgeous Jeameses in silk stockings and velvet coats, up behind, and powdered coachmen in front. Smart maids, with the rosiest children I ever saw; handsome girls, looking half asleep; dandies, in queer English hats and lavender kids, lounging about, and tall soldiers, in short red jackets and muffin caps stuck on one side, looking so funy, I longed to sketch them.

Rotten Row means "*Route de Roi,*" or the king's way; but now it's more like a riding school than anything else. The horses are splendid, and the men, especially the grooms, ride well, but the women are stiff, and bounce, which isn't according to our rules. I longed to show them a tearing American gallop, for they trotted solemnly up and down in their scant habits and high hats, looking like the women in a toy Noah's Ark. Every one rides – old men, stout ladies, little children, and the young folks do a deal of flirting here; I saw a pair exchange rosebuds, for it's the thing to wear one in the buttonhole, and I thought it rather a nice little idea.

In the P.M. to Westminster Abbey; but don't expect me to describe it, that's impossible – so I'll only say it was sublime! This evening we are going to see Fechter, which will be an appropriate end to the happiest day of my life.

Midnight.

It's very late, but I can't let my letter go in the morning without telling you what happened last evening. Who do you think came in, as we were at tea? Laurie's English friends, Fred and Frank Vaughn! I was *so* surprised, for I shouldn't have known them, but for the cards. Both are tall fellows, with whiskers; Fred handsome in the English style, and Frank much better, for he only limps slightly, and uses no crutches. They had heard from Laurie where we were to be, and came to ask us to their house, but uncle won't go, so we shall return the call, and see them as we can. They went to the theatre with us, and we did have *such* a good time, for Frank devoted himself to Flo, and Fred and I talked over past, present and future fun as if we had known each other all our days. Tell Beth Frank asked for her, and was sorry to hear of her ill health. Fred laughed when I spoke of Jo, and sent his "respectful compliments to the big hat." Neither of them had forgotten Camp Laurence, or the fun we had there. What ages ago it seems, don't it?

Aunt is tapping on the wall for the third time, so I *must* stop. I really feel like a dissipated London fine lady, writing here so late, with my room full of pretty things, and my head a jumble of parks, theatres, new gowns and gallant creatures, who say "Ah," and twirl their blond mustaches, with the true English lordliness. I long to see you all, and in spite of my nonsense am, as ever, your loving

AMY.

PARIS.

DEAR GIRLS:

In my last I told you about our London visit, — how kind the Vaughns were, and what pleasant parties they made for us. I enjoyed the trips to Hampton Court and the Kensington Museum, more than anything else, — for at Hampton I saw Raphael's Cartoons, and, at the Museum, rooms full of pictures by Turner, Lawrence, Reynolds, Hogarth, and the other great creatures. The day in Richmond Park was charming, — for we had a regular English picnic, — and I had more splendid oaks and groups of deer than I could copy; also heard a nightingale, and saw larks go up. We "did" London to our hearts' content, — thanks to Fred and Frank, — and were sorry to go away; for, though English people are slow to take you in, when they once make up their minds to do it they cannot be outdone in hospitality, *I* think. The Vaughns hope to meet us in Rome next winter, and I shall be dreadfully disappointed if they don't, for Grace and I are great friends, and the boys very nice fellows, – especially Fred.

Well, we were hardly settled here when he turned up again, saying he had come for a holiday, and was going to Switzerland. Aunt looked sober at first, but he was so cool about it she couldn't say a word; and now we get on nicely, and are very glad he came, for he speaks French like a native, and I don't know what we should do without him. Uncle don't know ten words, and insists on talking English very loud, as if that would make people understand him. Aunt's pronunciation is old-fashioned, and Flo and I, though we flattered ourselves that we knew a good deal, find we don't, and are very grateful to have Fred do the *'parley-vooing,'* as uncle calls it.

Such delightful times as we are having! sight-seeing from morning till night! stopping for nice lunches in the gay *cafés*, and meeting with all sorts of droll adventures. Rainy days I spend in the Louvre, revelling in pictures. Jo would turn up her naughty nose at some of the finest, because she has no soul for art; but I have, and I'm cultivating eye and taste as fast as I can. She would like the relics of great people better, but I've seen her Napoleon's cocked hat and gray coat, his baby's cradle and his old toothbrush; also Marie Antoinette's little shoe, the ring of Saint Denis, Charlemagne's sword, and many other interesting things. I'll talk for hours about them when I come, but haven't time to write.

The Palais Royale is a heavenly place, – so full of *bijouterie* and lovely things that I'm nearly distracted because I can't buy them. Fred wanted to get me some, but of course I didn't allow it. Then the Bois and the Champs Elysées are *tres magnifique*. I've seen the imperial family several times, – the Emperor an ugly, hard-looking man, the Empress pale and pretty, but dressed in horrid taste, *I* thought, – purple dress, green hat, and yellow gloves. Little Nap, is a handsome boy, who sits chatting to his tutor, and kisses his hand to the people as he passes in his four-horse barouche, with postilions in red satin jackets, and a mounted guard before and behind.

We often walk in the Tuileries gardens, for they are lovely, though the antique Luxembourg gardens suit me better. Pere la Chaise is very curious, – for many of the tombs are like small rooms, and, looking in, one sees a table, with images or pictures of the dead, and chairs for the mourners to sit in when they come to lament. That is so Frenchy, – *n'est ce pas?*

Our rooms are on the Rue de Rivoli, and, sitting in the balcony, we look up and down the long, brilliant street. It is so pleasant that we spend our evenings talking there, – when too tired with our day's work to go out. Fred is very entertaining, and is altogether the most agreeable young man I ever knew, - except Laurie, – whose manners are more charming. I wish Fred was dark, for I don't fancy light men; however, the Vaughns are very rich, and come of an excellent family, so I won't find fault with their yellow hair, as my own is yellower.

Next week we are off to Germany and Switzerland; and, as we shall travel fast, I shall only be able to give you hasty letters. I keep my diary, and try to "remember correctly and describe clearly all that I see and admire," as father advised. It is good practice for me, and, with my sketch-book, will give you a better idea of my tour than these scribbles.

Adieu; I embrace you tenderly.

Votre Amie.

HEIDELBERG.

MY DEAR MAMMA:

Having a quiet hour before we leave for Berne, I'll try to tell you what has happened, for some of it is very important, as you will see.

The sail up the Rhine was perfect, and I just sat and enjoyed it with all my might. Get father's old guide-books, and read about it; I haven't words beautiful enough to describe it. At Coblentz we had a lovely time, for some students from Bonn, with whom Fred got acquainted on the boat, gave us a serenade. It was a moonlight night, and, about one o'clock, Flo and I were waked by the most delicious music under our windows. We flew up, and hid behind the curtains; but sly peeps showed us Fred and the students singing away down below. It was the most romantic thing I ever saw; the river, the bridge of boats, the great fortress opposite, moonlight everywhere, and music fit to melt a heart of stone.

When they were done we threw down some flowers, and saw them scramble for them, kiss their hands to the invisible ladies, and go laughing away, – to smoke, and drink beer, I suppose. Next morning Fred showed me one of the crumpled flowers in his vest pocket, and looked very sentimental. I laughed at him, and said I didn't throw it, but Flo, – which seemed to disgust him. I'm afraid I'm going to have trouble with that boy, – it begins to look like it.

The baths at Nassau were very gay, so was Baden-Baden, where Fred lost some money, and I scolded him. He needs some one to look after him when Frank is not with him. Kate said once she hoped he'd marry soon, and I quite agree with her that it would be well for him. Frankfort was delightful; I saw Goethe's house, Schiller's statue, and Dannecker's famous "Ariadne." It was very lovely, but I should have enjoyed it more if I had known the story better. I didn't like to ask, as every one knew it, or pretended they did. I wish Jo would tell me all about it; I ought to have read more, for I find I don't know anything, and it mortifies me.

Now comes the serious part, — for it happened here, and Fred is just gone. He has been so kind and jolly that we all got quite fond of him; I never thought of anything but a travelling friendship, till the serenade night. Since then I've begun to feel that the moonlight walks, balcony talks, and daily adventures were something more to him than fun. I haven't flirted, mother, truly, — but remembered what you said to me, and have done my very best. I can't help it if people like me; I don't try to make them and it worries me if I don't care for them, though Jo says I haven't got any heart. Now I know mother will shake her head, and the girls say, "Oh, the mercenary little wretch!" but I've made up my mind, and, if Fred asks me, I shall accept him, though I'm not madly in love. I like him, and we get on comfortably together. He is handsome, young, clever enough, and very rich, — ever so much richer than the Laurences. I don't think his family would object, and I should be very happy, for they are all kind, well-bred, generous people, and they like me. Fred, as the eldest twin, will have the estate, I suppose, — and such a splendid one as it is! A city house, in a fashionable street, — not so showy as our big houses, but twice as comfortable, and full of solid luxury, such as English people believe in. I like it, for it's genuine; I've seen the plate, the family jewels, the old servants, and pictures of the country place with its park, great house, lovely grounds, and fine horses. Oh, it would be all I should ask! and I'd rather have it than any title such as girls snap up so readily, and find nothing behind. I may be mercenary, but I hate poverty, and don't mean to bear it a minute longer than I can help. One of us *must* marry well; Meg didn't, Jo won't, Beth can't, yet, — so I shall, and make everything cosy all round. I wouldn't marry a man I hated or despised. You may be sure of that; and, though Fred is not my model hero, he does very well, and, in time, I should get fond enough of him if he was very fond of me, and let me do just as I liked. So I've been turning the matter over in my mind the last week, – for it was impossible to help seeing Fred liked me. He said nothing, but little things showed it; he never goes with Flo, always gets on my side of the carriage, table, or promenade, looks sentimental when we are alone, and frowns at any one else who ventures to speak to me. Yesterday, at dinner, when an Austrian officer stared at us, and then said something to his friend, – a rakish-looking Baron, – about *"ein wonderschönes Blöndchen,"* Fred looked as fierce as a lion, and cut his meat so savagely, it nearly flew off his plate. He isn't one of the cool, stiff Englishmen, but is rather peppery, for he has Scotch blood in him, as one might guess from his bonnie blue eyes.

Well, last evening we went up to the castle about sunset, – at least all of us but Fred, who was to meet us there after going to the Poste Restante for letters. We had a charming time poking about the ruins, the vaults where the monster tun is, and the beautiful gardens made by the Elector, long ago, for his English wife. I liked the great terrace best, for the view was divine; so, while the rest went to see the rooms inside, I sat there trying to sketch the gray-stone lion's head on the wall, with scarlet woodbine sprays hanging round it. I felt as if I'd got into a romance, sitting there watching the Neckar rolling through the valley, listening to the music of the Austrian band below, and waiting for my lover, – like a real story-book girl. I had a feeling that something was going to happen, and I was ready for it. I didn't feel blushy or quakey, but quite cool, and only a little excited.

By and by I heard Fred's voice, and then he came hurrying through the great arch to find me. He looked so troubled that I forgot all about myself, and asked what the matter was. He said he'd just got a letter begging him to come home, for Frank was very ill; so he was going at once, in the night train, and only had time to say "good-by." I was very sorry for him, and disappointed for myself, – but only for a minute, – because he said, as he shook hands, – and said it in a way that I could not mistake, – "I shall soon come back, – you won't forget me, Amy?"

I didn't promise, but I looked at him and he seemed satisfied, – and there was no time for anything but messages and good-byes, for he was off in an hour, and we all miss him very much. I know he wanted to speak, but I think, from something he once hinted, that he had promised his father not to do anything of the sort yet awhile, – for he is a rash boy, and the old gentleman dreads a foreign daughter-in-law. We shall soon meet in Rome; and then, if I don't change my mind, I'll say "Yes, thank you," when he says, "Will you, please?"

Of course this is all *very private*, but I wished you to know what was going on. Don't be anxious about me; remember I am your "prudent Amy," and be sure I will do nothing rashly. Send me as much advice as you like; I'll use it if I can. I wish I could see you for a good talk, Marmee. Love and trust me.

Ever your

AMY.

CHAPTER THIRTY TWO

TENDER TROUBLES

~

"Jo, I'm anxious about Beth."

"Why, mother, she has seemed unusually well since the babies came."

"It's not her health that troubles me now; it's her spirits. I'm sure there is something on her mind, and I want you to discover what it is."

"What makes you think so, mother?"

"She sits alone a good deal, and doesn't talk to her father as much as she used. I found her crying over the babies the other day. When she sings, the songs are always sad ones, and now and then I see a look in her face that I don't understand. This isn't Beth, and it worries me."

"Have you asked her about it?"

"I have tried once or twice; but she either evaded my questions, or looked so distressed, that I stopped. I never force my children's confidence, and I seldom have to wait for it long."

Mrs. March glanced at Jo as she spoke, but the face opposite seemed quite unconscious of any secret disquietude but Beth's; and, after sewing thoughtfully for a minute, Jo said, –

"I think she is growing up, and so begins to dream dreams, and have hopes, and fears, and fidgets, without knowing why, or being able to explain them. Why, mother, Beth's eighteen; but we don't realize it, and treat her like a child, forgetting she's a woman."

"So she is; dear heart, how fast you do grow up," returned her mother, with a sigh and a smile.

"Can't be helped, Marmee; so you must resign yourself to all sorts of worries, and let your birds hop out of the nest, one by one. I promise never to hop very far, if that is any comfort to you."

"It is a great comfort, Jo; I always feel strong when you are at home, now Meg is gone. Beth is too feeble, and Amy too young to depend upon; but when the tug comes, you are always ready."

"Why, you know I don't mind hard jobs much, and there must always be one scrub in a family. Amy is splendid in fine works, and I'm not; but I feel in my element when all the carpets are to be taken up, or half the family fall sick at once. Amy is distinguishing herself abroad; but if anything is amiss at home, I'm your man."

"I leave Beth to your hands then, for she will open her tender, little heart to her Jo sooner than to any one else. Be very kind, and don't let her think any one watches or talks about her. If she only would get quite strong and cheerful again, I shouldn't have a wish in the world."

"Happy woman! I've got heaps."

"My dear, what are they?"

"I'll settle Bethy's troubles, and then I'll tell you mine. They are not very wearing, so they'll keep;" and Jo stitched away with a wise nod, which set her mother's heart at rest about her, for the present at least.

While apparently absorbed in her own affairs, Jo watched Beth; and, after many conflicting conjectures, finally settled upon one which seemed to explain the change in her. A slight incident gave Jo the clue to the mystery, she thought, and lively fancy, loving heart did the rest. She was affecting to write busily one Saturday afternoon, when she and Beth were alone together; yet, as she scribbled, she kept her eye on her sister, who seemed unusually quiet. Sitting at the window, Beth's work often dropped into her lap, and she leaned her head upon her hand, in a dejected attitude, while her eyes rested on the dull, autumnal landscape. Suddenly some one passed below, whistling like an operatic blackbird, and a voice called out, –

"All serene! Coming in to-night."

Beth started, leaned forward, smiled and nodded, watched the passer-by till his quick tramp died away, then said softly, as if to herself, –

"How strong, and well, and happy that dear boy looks."

"Hum!" said Jo, still intent upon her sister's face; for the bright color faded as quickly as it came, the smile vanished, and presently a tear lay shining on the window ledge. Beth whisked it off, and glanced apprehensively at Jo; but she was scratching away at a tremendous rate, apparently engrossed in "Olympia's Oath." The instant Beth turned, Jo began her watch again, saw Beth's hand go quietly to her eyes more than once, and, in her half-averted face, read a tender sorrow that made her own eyes fill. Fearing to betray herself, she slipped away, murmuring something about needing more paper.

"Mercy on me, Beth loves Laurie!" she said, sitting down in her own room, pale with the shock of the discovery which she believed she had just made. "I never dreamt of such a thing! What *will* mother say? I wonder if he – " there Jo stopped, and turned scarlet with a sudden thought. "If he shouldn't love back again, how dreadful it would be. He must; I'll make him!" and she shook her head threateningly at the picture of the mischievous looking boy laughing at her from the wall. "Oh, dear, we *are* growing up with a vengeance. Here's Meg married, and a ma, Amy flourishing away at Paris, and Beth in love. I'm the only one that has sense enough to keep out of mischief." Jo thought intently for a minute, with her eyes fixed on the picture; then she smoothed out her wrinkled forehead, and said, with a decided nod at the face opposite, – "No, thank you, sir! you're very charming, but you've no more stability than a weather-cock; so you needn't write touching notes, and smile in that insinuating way, for it won't do a bit of good, and I won't have it."

Then she sighed, and fell into a reverie, from which she did not wake till the early twilight sent her down to take new observations, which only confirmed her suspicion. Though Laurie flirted with Amy, and joked with Jo, his manner to Beth had always been peculiarly kind and gentle, but so was everybody's; therefore, no one thought of imagining that he cared more for her than for the others. Indeed, a general impression had prevailed in the family, of late, that "our boy" was getting fonder than ever of Jo, who, however, wouldn't hear a word upon the subject, and scolded violently if any one dared to suggest it. If they had known the various tender passages of the past year, or rather attempts at tender passages, which had been nipped in the bud, they would have had the immense satisfaction of saying, "I told you so." But Jo hated "philandering," and wouldn't allow it, always having a joke or a frown ready at the least sign of impending danger.

When Laurie first went to college, he fell in love about once a month; but these small flames were as brief as ardent, did no damage, and much amused Jo, who took great interest in the alternations of hope, despair, and resignation, which were confided to her in their weekly conferences. But there came a time when Laurie ceased to worship at many shrines, hinted darkly at one all-absorbing passion, and indulged occasionally in Byronic fits of gloom. Then he avoided the tender subject altogether, wrote philosophical notes to Jo, turned studious, and gave out that he was going to "dig," intending to graduate in a blaze of glory. This suited the young lady better than twilight confidences, tender pressures of the hand, and eloquent glances of the eye; for which Jo, brain developed earlier than heart, and she preferred imaginary heroes to real ones, because, when tired of them, the former could be shut up in the tin-kitchen till called for, and the latter were less manageable.

Things were in this state when the grand discovery was made, and Jo watched Laurie that night as she had never done before. If she had not got the new idea into her head, she would have seen nothing unusual in the fact, that Beth was very quiet, and Laurie very kind to her. But having given the rein to her lively fancy, it galloped away with her at a great pace; and common sense, being rather weakened by a long course of romance writing, did not come to the rescue. As usual, Beth lay on the sofa, and Laurie sat in a low chair close by, amusing her with all sorts of gossip; for she depended on her weekly "spin," and he never disappointed her. But that evening, Jo fancied that Beth's eyes rested on the lively, dark face beside her with peculiar pleasure, and that she listened with intense interest to an account of some exciting cricket match, though the phrases, "caught off a tice," "stumped off his ground," and "the leg hit for three," were as intelligible to her as Sanscrit. She also fancied, having set her heart upon seeing it, that she saw a certain increase of gentleness in Laurie's manner, that he dropped his voice now and then, laughed less than usual, was a little absent-minded, and settled the afghan over Beth's feet with an assiduity that was really almost tender.

"Who knows! stranger things have happened," thought Jo, as she fussed about the room. "She will make quite an angel of him, and he will make life delightfully easy and pleasant for the dear, if they only love each other. I don't see how he can help it; and I do believe he would if the rest of us were out of the way."

As every one *was* out of the way but herself, Jo began to feel that she ought to dispose of herself with all speed. But where should she go? and burning to lay herself upon the shrine of sisterly devotion, she sat down to settle that point.

Now the old sofa was a regular patriarch of a sofa — long, broad, well-cushioned and low. A trifle shabby, as well it might be, for the girls had slept and sprawled on it as babies, fished over the back, rode on the arms, and had menageries under it as children, and rested tired heads, dreamed dreams, and listened to tender talk on it as young women. They all loved it, for it was a family refuge, and one corner had always been Jo's favorite lounging place. Among the many pillows that adorned the venerable couch was one, hard, round, covered with prickly horse-hair, and furnished with a knobby button at each end; this repulsive pillow was her especial property, being used as a weapon of defence, a barricade, or a stern preventive of too much slumber.

Laurie knew this pillow well, and had cause to regard it with deep aversion; having been unmercifully pummelled with it in former days, when romping was allowed, and now frequently debarred by it from taking the seat he most coveted, next to Jo in the sofa corner. If "the sausage," as they called it, stood on end, it was a sign that he might approach and repose; but if it laid flat across the sofa, woe to the man, woman or child who dared disturb it. That evening Jo forgot to barricade her corner, and had not been in her seat five minutes, before a massive form appeared beside her, and with both arms spread over the sofa-back, both long legs stretched out before him, Laurie exclaimed with a sigh of satisfaction, —

"Now *this* is filling at the price!"

"No slang," snapped Jo, slamming down the pillow. But it was too late — there was no room for it; and coasting on to the floor, it disappeared in a most mysterious manner.

"Come, Jo, don't be thorny. After studying himself to a skeleton all the week, a fellow deserves petting, and ought to get it."

"Beth will pet you, I'm busy."

"No, she's not to be bothered with me; but you like that sort of thing, unless you've suddenly lost your taste for it. Have you? Do you hate your boy, and want to fire pillows at him?"

Anything more wheedlesome than that touching appeal was seldom seen, but Jo quenched "her boy" by turning on him with the stern query, —

"How many bouquets have you sent Miss Randal this week?"

"Not one, upon my word! She's engaged. Now then."

"I'm glad of it; that's one of your foolish extravagances, sending flowers and things to girls, for whom you don't care two pins," continued Jo, reprovingly.

"Sensible girls, for whom I do care whole papers of pins, won't let me send them 'flowers and things,' so what can I do? my feelings must have a *went*."

"Mother doesn't approve of flirting, even in fun; and you do flirt desperately, Teddy."

"I'd give anything if I could answer, 'So do you.' As I can't, I'll merely say that I don't see any harm in that pleasant little game, if all parties understand that it's only play."

"Well, it does look pleasant, but I can't learn how it's done. I've tried, because one feels awkward in company, not to do as everybody else is doing; but I don't seem to get on," said Jo, forgetting to play Mentor.

"Take lessons of Amy; she has a regular talent for it."

"Yes, she does it very prettily, and never seems to go too far. I suppose it's natural to some people to please without trying, and others to always say and do the wrong thing in the wrong place."

"I'm glad you can't flirt; it's really refreshing to see a sensible, straightforward girl, who can be jolly and kind without making a fool of herself. Between ourselves, Jo, some of the girls I know really do go on at such a rate I'm ashamed of them. They don't mean any harm, I'm sure; but if they knew how we fellows talked about them afterward, they'd mend their ways, I fancy."

"They do the same; and, as their tongues are the sharpest, you fellows get the worse of it, for you are as silly as they, every bit. If you behaved properly, they would; but, knowing you like their nonsense, they keep it up, and then you blame them."

"Much you know about it, ma'am!" said Laurie, in a superior tone. "We don't like romps and flirts, though we may act as if we did sometimes. The pretty, modest girls are never talked about, except respectfully, among gentlemen. Bless your innocent soul, if you could be in my place for a month you'd see things that would astonish you a trifle. Upon my word, when I see one of those harum-scarum girls, I always want to say with our friend Cock Robin:

"'Out upon you, fie upon you,
Bold-faced jig!'"

It was impossible to help laughing at the funny conflict between Laurie's chivalrous reluctance to speak ill of womankind, and his very natural dislike of the unfeminine folly of which fashionable society showed him many samples. Jo knew that "young Laurence" was regarded as a most eligible *parti* by worldly mammas, was much smiled upon by their daughters, and flattered enough by ladies of all ages to make a cockscomb of him; so she watched him rather jealously, fearing he would be spoilt, and rejoiced more than she confessed to find that he still believed in modest girls. Returning suddenly to her admonitory tone, she said, dropping her voice, "If you *must* have a 'went,' Teddy, go and devote yourself to one of the 'pretty modest girls' whom you do respect, and not waste your time with the silly ones."

"You really advise it?" and Laurie looked at her with an odd mixture of anxiety and merriment in his face.

"Yes, I do; but you'd better wait till you are through college, on the whole, and be fitting yourself for the place meantime. You're not half good enough for – well, whoever the modest girl may be;" and Jo looked a little queer likewise, for a name had almost escaped her.

"That I'm not!" acquiesced Laurie, with an expression of humility quite new to him, as he dropped his eyes, and absently wound Joe's apron tassel round his finger.

"Mercy on us, this will never do," thought Jo; adding aloud, "Go and sing to me. I'm dying for some music, and always like yours."

"I'd rather stay here, thank you."

"Well, you can't; there isn't room. Go and make yourself useful, since you are too big to be ornamental. I thought you hated to be tied to a woman's apron-string," retorted Jo, quoting certain rebellious words of his own.

"Ah, that depends on who wears the apron!" and Laurie gave an audacious tweak at the tassel.

"Are you going?" demanded Jo, diving for the pillow.

He fled at once, and the minute it was well "Up with the bonnets of bonnie Dundee," she slipped away, to return no more till the young gentleman had departed in high dudgeon.

Jo lay long awake that night, and was just dropping off when the sound of a stifled sob made her fly to Beth's bedside, with the anxious inquiry, "What is it, dear?"

"I thought you were asleep," sobbed Beth.

"Is it the old pain, my precious?"

"No; it's a new one; but I can't bear it," and Beth tried to check her tears.

"Tell me all about it, and let me cure it as I often did the other."

"You can't; there is no cure." There Beth's voice gave way, and, clinging to her sister, she cried so despairingly that Jo was frightened.

"Where is it? Shall I call mother?"

Beth did not answer the first question; but in the dark one hand went involuntarily to her heart, as if the pain were there; with the other she held Jo fast, whispering eagerly, "No, no, don't call her; don't tell her! I shall be better soon. Lie down here and 'poor' my head. I'll be quiet, and go to sleep; indeed I will."

Jo obeyed; but as her hand went softly to and fro across Beth's hot forehead and wet eyelids, her heart was very full, and she longed to speak. But young as she was Jo had learned that hearts, like flowers, cannot be rudely handled, but must open naturally; so, though she believed she knew the cause of Beth's new pain, she only said, in her tenderest tone, "Does anything trouble you, deary?"

"Yes, Jo!" after a long pause.

"Wouldn't it comfort you to tell me what it is?"

"Not now, not yet."

"Then I won't ask; but remember, Bethy, that mother and Jo are always glad to hear and help you, if they can."

"I know it. I'll tell you by and by."

"Is the pain better now?"

"Oh, yes, much better; you are so comfortable, Jo!"

"Go to sleep, dear; I'll stay with you."

So cheek to cheek they fell asleep, and on the morrow Beth seemed quite herself again; for, at eighteen, neither heads nor hearts ache long, and a loving word can medicine most ills.

But Jo had made up her mind, and, after pondering over a project for some days, she confided it to her mother.

"You asked me the other day what my wishes were. I'll tell you one of them, Marmee," she began, as they sat alone together. "I want to go away somewhere this winter for a change."

"Why, Jo?" and her mother looked up quickly, as if the words suggested a double meaning.

With her eyes on her work, Jo answered soberly, "I want something new; I feel restless, and anxious to be seeing, doing, and learning more than I am. I brood too much over my own small affairs, and need stirring up, so, as I can be spared this winter I'd like to hop a little way and try my wings."

"Where will you hop?"

"To New York. I had a bright idea yesterday, and this is it. You know Mrs. Kirke wrote to you for some respectable young person to teach her children and sew. It's rather hard to find just the thing, but I think I should suit if I tried."

"My dear, go out to service in that great boarding-house!" and Mrs. March looked surprised, but not displeased.

"It's not exactly going out to service; for Mrs. Kirke is your friend, – the kindest soul that ever lived, – and would make things pleasant for me, I know. Her family is separate from the rest, and no one knows me there. Don't care if they do; it's honest work, and I'm not ashamed of it."

"Nor I; but your writing?"

"All the better for the change. I shall see and hear new things, get new ideas, and, even if I haven't much time there, I shall bring home quantities of material for my rubbish."

"I have no doubt of it; but are these your only reasons for this sudden fancy?"

"No, mother."

"May I know the others?"

Jo looked up and Jo looked down, then said slowly, with sudden color in her cheeks, "It may be vain and wrong to say it, but – I'm afraid – Laurie is getting too fond of me."

"Then you don't care for him in the way it is evident he begins to care for you?" and Mrs. March looked anxious as she put the question.

"Mercy, no! I love the dear boy as I always have, and am immensely proud of him; but as for anything more, it's out of the question."

"I'm glad of that, Jo!"

"Why, please?"

"Because, dear, I don't think you are suited to one another. As friends, you are very happy, and your frequent quarrels soon blow over; but I fear you would both rebel if you were mated for life. You are too much alike, and too fond of freedom, not to mention hot tempers and strong wills, to get on happily together, in a relation which needs infinite patience and forbearance, as well as love."

"That's just the feeling I had, though I couldn't express it. I'm glad you think he is only beginning to care for me. It would trouble me sadly to make him unhappy; for I couldn't fall in love with the dear old fellow merely out of gratitude, could I?"

"You are sure of his feeling for you?"

The color deepened in Jo's cheeks, as she answered with the look of mingled pleasure, pride, and pain which young girls wear when speaking of first lovers, –

"I'm afraid it is so, mother; he hasn't said anything, but he looks a great deal. I think I had better go away before it comes to anything."

"I agree with you, and if it can be managed you shall go."

Jo looked relieved, and, after a pause, said, – smiling, –

"How Mrs. Moffat would wonder at your want of management, if she knew; and how she will rejoice that Annie still may hope."

"Ah, Jo, mothers may differ in their management, but the hope is the same in all – the desire to see their children happy. Meg is so, and I am content with her success. You I leave to enjoy your liberty till you tire of it; for only then will you find that there is something sweeter. Amy is my chief care now, but her good sense will help her. For Beth, I indulge no hopes except that she may be well. By the way, she seems brighter this last day or two. Have you spoken to her?"

"Yes; she owned she had a trouble, and promised to tell me by and by. I said no more, for I think I know it;" and Jo told her little story.

Mrs. March shook her head, and did not take so romantic a view of the case, but looked grave, and repeated her opinion that, for Laurie's sake, Jo should go away for a time.

"Let us say nothing about it to him till the plan is settled; then I'll run away before he can collect his wits and be tragical. Beth must think I'm going to please myself, as I am, for I can't talk about Laurie to her; but she can pet and comfort him after I'm gone, and so cure him of this romantic notion. He's been through so many little trials of the sort, he's used to it, and will soon get over his love-lornity."

Jo spoke hopefully, but could not rid herself of the foreboding fear that this "little trial" would be harder than the others, and that Laurie would not get over his "love-lornity" as easily as heretofore.

The plan was talked over in a family council, and agreed upon; for Mrs. Kirke gladly accepted Jo, and promised to make a pleasant home for her. The teaching would render her independent; and such leisure as she got might be made profitable by writing, while the new scenes and society would be both useful and agreeable. Jo liked the prospect, and was eager to be gone, for the home-nest was growing too narrow for her restless nature and adventurous spirit. When all was settled, with fear and trembling she told Laurie; but, to her surprise, he took it very quietly. He had been graver than usual of late, but very pleasant; and, when jokingly accused of turning over a new leaf, he answered, soberly, "So I am; and I mean this one shall stay turned."

Jo was very much relieved that one of his virtuous fits should come on just then, and made her preparations with a lightened heart, – for Beth seemed more cheerful, – and hoped she was doing the best for all.

"One thing I leave to your especial care," she said, the night before she left.

"You mean your papers?" asked Beth.

"No – my boy; be very good to him, won't you?"

"Of course I will; but I can't fill your place, and he'll miss you sadly."

"It won't hurt him; so remember, I leave him in your charge, to plague, pet, and keep in order."

"I'll do my best, for your sake," promised Beth, wondering why Jo looked at her so queerly.

When Laurie said "Good-by," he whispered, significantly, "It won't do a bit of good, Jo. My eye is on you; so mind what you do, or I'll come and bring you home."

CHAPTER THIRTY-THREE

JO'S JOURNAL

~

NEW YORK, NOV.

DEAR MARMEE AND BETH:

    I'm going to write you a regular volume, for I've got lots to tell, though I'm not a fine young lady travelling on the continent. When I lost sight of father's dear old face, I felt a trifle blue, and might have shed a briny drop or two, if an Irish lady with four small children, all crying more or less, hadn't diverted my mind; for I amused myself by dropping gingerbread nuts over the seat every time they opened their mouths to roar.

    Soon the sun came out; and taking it as a good omen, I cleared up likewise, and enjoyed my journey with all my heart.

    Mrs. Kirke welcomed me so kindly I felt at home at once, even in that big house full of strangers. She gave me a funny little sky parlor – all she had; but there is a stove in it, and a nice table in a sunny window, so I can sit here and write whenever I like. A fine view, and a church tower opposite, atone for the many stairs, and I took a fancy to my den on the spot. The nursery, where I am to teach and sew, is a pleasant room next Mrs. Kirke's private parlor, and the two little girls are pretty children – rather spoilt, I guess, but they took to me after telling them "The Seven Bad Pigs"; and I've no doubt I shall make a model governess.

I am to have my meals with the children, if I prefer it to the great table, and for the present I do, for I *am* bashful, though no one will believe it.

"Now my dear, make yourself at home," said Mrs. K. in her motherly way; "I'm on the drive from morning to night, as you may suppose, with such a family; but a great anxiety will be off my mind if I know the children are safe with you. My rooms are always open to you, and your own shall be as comfortable as I can make it. There are some pleasant people in the house, if you feel sociable, and your evenings are always free. Come to me if anything goes wrong, and be as happy as you can. There's the tea-bell; I must run and change my cap;" and off she bustled, leaving me to settle myself in my new nest.

As I went down stairs, soon after, I saw something I liked. The flights are very long in this tall house, and as I stood waiting at the head of the third one for a little servant girl to lumber up, I saw a queer-looking man come along behind her, take the heavy hod of coal out of her hand, carry it all the way up, put it down at a door near by, and walk away, saying, with a kind nod and a foreign accent, –

"It goes better so. The little back is too young to haf such heaviness."

Wasn't it good of him? I like such things; for, as father says, trifles show character. When I mentioned it to Mrs. K., that evening, she laughed, and said, –

"That must have been Professor Bhaer; he's always doing things of that sort."

Mrs. K. told me he was from Berlin; very learned and good, but poor as a church mouse, and gives lessons to support himself and two little orphan nephews whom he is educating here, according to the wishes of his sister, who married an American. Not a very romantic story, but it interested me; and I was glad to hear that Mrs. K. lends him her parlor for some of his scholars. There is a glass door between it and the nursery, and I mean to peep at him, and then I'll tell you how he looks. He's most forty, so it's no harm, Marmee.

After tea and a go-to-bed romp with the little girls, I attacked the big work-basket, and had a quiet evening chatting with my new friend. I shall keep a journal-letter, and send it once a week; so good-night, and more to-morrow.

Tuesday Eve.

Had a lively time in my seminary, this morning, for the children acted like Sancho; and at one time I really thought I should shake them all round. Some good angel inspired me to try gymnastics, and I kept it up till they were glad to sit down and keep still. After luncheon, the girl took them out for a walk, and I went to my needle-work, like little Mabel, "with a willing mind." I was thanking my stars that I'd learned to make nice button-holes, when the parlor door opened, and shut, and some one began to hum, –

Kennst du das land,

like a big bumble-bee. It was dreadfully improper, I know, but I couldn't resist the temptation; and lifting one end of the curtain before the glass door, I peeped in. Professor Bhaer was there; and while he arranged his books, I took a good look at him. A regular German – rather stout, with brown hair tumbled all over his head, a bushy beard, droll nose, the kindest eyes I ever saw, and a splendid big voice that does one's ears good, after our sharp or slipshod American gabble. His clothes were rusty, his hands were large, and he hadn't a handsome feature in his face, except his beautiful teeth; yet I liked him, for he had a fine head; his linen was spandy nice, and he looked like a gentleman, though two buttons were off his coat, and there was a patch on one shoe. He looked sober in spite of his humming, till he went to the window to turn the hyacinth bulbs toward the sun, and stroke the cat, who received him like an old friend. Then he smiled; and when a tap came at the door, called out in a loud, brisk tone, –

"Herein!"

I was just going to run, when I caught sight of a morsel of a child carrying a big book, and stopped to see what was going on.

"Me wants my Bhaer," said the mite, slamming down her book, and running to meet him.

The Professor caught Tina up with a laugh.

"Thou shalt haf thy Bhaer; come, then, and take a goot hug from him, my Tina," said the Professor, catching her up, with a laugh, and holding her so high over his head that she had to stoop her little face to kiss him.

"Now me mus tuddy my lessin," went on the funny little thing; so he put her up at the table, opened the great dictionary she had brought, and gave her a paper and pencil, and she scribbed away, turning a leaf now and then, and passing her little fat finger down the page, as if finding a word, so soberly, that I nearly betrayed myself by a laugh, while Mr. Bhaer stood stroking her pretty hair, with a fatherly look, that made me think she must be his own, though she looked more French than German.

Another knock, and the appearance of two young ladies sent me back to my work, and there I virtuously remained through all the noise and gabbling that went on next door. One of the girls kept laughing affectedly, and saying "Now, Professor," in a coquettish tone, and the other pronounced her German with an accent that must have made it hard for him to keep sober.

Both seemed to try his patience sorely; for more than once I heard him say, emphatically, "No, no, it is *not* so; you haf not attend to what I say;" and once there was a loud rap, as if he struck the table with his book, followed by the despairing exclamation, "Prut! it all goes bad this day."

Poor man, I pitied him; and when the girls were gone, took just one more peep, to see if he survived it. He seemed to have thrown himself back in his chair, tired out, and sat there with his eyes shut, till the clock struck two, when he jumped up, put his books in his pocket, as if ready for another lesson, and, taking little Tina, who had fallen asleep on the sofa, in his arms, he carried her quietly away. I guess he has a hard life of it.

Mrs. Kirke asked me if I wouldn't go down to the five o'clock dinner; and, feeling a little bit home-sick, I thought I would, just to see what sort of people are under the same roof with me. So I made myself respectable, and tried to slip in behind Mrs. Kirke; but as she is short, and I'm tall, my efforts at concealment were rather a failure. She gave me a seat by her, and after my face cooled off, I plucked up courage, and looked about me. The long table was full, and every one intent on getting their dinner — the gentlemen especially, who seemed to be eating on time, for they *bolted* in every sense of the word, vanishing as soon as they were done. There was the usual assortment of young men, absorbed in themselves; young couples absorbed in each other; married ladies in their babies, and old gentlemen in politics. I don't think I shall care to have much to do with any of them, except one sweet-faced maiden lady, who looks as if she had something in her.

Cast away at the very bottom of the table was the Professor, shouting answers to the questions of a very inquisitive, deaf old gentleman on one side, and talking philosophy with a Frenchman on the other. If Amy had been here, she'd have turned her back on him forever, because, sad to relate, he had a great appetite, and shovelled in his dinner in a manner which would have horrified "her ladyship." I didn't mind, for I like "to see folks eat with a relish," as Hannah says, and the poor man must have needed a deal of food, after teaching idiots all day.

As I went up stairs after dinner, two of the young men were settling their beavers before the hall mirror and I heard one say low to the other, "Who's the new party?"

"Governess, or something of that sort."

"What the deuce is she at our table for?"

"Friend of the old lady's."

"Handsome head, but no style."

"Not a bit of it. Give us a light and come on."

I felt angry at first, and then I didn't care, for a governess is as good as a clerk, and I've got sense, if I haven't style, which is more than some people have, judging from the remarks of the elegant beings who clattered away, smoking like bad chimneys. I hate ordinary people!

Thursday.

Yesterday was a quiet day, spent in teaching, sewing, and writing in my little room, – which is very cosy, with a light and fire. I picked up a few bits of news, and was introduced to the Professor. It seems that Tina is the child of the Frenchwoman who does the fine ironing in the laundry here. The little thing has lost her heart to Mr. Bhaer, and follows him about the house like a dog whenever he is at home, which delights him, – as he is very fond of children, though a "bacheldore." Kitty and Minnie Kirke likewise regard him with affection, and tell all sorts of stories about the plays he invents, the presents he brings, and the splendid tales he tells. The young men quiz him, it seems, call him Old Fritz, Lager Beer, Ursa Major, and make all manner of jokes on his name. But he enjoys it like a boy, Mrs. K. says, and takes it so good-naturedly that they all like him, in spite of his odd ways.

The maiden lady is a Miss Norton, — rich, cultivated, and kind. She spoke to me at dinner to-day (for I went to table again, it's such fun to watch people), and asked me to come and see her at her room. She has fine books and pictures, knows interesting persons, and seems friendly; so I shall make myself agreeable, for I *do* want to get into good society, only it isn't the same sort that Amy likes.

I was in our parlor last evening, when Mr. Bhaer came in with some newspapers for Mrs. Kirke. She wasn't there, but Minnie, who is a little old woman, introduced me very prettily: "This is mamma's friend, Miss March."

"Yes; and she's jolly, and we like her lots," added Kitty, who is an *"enfant terrible."*

We both bowed, and then we laughed, for the prim introduction and the blunt addition were rather a comical contrast.

"Ah, yes; I hear these naughty ones go to vex you, Mees Marsch. If so again, call at me and I come," he said, with a threatening frown that delighted the little wretches.

I promised I would, and he departed; but it seems as if I was doomed to see a good deal of him, for to-day, as I passed his door on my way out, by accident I knocked against it with my umbrella. It flew open, and there he stood in his dressing-gown, with a big blue sock on one hand and a darning needle in the other; he didn't seem at all ashamed of it, for when I explained and hurried on, he waved his hand, sock and all, saying, in his loud, cheerful way, —

"You haf a fine day to make your walk. *Bon voyage, mademoiselle.*"

I laughed all the way down stairs; but it was a little pathetic, also, to think of the poor man having to mend his own clothes. The German gentlemen embroider, I know, — but darning hose is another thing, and not so pretty.

Saturday.

Nothing has happened to write about, except a call on Miss Norton, who has a room full of lovely things, and who was very charming, for she showed me all her treasures, and asked me if I would sometimes go with her to lectures and concerts, as her escort, – if I enjoyed them. She put it as a favor; but I'm sure Mrs. Kirke has told her about us, and she does it out of kindness to me. I'm as proud as Lucifer, but such favors from such people don't burden me, and I accepted gratefully.

When I got back to the nursery there was such an uproar in the parlor that I looked in, and there was Mr. Bhaer down on his hands and knees, with Tina on his back, Kitty leading him with a jump-rope, and Minnie feeding two small boys with seed-cakes, as they roared and ramped in cages built of chairs.

"We are playing *nargerie*," explained Kitty.

"Dis is mine effalunt," added Tina, holding on by the Professor's hair.

"Mamma always allows us to do what we like Saturday afternoon, when Franz and Emil come, don't she, Mr. Bhaer?" said Minnie.

The "effalunt" sat up, looking as much in earnest as any of them, and said, soberly, to me, –

"I gif you my wort, it is so. If we make too large a noise you shall say 'hush!' to us, and we go more softly."

I promised to do so, but left the door open, and enjoyed the fun as much as they did, – for a more glorious frolic I never witnessed. They played tag, and soldiers, danced and sung, and when it began to grow dark they all piled on to the sofa about the Professor, while he told charming fairy stories of the storks on the chimney-tops, and the little "Kobolds," who ride the snowflakes as they fall. I wish Americans were as simple and natural as Germans, don't you?

I'm so fond of writing, I should go spinning on forever if motives of economy didn't stop me; for though I've used thin paper, and written fine, I tremble to think of the stamps this long letter will need. Pray forward Amy's as soon as you can spare them. My small news will sound very flat after her splendors, but you will like them, I know. Is Teddy studying so hard that he can't find time to write to his friends? Take good care of him for me, Beth, and tell me all about the babies, and give heaps of love to every one.

From your faithful

Jo.

P.S. On reading over my letter, it strikes me as rather Bhaery; but I'm always interested in odd people, and I really had nothing else to write about. Bless you.

Dec.

MY PRECIOUS BETSEY:

As this is to be a scribble-scrabble letter, I direct it to you, for it may amuse you, and give you some idea of my goings on; for, though quiet, they are rather amusing, for which, oh, be joyful! After what Amy would call Herculaneum efforts, in the way of mental and moral agriculture, my young ideas begin to shoot, and my little twigs to bend, as I could wish. They are not so interesting to me as Tina and the boys, but I do my duty by them, and they are fond of me. Franz and Emil are jolly little lads, quite after my own heart, for the mixture of German and American spirit in them produces a constant state of effervescence. Saturday afternoons are riotous times, whether spent in the house or out; for on pleasant days they all go to walk, like a seminary, with the Professor and myself to keep order; and then such fun!

We are very good friends now, and I've begun to take lessons. I really couldn't help it, and it all came about in such a funny way, that I must tell you. To begin at the beginning. Mrs. Kirke called to me, one day, as I passed Mr. Bhaer's room, where she was rummaging.

"Did you ever see such a den, my dear? Just come and help me put these books to rights, for I've turned everything upside down, trying to discover what he has done with the six new handkerchiefs I gave him, not long ago."

I went in, and while we worked I looked about me, for it was "a den," to be sure. Books and papers, everywhere; a broken meerschaum, and an old flute over the mantle-piece, as if done with; a ragged bird, without any tail, chirped on one window-seat, and a box of white mice adorned the other; half-finished boats, and bits of string, lay among the manuscripts; dirty little boots stood drying before the fire, and traces of the dearly beloved boys, for whom he makes a slave of himself, were to be seen all over the room. After a grand rummage three of the missing articles were found, – one over the bird-cage, one covered with ink, and a third burnt brown, having been used as a holder.

"Such a man!" laughed good-natured Mrs. K., as she put the relics in the rag-bag. "I suppose the others are torn up to rig ships, bandage cut fingers, or make kite tails. It's dreadful, but I can't scold him; he's so absent-minded and good-natured, he lets those boys ride over him rough-shod. I agreed to do his washing and mending, but he forgets to give out his things, and I forget to look them over, so he comes to a sad pass sometimes."

"Let me mend them," said I; "I don't mind it, and he needn't know. I'd like to, – he's so kind about bringing my letters, and lending books."

So I have got his things in order, and knit heels into two pairs of the socks, – for they were boggled out of shape with his queer darns. Nothing was said, and I hoped he wouldn't find it out, – but one day last week he caught me at it. Hearing the lessons he gives to others has interested and amused me so much, that I took a fancy to learn; for Tina runs in and out, leaving the door open, and I can hear. I had been sitting near this door, finishing off the last sock, and trying to understand what he said to a new scholar, who is as stupid as I am; the girl had gone, and I thought he had also, it was so still, and I was busily gabbling over a verb, and rocking to and fro in a most absurd way, when a little crow made me look up, and there was Mr. Bhaer looking and laughing quietly, when he made signs to Tina not to betray him.

"So," he said, as I stopped and stared like a goose, "you peep at me, I peep at you, and that is not bad; but see, I am not pleasanting when I say, haf you a wish for German?"

"Yes; but you are too busy; I am too stupid to learn," I blundered out, as red as a beet.

"Prut!' we will make the time, and we fail not to find the sense. At efening I shall gif a little lesson with much gladness; for, look you, Mees Marsch, I haf this debt to pay," and he pointed to my work. "'Yes!' they say to one another, these so kind ladies, 'he is a stupid old fellow; he will see not what we do; he will never opserve that his sock-heels go not in holes any more; he will think his buttons grow out new when they fall, and believe that strings make theirselves.' Ah! but I haf an eye, and I see much. I haf a heart and I feel the thanks for this. Come, – a little lesson then and now, or – no more good fairy works for me and mine."

Of course I couldn't say anything after that, and as it really is a splendid opportunity, I made the bargain, and we began. I took four lessons, and then I stuck fast in a grammatical bog. The Professor was very patient with me, but it must have been torment to him, and now and then he'd look at me with such an expression of mild despair, that it was a toss up with me whether to laugh or cry. I tried both ways; and when it came to a sniff of utter mortification and woe, he just threw the grammar on to the floor, and marched out of the room. I felt myself disgraced and deserted forever, but didn't blame him a particle, and was scrambling my papers together, meaning to rush up stairs and shake myself hard, when in he came, as brisk and beaming as if I'd covered my name with glory: –

"Now we shall try a new way. You and I will read these pleasant little Märchen together, and dig no more in that dry book, that goes in the corner for making us trouble."

He spoke so kindly, and opened Hans Andersen's fairy tales so invitingly before me, that I was more ashamed than ever, and went at my lesson in a neck-or-nothing style that seemed to amuse him immensely. I forgot my bashfulness, and pegged away (no other word will express it) with all my might, tumbling over long words, pronouncing according to the inspiration of the minute, and doing my very best. When I finished reading my first page, and stopped for breath, he clapped his hands and cried out, in his hearty way, "Das ist gute! Now we go well! My turn. I do him in German; gif me your ear." And away he went, rumbling out the words with his strong voice, and a relish which was good to see as well as hear. Fortunately, the story was the "Constant Tin Soldier," which is droll, you know, so I could laugh, – and I did, – though I didn't understand half he read, – for I couldn't help it, he was so earnest, I so excited, and the whole thing so comical.

After that we got on better, and now I read my lessons pretty well; for this way of studying suits me, and I can see that the grammar gets tucked into the tales and poetry, as one gives pills in jelly. I like it very much, and he don't seem tired of it yet, – which is very good of him, isn't it? I mean to give him something on Christmas, for I don't dare offer money. Tell me something nice, Marmee.

I'm glad Laurie seems so happy and busy, – that he has given up smoking, and lets his hair grow. You see Beth manages him better than I did. I'm not jealous, dear; do your best, only don't make a saint of him. I'm afraid I couldn't like him without a spice of human naughtiness. Read him bits of my letters. I haven't time to write much, and that will do just as well. Thank heaven, Beth continues so comfortable.

Jan.

A happy New Year to you all, my dearest family, which of course includes Mr. L. and a young man by the name of Teddy. I can't tell you how much I enjoyed your Christmas bundle, for I didn't get it till night, and had given up hoping. Your letter came in the morning, but you said nothing about a parcel, meaning it for a surprise; so I was disappointed, for I'd had a "kind of a feeling" that you wouldn't forget me. I felt a little low in my mind, as I sat up in my room, after tea; and when the big, muddy, battered-looking bundle was brought to me, I just hugged it, and pranced. It was so *homey* and refreshing, that I sat down on the floor, and read, and looked, and eat, and laughed and cried, in my usual absurd way. The things were just what I wanted, and all the better for being made instead of bought. Beth's new "ink-bib" was capital; and Hannah's box of hard gingerbread will be a treasure. I'll be sure and wear the nice flannels you sent, Marmee, and read carefully the books father has marked. Thank you all heaps and heaps!

Speaking of books, reminds me that I'm getting rich in that line; for, on New Year's day, Mr. Bhaer gave me a fine Shakespeare. It is one he values much, and I've often admired it, set up in the place of honor, with his German Bible, Plato, Homer, and Milton; so you may imagine how I felt when he brought it down, without its cover, and showed me my name in it, "from my friend Friedrich Bhaer."

"You say often you wish a library; here I gif you one; for between these two lids (he meant covers) is many books in one. Read him well, and he will help you much; for the study of character in this book will help you to read it in the world, and paint it with your pen."

I thanked him as well as I could, and talk now about "my library," as if I had a hundred books. I never knew how much there was in Shakespeare before; but then I never had a Bhaer to explain it to me. Now *don't* laugh at his horrid name; it isn't pronounced either Bear or Beer, as people *will* say it, but something between the two, as only Germans can do it. I'm glad you both like what I tell you about him, and hope you will know him some day. Mother would admire his warm heart, father his wise head. I admire both, and feel rich in my new "friend Friedrich Bhaer."

Not having much money, or knowing what he'd like, I got several little things, and put them about the room, where he would find them unexpectedly. They were useful, pretty, or funny — a new standish on his table, a little vase for his flower — he always has one — or a bit of green in a glass, to keep him fresh, he says; and a holder for his blower, so that he needn't burn up what Amy calls "mouchoirs." I made it like those Beth invented — a big butterfly with a fat body, and black and yellow wings, worsted feelers, and bead eyes. It took his fancy immensely, and he put it on his mantelpiece as an article of *virtu*; so it was rather a failure after all. Poor as he is, he didn't forget a servant or a child in the house; and not a soul here, from the French laundry-woman to Miss Norton, forgot him. I was so glad of that.

They got up a masquerade, and had a gay time, New Year's eve. I didn't mean to go down, having no dress; but, at the last minute, Mrs. Kirke remembered some old brocades, and Miss Norton lent me lace and feathers; so I rigged up as Mrs. Malaprop, and sailed in with a mask on. No one knew me, for I disguised my voice, and no one dreamed of the silent, haughty Miss March (for they think I am very stiff and cool, most of them; and so I am to whipper-snappers) could dance, and dress, and burst out into a "nice derangement of epitaphs, like an allegory on the banks of the Nile." I enjoyed it very much; and when we unmasked, it was fun to see them stare at me. I heard one of the young men tell another that he knew I'd been an actress; in fact, he thought he remembered seeing me at one of the minor theatres. Meg will relish that joke. Mr. Bhaer was Nick Bottom, and Tina was Titania — a perfect little fairy in his arms. To see them dance was "quite a landscape," to use a Teddyism.

I had a very happy New Year, after all, and when I thought it over in my room, I felt as if I was getting on a little in spite of my many failures; for I'm cheerful all the time now, work with a will, and take more interest in other people than I used to, which is satisfactory. Bless you all. Ever your loving

Jo.

CHAPTER THIRTY-FOUR

A FRIEND

~

Though very happy in the social atmosphere about her, and very busy with the daily work that earned her bread, and made it sweeter for the effort, Jo still found time for literary labors. The purpose which now took possession of her was a natural one to a poor and ambitious girl; but the means she took to gain her end were not the best. She saw that money conferred power; money and power, therefore, she resolved to have; not to be used for herself alone, but for those whom she loved more than self. The dream of filling home with comforts, giving Beth everything she wanted, from strawberries in winter to an organ in her bedroom; going abroad herself, and always having *more* than enough, so that she might indulge in the luxury of charity, had been for years Jo's most cherished castle in the air.

The prize-story experience had seemed to open a way which might, after long travelling, and much up-hill work, lead to this delightful *chateau en Espagne*. But the novel disaster quenched her courage for a time, for public opinion is a giant which has frightened stouter-hearted Jacks on bigger beanstalks than hers. Like that immortal hero, she reposed a while after the first attempt, which resulted in a tumble, and the least lovely of the giant's treasures, if I remember rightly. But the "up again and take another" spirit was as strong in Jo as in Jack; so she scrambled up on the shady side, this time, and got more booty, but nearly left behind her what was far more precious than the money-bags.

She took to writing sensation stories – for in those dark ages, even all-perfect America read rubbish. She told no one, but concocted a "thrilling tale," and boldly carried it herself to Mr. Dashwood, editor of the "Weekly Volcano." She had never read Sartor Resartus, but she had a womanly instinct that clothes possess an influence more powerful over many than the worth of character or the magic of manners. So she dressed herself in her best, and, trying to persuade herself that she was neither excited nor nervous, bravely climbed two pairs of dark and dirty stairs to find herself in a disorderly room, a cloud of cigar smoke, and the presence of three gentlemen sitting with their heels rather higher than their hats, which articles of dress none of them took the trouble to remove on her appearance. Somewhat daunted by this reception, Jo hesitated on the threshold, murmuring in much embarrassment, –

"Excuse me; I was looking for the 'Weekly Volcano' office; I wished to see Mr. Dashwood."

Down went the highest pair of heels, up rose the smokiest gentleman, and, carefully cherishing his cigar between his fingers, he advanced with a nod, and a countenance expressive of nothing but sleep. Feeling that she must get through with the matter somehow, Jo produced her manuscript, and, blushing redder and redder with each sentence, blundered out fragments of the little speech carefully prepared for the occasion.

"A friend of mine desired me to offer – a story – just as an experiment – would like your opinion – be glad to write more if this suits."

While she blushed and blundered, Mr. Dashwood had taken the manuscript, and was turning over the leaves with a pair of rather dirty fingers, and casting critical glances up and down the neat pages.

"Not a first attempt, I take it?" observing that the pages were numbered, covered only on one side, and not *tied* up with a ribbon – sure sign of a novice.

"No, sir; she has had some experience, and got a prize for a tale in the 'Blarneystone Banner.'"

"Oh, did she?" and Mr. Dashwood gave Jo a quick look, which seemed to take note of everything she had on, from the bow in her bonnet to the buttons on her boots. "Well, you can leave it, if you like; we've more of this sort of thing on hand than we know what to do with, at present; but I'll run my eye over it, and give you an answer next week."

Now Jo did *not* like to leave it, for Mr. Dashwood didn't suit her at all; but, under the circumstances, there was nothing for her to do but bow and walk away, looking particularly tall and dignified, as she was apt to do, when nettled or abashed. Just then she was both; for it was perfectly evident from the knowing glances exchanged among the gentlemen, that her little fiction of "my friend" was considered a good joke; and a laugh produced by some inaudible remark of the editor, as he closed the door, completed her discomfiture. Half resolving never to return, she went home, and worked off her irritation by stitching pinafores vigorously; and in an hour or two was cool enough to laugh over the scene, and long for next week.

When she went again, Mr. Dashwood was alone, whereat she rejoiced. Mr. Dashwood was much wider awake than before, – which was agreeable, – and Mr. Dashwood was not too deeply absorbed in a cigar to remember his manners, – so the second interview was much more comfortable than the first.

"We'll take this" (editors never say "I"), "if you don't object to a few alterations. It's too long, – but omitting the passages I've marked will make it just the right length," he said, in a businesslike tone.

Jo hardly knew her own MS. again, so crumpled and underscored were its pages and paragraphs; but, feeling as a tender parent might on being asked to cut off her baby's legs in order that it might fit it into a new cradle, she looked at the marked passages, and was surprised to find that all the moral reflections, – which she had carefully put in as ballast for much romance, – had all been stricken out.

"But, sir, I thought every story should have some sort of a moral, so I took care to have a few of my sinners repent."

Mr. Dashwood's editorial gravity relaxed into a smile, for Jo had forgotten her "friend," and spoken as only an author could.

"People want to be amused, not preached at, you know. Morals don't sell nowadays;" which was not quite a correct statement, by the way.

"You think it would do with these alterations, then?"

"Yes; it's a new plot, and pretty well worked up — language good, and so on," was Mr. Dashwood's affable reply.

"What do you — that is, what compensation — " began Jo, not exactly knowing how to express herself.

"Oh, yes, — well, we give from twenty-five to thirty for things of this sort. Pay when it comes out," returned Mr. Dashwood, as if that point had escaped him; such trifles often do escape the editorial mind, it is said.

"Very well; you can have it," said Jo, handing back the story, with a satisfied air; for, after the dollar-a-column work, even twenty-five seemed good pay.

"Shall I tell my friend you will take another if she has one better than this?" asked Jo, unconscious of her little slip of the tongue, and emboldened by her success.

"Well, we'll look at it; can't promise to take it; tell her to make it short and spicy, and never mind the moral. What name would your friend like to put to it?" in a careless tone.

"None at all, if you please; she doesn't wish her name to appear, and has no *nom de plume*," said Jo, blushing in spite of herself.

"Just as she likes, of course. The tale will be out next week; will you call for the money, or shall I send it?" asked Mr. Dashwood, who felt a natural desire to know who his new contributor might be.

"I'll call; good morning, sir."

As she departed, Mr. Dashwood put up his feet, with the graceful remark, "Poor and proud, as usual, but she'll do."

Following Mr. Dashwood's directions, and making Mrs. Northbury her model, Jo rashly took a plunge into the frothy sea of sensational literature; but, thanks to the life-preserver thrown her by a friend, she came up again, not much the worse for her ducking.

Like most young scribblers, she went abroad for her characters and scenery, and banditti, counts, gypsies, nuns, and duchesses appeared upon her stage, and played their parts with as much accuracy and spirit as could be expected. Her readers were not particular about such trifles as grammar, punctuation, and probability, and Mr. Dashwood graciously permitted her to fill his columns at the lowest prices, not thinking it necessary to tell her that the real cause of his hospitality was the fact that one of his hacks, on being offered higher wages, had basely left him in the lurch.

She soon became interested in her work, – for her emaciated purse grew stout, and the little hoard she was making to take Beth to the mountains next summer, grew slowly but surely, as the weeks passed. One thing disturbed her satisfaction, and that was that she did not tell them at home. She had a feeling that father and mother would not approve, – and preferred to have her own way first, and beg pardon afterward. It was easy to keep her secret, for no name appeared with her stories; Mr. Dashwood had, of course, found it out very soon, but promised to be dumb; and, for a wonder, kept his word.

She thought it would do her no harm, for she sincerely meant to write nothing of which she should be ashamed, and quieted all pricks of conscience by anticipations of the happy minute when she should show her earnings and laugh over her well-kept secret.

But Mr. Dashwood rejected any but thrilling tales; and, as thrills could not be produced except by harrowing up the souls of the readers, history and romance, land and sea, science and art, police records and lunatic asylums, had to be ransacked for the purpose. Jo soon found that her innocent experience had given her but few glimpses of the tragic world which underlies society; so, regarding it in a business light, she set about supplying her deficiencies with characteristic energy. Eager to find material for stories, and bent on making them original in plot, if not masterly in execution, she searched newspapers for accidents, incidents, and crimes; she excited the suspicions of public librarians by asking for works on poisons; she studied faces in the street, – and characters good, bad, and indifferent, all about her; she delved in the dust of ancient times, for facts or fictions so old that they were as good as new, and introduced herself to folly, sin, and misery, as well as her limited opportunities allowed. She thought she was prospering finely; but, unconsciously, she was beginning to desecrate some of the womanliest attributes of a woman's character. She was living in bad society; and, imaginary though it was, its influence affected her, for she was feeding heart and fancy on dangerous and unsubstantial food, and was fast brushing the innocent bloom from her nature by a premature acquaintance with the darker side of life, which comes soon enough to all of us.

She was beginning to feel rather than see this, for much describing of other people's passions and feelings set her to studying and speculating about her own, — a morbid amusement, in which healthy young minds do not voluntarily indulge. Wrong-doing always brings its own punishment; and, when Jo most needed hers, she got it.

I don't know whether the study of Shakespeare helped her to read character, or the natural instinct of a woman for what was honest, brave and strong; but while endowing her imaginary heroes with every perfection under the sun, Jo was discovering a live hero, who interested her in spite of many human imperfections. Mr. Bhaer, in one of their conversations, had advised her to study simple, true, and lovely characters, wherever she found them, as good training for a writer; Jo took him at his word, — for she coolly turned round and studied him, — a proceeding which would have much surprised him, had he known it, — for the worthy Professor was very humble in his own conceit.

Why everybody liked him was what puzzled Jo, at first. He was neither rich nor great, young nor handsome, — in no respect what is called fascinating, imposing, or brilliant; and yet he was as attractive as a genial fire, and people seemed to gather about him as naturally as about a warm hearth. He was poor, yet always appeared to be giving something away, — a stranger, yet every one was his friend; no longer young, — but as happy-hearted as a boy; plain and odd, — yet his face looked beautiful to many, and his oddities were freely forgiven for his sake. Jo often watched him, trying to discover the charm, and, at last, decided that it was benevolence which worked the miracle. If he had any sorrow "it sat with its head under its wing," and he turned only his sunny side to the world. There were lines upon his forehead, but Time seemed to have touched him gently, remembering how kind he was to others. The pleasant curves about his mouth were the memorials of many friendly words and cheery laughs; his eyes were never cold or hard, and his big hand had a warm, strong grasp that was more expressive than words.

His very clothes seemed to partake of the hospitable nature of the wearer. They looked as if they were at ease, and liked to make him comfortable; his capacious waistcoat was suggestive of a large heart underneath; his rusty coat had a social air, and the baggy pockets plainly proved that little hands often went in empty and came out full; his very boots were benevolent, and his collars never stiff and raspy like other people's.

"That's it!" said Jo to herself, when she at length discovered that genuine good-will toward one's fellowmen could beautify and dignify even a stout German teacher, who shovelled in his dinner, darned his own socks, and was burdened with the name of Bhaer.

Jo valued goodness highly, but she also possessed a most feminine respect for intellect, and a little discovery which she made about the Professor added much to her regard for him. He never spoke of himself, and no one ever knew that in his native city he had been a man much honored and esteemed for learning and integrity, till a countryman came to see him, and, in a conversation with Miss Norton, divulged the pleasing fact. From her Jo learned it, — and liked it all the better because Mr. Bhaer had never told it. She felt proud to know that he was an honored Professor in Berlin, though only a poor language-master in America, and his homely, hard-working life was much beautified by the spice of romance which this discovery gave it.

Another and a better gift than intellect was shown her in a most unexpected manner. Miss Norton had the *entrée* into literary society, which Jo would have had no chance of seeing but for her. The solitary woman felt an interest in the ambitious girl, and kindly conferred many favors of this sort both on Jo and the Professor. She took them with her, one night, to a select symposium, held in honor of several celebrities.

Jo went prepared to bow down and adore the mighty ones whom she had worshipped with youthful enthusiasm afar off. But her reverence for genius received a severe shock that night, and it took her some time to recover from the discovery that the great creatures were only men and women, after all. Imagine her dismay, on stealing a glance of timid admiration at the poet whose lines suggested an ethereal being fed on "spirit, fire, and dew," to behold him devouring his supper with an ardor which flushed his intellectual countenance. Turning as from a fallen idol, she made other discoveries which rapidly dispelled her romantic illusions. The great novelist vibrated between two decanters with the regularity of a pendulum; the famous divine flirted openly with one of the Madame de Staëls of the age, who looked daggers at another Corinne, who was amiably satirizing her, after out-manœuvring her in efforts to absorb the profound philosopher, who imbibed tea Johnsonianly and appeared to slumber, – the loquacity of the lady rendering speech impossible. The scientific celebrities, forgetting their mollusks and Glacial Periods, gossiped about art, while devoting themselves to oysters and ices with characteristic energy; the young musician, who was charming the city like a second Orpheus, talked horses; and the specimen of the British nobility present happened to be the most ordinary man of the party.

Before the evening was half over, Jo felt so completely *désillusionnée*, that she sat down in a corner to recover herself. Mr. Bhaer soon joined her, looking rather out of his element, and presently several of the philosophers, each mounted on his hobby, came ambling up to hold an intellectual tournament in the recess. The conversation was miles beyond Jo's comprehension, but she enjoyed it, though Kant and Hegel were unknown gods, the Subjective and Objective unintelligible terms; and the only thing "evolved from her inner consciousness," was a bad headache after it was all over. It dawned upon her gradually, that the world was being picked to pieces, and put together on new, and, according to the talkers, on infinitely better principles than before; that religion was in a fair way to be reasoned into nothingness, and intellect was to be the only God. Jo knew nothing about philosophy or metaphysics of any sort, but a curious excitement, half pleasurable, half painful, came over her, as she listened with a sense of being turned adrift into time and space, like a young balloon out on a holiday.

She looked round to see how the Professor liked it, and found him looking at her with the grimmest expression she had ever seen him wear. He shook his head, and beckoned her to come away, but she was fascinated, just then, by the freedom of Speculative Philosophy, and kept her seat, trying to find out what the wise gentlemen intended to rely upon after they annihilated all the old beliefs.

Now Mr. Bhaer was a diffident man, and slow to offer his own opinions, not because they were unsettled, but too sincere and earnest to be lightly spoken. As he glanced from Jo to several other young people attracted by the brilliancy of the philosophic pyrotechnics, he knit his brows, and longed to speak, fearing that some inflammable young soul would be led astray by the rockets, to find, when the display was over, that they had only an empty stick, or a scorched hand.

He bore it as long as he could; but when he was appealed to for an opinion, he blazed up with honest indignation, and defended religion with all the eloquence of truth – an eloquence which made his broken English musical, and his plain face beautiful. He had a hard fight, for the wise men argued well; but he didn't know when he was beaten, and stood to his colors like a man. Somehow, as he talked, the world got right again to Jo; the old beliefs that had lasted so long, seemed better than the new. God was not a blind force, and immortality was not a pretty fable, but a blessed fact. She felt as if she had solid ground under her feet again; and when Mr. Bhaer paused, out-talked, but not one whit convinced, Jo wanted to clap her hands and thank him.

She did neither; but she remembered this scene, and gave the Professor her heartiest respect, for she knew it cost him an effort to speak out then and there, because his conscience would not let him be silent. She began to see that character is a better possession than money, rank, intellect, or beauty; and to feel that if greatness is what a wise man has defined it to be, – "truth, reverence, and good-will," – then her friend Friedrich Bhaer was not only good, but great.

This belief strengthened daily. She valued his esteem, she coveted his respect, she wanted to be worthy of his friendship; and, just when the wish was sincerest, she came near losing everything. It all grew out of a cocked hat; for one evening the Professor came in to give Jo her lesson, with a paper soldier-cap on his head, which Tina had put there, and he had forgotten to take off.

"It's evident he doesn't prink at his glass before coming down," thought Jo, with a smile, as he said "Good efening," and sat soberly down, quite unconscious of the ludicrous contrast between his subject and his head-gear, for he was going to read her the "Death of Wallenstein."

She said nothing at first, for she liked to hear him laugh out his big, hearty laugh, when anything funny happened, so she left him to discover it for himself, and presently forgot all about it; for to hear a German read Schiller is rather an absorbing occupation. After the reading came the lesson, which was a lively one, for Jo was in a gay mood that night, and the cocked hat kept her eyes dancing with merriment. The Professor didn't know what to make of her, and stopped, at last, to ask with an air of mild surprise that was irresistible, –

"Mees Marsch, for what do you laugh in your master's face? Haf you no respect for me, that you go on so bad?"

"How can I be respectful, sir, when you forget to take your hat off?" said Jo.

Lifting his hand to his head, the absent-minded Professor gravely felt and removed the little cocked hat, looked at it a minute, and then threw back his head, and laughed like a merry bass-viol.

"Ah! I see him now; it is that imp Tina who makes me a fool with my cap. Well, it is nothing; but see you, if this lesson goes not well, you too shall wear him."

But the lesson did not go at all, for a few minutes, because Mr. Bhaer caught sight of a picture on the hat; and, unfolding it, said with an air of great disgust, —

"I wish these papers did not come in the house; they are not for children to see, nor young people to read. It is not well; and I haf no patience with those who make this harm."

Jo glanced at the sheet, and saw a pleasing illustration composed of a lunatic, a corpse, a villain, and a viper. She did not like it; but the impulse that made her turn it over was not one of displeasure, but fear, because, for a minute, she fancied the paper was the "Volcano." It was not, however, and her panic subsided as she remembered that, even if it had been, and one of her own tales in it, there would have been no name to betray her. She had betrayed herself, however, by a look and a blush; for, though an absent man, the Professor saw a good deal more than people fancied. He knew that Jo wrote, and had met her down among the newspaper offices more than once; but as she never spoke of it, he asked no questions, in spite of a strong desire to see her work. Now it occurred to him that she was doing what she was ashamed to own, and it troubled him. He did not say to himself, "It is none of my business; I've no right to say anything," as many people would have done; he only remembered that she was young and poor, a girl far away from mother's love and father's care; and he was moved to help her with an impulse as quick and natural as that which would prompt him to put out his hand to save a baby from a puddle. All this flashed through his mind in a minute, but not a trace of it appeared in his face; and by the time the paper was turned, and Jo's needle threaded, he was ready to say quite naturally, but very gravely, —

"Yes, you are right to put it from you. I do not like to think that good young girls should see such things. They are made pleasant to some, but I would more rather give my boys gunpowder to play with than this bad trash."

"All may not be bad – only silly, you know; and if there is a demand for it, I don't see any harm in supplying it. Many very respectable people make an honest living out of what are called sensation stories," said Jo, scratching gathers so energetically that a row of little slits followed her pin.

"There is a demand for whiskey, but I think you and I do not care to sell it. If the respectable people knew what harm they did, they would not feel that the living *was* honest. They haf no right to put poison in the sugar-plum, and let the small ones eat it. No; they should think a little, and sweep mud in the street before they do this thing!"

Mr. Bhaer spoke warmly, and walked to the fire, crumpling the paper in his hands. Jo sat still, looking as if the fire had come to her; for her cheeks burned long after the cocked hat had turned to smoke, and gone harmlessly up the chimney.

"I should like much to send all the rest after him," muttered the Professor, coming back with a relieved air.

Jo thought what a blaze her pile of papers, up stairs, would make, and her hard-earned money lay rather heavily on her conscience at that minute. Then she thought consolingly to herself, "Mine are not like that; they are only silly, never bad; so I won't be worrried;" and, taking up her book, she said, with a studious face, –

"Shall we go on, sir? I'll be very good and proper now."

"I shall hope so," was all he said, but he meant more than she imagined; and the grave, kind look he gave her, made her feel as if the words "Weekly Volcano" were printed in large type, on her forehead.

As soon as she went to her room, she got out her papers, and carefully re-read every one of her stories. Being a little short-sighted, Mr. Bhaer sometimes used eye-glasses, and Jo had tried them once, smiling to see how they magnified the fine print of her book; now she seemed to have got on the Professor's mental or moral spectacles also, for the faults of these poor stories glared at her dreadfully, and filled her with dismay.

"They *are* trash, and will soon be worse than trash if I go on; for each is more sensational than the last. I've gone blindly on, hurting myself and other people, for the sake of money; – I know it's so; for I can't read this stuff in sober earnest without being horribly ashamed of it; and *what should* I do if they were seen at home, or Mr. Bhaer got hold of them?"

Jo turned hot at the bare idea, and stuffed the whole bundle into her stove, nearly setting the chimney afire with the blaze.

"Yes, that's the best place for such inflammable nonsense; I'd better burn the house down, I suppose, than let the other people blow themselves up with my gunpowder," she thought, as she watched the "Demon of the Jura" whisk away, a little black cinder with fiery eyes.

But when nothing remained of all her three months' work, except a heap of ashes, and the money in her lap, Jo looked sober, as she sat on the floor, wondering what she ought to do about her wages.

"I think I haven't done much harm *yet*, and may keep this to pay for my time," she said, after a long meditation, adding, impatiently, "I almost wish I hadn't any conscience, it's so inconvenient. If I didn't care about doing right, and didn't feel uncomfortable when doing wrong, I should get on capitally. I can't help wishing, sometimes, that father and mother hadn't been so dreadfully particular about such things."

Ah, Jo, instead of wishing that, thank God that "father and mother *were* particular," and pity from your heart those who have no such guardians to hedge them round with principles which may seem like prison walls to impatient youth, but which will prove sure foundations to build character upon in womanhood.

Jo wrote no more sensational stories, deciding that the money did not pay for her share of the sensation; but, going to the other extreme, as is the way with people of her stamp, she took a course of Mrs. Sherwood, Miss Edgeworth and Hannah More; and then produced a tale which might have been more properly called an essay or a sermon, so intensely moral was it. She had her doubts about it from the beginning; for her lively fancy and girlish romance felt as ill at ease in the new style as she would have done masquerading in the stiff and cumbrous costume of the last century. She sent this didactic gem to several markets, but it found no purchaser; and she was inclined to agree with Mr. Dashwood, that morals didn't sell.

Then she tried a child's story, which she could easily have disposed of it she had not been mercenary enough to demand filthy lucre for it. The only person who offered enough to make it worth her while to try juvenile literature, was a worthy gentleman who felt it his mission to convert all the world to his particular belief. But much as she liked to write for children, Jo could not consent to depict all her naughty boys as being eaten by bears, or tossed by mad bulls, because they did not go to a particular Sabbath-school, nor all the good infants who did go, of course, as rewarded by every kind of bliss, from gilded ginger-bread to escorts of angels, when they departed this life, with psalms or sermons on their lisping tongues. So nothing came of these trials; and Jo corked up her inkstand, and said, in a fit of very wholesome humility, –

"I don't know anything; I'll wait till I do before I try again, and, meantime, 'sweep mud in the street,' if I can't do better – that's honest, any way;" which decision proved that her second tumble down the bean-stalk had done her some good.

While these internal revolutions were going on, her external life had been as busy and uneventful as usual; and if she sometimes looked serious, or a little sad, no one observed it but Professor Bhaer. He did it so quietly, that Jo never knew he was watching to see if she would accept and profit by his reproof; but she stood the test, and he was satisfied; for, though no words passed between them, he knew that she had given up writing. Not only did he guess it by the fact that the second finger of her right hand was no longer inky, but she spent her evenings down stairs, now, was met no more among newspaper offices, and studied with a dogged patience, which assured him that she was bent on occupying her mind with something useful, if not pleasant.

He helped her in many ways, proving himself a true friend, and Jo was happy; for while her pen lay idle, she was learning other lessons beside German, and laying a foundation for the sensation story of her own life.

It was a pleasant winter and a long one, for she did not leave Mrs. Kirke till June. Every one seemed sorry when the time came; the children were inconsolable, and Mr. Bhaer's hair stuck straight up all over his head – for he always rumpled it wildly when disturbed in mind.

"Going home! Ah, you are happy that you haf a home to go in," he said, when she told him, and sat silently pulling his beard, in the corner, while she held a little levee on that last evening.

She was going early, so she bade them all good-by over night; and when his turn came, she said warmly, –

"Now, sir, you won't forget to come and see us, if you ever travel our way, will you? I'll never forgive you, if you do, for I want them all to know my friend."

"Do you? Shall I come?" he asked, looking down at her with an eager expression, which she did not see.

"Yes, come next month; Laurie graduates then, and you'd enjoy Commencement as something new."

"That is your best friend, of whom you speak?" he said, in an altered tone.

"Yes, my boy Teddy; I'm very proud of him, and should like you to see him."

Jo looked up, then, quite unconscious of anything but her own pleasure, in the prospect of showing them to one another. Something in Mr. Bhaer's face suddenly recalled the fact that she might find Laurie more than a best friend, and simply because she particularly wished not to look as if anything was the matter, she involuntarily began to blush; and the more she tried not to, the redder she grew. If it had not been for Tina on her knee, she didn't know what would have become of her. Fortunately, the child was moved to hug her; so she managed to hide her face an instant, hoping the Professor did not see it. But he did, and his own changed again from that momentary anxiety to its usual expression, as he said, cordially, –

"I fear I shall not make the time for that, but I wish the friend much success, and you all happiness; Gott bless you!" and with that, he shook hands warmly, shouldered Tina, and went away.

But after the boys were abed, he sat long before his fire, with the tired look on his face, and the "*heimweh*," or homesickness lying heavily at his heart. Once when he remembered Jo, as she sat with the little child in her lap, and that new softness in her face, he leaned his head on his hands a minute, and then roamed about the room, as if in search of something that he could not find.

"It is not for me; I must not hope it now," he said to himself, with a sigh that was almost a groan; then, as if reproaching himself for the longing that he could not repress, he went and kissed the two towzled heads upon the pillow, took down his seldom-used meerschaum, and opened his Plato.

He did his best, and did it manfully; but I don't think he found that a pair of rampant boys, a pipe or even the divine Plato, were very satisfactory substitutes for wife and child, and home.

Early as it was, he was at the station, next morning, to see Jo off; and, thanks to him, she began her solitary journey with the pleasant memory of a familiar face smiling its farewell, a bunch of violets to keep her company, and, best of all, the happy thought, —

"Well, the winter's gone, and I've written no books — earned no fortune; but I've made a friend worth having, and I'll try to keep him all my life."

CHAPTER THIRTY-FIVE

HEARTACHE

~

Whatever his motive might have been, Laurie "dug" to some purpose that year, for he graduated with honor, and gave the Latin Oration with the grace of a Phillips, and the eloquence of a Demosthenes, – so his friends said. They were all there – his grandfather, oh, so proud! – Mr. and Mrs. March, John and Meg, Jo and Beth, and all exulted over him with the sincere admiration which boys make light of at the time, but fail to win from the world by any after-triumphs.

"I've got to stay for this confounded supper, – but I shall be home early to-morrow; you'll come and meet me as usual, girls?" Laurie said, as he put the sisters into the carriage after the joys of the day were over. He said "girls," but he meant Jo, – for she was the only one who kept up the old custom; she had not the heart to refuse her splendid, successful boy anything, and answered, warmly, –

"I'll come, Teddy, rain or shine, and march before you, playing '*Hail, the conquering hero comes*,' on a jews-harp."

Laurie thanked her with a look that made her think, in a sudden panic, "Oh, deary me! I know he'll say something, and then what shall I do?"

Evening meditation and morning work somewhat allayed her fears, and, having decided that she wouldn't be vain enough to think people were going to propose when she had given them every reason to know what her answer would be, she set forth at the appointed time hoping Teddy wouldn't go and make her hurt his poor little feelings. A call at Meg's, and a refreshing sniff and sip at the Daisy and Demijohn, still further fortified her for the *tête-a-tête*, but when she saw a stalwart figure looming in the distance, she had a strong desire to turn about and run away.

"Where's the jews-harp, Jo?" cried Laurie, as soon as he was within speaking distance.

"I forgot it;" and Jo took heart again, for that salutation could not be called lover-like.

She always used to take his arm on these occasions, now she did not, and he made no complaint, – which was a bad sign, – but talked on rapidly about all sorts of far-away subjects, till they turned from the road into the little path that led homeward through the grove. Then he walked more slowly, suddenly lost his fine flow of language, and, now and then, a dreadful pause occurred. To rescue the conversation from one of the wells of silence into which it kept falling, Jo said, hastily, –

"Now you must have a good, long holiday!"

"I intend to."

Something in his resolute tone made Jo look up quickly, to find him looking down at her with an expression that assured her the dreaded moment had come and made her put out her hand with an imploring, –

"No, Teddy, – please don't!"

"I will; and you *must* hear me. It's no use, Jo, we've got to have it out, and the sooner the better for both of us," he answered, getting flushed and excited all at once.

"Say what you like, then; I'll listen," said Jo, with a desperate sort of patience.

Laurie was a young lover, but he was in earnest, and meant to "have it out," if he died in the attempt; so he plunged into the subject with characteristic impetuosity, saying, in a voice that *would* get choky now and then, in spite of manful efforts to keep it steady, –

"I've loved you ever since I've known you, Jo, – couldn't help it, you've been so good to me, – I've tried to show it, but you wouldn't let me; now I'm going to make you hear, and give me an answer, for I *can't* go on so any longer."

"I wanted to save you this; I thought you'd understand – " began Jo, finding it a great deal harder than she expected.

"I know you did; but girls are so queer you never know what they mean. They say No, when they mean Yes; and drive a man out of his wits just for the fun of it," returned Laurie, entrenching himself behind an undeniable fact.

"*I* don't. I never wanted to make you care for me so, and I went away to keep you from it if I could."

"I thought so; it was like you, but it was no use. I only loved you all the more, and I worked hard to please you, and I gave up billiards and everything you didn't like, and waited and never complained, for I hoped you'd love me, though I'm not half good enough – " here there was a choke that couldn't be controlled, so he decapitated buttercups while he cleared his "confounded throat."

"Yes, you are; you're a great deal too good for me, and I'm so grateful to you, and so proud and fond of you, I don't see why I can't love you as you want me to. I've tried, but I can't change the feeling, and it would be a lie to say I do when I don't."

"Really, truly, Jo?"

He stopped short, and caught both her hands as he put his question with a look that she did not soon forget.

"Really, truly, dear!"

They were in the grove now, – close by the stile; and when the last words fell reluctantly from Jo's lips, Laurie dropped her hands and turned as if to go on, but for once in his life that fence was too much for him; so he just laid his head down on the mossy post, and stood so still that Jo was frightened.

"Oh, Teddy, I'm so sorry, so desperately sorry, I could kill myself if it would do any good! I wish you wouldn't take it so hard; I can't help it; you know it's impossible for people to make themselves love other people if they don't," cried Jo, inelegantly but remorsefully, as she softly patted his shoulder, remembering the time when he had comforted her so long ago.

"They do sometimes," said a muffled voice from the post.

"I don't believe it's the right sort of love, and I'd rather not try it," was the decided answer.

There was a long pause, while a blackbird sung blithely on the willow by the river, and the tall grass rustled in the wind. Presently Jo said, very soberly, as she sat down on the step of the stile, –

"Laurie, I want to tell you something."

He started as if he had been shot, threw up his head, and cried out, in a fierce tone, –

"*Don't* tell me that, Jo; I can't bear it now!"

"Tell what?" she asked, wondering at his violence.

"That you love that old man."

"What old man?" demanded Jo, thinking he must mean his grandfather.

"That devilish Professor you were always writing about. If you say you love him I know I shall do something desperate" – and he looked as if he would keep his word, as he clenched his hands with a wrathful spark in his eyes.

Jo wanted to laugh, but restrained herself, and said, warmly, for she, too, was getting excited with all this, –

"Don't swear, Teddy! He isn't old, nor anything bad, but good and kind, and the best friend I've got – next to you. Pray don't fly into a passion; I want to be kind, but I know I shall get angry if you abuse my Professor. I haven't the least idea of loving him, or anybody else."

"But you will after a while, and then what will become of me?"

"You'll love some one else, too, like a sensible boy, and forget all this trouble."

"I *can't* love any one else; and I'll never forget you, Jo, never! never!" with a stamp to emphasize his passionate words.

"What *shall* I do with him?" sighed Jo, finding that emotions were more unmanageable than she expected. "You haven't heard what I wanted to tell you. Sit down and listen; for indeed I want to do right, and make you happy," she said, hoping to soothe him with a little reason, – which proved that she knew nothing about love.

Seeing a ray of hope in that last speech, Laurie threw himself down on the grass at her feet, leaned his arm on the lower step of the stile, and looked up at her with an expectant face. Now that arrangement was not conducive to calm speech or clear thought on Jo's part; for how *could* she say hard things to her boy while he watched her with eyes full of love and longing, and lashes still wet with the bitter drop or two her hardness of heart had wrung from him? She gently turned his head away, saying, as she stroked the wavy hair which had been allowed to grow for her sake, – how touching that was to be sure! –

"I agree with mother, that you and I are not suited to each other, because our quick tempers and strong wills would probably make us very miserable, if we were so foolish as to – " Jo paused a little over the last word, but Laurie uttered it with a rapturous expression, -

"Marry, – no, we shouldn't! If you loved me, Jo, I should be a perfect saint, – for you can make me anything you like!"

"No, I can't. I've tried it and failed, and I won't risk our happiness by such a serious experiment. We don't agree, and we never shall; so we'll be good friends all our lives, but we won't go and do anything rash."

"Yes, we will if we get the chance," muttered Laurie, rebelliously.

"Now do be reasonable, and take a sensible view of the case," implored Jo, almost at her wit's end.

"I won't be reasonable; I don't want to take what you call 'a sensible view'; it won't help me, and it only makes you harder. I don't believe you've got any heart."

"I wish I hadn't!"

There was a little quiver in Jo's voice, and, thinking it a good omen, Laurie turned around, bringing all his persuasive powers to bear as he said, in the wheedlesome tone that had never been so dangerously wheedlesome before, –

"Don't disappoint us, dear! every one expects it. Grandpa has set his heart upon it, – your people like it, – and I can't get on without you. Say you will, and let's be happy! do, do!"

Not until months afterward did Jo understand how she had the strength of mind to hold fast to the resolution she had made when she decided that she did not love her boy, and never could. It was very hard to do, but she did it, knowing that delay was both useless and cruel.

"I can't say 'Yes' truly, so I won't say it at all. You'll see that I'm right, by and by, and thank me for it" – she began, solemnly.

"I'll be hanged if I do!" and Laurie bounced up off the grass, burning with indignation at the bare idea.

"Yes, you will!" persisted Jo; "you'll get over this after a while, and find some lovely, accomplished girl, who will adore you, and make a fine mistress for your fine house. I shouldn't. I'm homely, and awkward, and odd, and old, and you'd be ashamed of me, and we should quarrel, – we can't help it even now, you see, – and I shouldn't like elegant society and you would, and you'd hate my scribbling, and I couldn't get on without it, and we should be unhappy, and wish we hadn't done it, – and everything would be horrid!"

"Anything more?" asked Laurie, finding it hard to listen patiently to this prophetic burst.

"Nothing more, – except that I don't believe I shall ever marry; I'm happy as I am, and love my liberty too well to be in any hurry to give it up for any mortal man."

"I know better!" broke in Laurie, "you think so now; but there'll come a time when you *will* care for somebody, and you'll love him tremendously, and live and die for him. I know you will, – it's your way, – and I shall have to stand by and see it" – and the despairing lover cast his hat upon the ground with a gesture that would have seemed comical, if his face had not been so tragical.

"Yes, I *will* live and die for him, if he ever comes and makes me love him in spite of myself, and you must do the best you can," cried Jo, losing patience with poor Teddy. "I've done my best, but you *won't* be reasonable, and it's selfish of you to keep teasing for what I can't give. I shall always be fond of you, – very fond indeed, as a friend, – but I'll never marry you; and the sooner you believe it the better for both of us, – so now."

That speech was like fire to gunpowder. Laurie looked at her a minute, as if he did not quite know what to do with himself, then turned sharply away, saying, in a desperate sort of tone, –

"You'll be sorry some day, Jo."

"Oh, where are you going?" she cried, for his face frightened her.

"To the devil!" was the consoling answer.

For a minute Jo's heart stood still, as he swung himself down the bank, toward the river; but it takes much folly, sin, or misery to send a

young man to a violent death, and Laurie was not one of the weak sort, who
are conquered by a single failure. He had no thought of a melodramatic
plunge, but some blind instinct led him to fling hat and coat into his boat,
and row away with all his might, making better time up the river than he
had done in many a race. Jo drew a long breath, and unclasped her hands
as she watched the poor fellow trying to outstrip the trouble which he
carried in his heart.

"That will do him good, and he'll come home in such a tender, tender,
penitent state of mind, that I shan't dare to see him," she said; adding, as
she went slowly home, feeling as if she had murdered some innocent thing,
and buried it under the leaves, –

"Now I must go and prepare Mr. Laurence to be very kind to my
poor boy. I wish he'd love Beth; perhaps he may, in time, but I begin to
think I was mistaken about her. Oh dear! how can girls like to have lovers,
and refuse them. I think it's dreadful."

Being sure that no one could do it so well as herself, she went
straight to Mr. Laurence, told the hard story bravely through, and then
broke down, crying so dismally over her own insensibility, that the kind
old gentleman, though sorely disappointed, did not utter a reproach. He
found it difficult to understand how any girl could help loving Laurie, and
hoped she would change her mind, but he knew even better than Jo, that
love cannot be forced, so he shook his head sadly, and resolved to carry his
boy out of harm's way; for Young Impetuosity's parting words to Jo
disturbed him more than he would confess.

When Laurie came home, dead tired, but quite composed, his
grandfather met him as if he knew nothing, and kept up the delusion very
successfully, for an hour or two. But when they sat together in the twilight,
the time they used to enjoy so much, it was hard work for the old man to
ramble on as usual, and harder still for the young one to listen to praises of
the last year's success, which to him now seemed love's labor lost. He bore
it as long as he could, then went to his piano, and began to play. The
windows were open; and Jo, walking in the garden with Beth, for once
understood music better than her sister, for he played the "Sonata
Pathetique," and played it as he never did before.

"That's very fine, I dare say, but it's sad enough to make one cry; give
us something gayer, lad," said Mr. Laurence, whose kind old heart was full

of sympathy, which he longed to show, but knew not how.

Laurie dashed into a livelier strain, played stormily for several minutes, and would have got through bravely, if, in a momentary lull, Mrs. March's voice had not been heard calling, –

"Jo, dear, come in; I want you."

Just what Laurie longed to say, with a different meaning! As he listened, he lost his place; the music ended with a broken chord, and the musician sat silent in the dark.

"I can't stand this," muttered the old gentleman – up he got, groped his way to the piano, laid a kind hand on either of the broad shoulders, and said, as gently as a woman, –

"I know, my boy, I know."

No answer for an instant; then Laurie asked sharply, –

"Who told you?"

"Jo herself."

"Then there's an end of it!" and he shook off his grandfather's hands with an impatient motion; for, though grateful for the sympathy, his man's pride could not bear a man's pity.

"Not quite; I want to say one thing, and then there shall be an end of it," returned Mr. Laurence, with unusual mildness. "You won't care to stay at home, just now, perhaps?"

"I don't intend to run away from a girl. Jo can't prevent my seeing her, and I shall stay and do it as long as I like," interrupted Laurie, in a defiant tone.

"Not if you are the gentleman I think you. I'm disappointed, but the girl can't help it; and the only thing left for you to do, is to go away for a time. Where will you go?"

"Anywhere; I don't care what becomes of me;" and Laurie got up, with a reckless laugh, that grated on his grandfather's ear.

"Take it like a man, and don't do anything rash, for God's sake. Why not go abroad, as you planned, and forget it?"

"I can't."

"But you've been wild to go, and I promised you should, when you got through college."

"Ah, but I didn't mean to go alone!" and Laurie walked fast through the room, with an expression which it was well his grandfather did not see.

"I don't ask you to go alone; there's some one ready and glad to go with you, anywhere in the world."

"Who, sir?" stopping to listen.

"Myself."

Laurie came back as quickly as he went, and put out his hand, saying huskily, –

"I'm a selfish brute; but – you know – grandfather – "

"Lord help me, yes, I do know, for I've been through it all before, once in my own young days, and then with your father. Now, my dear boy, just sit quietly down, and hear my plan. It's all settled, and can be carried out at once," said Mr. Laurence, keeping hold of the young man, as if fearful that he would break away, as his father had done before him.

"Well, sir, what is it?" and Laurie sat down without a sign of interest in face or voice.

"There is business in London that needs looking after; I meant you should attend to it; but I can do it better myself, and things here will get on very well with Brooke to manage them. My partners do almost everything; I'm merely holding on till you take my place, and can be off at any time."

"But you hate travelling, sir; I can't ask it of you at your age," began Laurie, who was grateful for the sacrifice, but much preferred to go alone, if he went at all.

The old gentleman knew that perfectly well, and particularly desired to prevent it; for the mood in which he found his grandson, assured him that it would not be wise to leave him to his own devices. So, stifling a natural regret at the thought of the home comforts he would leave behind him, he said, stoutly, –

"Bless your soul, I'm not superannuated yet. I quite enjoy the idea; it will do me good, and my old bones won't suffer, for travelling nowadays is almost as easy as sitting in a chair."

A restless movement from Laurie suggested that *his* chair was not easy, or that he did not like the plan, and made the old man add, hastily, -

"I don't mean to be a marplot or a burden, I go because I think you'd feel happier than if I were left behind. I don't intend to gad about with you, but leave you free to go where you like, while I amuse myself in my own way. I've friends in London and Paris, and should like to visit them;

meantime, you can go to Italy, Germany, Switzerland, where you will, and enjoy pictures, music, scenery and adventures, to your heart's content."

Now, Laurie felt just then that his heart was entirely broken, and the world a howling wilderness; but, at the sound of certain words which the old gentleman artfully introduced into his closing sentence, the broken heart gave an unexpected leap, and a green oasis or two suddenly appeared in the howling wilderness. He sighed, and then said, in a spiritless tone, -

"Just as you like, sir; it doesn't matter where I go, *or* what I do."

"It does to me — remember that, my lad; I give you entire liberty, but I trust you to make an honest use of it. Promise me that, Laurie."

"Anything you like, sir."

"Good!" thought the old gentleman; "you don't care now, but there'll come a time when that promise will keep you out of mischief, or I'm much mistaken."

Being an energetic individual, Mr. Laurence struck while the iron was hot; and before the blighted being recovered spirit enough to rebel, they were off. During the time necessary for preparation, Laurie bore himself as young gentlemen usually do in such cases. He was moody, irritable, and pensive by turns; lost his appetite, neglected his dress, and devoted much time to playing tempestuously on his piano; avoided Jo, but consoled himself by staring at her from his window, with a tragical face that haunted her dreams by night, and oppressed her with a heavy sense of guilt by day. Unlike some sufferers, he never spoke of his unrequited passion, and would allow no one, not even Mrs. March, to attempt consolation, or offer sympathy. On some accounts, this was a relief to his friends; but the weeks before his departure were very uncomfortable, and every one rejoiced that the "poor, dear fellow was going away to forget his trouble, and come home happy." Of course he smiled darkly at their delusion, but passed it by, with the sad superiority of one who knew that his fidelity, like his love, was unalterable.

When the parting came he affected high spirits, to conceal certain inconvenient emotions which seemed inclined to assert themselves. This gayety did not impose upon anybody, but they tried to look as if it did, for his sake, and he got on very well till Mrs. Marsh kissed him, with a whisper full of motherly solicitude; then, feeling that he was going very fast, he hastily embraced them all round, not forgetting the afflicted Hannah, and ran down stairs as if for his life. Jo followed a minute after to wave her hand to him if he looked round. He did look round, came back, put his arms about her, as she stood on the step above him, and looked up at her with a face that made his short appeal both eloquent and pathetic.

"Oh, Jo, can't you?"

"Teddy, dear, I wish I could!"

That was all, except a little pause; then Laurie straightened himself up, said "It's all right, never mind," and went away without another word. Ah, but it wasn't all right, and Jo *did* mind; for while the curly head lay on her arm a minute after her hard answer, she felt as if she had stabbed her dearest friend; and when he left her, without a look behind him, she knew that the boy Laurie never would come again.

CHAPTER THIRTY-SIX

BETH'S SECRET

~

When Jo came home that spring, she had been struck with the change in Beth. No one spoke of it, or seemed aware of it, for it had come too gradually to startle those who saw her daily; but to eyes sharpened by absence it was very plain, and a heavy weight fell on Jo's heart as she saw her sister's face. It was no paler, and but little thinner than in the autumn; yet there was a strange, transparent look about it, as if the mortal was being slowly refined away, and the immortal shining through the frail flesh with an indescribably pathetic beauty. Jo saw and felt it, but said nothing at the time, and soon the first impression lost much of its power, for Beth seemed happy, — no one appeared to doubt that she was better; and, presently, in other cares, Jo for a time forgot her fear.

But when Laurie was gone, and peace prevailed again, the vague anxiety returned and haunted her. She had confessed her sins and been forgiven; but when she showed her savings and proposed the mountain trip, Beth had thanked her heartily, but, begged not to go so far away from

401

home. Another little visit to the seashore would suit her better, and, as grandma could not be prevailed upon to leave the babies, Jo took Beth down to the quiet place, where she could live much in the open air, and let the fresh sea breezes blow a little color into her pale cheeks.

It was not a fashionable place, but, even among the pleasant people there, the girls made few friends, preferring to live for one another. Beth was too shy to enjoy society, and Jo too wrapt up in her to care for any one else; so they were all in all to each other, and came and went, quite unconscious of the interest they excited in those about them, – who watched with sympathetic eyes the strong sister and the feeble one, always together, as if they felt instinctively that a long separation was not far away.

They did feel it, yet neither spoke of it; for often between ourselves and those nearest and dearest to us there exists a reserve which it is very hard to overcome. Jo felt as if a veil had fallen between her heart and Beth's; but when she put out her hand to lift it up there seemed something sacred in the silence, and she waited for Beth to speak. She wondered, and was thankful also, that her parents did not seem to see what she saw; and, during the quiet weeks, when the shadow grew so plain to her, she said nothing of it to those at home, believing that it would tell itself when Beth came back no better. She wondered still more if her sister really guessed the hard truth, and what thoughts were passing through her mind during the long hours when she lay on the warm rocks with her head in Jo's lap, while the winds blew healthfully over her, and the sea made music at her feet.

One day Beth told her. Jo thought she was asleep, she lay so still; and, putting down her book, sat looking at her with wistful eyes, – trying to see signs of hope in the faint color on Beth's cheeks. But she could not find enough to satisfy her, – for the cheeks were very thin, and the hands seemed too feeble to hold even the rosy little shells they had been gathering. It came to her then more bitterly than ever that Beth was slowly drifting away from her, and her arms instinctively tightened their hold upon the dearest treasure she possessed. For a minute her eyes were too dim for seeing, and, when they cleared, Beth was looking up at her so tenderly, that there was hardly any need for her to say, –

"Jo, dear, I'm glad you know it. I've tried to tell you, but I couldn't."

There was no answer except her sister's cheek against her own, – not even tears, – for when most deeply moved Jo did not cry. She was the weaker then, and Beth tried to comfort and sustain her with her arms about her, and the soothing words she whispered in her ear.

"I've known it for a good while, dear, and now I'm used to it, it isn't hard to think of or to bear. Try to see it so, and don't be troubled about me, because it's best; indeed it is."

"Is this what made you so unhappy in the autumn, Beth?" You did not feel it then, and keep it to yourself so long, did you?" asked Jo, refusing to see or say that it *was* best, but glad to know that Laurie had no part in Beth's trouble.

"Yes; I gave up hoping then, but I didn't like to own it; I tried to think it was a sick fancy, and would not let it trouble any one. But when I saw you all so well, and strong, and full of happy plans, it was hard to feel that I could never be like you, – and then I was miserable, Jo."

"Oh, Beth, and you didn't tell me, – didn't let me comfort and help you! How could you shut me out, and bear it all alone?"

Jo's voice was full of tender reproach, and her heart ached to think of the solitary struggle that must have gone on while Beth learned to say good-by to health, love, and life, and take up her cross so cheerfully.

"Perhaps it was wrong, but I tried to do right; I wasn't sure, no one said anything, and I hoped I was mistaken. It would have been selfish to frighten you all when Marmee was so anxious about Meg, and Amy away, and you so happy with Laurie, – at least I thought so then."

"And I thought that you loved him, Beth, and I went away because I couldn't," cried Jo, – glad to say all the truth.

Beth looked so amazed at the idea, that Jo smiled in spite of her pain, and added, softly, –

"Then you didn't, deary?" I was afraid it was so, and imagined your poor little heart full of love-lornity all that while."

"Why, Jo! how could I, when he was so fond of you?" asked Beth, as innocently as a child. "I do love him dearly; he is so good to me, how can I help it? But he never could be anything to me but a brother. I hope he truly will be, some time."

"Not through me," said Jo, decidedly. "Amy is left for him, and they would suit excellently, – but I have no heart for such things now. I don't care what becomes of anybody but you, Beth. You *must* get well."

"I want to, – oh, so much! I try, but every day I lose a little, and feel more sure that I shall never gain it back. It's like the tide, Jo, when it turns, – it goes slowly, but it can't be stopped."

"It *shall* be stopped, – your tide must not turn so soon, – nineteen is too young. Beth, I can't let you go. I'll work, and pray, and fight against it. I'll keep you in spite of everything; there must be ways, – it can't be too late. God won't be so cruel as to take you from me," cried poor Jo, rebelliously, – for her spirit was far less piously submissive than Beth's.

Simple, sincere people seldom speak much of their piety; it shows itself in acts, rather than in words, and has more influence than homilies or protestations. Beth could not reason upon or explain the faith that gave her courage and patience to give up life, and cheerfully wait for death. Like a confiding child, she asked no questions, but left everything to God and nature, Father and mother of us all, feeling sure that they, and they only, could teach and strengthen heart and spirit for this life and the life to come. She did not rebuke Jo with saintly speeches, only loved her better for her passionate affection, and clung more closely to the dear human love, from which our Father never means us to be weaned, but through which He draws us closer to Himself. She could not say, "I'm glad to go," for life was very sweet to her; she could only sob out, "I'll try to be willing," while she held fast to Jo, as the first bitter wave of this great sorrow broke over them together.

By and by Beth said, with recovered serenity, –

"You'll tell them this, when we go home?"

"I think they will see it without words," sighed Jo; for now it seemed to her that Beth changed every day.

"Perhaps not; I've heard that the people who love best are often blindest to such things. If they don't see it, you will tell them for me. I don't want any secrets, and it's kinder to prepare them. Meg has John and the babies to comfort her, but you must stand by father and mother, won't you, Jo?"

"If I can, but, Beth, I don't give up yet; I'm going to believe that it *is* a sick fancy, and not let you think it's true," said Jo, trying to speak cheerfully.

Beth lay a minute thinking, and then said in her quiet way, –

"I don't know how to express myself, and shouldn't try to any one but you, because I can't speak out, except to my old Jo. I only mean to say, that I have a feeling that it never was intended I should live long. I'm not like the rest of you; I never made any plans about what I'd do when I grew up; I never thought of being married, as you all did. I couldn't seem to imagine myself anything but stupid little Beth, trotting about at home, of no use anywhere but there. I never wanted to go away, and the hard part now is the leaving you all. I'm not afraid, but it seems as if I should be homesick for you even in heaven."

Jo could not speak; and for several minutes there was no sound but the sigh of the wind, and the lapping of the tide. A white-winged gull flew by, with the flash of sunshine on its silvery breast; Beth watched it till it vanished, and her eyes were full of sadness. A little gray-coated sand-bird came tripping over the beach, "peeping" softly to itself, as if enjoying the sun and sea; it came quite close to Beth, looked at her with a friendly eye, and sat upon a warm stone, dressing its wet feathers, quite at home. Beth smiled, and felt comforted, for the tiny thing seemed to offer its small friendship, and remind her that a pleasant world was still to be enjoyed.

"Dear little bird! See, Jo, how tame it is. I like peeps better than the gulls, they are not so wild and handsome, but they seem happy, confiding little things. I used to call them my birds, last summer; and mother said they reminded her of me — busy, quaker-colored creatures, always near the shore, and always chirping that contented little song of theirs. You are the gull, Jo, strong and wild, fond of the storm and the wind, flying far out to sea, and happy all alone. Meg is the turtle-dove, and Amy is like the lark she writes about, trying to get up among the clouds, but always dropping down into its nest again. Dear little girl! she's so ambitious, but her heart is good and tender, and no matter how high she flies, she never will forget home. I hope I shall see her again, but she seems *so* far away."

"She is coming in the spring, and I mean that you shall be all ready to see and enjoy her. I'm going to have you well and rosy, by that time," began Jo, feeling that of all the changes in Beth, the talking change was the greatest, for it seemed to cost no effort now, and she thought aloud in a way quite unlike bashful Beth.

"Jo, dear, don't hope any more; it won't do any good, I'm sure of that. We won't be miserable, but enjoy being together while we wait. We'll have happy times, for I don't suffer much, and I think the tide will go out easily, if you help me."

Jo leaned down to kiss the tranquil face; and with that silent kiss, she dedicated herself soul and body to Beth.

She was right – there was no need of any words when they got home, for father and mother saw plainly, now, what they had prayed to be saved from seeing. Tired with her short journey, Beth went at once to bed, saying how glad she was to be at home; and when Jo went down, she found that she would be spared the hard task of telling Beth's secret. Her father stood leaning his head on the mantel-piece, and did not turn as she came in; but her mother stretched out her arms as if for help, and Jo went to comfort her without a word.

CHAPTER THIRTY-SEVEN

NEW IMPRESSIONS
~

At three o'clock in the afternoon, all the fashionable world at Nice may be seen on the Promenade des Anglais — a charming place; for the wide walk, bordered with palms, flowers, and tropical shrubs, is bounded on one side by the sea, on the other by the grand drive, lined with hotels and villas, while beyond lie orange orchards and the hills. Many nations are represented, many languages spoken, many costumes worn; and, on a sunny day, the spectacle is as gay and brilliant as a carnival. Haughty English, lively French, sober Germans, handsome Spaniards, ugly Russians, meek Jews, free-and-easy Americans, — all drive, sit, or saunter here, chatting over the news, and criticising the latest celebrity who has arrived — Ristori or Dickens, Victor Emanuel or the Queen of the Sandwich Islands. The equipages are as varied as the company, and attract as much attention, especially the low basket barouches in which ladies drive themselves, with a pair of dashing ponies, gay nets to keep their voluminous flounces from overflowing the diminutive vehicles, and little grooms on the perch behind.

Along this walk, on Christmas day, a tall young man walked slowly, with his hands behind him, and a somewhat absent expression of countenance. He looked like an Italian, was dressed like an Englishman, and had the independent air of an American — a combination which caused sundry pairs of feminine eyes to look approvingly after him, and sundry dandies in black velvet suits, with rose-colored neckties, buff gloves, and orange flowers in their buttonholes, to shrug their shoulders, and then envy him his inches. There were plenty of pretty faces to admire, but the young man took little notice of them, except to glance now and then at some blond girl or lady in blue. Presently he strolled out of the promenade, and stood a moment at the crossing, as if undecided whether to go and listen to the band in the Jardin Publique, or to wander along the beach toward Castle Hill. The quick trot of ponies' feet made him look up, as one of the little carriages, containing a single lady, came rapidly down the street. The lady was young, blond, and dressed in blue. He stared a minute, then his whole face woke up, and, waving his hat like a boy, he hurried forward to meet her.

"Oh, Laurie! is it really you? I thought you'd never come!" cried Amy, dropping the reins, and holding out both hands, to the great scandalization of a French mamma, who hastened her daughter's step, lest she should be demoralized by beholding the free manners of these "mad English."

"I was detained by the way, but I promised to spend Christmas with you, and here I am."

"How is your grandfather? When did you come? Where are you staying?"

"Very well — last night — at the Chauvain. I called at your hotel, but you were all out."

"*Mon Dieu!* I have so much to say, and don't know where to begin. Get in, and we can talk at our ease; I was going for a drive, and longing for company. Flo's saving up for to-night."

"What happens, then — a ball?"

"A Christmas party at our hotel. There are many Americans there, and they give it in honor of the day. You'll go with us, of course? aunt will be charmed."

"Thank you! where now?" asked Laurie, leaning back and folding his arms, a proceeding which suited Amy, who preferred to drive; for her parasol-whip and blue reins, over the white ponies' backs, afforded her infinite satisfaction.

"I'm going to the banker's first, for letters, and then to Castle Hill; the view is so lovely, and I like to feed the peacocks. Have you ever been there?"

"Often, years ago; but I don't mind having at look at it."

"Now tell me all about yourself. The last I heard of you, your grandfather wrote that he expected you from Berlin."

"Yes, I spent a month there, and then joined him in Paris, where he has settled for the winter. He has friends there, and finds plenty to amuse him; so I go and come, and we get on capitally."

"That's a sociable arrangement," said Amy, missing something in Laurie's manner, though she couldn't tell what.

"Why, you see, he hates to travel, and I hate to keep still; so we each suit ourselves, and there is no trouble. I am often with him, and he enjoys my adventures, while I like to feel that some one is glad to see me when I get back from my wanderings. Dirty old hole, isn't it?" he added, with a sniff of disgust, as they drove along the boulevard to the Place Napoleon, in the old city.

"The dirt is picturesque, so I don't mind. The river and the hills are delicious, and these glimpses of the narrow cross streets are my delight. Now we shall have to wait for that procession to pass; it's going to the church of St. John."

While Laurie listlessly watched the procession of priests under their canopies, white-veiled nuns bearing lighted tapers, and some brotherhood in blue, chanting as they walked, Amy watched him, and felt a new sort of shyness steal over her, for he was changed, and she couldn't find the merry-faced boy she left, in the moody-looking man beside her. He was handsomer than ever, and greatly improved, she thought; but now that the flush of pleasure at meeting her was over, he looked tired and spiritless — not sick, nor exactly unhappy, but older and graver than a year or two of prosperous life should have made him. She couldn't understand it, and did not venture to ask questions; so she shook her head, and touched up her ponies, as the procession wound away across the arches of the Paglioni bridge, and vanished in the church.

"*Que pensez vous?*" she said, airing her French, which had improved in quantity, if not in quality, since she came abroad.

"That mademoiselle has made good use of her time, and the result is charming," replied Laurie, bowing, with his hand on his heart, and an admiring look.

She blushed with pleasure, but, somehow, the compliment did not satisfy her like the blunt praises he used to give her at home, when he promenaded round her on festival occasions, and told her she was "altogether jolly," with a hearty smile and an approving pat on the head. She didn't like the new tone; for though not *blasé*, it sounded indifferent in spite of the look.

"If that's the way he's going to grow up, I wish he'd stay a boy," she thought, with a curious sense of disappointment and discomfort; trying, meantime, to seem quite easy and gay.

At Avigdor's she found the precious home letters, and, giving the reins to Laurie, read them luxuriously as they wound up the shady road between green hedges, where tea-roses bloomed as freshly as in June.

"Beth is very poorly, mother says. I often think I ought to go home, but they all say 'stay'; so I do, for I shall never have another chance like this," said Amy, looking sober over one page.

"I think you are right, there; you could do nothing at home, and it is a great comfort to them to know that you are well and happy, and enjoying so much, my dear."

He drew a little nearer, and looked more like his old self, as he said that; and the fear that sometimes weighed on Amy's heart was lightened, — for the look, the act, the brotherly "my dear," seemed to assure her that if any trouble did come, she would not be alone in a strange land. Presently she laughed, and showed him a small sketch of Jo in her scribbling suit, with the bow rampantly erect upon her cap, and issuing from her mouth the words, "Genius burns!"

Laurie smiled, took it, put it in his vest pocket 'to keep it from blowing away," and listened with interest to the lively letter Amy read him.

"This will be a regularly merry Christmas to me, with presents in the morning, you and letters in the afternoon, and a party at night," said Amy, as they alighted among the ruins of the old fort, and a flock of splendid peacocks came trooping about them, tamely waiting to be fed. While Amy stood laughing on the bank above him as she scattered crumbs to the brilliant birds, Laurie looked at her as she had looked at him, with a natural curiosity to see what changes time and absence had wrought. He found nothing to perplex or disappoint, much to admire and approve; for, overlooking a few little affectations of speech and manner, she was as sprightly and graceful as ever, with the addition of that indescribable something in dress and bearing which we call elegance. Always mature for her age, she had gained a certain *aplomb* in both carriage and conversation, which made her seem more of a woman of the world than she was; but her old petulance now and then showed itself, her strong will still held its own, and her native frankness was unspoiled by foreign polish.

Laurie did not read all this while he watched her feed the peacocks, but he saw enough to satisfy and interest him, and carried away a pretty little picture of a bright-faced girl standing in the sunshine, which brought out the soft hue of her dress, the fresh color of her cheeks, the golden gloss of her hair, and made her a prominent figure in the pleasant scene.

As they came up on to the stone plateau that crowns the hill, Amy waved her hand as if welcoming him to her favorite haunt, and said, pointing here and there, –

"Do you remember the Cathedral and the Corso, the fishermen dragging their nets in the bay, and the lovely road to Villa Franca, Schubert's Tower, just below, and, best of all, that speck far out to sea which they say is Corsica?"

"I remember; it's not much changed," he answered without enthusiasm.

"What Jo would give for a sight of that famous speck!" said Amy, feeling in good spirits, and anxious to see him so also.

"Yes," was all he said, but he turned and strained his eyes to see the island which a greater usurper than even Napoleon now made interesting in his sight.

"Take a good look at it for her sake, and then come and tell me what you have been doing with yourself all this while," said Amy, seating herself, ready for a good talk.

But she did not get it; for, though he joined her, and answered all her questions freely, she could only learn that he had roved about the continent and been to Greece. So, after idling away an hour, they drove home again; and, having paid his respects to Mrs. Carrol, Laurie left them, promising to return in the evening.

It must be recorded of Amy, that she deliberately "prinked" that night. Time and absence had done its work on both the young people; she had seen her old friend in a new light, – not as "our boy," but as a handsome and agreeable man, and she was conscious of a very natural desire to find favor in his sight. Amy knew her good points, and made the most of them, with the taste and skill which is a fortune to a poor and pretty woman.

Tarlatan and tulle were cheap at Nice, so she enveloped herself in them on such occasions, and, following the sensible English fashion of simple dress for young girls, got up charming little toilettes with fresh flowers, a few trinkets, and all manner of dainty devices, which were both inexpensive and effective. It must be confessed that the artist sometimes got possession of the woman, and indulged in antique *coiffures*, statuesque attitudes, and classic draperies. But, dear heart, we all have our little weaknesses, and find it easy to pardon such in the young, who satisfy our eyes with their comeliness, and keep our hearts merry with their artless vanities.

"I do want him to think I look well, and tell them so at home," said Amy to herself, as she put on Flo's old white silk ball dress, and covered it with a cloud of fresh illusion, out of which her white shoulders and golden head emerged with a most artistic effect. Her hair she had the sense to let alone, after gathering up the thick waves and curls into a Hebe-like knot at the back of her head.

"It's not the fashion, but it's becoming, and I can't afford to make a fright of myself," she used to say, when advised to frizzle, puff, or braid as the latest style commanded.

Having no ornaments fine enough for this important occasion, Amy looped her fleecy skirts with rosy clusters of azalea, and framed the white shoulders in delicate green vines. Remembering the painted boots, she surveyed her white satin slipper with girlish satisfaction, and *chasséed* down the room, admiring her aristocratic feet all by herself.

"My new fan just matches my flowers, my gloves fit to a charm, and the real lace on aunt's *mouchoir* gives an air to my whole dress. If I only had a classical nose and mouth I should be perfectly happy," she said, surveying herself with a critical eye, and a candle in each hand.

In spite of this affliction, she looked unusually gay and graceful as she glided away; she seldom ran, – it did not suit her style, she thought, – for, being tall, the stately and Junoesque was more appropriate than the sportive or piquante. She walked up and down the long saloon while waiting for Laurie, and once arranged herself under the chandelier, which had a good effect upon her hair; then she thought better of it, and went away to the other end of the room, – as if ashamed of the girlish desire to have the first view a propitious one. It so happened that she could not have done a better thing, for Laurie came in so quietly she did not hear him; and, as she stood at the distant window with her head half turned, and one hand gathering up her dress, the slender, white figure against the red curtains was as effective as a well-placed statue.

"Good evening, Diana!" said Laurie, with the look of satisfaction she liked to see in his eyes when they rested on her.

"Good evening, Apollo!" she answered, smiling back at him, – for he, too, looked unusually *débonnaire*, – and the thought of entering the ball-room on the arm of such a personable man, caused Amy to pity the four plain Misses Davis from the bottom of her heart.

"Here are your flowers! I arranged them myself, remembering that you didn't like what Hannah calls a 'sot-bookay,'" said Laurie, handing her a delicate nosegay, in a holder that she had long coveted as she daily passed it in Cardiglia's window.

"How kind you are!" she exclaimed, gratefully; "if I'd known you were coming I'd have had something ready for you to-day, – though not as pretty as this, I'm afraid."

"Thank you; it isn't what it should be, but you have improved it," he added, as she snapped the silver bracelet on her wrist.

"Please don't!"

"I thought you liked that sort of thing!"

"Not from you; it doesn't sound natural, and I like your old bluntness better."

"I'm glad of it!" he answered, with a look of relief; then buttoned her gloves for her, and asked if his tie was straight, just as he used to do when they went to parties together, at home.

The company assembled in the long *salle a manger*, that evening, was such as one sees nowhere but on the continent. The hospitable Americans had invited every acquaintance they had in Nice, and, having no prejudice against titles, secured a few to add lustre to their Christmas ball.

A Russian prince condescended to sit in a corner for an hour, and talk with a massive lady, dressed like Hamlet's mother, in black velvet, with a pearl bridle under her chin. A Polish count, aged eighteen, devoted himself to the ladies, who pronounced him "a fascinating dear," and a German Serene Something, having come for the supper alone, roamed vaguely about, seeking what he might devour. Baron Rothschild's private secretary, a large-nosed Jew, in tight boots, affably beamed upon the world, as if his master's name crowned him with a golden halo; a stout Frenchman, who knew the Emperor, came to indulge his mania for dancing, and Lady de Jones, a British matron, adorned the scene with her little family of eight. Of course, there were many light-footed, shrill-voiced American girls, handsome, lifeless looking English ditto, and a few plain but piquante French demoiselles. Likewise the usual set of travelling young gentlemen, who disported themselves gaily, while mammas of all nations lined the walls, and smiled upon them benignly when they danced with their daughters.

Any young girl can imagine Amy's state of mind when she "took the stage" that night, leaning on Laurie's arm. She knew she looked well, she loved to dance, she felt that her foot was on her native heath in a ball-room, and enjoyed the delightful sense of power which comes when young girls first discover the new and lovely kingdom they are born to rule by virtue of beauty, youth, and womanhood. She did pity the Davis girls, who were awkward, plain, and destitute of escort – except a grim papa and three grimmer maiden aunts – and she bowed to them in her friendliest manner, as she passed; which was good of her, as it permitted them to see her dress, and burn with curiosity to know who her distinguished-looking friend might be. With the first burst of the band, Amy's color rose, her eyes began to sparkle, and her feet to tap the floor impatiently; for she danced well, and wanted Laurie to know it; therefore, the shock she received can better be imagined than described, when he said, in a perfectly tranquil tone, –

"Do you care to dance?"

"One usually does at a ball!"

Her amazed look and quick answer caused Laurie to repair his error as fast as possible.

"I meant the first dance. May I have the honor?"

"I can give you one if I put off the Count. He dances divinely; but he will excuse me, as you are an old friend," said Amy, hoping that the name would have a good effect, and show Laurie that she was not to be trifled with.

"Nice little boy, but rather a short Pole to support the steps of

> A daughter of the gods
> Divinely tall, and most divinely fair,"

was all the satisfaction she got, however.

The set in which they found themselves was composed of English, and Amy was compelled to walk decorously through a cotillion, feeling all the while as if she could dance the Tarantula with a relish. Laurie resigned her to the "nice little boy," and went to do his duty to Flo, without securing Amy for the joys to come, which reprehensible want of forethought was properly punished, for she immediately engaged herself till supper, meaning to relent if he then gave any sign of penitence. She showed him her ball-book with demure satisfaction when he strolled, instead of rushing, up to claim her for the next, a glorious polka-redowa; but his polite regrets didn't impose upon her, and when she gallopaded away with the Count, she saw Laurie sit down by her aunt, with an actual expression of relief.

That was unpardonable; and Amy took no more notice of him for a long while, except a word now and then, when she came to her chaperon, between the dances, for a necessary pin or a moment's rest. Her anger had a good effect, however, for she hid it under a smiling face, and seemed unusually blithe and brilliant. Laurie's eyes followed her with pleasure, for she neither romped nor sauntered, but danced with spirit and grace, making the delightsome pastime what it should be. He very naturally fell to studying her from this new point of view; and before the evening was half over, had decided that "little Amy was going to make a very charming woman."

It was a lively scene, for soon the spirit of the social season took possession of every one, and Christmas merriment made all faces shine, hearts happy, and heels light. The musicians fiddled, tooted, and banged as if they enjoyed it; everybody danced who could, and those who couldn't admired their neighbors with uncommon warmth. The air was dark with Davises, and many Joneses gambolled like a flock of young giraffes. The golden secretary darted through the room like a meteor, with a dashing Frenchwoman, who carpeted the floor with her pink satin train. The Serene Teuton found the supper-table, and was happy, eating steadily through the bill of fare, and dismaying the garçons by the ravages he committed. But the Emperor's friend covered himself with glory, for he danced *everything*, whether he knew it or not, and introduced impromptu pirouettes when the figures bewildered him. The boyish abandon of that stout man was charming to behold; for, though he "carried weight," he danced like an India rubber ball. He ran, he flew, he pranced; his face glowed, his bald head shone, his coat tails waved wildly, his pumps actually twinkled in the air, and when the music stopped, he wiped the drops from his brow, and beamed upon his fellow-men like a French Pickwick without glasses.

Amy and her Pole distinguished themselves by equal enthusiasm, but more graceful agility; and Laurie found himself involuntarily keeping time to the rhythmic rise and fall of the white slippers, as they flew by, as indefatigably as if winged. When little Vladimir finally relinquished her, with assurances that he was "desolated to leave so early," she was ready to rest, and see how her recreant knight had borne his punishment.

It had been successful; for, at three-and-twenty, blighted affections find a balm in friendly society, and young nerves will thrill, young blood dance, and healthy young spirits rise, when subjected to the enchantment of beauty, light, music, and motion. Laurie had a waked-up look as he rose to give her his seat; and when he hurried away to bring her some supper, she said to herself, with a satisfied smile, —

"Ah, I thought that would do him good!"

"You look like Balzac's '*Femme piente par elle même*,' " he said, as he fanned her with one hand, and held her coffee-cup in the other.

"My rouge won't come off;" and Amy rubbed her brilliant cheek, and showed him her white glove, with a sober simplicity that made him laugh outright.

"What do you call this stuff?" he asked, touching a fold of her dress that had blown over his knee.

"Illusion."

"Good name for it; it's very pretty — new thing, isn't it?"

"It's as old as the hills; you have seen it on dozens of girls, and you never found out that it was pretty till now — *stupide!*"

"I never saw it on you, before, which accounts for the mistake, you see."

"None of that, it is forbidden; I'd rather take coffee than compliments, just now. No, don't lounge, it makes me nervous."

Laurie sat bolt upright, and meekly took her empty plate, feeling an odd sort of pleasure in having "little Amy" order him about; for she had lost her shyness now, and felt an irresistible desire to trample on him, as girls have a delightful way of doing when lords of creation show any signs of subjection.

"Where did you learn all this sort of thing?" he asked, with a quizzical look.

"As 'this sort of thing' is rather a vague expression, would you kindly explain?" returned Amy, knowing perfectly well what he meant, but wickedly leaving him to describe what is indescribable.

"Well — the general air, the style, the self-possession, the — the — illusion — you know," laughed Laurie, breaking down, and helping himself out of his quandary with the new word.

Amy was gratified, but, of course, didn't show it, and demurely answered, —

"Foreign life polishes one in spite of one's self; I study as well as play; and as for this" — with a little gesture toward her dress — "why, tulle is cheap; posies to be had for nothing, and I am used to making the most of my poor little things."

Amy rather regretted that last sentence, fearing it wasn't in good taste; but Laurie liked her the better for it, and found himself both admiring and respecting the brave patience that made the most of opportunity, and the cheerful spirit that covered poverty with flowers. Amy did not know why he looked at her so kindly, nor why he filled up her book with his own name, and devoted himself to her for the rest of the evening, in the most delightful manner; but the impulse that wrought this agreeable change was the result of one of the new impressions which both of them were unconsciously giving and receiving.

CHAPTER THIRTY-EIGHT

ON THE SHELF

~

In France the young girls have a dull time of it till they are married, when *"Vive la liberté"* becomes their motto. In America, as every one knows, girls early sign a declaration of independence, and enjoy their freedom with republican zest; but the young matrons usually abdicate with the first heir to the throne, and go into a seclusion almost as close as a French nunnery, though by no means as quiet. Whether they like it or not, they are virtually put upon the shelf as soon as the wedding excitement is over, and most of them might exclaim, as did a very pretty woman the other day, "I'm as handsome as ever, but no one takes any notice of me because I'm married."

Not being a belle, or even a fashionable lady, Meg did not experience this affliction till her babies were a year old, — for in her little world primitive customs prevailed, and she found herself more admired and beloved than ever.

As she was a womanly little woman, the maternal instinct was very strong, and she was entirely absorbed in her children, to the utter exclusion of everything and everybody else. Day and night she brooded over them with tireless devotion and anxiety, leaving John to the tender mercies of the help, — for an Irish lady now presided over the kitchen department. Being a domestic man, John decidedly missed the wifely attentions he had been accustomed to receive; but, as he adored his babies, he cheerfully relinquished his comfort for a time, supposing, with masculine ignorance, that peace would soon be restored. But three months passed, and there was no return of repose; Meg looked worn and nervous, — the babies absorbed every minute of her time, — the house was neglected, — and Kitty, the cook, who took life "aisy," kept him on short commons. When he went out in the morning he was bewildered by small commissions for the captive mamma; if he came gaily in at night, eager to embrace his family, he was quenched by a "Hush! they are just asleep after worrying all day." If he proposed a little amusement at home, "No, it would disturb the babies." If he hinted at a lecture or concert, he was answered with a reproachful look, and a decided — "Leave my children for pleasure, never!" His sleep was broken by infant wails and visions of a phantom figure pacing noiselessly to and fro, in the watches of the night; his meals were interrupted by the frequent flight of the presiding genius, who deserted him, half-helped, if a muffled chirp sounded from the nest above; and, when he read his paper of an evening, Demi's colic got into the shipping-list, and Daisy's fall affected the price of stocks, — for Mrs. Brooke was only interested in domestic news.

The poor man was very uncomfortable, for the children had bereft him of his wife; home was merely a nursery, and the perpetual "hushing" made him feel like a brutal intruder whenever he entered the sacred precincts of Babydom. He bore it very patiently for six months, and, when no signs of amendment appeared, he did what other paternal exiles do, — tried to get a little comfort elsewhere. Scott had married and gone to housekeeping not far off, and John fell into the way of running over for an hour or two of an evening, when his own parlor was empty, and his own wife singing lullabies that seemed to have no end. Mrs. Scott was a lively, pretty girl, with nothing to do but be agreeable, — and she performed her mission most successfully. The parlor was always bright and attractive, the chess-board ready, the piano in tune, plenty of gay gossip, and a nice little supper set forth in tempting style.

John would have preferred his own fireside if it had not been so lonely; but as it was, he gratefully took the next best thing, and enjoyed his neighbor's society.

Meg rather approved of the new arrangement at first, and found it a relief to know that John was having a good time instead of dozing in the parlor, or tramping about the house and waking the children. But by and by, when the teething worry was over, and the idols went to sleep at proper hours, leaving mamma time to rest, she began to miss John, and find her work-basket dull company, when he was not sitting opposite in his old dressing-gown, comfortably scorching his slippers on the fender. She would not ask him to stay at home, but felt injured because he did not know that she wanted him without being told, – entirely forgetting the many evenings he had waited for her in vain. She was nervous and worn out with watching and worry, and in that unreasonable frame of mind which the best of mothers occasionally experience when domestic cares oppress them, want of exercise robs them of cheerfulness, and too much devotion to that idol of American women, – the teapot, – makes them feel as if they were all nerve and no muscle.

"Yes," she would say, looking in the glass, "I'm getting old and ugly; John don't find me interesting any longer, so he leaves his faded wife and goes to see his pretty neighbor, who has no incumbrances. Well, the babies love me; they don't care if I am thin and pale, and haven't time to crimp my hair; they are my comfort, and some day John will see what I've gladly sacrificed for them, – won't he, my precious?"

To which pathetic appeal Daisy would answer with a coo, or Demi with a crow, and Meg would put by her lamentations for a maternal revel, which soothed her solitude for the time being. But the pain increased as politics absorbed John, who was always running over to discuss interesting points with Scott, quite unconscious that Meg missed him. Not a word did she say, however, till her mother found her in tears one day, and insisted on knowing what the matter was, – for Meg's drooping spirits had not escaped her observation.

"I wouldn't tell any one except you, mother; but I really do need advice, for, if John goes on so much longer I might as well be a widow," replied Mrs. Brooke, drying her tears on Daisy's bib, with an injured air.

"Goes on how, my dear?" asked her mother, anxiously.

"He's away all day, and at night, when I want to see him, he is continually going over to the Scotts'. It isn't fair that I should have the hardest work, and never any amusement. Men are very selfish, even the best of them."

"So are women; don't blame John till you see where you are wrong yourself."

"But it can't be right for him to neglect me."

"Don't you neglect him?"

"Why, mother; I thought you'd take my part!"

"So I do as far as sympathizing goes; but I think the fault is yours, Meg."

"I don't see how."

"Let me show you. Did John ever neglect you, as you call it, while you made it a point to give him your society of an evening, – his only leisure time?"

"No; but I can't do it now, with two babies to tend."

"I think you could, dear; and I think you ought. May I speak quite freely, and will you remember that it's mother who blames as well as mother who sympathizes?"

"Indeed I will! speak to me as if I was little Meg again. I often feel as if I needed teaching more than ever, since these babies look to me for everything."

Meg drew her low chair beside her mother's, and, with a little interruption in either lap, the two women rocked and talked lovingly together, feeling that the tie of motherhood made them more one than ever.

"You have only made the mistake that most young wives make, – forgotten your duty to your husband in your love for your children. A very natural and forgivable mistake, Meg, but one that had better be remedied before you take to different ways; for children should draw you nearer than ever, not separate you, – as if they were all yours, and John had nothing to do but support them. I've seen it for some weeks, but have not spoken, feeling sure it would come right, in time."

"I'm afraid it won't. If I ask him to stay he'll think I'm jealous; and I wouldn't insult him by such an idea. He don't see that I want him, and I don't know how to tell him without words."

"Make it so pleasant he won't want to go away. My dear, he's longing for his little home; but it isn't home without you, and you are always in the nursery."

"Oughtn't I to be there?"

"Not all the time; too much confinement makes you nervous, and then you are unfitted for everything. Besides, you owe something to John as well as to the children; don't neglect husband for children, – don't shut him out of the nursery, but teach him how to help in it. His place is there as well as yours, and the children need him; let him feel that he has his part to do, and he will do it gladly and faithfully, and it will be better for you all."

"You really think so, mother?"

"I know it, Meg, for I've tried it; and I seldom give advice unless I've proved its practicability. When you and Jo were little, I went on just as you do, feeling as if I didn't do my duty unless I devoted myself wholly to you. Poor father took to his books, after I had refused all offers of help, and left me to try my experiment alone. I struggled along as well as I could, but Jo was too much for me. I nearly spoilt her by indulgence. You were poorly, and I worried about you till I fell sick myself. Then father came to the rescue, quietly managed everything, and made himself so helpful that I saw my mistake, and never have been able to get on without him since. That is the secret of our home happiness; he does not let business wean him from the little cares and duties that affect us all, and I try not to let domestic worries destroy my interest in his pursuits. Each do our part alone in many things, but at home we work together, always."

"It is so, mother; and my great wish is to be to my husband and children what you have been to yours. Show me how; I'll do anything you say."

"You always were my docile daughter. Well, dear, if I were you I'd let John have more to do with the management of Demi, – for the boy needs training, and it's none too soon to begin. Then I'd do what I have often proposed, – let Hannah come and help you; she is a capital nurse, and you may trust the precious babies to her while you do more housework. You need the exercise, Hannah would enjoy the rest, and John would find his wife again. Go out more; keep cheerful as well as busy, – for you are the sunshine-maker of the family, and if you get dismal there is no fair weather. Then I'd try to take an interest in whatever John likes, talk with him, let him read to you, exchange ideas, and help each other in that way. Don't shut yourself up in a bandbox because you are a woman, but understand what is going on, and educate yourself to take your part in the world's work, for it all affects you and yours."

"John is so sensible, I'm afraid he will think I'm stupid if I ask questions about politics and things."

"I don't believe he would; love covers a multitude of sins, and of whom could you ask more freely than of him? Try it, and see if he doesn't find your society far more agreeable than Mrs. Scott's suppers."

"I will. Poor John! I'm afraid I *have* neglected him sadly, but I thought I was right, and he never said anything."

"He tried not to be selfish, but he *has* felt rather forlorn, I fancy. This is just the time, Meg, when young married people are apt to grow apart, and the very time when they ought to be most together; for the first tenderness soon wears off, unless care is taken to preserve it; and no time is so beautiful and precious to parents, as the first years of the little lives given them to train. Don't let John be a stranger to the babies, for they will do more to keep him safe and happy in this world of trial and temptation, than anything else, and through them you will learn to know and love one another as you should. Now, dear, good-by; think over mother's preachment, act upon it if it seems good, and God bless you all"

Meg did think it over, found it good, and acted upon it, though the first attempt was not made exactly as she planned to have it. Of course, the children tyrannized over her, and ruled the house as soon as they found out that kicking and squalling brought them whatever they wanted. Mamma was an abject slave to their caprices, but papa was not so easily subjugated, and occasionally afflicted his tender spouse, by an attempt at paternal discipline with his obstreperous son. For Demi inherited a trifle of his sire's firmness of character – we won't call it obstinacy – and when he made up his little mind to have or to do anything, all the king's horses, and all the king's men could not change that pertinacious little mind. Mamma thought the dear too young to be taught to conquer his prejudices, but papa believed that it never was too soon to learn obedience; so Master Demi early discovered, that when he undertook to "wrastle" with "parpar," he always got the worst of it; yet, like the Englishman, Baby respected the man who conquered him, and loved the father, whose grave, "No, no" was more impressive than all the mother's love pats.

A few days after the talk with her mother, Meg resolved to try a social evening with John; so she ordered a nice supper, set the parlor in order, dressed herself prettily, and put the children to bed early, that nothing should interfere with her experiment. But, unfortunately, Demi's most unconquerable prejudice was against going to bed, and that night he decided to go on a rampage; so poor Meg sung and rocked, told stories, and tried every sleep-provoking wile she could devise, but all in vain – the big eyes wouldn't shut; and long after Daisy had gone to byelow, like the chubby little bunch of good nature she was, naughty Demi lay staring at the light, with the most discouragingly wide-awake expression of countenance.

"Will Demi lie still, like a good boy, while mamma runs down and gives poor papa his tea?" asked Meg, as the hall door softly closed, and the well-known step went tip-toeing into the dining-room.

"Me has tea!" said Demi, preparing to join in the revel.

"No; but I'll save you some little cakies for breakfast, if you'll go bye-bye, like Daisy. Will you, lovey?"

"Iss!" and Demi shut his eyes tight, as if to catch sleep, and hurry the desired day.

Taking advantage of the propitious moment, Meg slipped away, and ran down to greet her husband with a smiling face, and the little blue bow in her hair, which was his especial admiration. He saw it at once, and said, with pleased surprise, –

"Why, little mother, how gay we are to-night. Do you expect company?"

"Only you, dear."

"Is it a birthday, anniversary, or anything?"

"No; I'm tired of being a dowdy, so I dressed up as a change. You always make yourself nice for table, no matter how tired you are; so, why shouldn't I, when I have the time?"

"I do it out of respect to you, my dear," said old-fashioned John.

"Ditto, ditto, Mr. Brooke," laughed Meg, looking young and pretty again, as she nodded to him over the teapot.

"Well, it's altogether delightful, and like old times. This tastes right; I drink to your health, dear!" and John sipped his tea with an air of reposeful rapture, which was of very short duration, however; for, as he put down his cup, the door handle rattled mysteriously, and a little voice was heard, saying, impatiently, –

"Opy doy; me's tumming!"

"It's that naughty boy; I told him to go to sleep alone, and here he is, down stairs, getting his death a-cold pattering over that canvas," said Meg, answering the call.

"Mornin' now," announced Demi, in a joyful tone, as he entered, with his long night-gown gracefully festooned over his arm, and every curl bobbing gaily, as he pranced about the table, eyeing the "cakies" with loving glances.

"No, it isn't morning yet; you must go to bed, and not trouble poor mamma; then you can have the little cake with sugar on it."

"Me loves parpar," said the artful one, preparing to climb the paternal knee, and revel in forbidden joys. But John shook his head, and said to Meg, –

"If you told him to stay up there, and go to sleep alone, make him do it, or he will never learn to mind you."

"Yes, of course; come, Demi!" and Meg led her son away, feeling a strong desire to spank the little marplot who hopped beside her, laboring under the delusion that the bribe was to be administered as soon as they reached the nursery.

Nor was he disappointed; for that short-sighted woman actually gave him a lump of sugar, tucked him into his bed, and forbade any more promenades till morning.

"Iss!" said Demi the perjured, blissfully sucking his sugar, and regarding his first attempt as eminently successful.

Meg returned to her place, and supper was progressing pleasantly, when the little ghost walked again, and exposed the maternal delinquencies, by boldly demanding, –

"More sudar, marmar."

"Now this won't do," said John, hardening his heart against the engaging little sinner. "We shall never know any peace till that child learns to go to bed properly. You have made a slave of yourself long enough; give him one lesson, and then there will be an end of it. Put him in his bed, and leave him, Meg."

"He won't stay there; he never does, unless I sit by him."

"I'll manage him. Demi, go up stairs, and get into your bed, as mamma bids you."

"S'ant!" replied the young rebel, helping himself to the coveted "cakie," and beginning to eat the same with calm audacity.

"You must never say that to papa; I shall carry you if you don't go yourself."

"Go 'way; me don't love parpar;" and Demi retired to his mother's skirts for protection.

But even that refuge proved unavailing, for he was delivered over to the enemy, with a "Be gentle with him, John," which struck the culprit with dismay; for when mamma deserted him, then the judgment-day was at hand. Bereft of his cake, defrauded of his frolic, and borne away by a strong hand to that detested bed, poor Demi could not restrain his wrath; but openly defied papa, and kicked and screamed lustily all the way upstairs. The minute he was put into bed on one side, he rolled out at the other, and made for the door, only to be ignominiously caught up by the tail of his little toga, and put back again, which lively performance was kept up till the young man's strength gave out, when he devoted himself to roaring at the top of his voice. This vocal exercise usually conquered Meg; but John sat as unmoved as the post, which is popularly believed to be deaf. No coaxing, no sugar, no lullaby, no story — even the light was put out, and only the red glow of the fire enlivened the "big dark" which Demi regarded with curiosity rather than fear. This new order of things disgusted him, and he howled dismally for "marmar," as his angry passions subsided, and recollections of his tender bond-woman returned to the captive autocrat. The plaintive wail which succeeded the passionate roar went to Meg's heart, and she ran up to say, beseechingly, —

"Let me stay with him; he'll be good, now, John."

"No, my dear, I've told him he must go to sleep, as you bid him; and he must, if I stay here all night."

"But he'll cry himself sick," pleaded Meg, reproaching herself for deserting her boy.

"No, he won't, he's so tired he will soon drop off, and then the matter is settled; for he will understand that he has got to mind. Don't interfere; I'll manage him."

"He's my child, and I can't have his spirit broken by harshness."

"He's my child, and I won't have his temper spoilt by indulgence. Go down, my dear, and leave the boy to me."

When John spoke in that masterful tone, Meg always obeyed, and never regretted her docility.

"Please let me kiss him once, John?"

"Certainly; Demi, say 'good-night' to mamma, and let her go and rest, for she is very tired with taking care of you all day."

Meg always insisted upon it, that this kiss won the victory; for, after it was given, Demi sobbed more quietly, and lay quite still at the bottom of the bed, whither he had wriggled in his anguish of mind.

"Poor little man! he's worn out with sleep and crying; I'll cover him up, and then go and set Meg's heart at rest," thought John, creeping to the bedside, hoping to find his rebellious heir asleep.

But he wasn't; for the moment his father peeped at him, Demi's eyes opened, his little chin began to quiver, and he put up his arms, saying, with a penitent hiccough, "Me's dood, now."

Sitting on the stairs, outside, Meg wondered at the long silence which followed the uproar; and, after imagining all sorts of impossible accidents, she slipped into the room, to set her fears at rest. Demi lay fast asleep; not in his usual spread-eagle attitude, but in a subdued bunch, cuddled close in the circle of his father's arm, and holding his father's finger, as if he felt that justice was tempered with mercy, and had gone to sleep a sadder and a wiser baby. So held, John had waited with womanly patience till the little hand relaxed his hold; and, while waiting, had fallen asleep, more tired by that tussle with his little son than with his whole day's work.

As Meg stood watching the two faces on the pillow, she smiled to herself, and then slipped away again, saying, in a satisfied tone, –

"I never need fear that John will be too harsh with my babies, he *does* know how to manage them, and will be a great help, for Demi *is* getting too much for me."

When John came down at last, expecting to find a pensive or reproachful wife, he was agreeably surprised to find Meg placidly trimming a bonnet, and to be greeted with the request to read something about the election, if he was not too tired. John saw in a minute that a revolution of some kind was going on, but wisely asked no questions, knowing that Meg was such a transparent little person, she couldn't keep a secret to save her life, and therefore the clue would soon appear. He read a long debate with the most amiable readiness, and then explained it in his most lucid manner, while Meg tried to look deeply interested, to ask intelligent questions, and keep her thoughts from wandering from the state of the nation to the state of her bonnet. In her secret soul, however, she decided that politics were as bad as mathematics, and that the mission of politicians seemed to be calling each other names; but she kept these feminine ideas to herself, and when John paused, shook her head, and said with what she thought diplomatic ambiguity, –

"Well, I really don't see what we are coming to."

John laughed, and watched her for a minute, as she poised a pretty little preparation of tulle and flowers on her hand, and regarded it with the genuine interest which his harrangue had failed to waken.

"She is trying to like politics for my sake, so I'll try and like millinery for hers – that's only fair," thought John the just, adding aloud, –

"That's very pretty; is it what you call a breakfast cap?"

"My dear man, it's a bonnet – my very best go-to-concert and theatre bonnet!"

"I beg your pardon; it was so very small, I naturally mistook it for one of the fly-away things you sometimes wear. How do you keep it on?"

"These bits of lace are fastened under the chin, with a rose-bud, so" – and Meg illustrated by putting on the bonnet, and regarding him with an air of calm satisfaction, that was irresistible.

"It's a love of a bonnet, but I prefer the face inside, for it looks young and happy again," and John kissed the smiling face, to the great detriment of the rose-bud under the chin.

"I'm glad you like it, for I want you to take me to one of the new concerts some night; I really need some music to put me in tune. Will you, please?"

"Of course I will, with all my heart, or anywhere else you like. You have been shut up so long, it will do you no end of good, and I shall enjoy it, of all things. What put it into your head, little mother?"

"Well, I had a talk with Marmee the other day, and told her how nervous, and cross, and out of sorts I felt, and she said I needed change, and less care; so Hannah is to help me with the children, and I'm to see to things about the house more, and now and then have a little fun, just to keep me from getting to be a fidgety, broken-down old woman before my time. It's only an experiment, John, and I want to try it for your sake, as much as for mine, because I've neglected you shamefully lately, and I'm going to make home what it used to be, if I can. You don't object, I hope?"

Never mind what John said, or what a very narrow escape the little bonnet had from utter ruin; all that we have any business to know, is that John did *not* appear to object, judging from the changes which gradually took place in the house and its inmates. It was not all Paradise by any means, but every one was better for the division of labor system; the children throve under the paternal rule, for accurate, steadfast John brought order and obedience into Babydom, while Meg recovered her spirits, and composed her nerves, by plenty of wholesome exercise, a little pleasure, and much confidential conversation with her sensible husband. Home grew home-like again, and John had no wish to leave it, unless he took Meg with him. The Scotts came to the Brookes now, and every one found the little house a cheerful place, full of happiness, content, and family love; even gay Sallie Moffat liked to go there. "It is always so quiet and pleasant here; it does me good, Meg," she used to say, looking about her with wistful eyes, as if trying to discover the charm, that she might use it in her great house, full of splendid loneliness, for there were not riotous, sunny-faced babies there, and Ned lived in a world of his own, where there was no place for her.

This household happiness did not come all at once, but John and Meg had found the key to it, and each year of married life taught them how to use it, unlocking the treasuries of real home love and mutual helpfulness, which the poorest may possess, and the richest cannot buy. This is the sort of shelf on which young wives and mothers may consent to be laid, safe from the restless fret and fever of the world, finding loyal lovers in the little sons and daughters who cling to them, undaunted by sorrow, poverty or age; walking side by side, through fair and stormy weather, with a faithful friend, who is, in the true sense of the good old Saxon word, the "house-band," and learning, as Meg learned, that a woman's happiest kingdom is home, her highest honor the art of ruling it — not as a queen, but as a wise wife and mother.

CHAPTER THIRTY-NINE

LAZY LAURENCE

~

Laurie went to Nice intending to stay a week, and remained a
month. He was tired of wandering about alone, and Amy's
familiar presence seemed to give a home-like charm to the foreign scenes in
which she bore a part. He rather missed the "muching" he used to receive,
and enjoyed a taste of it again, – for no attentions, however flattering, from
strangers, were half so pleasant as the sisterly adoration of the girls at home.
Amy never would pet him like the others, but she was very glad to see him
now, and quite clung to him, – feeling that he was the representative of the
dear family for whom she longed more than she would confess. They
naturally took comfort in each other's society, and were much together, –
riding, walking, dancing, or dawdling, – for, at Nice, no one can be very
industrious during the gay season. But, while apparently amusing
themselves in the most careless fashion, they were half consciously making
discoveries and forming opinions about each other. Amy rose daily in the
estimation of her friend, but he sunk in hers, and each felt the truth before

a word was spoken. Amy tried to please, and succeeded, – for she was grateful for the many pleasures he gave her, and repaid him with the little services to which womanly women know how to lend an indescribable charm. Laurie made no effort of any kind, but just let himself drift along as comfortably as possible, trying to forget, and feeling that all women owed him a kind word because one had been cold to him. It cost him no effort to be generous, and he would have given Amy all the trinkets in Nice if she would have taken them, – but, at the same time, he felt that he could not change the opinion she was forming of him, and he rather dreaded the keen eyes that seemed to watch him with such half-sorrowful, half-scornful surprise.

"All the rest have gone to Monaco for the day; I preferred to stay at home and write letters. They are done now, and I am going to Valrosa to sketch; will you come?" said Amy, as she joined Laurie one lovely day when he lounged in as usual, about noon.

"Well, yes; but isn't it rather warm for such a long walk?" he answered slowly, – for the shaded *salon* looked inviting, after the glare without.

"I'm going to have the little carriage, and Baptiste can drive, – so you'll have nothing to do but hold your umbrella and keep your gloves nice," returned Amy, with a sarcastic glance at the immaculate kids, which were a weak point with Laurie.

"Then I'll go with pleasure," and he put out his hand for her sketch-book. But she tucked it under her arm with a sharp –

"Don't trouble yourself; it's no exertion to me, but *you* don't look equal to it."

Laurie lifted his eyebrows, and followed at a leisurely pace as she ran down stairs; but when they got into the carriage he took the reins himself, and left little Baptiste nothing to do but fold his arms and fall asleep on his perch.

The two never quarrelled; Amy was too well bred, and just now Laurie was too lazy; so, in a minute he peeped under her hat-brim with an inquiring air; she answered with a smile, and they went on together in the most amicable manner.

It was a lovely drive, along winding roads rich in the picturesque scenes that delight beauty-loving eyes. Here an ancient monastery, whence the solemn chanting of the monks came down to them. There a barelegged shepherd, in wooden shoes, pointed hat, and rough jacket over one shoulder, sat piping on a stone, while his goats skipped among the rocks or lay at his feet. Meek, mouse-colored donkeys, laden with panniers of freshly-cut grass, passed by, with a pretty girl in a *capaline* sitting between the green piles, or an old woman spinning with a distaff as she went. Brown, soft-eyed children ran out from the quaint stone hovels to offer nosegays, or bunches of oranges still on the bough. Gnarled olive trees covered the hills with their dusky foliage, fruit hung golden in the orchard, and great scarlet anemones fringed the roadside; while beyond green slopes and craggy heights, the Maritime Alps rose sharp and white against the blue Italian sky.

Valrosa well deserved its name, — for in that climate of perpetual summer roses blossomed everywhere. They overhung the archway, thrust themselves between the bars of the great gate with a sweet welcome to passers-by, and lined the avenue, winding through lemon trees, and feathery palms up to the villa on the hill. Every shadowy nook, where seats invited one to stop and rest, was a mass of bloom; every cool grotto had its marble nymph smiling from a veil of flowers; and every fountain reflected crimson, white, or pale pink roses, leaning down to smile at their own beauty. Roses covered the walls of the house, draped the cornices, climbed the pillars, and ran riot over the balustrade of the wide terrace, whence one looked down on the sunny Mediterranean and the white-walled city on its shore.

"This is a regular honeymoon Paradise, isn't it? Did you ever see such roses?" asked Amy, pausing on the terrace to enjoy the view, and a luxurious whiff of perfume that came wandering by.

"No, nor felt such thorns," returned Laurie, with his thumb in his mouth, after a vain attempt to capture a solitary scarlet flower that grew just beyond his reach.

"Try lower down, and pick those that have no thorns," said Amy, deftly gathering three of the tiny cream-colored ones that starred the wall behind her. She put them in his button hole, as a peace offering, and he stood a minute looking down at them with a curious expression, for in the Italian part of his nature there was a touch of superstition, and he was just then in that state of half-sweet, half-bitter melancholy, when imaginative young men find significance in trifles, and food for romance everywhere. He had thought of Jo in reaching after the thorny red rose, – for vivid flowers became her, – and she had often worn ones like that, from the green-house at home. The pale roses Amy gave him were the sort that Italians lay in dead hands, – never in bridal wreaths, – and, for a moment, he wondered if the omen was for Jo or for himself. But the next instant his American common sense got the better of sentimentality, and he laughed a heartier laugh than Amy had heard since he came.

"It's good advice, – you'd better take it and save your fingers," she said, thinking her speech amused him.

"Thank you, I will!" he answered in jest, – and a few months later he did it in earnest.

"Laurie, when are you going to your grandfather?" she asked, presently, as she settled herself on a rustic seat.

"Very soon."

"You have said that a dozen times within the last three weeks."

"I dare say; short answers save trouble."

"He expects you, and you really ought to go."

"Hospitable creature! I know it."

"Then why don't you do it?"

"Natural depravity, I suppose."

"Natural indolence, you mean. It's really dreadful!" and Amy looked severe.

"Not so bad as it seems, for I should only plague him if I went, so I might as well stay, and plague you a little longer – you can bear it better; in fact, I think it agrees with you excellently!" and Laurie composed himself for a lounge on the broad ledge of the balustrade.

Amy shook her head, and opened her sketch-book with an air of resignation, but she had made up her mind to lecture "that boy," and in a minute she began again.

"What are you doing just now?"

"Watching lizards."

"No, no! I mean what do you intend, and wish to do?"

"Smoke a cigarette, if you'll allow me."

"How provoking you are! I don't approve of cigars, and I will only allow it on condition that you let me put you into my sketch; I need a figure."

"With all the pleasure in life. How will you have me? full length, or three-quarters; on my head or my heels? I should respectfully suggest a recumbent posture, then put yourself in also, and call it, '*Dolce far niente*.'"

"Stay as you are, and go to sleep if you like. I intend to work hard," said Amy, in her most energetic tone.

"What delightful enthusiasm!" and he leaned against a tall urn, with an air of entire satisfaction.

"What would Jo say if she saw you now?" asked Amy impatiently, hoping to stir him up by the mention of her still more energetic sister's name.

"As usual: 'Go away, Teddy, I'm busy!'" He laughed as he spoke, but the laugh was not natural, and a shade passed over his face, for the utterance of the familiar name touched the wound that was not healed yet. Both tone and shadow struck Amy, for she had seen and heard them before, and now she looked up in time to catch a new expression on Laurie's face — a hard, bitter look, full of pain, dissatisfaction and regret. It was gone before she could study it, and the listless expression back again. She watched him for a moment with artistic pleasure, thinking how like an Italian he looked, as he lay basking in the sun, with uncovered head, and eyes full of southern dreaminess; for he seemed to have forgotten her, and fallen into a reverie.

"You look like the effigy of a young knight asleep on his tomb," she said, carefully tracing the well-cut profile defined against the dark stone.

"Wish I was!"

"That's a foolish wish, unless you have spoilt your life. You are so changed I sometimes think — " there Amy stopped with a half-timid, half-wistful look, more significant than her unfinished speech.

Laurie saw and understood the affectionate anxiety which she hesitated to express, and looking straight into her eyes, said, just as he used to say it to her mother, —

"It's all right, ma'am!"

That satisfied her, and set at rest the doubts that had begun to worry her lately. It also touched her, and she showed that it did, by the cordial tone in which she said, —

"I'm glad of that! I didn't think you'd been a very bad boy, but I fancied you might have wasted money at that wicked Baden-Baden, lost your heart to some charming Frenchwoman with a husband, or got into some of the scrapes that young men seem to consider a necessary part of a foreign tour. Don't stay out there in the sun, come and lie on the grass here, and 'let us be friendly,' as Jo used to say when we got in the sofa-corner and told secrets."

Laurie obediently threw himself down on the turf, and began to amuse himself by sticking daisies into the ribbons of Amy's hat, that lay there.

"I'm all ready for the secrets," and he glanced up with a decided expression of interest in his eyes.

"I've none to tell; you may begin."

"Haven't one to bless myself with. I thought perhaps you'd had some news from home."

"You have heard all that has come lately. Don't you hear often? I fancied Jo would send you volumes."

"She's very busy; I'm roving about so, it's impossible to be regular, you know. When do you begin your great work of art, Raphaella?" he asked, changing the subject abruptly after another pause, in which he had been wondering if Amy knew his secret, and wanted to talk about it.

"Never!" she answered, with a despondent, but decided air. "Rome took all the vanity out of me, for after seeing the wonders there, I felt too insignificant to live, and gave up all my foolish hopes in despair."

"Why should you, with so much energy and talent?"

"That's just why, because talent isn't genius, and no amount of energy can make it so. I want to be great, or nothing. I won't be a commonplace dauber, so I don't intend to try any more."

"And what are you going to do with yourself now, if I may ask?"

"Polish up my other talents, and be an ornament to society, if I get the chance."

It was a characteristic speech, and sounded daring; but audacity becomes young people, and Amy's ambition had a good foundation. Laurie smiled, but he liked the spirit with which she took up a new purpose, when a long cherished one died, and spent no time lamenting.

"Good! and here is where Fred Vaughn comes in, I fancy."

Amy preserved a discreet silence, but there was a conscious look in her downcast face, that made Laurie sit up and say gravely, –

"Now I'm going to play brother, and ask questions. May I?"

"I don't promise to answer."

"Your face will, if your tongue don't. You aren't woman of the world enough yet to hide your feelings, my dear. I've heard rumors about Fred and you last year, and it's my private opinion, that if he had not been called home so suddenly, and detained too long, that something would have come of it – hey?"

"That's not for me to say," was Amy's prim reply; but her lips would smile, and there was a traitorous sparkle of the eye, which betrayed that she knew her power and enjoyed the knowledge.

"You are not engaged, I hope?" and Laurie looked very elder-brotherly and grave all of a sudden.

"No."

"But you will be, if he comes back and goes properly down upon his knees, won't you?"

"Very likely."

"Then you are fond of old Fred?"

"I could be if I tried."

"But you don't intend to try till the proper moment? Bless my soul, what unearthly prudence! He's a good fellow, Amy, but not the man I fancied you'd like."

"He is rich, a gentleman, and has delightful manners," – began Amy, trying to be quite cool and dignified, but feeling a little ashamed of herself, in spite of the sincerity of her intentions.

"I understand – queens of society can't get on without money, so you mean to make a good match and start in that way? Quite right and proper as the world goes, but it sounds odd from the lips of one of your mother's girls."

"True, nevertheless!"

A short speech, but the quiet decision with which it was uttered, contrasted curiously with the young speaker. Laurie felt this instinctively, and laid himself down again, with a sense of disappointment which he could not explain. His look and silence, as well as a certain inward self-disapproval, ruffled Amy – and made her resolve to deliver her lecture without delay.

"I wish you'd do me the favor to rouse yourself a little," she said, sharply.

"Do it for me, there's a dear girl!"

"I could if I tried," and she looked as if she would like doing it in the most summary style.

"Try then, I give you leave," returned Laurie, who enjoyed having some one to tease, after his long abstinence from his favorite pastime.

"You'd be angry in five minutes."

"I'm never angry with you. It takes two flints to make a fire; you are as cool and soft as snow."

"You don't know what I can do – snow produces a glow and a tingle, if applied rightly. Your indifference is half affectation, and a good stirring up would prove it."

"Stir away, it won't hurt me, and it may amuse you, as the big man said when his little wife beat him. Regard me in the light of a husband or a carpet, and beat till you are tired, if that sort of exercise agrees with you."

Being decidedly nettled herself, and longing to see him shake off the apathy that so altered him, Amy sharpened both tongue and pencil, and began, –

"Flo and I have got a new name for you; it's 'Lazy Laurence'; how do you like it?"

She thought it would annoy him, but he only folded his arms under his head, with an imperturbable – "That's not bad! thank you ladies."

"Do you want to know what I honestly think of you?"

"Pining to be told."

"Well, I despise you."

If she had even said "I hate you," in a petulant or coquettish tone, he would have laughed, and rather liked it; but the grave, almost sad accent of her voice, made him open his eyes, and ask quickly, –

"Why, if you please?"

"Because with every chance for being good, useful and happy, you are faulty, lazy and miserable."

"Strong language, mademoiselle."

"If you like it, I'll go on."

"Pray do, it's quite interesting."

"I thought you'd find it so; selfish people always like to talk about themselves."

"Am *I* selfish?" the question slipped out involuntarily, and in a tone of surprise, for the one virtue on which he prided himself was generosity.

"Yes, very selfish," continued Amy, in a calm, cool voice, twice as effective, just then, as an angry one. "I'll show you how, for I've studied you while we have been frolicking, and I'm not at all satisfied with you. Here you have been abroad nearly six months, and done nothing but waste time and money, and disappoint your friends."

"Isn't a fellow to have any pleasure after a four-years' grind?"

"You don't look as if you'd had much; at any rate you are none the better for it, as far as I can see. I said when we first me, that you had improved; now I take it all back, for I don't think you half so nice as when I left you at home. You have grown abominably lazy, you like gossip, and waste time on frivolous things; you are contented to be petted and admired by silly people, instead of being loved and respected by wise ones. With money, talent, position, health, and beauty, – ah, you like that, old vanity! but it's the truth, so I can't help saying it, – with all these splendid things to use and enjoy, you can find nothing to do but dawdle, and instead of being the man you might and ought to be, you are only – " there she stopped, with a look that had both pain and pity in it.

"Saint Laurence on a gridiron," added Laurie, blandly finishing the sentence. But the lecture began to take effect, for there was a wide-awake sparkle in his eyes now, and a half-angry, half-injured expression replaced the former indifference.

"I suppose you'd take it so. You men tell us we are angels, and say we can make you what we will; but the instant we honestly try to do you good, you laugh at us, and won't listen, which proves how much your flattery is worth." Amy spoke bitterly, and turned her back on the exasperating martyr at her feet.

In a minute a hand came down over the page, so that she could not draw, and Laurie's voice said, with a droll imitation of a penitent child, –

"I will be good! oh, I will be good!"

But Amy did not laugh, for she was in earnest; and, tapping on the outspread hand with her pencil, said soberly, –

"Aren't you ashamed of a hand like that? It's as soft and white as a woman's, and looks as if it never did anything but wear Jouvin's best gloves, and pick flowers for ladies. You are not a dandy, thank heaven! so I'm glad to see there are no diamonds or big seal rings on it, only the little old one Jo gave you so long ago. Dear soul! I wish she was here to help me."

"So do I!"

The hand vanished as suddenly as it came, and there was energy enough in the echo of her wish to suit even Amy. She glanced down at him with a new thought in her mind, — but he was lying with his hat half over his face, as if for shade, and his mustache hid his mouth. She only saw his chest rise and fall, with a long breath that might have been a sigh, and the hand that wore the ring nestle down into the grass, as if to hide something too precious or too tender to be spoken of. All in a minute various hints and trifles assumed shape and significance in Amy's mind, and told her what her sister never had confided to her. She remembered that Laurie never spoke voluntarily of Jo; she recalled the shadow on his face just now, the change in his character, and the wearing of the little old ring, which was no ornament to a handsome hand. Girls are quick to read such signs, and feel their eloquence; Amy had fancied that perhaps a love-trouble was at the bottom of the alteration, and now she was sure of it; her keen eyes filled, and, when she spoke again, it was in a voice that could be beautifully soft and kind when she chose to make it so.

"I know I have no right to talk so to you, Laurie; and if you weren't the sweetest-tempered fellow in the world, you'd be very angry with me. But we are all so fond and proud of you, I couldn't bear to think they should be disappointed in you at home as I have been, — though perhaps they would understand the change better than I do."

"I think they would," came from under the hat, in a grim tone, quite as touching as a broken one.

"They ought to have told me, and not let me go blundering and scolding, when I should have been more kind and patient than ever. I never did like that Miss Randal, and now I hate her!" said artful Amy, — wishing to be sure of her facts this time.

"Hang Miss Randal!" and Laurie knocked the hat off his face with a look that left no doubt of his sentiments toward that young lady.

"I beg pardon; I thought — " and there she paused diplomatically.

"No, you didn't; you knew perfectly well I never cared for any one but Jo." Laurie said that in his old, impetuous tone, and turned his face away as he spoke.

"I did think so; but as they never said anything about it, and you came away, I supposed I was mistaken. And Jo wouldn't be kind to you? Why, I was sure she loved you dearly."

"She *was* kind, but not in the right way; and it's lucky for her she didn't love me, if I'm the good-for-nothing fellow you think me. It's her fault, though, and you may tell her so."

The hard, bitter look came back again as he said that, and it troubled Amy, for she did not know what balm to apply.

"I was wrong; I didn't know; I'm very sorry I was so cross, but I can't help wishing you'd bear it better, Teddy, dear."

"Don't! that's her name for me," and Laurie put up his hand with a quick gesture to stop the words spoken in Amy's half-kind, half-reproachful tone. "Wait till you've tried it yourself," he added, in a low voice, as he pulled up the grass by the handful.

"I'd take it manfully, and be respected if I couldn't be loved," cried Amy, with the decision of one who knew nothing about it.

Now Laurie flattered himself that he *had* borne it remarkably well, — making no moan, asking no sympathy, and taking his trouble away to live it down alone. Amy's lecture put the matter in a new light, and for the first time it did look weak and selfish to lose heart at the first failure, and shut himself up in moody indifference. He felt as if suddenly shaken out of a pensive dream, and found it impossible to go to sleep again. Presently he sat up, and asked, slowly, —

"Do you think Jo would despise me as you do?"

"Yes, if she saw you now. She hates lazy people. Why don't you do something splendid, and *make* her love you?"

"I did my best, but it was no use."

"Graduating well, you mean? That was no more than you ought to have done, for your grandfather's sake. It would have been shameful to fail after spending so much time and money, when every one knew you *could* do well."

"I did fail, say what you will, for Jo wouldn't love me," began Laurie, leaning his head on his hand in a despondent attitude.

"No, you didn't, and you'll say so in the end, — for it did you good, and proved that you could do something if you tried. If you'd only set about another task of some sort, you'd soon be your hearty, happy self again, and forget your trouble."

"That's impossible!"

"Try it and see. You needn't shrug your shoulders, and think 'Much she knows about such things.' I don't pretend to be wise, but I *am* observing, and I see a great deal more than you'd imagine. I'm interested in other people's experiences and inconsistencies; and, though I can't explain, I remember and use them for my own benefit. Love Jo all your days, if you choose, – but don't let it spoil you, – for it's wicked to throw away so many good gifts because you can't have the one you want. There, – I won't lecture any more, for I know you'll wake up, and be a man in spite of that hard-hearted girl."

Neither spoke for several minutes. Laurie sat turning the little ring on his finger, and Amy put the last touches to the hasty sketch she had been working at while she talked. Presently she put it on his knee, merely saying, –

"How do you like that?"

He looked and then he smiled, – as he could not well help doing, for it was capitally done. The long, lazy figure on the grass, with listless face, half-shut eyes, and one hand holding a cigar, from which came the little wreath of smoke that encircled the dreamer's head.

"How well you draw!" he said, with genuine surprise and pleasure at her skill, adding, with a half laugh, –

"Yes, that's me."

"As you are, – this is as you were," and Amy laid another sketch beside the one he held.

It was not nearly so well done, but there was a life and spirit in it which atoned for many faults, and it recalled the past so vividly that a sudden change swept over the young man's face as he looked. Only a rough sketch of Laurie taming a horse; hat and coat were off, and every line of the active figure, resolute face and commanding attitude, was full of energy and meaning. The handsome brute, just subdued, stood arching his neck under the tightly-drawn rein, with one foot impatiently pawing the ground, and ears pricked up as if listening for the voice that had mastered him. In the ruffled mane, the rider's breezy hair and erect attitude, there was a suggestion of suddenly arrested motion, of strength, courage, and youthful buoyancy that contrasted sharply with the supine grace of the "*Dolce far niente*" sketch. Laurie said nothing; but, as his eye went from one to the other, Amy saw him flush up and fold his lips together as if he read and accepted the little lesson she had given him. That satisfied her; and, without waiting for him to speak, she said, in her sprightly way, –

"Don't you remember the day you played 'Rarey' with Puck, and we all looked on? Meg and Beth were frightened, but Jo clapped and pranced, and I sat on the fence and drew you. I found that sketch in my portfolio the other day, touched it up, and kept it to show you."

"Much obliged! You've improved immensely since then, and I congratulate you. May I venture to suggest in 'a honeymoon Paradise,' that five o"clock is the dinner hour at your hotel?"

Laurie rose as he spoke, returned the pictures with a smile and a bow, and looked at his watch, as if to remind her that even moral lectures should have an end. He tried to resume his former easy, indifferent air, but it *was* an affectation now, – for the rousing had been more efficacious than he would confess. Amy felt the shade of coldness in his manner, and said to herself, –

"Now I've offended him. Well, if it does him good, I'm glad, – if it makes him hate me, I'm sorry; but it's true, and I can't take back a word of it."

They laughed and chatted all the way home; and little Baptiste, up behind, thought that Monsieur and Mademoiselle were in charming spirits. But both felt ill at ease; the friendly frankness was disturbed, the sunshine had a shadow over it, and, despite their apparent gayety, there was a secret discontent in the heart of each.

"Shall we see you this evening, *mon frere?*" asked Amy, as they parted at her aunt's door.

"Unfortunately I have an engagement. *Au revoir, Mademoiselle,*" and Laurie bent as if to kiss her hand, in the foreign fashion, which became him better than many men. Something in his face made Amy say, quickly and warmly, –

"No; be yourself with me, Laurie, and part in the good old way. I'd rather have a hearty English hand-shake than all the sentimental salutations in France."

"Good-by, dear," and, with these words, uttered in the tone she liked, Laurie left her, after a hand-shake almost painful in its heartiness.

Next morning, instead of the usual call, Amy received a note which made her smile at the beginning, and sigh at the end:—

My Dear Mentor:

Please make my adieux to your aunt, and exult within yourself, for "Lazy Laurence" has gone to his grandpa like the best of boys. A pleasant winter to you, and may the gods grant you a blissful honeymoon at Valrosa. I think Fred would be benefited by a rouser. Tell him so, with my congratulations.

Yours gratefully,

TELEMACHUS.

"Good boy! I'm glad he's gone," said Amy, with an approving smile; the next minute her face fell as she glanced about the empty room, adding, with an involuntary sigh, —

"Yes, I *am* glad, — but how I shall miss him."

CHAPTER FORTY

THE VALLEY
OF THE SHADOW
~

When the first bitterness was over, the family accepted the inevitable, and tried to bear it cheerfully, helping one another by the increased affection which comes to bind households tenderly together in times of trouble. They put away their grief, and each did their part toward making that last year a happy one.

The pleasantest room in the house was set apart for Beth, and in it was gathered everything that she most loved – flowers, pictures, her piano, the little work-table, and the beloved pussies. Father's best books found their way there, mother's easy chair, Jo's desk, Amy's loveliest sketches; and every day Meg brought her babies on a loving pilgrimage, to make sunshine for Aunty Beth. John quietly set apart a little sum, that he might enjoy the pleasure of keeping the invalid supplied with the fruit she loved and longed for; old Hannah never wearied of concocting dainty dishes to tempt a capricious appetite, dropping tears as she worked; and, from across the sea, came little gifts and cheerful letters, seeming to bring breaths of warmth and fragrance from the lands that know no winter.

Here, cherished like a household saint in its shrine, sat Beth, tranquil and busy as ever; for nothing could change the sweet, unselfish nature; and even while preparing to leave life, she tried to make it happier for those who should remain behind. The feeble fingers were never idle, and one of her pleasures was to make little things for the school children daily passing to and fro. To drop a pair of mittens from her window for a pair of purple hands, a needle-book for some small mother of many dolls, pen-wipers for young penmen toiling through forests of pot-hooks, scrap-books for picture-loving eyes, and all manner of pleasant devices, till the reluctant climbers up the ladder of learning found their way strewn with flowers, as it were, and came to regard the gentle giver as a sort of fairy god-mother, who sat above there, and showered down gifts miraculously suited to their tastes and needs. If Beth had wanted any reward, she found it in the bright little faces always turned up to her window, with nods and smiles, and the droll little letters which came to her, full of blots and gratitude.

The first few months were very happy ones, and Beth often used to look round, and say "How beautiful this is," as they all sat together in her sunny room, the babies kicking and crowing on the floor, mother and sisters working near, and father reading in his pleasant voice, from the wise old books, which seemed rich in good and comfortable words, as applicable now as when written centuries ago – a little chapel, where a paternal priest taught his flock the hard lessons all must learn, trying to show them that hope can comfort love, and faith make resignation possible. Simple sermons, that went straight to the souls of those who listened; for the father's heart was in the minister's religion, and the frequent falter in the voice gave a double eloquence to the words he spoke or read.

It was well for all that this peaceful time was given them as preparation for the sad hours to come; for, by and by, Beth said the needle was "so heavy," and put it down forever; talking wearied her, faces troubled her, pain claimed her for its own, and her tranquil spirit was sorrowfully perturbed by the ills that vexed her feeble flesh. Ah me! such heavy days, such long, long nights, such aching hearts and imploring prayers, when those who loved her best were forced to see the thin hands stretched out to them beseechingly, to hear the bitter cry, "Help me, help me!" and to feel that there was no help. A sad eclipse of the serene soul, a sharp struggle of the young life with death; but both were mercifully brief, and then, the natural rebellion was over, the old peace returned more beautiful than ever. With the wreck of her frail body, Beth's soul grew strong; and, though she said little, those about her felt that she was ready, saw that the first pilgrim called was likewise the fittest, and waited with her on the shore, trying to see the Shining Ones coming to receive her when she crossed the river.

Jo never left her for an hour since Beth had said, "I feel stronger when you are here." She slept on a couch in the room, waking often to renew the fire, to feed, lift, or wait upon the patient creature who seldom asked for anything, and "tried not to be a trouble." All day she haunted the room, jealous of any other nurse, and prouder of being chosen then than of any honor her life ever brought her. Precious and helpful hours to Jo, for now her heart received the teaching that it needed; lessons in patience were so sweetly taught her, that she could not fail to learn them; charity for all, the lovely spirit that can forgive and truly forget unkindness, the loyalty to duty that makes the hardest easy, and the sincere faith that fears nothing, but trusts undoubtingly.

Often when she woke, Jo found Beth reading in her well-worn little book, heard her singing softly, to beguile the sleepless night, or saw her lean her face upon her hands, while slow tears dropped through the transparent fingers; and Jo would lie watching her, with thoughts too deep for tears, feeling that Beth, in her simple unselfish way, was trying to wean herself from the dear old life, and fit herself for the life to come, by sacred words of comfort, quiet prayers, and the music she loved so well.

Seeing this did more for Jo than the wisest sermons, the saintliest hymns, the most fervent prayers that any voice could utter; for, with eyes made clear by many tears, and a heart softened by the tenderest sorrow, she recognized the beauty of her sister's life – uneventful, unambitious, yet full of the genuine virtues which "smell sweet, and blossom in the dust"; the self-forgetfulness that makes the humblest on earth remembered soonest in heaven, the true success which is possible to all.

One night, when Beth looked among the books upon her table, to find something to make her forget the mortal weariness that was almost as hard to bear as pain, as she turned the leaves of her old favorite "Pilgrim's Progress," she found a little paper scribbled over, in Jo's hand. The name caught her eye, and the blurred look of the lines made her sure that tears had fallen on it.

"Poor Jo, she's fast asleep, so I won't wake her to ask leave; she shows me all her things, and I don't think she'll mind if I look at this," thought Beth, with a glance at her sister, who lay on the rug, with the tongs beside her, ready to wake up the minute the log fell apart.

MY BETH

Sitting patient in the shadow
Till the blessed light shall come,
A serene and saintly presence
Sanctifies our troubled home.
Earthly joys, and hopes, and sorrows,
Break like ripples on the strand
Of the deep and solemn river
Where her willing feet now stand.

Oh, my sister, passing from me,
Out of human care and strife,
Leave me, as a gift, those virtues
Which have beautified your life.
Dear, bequeath me that great patience
Which has power to sustain
A cheerful, uncomplaining spirit
In its prison-house of pain.

Give me, for I need it sorely,
Of that courage, wise and sweet,
Which has made the path of duty
Green beneath your willing feet.
Give me that unselfish nature,
That with charity divine
Can pardon wrong for love's dear sake —
Meek heart, forgive me mine!

Thus our parting daily loseth
  Something of its bitter pain,
And while learning this hard lesson,
  My great loss becomes my gain.
For the touch of grief will render
  My wild nature more serene,
Give to life new aspirations —
  A new trust in the unseen.

Henceforth, safe across the river,
  I shall see forever more
A beloved, household spirit
  Waiting for me on the shore.
Hope and faith, born of my sorrow,
  Guardian angels shall become,
And the sister gone before me,
  By their hands shall lead me home.

Blurred and blotty, faulty and feeble as the lines were, they brought a look of inexpressible comfort to Beth's face, for her one regret had been that she had done so little; and this seemed to assure her that her life had not been useless — that her death would not bring the despair she feared. As she sat with the paper folded between her hands, the charred log fell asunder. Jo started up, revived the blaze, and crept to the bedside, hoping Beth slept.

"Not asleep, but so happy, dear. See, I found this and read it; I knew you wouldn't care. Have I been all that to you, Jo?" she asked, with wistful, humble earnestness.

"Oh, Beth, so much, so much!" and Jo's head went down upon the pillow, beside her sister's.

"Then I don't feel as if I'd wasted my life. I'm not so good as you make me, but I *have* tried to do right; and now, when it's too late to begin even to do better, it's such a comfort to know that some one loves me so much, and feels as if I'd helped her."

"More than any one in the world, Beth. I used to think I couldn't let you go; but I'm learning to feel that I don't lose you; that you'll be more to me than ever, and death can't part us, though it seems to."

"I know it cannot, and I don't fear it any longer, for I'm sure I shall be your Beth still, to love and help you more than ever. You must take my place, Jo, and be everything to father and mother when I'm gone. They will turn to you — don't fail them; and if it's hard to work alone, remember that I don't forget you, and that you'll be happier in doing that, than writing splendid books, or seeing all the world; for love is the only thing that we can carry with us when we go, and it makes the end so easy."

"I'll try, Beth;" and then and there Jo renounced her old ambition, pledged herself to a new and better one, acknowledging the poverty of other desires, and feeling the blessed solace of a belief in the immortality of love.

So the spring days came and went, the sky grew clearer, the earth greener, the flowers were up fair and early, and the birds came back in time to say good-by to Beth, who, like a tired but trustful child, clung to the hands that had led her all her life, as father and mother guided her tenderly through the valley of the shadow, and gave her up to God.

Seldom, except in books, do the dying utter memorable words, see visions, or depart with beatified countenances; and those who have sped many parting souls know, that to most the end comes as naturally and simply as sleep. As Beth had hoped, the "tide went out easily"; and in the dark hour before the dawn, on the bosom where she had drawn her first breath, she quietly drew her last, with no farewell but one loving look and a little sigh.

With tears, and prayers, and tender hands, mother and sisters made her ready for the long sleep that pain would never mar again — seeing with grateful eyes the beautiful serenity that soon replaced the pathetic patience that had wrung their hearts so long, and feeling with reverent joy, that to their darling death was a benignant angel — not a phantom full of dread.

When morning came, for the first time in many months the fire was out, Jo's place was empty, and the room was very still. But a bird sang blithely on a budding bough, close by, the snowdrops blossomed freshly at the window, and the spring sunshine streamed in like a benediction over the placid face upon the pillow — a face so full of painless peace, that those who loved it best smiled through their tears, and thanked God that Beth was well at last.

CHAPTER FORTY-ONE

LEARNING TO FORGET

~

*A*my's lectures did Laurie good, though, of course, he did not own it till long afterward; men seldom do, – for when women are the advisers, the lords of creation don't take the advice till they have persuaded themselves that it is just what they intended to do; then they act upon it, and, if it succeeds, they give the weaker vessel half the credit of it; if it fails, they generously give her the whole. Laurie went back to his grandfather, and was so dutifully devoted for several weeks that the old gentleman declared the climate of Nice had improved him wonderfully, and he had better try it again. There was nothing the young gentleman would have liked better, – but elephants could not have dragged him back after the scolding he had received; pride forbid, – and whenever the longing grew very strong, he fortified his resolution by repeating the words that had made the deepest impression, – "I despise you;" "Go and do something splendid that will *make* her love you."

Laurie turned the matter over in his mind so often that he soon brought himself to confess that he *had* been selfish and lazy; but then when a man has a great sorrow, he should be indulged in all sorts of vagaries till he has lived it down. He felt that his blighted affections were quite dead now; and, though he should never cease to be a faithful mourner, there was no occasion to wear his weeds ostentatiously. Jo *wouldn't* love him, but he might *make* her respect and admire him by doing something which should prove that a girl's "No" had not spoilt his life. He had always meant to do something, and Amy's advice was quite unnecessary. He had only been waiting till the aforesaid blighted affections were decently interred; that being done, he felt that he was ready to "hide his stricken heart, and still toil on."

As Goethe, when he had a joy or a grief, put it into a song, so Laurie resolved to embalm his love-sorrow in music, and compose a Requiem which should harrow up Jo's soul and melt the heart of every hearer. So the next time the old gentleman found him getting restless and moody, and ordered him off, he went to Vienna, where he had musical friends, and fell to work with the firm determination to distinguish himself. But, whether the sorrow was too vast to be embodied in music, or music too ethereal to uplift a mortal woe, he soon discovered that the Requiem was beyond him, just at present. It was evident that his mind was not in working order yet, and his ideas needed clarifying; for often, in the middle of a plaintive strain, he would find himself humming a dancing tune that vividly recalled the Christmas ball at Nice, – especially the stout Frenchman, – and put an effectual stop to tragic composition for the time being.

Then he tried an Opera, – for nothing seemed impossible in the beginning, – but here, again, unforeseen difficulties beset him. He wanted Jo for his heroine, and called upon his memory to supply him with tender recollections and romantic visions of his love. But memory turned traitor; and, as if possessed by the perverse spirit of the girl, would only recall Jo's oddities, faults, and freaks, would only show her in the most unsentimental aspects, – beating mats with her head tied up in a bandanna, barricading herself with the sofa-pillow, or throwing cold water over his passion *à la* Gummidge, – and an irresistible laugh spoilt the pensive picture he was endeavoring to paint. Jo wouldn't be put into the Opera at any price, and he had to give up with a "Bless that girl, what a torment she is!" and a clutch at his hair, as became a distracted composer.

When he looked about him for another and a less intractable damsel to immortalize in melody, memory produced one with the most obliging readiness. This phantom wore many faces, but it always had golden hair, was enveloped in a diaphanous cloud, and floated airily before his mind's eye in a pleasing chaos of roses, peacocks, white ponies and blue ribbons. He did not give the complaisant wraith any name, but he took her for his heroine, and grew quite fond of her, as well he might, — for he gifted her with every gift and grace under the sun, and escorted her, unscathed, through trials which would have annihilated any mortal woman.

Thanks to this inspiration, he got on swimmingly for a time, but gradually the work lost its charm, and he forgot to compose, while he sat musing, pen in hand, or roamed about the gay city to get new ideas and refresh his mind, which seemed to be in a somewhat unsettled state that winter. He did not do much, but he thought a great deal, and was conscious of a change of some sort going on in spite of himself. "It's genius simmering, perhaps, — I'll let it simmer, and see what comes of it," he said, with a secret suspicion, all the while, that it wasn't genius, but something far more common. Whatever it was, it simmered to some purpose, for he grew more and more discontented with his desultory life, began to long for some real and earnest work to go at, soul and body, and finally came to the wise conclusion that every one who loved music was not a composer. Returned from one of Mozart's grand operas, splendidly performed at the Royal Theatre, he looked over his own, played a few of the best parts, sat staring up at the busts of Mendelssohn, Beethoven, and Bach, who stared benignly back again; then suddenly he tore up his music sheets, one by one, and, as the last fluttered out of his hand, he said soberly, to himself, —

"She is right! talent isn't genius, and you can't make it so. That music has taken the vanity out of me as Rome took it out of her, and I won't be a humbug any longer. Now what shall I do?"

That seemed a hard question to answer, and Laurie began to wish he had to work for his daily bread. Now, if ever, occurred an eligible opportunity for "going to the devil," as he once forcibly expressed it, — for he had plenty of money and nothing to do, — and Satan is proverbially fond of providing employment for full and idle hands. The poor fellow had temptations enough from without and from within, but he withstood them pretty well, — for much as he valued liberty he valued good faith and confidence more, – so his promise to his grandfather, and his desire to be able to look honestly into the eyes of the women who loved him, and say "All's well," kept him safe and steady.

Very likely some Mrs. Grundy will observe, "I don't believe it; boys will be boys, young men must sow their wild oats, and women must not expect miracles." I dare say *you* don't, Mrs. Grundy, but it's true, nevertheless. Women work a good many miracles, and I have a persuasion that they may perform even that of raising the standard of manhood by refusing to echo such sayings. Let the boys be boys, – the longer the better, – and let the young men sow their wild oats if they must, – but mothers, sisters, and friends may help to make the crop a small one, and keep many tares from spoiling the harvest, by believing, – and showing that they believe, – in the possibility of loyalty to the virtues which make men manliest in good women's eyes. If it *is* a feminine delusion, leave us to enjoy it while we may, – for without it half the beauty and the romance of life is lost, and sorrowful forebodings would embitter all our hopes of the brave, tender-hearted little lads, who still love their mothers better than themselves, and are not ashamed to own it.

Laurie thought that the task of forgetting his love for Jo would absorb all his powers for years; but, to his great surprise, he discovered it grew easier every day. He refused to believe it at first, – got angry with himself, and couldn't understand it; but these hearts of ours are curious and contrary things, and time and nature work their will in spite of us. Laurie's heart *wouldn't* ache; the wound persisted in healing with a rapidity that astonished him, and, instead of trying to forget, he found himself trying to remember. He had not foreseen this turn of affairs, and was not prepared for it. He was disgusted with himself, surprised at his own fickleness, and full of a queer mixture of disappointment and relief that he could recover from such a tremendous blow so soon. He carefully stirred up the embers of his lost love, but they refused to burst into a blaze; there was only a comfortable glow that warmed and did him good without putting him into a fever, and he was reluctantly obliged to confess that the boyish passion was slowly subsiding into a more tranquil sentiment, – very tender, a little sad and resentful still, – but that was sure to pass away in time, leaving a brotherly affection which would last unbroken to the end.

As the word "brotherly" passed through his mind in one of these reveries, he smiled, and glanced at the picture of Mozart that was before him, –

"Well, he was a great man; and when he couldn't have one sister he took the other, and was happy."

Laurie did not utter the words, but he thought them, and the next instant kissed the little old ring, saying to himself, –

"No, I won't! I haven't forgotten, I never can. I'll try again, and if that fails, why then –"

Leaving his sentence unfinished, he seized pen and paper and wrote to Jo, telling her that he could not settle to anything while there was the least hope of her changing her mind. Couldn't she, wouldn't she, – and let him come home and be happy? While waiting for an answer he did nothing, – but he did it energetically, for he was in a fever of impatience. It came at last, and settled his mind effectually on one point, – for Jo decidedly couldn't and wouldn't. She was wrapped up in Beth, and never wished to hear the word "love" again. Then she begged him to be happy with somebody else, but always to keep a little corner of his heart for his loving sister Jo. In a postscript she desired him not to tell Amy that Beth was worse; she was coming home in the spring, and there was no need of saddening the remainder of her stay. That would be time enough, please God, but Laurie must write to her often, and not let her feel lonely, homesick, or anxious.

"So I will, at once. Poor little girl; it will be a sad going home for her, I'm afraid;" and Laurie opened his desk, as if writing to Amy had been the proper conclusion of the sentence left unfinished some weeks before.

But he did not write the letter that day; for, as he rummaged out his best paper, he came across something which changed his purpose. Tumbling about in one part of his desk, among bills, passports, and business documents of various kinds, were several of Jo's letters, and in another compartment were three notes from Amy, carefully tied up with one of her blue ribbons, and sweetly suggestive of the little dead roses put away inside. With a half-repentant, half-amused expression, Laurie gathered up all Jo's letters, smoothed, folded, and put them neatly into a small drawer of the desk, stood a minute turning the ring thoughtfully on his finger, then slowly drew it off, laid it with the letters, locked the drawer, and went out to hear High Mass at Saint Stefan's, feeling as if there had been a funeral; and, though not overwhelmed with affliction, this seemed a more proper way to spend the rest of the day, than writing letters to charming young ladies.

The letter went very soon, however, and was promptly answered, for Amy *was* homesick, and confessed it in the most delightfully confiding manner. The correspondence flourished famously, and letters flew to and fro, with unfailing regularity, all through the early spring. Laurie sold his busts, made allumettes of his opera, and went back to Paris, hoping somebody would arrive before long. He wanted desperately to go to Nice, but would not till he was asked; and Amy would not ask him, for just then she was having little experiences of her own, which made her rather wish to avoid the quizzical eyes of "our boy."

Fred Vaughn had returned, and put the question to which she had once decided to answer "Yes, thank you;" but now she said, "No, thank you," kindly but steadily; for when the time came, her courage failed her, and she found that something more than money and position was needed to satisfy the new longing that filled her heart so full of tender hopes and fears. The words "Fred is a good fellow, but not at all the man I fancied you would ever like," and Laurie's face, when he uttered them, kept returning to her as pertinaciously as her own did, when she said in look, if not in words, "I shall marry for money." It troubled her to remember that now, she wished she could take it back, it sounded so unwomanly. She didn't want Laurie to think her a heartless, worldly creature; she didn't care to be a queen of society now half so much as she did to be a lovable woman; she was so glad he didn't hate her for the dreadful things she said, but took them so beautifully, and was kinder than ever. His letters were such a comfort — for the home letters were irregular, and were not half so satisfactory as his when they did come. It was not only a pleasure, but a duty to answer them, for the poor fellow was forlorn, and needed petting, since Jo persisted in being stony-hearted. She ought to have made an effort, and tried to love him — it couldn't be very hard — many people would be proud and glad to have such a dear boy care for them; but Jo never would act like other girls, so there was nothing to do but be very kind, and treat him like a brother.

If all brothers were treated as well as Laurie was at this period, they would be a much happier race of beings than they are. Amy never lectured now; she asked his opinion on all subjects; she was interested in everything he did, made charming little presents for him and sent him two letters a week, full of lively gossip, sisterly confidences, and captivating sketches of the lovely scenes about her. As few brothers are complimented by having their letters carried about in their sisters' pockets, read and re-read diligently, cried over when short, kissed when long, and treasured carefully, we will not hint that Amy did any of these fond and foolish things. But she certainly did grow a little pale and pensive that spring, lost much of her relish for society, and went out sketching alone a good deal. She never had much to show when she came home, but was studying nature, I dare say, while she sat for hours with her hands folded, on the terrace at Valrosa, or absently sketched any fancy that occurred to her — a stalwart knight carved on a tomb, a young man asleep in the grass, with his hat over his eyes, or a curly-haired girl in gorgeous array, promenading down a ball-room, on the arm of a tall gentleman, both faces being left a blur, according to the last fashion in art, which was safe, but not altogether satisfactory.

Her aunt thought that she regretted her answer to Fred; and, finding denials useless, and explanations impossible, Amy left her to think what she liked, taking care that Laurie should know that Fred had gone to Egypt. That was all, but he understood it, and looked relieved, as he said to himself, with a venerable air, —

"I was sure she would think better of it. Poor old fellow, I've been through it all, and I can sympathize."

With that he heaved a great sigh, and then, as if he had discharged his duty to the past, put his feet up on the sofa, and enjoyed Amy's letter luxuriously.

While these changes were going on abroad, trouble had come at home; but the letter telling that Beth was failing, never reached Amy; and when the next found her, the grass was green above her sister. The sad news met her at Vevey, for the heat had driven them from Nice in May, and they had travelled slowly to Switzerland by way of Genoa and the Italian lakes. She bore it very well, and quietly submitted to the family decree, that she should not shorten her visit, for, since it was too late to say good-by to Beth, she had better stay, and let absence soften her sorrow. But her heart was very heavy — she longed to be at home; and every day looked wistfully across the lake, waiting for Laurie to come and comfort her.

He did come very soon; for the same mail brought letters to them both, but he was in Germany, and it took some days to reach him. The moment he read it, he packed his knapsack, bade adieu to his fellow-pedestrians, and was off to keep his promise, with a heart full of joy and sorrow, hope and suspense.

He knew Vevey well; and as soon as the boat touched the little quay, he hurried along the shore to La Tour, where the Carrols were living *en pension*. The garçon was in despair that the whole family had gone to take a promenade on the lake – but no, the blonde mademoiselle might be in the chateau garden. If *monsieur* would give himself the pain of sitting down, a flash of time should present her. But monsieur could not wait even "a flash of time," and in the middle of the speech, departed to find mademoiselle himself.

A pleasant old garden on the borders of the lovely lake, with chestnuts rustling overhead, ivy climbing everywhere, and the black shadow of the tower falling far across the sunny water. At one corner of the wide, low wall was a seat, and here Amy often came to read or work, or console herself with the beauty all about her. She was sitting here that day, leaning her head on her hand, with a homesick heart and heavy eyes, thinking of Beth, and wondering why Laurie did not come. She did not hear him cross the courtyard beyond, nor see him pause in the archway that led from the subterranean path into the garden. He stood a minute, looking at her with new eyes, seeing what no one had ever seen before – the tender side of Amy's character. Everything about her mutely suggested love and sorrow; the blotted letters in her lap, the black ribbon that tied up her hair, the womanly pain and patience in her face; even the little ebony cross at her throat seemed pathetic to Laurie, for he had given it to her, and she wore it as her only ornament. If he had any doubts about the reception she would give him, they were set at rest the minute she looked up and saw him; for, dropping everything, she ran to him, exclaiming in a tone of unmistakable love and longing, –

"Oh, Laurie, Laurie! I knew you'd come to me!"

I think everything was said and settled then; for, as they stood together quite silent for a moment, with the dark head bent down protectingly over the light one, Amy felt that no one could comfort and sustain her so well as Laurie, and Laurie decided that Amy was the only woman in the world who could fill Jo's place, and make him happy. He did not tell her so; but she was not disappointed, for both felt the truth, were satisfied, and gladly left the rest to silence.

In a minute Amy went back to her place; and while she dried her tears, Laurie gathered up the scattered papers, finding in the sight of sundry well-worn letters and suggestive sketches, good omens for the future. As he sat down beside her, Amy felt shy again, and turned rosy red at the recollection of her impulsive greeting.

"I couldn't help it; I felt so lonely and sad, and was so very glad to see you. It was such a surprise to look up and find you, just as I was beginning to fear you wouldn't come," she said, trying in vain to speak quite naturally.

"I came the minute I heard. I wish I could say something to comfort you for the loss of dear little Beth, but I can only feel, and —" he could not get any farther, for he, too, turned bashful all of a sudden, and did not quite know what to say. He longed to lay Amy's head down on his shoulder and tell her to have a good cry, but did not dare, so took her hand instead, and gave it a sympathetic squeeze that was better than words.

"You needn't say anything, — this comforts me," she said, softly. "Beth is well and happy, and I mustn't wish her back, — but I dread going home, much as I long to see them all. We won't talk about it now, for it makes me cry, and I want to enjoy you while you stay. You needn't go right back, need you?"

"Not if you want me, dear."

"I do, so much! Aunt and Flo are very kind, but you seem like one of the family, and it would be so comfortable to have you for a little while."

Amy spoke and looked so like a homesick child whose heart was full, that Laurie forgot his bashfulness all at once, and gave her just what she wanted, — the petting she was used to, and the cheerful conversation she needed.

"Poor little soul! you look as if you'd grieved yourself half sick. I'm going to take care of you, so don't cry any more, but come and walk about with me, — the wind is too chilly for you to sit still," he said, in the half-caressing, half-commanding way that Amy liked, as he tied on her hat, drew her arm through his, and began to pace up and down the sunny walk, under the new-leaved chestnuts. He felt more at ease upon his legs, and

Amy found it very pleasant to have a strong arm to lean upon, a familiar face to smile at her, and a kind voice to talk delightfully for her alone.

The quaint old garden had sheltered many pairs of lovers, and seemed expressly made for them, so sunny and secluded was it, with nothing but the tower to overlook them, and the wide lake to carry away the echo of the words, as it rippled by below. For an hour this new pair walked and talked, or rested on the wall, enjoying the sweet influences which gave such a charm to time and place; and when an unromantic dinner-bell warned them away, Amy felt as if she left her burden of loneliness and sorrow behind her in the chateau garden.

The moment Mrs. Carrol saw the girl's altered face she was illuminated with a new idea, and exclaimed to herself, "Now I understand it all, – the child has been pining for young Laurence. Bless my heart! I never thought of such a thing!"

With praiseworthy discretion, the good lady said nothing, and betrayed no sign of enlightenment, but cordially urged Laurie to stay, and begged Amy to enjoy his society, for it would do her more good than so much solitude. Amy was a model of docility; and, as her aunt was a good deal occupied with Flo, she was left to entertain her friend, and did it with more than her usual success.

At Nice, Laurie had lounged and Amy had scolded; at Vevey, Laurie was never idle, but always walking, riding, boating, or studying, in the most energetic manner; while Amy admired everything he did, and followed his example as far and as fast as she could. He said the change was owing to the climate, and she did not contradict him, being glad of a like excuse for her own recovered health and spirits.

The invigorating air did them both good, and much exercise worked wholesome changes in minds as well as bodies. They seemed to get clearer views of life and duty up there among the everlasting hills; the fresh winds blew away desponding doubts, delusive fancies and moody mists; the warm spring sunshine brought out all sorts of aspiring ideas, tender hopes and happy thoughts, – the lake seemed to wash away the troubles of the past, and the grand old mountains to look benignly down upon them, saying, "Little children, love one another."

In spite of the new sorrow it was a very happy time, – so happy that Laurie could not bear to disturb it by a word. It took him a little while to recover from his surprise at the rapid cure of his first, and, as he had firmly believed, his last and only love. He consoled himself for the seeming disloyalty by the thought that Jo's sister was almost the same as Jo herself, and the conviction that it would have been impossible to love any other woman but Amy so soon and so well. His first wooing had been of the tempestuous order, and he looked back upon it as if through a long vista of years, with a feeling of compassion blended with regret. He was not ashamed of it, but put it away as one of the bitter-sweet experiences of his life, for which he could be grateful when the pain was over. His second wooing he resolved should be as calm and simple as possible; there was no need of having a scene, – hardly any need of telling Amy that he loved her; she knew it without words, and had given him his answer long ago. It all came about so naturally that no one could complain, and he knew that everybody would be pleased, – even Jo. But when our first little passion has been crushed, we are apt to be wary and slow in making a second trial; so Laurie let the days pass, enjoying every hour, and leaving them to chance the utterance of the word that would put an end to the first and sweetest part of his new romance.

He had rather imagined that the *denouément* would take place in the chateau garden by moonlight, and in the most graceful and decorous manner; but it turned out exactly the reverse, – for the matter was settled on the lake, at noonday, in a few blunt words. They had been floating about all the morning, from gloomy St. Gingolf to sunny Montreaux, with the Alps of Savoy on one side, Mont St. Bernard and the Dent du Midi on the other, pretty Vevey in the valley, and Lausanne upon the hill beyond, a cloudless blue sky overhead, and the bluer lake below, dotted with the picturesque boats that look like white-winged gulls.

They had been talking of Bonnivard as they glided past Chillon, and of Rousseau as they looked up at Clarens, where he wrote his Heloise. Neither had read it, but they knew it was a love story, and each privately wondered if it was half as interesting as their own. Amy had been dabbling her hand in the water during the little pause that fell between them, and, when she looked up, Laurie was leaning on his oars, with an expression in his eyes that made her say, hastily, – merely for the sake of saying something, –

"You must be tired, – rest a little, and let me row; it will do me good, for since you came I have been altogether lazy and luxurious."

"I'm not tired, but you may take an oar if you like. There's room enough, though I have to sit nearly in the middle, else the boat won't trim," returned Laurie, as if he rather liked the arrangement.

Feeling that she had not mended matters much, Amy took the offered third of a seat, shook her hair over her face, and accepted an oar. She rowed as well as she did many other things; and, though she used both hands, and Laurie but one, the oars kept time, and the boat went smoothly through the water.

"How well we pull together, don't we?" said Amy, who objected to silence just then.

"So well, that I wish we might always pull in the same boat. Will you, Amy?" very tenderly.

"Yes, Laurie!" very low.

Then they both stopped rowing, and unconsciously added a pretty little *tableau* of human love and happiness to the dissolving views reflected in the lake.

CHAPTER FORTY-TWO

ALL ALONE

~

*I*t was easy to promise self-abnegation when self was wrapt up in another, and heart and soul were purified by a sweet example; but when the helpful voice was silent, the daily lesson over, the beloved presence gone, and nothing remained but loneliness and grief, then Jo found her promise very hard to keep. How could she "comfort father and mother," when her own heart ached with a ceaseless longing for her sister; how could she "make the house cheerful," when all its light, and warmth, and beauty seemed to have deserted it when Beth left the old home for the new; and where, in all the world, could she "find some useful, happy work to do," that would take the place of the loving service which had been its own reward? She tried in a blind, hopeless way to do her duty, secretly rebelling against it all the while, for it seemed unjust that her few joys should be lessened, her burdens made heavier, and life get harder and harder as she toiled along. Some people seemed to get all sunshine, and some all shadow; it was not fair, for she tried more than Amy to be good, but never got any reward, — only disappointment, trouble, and hard work.

Poor Jo! these were dark days to her, for something like despair came over her when she thought of spending all her life in that quiet house, devoted to hum-drum cares, a few poor little pleasures, and the duty that never seemed to grow any easier. "I can't do it. I wasn't meant for a life like this, and I know I shall break away and do something desperate if somebody don't come and help me," she said to herself, when her first efforts failed, and she fell into the moody miserable state of mind which often comes when strong wills have to yield to the inevitable.

But some one did come and help her, though Jo did not recognize her good angels at once, because they wore familiar shapes, and used the simple spells best fitted to poor humanity. Often she started up at night, thinking Beth called her; and when the sight of the little empty bed made her cry with the bitter cry of an unsubmissive sorrow, "Oh, Beth! come back! come back!" she did not stretch out her yearning arms in vain; for, as quick to hear her sobbing as she had been to hear her sister's faintest whisper, her mother came to comfort her. Not with words only, but the patient tenderness that soothes by a touch, tears that were mute reminders of a greater grief than Jo's, and broken whispers, more eloquent than prayers, because hopeful resignation went hand-in-hand with natural sorrow. Sacred moments! when heart talked to heart in the silence of the night, turning affliction to a blessing, which chastened grief and strengthened love. Feeling this, Jo's burden seemed easier to bear, duty grew sweeter, and life looked more endurable, seen from the safe shelter of her mother's arms.

When aching heart was a little comforted, troubled mind likewise found help; for one day she went to the study, and, leaning over the good gray head lifted to welcome her with a tranquil smile, she said, very humbly, —

"Father, talk to me as you did to Beth. I need it more than she did, for I'm all wrong."

"My dear, nothing can comfort me like this," he answered, with a falter in his voice, and both arms round her, as if he, too, needed help, and did not fear to ask it.

Then, sitting in Beth's little chair close beside him, Jo told her troubles, the resentful sorrow for her loss, the fruitless efforts that discouraged her, the want of faith that made life look so dark, and all the sad bewilderment which we call despair. She gave him entire confidence, – he gave her the help she needed, and both found consolation in the act; for the time had come when they could talk together not only as father and daughter, but as man and woman, able and glad to serve each other with mutual sympathy as well as mutual love. Happy, thoughtful times there in the old study which Jo called "the church of one member," and from which she came with fresh courage, recovered cheerfulness, and a more submissive spirit, – for the parents who had taught one child to meet death without fear, were trying now to teach another to accept life without despondency or distrust, and to use its beautiful opportunities with gratitude and power.

Other helps had Jo, humble, wholesome duties and delights, that would not be denied their part in serving her, and which she slowly learned to see and value. Brooms and dishcloths never could be as distasteful as they once had been, for Beth had presided over both; and something of her housewifely spirit seemed to linger round the little mop and the old brush, that was never thrown away. As she used them, Jo found herself humming the songs Beth used to hum, imitating Beth's orderly ways, and giving the little touches here and there that kept everything fresh and cosy, which was the first step toward making home happy, though she didn't know it, till Hannah said with an approving squeeze of the hand, –

"You thoughtful creter, you're determined we shan't miss that dear lamb ef you can help it. We don't say much, but we see it, and the Lord will bless you for't, see ef He don't."

As they sat sewing together, Jo discovered how much improved her sister Meg was; how well she could talk, how much she knew about good, womanly impulses, thoughts and feelings, how happy she was in husband and children, and how much they were all doing for each other.

"Marriage is an excellent thing after all. I wonder if I should blossom out, half as well as you have, if I tried it, always *'perwisin'* I could," said Jo, as she constructed a kite for Demi, in the topsy-turvy nursery.

"It's just what you need to bring out the tender, womanly half of your nature, Jo. You are like a chestnut burr, prickly outside, but silky-soft within, and a sweet kernel, if one can only get at it. Love will make you show your heart some day, and then the rough burr will fall off."

"Frost opens chestnut burrs, ma'am, and it takes a good shake to bring them down. Boys go nutting, and I don't care to be bagged by them," returned Jo, pasting away at the kite, which no wind that blows would ever carry up, for Daisy had tied herself on as a bob.

Meg laughed, for she was glad to see a glimmer of Jo's old spirit, but she felt it her duty to enforce her opinion by every argument in her power; and the sisterly chats were not wasted, especially as two of Meg's most effective arguments were the babies, whom Jo loved tenderly. Grief is the best opener for some hearts, and Jo's was nearly ready for the bag; a little more sunshine to ripen the nut, then, not a boy's impatient shake, but a man's hand reached up to pick it gently from the burr, and find the kernel sound and sweet. If she had suspected this, she would have shut up tight, and been more prickly than ever; fortunately she wasn't thinking about herself, so, when the time came, down she dropped.

Now, if she had been the heroine of a moral storybook, she ought at this period of her life to have become quite saintly, renounced the world, and gone about doing good in a mortified bonnet, with tracts in her pocket. But you see Jo wasn't a heroine; she was only a struggling human girl, like hundreds of others, and she just acted out her nature, being sad, cross, listless or energetic, as the mood suggested. It's highly virtuous to say we'll be good, but we can't do it all at once, and it takes a long pull, a strong pull, and a pull all together, before some of us even get our feet set in the right way. Jo had got so far, she was learning to do her duty, and to feel unhappy if she did not; but to do it cheerfully – ah, that was another thing! She had often said she wanted to do something splendid, no matter how hard; and now she had her wish, – for what could be more beautiful than to devote her life to father and mother, trying to make home as happy to them as they had to her? And, if difficulties were necessary to increase the splendor of the effort, what could be harder for a restless, ambitious girl, than to give up her own hopes, plans and desires, and cheerfully live for others?

Providence had taken her at her word; here was the task, – not what she had expected, but better, because self had no part in it; now could she do it? She decided that she would try; and, in her first attempt, she found the helps I have suggested. Still another was given her, and she took it, – not as a reward, but as a comfort, as Christian took the refreshment afforded by the little arbor where he rested, as he climbed the hill called Difficulty.

"Why don't you write? that always used to make you happy," said her mother, once, when the desponding fit overshadowed Jo.

"I've no heart to write, and if I had, nobody cares for my things."

"We do; write something for us, and never mind the rest of the world. Try it dear; I'm sure it would do you good, and please us very much."

"Don't believe I can;" but Jo got out her desk, and began to overhaul her half-finished manuscripts.

An hour afterward her mother peeped in, and there she was scratching away, with her black pinafore on, and an absorbed expression, which caused Mrs. March to smile, and slip away, well pleased with the success of her suggestion. Jo never knew how it happened, but something got into that story that went straight to the hearts of those who read it; for, when her family had laughed and cried over it, her father sent it, much against her will, to one of the popular magazines, and, to her utter surprise, it was not only paid for, but others requested. Letters from several persons, whose praise was honor, followed the appearance of the little story, newspapers copied it, and strangers as well as friends admired it. For a small thing, it was a great success; and Jo was more astonished than when her novel was commended and condemned all at once.

"I don't understand it; what *can* there be in a simple little story like that, to make people praise it so?" she said, quite bewildered.

"There is truth in it, Jo, – that's the secret; humor and pathos make it alive, and you have found your style at last. You wrote with no thought of fame or money, and put your heart into it, my daughter; you have had the bitter, now comes the sweet; do your best, and grow as happy as we are in your success."

"If there *is* anything good or true in what I write, it isn't mine; I owe it all to you and mother, and to Beth," said Jo, more touched by her father's words than by any amount of praise from the world.

So taught by love and sorrow, Jo wrote her little stories, and sent them away to make friends for themselves and her, finding it a very charitable world to such humble wanderers, for they were kindly welcomed, and sent home comfortable tokens to their mother, like dutiful children, whom good fortune overtakes.

When Amy and Laurie wrote of their engagement, Mrs. March feared that Jo would find it difficult to rejoice over it, but her fears were soon set at rest; for, though Jo looked grave at first, she took it very quietly, and was full of hopes and plans for "the children," before she read the letter twice. It was a sort of written duet, wherein each glorified the other in lover-like fashion, very pleasant to read, and satisfactory to think of, for no one had any objection to make.

"You like it, mother?" said Jo, as they laid down the closely-written sheets, and looked at one another.

"Yes, I hoped it would be so, ever since Amy wrote that she had refused Fred. I felt sure then that something better than what you call 'the mercenary spirit' had come over her, and a hint here and there in her letters made me suspect that love and Laurie would win the day."

"How sharp you are, Marmee, and how silent; you never said a word to me."

"Mothers have need of sharp eyes and discreet tongues, when they have girls to manage. I was half afraid to put the idea into your head, lest you should write, and congratulate them before the thing was settled."

"I'm not the scatter-brain I was; you may trust me, I'm sober and sensible enough for any one's *confidante* now."

"So you are, dear, and I should have made you mine, only I fancied it might pain you to learn that your Teddy loved any one else."

"Now, mother, did you really think I could be so silly and selfish, after I'd refused his love, when it was freshest, if not best?"

"I knew you were sincere then, Jo, but lately I have thought that if he came back, and asked again, you might, perhaps, feel like giving another answer. Forgive me, dear, I can't help seeing that you are very lonely, and sometimes there is a hungry look in your eyes that goes to my heart; so I fancied that your boy might fill the empty place, if he tried now."

"No, mother, it is better as it is, and I'm glad Amy has learned to love him. But you are right in one thing; I *am* lonely, and perhaps if Teddy had tried again, I might have said 'Yes,' not because I love him any more, but because I care more to be loved, than when he went away."

"I'm glad of that, Jo, for it shows that you are getting on. There are plenty to love you, so try to be satisfied with father and mother, sisters and brothers, friends and babies, till the best lover of all comes to give you your reward."

"Mothers are the *best* lovers in the world; but, I don't mind whispering to Marmee, that I'd like to try all kinds. It's very curious, but the more I try to satisfy myself with all sorts of natural affections, the more I seem to want. I'd no idea hearts could take in so many – mine is so elastic, it never seems full now, and I used to be quite contented with my family; I don't understand it."

"I do," and Mrs. March, smiled her wise smile, as Jo turned back the leaves to read what Amy said of Laurie.

"It is so beautiful to be loved as Laurie loves me; he isn't sentimental; doesn't say much about it, but I see and feel it in all he says and does, and it makes me happy and so humble, that I don't seem to be the same girl I was. I never knew how good, and generous, and tender he was till now, for he lets me read his heart, and I find it full of noble impulses, and hopes, and purposes, and am so proud to know it's mine. He says he feels as if he 'could make a prosperous voyage now with me aboard as mate, and lots of love for ballast.' I pray he may, and try to be all he believes me, for I love my gallant captain with all my heart, and soul, and might, and never will desert him, while God lets us be together. Oh, mother, I never knew how much like heaven this world could be, when two people love and live for one another!"

"And that's out cool, reserved, and worldly Amy! Truly love does work miracles. How very, very happy they must be!" and Jo laid the rustling sheets together with a careful hand, as one might shut the covers of a lovely romance, which holds the reader fast till the end comes, and he finds himself alone in the work-a-day world again.

By and by, Jo roamed away up stairs, for it was rainy, and she could not walk. A restless spirit possessed her, and the old feeling came again, not bitter as it once was, but a sorrowfully patient wonder why one sister should have all she asked, the other nothing. It was not true; she knew that, and tried to put it away, but the natural craving for affection was strong, and Amy's happiness woke the hungry longing for some one to "love with heart and soul, and cling to, while God let them be together."

Up in the garret, where Jo's unquiet wanderings ended, stood four little wooden chests in a row, each marked with its owner's name, and each filled with relics of the childhood and girlhood ended now for all. Jo glanced into them, and when she came to her own, leaned her chin on the edge, and stared absently at the chaotic collection, till a bundle of old exercise-books caught her eye. She drew them out, turned them over, and re-lived that pleasant winter at kind Mrs. Kirke's. She had smiled at first, then she looked thoughtful, next sad, and when she came to a little message written in the Professor's hand, her lips began to tremble, the books slid out of her lap, and she sat looking at the friendly words as if they took a new meaning, and touched a tender spot in her heart.

"Wait for me, my friend, I may be a little late, but I shall surely come."

"Oh, if only he would! So kind, so good, so patient with me always; my dear old Fritz, I didn't value him half enough when I had him, but now how I should love to see him, for every one seems to be going away from me, and I'm all alone."

And holding the little paper fast, as if it were a promise yet to be fulfilled, Jo laid her head down on a comfortable rag-bag, and cried, as if in opposition to the rain pattering on the roof.

Was it all self-pity, loneliness, or low spirits? or was it the waking up of a sentiment which had bided its time as patiently as its inspirer? Who shall say.

SURPRISES

~

Jo was alone in the twilight, lying on the old sofa, looking at the fire, and thinking. It was her favorite way of spending the hour of dusk; no one disturbed her, and she used to lie there on Beth's little red pillow, planning stories, dreaming dreams, or thinking tender thoughts of the sister who never seemed far away. Her face looked tired, grave, and rather sad; for to-morrow was her birthday, and she was thinking how fast the years went by, how old she was getting, and how little she seemed to have accomplished. Almost twenty-five, and nothing to show for it, – Jo was mistaken in that; there was a good deal to show, and by and by she saw, and was grateful for it.

"An old maid – that's what I'm to be. A literary spinster, with a pen for a spouse, a family of stories for children, and twenty years hence a morsel of fame, perhaps; when, like poor Johnson, I'm old, and can't enjoy it – solitary, and can't share it, independent, and don't need it. Well, I needn't be a sour saint nor a selfish sinner; and, I dare say, old maids are very comfortable when they get used to it; but –" and there Jo sighed, as if the prospect was not inviting.

It seldom is, at first, and thirty seems the end of all things to five-and-twenty; but it's not so bad as it looks, and one can get on quite happily if one has something in one's self to fall back upon. At twenty-five, girls begin to talk about being old maids, but secretly resolve that they never will; at thirty, they say nothing about it, but quietly accept the fact; and, if sensible, console themselves by remembering that they have twenty more useful, happy years, in which they may be learning to grow old gracefully. Don't laugh at the spinsters, dear girls, for often very tender, tragical romances are hidden away in the hearts that beat so quietly under the sober gowns, and many silent sacrifices of youth, health, ambition, love itself, make the faded faces beautiful in God's sight. Even the sad, sour sisters should be kindly dealt with, because they have missed the sweetest part of life if for no other reason; and, looking at them with compassion; not contempt, girls in their bloom should remember that they too may miss the blossom time – that rosy cheeks don't last forever, the silver threads will come in the bonnie brown hair, and, that by and by, kindness and respect will be as sweet as love and admiration now.

Gentlemen, which means boys, be courteous to the old maids, no matter how poor and plain and prim, for the only chivalry worth having is that which is the readiest to pay deference to the old, protect the feeble, and serve womankind, regardless of rank, age, or color. Just recollect the good aunts who have not only lectured and fussed, but nursed and petted, too often without thanks – the scrapes they have helped you out of, the "tips" they have given you from their small store, the stitches the patient old fingers have set for you, the steps the willing old feet have taken, and gratefully pay the dear old ladies the little attentions that women love to receive as long as they live. The bright-eyed girls are quick to see such traits, and will like you all the better for them; and, if death, almost the only power that can part mother and son, should rob you of yours, you will be sure to find a tender, welcome, and maternal cherishing from some Aunt Priscilla, who has kept the warmest corner of her lonely old heart for "the best nevvy in the world."

Jo must have fallen asleep (as I dare say my reader has during this little homily), for, suddenly, Laurie's ghost seemed to stand before her. A substantial, life-like ghost leaning over her, with the very look he used to wear when he felt a good deal, and didn't like to show it. But, like Jenny in the ballad, –

She could not think it he,

and lay staring up at him, in startled silence, till he stooped and kissed her. Then she knew him, and flew up, crying joyfully, –

"Oh, my Teddy! Oh, my Teddy!"

"Dear Jo, you are glad to see me, then?"

"Glad! my blessed boy, words can't express my gladness. Where's Amy?"

"Your mother has got her, down at Meg's. We stopped there by the way, and there was no way of getting my wife out of their clutches."

"Your what?" cried Jo – for Laurie uttered those two words with an unconscious pride and satisfaction, which betrayed him.

"Oh, the dickens! now I've done it;" and he looked so guilty that Jo was down upon him like a flash.

"You've gone and got married?"

"Yes, please, but I never will again;" and he went down upon his knees with a penitent clasping of hands, and a face full of mischief, mirth, and triumph.

"Actually married?"

"Very much so, thank you."

"Mercy on us; what dreadful thing will you do next?" and Jo fell into her seat, with a gasp.

"A characteristic, but not exactly complimentary congratulation," returned Laurie, still in an abject attitude, but beaming with satisfaction.

"What can you expect, when you take one's breath away, creeping in like a burglar, and letting cats out of bags like that? Get up, you ridiculous boy, and tell me all about it."

"Not a word, unless you let me come in my old place, and promise not to barricade."

Jo laughed at that as she had not done for many a long day, and patted the sofa invitingly, as she said, in a cordial tone, –

"The old pillow is up garret, and we don't need it now; so, come and 'fess, Teddy."

"How good it sounds to hear you say 'Teddy'; no one ever calls me that but you;" and Laurie sat down with an air of great content.

"What does Amy call you?"

"My lord."

"That's like her – well, you look it;" and Jo's eyes plainly betrayed that she found her boy comelier than ever.

The pillow was gone, but there *was* a barricade, nevertheless; a natural one raised by time, absence, and change of heart. Both felt it, and for a minute looked at one another as if that invisible barrier cast a little shadow over them. It was gone directly, however, for Laurie said, with a vain attempt at dignity, –

"Don't I look like a married man, and the head of a family?"

"Not a bit, and you never will. You've grown bigger and bonnier, but you are the same scapegrace as ever."

"Now, really, Jo, you ought to treat me with more respect," began Laurie, who enjoyed it all immensely.

"How can I, when the mere idea of you, married and settled, is so irresistibly funny that I can't keep sober," answered Jo, smiling all over her face, so infectiously, that they had another laugh, and then settled down for a good talk, quite in the pleasant old fashion.

"It's no use your going out in the cold to get Amy, for they are all coming up, presently; I couldn't wait; I wanted to be the one to tell you the grand surprise, and have 'first skim,' as we used to say, when we squabbled about the cream."

"Of course you did, and spoilt your story by beginning at the wrong end. Now, start right, and tell me how it all happened; I'm pining to know."

"Well, I did it to please Amy," began Laurie, with a twinkle, that made Jo exclaim, –

"Fib number one; Amy did it to please you. Go on, and tell the truth, if you can, sir."

"Now she's beginning to marm it, isn't it jolly to hear her?" said Laurie to the fire, and the fire glowed and sparkled as if it quite agreed. "It's all the same, you know, she and I being one. We planned to come home with the Carrols, a month or more ago, but they suddenly changed their minds, and decided to pass another winter in Paris. But grandpa wanted to come home; he went to please me, and I couldn't let him go alone, neither could I leave Amy; and Mrs. Carrol had got English notions about chaperons, and such nonsense, and wouldn't let Amy come with us. So I just settled the difficulty, by saying, 'Let's be married, and then we can do as we like.'"

"Of course you did; you always have things to suit you."

"Not always;" and something in Laurie's voice made Jo say, hastily, —

"How did you ever get aunt to agree?"

"It was hard work; but, between us, we talked her over, for we had heaps of good reasons on our side. There wasn't time to write and ask leave, but you all liked it, and had consented to it by and by — and it was only 'taking time by the fetlock,' as my wife says."

"Aren't we proud of those two words, and don't we like to say them?" interrupted Jo, addressing the fire in her turn, and watching with delight the happy light it seemed to kindle in the eyes that had been so tragically gloomy when she saw them last.

"A trifle, perhaps; she's such a captivating little woman I can't help being proud of her. Well, then, uncle and aunt were there to play propriety; we were so absorbed in one another we were of no mortal use apart, and that charming arrangement would make everything easy all round; so we did it."

"When, where, how?" asked Jo, in a fever of feminine interest and curiosity, for she could not realize it a particle.

"Six weeks ago, at the American consul's, in Paris — a very quiet wedding, of course; for even in our happiness we didn't forget dear little Beth."

Jo put her hand in his as he said that, and Laurie gently smoothed the little red pillow, which he remembered well.

"Why didn't you let us know afterward?" asked Jo, in a quieter tone, when they had sat quite still a minute.

"We wanted to surprise you; we thought we were coming directly home, at first, but the dear old gentleman, as soon as we were married, found he couldn't be ready under a month, at least, and sent us off to spend our honeymoon wherever we liked. Amy had once called Valrosa a regular honeymoon home, so we went there, and were as happy as people are but once in their lives. My faith, wasn't it love among the roses!"

Laurie seemed to forget Jo, for a minute, and Jo was glad of it; for the fact that he told her these things so freely and naturally, assured her that he had quite forgiven and forgotten. She tried to draw away her hand; but, as if he guessed the thought that prompted the half involuntary impulse, Laurie held it fast, and said, with a manly gravity she had never seen in him before, –

"Jo, dear, I want to say one thing, and then we'll put it by forever. As I told you, in my letter, when I wrote that Amy had been so kind to me, I never shall stop loving you; but the love is altered, and I have learned to see that it is better as it is. Amy and you change places in my heart, that's all. I think it was meant to be so, and would have come about naturally, if I had waited, as you tried to make me; but I never could be patient, and so I got a heartache. I was a boy then – headstrong and violent; and it took a hard lesson to show me my mistake. For it *was* one, Jo, as you said, and I found it out, after making a fool of myself. Upon my word, I was so tumbled up in my mind, at one time, that I didn't know which I loved best – you or Amy, and tried to love both alike; but I couldn't; and when I saw her in Switzerland, everything seemed to clear up all at once. You both got into your right places, and I felt sure that it was well off with the old love, before it was on with the new; that I could honestly share my heart between sister Jo and wife Amy, and love them both dearly. Will you believe it, and go back to the happy old times, when we first knew one another?"

"I'll believe it, with all my heart; but Teddy, we never can be boy and girl again – the happy old times can't come back, and we mustn't expect it. We are man and woman now, with sober work to do, for play-time is over, and we must give up frolicking. I'm sure you feel this; I see the change in you, and you'll find it in me; I shall miss my boy, but I shall love the man as much, and admire him more, because he means to be what I hoped he would. We can't be little playmates any longer, but we will be brother and sister, to love and help one another all our lives, won't we, Laurie?"

He did not say a word, but took the hand she offered him, and laid his face down on it for a minute, feeling that out of the grave of a boyish passion, there had risen a beautiful, strong friendship to bless them both. Presently Jo said cheerfully, for she didn't want the coming home to be a sad one, –

"I can't make it true that you children are really married, and going to set up housekeeping. Why, it seems only yesterday that I was buttoning Amy's pinafore, and pulling your hair when you teased. Mercy me, how time does fly!"

"As one of the children is older than yourself, you needn't talk so like a grandma. I flatter myself I'm a 'gentleman growed,' as Peggoty said of David; and when you see Amy, you'll find her rather a precocious infant," said Laurie, looking amused at her maternal air.

"You may be a little older in years, but I'm ever so much older in feeling, Teddy. Women always are; and this last year has been such a hard one, that I feel forty."

"Poor Jo! we left you to bear it alone, while we went pleasuring. You *are* older; here's a line, and there's another; unless you smile, your eyes look sad, and when I touched the cushion, just now, I found a tear on it. You've had a great deal to bear, and had to bear it all alone; what a selfish beast I've been!" and Laurie pulled his own hair, with a remorseful look.

But Jo only turned over the traitorous pillow, and answered in a tone which she tried to make quite cheerful, –

"No, I had father and mother to help me, the dear babies to comfort me, and the thought that you and Amy were safe and happy, to make the troubles here easier to bear. I *am* lonely, sometimes, but I dare say it's good for me, and –"

"You never shall be again," broke in Laurie, putting his arm about her, as if to fence out every human ill. "Amy and I can't get on without you, so you must come and teach the children to keep house, and go halves in everything, just as we used to do, and let us pet you, and all be blissfully happy and friendly together."

"If I shouldn't be in the way, it would be very pleasant. I begin to feel quite young already; for, somehow, all my troubles seemed to fly away when you came. You always were a comfort, Teddy;" and Jo leaned her head on his shoulder, just as she did years ago, when Beth lay ill, and Laurie told her to hold on to him.

He looked down at her, wondering if she remembered the time, but Jo was smiling to herself, as if, in truth, her troubles *had* all vanished at his coming.

"You are the same Jo still, dropping tears about one minute, and laughing the next. You look a little wicked now; what is it, grandma?"

"I was wondering how you and Amy get on together."

"Like angels!"

"Yes, of course, at first — but which rules?"

"I don't mind telling you that she does, now; at least I let her think so, — it pleases her, you know. By and by we shall take turns, for marriage, they say, halves one's rights and doubles one's duties."

"You'll go on as you begin, and Amy will rule you all the days of your life."

"Well, she does it so imperceptibly that I don't think I shall mind much. She is the sort of woman who knows how to rule well; in fact, I rather like it, for she winds one round her finger as softly and prettily as a skein of silk, and makes you feel as if she was doing you a favor all the while."

"That ever I should live to see you a henpecked husband and enjoying it!" cried Jo, with uplifted hands.

It was good to see Laurie square his shoulders, and smile with masculine scorn at that insinuation, as he replied, with his "high and mighty" air, —

"Amy is too well-bred for that, and I am not the sort of man to submit to it. My wife and I respect ourselves and one another too much ever to tyrannize or quarrel."

Jo liked that, and thought the new dignity very becoming, but the boy seemed changing very fast into the man, and regret mingled with her pleasure.

"I am sure of that; Amy and you never did quarrel as we used to. She is the sun, and I the wind, in the fable, and the sun managed the man best, you remember."

"She can blow him up as well as shine on him," laughed Laurie. "Such a lecture as I got at Nice! I give you my word it was a deal worse than any of your scoldings. A regular rouser; I'll tell you all about it some time, — *she* never will, because, after telling me that she despised me and was ashamed of me, she lost her heart to the despicable party, and married the good-for-nothing."

"What baseness! Well, if she abuses you come to me, and I'll defend you!"

"I look as if I needed it, don't I?" said Laurie, getting up and striking an attitude which suddenly changed from the imposing to the rapturous, as Amy's voice was heard calling, –

"Where is she? where's my dear old Jo?"

In trooped the whole family, and every one was hugged and kissed all over again, and, after several vain attempts, the three wanderers were set down to be looked at and exulted over. Mr. Laurence, hale and hearty as ever, was quite as much improved as the others by his foreign tour, – for the crustiness seemed to be nearly gone, and the old-fashioned courtliness had received a polish which made it kindlier than ever. It was good to see him beam at "my children," as he called the young pair; it was better still to see Amy pay him the daughterly duty and affection which completely won his old heart; and, best of all, to watch Laurie revolve about the two as if never tired of enjoying the pretty picture they made.

The minute she put her eyes upon Amy, Meg became conscious that her own dress hadn't a Parisian air, – that young Mrs. Moffat would be entirely eclipsed by young Mrs. Laurence, and that "her ladyship" was altogether a most elegant and graceful woman. Jo thought, as she watched the pair, "How well they look together! I was right, and Laurie has found the beautiful, accomplished girl who will become his home better than clumsy old Jo, and be a pride, not a torment to him." Mrs. March and her husband smiled and nodded at each other with happy faces, – for they saw that their youngest had done well, not only in worldly things, but the better wealth of love, confidence, and happiness.

For Amy's face was full of the soft brightness which betokens a peaceful heart, her voice had a new tenderness in it, and the cool, prim carriage was changed to a gentle dignity, both womanly and winning. No little affectations marred it, and the cordial sweetness of her manner was more charming than the new beauty or the old grace, for it stamped her at once with the unmistakable sign of the true gentlewoman she had hoped to become.

"Love has done much for our little girl," said her mother, softly.

"She has had a good example before her all her life, my dear," Mr. March whispered back, with a loving look at the worn face and gray head beside him.

Daisy found it impossible to keep her eyes off her "pitty aunty," but attached herself like a lap-dog to the wonderful châtelaine full of delightful charms. Demi paused to consider the new relationship before he compromised himself by the rash acceptance of a bribe, which took the tempting form of a family of wooden bears, from Berne. A flank movement produced an unconditional surrender, however, for Laurie knew where to have him: —

"Young man, when I first had the honor of making your acquaintance you hit me in the face; now I demand the satisfaction of a gentleman!" and with that the tall uncle proceeded to toss and tousle the small nephew in a way that damaged his philosophical dignity as much as it delighted his boyish soul.

"Blest if she ain't in silk from head to foot; ain't it a relishin' sight to see her settin' there as fine as a fiddle, and hear folks calling little Amy 'Mis Laurence!'" muttered old Hannah, who could not resist frequent "peeks" through the slide as she set the table in a most decidedly promiscuous manner.

Mercy on us, how they did talk! first one, then the other, then all burst out together, — trying to tell the history of three years in half an hour. It was fortunate that tea was at hand, to produce a lull and provide refreshment, — for they would have been hoarse and faint if they had gone on much longer. Such a happy procession as filed away into the little dining-room! Mr. March proudly escorted "Mrs. Laurence"; Mrs. March as proudly leaned on the arm of "my son"; the old gentleman took Jo with a whispered "You must be my girl now," and a glance at the empty corner by the fire, that made Jo whisper back, with trembling lips, "I'll try to fill her place, sir."

The twins pranced behind, feeling that the millennium was at hand, — for every one was so busy with the new comers that they were left to revel at their own sweet will, and you may be sure they made the most of the opportunity. Didn't they steal sips of tea, stuff gingerbread *ad libitum*, get a hot biscuit apiece, and, as a crowning trespass, didn't they each whisk a captivating little tart into their tiny pockets, there to stick and crumble treacherously, — teaching them that both human nature and pastry are frail! Burdened with the guilty consciousness of the sequestered tarts, and fearing Dodo's sharp eyes would pierce the thin disguise of cambric and

Jo laid her head down and cried. (Chapter 42)

There stood a stout, bearded gentleman.
(Chapter 43)

merino which hid their booty, the little sinners attached themselves to "Dranpa," who hadn't his spectacles on. Amy, who was handed about like refreshments, returned to the parlor on Father Laurence's arm; the others paired off as before, and this arrangement left Jo companionless. She did not mind it at the minute, for she lingered to answer Hannah's inquiry, —

"Will Miss Amy ride in her coop (*coupé*), and use all them lovely silver dishes that's stored away over yander?"

"Shouldn't wonder if she drove six white horses, ate off gold plate, and wore diamonds and point-lace every day. Teddy thinks nothing too good for her," returned Jo, with infinite satisfaction.

"No more there is! Will you have hash or fishballs for breakfast?" asked Hannah, who wisely mingled poetry with prose.

"I don't care," and Jo shut the door, feeling that food was an uncongenial topic just then. She stood a minute looking at the party vanishing above, and, as Demi's short plaid legs toiled up the last stair, a sudden sense of loneliness came over her, so strongly that she looked about her with dim eyes, as if to find something to lean upon, — for even Teddy had deserted her. If she had known what birthday gift was coming every minute nearer and nearer, she would not have said to herself "I'll weep a little weep when I go to bed; it won't do to be dismal now." Then she drew her hand over her eyes, — for one of her boyish habits was never to know where her handkerchief was, — and had just managed to call up a smile, when there came a knock at the porch door.

She opened it with hospitable haste, and started as if another ghost had come to surprise her, — for there stood a stout, bearded gentleman, beaming on her from the darkness like a midnight sun.

"Oh, Mr. Bhaer, I *am* so glad to see you!" cried Jo, with a clutch, as if she feared the night would swallow him up before she could get him in.

"And I to see Miss Marsch, — but no, you haf a party —" and the Professor paused as the sound of voices and the tap of dancing feet came down to them.

"No, we haven't, — only the family. My brother and sister have just come home, and we are all very happy. Come in, and make one of us."

Though a very social man, I think Mr. Bhaer would have gone decorously away, and come again another day; but how could he when Jo shut the door behind him, and bereft him of his hat? Perhaps her face had something to do with it, for she forgot to hide her joy at seeing him, and showed it with a frankness that proved irresistible to the solitary man, whose welcome far exceeded his boldest hopes.

"If I shall not be Monsieur De Trop I will so gladly see them all. You haf been ill, my friend?"

He put the question abruptly, for, as Jo hung up his coat, the light fell on her face, and he saw a change in it.

"Not ill, but tired and sorrowful; we have had trouble since I saw you last."

"Ah, yes, I know! my heart was sore for you when I heard that;" and he shook hands again with such a sympathetic face, that Jo felt as if no comfort could equal the look of the kind eyes, the grasp of the big, warm hand.

"Father, mother, this is my friend, Professor Bhaer," she said, with a face and tone of such irrepressible pride and pleasure, that she might as well have blown a trumpet and opened the door with a flourish.

If the stranger had had any doubts about his reception, they were set at rest in a minute by the cordial welcome he received. Every one greeted him kindly, for Jo's sake, at first, but very soon they liked him for his own. They could not help it, for he carried the talisman that opens all hearts, and these simple people warmed to him at once, feeling even more friendly because he was poor, – for poverty enriches those who live above it, and is a sure passport to truly hospitable spirits. Mr. Bhaer sat looking about him with the air of a traveller who knocks at a strange door, and, when it opens, finds himself at home. The children went to him like bees to a honey-pot; and, establishing themselves on each knee, proceeded to captivate him by rifling his pockets, pulling his beard, and investigating his watch, with juvenile audacity. The women telegraphed their approval to one another, and Mr. March, feeling that he had got a kindred spirit, opened his choicest stores for his guest's benefit, while silent John listened and enjoyed the talk, but said not a word, and Mr. Laurence found it impossible to go to sleep.

If Jo had not been otherwise engaged, Laurie's behavior would have amused her; for a faint twinge, not of jealousy, but something like suspicion, caused that gentleman to stand aloof at first, and observe the new comer with brotherly circumspection. But it did not last long; he got interested in spite of himself, and, before he knew it, was drawn into the circle, for Mr. Bhaer talked well in this genial atmosphere, and did himself justice. He seldom spoke to Laurie, but he looked at him often, and a shadow would pass across his face, as if regretting his own lost youth, as he watched the young man in his prime. Then his eye would turn to Jo so wistfully, that she would have surely answered the mute inquiry if she had seen it; but Jo had her own eyes to take care of, and, feeling that they could not be trusted, she prudently kept them on the little sock she was knitting, like a model maiden aunt.

A stealthy glance now and then refreshed her like sips of fresh water after a dusty walk, for the sidelong peeps showed her several propitious omens. Mr. Bhaer's face had lost the absent-minded expression, and looked all alive with interest in the present moment — actually young and handsome, she thought, forgetting to compare him with Laurie, as she usually did strange men, to their great detriment. Then he seemed quite inspired; though the burial customs of the ancients, to which the conversation had strayed, might not be considered an exhilarating topic. Jo quite glowed with triumph when Teddy got quenched in an argument, and thought to herself, as she watched her father's absorbed face, "How he would enjoy having such a man as my Professor to talk with every day!" Lastly, Mr. Bhaer was dressed in a spandy-new suit of black, which made him look more like a gentleman than ever. His bushy hair had been cut, and smoothly brushed, but didn't stay in order long, for, in exciting moments, he rumpled it up in the droll way he used to do, and Jo liked it rampantly erect, better than flat, because she thought it gave his fine forehead a Jove-like aspect. Poor Jo! how she did glorify that plain man, as she sat knitting away so quietly, yet letting nothing escape her — not even the fact that Mr. Bhaer actually had gold sleeve-buttons in his immaculate wristbands.

"Dear old fellow; he couldn't have got himself up with more care, if he'd been going a-wooing," said Jo to herself; and then a sudden thought, born of the words, made her blush so dreadfully, that she had to drop her ball, and go down after it, to hide her face.

The manœuvre did not succeed as well as she expected, however; for, though just in the act of setting fire to a funeral pile, the Professor dropped his torch, metaphorically speaking, and made a dive after the little blue ball. Of course they bumped their heads smartly together, saw stars, and both came up flushed and laughing, without the ball, to resume their seats, wishing they had not left them.

Nobody knew where the evening went to, for Hannah skilfully abstracted the babies at an early hour, nodding like two rosy poppies, and Mr. Laurence went home to rest. The others sat round the fire, talking away, utterly regardless of the lapse of time, till Meg, whose maternal mind was impressed with a firm conviction that Daisy had tumbled out of bed, and Demi set his night-gown afire, studying the structure of matches, made a move to go.

"We must have our sing in the good old way, for we are all together again, once more," said Jo, feeling that a good shout would be a safe and pleasant vent for the jubilant emotions of her soul.

They were not *all* there, but no one found the words thoughtless or untrue; for Beth still seemed among them – a peaceful presence – invisible, but dearer than ever; since death could not break the household league that love made indissoluble. The little chair stood in its old place; the tidy basket, with the bit of work she left unfinished when the needle grew so heavy, was still on its accustomed shelf; the beloved instrument, seldom touched now, had not been moved; and above it, Beth's face, serene and smiling, as in the early days, looked down upon them, seeming to say, "Be happy! I am here."

"Play something, Amy; let them hear how much you have improved," said Laurie, with pardonable pride in his promising pupil.

But Amy whispered, with full eyes, as she twirled the faded stool, – "Not to-night, dear; I can't show off to-night."

But she did show something better than brilliancy or skill, for she sung Beth's songs, with a tender music in her voice which the best master could not have taught, and touched the listeners' hearts with a sweeter power than any other inspiration could have given her. The room was very still when the clear voice failed suddenly, at the last line of Beth's favorite hymn. It was hard to say, –

Earth has no sorrow that heaven cannot heal;

and Amy leaned against her husband, who stood behind her, feeling that her welcome home was not quite perfect without Beth's kiss.

"Now we must finish with Mignon's song, for Mr. Bhaer sings that," said Jo, before the pause grew painful; and Mr. Bhaer cleared his throat with a gratified "hem," as he stepped into the corner where Jo stood, saying, –

"You will sing with me; we go excellently well together."

A pleasing fiction, by the way, for Jo had no more idea of music than a grasshopper; but she would have consented, if he had proposed to sing a whole opera, and warbled away, blissfully regardless of time and tune. It didn't much matter, for Mr. Bhaer sang like a true German, heartily and well; and Jo soon subsided into a subdued hum, that she might listen to the mellow voice that seemed to sing for her alone.

Know'st thou the land where the citron blooms,

used to be the Professor's favorite line; for "das land" meant Germany to him; but now he seemed to dwell, with peculiar warmth and melody, upon the words, –

There, oh there, might I with thee,
Oh my beloved go;

and one listener was so thrilled by the tender invitation, that she longed to say she did know the land, and would joyfully depart thither, whenever he liked.

The song was considered a great success, and the singer bashfully retired, covered with laurels. But a few minutes afterwards, he forgot his manners entirely, and stared at Amy putting on her bonnet – for she had been introduced simply as "my sister," and no one had called her by her new name since he came. He forgot himself, still farther, when Laurie said, in his most gracious manner, at parting, –

"My wife and I are very glad to meet you, sir; please remember that there is always a welcome waiting for you, over the way."

Then the Professor thanked him so heartily, and looked so suddenly illuminated with satisfaction, that Laurie thought him the most delightfully demonstrative old fellow he ever met.

"I too shall go; but I shall gladly come again, if you will give me leave, dear madame, for a little business in the city will keep me here some days."

He spoke to Mrs. March, but he looked at Jo; and the mother's voice gave as cordial an assent as did the daughter's eyes; for Mrs. March was not so blind to her children's interest as Mrs. Moffat supposed.

"I suspect that is a wise man," remarked Mr. March, with placid satisfaction, from the hearth-rug, after the last guest had gone.

"I know he is a good one," added Mrs. March, with decided approval, as she wound up the clock.

"I thought you'd like him," was all Jo said, as she slipped away to her bed.

She wondered what the business was that brought Mr. Bhaer to the city, and finally decided that he had been appointed to some great honor, somewhere, but had been too modest to mention the fact. If she had seen his face when, safe in his own room, he looked at the picture of a severe and rigid young lady, with a good deal of hair, who appeared to be gazing darkly into futurity, it might have thrown some light upon the subject, especially when he turned off the gas, and kissed the picture in the dark.

CHAPTER FORTY-FOUR

MY LORD AND LADY

~

"Please, Madam Mother, could you lend me my wife for half an hour? The luggage has come, and I've been making hay of Amy's Paris finery, trying to find some things I want," said Laurie, coming in the next day to find Mrs. Laurence sitting in her mother's lap, as if being made "the baby" again.

"Certainly; go, dear; I forget that you have any home but this," and Mrs. March pressed the white hand that wore the wedding ring, as if asking pardon for her maternal covetousness.

"I shouldn't have come over if I could have helped it; but I can't get on without my little woman any more than a —"

"Weathercock can without wind," suggested Jo, as he paused for a simile; Jo had grown quite her old saucy self again since Teddy came home.

"Exactly; for Amy keeps me pointing due west most of the time, with only an occasional whiffle round to the south, and I haven't had an easterly spell since I was married; don't know anything about the north, but am altogether salubrious and balmy, — hey, my lady?"

"Lovely weather so far; I don't know how long it will last, but I'm not afraid of storms, for I'm learning how to sail my ship. Come home, dear, and I'll find your bootjack; I suppose that's what you are rummaging after among my things. Men are *so* helpless, mother," said Amy, with a matronly air, which delighted her husband.

"What are you going to do with yourselves after you get settled?" asked Jo, buttoning Amy's cloak as she used to button her pinafores.

"We have our plans; we don't mean to say much about them yet, because we are such very new brooms, but we don't intend to be idle. I'm going into business with a devotion that shall delight grandpa, and prove to him that I'm not spoilt. I need something of the sort to keep me steady. I'm tired of dawdling, and mean to work like a man."

"And Amy, what is she going to do?" asked Mrs. March, well pleased at Laurie's decision, and the energy with which he spoke.

"After doing the civil all round, and airing our best bonnet, we shall astonish you by the elegant hospitalities of our mansion, the brilliant society we shall draw about us, and the beneficial influence we shall exert over the world at large. That's about it, isn't it, Madame Recamier?" asked Laurie, with a quizzical look at Amy.

"Time will show. Come away, Impertinence, and don't shock my family by calling me names before their faces," answered Amy, resolving that there should be a home with a good wife in it before she set up a *salon* as a queen of society.

"How happy those children seem together!" observed Mr. March, finding it difficult to become absorbed in his Aristotle after the young couple had gone.

"Yes, and I think it will last," added Mrs. March, with the restful expression of a pilot who had brought a ship safely into port.

"I know it will. Happy Amy!" and Jo sighed, then smiled brightly as Professor Bhaer opened the gate with an impatient push.

Later in the evening, when his mind had been set to rest about the bootjack, Laurie said suddenly to his wife, who was flitting about, arranging her new art treasures, —

"Mrs. Laurence."

"My lord!"

"That man intends to marry our Jo!"

"I hope so; don't you, dear?"

"Well, my love, I consider him a trump, in the fullest sense of that expressive word, but I do wish he was a little younger and a good deal richer."

"Now, Laurie, don't be too fastidious and worldly-minded. If they love one another it doesn't matter a particle how old they are, nor how poor. Women *never* should marry for money – " Amy caught herself up short as the words escaped her, and looked at her husband, who replied, with malicious gravity, –

"Certainly not, though you do hear charming girls say that they intend to do it sometimes. If my memory serves me, you once thought it your duty to make a rich match; that accounts, perhaps, for your marrying a good-for-nothing like me."

"Oh, my dearest boy, don't, don't say that! I forgot you were rich when I said 'Yes.' I'd have married you if you hadn't a penny, and I sometimes wish you *were* poor that I might show how much I love you;" and Amy, who was very dignified in public and very fond in private, gave convincing proofs of the truth of her words.

"You don't really think I am such a mercenary creature as I tried to be once, do you? It would break my heart, if you didn't believe that I'd gladly pull in the same boat with you, even if you had to get your living by rowing on the lake."

"Am I an idiot and a brute? How could I think so, when you refused a richer man for me, and won't let me give you half I want to now, when I have the right? Girls do it every day, poor things, and are taught to think it is their only salvation; but you had better lessons, and, though I trembled for you at one time, I was not disappointed, – for the daughter was true to the mother's teaching. I told mamma so yesterday, and she looked as glad and grateful as if I'd given her a check for a million, to be spent in charity. You are not listening to my moral remarks, Mrs. Laurence," – and Laurie paused, for Amy's eyes had an absent look, though fixed upon his face.

"Yes, I am, and admiring the dimple in your chin at the same time. I don't wish to make you vain, but I must confess that I'm prouder of my handsome husband than of all his money. Don't laugh, – but your nose is *such* a comfort to me," and Amy softly caressed the well-cut feature with artistic satisfaction.

Laurie had received many compliments in his life, but never one that suited him better, as he plainly showed, though he did laugh at his wife's peculiar taste, while she said slowly, —

"May I ask you a question, dear?"

"Of course you may."

"Shall you care if Jo does marry Mr. Bhaer?"

"Oh, that's the trouble, is it? I thought there was something in the dimple that didn't suit you. Not being a dog in the manger, but the happiest fellow alive, I assure you I can dance at Jo's wedding with a heart as light as my heels. Do you doubt it, *ma amie?*"

Amy looked up at him, and was satisfied; her last little jealous fear vanished forever, and she thanked him, with a face full of love and confidence.

"I wish we could do something for that capital old Professor. Couldn't we invent a rich relation, who shall obligingly die out there in Germany, and leave him a tidy little fortune?" said Laurie, when they began to pace up and down the long drawing-room, arm in arm, as they were fond of doing, in memory of the chateau garden.

"Jo would find us out, and spoil it all; she is very proud of him, just as he is, and said yesterday that she thought poverty was a beautiful thing."

"Bless her dear heart, she won't think so when she has a literary husband, and a dozen little professors and professorins to support. We won't interfere now, but watch our chance, and do them a good turn in spite of themselves. I owe Jo for a part of my education, and she believes in people's paying their honest debts, so I'll get round her in that way."

"How delightful it is to be able to help others, isn't it? That was always one of my dreams, to have the power of giving freely; and, thanks to you, the dream has come true."

"Ah, we'll do lots of good, won't we? There's one sort of poverty that I particularly like to help. Out-and-out beggars get taken care of, but poor gentlefolk fare badly, because they won't ask, and people don't dare to offer charity; yet there are a thousand ways of helping them, if one knows how to do it so delicately that it don't offend. I must say, I like to serve a decayed gentleman better than a blarneying beggar; I suppose it's wrong, but I do, though it is harder."

"Because it takes a gentleman to do it," added the other member of the domestic admiration society.

"Thank you, I'm afraid I don't deserve that pretty compliment. But I was going to say, that while I was dawdling about abroad, I saw a good many talented young fellows making all sorts of sacrifices, and enduring real hardships, that they might realize their dreams. Splendid fellows, some of them, working like heroes, poor and friendless, but so full of courage, patience and ambition, that I was ashamed of myself, and longed to give them a right good lift. Those are people whom it's a satisfaction to help, for if they've got genius, it's an honor to be allowed to serve them, and not let it be lost or delayed for want of fuel to keep the pot boiling; if they haven't, it's a pleasure to comfort the poor souls, and keep them from despair, when they find it out."

"Yes, indeed; and there's another class who can't ask, and who suffer in silence; I know something of it, for I belonged to it, before you made a princess of me, as the king does the beggar-maid in the old story. Ambitious girls have a hard time, Laurie, and often have to see youth, health, and precious opportunities go by, just for want of a little help at the right minute. People have been very kind to me, and whenever I see girls struggling along, as we used to do, I want to put out my hand and help them, as I was helped."

"And so you shall, like an angel as you are!" cried Laurie, resolving, with a glow of philanthropic zeal, to found and endow an institution, for the express benefit of young women with artistic tendencies. "Rich people have no right to sit down and enjoy themselves, or let their money accumulate for others to waste. It's not half so sensible to leave a lot of legacies when one dies, as it is to use the money wisely while alive, and enjoy making one's fellow-creatures happy with it. We'll have a good time ourselves, and add an extra relish to our own pleasure, by giving other people a generous taste. Will you be a little Dorcas, going about emptying a big basket of comforts, and filling it up with good deeds?"

"With all my heart, if you will be a brave St. Martin, stopping, as you ride gallantly through the world, to share your cloak with the beggar."

"It's a bargain, and we shall get the best of it!"

So the young pair shook hands upon it, and then paced happily on again, feeling that their pleasant home was more home-like, because they hoped to brighten other homes, believing that their own feet would walk more uprightly along the flowery path before them, if they smoothed rough ways for other feet, and feeling that their hearts were more closely knit together by a love which could tenderly remember those less blest than they.

CHAPTER FORTY-FIVE

DAISY AND DEMI

~

*I*cannot feel that I have done my duty as humble historian of the March family, without devoting at least one chapter to the two most precious and important members of it. Daisy and Demi had now arrived at years of discretion; for in this fast age babies of three or four assert their rights, and get them, too, which is more than many of their elders do. If there ever were a pair of twins in danger of being utterly spoilt by adoration, it was these prattling Brookes. Of course they were the most remarkable children ever born; as will be shown when I mention that they walked at eight months, talked fluently at twelve months, and at two years they took their places at table, and behaved with a propriety which charmed all beholders. At three Daisy demanded a "needler," and actually made a bag with four stitches in it; she likewise set up housekeeping in the sideboard, and managed a microscopic cooking stove with a skill that brought tears of pride to Hannah's eyes, while Demi learned his letters with his grandfather, who invented a new mode of teaching the alphabet by forming the letters with his arms and legs, – thus uniting gymnastics for head and heels. The boy early developed a mechanical genius which delighted his father; and distracted his mother, for he tried to imitate every machine he saw, and kept the nursery in a chaotic condition, with his "sewing-sheen," – a mysterious structure of string, chairs, clothes-pins and spools, for wheels to go "wound and wound"; also a basket hung over the back of a big chair, in which he vainly tried to hoist his too confiding sister, who, with feminine devotion, allowed her little head to be bumped till rescued, when the young inventor indignantly remarked, "Why, marmar, dats mine lellywaiter, and me's trying to pull her up."

Though utterly unlike in character, the twins got on remarkably well together, and seldom quarrelled more than thrice a day. Of course, Demi tyrannized over Daisy, and gallantly defended her from every other aggressor; while Daisy made a galley slave of herself, and adored her brother, as the one perfect being in the world. A rosy, chubby, sunshiny little soul was Daisy, who found her way to everybody's heart, and nestled there. One of the captivating children, who seem made to be kissed and cuddled, adorned and adored like little goddesses, and produced for general approval on all festive occasions. Her small virtues were so sweet, that she would have been quite angelic, if a few small naughtinesses had not kept her delightfully human. It was all fair weather in her world, and every morning she scrambled up to the window in her little night-gown to look out, and say, no matter whether it rained or shone, "Oh, pitty day; oh, pitty day!" Every one was a friend, and she offered kisses to a stranger so confidingly, that the most inveterate bachelor relented and baby-lovers became faithful worshippers.

"Me loves evvybody," she once said, opening her arms, with her spoon in one hand, and her mug in the other, as if eager to embrace and nourish the whole world.

As she grew, her mother began to feel that the Dove-cote would be blest by the presence of an inmate as serene and loving as that which had helped to make the old house home, and to pray that she might be spared a loss like that which had lately taught them how long they had entertained an angel unawares. Her grandfather often called her "Beth," and her grandmother watched over her with untiring devotion, as if trying to atone for some past mistake, which no eye but her own could see.

Demi, like a true Yankee, was of an inquiring turn, wanting to know everything, and often getting much disturbed, because he could not get satisfactory answers to his perpetual "What for?"

He also possessed a philosophic bent, to the great delight of his grandfather, who used to hold Socratic conversations with him, in which the precocious pupil occasionally posed his teacher to the undisguised satisfaction of the women folk.

"What makes my legs go, Dranpa?" asked the young philosopher, surveying those active portions of his frame with a meditative air, while resting after a go-to-bed frolic one night.

"It's your little mind, Demi," replied the sage, stroking the yellow head respectfully.

"What is a little mine?"

"It is something which makes your body move, as the spring made the wheels go in my watch when I showed it to you."

"Open me; I want to see it go wound."

"I can't do that any more than you could open the watch. God winds you up, and you go till He stops you."

"Does I?" and Demi's brown eyes grew big and bright as he took in the new thought. "Is I wounded up like the watch?"

"Yes; but I can't show you how; for it is done when we don't see."

Demi felt of his back, as if expecting to find it like that of the watch, and then gravely remarked, –

"I dess Dod does it when I's asleep."

A careful explanation followed, to which he listened so attentively that his anxious grandmother said, –

"My dear, do you think it wise to talk about such things to that baby? He's getting great bumps over his eyes, and learning to ask the most unanswerable questions."

"If he is old enough to ask the questions he is old enough to receive true answers. I am not putting the thoughts into his head, but helping him unfold those already there. These children are wiser than we are, and I have no doubt the boy understands every word I have said to him. Now, Demi, tell me where you keep your mind?"

If the boy had replied like Alcibiades, "By the gods, Socrates, I cannot tell," his grandfather would not have been surprised; but when, after standing a moment on one leg, like a meditative young stork, he answered, in a tone of calm conviction, "In my little belly," the old gentleman could only join in grandma's laugh, and dismiss the class in metaphysics.

There might have been cause for maternal anxiety, if Demi had not given convincing proofs that he was a true boy, as well as a budding philosopher; for, often, after a discussion which caused Hannah to prophesy, with ominous nods, "that child ain't long for this world," he would turn about and set her fears at rest by some of the pranks with which dear, dirty, naughty little rascals distract and delight their parents' souls.

Meg made many moral rules, and tried to keep them; but what mother was ever proof against the winning wiles, the ingenious evasions, or the tranquil audacity of the miniature men and women who so early show themselves accomplished Artful Dodgers?

"No more raisins, Demi, they'll make you sick," says mamma to the young person who offers his services in the kitchen with unfailing regularity on plum-pudding day.

"Me likes to be sick."

"I don't want to have you, – so run away and help Daisy make patty-cakes."

He reluctantly departs, but his wrongs weigh upon his spirit; and, by and by, when an opportunity comes to redress them, he outwits mamma by a shrewd bargain.

"Now you have been good children, and I'll play anything you like," says Meg, as she leads her assistant cooks up stairs, when the pudding is safely bouncing in the pot.

"Truly, marmar?" asks Demi, with a brilliant idea in his well-powdered head.

"Yes, truly; anything you say," replied the short-sighted parent, preparing herself to sing "The Three Little Kittens" half a dozen times over, or to take her family to "Buy a penny bun," regardless of wind or limb. But Demi corners her by the cool reply, –

"Then we'll go and eat up all the raisins."

Aunt Dodo was chief playmate and *confidante* of both children, and the trio turned the little house topsy-turvy. Aunt Amy was as yet only a name to them, Aunt Beth soon faded into a pleasantly vague memory, but

Aunt Dodo was a living reality, and they made the most of her, – for which compliment she was deeply grateful. But when Mr. Bhaer came, Jo neglected her playfellows, and dismay and desolation fell upon their little souls. Daisy, who was fond of going about peddling kisses, lost her best customer and became bankrupt; Demi, with infantile penetration, soon discovered that Dodo liked to play with "the bear-man" better than she did with him; but, though hurt, he concealed his anguish, for he hadn't the heart to insult a rival who kept a mine of chocolate drops in his waistcoat pocket, and a watch that could be taken out of its case and freely shaken by ardent admirers.

Some persons might have considered these pleasing liberties as bribes; but Demi didn't see it in that light, and continued to patronize the "bear-man" with pensive affability, while Daisy bestowed her small affections upon him at the third call, and considered his shoulder her throne, his arm her refuge, his gifts treasures of surpassing worth.

Gentlemen are sometimes seized with sudden fits of admiration for the young relatives of ladies whom they honor with their regard; but this counterfeit philoprogenitiveness sits uneasily upon them, and does not deceive anybody a particle. Mr. Bhaer's devotion was sincere, however, likewise effective, – for honesty is the best policy in love as in law; he was one of the men who are at home with children, and looked particularly well when little faces made a pleasant contrast with his manly one. His business, whatever it was, detained him from day to day, but evening seldom failed to bring him out to see – well, he always asked for Mr. March, so I suppose *he* was the attraction. The excellent papa labored under the delusion that he was, and revelled in long discussions with the kindred spirit, till a chance remark of his more observing grandson suddenly enlightened him.

Mr. Bhaer came in one evening to pause on the threshold of the study, astonished by the spectacle that met his eye. Prone upon the floor lay Mr. March, with his respectable legs in the air, and beside him, likewise prone, was Demi, trying to imitate the attitude with his own short, scarlet-stockinged legs, both grovellers so seriously absorbed that they were unconscious of spectators, till Mr. Bhaer laughed his sonorous laugh, and Jo cried out, with a scandalized face, –

"Father, father! here's the Professor!"

Down went the black legs and up came the gray head, as the

preceptor said, with undisturbed dignity, –

"Good evening, Mr. Bhaer. Excuse me for a moment, – we are just finishing our lesson. Now, Demi, make the letter and tell its name."

"I knows him," and, after a few convulsive efforts, the red legs took the shape of a pair of compasses, and the intelligent pupil triumphantly shouted "It's a We, Dranpa, it's a We!"

"He's a born Weller," laughed Jo, as her parent gathered himself up, and her nephew tried to stand on his head, as the only mode of expressing his satisfaction that school was over.

"What have you been at to-day, bübchen?" asked Mr. Bhaer, picking up the gymnast.

"Me went to see little Mary."

"And what did you there?"

"I kissed her," began Demi, with artless frankness.

"Prut! thou beginnest early. What did the little Mary say to that?" asked Mr. Bhaer, continuing to confess the young sinner, who stood upon his knee, exploring the waistcoat pocket.

"Oh, she liked it, and she kissed me, and I liked it. *Don't* little boys like little girls?" added Demi, with his mouth full, and an air of bland satisfaction.

"You precocious chick, – who put that into your head?" said Jo, enjoying the innocent revelations as much as the Professor.

"'Tisn't in mine head, it's in mine mouf," answered literal Demi, putting out his tongue with a chocolate drop on it, – thinking she alluded to confectionery, not ideas.

"Thou shouldst save some for the little friend; sweets to the sweet, mannling," and Mr. Bhaer offered Jo some with a look that made her wonder if chocolate was not the nectar drunk by the gods. Demi also saw the smile, was impressed by it, and artlessly inquired, –

"Do great boys like great girls too, 'Fessor?"

Like young Washington, Mr. Bhaer "couldn't tell a lie"; so he gave the somewhat vague reply, that he believed they did, sometimes, in a tone that made Mr. March put down his clothes-brush, glance at Jo's retiring face, and then sink into his chair, looking as if the "precocious chick" had put an idea into *his* head that was both sweet and sour.

Why, Dodo, when she caught him in the china-closet half an hour afterward, nearly squeezed the breath out of his little body with a tender embrace, instead of shaking him for being there, and why she followed up this novel performance by the unexpected gift of a big slice of bread and jelly, remained one of the problems over which Demi puzzled his small wits, and was forced to leave unsolved forever.

CHAPTER FORTY-SIX

UNDER THE UMBRELLA

~

While Laurie and Amy were taking conjugal strolls over velvet carpets, as they set their house in order, and planned a blissful future, Mr. Bhaer and Jo were enjoying promenades of a different sort, along muddy roads and sodden fields.

"I always do take a walk toward evening, and I don't know why I should give it up, just because I often happen to meet the Professor on his way out," said Jo to herself, after two or three encounters; for, though there were two paths to Meg's, whichever one she took she was sure to meet him, either going or returning. He was always walking rapidly, and never seemed to see her till quite close, when he would look as if his short-sighted eyes had failed to recognize the approaching lady till that moment. Then, if she was going to Meg's, he always had something for the babies; if her face was turned homeward, he had merely strolled down to see the river, and was just about returning, unless they were tired of his frequent calls.

Under the circumstances, what could Jo do but greet him civilly, and invite him in? If she *was* tired of his visits, she concealed her weariness with perfect skill, and took care that there should be coffee for supper, "as Friedrich – I mean Mr. Bhaer – don't like tea."

By the second week, every one knew perfectly well what was going on, yet every one tried to look as if they were stone-blind to the changes in Jo's face – never asked why she sang about her work, did up her hair three times a day, and got so blooming with her evening exercise; and no one seemed to have the slightest suspicion that Professor Bhaer, while talking philosophically with her father, was giving the daughter lessons in love.

Jo couldn't even lose her heart in a decorous manner, but sternly tried to quench her feelings; and, failing to do so, led a somewhat agitated life. She was mortally afraid of being laughed at for surrendering, after her many and vehement declarations of independence. Laurie was her especial dread; but, thanks to the new manager, he behaved with praiseworthy propriety, never called Mr. Bhaer "a capital old fellow" in public, never alluded, in the remotest manner, to Jo's improved appearance, or expressed the least surprise at seeing the Professor's hat on the Marches' hall-table, nearly every evening. But he exulted in private, and longed for the time to come when he could give Jo a piece of plate, with a bear and a ragged staff on it as an appropriate coat of arms.

For a fortnight, the Professor came and went with lover-like regularity; then he stayed away for three whole days, and made no sign – a proceeding which caused everybody to look sober, and Jo to become pensive, at first, and then, – alas for romance, – very cross.

"Disgusted, I dare say, and gone home as suddenly as he came. It's nothing to me, of course; but I *should* think he would have come and bid us good-by, like a gentleman," she said to herself, with a despairing look at the gate, as she put on her things for the customary walk, one dull afternoon.

"You'd better take the little umbrella, dear; it looks like rain," said her mother, observing that she had on her new bonnet, but not alluding to the fact.

"Yes, Marmee; do you want anything in town? I've got to run in and get some paper," returned Jo, pulling out the bow under her chin, before the glass, as an excuse for not looking at her mother.

"Yes; I want some twilled silesia, a paper of number nine needles, and two yards of narrow lavender ribbon. Have you got your thick boots on, and something warm under your cloak?"

"I believe so," answered Jo, absently.

"If you happen to meet Mr. Bhaer, bring him home to tea; I quite long to see the dear man," added Mrs. March.

Jo heard *that*, but made no answer, except to kiss her mother, and walk rapidly away, thinking with a glow of gratitude, in spite of her heartache, —

"How good she is to me! What *do* girls do who haven't any mothers to help them through their troubles?"

The dry goods stores were not down among the counting houses, banks, and wholesale warerooms, where gentlemen most do congregate; but Jo found herself in that part of the city before she did a single errand, loitering along as if waiting for some one, examining engineering instruments in one window, and samples of wool in another, with most unfeminine interest; tumbling over barrels, being half-smothered by descending bales, and hustled unceremoniously by busy men, who looked as if they wondered "how the deuce she got there." A drop of rain on her cheek recalled her thoughts from baffled hopes to ruined ribbons; for the drops continued to fall, and, being a woman as well as a lover, she felt that, though it was too late to save her heart, she might her bonnet. Now she remembered the little umbrella, which she had forgotten to take in her hurry to be off; but regret was unavailing, and nothing could be done but borrow one, or submit to a drenching. She looked up at the lowering sky, down at the crimson bow, already flecked with black, forward along the muddy street, then one long, lingering look behind, at a certain grimy warehouse, with "Hoffmann, Swartz & Co." over the door, and said to herself, with a sternly reproachful air, —

"It serves me right! What business had I to put on all my best things, and come philandering down here, hoping to see the Professor? Jo, I'm ashamed of you! No, you shall *not* go there and borrow an umbrella, or find out where he is, from his friends. You shall slop away, and do your errands in the rain; and if you catch your death, and ruin your bonnet, it's no more than you deserve. Now then!"

With that she rushed across the street so impetuously, that she narrowly escaped annihilation from a passing truck, and precipitated herself into the arms of a stately old gentleman, who said, "I beg pardon, ma'am," and looked mortally offended. Somewhat daunted, Jo righted herself, spread her handkerchief over the devoted ribbons, and putting temptation behind her, hurried on, with increasing dampness about the ankles, and much clashing of umbrellas overhead. The fact that a somewhat dilapidated blue one remained stationary above the unprotected bonnet, attracted her attention; and, looking up, she saw Mr. Bhaer looking down.

"I feel I know the strong-minded lady who goes so bravely under many horse noses, and so fast through much mud. What do you down here, my friend?"

"I'm shopping."

Mr. Bhaer smiled, as he glanced from the pickle-factory on one side, to the wholesale hide and leather concern on the other; but he only said, politely, –

"You haf no umbrella; may I go also, and take for you the bundles?"

"Yes, thank you."

Jo's cheeks were as red as her ribbon, and she wondered what he thought of her; but she didn't care, for in a minute she found herself walking away, arm-in-arm with her Professor, feeling as if the sun had suddenly burst out with uncommon brilliancy, that the world was all right again, and that one thoroughly happy woman was paddling through the wet that day.

"We thought you had gone," said Jo, hastily, for she knew he was looking at her, – her bonnet wasn't big enough to hide her face, and she feared he might think the joy it betrayed unmaidenly.

"Did you believe that I should go with no farewell to those who haf been so heavenly kind to me?" he asked, so reproachfully, that she felt as if she had insulted him by the suggestion, and answered, heartily, –

"No, *I* didn't; I knew you were busy about your own affairs, but we rather missed you, – father and mother especially."

"And you?"

"I'm always glad to see you, sir."

In her anxiety to keep her voice quite calm, Jo made it rather cool, and the frosty little monosyllable at the end seemed to chill the Professor, for his smile vanished, as he said, gravely, –

"I thank you, and come one time more before I go."

"You *are* going then?"

"I haf no longer any business here; it is done."

"Successfully, I hope?" said Jo, for the bitterness of disappointment was in that short reply of his.

"I ought to think so, for I haf a way opened to me by which I can make my bread and gif my Jünglings much help."

"Tell me, please! I like to know all about the – the boys," said Jo eagerly.

"That is so kind, I gladly tell you. My friends find for me a place in a college, where I teach as at home, and earn enough to make the way smooth for Franz and Emil. For this I should be grateful, should I not?"

"Indeed you should! How splendid it will be to have you doing what you like, and be able to see you often, and the boys – " cried Jo, clinging to the lads as an excuse for the satisfaction she could not help betraying.

"Ah, but we shall not meet often, I fear; this place is at the West."

"So far away!" and Jo left her skirts to their fate, as if it didn't matter now what became of her clothes or herself.

Mr. Bhaer could read several languages, but he had not learned to read women yet. He flattered himself that he knew Jo pretty well, and was, therefore, much amazed by the contradictions of voice, face, and manner, which she showed him in rapid succession that day, – for she was in half a dozen different moods in the course of half an hour. When she met him she looked surprised, though it was impossible to help suspecting that she had come for that express purpose. When he offered her his arm, she took it with a look that filled him with delight; but when he asked if she missed him, she gave such a chilly, formal reply, that despair fell upon him. On learning his good fortune she almost clapped her hands, – was the joy all for the boys? Then, on hearing his destination, she said, "So far away!" in a tone of despair that lifted him on to a pinnacle of hope; but the next minute she tumbled him down again by observing, like one entirely absorbed in the matter, –

"Here's the place for my errands; will you come in? It won't take long."

Jo prided herself upon her shopping capabilities, and particularly wished to impress her escort with the neatness and despatch with which she would accomplish the business. But, owing to the flutter she was in, everything went amiss; she upset the tray of needles, forgot the silesia was to be "twilled" till it was cut off, gave the wrong change, and covered herself with confusion by asking for lavender ribbon at the calico counter. Mr. Bhaer stood by, watching her blush and blunder; and, as he watched, his own bewilderment seemed to subside, for he was beginning to see that on some occasions women, like dreams, go by contraries.

When they came out, he put the parcel under his arm with a more cheerful aspect, and splashed through the puddles as if he rather enjoyed it, on the whole.

"Should we not do a little what you call shopping for the babies, and haf a farewell feast to-night if I go for my last call at your so pleasant home?" he asked, stopping before a window full of fruit and flowers.

"What will we buy?" said Jo, ignoring the latter part of his speech, and sniffing the mingled odors with an affectation of delight, as they went in.

"May they haf oranges and figs?" asked Mr. Bhaer, with a paternal air.

"They eat them when they can get them."

"Do you care for nuts?"

"Like a squirrel."

"Hamburg grapes; yes, we shall surely drink to the Fatherland in those?"

Jo frowned upon that piece of extravagance, and asked why he didn't buy a frail of dates, a cask of raisins, and a bag of almonds, and done with it? Whereat Mr. Bhaer confiscated her purse, produced his own, and finished the marketing by buying several pounds of grapes, a pot of rosy daisies, and a pretty jar of honey, to be regarded in the light of a demijohn. Then, distorting his pockets with the knobbly bundles, and giving her the flowers to hold, he put up the old umbrella, and they travelled on again.

"Miss Marsch, I haf a great favor to ask you," began the Professor, after a moist promenade of half a block.

"Yes, sir," and Jo's heart began to beat so hard she was afraid he would hear it.

"I am bold to say it in spite of the rain, because so short a time remains to me."

"Yes, sir," and Jo nearly smashed the small flower-pot with the sudden squeeze she gave it.

"I wish to get a little dress for my Tina, and I am too stupid to go alone. Will you kindly gif me a word of taste and help?"

"Yes, sir," and Jo felt as calm and cool all of a sudden, as if she had stepped into a refrigerator.

"Perhaps also a shawl for Tina's mother, she is so poor and sick, and the husband is such a care, — yes, yes, a thick, warm shawl would be a friendly thing to take the little mother."

"I'll do it with pleasure, Mr. Bhaer. I'm going very fast, and he's getting dearer every minute," added Jo to herself; then, with a mental shake, she entered into the business with an energy which was pleasant to behold.

Mr. Bhaer left it all to her, so she chose a pretty gown for Tina, and then ordered out the shawls. The clerk, being a married man, condescended to take an interest in the couple, who appeared to be shopping for their family.

"Your lady may prefer this; it's a superior article, a most desirable color, quite chaste and genteel," he said, shaking out a comfortable gray shawl, and throwing it over Jo's shoulders.

"Does it suit you, Mr. Bhaer?" she asked, turning her back to him, and feeling deeply grateful for the chance of hiding her face.

"Excellently well, we will haf it," answered the Professor, smiling to himself, as he paid for it, while Jo continued to rummage the counters, like a confirmed bargain hunter.

"Now shall we go home?" he asked, as if the words were very pleasant to him.

"Yes, it's late, and I'm *so* tired." Jo's voice was more pathetic than she knew, for now the sun seemed to have gone in as suddenly as it came out, the world grew muddy and miserable again, and for the first time she discovered that her feet were cold, her head ached, and that her heart was colder than the former, fuller of pain than the latter. Mr. Bhaer was going away; he only cared for her as a friend, it was all a mistake, and the sooner it was over the better. With this idea in her head, she hailed an approaching omnibus with such a hasty gesture that the daisies flew out of the pot, and were badly damaged.

"That is not omniboos," said the Professor, waving the loaded vehicle away, and stopping to pick up the poor little posies.

"I beg your pardon, I didn't see the name distinctly. Never mind, I can walk, I'm used to plodding in the mud," returned Jo, winking hard, because she would have died rather than openly wipe her eyes.

Mr. Bhaer saw the drops on her cheeks, though she turned her head away; the sight seemed to touch him very much, for suddenly stooping down, he asked in a tone that meant a great deal, –

"Heart's dearest, why do you cry?"

Now if Jo had not been new to this sort of thing she would have said she wasn't crying, had a cold in her head, or told any other feminine fib proper to the occasion; instead of which that undignified creature answered, with an irrepressible sob, –

"Because you are going away."

"Ah, my Gott, that is *so* good!" cried Mr. Bhaer, managing to clasp his hands in spite of the umbrella and the bundles. "Jo, I haf nothing but much love to gif you; I came to see if you could care for it, and I waited to be sure that I was something more than a friend. Am I? Can you make a little place in your heart for old Fritz?" he added, all in one breath.

"Oh, yes!" said Jo, and he was quite satisfied, for she folded both hands over his arm, and looked up at him with an expression that plainly showed how happy she would be to walk through life beside him, even though she had no better shelter than the old umbrella, if he carried it.

It was certainly proposing under difficulties, for even if he had desired to do so, Mr. Bhaer could not go down upon his knees, on account of the mud, neither could he offer Jo his hand, except figuratively, for both were full; much less could he indulge in tender demonstrations in the open street, though he was near it; so the only way in which he could express his rapture was to look at her, with an expression which glorified his face to such a degree that there actually seemed to be little rainbows in the drops that sparkled on his beard. If he had not loved Jo very much, I don't think he could have done it *then*, for she looked far from lovely, with her skirts in a deplorable state, her rubber boots splashed to the ankle, and her bonnet a ruin. Fortunately, Mr. Bhaer considered her the most beautiful woman living, and she found him more "Jove-like" than ever, though his hat-brim was quite limp with the little rills trickling thence upon his shoulders (for he held the umbrella all over Jo), and every finger of his gloves needed mending.

Passers-by probably thought them a pair of harmless lunatics, for they entirely forgot to hail a 'bus, and strolled leisurely along, oblivious of deepening dusk and fog. Little they cared what anybody thought, for they were enjoying the happy hour that seldom comes but once in any life – the magical moment which bestows youth on the old, beauty on the plain, wealth on the poor, and gives human hearts a foretaste of heaven. The Professor looked as if he had conquered a kingdom, and the world had nothing more to offer him in the way of bliss, while Jo trudged beside him, feeling as if her place had always been there, and wondering how she ever could have chosen any other lot. Of course, she was the first to speak – intelligibly, I mean, for the emotional remarks which followed her impetuous "Oh, yes!" were not of a coherent or reportable character.

"Friedrich, why didn't you –"

"Ah, heaven! she gifs me the name that no one speaks since Minna died!" cried the Professor, pausing in a puddle to regard her with grateful delight.

"I always call you that to myself – I forgot; but I won't, unless you like it."

"Like it! it is more sweet to me than I can tell. Say 'thou,' also, and I shall say your language is almost as beautiful as mine."

"Isn't 'thou' a little sentimental?" asked Jo, privately thinking it a lovely monosyllable.

"Sentimental? yes; thank Gott, we Germans believe in sentiment, and keep ourselves young mit it. Your English 'you' is so cold – say 'thou,' heart's dearest, it means so much to me," pleaded Mr. Bhaer, more like a romantic student than a grave professor.

"Well, then, why didn't thou tell me all this sooner?" asked Jo, bashfully.

"Now I shall haf to show thee all my heart, and I so gladly will, because thou must take care of it hereafter. See, then, my Jo – ah, the dear, funny little name! – I had a wish to tell something the day I said good-by, in New York; but I thought the handsome friend was betrothed to thee, and so I spoke not. Would'st thou have said 'Yes,' then, if I *had* spoken?"

"I don't know; I'm afraid not, for I didn't have any heart, just then."

"Prut! that I do not believe. It was asleep till the fairy prince came through the wood, and waked it up. Ah well, '*Die erste Liebe ist die beste*'; but that I should not expect."

"Yes, the first love *is* the best; so be contented, for I never had another. Teddy was only a boy, and soon got over his little fancy," said Jo, anxious to correct the Professor's mistake.

"Good! then I shall rest happy, and be sure that thou givest me all. I haf waited so long, I am grown selfish, as thou wilt find, Professorin."

"I like that," cried Jo, delighted with her new name. "Now tell me what brought you, at last, just when I most wanted you?"

"This," – and Mr. Bhaer took a worn little paper out of his waistcoat pocket.

Jo unfolded it, and looked much abashed, for it was one of her own contributions to a paper that paid for poetry, which accounted for her sending it an occasional attempt.

"How could that bring you?" she asked, wondering what he meant.

"I found it by chance; I knew it by the names and the initials, and in it there was one little verse that seemed to call me. Read and find him; I will see that you go not in the wet."

Jo obeyed, and hastily skimmed through the lines which she had christened –

IN THE GARRET

Four little chests all in a row,
  Dim with dust, and worn by time,
All fashioned and filled, long ago,
  By children now in their prime.
Four little keys hung side by side,
  With faded ribbons, brave and gay,
When fashioned there with childish pride,
  Long ago, on a rainy day.
Four little names, one on each lid,
Carved out by a boyish hand,
  And underneath, there lieth hid
Histories of the happy band
  Once playing here, and pausing oft
To hear the sweet refrain,
  That came and went on the roof aloft,
In the falling summer rain.

"Meg" on the first lid, smooth and fair,
  I look in with loving eyes,

For folded here, with well-known care,
    A goodly gathering lies —
The record of a peaceful life,
    Gifts to gentle child and girl,
A bridal gown, lines to a wife,
    A tiny shoe, a baby curl.
No toys in this first chest remain,
    For all are carried away,
In their old age, to join again
    In another small Meg's play.
Ah, happy mother! well I know
    You hear like a sweet refrain,
Lullabies ever soft and low,
    In the falling summer rain.

"Jo" on the next lid, scratched and worn,
    And within a motley store
Of headless dolls, of school-books torn,
    Birds and beasts that speak no more.
Spoils brought home from fairy ground
    Only trod by youthful feet,
Dreams of a future never found,
    Memories of a past still sweet;
Half-writ poems, stories wild,
    April letters, warm and cold,
Diaries of a wilful child,
    Hints of a woman early old;
A woman in a lonely home,
    Hearing like a sad refrain, —
"Be worthy love, and love will come,"
    In the falling summer rain.

My "Beth!" the dust is always swept
    From the lid that bears your name,
As if by loving eyes that wept,
    By careful hands that often came.
Death canonized for us one saint,
    Ever less human than divine,
And still we lay, with tender plaint,
    Relics in this household shrine.
The silver bell, so seldom rung,
    The little cap which last she wore,
The fair, dead Catherine that hung
    By angels borne above her door;

The songs she sang without lament,
In her prison-house of pain,
Forever are they sweetly blent
With the falling summer rain.

Upon the last lid's polished field –
Legend now both fair and true –
A gallant knight bears on his shield,
"Amy," in letters gold and blue.
Within the snoods that bound her hair,
Slippers that have danced their last,
Faded flowers laid by with care,
Fans whose airy toils are past –
Gay valentines all ardent flames,
Trifles that have borne their part
In girlish hopes, and fears, and shames.
The record of a maiden heart,
Now learning fairer, truer spells,
Hearing, like a blithe refrain,
The silver sound of bridal bells
In the falling summer rain.

Four little chests all in a row,
Dim with dust, and worn by time,
Four women, taught by weal and woe,
To love and labor in their prime
Four sisters, parted for an hour, –
None lost, one only gone before,
Made by love's immortal power,
Nearest and dearest evermore.
Oh, when these hidden stores of ours
Lie open to the Father's sight,
May they be rich in golden hours, –
Deeds that show fairer for the light.
Lives whose brave music long shall ring
Like a spirit-stirring strain,
Souls that shall gladly soar and sing
In the long sunshine, after rain.

J.M.

"It's very bad poetry, but I felt it when I wrote it one day when I was very lonely, and had a good cry on a rag-bag. I never thought it would go where it could tell tales," said Jo, tearing up the verses the Professor had treasured so long.

"Let it go, – it has done its duty, – and I will haf a fresh one when I read all the brown book in which she keeps her little secrets," said Mr. Bhaer with a smile, as he watched the fragments fly away on the wind. "Yes," he added earnestly, "I read that, and I think to myself, 'She has a sorrow, she is lonely, she would find comfort in true love.' I haf a heart full, full for her; shall I not go and say, 'If this is not too poor a thing to gif for what I shall hope to receive, take it, in Gott's name.'"

"And so you came to find that it was not too poor, but the one precious thing I needed," whispered Jo.

"I had no courage to think that at first, heavenly kind as was your welcome to me. But soon I began to hope, and then I said, 'I will haf her if I die for it,' and so I will!" cried Mr. Bhaer, with a defiant nod, as if the walls of mist closing round them were barriers which he was to surmount or valiantly knock down.

Jo thought that was splendid, and resolved to be worthy of her knight, though he did not come prancing on a charger in gorgeous array.

"What made you stay away so long?" she asked presently, finding it so pleasant to ask confidential questions, and get delightful answers, that she could not keep silent.

"It was not easy, but I could not find the heart to take you from that so happy home until I could haf a prospect of one to give you, after much time perhaps, and hard work. How could I ask you to gif up so much for a poor old fellow, who has no fortune but a little learning?"

"I'm glad you *are* poor; I couldn't bear a rich husband!" said Jo, decidedly, adding, in a softer tone, "don't fear poverty; I've known it long enough to lose my dread, and be happy working for those I love; and don't call yourself old, – I never think of it, – I couldn't help loving you if you were seventy!"

The Professor found that so touching that he would have been glad of his handkerchief if he could have got at it; as he couldn't, Jo wiped his eyes for him, and said, laughing, as she took away a bundle or two, –

"I may be strong-minded, but no one can say I'm out of my sphere now, – for woman's special mission is supposed to be drying tears and bearing burdens. I'm to carry my share, Friedrich, and help to earn the home. Make up your mind to that, or I'll never go," she added, resolutely, as he tried to reclaim his load.

"We shall see. Haf you patience to wait a long time, Jo? I must go away and do my work alone; I must help my boys first, because even for you I may not break my word to Minna. Can you forgif that, and be happy, while we hope and wait?"

"Yes, I know I can; for we love one another, and that makes all the rest easy to bear. I have my duty also, and my work. I couldn't enjoy myself if I neglected them even for you, – so there's no need of hurry or impatience. You can do your part out West, – I can do mine here, – and both be happy, hoping for the best, and leaving the future to be as God wills."

"Ah! thou gifest me such hope and courage, and I haf nothing to gif back but a full heart and these empty hands," cried the Professor, quite overcome.

Jo never, never would learn to be proper; for when he said that as they stood upon the steps, she just put both hands into his, whispering tenderly, "Not empty now;" and, stooping down, kissed her Friedrich under the umbrella. It was dreadful, but she would have done it if the flock of draggle-tailed sparrows on the hedge had been human beings, – for she was very far gone indeed, and quite regardless of everything but her own happiness. Though it came in such a very simple guise, that was the crowning moment of both their lives, when, turning from the night, and storm, and loneliness, to the household of light, and warmth, and peace, waiting to receive them with a glad "Welcome home," Jo led her lover in, and shut the door.

CHAPTER FORTY-SEVEN

HARVEST TIME

~

For a year Jo and her Professor worked and waited, hoped and loved; met occasionally, and wrote such voluminous letters, that the rise in the price in paper was accounted for, Laurie said. The second year began rather soberly, for their prospect did not brighten, and Aunt March died suddenly. But when their first sorrow was over, – for they loved the old lady in spite of her sharp tongue, – they found they had cause for rejoicing, for she had left Plumfield to Jo, which made all sorts of joyful things possible.

"It's a fine old place, and will bring a handsome sum, for of course you intend to sell it?" said Laurie, as they were all talking the matter over, some weeks later.

"No, I don't," was Jo's decided answer, as she petted the fat poodle, whom she had adopted, out of respect to his former mistress.

"You don't mean to live there?"

"Yes, I do."

"But, my dear girl, it's an immense house, and will take a power of money to keep it in order. The garden and orchard alone need two or three men, and farming isn't in Bhaer's line, I take it."

"He'll try his hand at it there, if I propose it."

"And you expect to live on the produce of the place? Well, that sounds Paradisiacal, but you'll find it desperate hard work."

"The crop we are going to raise is a profitable one;" and Jo laughed.

"Of what is this fine crop to consist, ma'am?"

"Boys! I want to open a school for little lads – a good, happy, homelike school, with me to take care of them, and Fritz to teach them."

"There's a truly Joian plan for you! Isn't that just like her?" cried Laurie, appealing to the family, who looked as much surprised as he.

"I like it," said Mrs. March, decidedly.

"So do I," added her husband, who welcomed the thought of a chance for trying the Socratic method of education on modern youth.

"It will be an immense care for Jo," said Meg, stroking the head of her one all-absorbing son.

"Jo can do it, and be happy in it. It's a splendid idea – tell us all about it,"cried Mr. Laurence, who had been longing to lend the lovers a hand, but knew they would refuse his help.

"I knew you'd stand by me, sir. Amy does too – I see it in her eyes, though she prudently waits to turn it over in her mind before she speaks. Now, my dear people," continued Jo, earnestly, "just understand that this isn't a new idea of mine, but a long-cherished plan. Before my Fritz came, I used to think how, when I'd made my fortune, and no one needed me at home, I'd hire a big house, and pick up some poor, forlorn little lads, who hadn't any mothers, and take care of them, and make life jolly for them before it was too late. I see so many going to ruin for want of help, at the right minute; I love so to do anything for them; I seem to feel their wants, and sympathize with their troubles; and, oh, I should *so* like to be a mother to them!"

Mrs. March held out her hand to Jo, who took it smiling, with tears in her eyes, and went on in the old enthusiastic way, which they had not seen in a long while.

"I told my plan to Fritz once, and he said it was just what he would like, and agreed to try it when we got rich. Bless his dear heart, he's been doing it all his life, —helping poor boys, I mean, — not getting rich; that he'll never be — money don't stay in his pocket long enough to lay up any. But now, thanks to my good old aunt, who loved me better than I ever deserved, *I'm* rich — at least I feel so, and we can live at Plumfield, perfectly well, if we have a flourishing school. It's just the place for boys — the house is big, and the furniture strong and plain. There's plenty of room for dozens inside, and splendid grounds outside. They could help in the garden and orchard — such work is healthy, isn't it, sir? Then Fritz can train and teach in his own way, and father will help him. I can feed, and nurse, and pet, and scold them; and mother will be my stand-by. I've always longed for lots of boys, and never had enough; now I can fill the house full, and revel in the little dears to my heart's content. Think what luxury; Plumfield my own, and a wilderness of boys to enjoy it with me!"

As Jo waved her hands, and gave a sigh of rapture, the family went off into a gale of merriment, and Mr. Laurence laughed till they thought he'd have an apoplectic fit.

"I don't see anything funny," she said, gravely, when she could be heard. "Nothing could be more natural or proper than for my Professor to open a school, and for me to prefer to reside on my own estate."

"She is putting on airs already," said Laurie, who regarded the idea in the light of a capital joke. "But may I inquire how you intend to support the establishment? If all the pupils are little ragamuffins, I'm afraid your crop won't be profitable, in a worldly sense, Mrs. Bhaer."

"Now don't be a wet blanket, Teddy. Of course, I shall have rich pupils, also, — perhaps begin with such altogether; then, when I've got a start, I can take a ragamuffin or two, just for a relish. Rich people's children often need care and comfort, as well as poor. I've seen unfortunate little creatures left to servants, or backward ones pushed forward, when it's real cruelty. Some are naughty through mismanagement or neglect, and some lose their mothers. Besides, the best have to get through the hobbledehoy age, and that's the very time they need most patience and kindness. People laugh at them, and hustle them about, try to keep them out of sight, and expect them to turn, all at once, from pretty children into fine young men. They don't complain much, — plucky little souls, — but they feel it. I've been through something of it, and I know all about it. I've a special interest in such young bears, and like to show them that I see the warm, honest, well-meaning boy-hearts, in spite of the clumsy arms and legs, and the topsy-turvy heads. I've had experience, too, for haven't I brought up one boy to be a pride and honor to his family?"

"I'll testify that you tried to do it," said Laurie, with a grateful look.

"And I've succeeded beyond my hopes; for here you are, a steady, sensible, business man, doing lots of good with your money, and laying up the blessings of the poor, instead of dollars. But you aren't merely a business man, — you love good and beautiful things, enjoy them yourself, and let others go halves, as you always did in the old times. I *am* proud of you, Teddy, for you get better every year, and every one feels it, though you won't let them say so. Yes, and when I have my flock, I'll just point to you, and say, 'There's your model, my lads.'"

Poor Laurie didn't know where to look, for, man though he was, something of the old bashfulness came over him, as this burst of praise made all faces turn approvingly upon him.

"I say, Jo, that's rather too much," he began, just in his old boyish way. "You have all done more for me than I can ever thank you for, except by doing my best not to disappoint you. You have rather cast me off lately, Jo, but I've had the best of help, nevertheless; so, if I've got on at all, you may thank these two for it," — and he laid one hand gently on his grandfather's white head, the other on Amy's golden one, for the three were never far apart.

"I do think that families are the most beautiful things in all the world!" burst out Jo, who was in an unusually uplifted frame of mind, just then. "When I have one of my own, I hope it will be as happy as the three I know and love the best. If John and my Fritz were only here, it would be quite the little heaven on earth," she added more quietly. And that night, when she went to her room, after a blissful evening of family counsels, hopes and plans, her heart was so full of happiness, that she could only calm it by kneeling beside the empty bed always near her own, and thinking tender thoughts of Beth.

It was a very astonishing year, altogether, for things seemed to happen in an unusually rapid and delightful manner. Almost before she knew where she was, Jo found herself married and settled at Plumfield. Then a family of six or seven boys sprung up like mushrooms, and flourished surprisingly. Poor boys, as well as rich, — for Mr. Laurence was continually finding some touching case of destitution, and begging the Bhaers to take pity on the child, and he would gladly pay a trifle for its support. In this way the sly old gentleman got round proud Jo, and furnished her with the style of boy in which she most delighted.

Of course it was up-hill work at first, and Jo made queer mistakes; but the wise Professor steered her safely into calmer waters, and the most rampant ragamuffin was conquered in the end. How Jo did enjoy her "wilderness of boys," and how poor, dear Aunt March would have lamented had she been there to see the sacred precincts of prim, well-ordered Plumfield overrun with Toms, Dicks, and Harrys. There was a sort of poetic justice about it after all, — for the old lady had been the terror of all the boys for miles round; and now the exiles feasted freely on forbidden plums, kicked up the gravel with profane boots unreproved, and played cricket in the big field where the irritable "cow with a crumpled horn" used to invite rash youths to come and be tossed. It became a sort of boys' paradise, and Laurie suggested that it should be called the "Bhaer-garten," as a compliment to its master, and appropriate to its inhabitants.

It was never a fashionable school, and the Professor did not lay up a fortune, but it *was* just what Jo intended it to be, "a happy, home-like place for boys who needed teaching, care, and kindness." Every room in the big house was soon full, every little plot in the garden soon had its owner, a regular menagerie appeared in barn and shed, — for pet animals were allowed, — and, three times a day, Jo smiled at her Fritz from the head of a long table lined on either side with rows of happy young faces, which all turned to her with affectionate eyes, confiding words, and grateful hearts full of love for "Mother Bhaer." She had boys enough now, and did not tire of them, though they were not angels by any means, and some of them caused both Professor and Professorin much trouble and anxiety. But her faith in the good spot which exists in the heart of the naughtiest, sauciest, most tantalizing little ragamuffin gave her patience, skill, and, in time, success, — for no mortal boy could hold out long with Father Bhaer shining on him as benevolently as the sun, and Mother Bhaer forgiving him seventy times seven. Very precious to Jo was the friendship of the lads, their penitent sniffs and whispers after wrong-doing, their droll or touching little confidences, their pleasant enthusiasms, hopes, and plans; even their misfortunes, — for they only endeared them to her all the more. There were slow boys and bashful boys, feeble boys and riotous boys, boys that lisped and boys that stuttered, one or two lame ones, and a merry little quadroon, who could not be taken in elsewhere, but who was welcome to the "Bhaer-garten," though some people predicted that his admission would ruin the school.

Yes, Jo was a very happy woman there, in spite of hard work, much anxiety, and a perpetual racket. She enjoyed it heartily, and found the applause of her boys more satisfying than any praise of the world, – for now she told no stories except to her flock of enthusiastic believers and admirers. As the years went on, two little lads of her own came to increase her happiness. Rob, named for grandpa, and Teddy, – a happy-go-lucky baby, who seemed to have inherited his papa's sunshiny temper as well as his mother's lively spirit. How they ever grew up alive in that whirlpool of boys, was a mystery to their grandma and aunts; but they flourished like dandelions in spring, and their rough nurses loved and served them well.

There were a great many holidays at Plumfield, and one of the most delightful was the yearly apple-picking, – for then the Marches, Laurences, Brookeses, and Bhaers turned out in full force, and made a day of it. Five years after Jo's wedding one of these fruitful festivals occurred. A mellow October day, when the air was full of an exhilarating freshness which made the spirits rise, and the blood dance healthily in the veins. The old orchard wore its holiday attire; golden-rod and asters fringed the mossy walls; grasshoppers skipped briskly in the sere grass, and crickets chirped like fairy pipers at a feast. Squirrels were busy with their small harvesting, birds twittered their adieux from the alders in the lane, and every tree stood ready to send down its shower of red or yellow apples at the first shake. Everybody was there, – everybody laughed and sang, climbed up and tumbled down; everybody declared that there never had been such a perfect day or such a jolly set to enjoy it, – and every one gave themselves up to the simple pleasures of the hour as freely as if there were no such things as care or sorrow in the world.

Mr. March strolled placidly about, quoting Tusser, Cowley, and Columella to Mr. Laurence, while enjoying –

The gentle apple's winey juice.

The Professor charged up and down the green aisles like a stout Teutonic knight, with a pole for a lance, leading on the boys, who made a hook and ladder company of themselves, and performed wonders in the way of ground and lofty tumbling. Laurie devoted himself to the little ones, rode his small daughter in a bushel basket, took Daisy up among the birds' nests, and kept adventurous Rob from breaking his neck. Mrs. March and Meg sat among the apple piles like a pair of Pomonas, sorting the contributions that kept pouring in; while Amy, with a beautiful motherly expression in her face, sketched the various groups, and watched over one pale lad who sat adoring her with his little crutch beside him.

Jo was in her element that day, and rushed about with her gown pinned up, her hat anywhere but on her head, and her baby tucked under her arm, ready for any lively adventure which might turn up. Little Teddy bore a charmed life, for nothing ever happened to him, and Jo never felt any anxiety when he was whisked up into a tree by one lad, galloped off on the back of another, or supplied with sour russets by his indulgent papa, who labored under the Germanic delusion that babies could digest anything, from pickled cabbage to buttons, nails, and their own small shoes. She knew that little Ted would turn up again in time, safe and rosy, dirty and serene, and she always received him back with a hearty welcome, – for Jo loved her babies tenderly.

At four o'clock a lull took place, and baskets remained empty, while the apple-pickers rested, and compared rents and bruises. Then Jo and Meg, with a detachment of the bigger boys, set forth the supper on the grass, – for an out-of-door tea was always the crowning joy of the day. The land literally flowed with milk and honey on such occasions, – for the lads were not required to sit at table, but allowed to partake of refreshments as they liked, – freedom being the sauce best beloved by the boyish soul. They availed themselves of the rare privilege to the fullest extent, for some tried the pleasing experiment of drinking milk while standing on their heads, others lent a charm to leap-frog by eating pie in the pauses of the game, cookies were sown broadcast over the field, and apple turn-overs roosted in the trees like a new style of bird. The little girls had a private tea-party, and Ted roved among the edibles at his own sweet will.

When no one could eat any more, the Professor proposed the first regular toast, which was always drunk at such times, – "Aunt March, God bless her!" A toast heartily given by the good man, who never forgot how much he owed her, and quietly drunk by the boys, who had been taught to keep her memory green.

"Now, grandma's sixtieth birthday! Long life to her, with three times three!"

That was given with a will, as you may well believe; and the cheering once begun, it was hard to stop it. Everybody's health was proposed, from Mr. Laurence, who was considered their special patron, to the astonished guinea pig, who had strayed from its proper sphere in search of its young master. Demi, as the oldest grandchild, then presented the queen of the day with various gifts, so numerous that they were transported to the festive scene in a wheelbarrow. Funny presents, some of them, but what would have been defects to other eyes were ornaments to grandma's, – for the children's gifts were all their own. Every stitch Daisy's patient little fingers had put into the handkerchiefs she hemmed, was better than embroidery to Mrs. March; Demi's shoe box was a miracle of mechanical skill, though the cover wouldn't shut; Rob's footstool had a wiggle in its uneven legs, that she declared was very soothing; and no page of the costly book Amy's child gave her, was so fair as that on which appeared, in tipsy capitals, the words, – "To dear Grandma, from her little Beth."

During the ceremony the boys had mysteriously disappeared; and, when Mrs. March had tried to thank her children, and broken down, while Teddy wiped her eyes on his pinafore, the Professor suddenly began to sing. Then, from above him, voice after voice took up the words, and from tree to tree echoed the music of the unseen choir, as the boys sung, with all their hearts, the little song Jo had written, Laurie set to music, and the Professor trained his lads to give with the best effect. This was something altogether new, and it proved a grand success, for Mrs. March couldn't get over her surprise, and insisted on shaking hands with every one of the featherless birds, from tall Franz and Emil to the little quadroon, who had the sweetest voice of all.

After this, the boys dispersed for a final lark, leaving Mrs. March and her daughters under the festival tree.

"I don't think I ever ought to call myself 'Unlucky Jo' again, when my greatest wish has been so beautifully gratified," said Mrs. Bhaer, taking Teddy's little fist out of the milk pitcher, in which he was rapturously churning.

"And yet your life is very different from the one you pictured so long ago. Do you remember our castles in the air?" asked Amy, smiling as she watched Laurie and John playing cricket with the boys.

"Dear fellows! It does my heart good to see them forget business, and frolic for a day," answered Jo, who now spoke in a maternal way of all mankind. "Yes, I remember; but the life I wanted then seems selfish, lonely and cold to me now. I haven't given up the hope that I may write a good book yet, but I can wait, and I'm sure it will be all the better for such experiences and illustrations as these;" and Jo pointed from the lively lads in the distance to her father, leaning on the Professor's arm, as they walked to and fro in the sunshine, deep in one of the conversations which both enjoyed so much, and then to her mother, sitting enthroned among her daughters, with their children in her lap and at her feet, as if all found help and happiness in the face which never could grow old to them.

"My castle was the most nearly realized of all. I asked for splendid things, to be sure, but in my heart I knew I should be satisfied, if I had a little home, and John, and some dear children like these. I've got them all, thank God, and am the happiest woman in the world;" and Meg laid her hand on her tall boy's head, with a face full of tender and devout content.

"My castle is very different from what I planned, but I would not alter it, though, like Jo, I don't relinquish all my artistic hopes, or confine myself to helping others fulfil their dreams of beauty. I've begun to model a figure of a baby, and Laurie says it is the best thing I've ever done. I think so myself, and mean to do it in marble, so that whatever happens, I may at least keep the image of my little angel."

As Amy spoke, a great tear dropped on the golden hair of the sleeping child in her arms; for her one well-beloved daughter was a frail little creature, and the dread of losing her was the shadow over Amy's sunshine. This cross was doing much for both father and mother, for one love and sorrow bound them closely together. Amy's nature was growing sweeter, deeper and more tender; Laurie was growing more serious, strong and firm, and both were learning that beauty, youth, good fortune, even love itself, cannot keep care and pain, loss and sorrow, from the most blest; for —

Into each life some rain must fall,
Some days must be dark, and sad, and dreary.

"She is growing better, I am sure of it, my dear; don't despond, but hope, and keep happy," said Mrs. March, as tender-hearted Daisy stooped from her knee, to lay her rosy cheek against her little cousin's pale one.

"I never ought to, while I have you to cheer me up, Marmee, and Laurie to take more than half of every burden," replied Amy, warmly. "He never lets me see his anxiety, but is so sweet and patient with me, so devoted to Beth, and such a stay and comfort to me always, that I can't love him enough. So, in spite of my one cross, I can say with Meg, 'Thank God, I'm a happy woman.'"

"There's no need for me to say it, for every one can see that I'm far happier than I deserve," added Jo, glancing from her good husband to her chubby children, tumbling on the grass beside her. "Fritz is getting gray and stout, I'm growing as thin as a shadow, and am over thirty; we never shall be rich, and Plumfield may burn up any night, for that incorrigible Tommy Bangs *will* smoke sweetfern cigars under the bed-clothes, though he's set himself afire three times already. But in spite of these unromantic facts, I have nothing to complain of, and never was so jolly in my life. Excuse the remark, but living among the boys, I can't help using their expressions now and then."

"Yes, Jo, I think your harvest will be a good one," began Mrs. March, frightening away a big black cricket, that was staring Teddy out of countenance.

"Not half so good as yours, mother. Here it is, and we never can thank you enough for the patient sowing and reaping you have done," cried Jo, with the loving impetuosity which she never could outgrow.

"I hope there will be more wheat and fewer tares every year," said Amy, softly.

"A large sheaf, but I know there's room in your heart for it, Marmee dear," added Meg's tender voice.

Touched to the heart, Mrs. March could only stretch out her arms, as if to gather children and grandchildren to herself, and say, with face and voice full of motherly love, gratitude, and humility, —

"Oh, my girls, however long you may live, I never can wish you a greater happiness than this!"

Little Men

Life at Plumfield
With Jo's Boys

~

Louisa May Alcott

Illustrated by
Clara M. Burd

Contents

TO
FREDDY AND JOHNNY
THE LITTLE MEN
TO WHOM SHE OWES SOME OF THE BEST AND HAPPIEST
HOURS OF HER LIFE,
THIS BOOK IS GRATEFULLY DEDICATED
BY THEIR LOVING
"AUNT WEEDY"

ILLUSTRATIONS

"Please, sir, is this Plumfield?"

CHAPTER ONE

NAT

~

"Please, sir, is this Plumfield?" asked a ragged boy of the man who opened the great gate at which the omnibus left him.

"Yes; who sent you?"

"Mr. Laurence. I have a letter for the lady."

"All right; go up to the house, and give it to her; she'll see to you, little chap."

The man spoke pleasantly, and the boy went on, feeling much cheered by the words. Through the soft spring rain that fell on sprouting grass and budding trees, Nat saw a large square house before him — a hospitable-looking house, with an old-fashioned porch, wide steps, and lights shining in many windows. Neither curtains nor shutters hid the cheerful glimmer; and, pausing a moment before he rang, Nat saw many shadows dancing on the walls, heard the pleasant hum of young voices, and felt that it was hardly possible that the light and warmth and comfort within could be for a homeless "little chap" like him.

"I hope the lady *will* see to me," he thought; and gave a timid rap with the great bronze knocker, which was a jovial griffin's head.

A rosy-faced servant maid opened the door, and smiled as she took the letter which he silently offered. She seemed used to receiving strange boys, for she pointed to a seat in the hall, and said, with a nod, –

"Sit there and drip on the mat a bit, while I take this in to madam."

Nat found plenty to amuse him while he waited, and stared about him curiously, enjoying the view, yet glad to do so unobserved in the dusky recess by the door.

The house seemed swarming with boys, who were beguiling the rainy twilight with all sorts of amusements. There were boys everywhere, "up stairs and down stairs and in the lady's chamber," apparently, for various open doors showed pleasant groups of big boys, little boys, and middle-sized boys in all stages of evening relaxation, not to say effervescence. Two large rooms on the right were evidently schoolrooms, for desks, maps, blackboards, and books were scattered about. An open fire burned on the hearth, and several indolent lads lay on their backs before it, discussing a new cricket ground with such animation that their boots waved in the air. A tall youth was practising on the flute in one corner, quite undisturbed by the racket all about him. Two or three others were jumping over the desks, pausing, now and then, to get their breath, and laugh at the droll sketches of a little wag who was caricaturing the whole household on a blackboard.

In the room on the left a long supper table was seen, set forth with great pitchers of new milk, piles of brown and white bread, and perfect stacks of the shiny gingerbread so dear to boyish souls. A flavor of toast was in the air, also suggestions of baked apples, very tantalizing to one hungry little nose and stomach.

The hall, however, presented the most inviting prospect of all, for a brisk game of tag was going on in the upper entry. One landing was devoted to marbles, the other to checkers, while the stairs were occupied by a boy reading, a girl singing lullaby to her doll, two puppies, a kitten, and a constant succession of small boys sliding down the banisters, to the great detriment of their clothes, and danger to their limbs.

So absorbed did Nat become in this exciting race, that he ventured farther and farther out of his corner; and when one very lively boy came down so swiftly that he could not stop himself, but fell off the banisters, with a crash that would have broken any head but one rendered nearly as hard as a cannon-ball by eleven years of constant bumping, Nat forgot himself and ran up to the fallen rider, expecting to find him half-dead. The boy, however, only winked rapidly for a second, then lay calmly looking up at the new face with a surprised, "Hullo!"

"Hullo!" returned Nat, not knowing what else to say, and thinking that form of reply both brief and easy.

"Are you a new boy?" asked the recumbent youth, without stirring.

"Don't know yet."

"What's your name?"

"Nat Blake."

"Mine's Tommy Bangs; come up and have a go, will you?" and Tommy got upon his legs, as if he suddenly remembered the duties of hospitality.

"Guess I won't, till I see whether I'm going to stay or not," returned Nat, feeling the desire to stay increase every moment.

"I say, Demi, here's a new one. Come and see to him," and the lively Thomas returned to his sport with unabated relish.

At his call, the boy reading on the stairs looked up with a pair of big brown eyes, and after an instant's pause, as if a little shy, he put the book under his arm, and came soberly down to greet the newcomer, who found something very attractive in the pleasant face of this slender, mild-eyed boy.

"Have you seen Aunt Jo?" he asked, as if that were some sort of important ceremony.

"I haven't seen anybody yet but you boys; I'm waiting," answered Nat.

"Did Uncle Laurie send you?" proceeded Demi, politely, but gravely.

"Mr. Laurence did."

"He is Uncle Laurie; and he always sends nice boys."

Nat looked gratified at the remark, and smiled in a way that made his thin face very pleasant. He did not know what to say next, so the two stood staring at one another in friendly silence, till the little girl came up, with her doll in her arms. She was very like Demi, only not so tall, and had a rounder, rosier face, and blue eyes.

"This is my sister Daisy," announced Demi, as if presenting a rare and precious creature.

The children nodded to one another; and the little girl's face dimpled with pleasure, as she said, affably, —

"I hope you'll stay. We have such good times here; don't we, Demi?"

"Of course, we do; that's what Aunt Jo has Plumfield for."

"It seems a very nice place indeed," observed Nat, feeling that he must respond to these amiable young persons.

"It's the nicest place in the world; isn't it, Demi?" said Daisy, who evidently regarded her brother as authority on all subjects.

"No; I think Greenland, where the icebergs and seals are, is more interesting. But I'm fond of Plumfield, and it *is* a very nice place to be in,' returned Demi, who was interested just now in a book on Greenland. He was about to offer to show Nat the pictures and explain them, when the servant returned, saying, with a nod toward the parlor door, —

"All right; you are to stop."

"I'm glad; now come to Aunt Jo." And Daisy took him by the hand with a pretty protecting air, which made Nat feel at home at once.

Demi returned to his beloved book, while his sister led the newcomer into a back room, where a stout gentleman was frolicking with two little boys on the sofa, and a thin lady was just finishing the letter which she seemed to have been rereading.

"Here he is, Aunty!" cried Daisy.

"So this is my new boy? I am glad to see you, my dear, and hope you'll be happy here," said the lady, drawing him to her, and stroking back the hair from his forehead with a kind hand and a motherly look, which made Nat's lonely little heart yearn toward her.

She was not at all handsome, but she had a merry sort of face, that never seemed to have forgotten certain childish ways and looks, any more than her voice and manner had; and these things, hard to describe but very plain to see and feel, made her a genial, comfortable kind of person, easy to get on with, and generally "jolly," as boys would say. She saw the little tremble of Nat's lips as she smoothed his hair, and her keen eyes grew softer, but she only drew the shabby figure nearer and said, laughing, —

"I am Mother Bhaer, that gentleman is Father Bhaer, and these are the two little Bhaers. Come here, boys, and see Nat."

The three wrestlers obeyed at once; and the stout man, with a chubby child on each shoulder, came up to welcome the new boy. Rob and Teddy merely grinned at him, but Mr. Bhaer shook hands, and pointing to a low chair near the fire, said, in a cordial voice, —

"There is a place all ready for thee, my son; sit down and dry thy wet feet at once."

"Wet? so they are! My dear, off with your shoes this minute, and I'll have some dry things ready for you in a jiffy," cried Mrs. Bhaer, bustling about so energetically that Nat found himself in the cosy little chair, with dry socks and warm slippers on his feet, before he would have had time to say Jack Robinson, if he had wanted to try. He said, "Thank you, ma'am," instead; and said it so gratefully, that Mrs. Bhaer's eyes grew soft again, and she said something merry, because she felt so tender, which was a way she had.

"These are Tommy Bangs' slippers; but he never will remember to put them on in the house; so he shall not have them. They are too big; but that's all the better; you can't run away from us so fast as if they fitted."

"I don't want to run away, ma'am." And Nat spread his grimy little hands before the comfortable blaze, with a long sigh of satisfaction.

"That's good! Now I am going to toast you well, and try to get rid of that ugly cough. How long have you had it, dear?" asked Mrs. Bhaer, as she rummaged in her big basket for a strip of flannel.

"All winter. I got cold, and it wouldn't get better, somehow."

"No wonder, living in that damp cellar with hardly a rag to his poor dear back!" said Mrs. Bhaer, in a low tone to her husband, who was looking at the boy with a skilful pair of eyes, that marked the thin temples and feverish lips, as well as the hoarse voice and frequent fits of coughing that shook the bent shoulders under the patched jacket.

"Robin, my man, trot up to Nursey, and tell her to give thee the cough bottle and the liniment," said Mr. Bhaer, after his eyes had exchanged telegrams with his wife's.

Nat looked a little anxious at the preparations, but forgot his fears, in a hearty laugh, when Mrs. Bhaer whispered to him, with a droll look, —

"Hear my rogue Teddy try to cough. The sirup I'm going to give you has honey it in; and he wants some."

Little Ted was red in the face with his exertions by the time the bottle came, and was allowed to lick the spoon, after Nat had manfully taken a dose, and had the bit of flannel put about his throat.

These first steps toward a cure were hardly completed, when a great bell rang, and a loud tramping through the hall announced supper. Bashful Nat quaked at the thought of meeting many strange boys, but Mrs. Bhaer held out her hand to him, and Rob said, patronizingly, "Don't be 'fraid; I'll take care of you."

Twelve boys, six on a side, stood behind their chairs, prancing with impatience to begin, while the tall flute-playing youth was trying to curb their ardor. But no one sat down till Mrs. Bhaer was in her place behind the teapot, with Teddy on her left, and Nat on her right.

"This is our new boy, Nat Blake. After supper you can say, How do you do? Gently, boys, gently."

As she spoke every one stared at Nat, and then whisked into their seats, trying to be orderly, and failing utterly. The Bhaers did their best to have the lads behave well at mealtimes, and generally succeeded pretty well, for their rules were few and sensible, and the boys, knowing that they tried to make things easy and happy, did their best to obey. But there *are* times when hungry boys cannot be repressed without real cruelty, and Saturday evening, after a half holiday, was one of those times.

"Dear little souls, do let them have one day in which they can howl and racket and frolic, to their hearts' content. A holiday isn't a holiday without plenty of freedom and fun; and they shall have full swing once a week," Mrs. Bhaer used to say, when prim people wondered why banister sliding, pillow fights, and all manner of jovial games were allowed under the once decorous roof of Plumfield.

It did seem at times as if the aforesaid roof was in danger of flying off; but it never did, for a word from Father Bhaer could at any time produce a lull, and the lads had learned that liberty must not be abused. So, in spite of many dark predictions, the school flourished, and manners and morals were insinuated, without the pupils exactly knowing how it was done.

Nat found himself very well off behind the tall pitchers, with Tommy Bangs just round the corner, and Mrs. Bhaer close by, to fill up plate and mug as fast as he could empty them.

"Who is that boy next the girl down at the other end?" whispered Nat to his young neighbor under cover of a general laugh.

"That's Demi Brooke. Mr. Bhaer is his uncle."

"What a queer name!"

"His real name is John, but they call him Demi-John, because his father is John too. That's a joke, don't you see?" said Tommy, kindly explaining. Nat did not see, but politely smiled, and asked, with interest, –

"Isn't he a very nice boy?"

"I bet you he is; knows lots and reads like anything."

"Who is the fat one next to him?"

"Oh, that's Stuffy Cole. His name is George, but we call him Stuffy 'cause he eats so much. The little fellow next Father Bhaer is his boy Rob, and then there's big Franz his nephew; he teaches some, and kind of sees to us."

"He plays the flute, don't he?" asked Nat as Tommy rendered himself speechless by putting a whole baked apple into his mouth at one blow.

Tommy nodded, and said, sooner than one would have imagined possible under the circumstances, "Oh, don't he, though? And we dance sometimes, and do gymnastics to music. I like a drum myself, and mean to learn as soon as ever I can."

"I like a fiddle best; I can play one, too," said Nat, getting confidential on this attractive subject.

"Can you?" and Tommy stared over the rim of his mug with round eyes, full of interest. "Mr. Bhaer's got an old fiddle, and he'll let you play on it if you want to."

"Could I? Oh, I would like it ever so much. You see I used to go round fiddling with my father, and another man, till he died."

"Wasn't that fun?" cried Tommy, much impressed.

"No, it was horrid; so cold in winter, and hot in summer. And I got tired; and they were cross sometimes; and I didn't have enough to eat." Nat paused to take a generous bite of gingerbread, as if to assure himself that the hard times were over; and then he added regretfully, "But I did love my little fiddle, and I miss it. Nicolo took it away when father died, and wouldn't have me any longer, 'cause I was sick."

"You'll belong to the band if you play good. See if you don't."

"Do you have a band here?" And Nat's eyes sparkled.

"Guess we do; a jolly band, all boys; and they have concerts and things. You just see what happens to-morrow night."

After this pleasantly exciting remark, Tommy returned to his supper, and Nat sank into a blissful reverie over his full plate.

Mrs. Bhaer had heard all they said, while apparently absorbed in filling mugs, and overseeing little Ted, who was so sleepy that he put his spoon in his eye, nodded like a rosy poppy, and finally fell fast asleep, with his cheek pillowed on a soft bun. Mrs. Bhaer had put Nat next to Tommy, because that roly-poly boy had a frank and social way with him, very attractive to shy persons. Nat felt this, and had made several small confidences during supper, which gave Mrs. Bhaer the key to the new boy's character, better than if she had talked to him herself.

In the letter which Mr. Laurence had sent with Nat, he had said, —

DEAR JO: Here is a case after your own heart. This poor lad is an orphan now, sick and friendless. He had been a street musician; and I found him in a cellar, mourning for his dead father, and his lost violin. I think there is something in him, and have a fancy that between us we may give this little man a lift. You cure his overtasked body, Fritz help his neglected mind, and when he is ready I'll see if he is a genius or only a boy with a talent which may earn his bread for him. Give him a trial, for the sake of your own boy,

TEDDY.

"Of course we will!" cried Mrs. Bhaer, as she read the letter; and when she saw Nat, she felt at once that whether he was a genius or not, here was a lonely, sick boy, who needed just what she loved to give, a home and motherly care. Both she and Mr. Bhaer observed him quietly; and in spite of ragged clothes, awkward manners, and a dirty face, they saw much about Nat that pleased them. He was a thin, pale boy, of twelve, with blue eyes, and a good forehead under the rough, neglected hair; an anxious, scared face, at times, as if he expected hard words, or blows; and a sensitive mouth, that trembled when a kind glance fell on him; while a gentle speech called up a look of gratitude, very sweet to see. "Bless the poor dear, he shall fiddle all day long if he likes," said Mrs. Bhaer to herself, as she saw the eager, happy expression on his face when Tommy talked of the band.

So, after supper, when the lads flocked into the schoolroom for more "high jinks," Mrs. Jo appeared with a violin in her hand, and after a word with her husband, went to Nat, who sat in a corner watching the scene with intense interest.

"Now, my lad, give us a little tune. We want a violin in our band, and I think you will do it nicely."

She expected that he would hesitate; but he seized the old fiddle at once, and handled it with such loving care, it was plain to see that music was his passion.

"I'll do the best I can, ma'am," was all he said; and then drew the bow across the strings, as if eager to hear the dear notes again.

There was a great clatter in the room, but as if deaf to any sounds but those he made, Nat played softly to himself, forgetting everything in his delight. It was only a simple negro melody, such as street musicians play, bit it caught the ears of the boys at once, and silenced them, till they stood listening with surprise and pleasure. Gradually they got nearer and nearer, and Mr. Bhaer came up to watch the boy; for, as if was in his element now, Nat played away and never minded any one, while his eyes shone, his cheeks reddened, and his thin fingers flew, as he hugged the old fiddle and made it speak to all their hearts the language that he loved.

A hearty round of applause rewarded him better than a shower of pennies, when he stopped and glanced about him, as if to say, —

"I've done my best; please like it."

"I say, you do that first-rate," cried Tommy, who considered Nat his protégé.

"You shall be first fiddle in my band," added Franz, with an approving smile.

Mrs. Bhaer whispered to her husband, —

"Teddy is right: there's something in the child." And Mr. Bhaer nodded his head emphatically, as he clapped Nat on the shoulder, saying, heartily, —

"You play well, my son. Come now and play something which we can sing."

It was the proudest, happiest minute of the poor boy's life when he was led to the place of honor by the piano, and the lads gathered round, never heeding his poor clothes, but eyeing him respectfully, and waiting eagerly to hear him play again.

They chose a song he knew; and after one or two false starts they got going, and violin, flute, and piano led a chorus of boyish voices that made the old roof ring again. It was too much for Nat, more feeble than he knew; and as the final shout died away, his face began to work, he dropped the fiddle, and turning to the wall, sobbed like a little child.

"My dear, what is it?" asked Mrs. Bhaer, who had been singing with all her might, and trying to keep little Rob from beating time with his boots.

"You are all so kind, – and it's so beautiful, – I can't help it," sobbed Nat, coughing till he was breathless.

"Come with me, dear; you must go to bed and rest; you are worn out, and this is too noisy a place for you," whispered Mrs. Bhaer; and took him away to her own parlor, where she let him cry himself quiet.

Then she won him to tell her all his troubles, and listened to the little story with tears in her own eyes, though it was not a new one to her.

"My child, you have got a father and a mother now, and this is home. Don't think of those sad times any more, but get well and happy; and be sure you shall never suffer again, if we can help it. This place is made for all sorts of boys to have a good time in, and to learn how to help themselves and be useful men, I hope. You shall have as much music as you want, only you must get strong first. Now come up to Nursey and have a bath, and then go to bed, and tomorrow we will lay some nice little plans together."

Nat held her hand fast in his, but had not a word to say, and let his grateful eyes speak for him, as Mrs. Bhaer led him up to a big room, where they found a stout German woman with a face so round and cheery that it looked like a sort of sun, with the wide frill of her cap for rays.

"This is Nursey Hummel, and she will give you a nice bath, and cut your hair, and make you all 'comfy,' as Rob says. That's the bathroom in there; and on Saturday nights we scrub all the little lads first, and pack them away in bed before the big ones get through singing. Now then, Rob, in with you."

As she talked, Mrs. Bhaer had whipped off Rob's clothes and popped him into a long bathtub in the little room opening into the nursery.

There were two tubs, besides foot baths, basins, and all manner of contrivances for cleanliness. Nat was soon luxuriating in the other bath; and while simmering there, he watched the performances of the two women, who scrubbed, clean nightgowned, and bundled into bed four or five small boys, who, of course, cut up all sorts of capers during the operation, and kept every one in a gale of merriment till they were extinguished in their beds.

By the time Nat was washed and done up in a blanket by the fire, while Nursey cut his hair, a new detachment of boys arrived and were shut into the bathroom, where they made as much splashing and noise as a school of young whales at play.

"Nat had better sleep here, so that if his cough troubles him in the night you can see that he takes a good draught of flaxseed tea," said Mrs. Bhaer, who was flying about like a distracted hen with a large brood of lively ducklings.

Nursey approved the plan, finished Nat off with a flannel night-gown, a drink of something warm and sweet, and then tucked him into one of the three little beds standing in the room, where he lay looking like a contented mummy, and feeling that nothing more in the way of luxury could be offered him. Cleanliness in itself was a new and delightful sensation; flannel gowns were unknown comforts in his world; sips of "good stuff" soothed his cough as pleasantly as kind words did his lonely heart; and the feeling that somebody cared for him made than plain room seem a sort of heaven to the homeless child. It was like a cosy dream; and he often shut his eyes to see if it would not vanish when he opened them again. It was too pleasant to let him sleep, and he could not have done so if he had tried, for in a few minutes one of the peculiar institutions of Plumfield was revealed to his astonished but appreciative eyes.

A momentary lull in the aquatic exercises was followed by the sudden appearance of pillows flying in all directions, hurled by white goblins, who came rioting out of their beds. The battle raged in several rooms, all down the upper hall, and even surged at intervals into the nursery, when some hard-pressed warrior took refuge there. No one seemed to mind this explosion in the least; no one forbade it, or even looked surprised. Nursey went on hanging up towels, and Mrs. Bhaer looked out clean clothes, as calmly as if the most perfect order reigned. Nay, she even chased one daring boy out of the room, and fired after him the pillow he had slyly thrown at her.

"Won't they hurt them?" asked Nat, who lay laughing with all his might.

"Oh dear, no! we always allow one pillow fight Saturday night. The cases are changed tomorrow; and it gets up a glow after the boys' baths; so I rather like it myself," said Mrs. Bhaer, busy again among her dozen pairs of socks.

"What a very nice school this is!" observed Nat, in a burst of admiration.

"It's an odd one," laughed Mrs. Bhaer; "but you see we don't believe in making children miserable by too many rules, and too much study. I forbade nightgown parties at first; but, bless you, it was of no use. I could no more keep those boys in their beds, than so many jacks in the box. So I made an agreement with them: I was to allow a fifteen-minute pillow fight, every Saturday night; and they promised to go properly to bed every other night. I tried it, and it worked well. If they don't keep their word, no frolic; if they do, I just turn the glasses round, put the lamps in safe places, and let them rampage as much as they like."

"It's a beautiful plan," said Nat, feeling that he should like to join in the fray, but not venturing to propose it the first night. So he lay enjoying the spectacle, which certainly was a lively one.

Tommy Bangs led the assailing party, and Demi defended his own room with a dogged courage, fine to see, collecting pillows behind him as fast as they were thrown, till the besiegers were out of ammunition, when they would charge upon him in a body, and recover their arms. A few slight accidents occurred, but nobody minded, and gave and took sounding thwacks with perfect good humor, while pillows flew like big snowflakes, till Mrs. Bhaer looked at her watch, and called out,

"Time is up, boys. Into bed, every man Jack, or pay the forfeit!"

"What is the forfeit?" asked Nat, sitting up in his eagerness to know what happened to those wretches who disobeyed this most peculiar, but public-spirited schoolma'am.

"Lose their fun next time," answered Mrs. Bhaer. "I give them five minutes to settle down, then put out the lights, and expect order. They are honorable lads, and they keep their word."

That was evident, for the battle ended as abruptly as it began — a parting shot or two, a final cheer, as Demi fired the seventh pillow at the retiring foe, a few challenges for next time, then order prevailed; and nothing but an occasional giggle, or a suppressed whisper, broke the quiet which followed the Saturday-night frolic, as Mother Bhaer kissed her new boy, and left him to happy dreams of life at Plumfield.

THE BOYS

~

While Nat takes a good long sleep, I will tell my little readers something about the boys, among whom he found himself when he woke up.

To begin with our old friends. Franz was a tall lad, of sixteen now, a regular German, big, blond, and bookish, also very domestic, amiable, and musical. His uncle was fitting him for college, and his aunt for a happy home of his own hereafter, because she carefully fostered in him gentle manners, love of children, respect for women, old and young, and helpful ways about the house. He was her right-hand man on all occasions, steady, kind, and patient; and he loved his merry aunt as a mother, for such she had tried to be to him.

Emil was quite different, being quick-tempered, restless, and enterprising, bent on going to sea, for the blood of the old vikings stirred in his veins, and could not be tamed. His uncle promised that he should go when he was sixteen, and set him to studying navigation, gave him stories of good and famous admirals and heroes to read, and let him lead the life of a frog in river, pond, and brook, when lessons were done. His room looked like the cabin of a man-of-war, for everything was nautical, military, and shipshape. Captain Kidd was his delight, and his favorite amusement was to rig himself up like that piratical gentleman, and roar out sanguinary sea songs at the top of his voice. He would dance nothing but sailors' hornpipes, rolled in his gait, and was as nautical in conversation as his uncle would permit. The boys called him "Commodore," and took great pride in his fleet, which whitened the pond and suffered disasters that would have daunted any commander but a sea-struck boy.

Demi was one of the children who show plainly the effect of intelligent love and care, for soul and body worked harmoniously together. The natural refinement which nothing but home influence can teach, gave him sweet and simple manners: his mother had cherished an innocent and loving heart in him; his father had watched over the physical growth of the boy, and kept the little body straight and strong on wholesome food and exercise and sleep, while Grandpa March cultivated the little mind with the tender wisdom of a modern Pythagoras – not tasking it with long, hard lessons, parrot-learned, but helping it to unfold as naturally and beautifully as sun and dew help roses bloom. He was not a perfect child, by any means, but his faults were of the better sort; and being early taught the secret of self-control, he was not left at the mercy of appetites and passions, as some poor little mortals are, and then punished for yielding to the temptations against which they have no armor. A quiet, quaint boy was Demi, serious, yet cheery, quite unconscious that he was unusually bright and beautiful, yet quick to see and love intelligence or beauty in other children. Very fond of books, and full of lively fancies, born of a strong imagination and a spiritual nature, these traits made his parents anxious to balance them with useful knowledge and healthful society, lest they should make him one of those pale, precocious children who amaze and delight a family sometimes, and fade away like hothouse flowers, because the young soul blooms too soon, and has not a hearty body to root it firmly in the wholesome soil of this world.

So Demi was transplanted to Plumfield, and took so kindly to the life there that Meg and John and grandpa felt satisfied that they had done well. Mixing with other boys brought out the practical side of him, roused his spirit, and brushed away the pretty cobwebs he was so fond of spinning in that little brain of his. To be sure, he rather shocked his mother when he came home, by banging doors, saying "by George" emphatically, and demanding tall, thick boots "that clumped like papa's." But John rejoiced over him, laughed at his explosive remarks, got the boots, and said contentedly, "He is doing well; so let him clump. I want my son to be a manly boy, and this temporary roughness won't hurt him. We can polish him up by and by; and as for learning, he will pick that up as pigeons do peas. So don't hurry him."

Daisy was as sunshiny and charming as ever, with all sorts of little womanlinesses budding in her, for she was like her gentle mother, and delighted in domestic things. She had a family of dolls, whom she brought up in the most exemplary manner; she could not get on without her little work basket and bits of sewing, which she did so nicely, that Demi frequently pulled out his handkerchief to display her neat stitches, and Baby Josy had a flannel petticoat beautifully made by Sister Daisy. She liked to quiddle about the china closet, prepare the salt cellars, put the spoons straight on the table; and every day went round the parlor with her brush, dusting chairs and tables. Demi called her a "Betty," but was very glad to have her keep his things in order, lend him her nimble fingers in all sorts of work, and help him with his lessons, for they kept abreast there, and had no thought of rivalry.

The love between them was as strong as ever; and no one could laugh Demi out of his affectionate ways with Daisy. He fought her battles valiantly, and never could understand why boys should be ashamed to say "right out," that they loved their sisters. Daisy adored her twin, thought "my brother" the most remarkable boy in the world, and every morning, in her little wrapper, trotted to tap at his door with a motherly "Get up, my dear, it's 'most breakfast time; and here's your clean collar."

Rob was an energetic morsel of a boy, who seemed to have discovered the secret of perpetual motion, for he never was still. Fortunately, he was not mischievous, nor very brave; so he kept out of trouble pretty well, and vibrated between father and mother like an affectionate little pendulum with a lively tick, for Rob was a chatterbox.

Teddy was too young to play a very important part in the affairs of Plumfield, yet he had his little sphere, and filled it beautifully. Every one felt the need of a pet at times, and Baby was always ready to accommodate, for kissing and cuddling suited him excellently. Mrs. Jo seldom stirred without him; so he had his little finger in all the domestic pies, and everyone found them all the better for it, for they believed in babies at Plumfield.

Dick Brown, and Adolphus or Dolly Pettingill, were two eight-year-olds. Dolly stuttered badly, but was gradually getting over it, for no one was allowed to mock him and Mr. Bhaer tried to cure it, by making him talk slowly. Dolly was a good little lad, quite uninteresting and ordinary, but he flourished here, and went through his daily duties and pleasures with placid content and propriety.

Dick Brown's affliction was a crooked back, yet he bore his burden so cheerfully that Demi once asked in his queer way, "Do humps make people good-natured? I'd like one if they do."Dick was always merry, and did his best to be like other boys, for a plucky spirit lived in the feeble little body. When he first came, he was very sensitive about his misfortune, but soon learned to forget it, for no one dared remind him of it, after Mr. Bhaer had punished one boy for laughing at him.

"God don't care; for my soul is straight if my back isn't," sobbed Dick to his tormentor on that occasion; and, by cherishing this idea, the Bhaers soon led him to believe that people also loved his soul, and did not mind his body, except to pity and help him to bear it.

Playing menagerie once with the others, some one said, "What animal will you be, Dick?"

"Oh, I'm the dromedary; don't you see the hump on my back?" was the laughing answer.

"So you are, my nice little one that doesn't carry loads, but marches beside the elephant first in the procession," said Demi, who was arranging the spectacle.

"I hope others will be as kind to the poor dear as my boys have learned to be," said Mrs. Jo, quite satisfied with the success of her teaching, as Dick ambled past her, looking like a very happy, but a very feeble little dromedary, beside stout Stuffy, who did the elephant with ponderous propriety.

Jack Ford was a sharp, rather sly lad, who was sent to this school because it was cheap. Many men would have thought him a smart boy, but

Mr. Bhaer did not like his way of illustrating that Yankee word, and thought his unboyish keenness and money loving as much of an affliction as Dolly's stutter, or Dick's hump.

Ned Barker was like a thousand other boys of fourteen, all legs, blunder, and bluster. Indeed, the family called him the "Blunderbuss," and always expected to see him tumble over the chairs, bump against the tables and knock down any small articles near him. He bragged a good deal about what he could do, but seldom did anything to prove it, was not brave, and a little given to taletelling. He was apt to bully the small boys, and flatter the big ones, and without being at all bad, was just the sort of fellow who could very easily be led astray.

George Cole had been spoilt by an overindulgent mother, who stuffed him with sweetmeats till he was sick, and then thought him too delicate to study, so that at twelve years old, he was a pale, puffy boy, dull, fretful, and lazy. A friend persuaded her to send him to Plumfield, and there he soon waked up, for sweet things were seldom allowed, much exercise required, and study made so pleasant, that Stuffy was gently lured along, till he quite amazed his anxious mamma by his improvement, and convinced her that there was really something remarkable in Plumfield air.

Billy Ward was what the Scotch tenderly call an "innocent," for though thirteen years old, he was like a child of six. He had been an unusually intelligent boy, and his father had hurried him on too fast, giving him all sorts of hard lessons, keeping him at his books six hours a day, and expecting him to absorb knowledge as a Strassburg goose does the food crammed down its throat. He thought he was doing his duty, but he nearly killed the boy, for a fever gave the poor child a sad holiday, and when he recovered, the overtasked brain gave out, and Billy's mind was like a slate over which a sponge has passed, leaving it blank.

It was a terrible lesson to his ambitious father; he could not bear the sight of his promising child, changed to a feeble idiot, and he sent him away to Plumfield, scarcely hoping that he could be helped, but sure that he would be kindly treated. Quite docile and harmless was Billy, and it was pitiful to see how hard he tried to learn, as if groping dimly after the lost knowledge which had cost him so much. Day after day, he pored over the alphabet, proudly said A and B, and thought that he knew them, but on the morrow they were gone, and all the work was to be done over again. Mr.

Bhaer had infinite patience with him, and kept on in spite of the apparent hopelessness of the task, not caring for book lessons, but trying gently to clear away the mists from the darkened mind, and give it back intelligence enough to make the boy less a burden and an affliction.

Mrs. Bhaer strengthened his health by every aid she could invent, and the boys all pitied and were kind to him. He did not like their active plays, but would sit for hours watching the doves, would dig holes for Teddy till even that ardent grubber was satisfied, or follow Silas, the man, from place to place seeing him work, for honest Si was very good to him, and though he forgot his letters Billy remembered friendly faces.

Tommy Bangs was the scapegrace of the school, and the most trying little scapegrace that ever lived. As full of mischief as a monkey, yet so good-hearted that one could not help forgiving his tricks; so scatter-brained that words went by him like the wind, yet so penitent for every misdeed, that it was impossible to keep sober when he vowed tremendous vows of reformation, or proposed all sorts of queer punishments to be inflicted upon himself. Mr. and Mrs. Bhaer lived in a state of preparation for any mishap, from the breaking of Tommy's own neck, to the blowing up of the entire family with gunpowder; and Nursey had a particular drawer in which she kept bandages, plasters, and salves for his especial use, for Tommy was always being brought in half dead; but nothing ever killed him, and he rose from every downfall with redoubled vigor.

The first day he came, he chopped the top off one finger in the hay cutter, and during the week, fell from the shed roof, was chased by an angry hen who tried to pick his eyes out because he examined her chickens, got run away with, and had his ears boxed violently by Asia, who caught him luxuriously skimming a pan of cream with half a stolen pie. Undaunted, however, by any failures or rebuffs, this indomitable youth went on amusing himself with all sorts of tricks till no one felt safe. If he did not know his lessons, he always had some droll excuse to offer, and as he was usually clever at his books, and as bright as a button in composing answers when he did not know them, he got on pretty well at school. But out of school, believe me, Tommy was a real boy.

He wound fat Asia up in her own clothes line against the post, and left her there to fume and scold for half an hour one busy Monday morning. He dropped a hot cent down Mary Ann's back as that pretty maid was waiting at table one day when there were gentlemen to dinner, whereat the poor girl upset the soup and rushed out of the room in dismay, leaving the family to think that she had gone made. He fixed a pail of water up in a tree, with a bit of ribbon fastened to the handle, and when Daisy, attracted by the gay streamer, tried to pull it down, she got a bath that spoiled her clean frock and hurt her little feelings very much. He put rough white pebbles in the sugar-bowl when his grandmother came to tea, and the poor old lady wondered why they didn't melt in her cup, but was too polite to say anything. He passed round snuff in church so that five of the boys sneezed with such violence they had to go out. He dug paths in winter time, and then privately watered them so that people should tumble down. He drove poor Silas nearly wild by hanging his big boots in conspicuous places, for his feet were enormous, and he was very much ashamed of them. He persuaded confiding little Dolly to tie a thread to one of his loose teeth, and leave the string hanging from his mouth when he went to sleep, so that Tommy could pull it out without his feeling the dreaded operation. But the tooth wouldn't come at the first tweak, and poor Dolly woke up in great anguish of spirit, and lost all faith in Tommy from that day forth. The last prank had been to give the hens bread soaked in rum, which made them tipsy and scandalized all the other fowls, for the respectable old biddies went staggering about, pecking and clucking in the most maudlin manner, while the family were convulsed with laughter at their antics, till Daisy took pity on them and shut them up in the hen-house to sleep off their intoxication.

These were the boys, and they lived together as happily as twelve lads could, studying and playing, working and squabbling, fighting faults and cultivating virtues in the good old-fashioned way. Boys at other schools probably learned more from books, but less of that better wisdom which makes good men. Latin, Greek, and mathematics were all very well, but in Professor Bhaer's opinion, self-knowledge, self-help, and self-control were more important, and he tried to teach them carefully. People shook their heads sometimes at his ideas, even while they owned that the boys improved wonderfully in manners and morals. But then, as Mrs. Jo said to Nat, it was an "odd school."

CHAPTER THREE

SUNDAY

~

The moment the bell rang next morning Nat flew out of bed, and dressed himself with great satisfaction in the suit of clothes he found on the chair. They were not new, being half-worn garments of one of the well-to-do boys; but Mrs. Bhaer kept all such cast-off feathers for the picked robins who strayed into her nest. They were hardly on when Tommy appeared in a high state of clean collar, and escorted Nat down to breakfast.

The sun was shining into the dining room on the well-spread table, and the flock of hungry, hearty lads who gathered round it. Nat observed that they were much more orderly than they had been the night before, and everyone stood silently behind his chair while little Rob, standing beside his father at the head of the table, folded his hands, reverently bent his curly head, and softly repeated a short grace in the devout German fashion, which Mr. Bhaer loved and taught his little son to honor. Then they all sat down to enjoy the Sunday-morning breakfast of coffee, steak, and baked potatoes, instead of the bread and milk fare with which they usually satisfied their young appetites. There was much pleasant talk while the knives and forks rattled briskly, for certain Sunday lessons were to be learned, the Sunday walk settled, and plans for the week discussed. As he listened, Nat thought it seemed as if this day must be a very pleasant one, for he loved quiet, and there was a cheerful sort of hush over everything that pleased him very much; because, in spite of his rough life, the boy possessed the sensitive nerves which belong to a music-loving nature.

"Now, my lads, get your morning jobs done, and let me find you ready for church when the 'bus comes round," said Father Bhaer, and set the example by going into the schoolroom to get books ready for the morrow.

Every one scattered to his or her task, for each had some little daily duty, and was expected to perform it faithfully. Some brought wood and water, brushed the steps, or ran errands for Mrs. Bhaer. Others fed the pet animals, and did chores about the barn with Franz. Daisy washed the cups, and Demi wiped them, for the twins liked to work together, and Demi had been taught to make himself useful in the little house at home. Even baby Teddy had his small job to do, and trotted to and fro, putting napkins away, and pushing chairs into their places. For half an hour the lads buzzed about like a hive of bees, then the 'bus drove round, Father Bhaer and Franz with the eight older boys piled in, and away they went for a three-mile drive to church in town.

Because of the troublesome cough Nat preferred to stay at home with the four small boys, and spent a happy morning in Mrs. Bhaer's room, listening to the stories she read them, learning the hymn she taught them, and then quietly employing himself pasting pictures into an old ledger.

"This is my Sunday closet," she said, showing him shelves filled with picture books, paint boxes, architectural books, little diaries, and materials for letter writing. "I want my boys to love Sunday, to find it a peaceful, pleasant day, when they can rest from common study and play, yet enjoy quiet pleasures, and learn, in simple ways, lessons more important that any taught in school. Do you understand me?" she asked, watching Nat's attentive face.

"You mean to be good?" he said, after hesitating a minute.

"Yes; to be good, and to love to be good. It is hard work sometimes, I know very well; but we all help one another, and so we get on. This is one of the ways in which I try to help my boys," and she took down a thick book, which seemed half full of writing, and opened at a page on which there was one word at the top.

"Why, that's my name!" cried Nat, looking both surprised and interested.

"Yes; I have a page for each boy. I keep a little account of how he gets on through the week, and Sunday night I show him the record. If it is bad I am sorry and disappointed, if it is good I am glad and proud; but, whichever it is, the boys know I want to help them, and they try to do their best for love of me and Father Bhaer."

"I should think they would," said Nat, catching a glimpse of Tommy's name opposite his own, and wondering what was written under it.

Mrs. Bhaer saw his eye on the words, and shook her head, saying as she turned a leaf, —

"No, I don't show my records to any but the one to whom each belongs. I call this my conscience book; and only you and I will ever know what is to be written on the page below your name. Whether you will be pleased or ashamed to read it next Sunday depends on yourself. I think it will be a good report; at any rate, I shall try to make things easy for you in this new place, and shall be quite contented if you keep our few rules, live happily with the boys, and learn something."

"I'll try, ma'am"; and Nat's thin face flushed up with the earnestness of his desire to make Mrs. Bhaer "glad and proud," not "sorry and disappointed." "It must be a great deal of trouble to write about so many," he added, as she shut the book and gave Nat an encouraging pat on the shoulder.

"Not to me, for I really don't know which I like best, writing or boys," she said, laughing to see Nat stare with astonishment at the last item. "Yes, I know many people think boys are a nuisance, but that is because they don't understand them. I do; and I never saw the boy yet whom I could not get on capitally with after I had once found the soft spot in his heart. Bless me, I couldn't get on at all without my flock of dear, noisy, naughty, harum-scarum little lads, could I, my Teddy?" and Mrs. Bhaer hugged the young rogue, just in time to save the big inkstand from going into his pocket.

Nat, who had never heard anything like this before, really did not know whether Mother Bhaer was a trifle crazy, or the most delightful woman he had ever met. He rather inclined to the latter opinion, in spite of her peculiar tastes, for she had a way of filling up a fellow's plate before he asked, of laughing at his jokes, gently tweaking him by the ear, or clapping him on the shoulder, that Nat found very engaging.

"Now, I think you would like to go into the schoolroom and practise some of the hymns we are to sing tonight," she said, rightly guessing the thing of all others that he wanted to do.

Alone with the beloved violin and the music book propped up before him in the sunny window, while spring beauty filled the world outside, the Sabbath silence reigned within, Nat enjoyed an hour or two of genuine happiness, learning the sweet old tunes, and forgetting the hard past in the cheerful present.

When the churchgoers came back and dinner was over, every one read, wrote letters home, said his Sunday lessons, or talked quietly to one another, sitting here and there about the house. At three o'clock the entire family turned out to walk, for all the active young bodies must have exercise; and in these walks the active young minds were taught to see and love the providence of God in the beautiful miracles which Nature was working before their eyes. Mr. Bhaer always went with them, and in his simple, fatherly way, found for his flock "Sermons in stones, books in the running brooks, and good in everything."

Mrs. Bhaer with Daisy and her own two boys drove into town, to pay the weekly visit to grandma, which was busy Mother Bhaer's one holiday and greatest pleasure. Nat was not strong enough for the long walk, and asked to stay at home with Tommy, who kindly offered to do the honors of Plumfield. "You've seen the house, so come out and have a look at the garden, and the barn, and the menagerie," said Tommy, when they were left alone with Asia, to see that they didn't get into mischief; for, though Tommy was one of the best-meaning boys who ever adorned knickerbockers, accidents of the most direful nature were always happening to him, no one could exactly tell how.

"What is your menagerie?" asked Nat, as they trotted along the drive that encircled the house.

"We all have pets, you see, and we keep them in the corn barn, and call it the menagerie. Here you are. Isn't my guinea pig a beauty?" and

Tommy proudly presented one of the ugliest specimens of that pleasing animal that Nat ever saw.

"I know a boy with a dozen of them, and he said he'd give me one, only I hadn't any place to keep it, so I couldn't have it. It was white, with black spots, a regular rouser, and maybe I could get it for you if you'd like it," said Nat, feeling it would be a delicate return for Tommy's attentions.

"I'd like it ever so much, and I'll give you this one, and they can live together if they don't fight. Those white mice are Rob's, Franz gave them to him. The rabbits are Ned's, and the bantams outside are Stuffy's. That box thing is Demi's turtle tank, only he hasn't begun to get them yet. Last year he had sixty-two, whackers some of them. He stamped one of them with his name and the year, and let it go; and he says maybe he will find it ever so long after and know it. He read about a turtle being found that had a mark on it that showed it must be hundreds of years old. Demi's such a funny chap."

"What is in this box?" asked Nat, stopping before a large deep one, half full of earth.

"Oh, that's Jack Ford's worm shop. He digs heaps of them and keeps them here, and when we want any to go a fishing with, we buy some from him. It save lots of trouble, only he charges too much for them. Why, last time we traded I had to pay two cents a dozen, and then got little ones. Jack's mean sometimes, and I told him I'd dig for myself if he didn't lower his prices. Now, I own two hens, those gray ones with topknots, first-rate ones they are too, and I sell Mrs. Bhaer the eggs, but I never ask her more than twenty-five cents a dozen, never! I'd be ashamed to do it," cried Tommy with a glance of scorn at the worm shop.

"Who owns the dog?" asked Nat, much interested in these commercial transactions, and feeling that T. Bangs was a man whom it would be a privilege and a pleasure to patronize.

"The big dog is Emil's. His name is Christopher Columbus. Mrs. Bhaer named him because she likes to say Christopher Columbus, and no one minds it if she means the dog," answered Tommy, in the tone of a showman displaying his menagerie. "The white pup is Rob's, and the yellow one is Teddy's. A man was going to drown them in our pond and Pa Bhaer wouldn't let him. They do well enough for the little chaps, I don't think much of 'em myself. Their names are Castor and Pollux."

"I'd like Toby the donkey best, if I could have anything; it's so nice to ride, and he's so little and good," said Nat, remembering the weary tramps he had taken on his own tired feet.

"Mr. Laurie sent him out to Mrs. Bhaer, so she don't have to carry Teddy on her back when we go for a walk. We're all fond of Toby, and he's a first-rate donkey, sir. Those pigeons belong to the whole lot of us; we each have our pet one, and go shares in all the little ones as they come along. Squabs are great fun; there ain't any now, but you can go up and take a look at the old fellows, while I see if Cockleton and Granny have laid any eggs."

Nat climbed up a ladder, put his head through a trap door and took a long look at the pretty doves billing and cooing in their spacious loft — some on their nests, some bustling in and out, and some sitting at their doors, while many went flying from the sunny housetop to the straw-strewn farmyard, where six sleek cows were placidly ruminating.

"Everybody has got something but me. I wish I had a dove, or a hen, or even a turtle, all my own," thought Nat, feeling very poor as he saw the interesting treasures of the other boys. "How do you get these things?" he asked, when he joined Tommy in the barn.

"We find them, or buy them, or folks give them to us. My father sends me mine; but as soon as I get egg money enough, I'm going to buy a pair of ducks. There's a nice little pond for them behind the barn, and people pay well for duck eggs, and the little duckies are pretty, and it's fun to see them swim," said Tommy, with the air of a millionaire.

Nat sighed, for he had neither father nor money, nothing in the wide world but an old empty pocketbook, and the skill that lay in his ten finger tips. Tommy seemed to understand the question and the sigh which followed his answer, for after a moment of deep thought, he suddenly broke out, —

"Look here, I'll tell you what I'll do. If you will hunt eggs for me, — I hate it, — I'll give you one egg out of every dozen. You keep account, and when you have twelve, Mother Bhaer will give you twenty-five cents for them, and then you can buy what you like, don't you see?"

"I'll do it! What a kind fellow you are, Tommy!" cried Nat, quite dazzled by this brilliant offer.

"Pooh! that is not anything. You begin now and rummage the barn, and I'll wait here for you. Granny is cackling, so you're sure to find one somewhere," and Tommy threw himself down on the hay with a luxurious sense of having made a good bargain, and done a friendly thing.

Nat joyfully began his search, and went rustling from loft to loft till he found two fine eggs, one hidden under a beam, and the other in an old peck measure, which Mrs. Cockletop had appropriated.

"You may have one and I'll have the other, that will just make up my last dozen, and tomorrow we'll start fresh. Here, you chalk your accounts up near mine, and then we'll be all straight," said Tommy, showing a row of mysterious figures on the smooth side of an old winnowing machine.

With a delightful sense of importance, the proud possessor of one egg opened his account with his friend, who laughingly wrote above the figures these imposing words, –

"T. Bangs & Co."

Poor Nat found them so fascinating that he was with difficulty persuaded to go and deposit his first piece of portable property in Asia's storeroom. Then they went on again, and having made the acquaintance of the two horses, six cows, three pigs, and one Alderney "Bossy," as calves are called in New England, Tommy took Nat to a certain old willow tree that overhung a noisy little brook. From the fence it was an easy scramble into a wide niche between the three big branches, which had been cut off to send out from year to year a crowd of slender twigs, till a green canopy rustled overhead. Here little seats had been fixed, and in a hollow place a closet made big enough to hold a book or two, a dismantled boat, and several half-finished whistles.

"This is Demi's and my private place; we made it, and nobody can come up unless we let them, except Daisy; we don't mind her," said Tommy, as Nat looked with delight from the babbling brown water below to the green arch above, where bees were making a musical murmur as they feasted on the long yellow blossoms that filled the air with sweetness.

"Oh, it's just beautiful!" cried Nat. "I do hope you'll let me up sometimes. I never saw such a nice place in all my life. I'd like to be a bird, and live here always."

"It is pretty nice. You can come if Demi don't mind, and I guess he won't, because he said last night that he liked you."

"Did he?" and Nat smiled with pleasure, for Demi's regard seemed to be valued by all the boys, partly because he was Father Bhaer's nephew, and partly because he was such a sober, conscientious little fellow.

"Yes; Demi likes quiet chaps, and I guess he and you will get on if you care about reading as he does."

Poor Nat's flush of pleasure deepened to a painful scarlet at those last words, and he stammered out, —

"I can't read very well; I never had any time; I was always fiddling round, you know."

"I don't love it myself, but I can do it well enough when I want to," said Tommy, after a surprised look, which said as plainly as words, "A boy twelve years old and can't read!"

'I can read music, anyway," added Nat, rather ruffled at having to confess his ignorance.

"I can't," and Tommy spoke in a respectful tone, which emboldened Nat to say firmly, —

"I mean to study real hard and learn everything I can, for I never had a chance before. Does Mr. Bhaer give hard lessons?"

"No, he isn't a bit cross; he sort of explains and gives you a boost over the hard places. Some folks don't; my other master didn't. If we missed a word, didn't we get raps on the head!" and Tommy rubbed his own pate as if it tingled yet with the liberal supply of raps, the memory of which was the only thing he brought away after a year with his "other master."

"I think I could read this," said Nat, who had been examining the books.

"Read a bit, then; I'll help you," resumed Tommy, with a patronizing air.

So Nat did his best, and floundered through a page with many friendly "boosts" from Tommy, who told him he would soon "go it" as well as anybody. Then they sat and talked boy fashion about all sorts of things, among others, gardening; for Nat, looking down from his perch, asked what was planted in the many little patches lying below them on the other side of the brook.

"These are our farms," said Tommy. "We each have our own patch, and raise what we like in it, only we have to choose different things, and can't change till the crop is in, and we must keep it in order all summer."

"What are you going to raise this year?"

"Wal, I *cattle*ated to hev beans, as they are about the easiest crop a- goin'."

Nat could not help laughing, for Tommy had pushed back his hat, put his hands in his pockets, and drawled out his words in unconscious imitation of Silas, the man who managed the place for Mr. Bhaer.

"Come, you needn't laugh; beans *are* ever so much easier than corn or potatoes. I tried melons last year, but the bugs were a bother, and the old things wouldn't get ripe before the frost, so I didn't have but one good water and two little 'mush mellions,'" said Tommy, relapsing into a "Silasism" with the last word.

"Corn looks pretty growing," said Nat, politely, to atone for his laugh.

"Yes, but you have to hoe it over and over again. Now, six weeks' beans only have to be done once or so, and they get ripe soon. I'm going to try them, for I spoke first. Stuffy wanted them, but he's got to take peas; they only have to be picked, and he ought to do it, he eats such a lot."

"I wonder if I shall have a garden?" said Nat, thinking that even corn hoeing must be pleasant work.

"Of course you will," said a voice from below, and there was Mr. Bhaer returned from his walk, and come to find them, for he managed to have a little talk with every one of the lads some time during the day, and found that these chats gave them a good start for the coming week.

Sympathy is a sweet thing, and it worked wonders here, for each boy knew that Father Bhaer was interested in him, and some were readier to open their hearts to him than to a woman, especially the older ones, who liked to talk over their hopes and plans, man to man. When sick or in trouble they instinctively turned to Mrs. Jo, while the little ones made her their mother-confessor on all occasions.

In descending from their nest, Tommy fell into the brook; being used to it he calmly picked himself out and retired to the house to be dried. This left Nat to Mr. Bhaer, which was just what he wished, and, during the stroll they took among the garden plots, he won the lad's heart by giving him a little "farm," and discussing crops with him as gravely as if the food for the family depended on the harvest. From this pleasant topic they went to others, and Nat had many new and helpful thoughts put into a mind that received them as gratefully as the thirsty earth had received the warm spring rain. All supper time he brooded over them, often fixing his eyes on Mr. Bhaer with an inquiring look, that seemed to say, "I like that, do it again, sir." I don't know whether the man understood the child's mute language or not, but when the boys were all gathered together in Mrs. Bhaer's parlor for the Sunday evening talk, he chose a subject which might have been suggested by the walk in the garden.

As he looked about him Nat thought it seemed more like a great family than a school, for the lads were sitting in a wide half-circle round the fire, some on chairs, some on the rug, Daisy and Demi on the knees of Uncle Fritz, and Rob snugly stowed away in the back of his mother's easy chair, where he could nod unseen if the talk got beyond his depth. Every one looked quite comfortable and listened attentively, for the long walk made rest agreeable, and as every boy there knew that he would be called upon for his views he kept his wits awake to be ready with an answer.

"Once upon a time," began Mr. Bhaer, in the dear old-fashioned way, "there was a great and wise gardener who had the largest garden ever seen. A wonderful and lovely place it was, and he watched over it with the greatest skill and care, and raised all manner of excellent and useful things. But weeds would grow even in this fine garden; often the ground was bad and the good seeds sown in it would not spring up. He had many under gardeners to help him. Some did their duty and earned the rich wages he gave them; but others neglected their parts and let them run to waste, which displeased him much. But he was very patient, and for thousands and thousands of years he worked and waited for his great harvest."

"He must have been pretty old," said Demi, who was looking straight into Uncle Fritz's face, as if to catch every word.

"Hush, Demi, it's a fairy story," whispered Daisy.

"No, I think it's a arrygory," said Demi.

"What is a arrygory?" called out Tommy, who was of an inquiring turn.

"Tell him, Demi, if you can, and don't use words unless you are quite sure you know what they mean,' said Mr. Bhaer.

'I do know; grandpa told me! A fable is a arrygory; it's a story that means something. My 'story without an end' is one, because the child in it means a soul; don't it, Aunty?" cried Demi, eager to prove himself right.

"That's it, dear; and uncle's story is an allegory, I am quite sure; so listen and see what it means," returned Mrs. Jo, who always took part in whatever was going on, and enjoyed it as much as any boy among them.

Demi composed himself, and Mr. Bhaer went on in his best English, for he had improved much in the last five years, and said the boys did it.

"This great gardener gave a dozen or so of little plots to one of his servants, and told him to do his best and see what he could raise. Now this servant was not rich, nor wise, nor very good, but he wanted to help because the gardener had been very kind to him in many ways. So he gladly took the little plots and fell to work. They were all sorts of shapes and sizes, and some were very good soil, some rather stony, and all of them needed much care, for in the rich soil the weeds grew fast, and in the poor soil there were many stones."

"What was growing in them beside the weeds, and stones?" asked Nat; so interested he forgot his shyness and spoke before them all.

"Flowers," said Mr. Bhaer, with a kind look. "Even the roughest, most neglected little bed had a bit of heart's-ease or a sprig of mignonette in it. One had roses, sweet peas, and daisies in it" — here he pinched the plump cheek of the little girl leaning on his arm. "Another had all sorts of curious plants in it, bright pebbles, a vine that went climbing up like Jack's beanstalk, and many good seeds just beginning to sprout; for, you see, *this* bed had been taken fine care of by a wise old man, who had worked in gardens of this sort all his life."

At this part of the "arrygory," Demi put his head on one side like an inquisitive bird, and fixed his bright eye on his uncle's face, as if he suspected something and was on the watch. But Mr. Bhaer looked perfectly innocent, and went on glancing from one young face to another, with a grave, wistful look, that said much to his wife, who knew how earnestly he desired to do his duty in these little garden plots.

"As I tell you, some of these beds were easy to cultivate, — that means to take care of, Daisy, — and others were very hard. There was one particularly sunshiny little bed, that might have been full of fruits and vegetables as well as flowers, only it wouldn't take any pains, and when the man sowed, well, we'll say melons in this bed, they came to nothing, because the little bed neglected them. The man was sorry, and kept on trying, though every time the crop failed, all the bed said, was, 'I forgot.'"

Here a general laugh broke out, and every one looked at Tommy, who had pricked up his ears at the word "melons," and hung down his head at the sound of his favorite excuse.

"I knew he meant us!" cried Demi, clapping his hands. "You are the man, and we are the little gardens; aren't we, Uncle Fritz?"

"You have guessed it. Now each of you tell me what crop I shall try to sow in you this spring, so that next autumn I may get a good harvest out of my twelve, no, thirteen, plots," said Mr. Bhaer, nodding at Nat as he corrected himself.

"You can't sow corn and beans and peas in us. Unless you mean we are to eat a great many and get fat," said Stuffy, with a sudden brightening of his round, dull face as the pleasing idea occurred to him.

"He don't mean that kind of seeds. He means things to make us good; and the weeds are faults," cried Demi, who usually took the lead in these talks, because he was used to this sort of thing, and liked it very much.

"Yes, each of you think what you need most, and tell me, and I will help you to grow it; only, you must do your best, or you will turn out like Tommy's melons – all leaves and no fruit. I will begin with the oldest, and ask the mother what she will have in her plot, for we are all parts of the beautiful garden, and may have rich harvests for our Master if we love Him enough," said Father Bhaer.

"I shall devote the whole of *my* plot to the largest crop of patience I can get, for that is what I need most," said Mrs. Jo, so soberly that the lads fell to thinking in good earnest what they should say when their turns came, and some among them felt a twinge of remorse, that they had helped to use up Mother Bhaer's stock of patience so fast.

Franz wanted perseverance, Tommy steadiness, Ned went in for good temper, Daisy for industry, Demi for "as much wiseness as grandpa," and Nat timidly said he wanted so many things he would let Mr. Bhaer choose for him. The others chose much the same things, and patience, good temper, and generosity seemed the favorite crops. One boy wished to like to get up early, but did not know what name to give that sort of seed; and poor Stuffy sighed out, –

"I wish I loved my lessons as much as I do my dinner, but I can't."

"We will plant self-denial, and hoe it and water it, and make it grow so well that next Christmas no one will get ill by eating too much dinner. If you exercise your mind, George, it will get hungry just as your body does, and you will love books almost as much as my philosopher here," said

Mr. Bhaer; adding, as he stroked the hair off Demi's fine forehead, "you are greedy also, my son, and you like to stuff your little mind full of fairy tales and fancies, as well as George likes to fill his little stomach with cake and candy. Both are bad, and I want you to try something better. Arithmetic is not half so pleasant as "Arabian Nights," I know, but it is a very useful thing, and now is the time to learn it, else you will be ashamed and sorry by and by."

"But, 'Harry and Lucy,' and 'Frank,' are not fairy books, and they are all full of barometers, and bricks, and shoeing horses, and useful things, and I'm fond of them; ain't I, Daisy?" said Demi, anxious to defend himself.

"So they are; but I find you reading 'Roland and Maybird' a great deal oftener than 'Harry and Lucy,' and I think you are not half as fond of 'Frank' as you are of 'Sinbad.' Come, I shall make a little bargain with you both — George shall eat but three times a day, and you shall read but one story book a week, and I will give you the new cricket ground; only you must promise to play in it," said Uncle Fritz in his persuasive way, for Stuffy hated to run about, and Demi was always reading in play hours.

"But we don't like cricket," said Demi.

"Perhaps not *now*, but you will when you know it. Besides, you do like to be generous, and the other boys want to play, and you can give them the new ground if you choose."

This was taking them both on the right side, and they agreed to the bargain, to the great satisfaction of the rest.

There was a little more talk about the gardens, and then they all sang together. The band delighted Nat, for Mrs. Bhaer played the piano, Franz the flute, Mr. Bhaer a bass viol, and he himself the violin. A very simple little concert, but all seemed to enjoy it, and old Asia, sitting in the corner, joined at times with the sweetest voice of any, for in this family, master and servant, old and young, black and white, shared in the Sunday song, which went up to the Father of them all. After this they each shook hands with Father Bhaer; Mother Bhaer kissed them every one from sixteen-year-old Franz to little Rob, who kept the tip of her nose for his own particular kisses, and then they trooped up to bed.

The light of the shaded lamp that burned in the nursery shone softly on a picture hanging at the foot of Nat's bed. There were several others on the walls, but the boy thought there must be something peculiar about this one, for it had a graceful frame of moss and cones about it, and on a little bracket underneath stood a vase of wild flowers freshly gathered from the spring woods. It was the most beautiful picture of them all, and Nat lay looking at it, dimly feeling what it meant, and wishing he knew all about it.

"That's my picture," said a little voice in the room. Nat popped up his head, and there was Demi in his nightgown pausing on his way back from Aunt Jo's chamber, whither he had gone to get a cot for a cut finger.

"What is he doing to the children?" asked Nat.

"That is Christ, the Good Man, and He is blessing the children. Don't you know about Him?" said Demi, wondering.

"Not much, but I'd like to, He looks so kind," answered Nat, whose chief knowledge of the Good Man consisted in hearing His name taken in vain.

"I know all about it, and I like it very much, because it is true," said Demi.

"Who told you?"

"My grandpa, he knows *everything*, and tells the best stories in the world. I used to play with his big books, and make bridges, and railroads, and houses, when I was a little boy," began Demi.

"How old are you now?" asked Nat, respectfully.

"Most ten."

"You know a lot of things, don't you?"

"Yes; you see my head is pretty big, and grandpa says it will take a good deal to fill it, so I keep putting pieces of wisdom into it as fast as I can," returned Demi, in his quaint way.

Nat laughed, and then said soberly, "Tell on, please."

And Demi gladly told on without pause or punctuation, "I found a very pretty book one day and wanted to play with it, but grandpa said I mustn't, and showed me the pictures, and told me about them, and I liked the stories very much, all about Joseph and his bad brothers, and the frogs that came up out of the sea, and dear little Moses in the water, and ever so many more lovely ones, but I liked about the Good Man best of all, and grandpa told it to me so many times that I learned it by heart, and he gave me this picture so I shouldn't forget, and it was put up here once when I was sick, and I left it for other sick boys to see."

"What makes Him bless the children?" asked Nat, who found something very attractive in the chief figure of the group.

"Because He loved them."

"Were they poor children?" asked Nat, wistfully.

"Yes, I think so; you see some haven't got hardly any clothes on, and the mother's don't look like rich ladies. He liked poor people, and was very good to them. He made them well, and helped them, and told rich people they must not be cross to them, and they loved Him dearly, dearly," cried Demi with enthusiasm.

"Was He rich?"

"Oh no! He was born in a barn, and was so poor. He hadn't any house to live in when He grew up, and nothing to eat sometimes, but what people gave Him, and He went round preaching to everybody, and trying to make them good, till the bad men killed Him."

"What for?" and Nat sat up in his bed to look and listen, so interested was he in this man who cared for the poor so much.

"I'll tell you all about it; Aunt Jo won't mind;" and Demi settled himself on the opposite bed, glad to tell his favorite story to so good a listener.

Nursey peeped in to see if Nat was asleep, but when she saw what was going on, she slipped away again, and went to Mrs. Bhaer, saying with her kind face full of motherly emotion, –

"Will the dear lady come and see a pretty sight? It's Nat listening with all his heart to Demi telling the story of the Christ-child, like a little white angel as he is."

Mrs. Bhaer had meant to go and talk with Nat a moment before he slept, for she had found that a serious word spoken at this time often did much good. But when she stole to the nursery door, and saw Nat eagerly drinking in the words of his little friend, while Demi told the sweet and solemn story as it had been taught him, speaking softly as he sat with his beautiful eyes fixed on the tender face above them, her own filled with tears, and she went silently away, thinking to herself, –

"Demi is unconsciously helping the poor boy better than I can; I will not spoil it by a single word."

The murmur of the childish voice went on for a long time, as one innocent heart preached that great sermon to another, and no one hushed it. When it ceased at last, and Mrs. Bhaer went to take away the lamp, Demi was gone and Nat fast asleep, lying with his face toward the picture, as if he had already learned to love the Good Man who loved little children, and was a faithful friend to the poor. The boy's face was very placid, and as she looked at it she felt that if a single day of care and kindness had done so much, a year of patient cultivation would surely bring a grateful harvest from his neglected garden, which was already sown with the best of all seed by the little missionary in the nightgown.

CHAPTER FOUR

STEPPING-STONES

~

When Nat went into school on Monday morning, he quaked inwardly, for now he thought he should have to display his ignorance before them all. But Mr. Bhaer gave him a seat in the deep window, where he could turn his back on the others, and Franz heard him say his lessons there, so no one could hear his blunders or see how he blotted his copy book. He was truly grateful for this, and toiled away so diligently that Mr. Bhaer said, smiling, when he saw his hot face and inky fingers, –

"Don't work so hard, my boy; you will tire yourself out, and there is time enough."

"But I *must* work hard, or I can't catch up with the others. They know heaps, and I don't know anything," said Nat, who had been reduced to a state of despair by hearing the boys recite their grammar, history, and geography with what he thought amazing ease and accuracy.

"You know a good many things which they don't," said Mr. Bhaer, sitting down beside him, while Franz led a class of small students through the intricacies of the multiplication table.

"Do I?" and Nat looked utterly incredulous.

"Yes; for one thing, you can keep your temper, and Jack, who is quick at numbers, cannot; that is an excellent lesson, and I think you have learned it well. Then, you can play the violin, and not one of the lads can, though they want to do it very much. But, best of all, Nat, you really care to learn something, and that is half the battle. It seems hard at first, and you will feel discouraged, but plod away, and things will get easier and easier as you go on."

Nat's face had brightened more and more as he listened, for, small as the list of his learning was, it cheered him immensely to feel that he had anything to fall back upon. "Yes, I can keep my temper — father's beating taught me that; and I can fiddle, though I don't know where the Bay of Biscay is," he thought, with a sense of comfort impossible to express. Then he said aloud, and so earnestly that Demi heard him, —

"I *do* want to learn, and I *will* try. I never went to school, but I couldn't help it; and if the fellows don't laugh at me, I guess I'll get on first-rate — you and the lady are so good to me."

"They shan't laugh at you; if they do, I'll — I'll — tell them not to," cried Demi, quite forgetting where he was.

The class stopped in the middle of 7 times 9, and every one looked up to see what was going on.

Thinking that a lesson in learning to help one another was better than arithmetic just then, Mr. Bhaer told them about Nat, making such an interesting and touching little story out of it that the good-hearted lads all promised to lend him a hand, and felt quite honored to be called upon to impart their stores of wisdom to the chap who fiddled so capitally. This appeal established the right feeling among them, and Nat had few hindrances to struggle against, for every one was glad to give him a "boost" up the ladder of learning.

Till he was stronger, much study was not good for him, however, and Mrs. Jo found various amusements in the house for him while others were at their books. But his garden was his best medicine, and he worked away like a beaver, preparing his little farm, sowing his beans, watching eagerly to see them grow, and rejoicing over each green leaf and slender stalk that shot up and flourished in the warm spring weather. Never was a garden more faithfully hoed; Mr. Bhaer really feared that nothing would find time to grow, Nat kept up such a stirring of the soil; so he gave him easy jobs in the flower garden or among the strawberries, where he worked and hummed as busily as the bees booming all about him.

"This is the crop I like best," Mrs. Bhaer used to say, as she pinched the once thin cheeks now getting plump and ruddy, or stroked the bent shoulders that were slowly straightening up with healthful work, good food, and the absence of that heavy burden, poverty.

Demi was his little friend, Tommy his patron, and Daisy the comforter of all his woes; for, though the children were younger than he, his timid spirit found a pleasure in their innocent society, and rather shrunk from the rough sports of the elder lads. Mr. Laurence did not forget him, but sent clothes and books, music and kind messages, and now and then came out to see how his boy was getting on, or took him into town to a concert; on which occasions Nat felt himself translated into the seventh heaven of bliss, for he went to Mr. Laurence's great house, saw his pretty wife and little fairy of a daughter, had a good dinner, and was made so comfortable, that he talked and dreamed of it for days and nights afterward.

It takes so little to make a child happy, that it is a pity in a world full of sunshine and pleasant things, that there should be any wistful faces, empty hands, or lonely little hearts. Feeling this, the Bhaers gathered up all the crumbs they could find to feed their flock of hungry sparrows, for they were not rich, except in charity. Many of Mrs. Jo's friends who had nurseries sent her the toys of which their children so soon tired, and in mending these Nat found an employment that just suited him. He was very neat and skilful with those slender fingers of his, and passed many a rainy afternoon with his gum bottle, paintbox, and knife, repairing furniture, animals, and games, while Daisy was dressmaker to the dilapidated dolls. As fast as the toys were mended, they were put carefully away in a certain drawer which was to furnish forth a Christmas tree for all the poor children of the neighborhood, that being the way the Plumfield boys celebrated the birthday of Him who loved the poor and blessed the little ones.

Demi was never tired of reading and explaining his favorite books, and many a pleasant hour did they spend in the old willow, reveling over "Robinson Crusoe," "Arabian Nights," "Edgeworth's Tales," and the other dear immortal stories that will delight children for centuries to come. This opened a new world to Nat, and his eagerness to see what came next in the story helped him on till he could read as well as anybody, and felt so rich and proud with his new accomplishment, that there was danger of his being as much of a bookworm as Demi.

Another helpful thing happened in a most unexpected and agreeable manner. Several of the boys were "in business," as they called it, for most of them were poor, and knowing that they would have their own way to make by and by, the Bhaers encouraged any efforts at independence. Tommy sold his eggs; Jack speculated in live stock; Franz helped in the teaching, and was paid for it; Ned had a taste for carpentry, and a turning lathe was set up for him in which he turned all sorts of useful or pretty things, and sold them; while Demi constructed water mills, whirligigs, and unknown machines of an intricate and useless nature, and disposed of them to the boys.

"Let him be a mechanic if he likes," said Mr. Bhaer. "Give a boy a trade, and he is independent. Work is wholesome, and whatever talent these lads possess, be it for poetry, or plowing, it shall be cultivated and made useful to them if possible."

So when Nat came running to him one day to ask with an excited face, —

"Can I go and fiddle for some people who are to have a picnic in our woods? They will pay me, and I'd like to earn some money as the other boys do, and fiddling is the only way I know how to do it."

Mr. Bhaer answered readily, —

"Go, and welcome. It is an easy and a pleasant way to work, and I am glad it is offered you."

Nat went, and did so well, that when he came home he had two dollars in his pocket, which he displayed with intense satisfaction, as he told how much he had enjoyed the afternoon, how kind the young people were, and how they had praised his dance music, and promised to have him again.

"It is so much nicer than fiddling in the street, for then I got none of the money, and now I have it all, and a good time besides. I'm in business now as well as Tommy and Jack, and I like it ever so much," said Nat, proudly patting the old pocketbook, and feeling like a millionaire already.

He *was* in business truly, for picnics were plenty as summer opened, and Nat's skill was in great demand. He was always at liberty to go if lessons were not neglected, and if the picnickers were respectable young people. For Mr. Bhaer explained to him that a good plain education is necessary for every one, and that no amount of money should hire him to go where he might be tempted to do wrong. Nat quite agreed to this, and it was a pleasant sight to see the innocent-hearted lad go driving away in the gay wagons that stopped at the gate for him, or to hear him come fiddling home tired but happy, with his well-earned money in one pocket, and some "goodies" from the feast for Daisy or little Ted, whom he never forgot.

"I'm going to save up till I get enough to buy a violin for myself, and then I can earn my own living, can't I?" he used to say, as he brought his dollars to Mr. Bhaer to keep.

"I hope so, Nat; but we must get you strong and hearty first, and put a little more knowledge into this musical head of yours. Then Mr. Laurie will find you a place somewhere, and in a few years we will all come to hear you play in public."

With much congenial work, encouragement, and hope, Nat found life getting easier and happier every day, and made such progress in his music lessons, that his teacher forgave his slowness in some other things, knowing very well that where the heart is the mind works best. The only punishment the boy ever needed for neglect of more important lessons was to hang up the fiddle and the bow for a day. The fear of losing his bosom friend entirely made him go at his books with a will; and having proved that he *could* master the lessons, what was the use of saying "I can't"?

Daisy had a great love of music, and a great reverence for any one who could make it, and she was often found sitting on the stairs outside Nat's door while he was practising. This pleased him very much, and he played his best for that one quiet little listener; for she never would come in, but preferred to sit sewing her gay patchwork, or tending one of her many dolls, with an expression of dreamy pleasure on her face that made Aunt Jo say, with tears in her eyes, —

"So like my Beth," and go softly by, lest even her familiar presence mar the child's sweet satisfaction.

Nat was very fond of Mrs. Bhaer, but found something even more attractive in the good professor, who took fatherly care of the shy, feeble boy, who had barely escaped with his life from the rough sea on which his little boat had been tossing rudderless for twelve years. Some good angel must have watched over him, for though his body had suffered, his soul seemed to have taken little harm, and came ashore as innocent as a shipwrecked baby. Perhaps his love of music kept it sweet in spite of the discord all about him; Mr. Laurie said so, and he ought to know. However that might be, Father Bhaer took real pleasure in fostering poor Nat's virtues, and in curing his faults, finding his new pupil as docile and affectionate as a girl. He often called Nat his "daughter" when speaking of him to Mrs. Jo, and she used to laugh at his fancy, for Madame liked manly boys, and thought Nat amiable but weak, though you never would have guessed it, for she petted him as she did Daisy, and he thought her a very delightful woman.

One fault of Nat's gave the Bhaers much anxiety, although they saw how it had been strengthened by fear and ignorance. I regret to say that Nat sometimes told lies. Not very black ones, seldom getting deeper than grey, and often the mildest of white fibs; but that did not matter, a lie is a lie, and though we all tell many polite untruths in this queer world of ours, it is not right, and everybody knows it.

"You cannot be too careful; watch your tongue, and eyes, and hands, for it is easy to tell, and look, and act untruth," said Mr. Bhaer, in one of the talks he had with Nat about his chief temptation.

"I know it, and I don't mean to , but it's so much easier to get along if you ain't very fussy about being exactly true. I used to tell them because I was afraid of father and Nicolo, and now I do sometimes because the boys laugh at me. I know it's bad, but I forget,' and Nat looked much depressed by his sins.

"When I was a little lad I used to tell lies! Ach! what fibs they were, and my old grandmother cured me of it – how, do you think? My parents had talked, and cried, and punished, but still did I forget as you. Then said the dear old grandmother, 'I shall help you to remember, and put a check on this unruly part,' with that she drew out my tongue and snipped the end with her scissors till the blood ran. That was terrible, you may believe, but it did me much good, because it was sore for days, and every word I said came so slowly that I had time to think. After that I was more careful, and

The end of the pillow frolic. (Chapter 1)

*Demi settled himself on the opposite bed, glad to
tell his story to so good a listener. (Chapter 3)*

got on better, for I feared the big scissors. Yet the dear grandmother was most kind to me in all things, and when she lay dying far away in Nuremberg, she prayed that little Fritz might love God and tell the truth."

"I never had any grandmothers, but if you think it will cure me, I'll let you snip my tongue," said Nat, heroically, for he dreaded pain, yet did wish to stop fibbing.

Mr. Bhaer smiled, but shook his head.

"I have a better way than that; I tried it once before and it worked well. See now, when you tell a lie I will not punish you, but you shall punish me."

"How?" asked Nat, startled at the idea.

"You shall ferule me in the good old-fashioned way; I seldom do it myself, but it may make you remember better to give me pain than to feel it yourself."

"Strike you? Oh, I couldn't!" cried Nat.

"Then mind that tripping tongue of thine. I have no wish to be hurt, but I would gladly bear much pain to cure this fault."

This suggestion made such an impression on Nat, that for a long time he set a watch upon his lips and was desperately accurate, for Mr. Bhaer judged rightly, that love of him would be more powerful with Nat than fear for himself. But alas! one sad day Nat was off his guard, and when peppery Emil threatened to thrash him, if it was he who had run over his garden and broken down his best hills of corn, Nat declared he didn't, and then was ashamed to own up that he did do it, when Jack was chasing him the night before.

He thought no one would find it out, but Tommy happened to see him, and when Emil spoke of it a day or two later, Tommy gave his evidence, and Mr. Bhaer heard it. School was over, and they were all standing about in the hall, and Mr. Bhaer had just sat down on the straw settee, to enjoy his frolic with Teddy; but when he heard Tommy, and saw Nat turn scarlet, and look at him with a frightened face, he put the little boy down, saying, "Go to thy mother, bübchen, I will come soon," and taking Nat by the hand led him into the school, and shut the door.

The boys looked at one another in silence for a minute, then Tommy slipped out and peeping in at the half-closed blinds, beheld a sight that quite bewildered him. Mr. Bhaer had just taken down the long rule that hung over his desk, so seldom used that it was covered with dust.

"My eye! he's going to come down heavy on Nat this time. Wish I hadn't told," thought good-natured Tommy, for to be feruled was the deepest disgrace at this school.

"You remember what I told you last time?" said Mr. Bhaer, sorrowfully, not angrily.

"Yes; but please don't make me, I can't bear it," cried Nat, backing up against the door with both hands behind him, and a face full of distress.

"Why don't he up and take it like a man? I would," thought Tommy, though his heart beat fast at the sight.

"I shall keep my word, and you must remember to tell the truth. Obey me, Nat, take this and give me six good strokes."

Tommy was so staggered by this last speech that he nearly tumbled down the bank, but saved himself, and hung on to the window ledge, staring in with eyes as round as the stuffed owl's on the chimney piece.

Nat took the rule, for when Mr. Bhaer spoke in that tone every one obeyed him, and looking as scared and guilty as if about to stab his master, he gave two feeble blows on the broad hand held out to him. Then he stopped and looked up half-blind with tears, but Mr. Bhaer said steadily, —

"Go on, and strike harder."

As if seeing that it must be done, and eager to have the hard task soon over, Nat drew his sleeve across his eyes and gave two more quick hard strokes that reddened the hand, yet hurt the giver more.

"Isn't that enough?" he asked in a breathless sort of tone.

"Two more," was all the answer, and he gave them, hardly seeing where they fell, then threw the rule across the room, and hugging the kind hand in both his own, laid his face down on it sobbing out in a passion of love, and shame, and penitence, —

"I will remember! Oh! I will!"

Then Mr. Bhaer put an arm about him, and said in a tone as compassionate as it had just now been firm, —

"I think you will. Ask the dear God to help you, and try to spare us both another scene like this."

Tommy saw no more, for he crept back to the hall, looking so excited and sober that the boys crowded round him to ask what was being done to Nat.

In a most impressive whisper Tommy told them, and they looked as if the sky were about to fall, for this reversing the order of things almost took their breath away.

"He made me do the same thing once," said Emil, as if confessing a crime of the deepest dye.

"And you hit him? dear old Father Bhaer? By thunder, I'd just like to see you do it now!" said Ned, collaring Emil in a fit of righteous wrath.

"It was ever so long ago. I'd rather have my head cut off than do it now," and Emil mildly laid Ned on his back instead of cuffing him, as he would have felt it his duty to do on any less solemn occasion.

"How could you?" said Demi, appalled at the idea.

"I was hopping mad at the time, and thought I shouldn't mind a bit, rather like it perhaps. But when I'd hit Uncle one good crack, everything he had ever done for me came into my head all at once somehow, and I couldn't go on. No, sir! if he'd laid me down and walked on me, I wouldn't have minded, I felt so mean," and Emil gave himself a good thump in the chest to express his sense of remorse for the past.

"Nat's crying like anything, and feels no end sorry, so don't let's say a word about it; will we?" said tender-hearted Tommy.

"Of course we won't, but it's awful to tell lies," and Demi looked as if he found the awfulness much increased when the punishment fell not upon the sinner, but his best Uncle Fritz.

"Suppose we all clear out, so Nat can cut upstairs if he wants to," proposed Franz, and led the way to the barn, their refuge in troublous times.

Nat did not come to dinner, but Mrs. Jo took some up to him, and said a tender word, which did him good, though he could not look at her. By and by the lads playing outside heard the violin, and said among themselves, "He's all right now." He was all right, but felt shy about going down, till, opening his door to slip away into the woods, he found Daisy sitting on the stairs with neither work nor doll, only her little handkerchief in her hand, as if she had been mourning for her captive friend.

"I'm going to walk; want to come?" asked Nat, trying to look as if nothing was the matter, yet feeling very grateful for her silent sympathy, because he fancied every one must look upon him as a wretch.

"Oh, yes!" and Daisy ran for her hat, proud to be chosen as a companion by one of the big boys.

The others saw them go, but no one followed, for boys have a great deal more delicacy than they get credit for, and the lads instinctively felt that, when in disgrace, gentle little Daisy was their most congenial friend.

The walk did Nat good, and he came home quieter than usual, but looking cheerful again, and hung all over with daisy chains, made by his little playmate while he lay on the grass and told her stories.

No one said a word about the scene of the morning, but its effect was all the more lasting for that reason, perhaps. Nat tried his very best, and found much help, not only from the earnest little prayers he prayed to his Friend in heaven, but also in the patient care of the earthly friend, whose kind hand he never touched without remembering that it had willingly borne pain for his sake.

CHAPTER FIVE

PATTY PANS

~

"What's the matter, Daisy?"

"The boys won't let me play with them."

"Why not?"

"They say girls can't play football."

"They can, for I've done it!" and Mrs. Bhaer laughed at the remembrance of certain youthful frolics.

"I know I can play; Demi and I used to, and have nice times, but he won't let me now because the other boys laugh at him," and Daisy looked deeply grieved at her brother's hardness of heart.

"On the whole, I think he is right, deary. It's all very well when you two are alone, but it is too rough a game for you with a dozen boys; so I'd find some nice little play for myself."

"I'm tired of playing alone!" and Daisy's tone was very mournful.

"I'll play with you by and by, but just now I must fly about and get things ready for a trip into town. You shall go with me and see mamma, and if you like you can stay with her."

"I should like to go and see her and baby Josy, but I'd rather come back, please. Demi would miss me, and I love to be here, Aunty.'"

"You can't get on without your Demi, can you?" and Aunt Jo looked as if she quite understood the love of the little girl for her only brother.

"'Course I can't; we're twins, and so we love each other more than other people," answered Daisy, with a brightening face, for she considered being a twin one of the highest honors she could ever receive.

"Now, what will you do with your little self while I fly round?" asked Mrs. Bhaer, who was whisking piles of linen into a wardrobe with great rapidity.

"I don't know, I'm tired of dolls and things; I wish you'd make up a new play for me, Aunty Jo," said Daisy, swinging listlessly on the door.

"I shall have to think of a brand new one, and it will take me some time; so suppose you go down and see what Asia has for your lunch," suggested Mrs. Bhaer, thinking that would be a good way in which to dispose of the little hindrance for a time.

"Yes, I think I'd like that, if she isn't cross," and Daisy slowly departed to the kitchen, where Asia, the black cook, reigned undisturbed.

In five minutes Daisy was back again, with a wide-awake face, a bit of dough in her hand and dab of flour on her little nose.

"O Aunty! please could I make gingersnaps and things? Asia isn't cross, and she says I may, and it would be such fun, please do," cried Daisy, all in one breath.

"Just the thing, go and welcome, make what you like, and stay as long as you please," answered Mrs. Bhaer, much relieved, for sometimes the one little girl was harder to amuse than the dozen boys.

Daisy ran off, and while she worked, Aunt Jo racked her brain for a new play. Suddenly she seemed to have an idea, for she smiled to herself, slammed the doors of the wardrobe, and walked briskly away, saying, "I'll do it, if it's a possible thing!"

What it was no one found out that day, but Aunt Jo's eyes twinkled so when she told Daisy she had thought of a new play, and was going to buy it, that Daisy was much excited and asked questions all the way into town, without getting answers that told her anything. She was left at home to play with the new baby and delight her mother's eyes, while Aunt Jo went off shopping. When she came back with all sorts of queer parcels in corners of the carryall, Daisy was so full of curiosity that she wanted to go back to Plumfield at once. But her aunt would not be hurried, and made a long call in mamma's room, sitting on the floor with baby in her lap, making Mrs. Brooke laugh at the pranks of the boys, and all sorts of droll nonsense.

How her aunt told the secret Daisy could not imagine, but her mother evidently knew it, for she said, as she tied on the little bonnet and kissed the rosy little face inside, "Be a good child, my Daisy, and learn the nice new play Aunty has got for you. It's a most useful and interesting one, and it is very kind of her to play it with you, because she does not like it very well herself."

This last speech made the two ladies laugh heartily, and increased Daisy's bewilderment. As they drove away something rattled in the back of the carriage.

"What's that?" asked Daisy, pricking up her ears.

"The new play." answered Mrs. Jo, solemnly.

"What is it made of?" cried Daisy.

"Iron, tin, wood, brass, sugar, salt, coal, and a hundred other things."

"How strange! What color is it?"

"All sorts of colors."

"Is it large?"

"Part of it is, and a part isn't.'

"Did I ever see one?"

"Ever so many, but never one as nice as this."

"Oh! what can it be? I can't wait. When *shall* I see it?" and Daisy bounced up and down with impatience.

"Tomorrow morning, after lessons."

"Is it for the boys too?"

"No, all for you and Bess. The boys will like to see it, and want to play one part of it. But you can do as you like about letting them."

"I'll let Demi, if he wants to."

"No fear that they won't all want to, especially Stuffy," and Mrs. Bhaer's eyes twinkled more than ever, as she patted a queer, knobby bundle in her lap.

"Let me feel just once," prayed Daisy.

"Not a feel; you'd guess in a minute and spoil the fun."

Daisy groaned and then smiled all over her face, for through a little hole in the paper she caught a glimpse of something bright.

"How *can* I wait so long? Couldn't I see it today?"

"Oh dear, no! it has got to be arranged, and ever so many parts fixed in their places. I promised Uncle Teddy that you shouldn't see it till it was all in apple-pie order."

"If Uncle knows about it then it *must* be splendid!" cried Daisy, clapping her hands; for this kind, rich, jolly uncle of hers was as good as a fairy godmother to the children, and was always planning merry surprises, pretty gifts, and droll amusements for them.

"Yes; Teddy went and bought it with me, and we had such fun in the shop choosing the different parts. He would have everything fine and large, and my little plan got regularly splendid when he took hold. You must give him your very best kiss when he comes, for he is the kindest uncle that ever went and bought a charming little coo – Bless me! I nearly told you what it was!" and Mrs. Bhaer cut that most interesting word short off in the middle, and began to look over her bills as if afraid she would let the cat out of the bag if she talked any more. Daisy folded her hands with an air of resignation, and sat quite still trying to think what play had a "coo" in it.

When they got home she eyed every bundle that was taken out, and one large heavy one, which Franz took straight up stairs and hid in the nursery, filled her with amazement and curiosity. Something very mysterious went on up there that afternoon, for Franz was hammering, and Asia trotting up and down, and Aunt Jo flying around like a will-o'-the-wisp, with all sorts of things under her apron, while little Ted, who was the only child admitted, because he couldn't talk plain, babbled and laughed, and tried to tell what the "sumpin pitty" was.

All this made Daisy half wild, and her excitement spread among the boys, who quite overwhelmed Mother Bhaer with offers of assistance, which she declined by quoting their own words to Daisy,

"Girls can't play with boys. This is for Daisy, and Bess, and me, so we don't want you." Whereupon the young gentlemen meekly retired, and invited Daisy to a game of marbles, horse, football, anything she liked, with a sudden warmth and politeness which astonished her innocent little soul.

Thanks to these attentions, she got through the afternoon, went early to bed, and next morning did her lessons with an energy which made Uncle Fritz wish that a new game could be invented every day. Quite a thrill pervaded the schoolroom when Daisy was dismissed at eleven o'clock, for every one knew that *now* she was going to have the new and mysterious play.

Many eyes followed her as she ran away, and Demi's mind was so distracted by this event that when Franz asked him where the desert of Sahara was, he mournfully replied, "In the nursery," and the whole school laughed at him.

"Aunt Jo, I've done all my lessons, and I can't wait one single minute more!" cried Daisy, flying into Mrs. Bhaer's room.

"It's all ready, come on," and tucking Ted under one arm, and her work basket under the other, Aunt Jo promptly led the way upstairs.

"I don't see anything," said Daisy, staring about her as she got inside the nursery door.

"Do you hear anything?" asked Aunt Jo, catching Ted back by his little frock as he was making straight for one side of the room.

Daisy did hear an odd crackling, and then a purry little sound as of a kettle singing. These noises came from behind a curtain drawn before a deep bay window. Daisy snatched it back, gave one joyful "Oh!" and then stood gazing with delight at — what do you think?

A wide seat ran round the three sides of the window; on one side hung and stood all sorts of pots and pans, gridirons and skillets; on the other side a small dinner and tea set, and on the middle part a cooking stove. Not a tin one, that was of no use, but a real iron stove, big enough to cook for a large family of very hungry dolls. But the best of it was that a real fire burned in it, real steam came out of the nose of the little teakettle, and the lid of the little boiler actually danced a jig, the water inside bubbled so hard. A pane of glass had been taken out and replaced by a sheet of tin, with a hole for the small funnel, and real smoke went sailing away outside so naturally, that it did one's heart good to see it. The box of wood with a hod of charcoal stood near by; just above hung dustpan, brush and broom; a little market basket was on the low table at which Daisy used to play, and over the back of the little chair hung a white apron with a bib, and a droll mob cap. The sun shone in as if he enjoyed the fun, the little stove roared beautifully, the kettle steamed, the new tins sparkled on the walls, the pretty china stood in tempting rows, and it was altogether as cheery and complete a kitchen as any child could desire.

Daisy stood quite still after the first glad "Oh!" but her eyes went quickly from one charming object to another, brightening as they looked, till they came to Aunt Jo's merry face; there they stopped as the happy little girl hugged her, saying gratefully, –

"Oh, Aunty, it's a splendid new play! can I really cook at the dear stove, and have parties and sweep, and make fires that truly burn? I like it so much! What made you think of it?'

"Your liking to make gingersnaps with Asia made me think of it," said Mrs. Bhaer, holding Daisy, who frisked as if she would fly. "I knew Asia wouldn't let you mess in her kitchen very often, and it wouldn't be safe at this fire up here, so I thought I'd see if I could find a little stove for you, and teach you to cook; that would be fun, and useful too. So I traveled round among the toy shops, but everything large cost too much and I was thinking I should have to give it up, when I met Uncle Teddy. As soon as he knew what I was about, he said he wanted to help, and insisted on buying the biggest toy stove we could find. I scolded, but he only laughed, and teased me about my cooking when we were young, and said I must teach Bess as well as you, and went on buying all sorts of nice little things for my 'cooking class', as he called it."

"I'm so glad you met him!" said Daisy, as Mrs. Jo stopped to laugh at the memory of the funny time she had with Uncle Teddy.

"You must study hard and learn to make all kinds of things, for he says he shall come out to tea very often, and expects something uncommonly nice."

"It's the sweetest, dearest kitchen in the world, and I'd rather study with it than do anything else. Can't I learn pies, and cake, and macaroni, and everything?" cried Daisy, dancing round the room with a new saucepan in one hand and the tiny poker in the other.

"All in good time. This is to be a useful play, I am to help you, and you are to be my cook, so I shall tell you what to do, and show you how. Then we shall have things fit to eat, and you will be really learning how to cook on a small scale. I'll call you Sally, and say you are a new girl just come," added Mrs. Jo, setting down to work, while Teddy sat on the floor sucking his thumb, and staring at the stove as if it were a live thing, whose appearance deeply interested him.

"That will be *so* lovely! What shall I do first?" asked Sally, with such a happy face and willing air that Aunt Jo wished all new cooks were half as pretty and pleasant.

"First of all, put on this clean cap and apron. I am rather old-fashioned, and I like my cook to be very tidy."

Sally tucked her curly hair into the round cap, and put on the apron without a murmur, though usually she rebelled against bibs.

"Now you can put things in order, and wash up the new china. The old set needs washing also, for my last girl was apt to leave it in a sad state after a party."

Aunt Jo spoke quite soberly, but Sally laughed, for she knew who the untidy girl was who had left the cups sticky. Then she turned up her cuffs, and with a sigh of satisfaction began to stir about her kitchen, having little raptures now and then over the "sweet rolling pin," the "darling dish-tub," or the "cunning pepper pot."

"Now, Sally, take your basket and go market; here is the list of things I want for dinner,' said Mrs. Jo, giving her a bit of paper when the dishes were all in order.

"Where is the market?" asked Daisy, thinking that the new play got more and more interesting every minute.

"Asia is the market."

Away went Sally, causing another stir in the schoolroom as she passed the door in her new costume, and whispered to Demi, with a face full of delight, "It's a perfectly splendid play!"

Old Asia enjoyed the joke as much as Daisy, and laughed jollily as the little girl came flying into the room with her cap all on one side, the lids of her basket rattling like castanets, and looking like a very crazy little cook.

"Mrs. Aunt Jo wants these things, and I must have them right away," said Daisy, importantly.

"Let's see, honey; here's two pounds of steak, potatoes, squash, apples, bread, and butter. The meat ain't come yet; when it does I'll send it up. The other things are all handy."

Then Asia packed one potato, one apple, a bit of squash, a little pat of butter, and a roll, into the basket, telling Sally to be on the watch for the butcher's boy, because he sometimes played tricks.

"Who he is?" and Daisy hoped it would be Demi.

"You'll see," was all Asia would say; and Sally went off in great spirits, signing a verse from dear Mary Howitt's sweet story in rime, —

> *"Away went little Mabel,*
> *With the wheaten cake so fine,*
> *The new made pot of butter,*
> *And the little flask of wine."*

"Put everything but the apple into the store closet for the present," said Mrs. Jo, when the cook got home.

There was a cupboard under the middle shelf, and on opening the door fresh delights appeared. One half was evidently the cellar, for wood, coal, and kindlings were piled there. The other half was full of little jars, boxes, and all sorts of droll contrivances for holding small quantities of flour, meal, sugar, salt, and other household stores. A pot of jam was there, a little tin box of gingerbread, a cologne bottle full of currant wine, and a tiny canister of tea. But the crowning charm was two doll's pans of new milk with cream actually rising on it, and a wee skimmer all ready to skim it with. Daisy clasped her hands at this delicious spectacle, and wanted to skim immediately. But Aunt Jo said, —

"Not yet; you will want the cream to eat on your apple pie at dinner, and must not disturb it till then."

"Am I going to have pie?" cried Daisy, hardly believing that such bliss could be in store for her.

"Yes; if your oven does well we will have two pies, one apple and one strawberry," said Mrs. Jo, who was nearly as interested in the new play as Daisy herself.

"Oh, what next?" asked Sally, all impatience to begin.

"Shut the lower draught of the stove, so that the oven may heat. Then wash your hands and get out the flour, sugar, salt, butter and cinnamon. See if the pie board is clean, and pare your apple ready to put in."

Daisy got things together with as little noise and spilling as could be expected, from so young a cook.

"I really don't know how to measure for such tiny pies; I must guess at it, and if these don't succeed, we must try again," said Mrs. Jo, looking rather perplexed, and very much amused with the small concern before her. "Take that little pan full of flour, put in a pinch of salt, and then rub in as much butter as will go on that plate. Always remember to put your dry things together first, and then the wet. It mixes better so."

"I know how; I saw Asia do it. Don't I butter the pie plates too? She did, the first thing," said Daisy, whisking the flour about at a great rate.

"Quite right! I do believe you have a gift for cooking, you take to it so cleverly," said Aunt Jo, approvingly. "Now a dash of cold water, just enough to wet it; then scatter some flour on the board, work in a little, and roll the paste out; yes, that's the way. Now put dabs of butter all over it, and roll it out again. We won't have our pastry very rich, or the dolls will get dyspeptic."

Daisy laughed at the idea, and scattered the dabs with a liberal hand. Then she rolled and rolled with her delightful little pin, and having got her paste ready proceeded to cover the plates with it. Next the apple was sliced in, sugar and cinnamon lavishly sprinkled over it, and then the top crust put on with breathless care.

"I always wanted to cut them round, and Asia never would let me. How nice it is to do it all my own self!" said Daisy, as the little knife went clipping round the doll's plate poised on her hand.

All cooks, even the best, meet with mishaps sometimes, and Sally's first one occurred then, for the knife went so fast that the plate slipped, turned a somersault in the air, and landed the dear little pie upside down on the floor. Sally screamed, Mrs. Jo laughed, Teddy scrambled to get it, and for a moment confusion reigned in the new kitchen.

"It didn't spill or break, because I pinched the edges together so hard; it isn't hurt a bit, so I'll prick holes in it, and then it will be ready," said Sally, picking up the capsized treasure and putting it into shape with a childlike disregard of the dust it had gathered in its fall.

"My new cook has a good temper, I see, and that is such a comfort," said Mrs. Jo. "Now open the jar of strawberry jam, fill the uncovered pie, and put some strips of paste over the top as Asia does."

"I'll make a D in the middle and have zigzags all round, that will be so interesting when I come to eat it," said Sally, loading her pie with quirls and flourishes that would have driven a real pastry cook wild. "*Now* I put them in!" she exclaimed; when the last grimy knob had been carefully planted in the red field of jam, and with an air of triumph she shut them into the little oven.

"Clear up your things; a good cook never lets her utensils collect. Then pare your squash and potatoes.'

"There is only one potato," giggled Sally.

"Cut it in four pieces, so it will go into the little kettle, and put the bits into cold water till it is time to cook them."

"Do I soak the squash too?"

"No, indeed! just pare it and cut it up, and put it into the steamer over the pot. It is drier so, though it takes longer to cook.'

Here a scratching at the door caused Sally to run and open it, when Kit appeared with a covered basket in his mouth.

"Here the butcher's boy!" cried Daisy, much tickled at the idea, as she relieved him of his load, whereat he licked his lips and began to beg, evidently thinking that it was his own dinner, for he often carried it to his master in that way. Being undeceived, he departed in great wrath and barked all the way down stairs to ease his wounded feelings.

In the basket were two bits of steak (doll's pounds), a baked pear, a small cake, and paper with them on which Asia had scrawled, "For Missy's lunch, if her cookin' don't turn out well."

"I don't want any of her old pears and things; my cooking *will* turn out well, and I'll have a splendid dinner; see if I don't!" cried Daisy, indignantly.

"We may like them if company should come. It is always well to have something in the storeroom," said Aunt Jo, who had been taught this valuable fact by a series of domestic panics.

"Me is hundry," announced Teddy, who began to think what with so much cooking going on it was about time for somebody to eat something. His mother gave him her work basket to rummage, hoping to keep him quiet till dinner was ready, and returned to her housekeeping.

"Put on your vegetables, set the table, and then have some coals kindling ready for the steak."

What a thing it was to see the potatoes bobbing about in the little pot; to peep at the squash getting soft so fast in the tiny steamer; to whisk open the oven door every five minutes to see how the pies got on, and at last when the coals were red and glowing, to put two real steaks on a finger-long gridiron and proudly turn them with a fork. The potatoes were done first, and no wonder, for they had boiled frantically all the while. They were pounded up with a little pestle, had much butter and no salt put in (cook forgot it in the excitement of the moment), then it was made into a mound in a gay, red dish, smoothed over with a knife dipped in milk, and put in the oven to brown.

So absorbed in these last performances had Sally been, that she forgot her pastry till she opened the door to put in the potato, then a wail arose, for, alas! alas! the little pies were burnt black!

"Oh, my pies! my darling pies! they are all spoiled!" cried poor Sally, wringing her dirty little hands as she surveyed the ruin of her work. The tart was especially pathetic, for the quirls and zigzags stuck up in all directions from the blackened jelly, like the walls and chimney of a house after a fire.

"Dear, dear, I forgot to remind you to take them out; it's just my luck," said Aunt Jo, remorsefully. "Don't cry, darling, it was my fault; we'll try again after dinner,' she added, as a great tear dropped from Sally's eyes and sizzled on the hot ruins of the tart.

More would have followed, if the steak had not blazed up just then, and so occupied the attention of cook, that she quickly forgot the lost pastry.

"Put the meat-dish and your own plates down to warm, while you mash the squash with butter, salt, and a little pepper on the top," said Mrs. Jo, devoutly hoping that the dinner would meet with no further disasters.

The "cunning pepper pot" soothed Sally's feelings, and she dished up her squash in fine style. The dinner was safely put upon the table; the six dolls were seated three on a side; Teddy took the bottom, and Sally the top. When all were settled, it was a most imposing spectacle, for one doll was in full ball costume, another in her night-gown; Jerry, the worsted boy, wore his red winter suit, while Annabella, the noseless darling, was airily attired in nothing but her own kid skin. Teddy, as father of the family, behaved with great propriety, for he smilingly devoured everything offered him, and did not find a single fault. Daisy beamed upon her company like the weary, warm, but hospitable hostess, so often to be seen at larger tables than this, and did the honors with an air of innocent satisfaction, which we do *not* often see elsewhere.

The steak was so tough, that the little carving knife would not cut it; the potato did not go round, and the squash was very lumpy; but the guests appeared politely unconscious of these trifles; and the master and mistress of the house cleared the table with appetites that any one might envy them. The joy of skimming a jug full of cream mitigated the anguish felt for the loss of the pies, and Asia's despised cake proved a treasure in the way of dessert.

"That is the nicest lunch I ever had; can't I do it every day?" asked Daisy as she scraped up and ate the leavings all round.

"You can cook things every day after lessons, but I prefer that you should eat your dishes at your regular meals, and only have a bit of gingerbread for lunch. To-day, being the first time, I don't mind, but we must keep our rules. This afternoon you can make something for tea if you like," said Mrs. Jo, who had enjoyed the dinner party very much, though no one had invited her to partake.

"Do let me make flapjacks for Demi, he loves them so, and it's such fun to turn them and put sugar in between," cried Daisy, tenderly wiping a yellow stain off Annabella's broken nose, for Bella had refused to eat squash when it was pressed upon her as good for "lumatism," a complaint which it is no wonder she suffered from, considering the lightness of her attire.

"But if you give Demi goodies, all the others will expect some also, and then you will have your hands full."

"Couldn't I have Demi come up to tea alone just this one time, and after that I could cook things for the others if they were good," proposed Daisy, with sudden inspiration.

"That is a capital idea, Posy! We will make your little messes rewards for the good boys, and I don't know one among them who would not like something nice to eat more than almost anything else. If little men are like big ones, good cooking will touch their hearts and soothe their tempers delightfully," added Aunt Jo, with a merry nod toward the door, where stood Papa Bhaer, surveying the scene with a face full of amusement.

"That last hit was for me, sharp woman. I accept it, for it is true; but if I had married thee for thy cooking, heart's dearest, I should have fared badly all these years," answered the professor, laughing, as he tossed Teddy, who became quite apopletic in his endeavors to describe the feast he had just enjoyed.

Daisy proudly showed her kitchen, and rashly promised Uncle Fritz as many flapjacks as he could eat. She was just telling about the new rewards when the boys, headed by Demi, burst into the room snuffing the air like a pack of hungry hounds, for school was out, dinner was not ready, and the fragrance of Daisy's steak led them straight to the spot.

A prouder little damsel was never seen than Sally as she displayed her treasures and told the lads what was in store for them. Several rather scoffed at the idea of her cooking anything fit to eat, but Stuffy's heart was won at once, Nat and Demi had firm faith in her skill, and the others said they would wait and see. All admired the kitchen, however, and examined the stove with deep interest. Demi offered to buy the boiler on the spot, to be used in a steam engine which he was constructing; and Ned declared that the best and biggest saucepan was just the thing to melt his lead in when he ran bullets, hatchets and such trifles.

Daisy looked so alarmed at these proposals, that Mrs. Jo then and there made and proclaimed a law that no boy should touch, use, or even approach the sacred stove without a special permit from the owner thereof. This increased its value immensely in the eyes of the gentlemen, especially as any infringement of the law would be punished by the forfeiture of all right to partake of the delicacies promised to the virtuous.

At this point the bell rang, and the entire population went down to dinner, which meal was enlivened by each of the boys giving Daisy a list of things he would like to have cooked for him as fast as he earned them. Daisy, whose faith in her stove was unlimited, promised everything, if Aunt Jo would tell her how to make them. This suggestion rather alarmed Mrs. Jo, for some of the dishes were quite beyond her skill — wedding cake, for instance, bull's-eye candy, and cabbage soup with herrings and cherries in it, which Mr. Bhaer proposed as his favorite, and immediately reduced his wife to despair, for German cookery was beyond her.

Daisy wanted to begin again the minute dinner was over, but she was only allowed to clear up, fill the kettle ready for tea, and wash out her apron, which looked as if she had cooked a Christmas feast. She was then sent out to play till five o'clock, for Uncle Fritz said that too much study, even at cooking stoves, was bad for little minds and bodies, and Aunt Jo

Demi stuffed like any carnal boy.

knew by long experience how soon new toys lose their charm if they are not prudently used.

Every one was very kind to Daisy that afternoon. Tommy promised her the first fruits of his garden, though the only visible crop just then was pigweed; Nat offered to supply her with wood, free of charge; Stuffy quite worshipped her; Ned immediately fell to work on a little refrigerator for her kitchen; and Demi, with a punctuality beautiful to see in one so young, escorted her to the nursery just as the clock struck five. It was not time for the party to begin, but he begged so hard to come in and help that he was allowed privileges few visitors enjoy, for he kindled the fire, ran errands, and watched the progress of his supper with intense interest. Mrs. Jo directed the affair as she came and went, being very busy putting up clean curtains all over the house.

"Ask Asia for a cup of sour cream, then your cakes will be light without much soda, which I don't like," was the first order.

Demi tore down stairs, and returned with the cream, also a puckered-up face, for he had tasted it on his way, and found it so sour that he predicted the cakes would be uneatable. Mrs. Jo took this occasion to deliver a short lecture from the step-ladder on the chemical properties of soda, to which Daisy did not listen, but Demi did, and understood it, as he proved by the brief but comprehensive reply,

"Yes I see, soda turns sour things sweet, and the fizzling up makes them light. Let's see you do it, Daisy."

"Fill that bowl nearly full of flour and add a little salt to it," continued Mrs. Jo.

"Oh dear, everything has to have salt in it, seems to me," said Sally, who was tired of opening the pill-box in which it was kept.

"Salt is like good humor, and nearly everything is better for a pinch of it, Posy," and Uncle Fritz stopped as he passed, hammer in hand, to drive up two or three nails for Sally's little pans to hang on.

"You are not invited to tea, but I'll give you some cakes, and I won't be cross," said Daisy, putting up her floury little face to thank him with a kiss.

"Fritz, you must not interrupt my cooking class, or I'll come in and moralize when you are teaching Latin. How would you like that?" said Mrs. Jo, throwing a great chintz curtain down on his head.

"Very much, try it and see," and the amiable Father Bhaer went singing and tapping about the house like a mammoth woodpecker.

"Put the soda into the cream, and when it 'fizzles,' as Demi says, stir it into the flour, and beat it up as hard as ever you can. Have your griddle hot, butter it well, and then fry away till I come back," and Aunt Jo vanished also.

Such a clatter as the little spoon made, and such a beating as the batter got, it quite foamed, I assure you; and when Daisy poured some on to the griddle, it rose like magic into a puffy flapjack, that made Demi's mouth water. To be sure, the first one stuck and scorched, because she forgot the butter, but after that first failure all went well, and six capital little cakes were safely landed in a dish.

"I think I'd like maple sirup better than sugar," said Demi from his armchair, where he had settled himself after setting the table in a new and peculiar manner.

"Then go and ask Asia for some," answered Daisy, going into the bathroom to wash her hands.

While the nursery was empty something dreadful happened. You see, Kit had been feeling hurt all day because he had carried meat safely and yet got none to pay him. He was not a bad dog, but he had his little faults like the rest of us, and could not always resist temptation. Happening to stroll into the nursery at that moment, he smelt the cakes, saw them unguarded on the low table, and never stopping to think of consequences, swallowed all six at one mouthful. I am glad to say that they were very hot, and burned him so badly that he could not repress a surprised yelp. Daisy heard it, ran in, saw the empty dish, also the end of a yellow tail disappearing under the bed. Without a word she seized that tail, pulled out the thief, and shook him till his ears flapped wildly, then bundled him down stairs to the shed, where he spent a lonely evening in the coal bin.

Cheered by the sympathy which Demi gave her, Daisy made another bowl full of batter, and fried a dozen cakes, which were even better than the others. Indeed, Uncle Fritz after eating two sent up word that he had never tasted any so nice, and every boy at the table below envied Demi at the flapjack party above.

It was a truly delightful supper, for the little teapot lid only fell off three times, and the milk jug upset but once; the cakes floated in sirup, and the toast had a delicious beefsteak flavor, owing to cook's using the gridiron to make it on. Demi forgot philosophy, and stuffed like any carnal boy, while Daisy planned sumptuous banquets, and the dolls looked on smiling affably.

"Well, dearies, have you had a good time?" asked Mrs. Jo, coming up with Teddy on her shoulder.

"A *very* good time. I shall come again *soon*," answered Demi, with emphasis.

"I'm afraid you have eaten too much, by the look of the table."

"No, I haven't; I only ate fifteen cakes, and they were very little ones," protested Demi, who had kept his sister busy supplying his plate.

"They won't hurt him, they are so nice," said Daisy, with such a funny mixture of maternal fondness, and housewifely pride, that Aunt Jo could only smile and say, —

"Well, on the whole, the new game is a success, then?"

"*I* like it," said Demi, as if his approval was all that was necessary.

"It is the dearest play ever made!" cried Daisy, hugging her little dish tub as she proposed to wash up the cups. "I just wish everybody had a sweet cooking stove like mine," she added, regarding it with affection.

"This play ought to have a name," said Demi, gravely removing the sirup from his countenance with his tongue.

"It has."

"Oh, what?" asked both children eagerly.

"Well, I think we will call it Patty pans," and Aunt Jo retired, satisfied with the success of her last trap to catch a sunbeam.

CHAPTER SIX

A FIREBRAND

~

"Please, ma'am, could I speak to you? It is something *very* important," said Nat, popping his head in at the door of Mrs. Bhaer's room.

It was the fifth head which had popped in during the last half hour; but Mrs. Jo was used to it, so she looked up, and said briskly, –

"What is it, my lad?"

Nat came in, shut the door carefully behind him, and said in an eager, anxious tone, –

"Dan has come."

"Who is Dan?"

"He's a boy I used to know when I fiddled round the streets. He sold papers, and he was kind to me and I saw him the other day in town, and told him how nice it was here, and he's come."

"But, my dear, that is rather a sudden way to pay a visit."

"Oh, it isn't a visit; he wants to stay if you will let him!" said Nat, innocently.

"Well, but I don't know about that," began Mrs. Bhaer, rather startled by the coolness of the proposition.

"Why, I thought you liked to have poor boys come and live with you, and be kind to them as you were to me," said Nat, looking surprised and alarmed.

"So I do, but I like to know something about them first. I have to choose them, because there are so many. I have not room for all. I wish I had."

"I told him to come because I thought you'd like it, but if there ain't room he can go away again," said Nat, sorrowfully.

The boy's confidence in her hospitality touched Mrs. Bhaer, and she could not find the heart to disappoint his hope, and spoil his kind little plan, so she said, –

"Tell me about this Dan."

"I don't know anything, only he hasn't got any folks, and he's poor, and he was good to me, so I'd like to be good to him if I could."

"Excellent reasons every one; but really, Nat, the house is full, and I don't know where I could put him," said Mrs. Bhaer, more and more inclined to prove herself the haven of refuge he seemed to think her.

"He could have my bed, and I could sleep in the barn. It isn't cold now, and I don't mind, I used to sleep anywhere with father," said Nat, eagerly.

Something in his speech and face made Mrs. Jo put her hand on his shoulder, and say in her kindest tone, –

"Bring in your friend, Nat; I think we must find room for him without giving him your place."

Nat joyfully ran off, and soon returned followed by a most unprepossessing boy, who slouched in and stood looking about him, with a half bold, half sullen look, which made Mrs. Bhaer say to herself, after one glance, –

"A bad specimen, I am afraid."

"This is Dan," said Nat, presenting him as if sure of his welcome.

"Nat tells me you would like to come and stay with us," began Mrs. Jo, in a friendly tone.

"Yes," was the gruff reply.

"Have you no friends to take care of you?"

"No."

"Say, 'No, ma'am,'" whispered Nat.

"Shan't either," muttered Dan.

"How old are you?"

"About fourteen."

"You look older. What can you do?"

"'Most anything."

"If you stay here we shall want you to do as the others do, work and study as well as play. Are you willing to agree to that?"

"Don't mind trying."

"Well, you can stay a few days, and we will see how we get on together. Take him out, Nat, and amuse him till Mr. Bhaer comes home, when we will settle about the matter," said Mrs. Jo, finding it rather difficult to get on with this cool young person, who fixed his big black eyes on her with a hard, suspicious expression, sorrowfully unboyish.

"Come on, Nat," he said, and slouched out again.

"Thank you, ma'am," added Nat, as he followed him, feeling without quite understanding the difference in the welcome given to him and to his ungracious friend.

"The fellows are having a circus out in the barn; don't you want to come and see it?" he asked, as they came down the wide steps on to the lawn.

"Are they big fellows?" said Dan.

"No; the big ones have gone fishing."

"Fire away, then," said Dan.

Nat led him to the great barn and introduced him to his set, who were disporting themselves among the half empty lofts. A large circle was marked out with hay on the wide floor, and in the middle stood Demi with a long whip, while Tommy, mounted on the much enduring Toby, pranced about the circle playing being a monkey.

"You must pay a pin apiece, or you can't see the show," said Stuffy, who stood by the wheelbarrow in which sat the band, consisting of a pocket comb blown upon by Ned, and toy drum beaten spasmodically by Rob.

"He's company, so I'll pay for both," said Nat, handsomely, as he stuck two crooked pins in the dried mushrooms which served as moneybox.

With a nod to the company they seated themselves on a couple of boards, and the performance went on. After the monkey act, Ned gave them a fine specimen of his agility of jumping over an old chair, and running up and down ladders, sailor fashion. Then Demi danced a jig with a gravity beautiful to behold. Nat was called upon to wrestle with Stuffy, and speedily laid that stout youth upon the ground. After this, Tommy proudly advanced to turn a somersault, an accomplishment which he had acquired by painful perseverance, practising in private till every joint of his little frame was black and blue. His feats were received with great applause, and he was about to retire, flushed with pride and a rush of blood to the head, when a scornful voice in the audience was heard to say, "Ho! that ain't anything!"

"Say that again, will you?" and Tommy bristled up like an angry turkey cock.

"Do you want to fight?" said Dan, promptly descending from the barrel and doubling up his fists in a business-like manner.

"No, I don't," and the candid Thomas retired a step, rather taken aback by the proposition.

"Fighting isn't allowed!" cried the others, much excited.

"You're a nice lot," sneered Dan.

"Come, if you don't behave, you shan't stay," said Nat, firing up at that insult to his friends.

"I'd like to see him do better than I did, that's all," observed Tommy, with a swagger.

"Clear the way, then," and without the slightest preparation Dan turned three somersaults one after the other and came up on his feet.

"You can't beat that, Tom; you always hit your head and tumble flat," said Nat, pleased at his friend's success.

Before he could say any more the audience were electrified by three more somersaults backwards, and a short promenade on the hands, head down, feet up. This brought down the house, and Tommy joined in the admiring cries which greeted the accomplished gymnast as he righted himself, and looked at them with an air of calm superiority.

"Do you think I could learn to do it without its hurting me very much?" Tom meekly asked, as he rubbed the elbows which still smarted after the last attempt.

"What will you give me if I'll teach you?" said Dan.

"My new jackknife; it's got five blades, and only one is broken."

"Give it here then."

Tommy handed it over with an affectionate look at its smooth handle. Dan examined it carefully, then putting it into his pocket, walked off, saying with a wink, "Keep it up till you learn, that's all."

A howl of wrath from Tommy was followed by a general uproar, which did not subside till Dan, finding himself in a minority, proposed that they should play stick knife, and which ever won should have the treasure. Tommy agreed, and the game was played in a circle of excited faces, which all wore an expression of satisfaction, when Tommy won and secured the knife in the depth of his safest pocket.

"You come with me, and I'll show you round," said Nat, feeling that he must have a little serious conversation with his friend in private.

What passed between them no one knew, but when they appeared again, Dan was more respectful to every one, though still gruff in his speech, and rough in his manner; and what else could be expected of the poor lad who had been knocking about the world all his short life with no one to teach him any better?

The boys had decided that they did not like him, and so they left him to Nat, who soon felt rather oppressed by the responsibility, but was too kind-hearted to desert him.

Tommy, however, felt that in spite of the jackknife transaction, there was a bond of sympathy between them, and longed to return to the interesting subject of somersaults. He soon found an opportunity, for Dan, seeing how much he admired him, grew more amiable, and by the end of the first week was quite intimate with the lively Tom.

Mr. Bhaer, when he heard the story and saw Dan, shook his head, but only said quietly, –

"The experiment may cost us something, but we will try it."

If Dan felt any gratitude for his protection, he did not show it, and took without thanks all that was given him. He was ignorant, but very quick to learn when he chose; had sharp eyes to watch what went on about him; a saucy tongue, rough manners, and a temper that was fierce and sullen by turns. He played with all his might, and played well at almost all the games. He was silent and gruff before grown people, and only now and then was thoroughly social among the lads. Few of them really liked him, but few could help admiring his courage and strength, for nothing daunted him, and he knocked tall Franz flat on one occasion with an ease that caused all the others to keep at a respectful distance from his fists. Mr. Bhaer watched him silently, and did his best to tame the "Wild Boy," as they called him, but in private the worthy man shook his head, and said soberly, "I *hope* the experiment will turn out well, but I am a little afraid it may cost too much."

Mrs. Bhaer lost her patience with him half a dozen times a day, yet never gave him up, and always insisted that there was something good in the lad, after all; for he was kinder to animals than to people, he liked to rove about in the woods, and, best of all, little Ted was fond of him. What the secret was no one could discover, but Baby took to him at once, — gabbled and crowed whenever he saw him, — preferred his strong back to ride on to any of the others — and called him "My Danny" out of his own little head. Teddy was the only creature to whom Dan showed any affection, and this was only manifested when he thought no one else could see it; but mothers' eyes are quick, and motherly hearts instinctively divine who love their babies. So Mrs. Jo soon saw and felt that there *was* a soft spot to rough Dan, and bided her time to touch and win him.

But an unexpected and decidedly alarming event upset all their plans, and banished Dan from Plumfield.

Tommy, Nat, and Demi began by patronizing Dan, because the other lads rather slighted him; but soon they each felt there was a certain fascination about the bad boy, and from looking down upon him they came to looking up, each for a different reason. Tommy admired his skill and courage; Nat was grateful for past kindness; and Demi regarded him as a sort of animated story book, for when he chose, Dan could tell his adventures in a most interesting way. It pleased Dan to have the three favorites like him, and he exerted himself to be agreeable, which was the secret of his success.

The Bhaers were surprised, but hoped the lads would have a good influence over Dan, and waited with some anxiety, trusting that no harm would come of it.

Dan felt they did not quite trust him, and never showed them his best side, but took a wilful pleasure in trying their patience and thwarting their hopes as far as he dared.

Mr. Bhaer did not approve of fighting, and did not think it a proof of either manliness or courage for two lads to pommel each other for the amusement of the rest. All sorts of hardy games and exercises were encouraged, and the boys were expected to take hard knocks and tumbles without whining; but black eyes and bloody noses given for the fun of it were forbidden as a foolish and a brutal play.

Dan laughed at this rule, and told such exciting tales of his own valor, and the many frays that he had been in, that some of the lads were fired with a desire to have a regular good "mill."

"Don't tell, and I'll show you how," said Dan; and, getting half a dozen of the lads together behind the barn, he gave them a lesson in boxing, which quite satisfied the ardor of most of them. Emil, however, could not submit to be beaten by a fellow younger than himself, – for Emil was past fourteen, and a plucky fellow, – so he challenged Dan to a fight. Dan accepted at once, and the others looked on with intense interest.

What little bird carried the news to headquarters no one ever knew, but, in the very hottest of the fray, when Dan and Emil were fighting like a pair of young bulldogs, and the others with fierce, excited faces were cheering them on, Mr. Bhaer walked into the ring, plucked the combatants apart with a strong hand, and said, in the voice they seldom heard, –

"I can't allow this, boys! Stop it at once; and never let me see it again. I keep a school for boys, not for wild beasts. Look at each other and be ashamed of yourselves."

"You let me go, and I'll knock him down again," shouted Dan, sparring away in spite of the grip on his collar.

"Come on, come on, I ain't thrashed yet!" cried Emil, who had been down five times, but did not know when he was beaten.

"They are playing be gladdy – what-you-call-'ems, like the Romans, Uncle Fritz," called out Demi, whose eyes were bigger than ever with the excitement of this new pastime.

"They were a fine set of brutes; but we have learned something since then, I hope, and I cannot have you make my barn a Colosseum. Who proposed this?" asked Mr. Bhaer.

"Dan," answered several voices.

"Don't you know that it is forbidden?"

"Yes," growled Dan, sullenly.

"Then why break the rule?"

"They'll all be mollycoddles, if they don't know how to fight."

"Have you found Emil a mollycoddle? He doesn't look much like one," and Mr. Bhaer brought the two face to face. Dan had a black eye, and his jacket was torn to rags; but Emil's face was covered with blood from a cut lip and a bruised nose, while a bump on his forehead was already as purple as a plum. In spite of his wounds however, he still glared upon his foe, and evidently panted to renew the fight.

"He'd make a first-rater if he were taught," said Dan, unable to withhold the praise from the boy who made it necessary for him to do his best.

"He'll be taught to fence and box by and by, and till then I think he will do very well without any lessons in mauling. Go and wash your faces; and remember, Dan, if you break any more of the rules again, you will be sent away. That was the bargain; do your part and we will do ours."

The lads went off, and after a few more words to the spectators, Mr. Bhaer followed to bind up the wounds of the young gladiators. Emil went to bed sick, and Dan was an unpleasant spectacle for a week.

But the lawless lad had no thought of obeying, and soon transgressed again.

One Saturday afternoon as a party of the boys went out to play, Tommy said, —

"Let's go down to the river, and cut a lot of new fish-poles."

"Take Toby to drag them back, and one of us can ride him down," proposed Stuffy, who hated to walk.

"That means *you*, I suppose; well, hurry up, lazybones," said Dan.

Away they went, and having got the poles were about to go home, when Demi unluckily said to Tommy, who was on Toby with a long rod in his hand,

"You look like the picture of the man in the bull fight, only you haven't got a red cloth, or pretty clothes on."

"I'd like to see one; wouldn't you?" said Tommy, shaking his lance.

"Let's have one; there's old Buttercup in the big meadow. Ride at her, Tom, and see her run," proposed Dan, bent on mischief.

"No, you mustn't," began Demi, who was learning to distrust Dan's propositions.

"Why not, little fuss button?" demanded Dan.

"I don't think Uncle Fritz would like it."

"Did he ever say we must not have a bull fight?"

"No, I don't think he ever did," admitted Demi.

"Then hold your tongue. Drive on, Tom, and here's a red rag to flap at the old thing. I'll help you to stir her up," and over the wall went Dan, full of the new game, and the rest followed like a flock of sheep; even Demi, who sat upon the bars, and watched the fun with interest.

Poor Buttercup was not in a very good mood, for she had been lately bereft of her calf, and mourned for the little thing most dismally. Just now she regarded all mankind as her enemies (and I do not blame her), so when the matadore came prancing toward her with the red handkerchief flying at the end of his long lance, she threw up her head, and gave a most appropriate "Moo!" Tommy rode gallantly at her, and Toby, recognizing an old friend, was quite willing to approach; but when the lance came down on her back with a loud whack, both cow and donkey were surprised and disgusted. Toby backed with a bray of remonstrance, and Buttercup lowered her horns angrily.

"At her again, Tom; she's jolly cross, and will do it capitally!" called Dan, coming up behind with another rod, while Jack and Ned followed his example.

Seeing herself thus beset, and treated with such disrespect, Buttercup trotted round the field, getting more and more bewildered and excited every moment, for which ever way she turned, there was a dreadful boy, yelling and brandishing a new and very disagreeable sort of whip. It was great fun for them, but real misery for her, till she lost patience and turned the tables in the most unexpected manner. All at once she wheeled short around, and charged full at her old friend Toby, whose conduct cut her to the heart. Poor slow Toby backed so precipitately that he tripped over a stone, and down went horse, matadore, and all, in one ignominious heap, while distracted Buttercup took a surprising leap over the wall, and galloped wildly out of sight down the road.

"Catch her, stop her, head her off! run, boys, run!" shouted Dan, tearing after her at his best pace, for she was Mr. Bhaer's pet Alderney, and if anything happened to her, Dan feared it would be all over with him. Such a running and racing and bawling and puffing as there was before she was caught! The fish poles were left behind; Toby was trotted nearly off his legs in the chase; and every boy was red, breathless, and scared. They found poor Buttercup at last in a flower garden, where she had taken refuge, worn out with the long run. Borrowing a rope for a halter, Dan led her home, followed by a party of very sober young gentlemen, for the cow was in a sad state, having strained her shoulder in jumping, so that she limped, her eyes looked wild, and her glossy coat was wet and muddy.

"You'll catch it this time, Dan," said Tommy, as he led the wheezing donkey beside the maltreated cow.

"So will you, for you helped."

"We all did, but Demi," added Jack.

"He put it into our heads," said Ned.

"I told you not to do it," cried Demi, who was most broken-hearted at poor Buttercup's state.

"Old Bhaer will send me off, I guess. Don't care if he does," muttered Dan, looking worried in spite of his words.

"We'll ask him not to, all of us," said Demi, and the others assented with the exception of Stuffy, who cherished the hope that all the punishment might fall on one guilty head. Dan only said, "Don't bother about me," but he never forgot it, even though he led the lads astray again, as soon as the temptation came.

When Mr. Bhaer saw the animal, and heard the story, he said very little, evidently fearing that he should say too much in the first moments of impatience. Buttercup was made comfortable in her stall, and the boys sent to their rooms till supper time. This brief respite gave them time to think the matter over, to wonder what the penalty would be, and to try to imagine where Dan would be sent. He whistled briskly in his room, so that no one should think he cared a bit; but while he waited to know his fate, the longing to stay grew stronger and stronger, the more he recalled the comfort and kindness he had known here, the hardship and neglect he had felt elsewhere. He knew they tried to help him, and at the bottom of his heart he was grateful, but his rough life had made him hard and careless, suspicious and wilful. He hated restraint of any sort, and fought against it like an untamed creature, even while he knew it was kindly meant, and dimly felt that he would be the better for it. He made up his mind to be turned adrift again, to knock about the city as he had done nearly all his life; a prospect that made him knit his black brows, and look about the cosy little room with a wistful expression that would have touched a much harder heart than Mr. Bhaer's if he had seen it. It vanished instantly, however, when the good man came in, and said in his accustomed grave way, –

"I have heard all about it, Dan, and though you have broken the rules again, I am going to give you one more trial, to please Mother Bhaer."

Dan flushed up to his forehead at this unexpected reprieve, but he only said in his gruff way, –

"I didn't know there was any rule about bull fighting."

"As I never expected to have any at Plumfield, I never did make such a rule," answered Mr. Bhaer, smiling in spite of himself at the boy's excuse. Then he added gravely, "But one of the first and most important of our few laws is the law of kindness to every dumb creature on the place. I want everybody and everything to be happy here, to love, and trust, and serve us, as we try to love and trust and serve them faithfully and willingly. I have often said that you were kinder to the animals than any of the other boys, and Mrs. Bhaer liked that trait in you very much, because she thought it showed a good heart. But you have disappointed us in that, and we are sorry, for we hoped to make you quite one of us. Shall we try again?"

Dan's eyes had been on the floor, and his hands nervously picking at the bit of wood he had been whittling as Mr. Bhaer came in, but when he heard the kind voice ask the question, he looked up quickly, and said in a more respectful tone than he had ever used before, –

"Yes, please."

"Very well, then, we will say no more, only you will stay at home from the walk to-morrow, as the other boys will and all of you must wait on poor Buttercup till she is well again."

"I will."

"Now, go down to supper, and do your best, my boy, more for your own sake than for ours." Then Mr. Bhaer shook hands with him, and Dan went down more tamed by kindness than he would have been by the good whipping which Asia had strongly recommended.

Dan did try for a day or two, but not being used to it, he soon tired and relapsed into his old wilful ways. Mr. Bhaer was called from home on business one day, and the boys had no lessons. They liked this, and played hard till bedtime, when most of them turned in and slept like dormice. Dan, however, had a plan in his head, and when he and Nat were alone, he unfolded it.

"Look here!" he said, taking from under his bed a bottle, a cigar, and a pack of cards, "I'm going to have some fun, and do as I used to with the fellows in town. Here's some beer, I got it off the old man at the station, and this cigar; you can pay for them, or Tommy will, he has heaps of money, and I haven't a cent. I'm going to ask him in; no, you go, they won't mind you."

"The folks won't like it," began Nat.

"They won't know. Daddy Bhaer is away, and Mrs. Bhaer's busy with Ted; he's got croup or something, and she can't leave him. We shan't sit up late or make any noise, so where's the harm?"

"Asia will know if we burn the lamp long, she always does."

"No, she won't, I've got the dark lantern on purpose; it don't give much light, and we can shut it quick if we hear any one coming," said Dan.

This idea struck Nat as a fine one, and lent an air of romance to the thing. He started off to tell Tommy, but put his head in again to say, —

"You want Demi, too, don't you?"

"No, I don't; the Deacon will roll up eyes and preach if you tell him. He will be asleep, so just tip the wink to Tom and cut back again."

Nat obeyed, and returned in a minute with Tommy half dressed, rather tousled about the head and very sleepy, but quite ready for fun as usual.

"Now, keep quiet, and I'll show you how to play a first-rate game called 'Poker,'" said Dan, as the three revelers gathered round the table, on which were set forth the bottle, the cigar, and the cards. "First we'll all have a drink, then we'll take a go at the 'weed,' and then we'll play. That's the way men do, and it's jolly fun."

The beer circulated in a mug, and all three smacked their lips over it, though Nat and Tommy did not like the bitter stuff. The cigar was worse still, but they dared not say so, and each puffed away till he was dizzy or choked, when he passed the 'weed' on to his neighbor. Dan liked it, for it seemed like old times when he now and then had a chance to imitate the low men who surrounded him. He drank, and smoked, and swaggered as much like them as he could, and, getting into the spirit of the part he assumed, he soon began to swear under his breath for fear someone should hear him. "You mustn't; it's wicked to say 'Damn!'" cried Tommy, who had followed his leader so far.

"Oh, hang! don't you preach, but play away; it's part of the fun to swear."

"I'd rather say 'thunder-turtles,'" said Tommy, who had composed this interesting exclamation and was very proud of it.

"And I'll say 'The Devil;' that sounds well," added Nat, much impressed by Dan's manly ways.

Dan scoffed at their "nonsense," and swore stoutly as he tried to teach them the new game.

But Tommy was very sleepy, and Nat's head began to ache with the beer and the smoke, so neither of them was very quick to learn, and the game dragged. The room was nearly dark, for the lantern burned badly; they could not laugh loud nor move about much, for Silas slept next door in the shed chamber, and altogether the party was dull. In the middle of a deal Dan stopped suddenly, called out, "Who's that?" in a startled tone, and at the same moment drew the slide over the light. A voice in the darkness said tremulously, "I can't find Tommy," and then there was the quick patter of bare feet running away down the entry that led from the wing to the main house.

"It's Demi! he's gone to call someone; cut into bed, Tom, and don't tell!" cried Dan, whisking all signs of the revel out of sight, and beginning to tear off his clothes, while Nat did the same.

Tommy flew to his room and dived into bed, where he lay laughing till something burned his hand, when he discovered that he was still clutching the stump of the festive cigar, which he happened to be smoking when the revel broke up.

It was nearly out, and he was about to extinguish it carefully when Nursey's voice was heard, and fearing it would betray him if he hid it in the bed, he threw it underneath, after a final pinch which he thought finished it.

Nursey came in with Demi, who looked much amazed to see the red face of Tommy reposing peacefully upon his pillow.

"He wasn't there just now, because I woke up and could not find him anywhere," said Demi, pouncing on him.

"What mischief are you at now, bad child?" asked Nursey, with a good-natured shake, which made the sleeper open his eyes to say meekly,

"I only ran into Nat's room to see him about something. Go away, and let me alone; I'm awfully sleepy."

Nursey tucked Demi in, and went off to reconnoitre, but only found two boys slumbering peacefully in Dan's room. "Some little frolic," she thought, and as there was no harm done she said nothing to Mrs. Bhaer who was busy and worried over little Teddy.

Tommy was sleepy, and telling Demi to mind his own business and not ask questions, he was snoring in ten minutes, little dreaming what was going on under his bed. The cigar did not go out, but smouldered away on the straw carpet till it was nicely on fire, and a hungry little flame went creeping along till the dimity bedcover caught, then the sheets, and then the bed itself. The beer made Tommy sleep heavily, and the smoke stupefied Demi, so they slept on till the fire began to scorch them, and they were in danger of being burned to death.

Franz was sitting up to study, and as he left the schoolroom he smelled the smoke, dashed upstairs and saw it coming in a cloud from the left wing of the house. Without stopping to call any one, he ran into the room, dragged the boys from the blazing bed, and splashed all the water he could find at hand on to the flames. It checked but did not quench the fire, and the children, wakened on being tumbled topsy-turvy into a cold hall, began to roar at the top of their voices. Mrs. Bhaer instantly appeared, and a minute after Silas burst out of his room shouting "Fire!" in a tone that raised the whole house. A flock of white goblins with scared faces crowded into the hall, and for a minute every one was panic-stricken.

Then Mrs. Bhaer found her wits, bade Nursey to see to the burnt boys, and sent Franz and Silas down stairs for some tubs of wet clothes which she flung on to the bed, over the carpet, and up against the curtains, now burning finely, and threatening to kindle the walls.

Most of the boys stood dumbly looking on, but Dan and Emil worked bravely, running to and fro with water from the bathroom, and helping to pull down the dangerous curtains.

The peril was soon over, and ordering the boys all back to bed, and leaving Silas to watch lest the fire broke out again, Mrs. Bhaer and Franz went to see how the poor boys got on. Demi had escaped with one burn and a grand scare, but Tommy had not only most of his hair scorched off his head, but a great burn on his arm, that made him half crazy with the pain. Demi was soon made cosy, and Franz took him away to his own bed, where the kind lad soothed his fright and hummed him to sleep as cosily as a woman. Nursey watched over poor Tommy all night, trying to ease his misery, and Mrs. Bhaer vibrated between him and little Teddy with oil and cotton, paregoric and squills, saying to herself from time to time, as if she found great amusement in the thought, "I always *knew* Tommy would set the house on fire, and now he has done it!"

When Mr. Bhaer got home next morning he found a nice state of things. Tommy in bed, Teddy wheezing like a little grampus, Mrs. Jo quite used up and the whole flock of boys so excited that they all talked at once, and almost dragged him by main force to view the ruins. Under his quiet management things soon fell into order, for every one felt that he was equal to a dozen conflagrations, and worked with a will at what ever task he gave them.

There was no school that morning, but by afternoon the damaged room was put to rights, the invalids were better, and there was time to hear and judge the little culprits quietly. Nat and Tommy told their parts in the mischief, and were honestly sorry for the danger they had brought to the dear old house and all in it. But Dan put on his devil-may-care look, and would not own that there was much harm done.

Now, of all things, Mr. Bhaer hated drinking, gambling, and swearing; smoking he had given up that the lads might not be tempted to try it, and it grieved and angered him deeply to find that the boy, with whom he had tried to be most forbearing, should take advantage of his absence to introduce these forbidden vices, and teach his innocent little lads to think it manly and pleasant to indulge in them. He talked long and earnestly to the assembled boys, and ended by saying, with an air of mingled firmness and regret, —

"I think Tommy is punished enough, and that scar on his arm will remind him for a long time to let these things alone. Nat's fright will do for him, for he is really sorry, and does try to obey me. But you, Dan, have been many times forgiven, and yet it does no good. I cannot have my boys hurt by your bad example, nor my time wasted in talking to deaf ears, so you can say good-by to them all, and tell Nursey to put up your things in my little black bag."

"Oh! sir, where is he going?" cried Nat.

"To a pleasant place up in the country, where I sometimes send boys when they don't do well here. Mr. Page is a kind man, and Dan will be happy there if he chooses to do his best."

"Will he ever come back?" asked Demi.

"That will depend on himself; I hope so."

As he spoke, Mr. Bhaer left the room to write his letter to Mr. Page, and the boys crowded round Dan very much as people do about a man who is going on a long and perilous journey to unknown regions.

"I wonder if you'll like it," began Jack.

"Shan't stay if I don't," said Dan, coolly.

"Where will you go?" asked Nat.

"I may go to sea, or out west, or take a look at California," answered Dan, with a reckless air that quite took away the breath of the little boys.

"Oh, don't! stay with Mr. Page awhile and then come back here; do, Dan," pleaded Nat, much affected at the whole affair.

"I don't care where I go, or how long I stay, and I'll be hanged if I ever come back here," with which wrathful speech Dan went away to put up his things, every one of which Mr. Bhaer had given him.

That was the only good-by he gave the boys, for they were all talking the matter over in the barn when he came down, and he told Nat not to call them. The wagon stood at the door, and Mrs. Bhaer came out to speak to Dan, looking so sad that his heart smote him, and he said in a low tone,

"May I say good-by to Teddy?"

"Yes, dear; go in and kiss him, he will miss his Danny very much."

No one saw the look in Dan's eyes as he stooped over the crib, and saw the little face light up at first sight of him, but he heard Mrs. Bhaer say pleadingly, –

"Can't we give the poor lad *one* more trial, Fritz?" and Mr. Bhaer answer in his steady way, –

"My dear, it is not best, so let him go where he can do no harm to others, while they do good for him, and by and by he shall come back, I promise you."

"He's the only boy we ever failed with, and I am so grieved, for I thought there was the making of a fine man in him, in spite of his faults."

Dan heard Mrs. Bhaer sigh, and he wanted to ask for *one more* trial himself, but his pride would not let him, and he came out with the hard look on his face, shook hands without a word, and drove away with Mr. Bhaer, leaving Nat and Mrs. Jo to look after him with tears in their eyes.

A few days afterwards they received a letter from Mr. Page, saying that Dan was doing well, whereat they all rejoiced. But three weeks later came another letter, saying that Dan had run away, and nothing had been heard of him, whereat they all looked sober, and Mr. Bhaer said, –

"Perhaps I ought to have given him another chance."

Mrs. Bhaer, however, nodded wisely and answered, "Don't be troubled, Fritz; the boy will come back to us, I'm sure of it."

But time went on and no Dan came.

CHAPTER SEVEN

NAUGHTY NAN

~

"*F*ritz, I've got a new idea," cried Mrs. Bhaer, as she met her husband one day after school.

"Well, my dear, what is it?" and he waited willingly to hear the new plan, for some of Mrs. Jo's ideas were so droll, it was impossible to help laughing at them, though usually they were quite sensible, and he was glad to carry them out.

"Daisy needs a companion and the boys would be all the better for another girl among them; you know we believe in bringing up little men and women together, and it is high time we acted up to our belief. They pet and tyrannize over Daisy by turns, and she is getting spoiled. Then they must learn gentle ways, and improve their manners, and having girls about will do it better than anything else."

"You are right, as usual. Now, whom shall we have?" asked Mr. Bhaer, seeing by the look in her eye that Mrs. Jo had someone all ready to propose.

"Little Annie Harding."

"What! Naughty Nan, as the lads call her?" cried Mr. Bhaer, looking very much amused.

"Yes, she is running wild at home since her mother died, and is too bright a child to be spoiled by servants. I have had my eye on her for some time, and when I met her father in town the other day I asked him why he did not send her to school. He said he would gladly if he could find as good a school for girls as ours was for boys. I know he would rejoice to have her come; so suppose we drive over this afternoon and see about it."

"Have not you cares enough now, my Jo, without this little gypsy to torment you?" asked Mr. Bhaer, patting the hand that lay on his arm.

"Oh dear, no," said Mother Bhaer, briskly. "I like it, and never was happier than since I had my wilderness of boys. You see, Fritz, I feel a great sympathy for Nan, because I was such a naughty child myself that I know all about it. She is full of spirits, and only needs to be taught what to do with them to be as nice a little girl as Daisy. Those quick wits of hers would enjoy lessons if they were rightly directed, and what is now a tricksy midget would soon become a busy, happy child. I know how to manage her, for I remember how my blessed mother managed me, and" –

"And if you succeed half as well as she did, you will have done a magnificent work," interrupted Mr. Bhaer, who labored under the delusion that Mrs. B. was the best and most charming woman alive.

"Now, if you make fun of my plan I'll give you bad coffee for a week, and then where are you, sir?" cried Mrs. Jo, tweaking him by the ear just as if he was one of the boys.

"Won't Daisy's hair stand erect with horror at Nan's wild ways?" asked Mr. Bhaer, presently, when Teddy had swarmed up his waistcoat, and Rob up his back, for they always flew at their father the minute school was done.

"At first, perhaps, but it will do Posy good. She is getting prim and Bettyish, and needs stirring up a bit. She always has a good time when Nan comes over to play, and the two will help each other without knowing it. Dear me, half the science of teaching is knowing how much children do for one another, and when to mix them."

"I only hope she won't turn out another firebrand."

"My poor Dan! I never can quite forgive myself for letting him go," sighed Mrs. Bhaer.

At the sound of the name, little Teddy, who had never forgotten his friend, struggled down from his father's arms, and trotted to the door, looked out over the sunny lawn with a wistful face, and then trotted back again, saying, as he always did when disappointed of the longed-for sight, –

"My Danny's tummin' soon."

"I really think we ought to have kept him, if only for Teddy's sake, he was so fond of him, and perhaps baby's love would have done for him what we failed to do."

"I've sometimes felt that myself; but after keeping the boys in a ferment, and nearly burning up the whole family, I thought it safer to remove the firebrand, for a time at least," said Mr. Bhaer.

"Dinner's ready, let me ring the bell," and Rob began a solo upon that instrument which made it impossible to hear oneself speak.

"Then I may have Nan, may I?" asked Mrs. Jo.

"A dozen Nans if you want them, my dear," answered Mr. Bhaer, who had room in his fatherly heart for all the naughty neglected children in the world.

When Mrs. Bhaer returned from her drive that afternoon, before she could unpack the load of little boys, without whom she seldom moved, a small girl of ten skipped out at the back of the carryall, and ran into the house, shouting, –

"Hi, Daisy! where are you?"

Daisy came, and looked pleased to see her guest, but also a trifle alarmed, when Nan said, still prancing, as if it was impossible to keep still, –

"I'm going to stay here always, papa say I may, and my box is coming to-morrow, all my things had to be washed and mended, and your aunt came and carried me off. Isn't it great fun?"

"Why, yes. Did you bring your big doll?" asked Daisy, hoping she had, for on the last visit Nan had ravaged the baby house, and insisted on washing Blanche Matilda's plaster face, which spoilt the poor dear's complexion for ever.

"Yes, she's somewhere round," returned Nan, with unmaternal carelessness. "I made you a ring coming along, and pulled the hairs out of Dobbin's tail. Don't you want it?" and Nan presented a horsehair ring in token of friendship, as they had both vowed they would never speak to one another again when they last parted.

Won by the beauty of the offering, Daisy grew more cordial, and proposed retiring to the nursery, but Nan said, "No, I want to see the boys, and the barn," and ran off, swinging her hat by one string till it broke, when she left it to its fate on the grass.

"Hullo! Nan!" cried the boys as she bounced in among them with the announcement, —

"I'm going to stay."

"Hooray!" bawled Tommy from the wall on which he was perched, for Nan was a kindred spirit, and he foresaw "larks" in the future.

"I can bat; let me play," said Nan, who could turn her hand to anything, and did not mind hard knocks.

"We ain't playing now, and our side beat without you."

"I can beat you in running, anyway," returned Nan, falling back on her strong point.

"Can she?" asked Nat of Jack.

"She runs very well for a girl," answered Jack, who looked down upon Nan with condescending approval.

"Will you try?" said Nan, longing to display her powers.

"It's too hot," and Tommy languished against the wall as if quite exhausted.

"What's the matter with Stuffy?" asked Nan, whose quick eyes were roving from face to face.

"Ball hurt his hand; he howls at everything," answered Jack, scornfully.

"I don't, I never cry, no matter how much I'm hurt; it's babyish," said Nan, loftily.

"Pooh! I could make you cry in two minutes," returned Stuffy, rousing up.

"See if you can."

"Go and pick that bunch of nettles, then," and Stuffy pointed to a sturdy specimen of that prickly plant growing by the wall.

Nan instantly "grasped the nettle," pulled it up, and held it with a defiant gesture, in spite of the almost unbearable sting.

"Good for you," cried the boys, quick to acknowledge courage even in one of the weaker sex.

More nettled than she was, Stuffy determined to get a cry out of her somehow, and he said tauntingly, "You are used to poking your hands into everything, so that isn't fair. Now go and bump your head real hard against the barn, and see if you don't howl then."

"Don't do it," said Nat, who hated cruelty.

But Nan was off, and running straight at the barn, she gave her head a blow that knocked her flat, and sounded like a battering-ram. Dizzy, but undaunted, she staggered up, saying stoutly, though her face was drawn with pain,

"That hurt, but I don't cry."

"Do it again," said Stuffy, angrily; and Nan would have done it, but Nat held her; and Tommy, forgetting the heat, flew at Stuffy like a little gamecock, roaring out, —

"Stop it, or I'll throw you over the barn!" and so shook and hustled poor Stuffy, that for a minute he did not know whether he was on his head or his heels.

"She told me to," was all he could say, when Tommy let him alone.

"Never mind if she did; it is awfully mean to hurt a little girl," said Demi, reproachfully.

"Ho! I don't mind; I ain't a little girl, I'm older than you and Daisy; so now," cried Nan, ungratefully.

"Don't preach, Deacon, you bully Posy every day of your life," called out the Commodore, who just then hove in sight.

"I don't hurt her; do I Daisy?" and Demi turned to his sister, who was "pooring" Nan's tingling hands, and recommending water for the purple lump rapidly developing itself on her forehead.

"You are the best boy in the world," promptly answered Daisy; adding, as truth compelled her to do, "you do hurt me sometimes, but you don't mean to."

"Put away the bats and things, and mind what you are about, my hearties. No fighting allowed aboard this ship," said Emil, who rather lorded it over the others.

"How do you do, Madge Wildfire?" said Mr. Bhaer, as Nan came in with the rest to supper. "Give the right hand, little daughter, and mind thy manners," he added, as Nan offered him her left.

"The other hurts me."

"The poor little hand! What has it been doing to get those blisters?" he asked, drawing it from behind her back, where she had put it with a look which made him think she had been in mischief.

Before Nan could think of any excuse, Daisy burst out with the whole story, during which Stuffy tried to hide his face in a bowl of bread and milk. When the tale was finished, Mr. Bhaer looked down the long table toward his wife, and said with a laugh in his eyes, –

"This rather belongs to your side of the house, so I won't meddle with it, my dear."

Mrs. Jo knew what he meant, but she liked her little black sheep all the better for her pluck, though she only said in her soberest way, –

"Do you know why I asked Nan to come here?"

"To plague me," muttered Stuffy, with his mouth full.

"To help me make little gentlemen of you, and I think you have shown that some of you need it."

Here Stuffy retired into his bowl again, and did not emerge till Demi made them all laugh by saying, in his slow wondering way, –

"How can she, when she's such a tomboy!"

"That's just it, she needs help as much as you, and I expect you to set her an example of good manners."

"Is she going to be a little gentlemen too?" asked Rob.

"She'd like it; wouldn't you, Nan?" added Tommy.

"No, I shouldn't; I hate boys!" said Nan, fiercely, for her hand still smarted, and she began to think that she might have shown her courage in some wiser way.

"I am sorry you hate my boys, because they *can* be well-mannered, and most agreeable when they choose. Kindness in looks and words and ways is true politeness, and any one can have it if they only try to treat other people as he likes to be treated himself."

Mrs. Bhaer had addressed herself to Nan, but the boys nudged one another, and appeared to take the hint, for that time at least, and passed the butter; said "please," and "thank you," "yes, sir," and "no, ma'am," with unusual elegance and respect. Nan said nothing, but kept herself quiet and refrained from tickling Demi, though strongly tempted to do so, because of the dignified airs he put on. She also appeared to have forgotten her hatred of boys, and played "I spy" with them till dark. Stuffy was observed to offer her frequent sucks of his candy ball during the game, which evidently sweetened her temper, for the last thing she said on going to bed was, —

"When my battledore and shuttlecock come, I'll let you all play with them."

Her first remark in the morning was "Has my box come?" and when told that it would arrive some time during the day, she fretted and fumed, and whipped her doll, till Daisy was shocked. She managed to exist, however, till five o'clock, when she disappeared, and was not missed till supper time, because those at home thought she had gone to the hill with Tommy and Demi.

"I saw her going down the avenue alone as hard as she could pelt," said Mary Ann, coming in with the hasty pudding, and finding every one asking, "Where is Nan?"

"She has run home, little gypsy!" cried Mrs. Bhaer, looking anxious.

"Perhaps she has gone to the station to look after her luggage," suggested Franz.

"That is impossible, she does not know the way, and if she found it she could never carry the box a mile," said Mrs. Bhaer, beginning to think that her new idea might be rather a hard one to carry out.

"It would be like her," and Mr. Bhaer caught up his hat to go to find the child, when a shout from Jack, who was at the window, made every one hurry to the door.

There was Miss Nan, to be sure, tugging along a large bandbox tied up in a linen bag. Very hot and dusty and tired did she look, but marched stoutly along, and came puffing up to the steps, where she dropped her load with a sigh of relief, and sat down upon it, observing as she crossed her tired arms, "I couldn't wait any longer, so I went and got it."

"But you did not know the way," said Tommy, while the rest stood round enjoying the joke.

"Oh, I found it, I never get lost."

"It's a mile, how could you go so far?"

"Well, it was pretty far, but I rested a good deal."

"Wasn't that thing very heavy?"

"It's so round, I couldn't get hold of it good, and I thought my arms would break right off."

"I don't see how the station master let you have it," said Tommy.

"I didn't say anything to him. He was in the little ticket place, and didn't see me, so I just took it."

"Run down and tell him it is all right, Franz, or old Dodd will think it is stolen," said Mr. Bhaer, joining in the shout of laughter at Nan's coolness.

"I told you we would send for it if it did not come. Another time you must wait, for you will get into trouble if you run away. Promise me this, or I shall not dare to trust you out of my sight," said Mrs. Bhaer, wiping the dust off Nan's little hot face.

"Well, I won't, only papa tells me not to put off doing things, so I don't."

"That is rather a poser; I think you had better give her some supper now, and a private lecture by and by," said Mr. Bhaer, too much amused to be angry at the young lady's exploit.

The boys thought it "great fun," and Nan entertained them all supper time with an account of her adventures; for a big dog had barked at her, a man had laughed at her, a woman had given her a doughnut, and her hat had fallen into the brook when she stopped to drink, exhausted with her exertion.

"I fancy you will have your hands full now, my dear, Tommy and Nan are quite enough for one woman," said Mr. Bhaer, half an hour later.

"I know it will take some time to tame the child, but she is such a generous, warm-hearted little thing, I should love her even if she were twice as naughty," answered Mrs. Jo, pointing to the merry group, in the middle of which stood Nan, giving away her things right and left, as lavishly as if the big bandbox had no bottom.

It was those good traits that soon made little "Giddy-gaddy," as they called her, a favorite with every one. Daisy never complained of being dull again, for Nan invented the most delightful plays, and her pranks rivaled Tommy's, to the amusement of the whole school. She buried her big doll and forgot it for a week, and found it well mildewed when she dug it up. Daisy was in despair, but Nan took it to the painter who was at work about the house, got him to paint it brick red, with staring black eyes, then she dressed it up with feathers, and scarlet flannel, and one of Ned's leaden hatchets; and in the character of an Indian chief, the late Poppydilla tomahawked all the other dolls, and caused the nursery to run red with imaginary gore. She gave away her new shoes to a beggar child, hoping to be allowed to go barefoot, but found it impossible to combine charity and comfort, and was ordered to ask leave before disposing of her clothes. She delighted the boys by making a fire ship out of a shingle with two large sails wet with turpentine, which she lighted, and then sent the little vessel floating down the brook at dusk. She harnessed the old turkey cock to a straw wagon, and made him trot round the house at a tremendous pace. She gave her coral necklace for four unhappy kittens, which had been tormented by some heartless lads, and tended them for days as gently as a mother, dressing their wounds with cold cream, feeding them with a doll's spoon, and mourning over them when they died, till she was consoled by one of Demi's best turtles. She made Silas tattoo an anchor on her arm like his, and begged hard to have a blue star on each cheek, but he dared not do it, though she coaxed and scolded till the soft-hearted fellow longed to give in. She rode every animal on the place, from the big horse Andy to the cross pig, from whom she was rescued with difficulty. Whatever the boys dared her to do she instantly attempted, no matter how dangerous it might be, and they were never tired of testing her courage.

Mr. Bhaer suggested that they should see who would study best, and Nan found as much pleasure in using her quick wits and fine memory as her active feet and merry tongue, while the lads had to do their best to keep their places, for Nan showed them that girls could do most things as well as boys, and some things better. There were no rewards in school, but Mr. Bhaer's "Well done!" and Mrs. Bhaer's good report in the conscience book taught them to love duty for its own sake, and try to do it faithfully, sure that sooner or later the recompense would come. Little Nan was quick to feel the new atmosphere, to enjoy it, to show that it was what she needed; for this little garden was full of sweet flowers, half hidden by the weeds; and when kind hands gently began to cultivate it, all sorts of green shoots sprung up, promising to blossom beautifully in the warmth of love and care, the best climate for young hearts and souls all the world over.

CHAPTER EIGHT

Pranks and Plays

~

As there is no particular plan to this story, except to describe a few scenes in the life of Plumfield for the amusement of certain little persons, we will gently ramble along in this chapter and tell some of the pastimes of Mrs. Jo's boys. I beg leave to assure my honored readers that most of the incidents are taken from real life, and that the oddest are the truest; for no person, no matter how vivid an imagination he may have, can invent anything half so droll as the freaks and fancies that originate in the lively brains of little people.

Daisy and Demi were full of these whims, and lived in a world of their own, peopled with lovely or grotesque creatures, to whom they gave the queerest names, and with whom they played the queerest games. One of these nursery inventions was an invisible sprite called "The Naughty Kitty-mouse," whom the children had believed in, feared, and served for a long time. They seldom spoke of it to any one else, kept their rites as private as possible; and, as they never tried to describe it even to

627

themselves, this being had a vague mysterious charm very agreeable to Demi, who delighted in elves and goblins. A most whimsical and tyrannical imp was the Naughty Kitty-mouse, and Daisy found a fearful pleasure in its service, blindly obeying its most absurd demands, which were usually proclaimed from the lips of Demi, whose powers of invention were great. Rob and Teddy sometimes joined in these ceremonies, and considered them excellent fun, although they did not understand half that went on.

One day after school Demi whispered to his sister, with an ominous wag of the head, —

"The Kitty-mouse wants us this afternoon."

"What for?" asked Daisy, anxiously.

"A *sackerryfice*," answered Demi, solemnly. "There must be a fire behind the big rock at two o'clock, and we must all bring the things we like best, and burn them!" he added, with an awful emphasis on the last words.

"Oh, dear! I love the new paper dollies Aunt Amy painted for me best of anything; must I burn them up?" cried Daisy, who never thought of denying the unseen tyrant anything it demanded.

"Every one. I shall burn my boat, my best scrapbook, and *all* my soldiers," said Demi, firmly.

"Well, I will; but it's too bad of Kitty-mouse to want our very nicest things," sighed Daisy.

"A *sackerryfice* means to give up what you are fond of, so we *must*," explained Demi, to whom the new idea had been suggested by hearing Uncle Fritz describe the customs of the Greeks to the big boys who were reading about them in school.

"Is Rob coming too?" asked Daisy.

"Yes, and he is going to bring his toy village; it is all made of wood, you know, and will burn nicely. We'll have a grand bonfire, and see them blaze up, won't we?"

This brilliant prospect consoled Daisy, and she ate her dinner with a row of paper dolls before her, as a sort of farewell banquet.

At the appointed hour the sacrificial train set forth, each child bearing the treasures demanded by the insatiable Kitty-mouse. Teddy insisted on going also, and seeing that all the others had toys, he tucked a squeaking lamb under one arm, and old Annabella under the other, little dreaming what anguish the latter idol was to give him.

"Where are you going, my chickens?" asked Mrs. Jo, as the flock passed her door.

"To play by the big rock; can't we?"

"Yes, only don't go near the pond, and take good care of baby."

"I always do," said Daisy, leading forth her charge with a capable air.

"Now, you must all sit round, and not move till I tell you. This flat stone is an altar, and I am going to make a fire on it."

Demi then proceeded to kindle up a small blaze, as he had seen the boys do at picnics. When the flame burned well, he ordered the company to march round it three times and then stand in a circle.

"I shall begin, and as fast as my things are burnt, you must bring yours."

With that he solemnly laid on a little paper book full of pictures, pasted in by himself; this was followed by a dilapidated boat, and then one by one the unhappy leaden soldiers marched to death. Not one faltered or hung back, from the splendid red and yellow captain to the small drummer who had lost his legs; all vanished in the flames and mingled in one common pool of melted lead.

"Now, Daisy!" called the high priest of Kitty-mouse, when his rich offerings had been consumed, to the great satisfaction of the children.

"My dear dollies, how *can* I let them go?" moaned Daisy, hugging the entire dozen with a face full of maternal woe.

"You must," commanded Demi; and with a farewell kiss to each, Daisy laid her blooming dolls upon the coals.

"Let me keep one, the dear blue thing, she is *so* sweet," besought the poor little mamma, clutching her last in despair.

"More! more!" growled an awful voice, and Demi cried, "That's the Kitty-mouse! she must have every one, quick, or she will scratch us."

In went the precious blue belle, flounces, rosy hat, and all, and nothing but a few black flakes remained of that bright band.

"Stand the houses and trees round, and let them catch themselves; it will be like a real fire then," said Demi, who liked variety in his "sackerryfices."

Charmed by this suggestion, the children arranged the doomed village, laid a line of coals along the main street, and then sat down to watch the conflagration. It was somewhat slow to kindle owing to the paint, but at last one ambitious little cottage blazed up, fired a tree of the palm species, which fell on to the roof of a large family mansion, and in a few minutes the entire town was burning merrily. The wooden population stood and stared at the destruction like blockheads, as they were, till they also caught and blazed away without a cry. It took some time to reduce the town to ashes, and the lookers-on enjoyed the spectacle immensely, cheering as each house fell, dancing like wild Indians when the steeple flamed aloft, and actually casting one wretched little churn-shaped lady, who had escaped to the suburbs, into the very heart of the fire.

The superb success of this last offering excited Teddy to such a degree, that he first threw his lamb into the conflagration, and before it had time even to roast, he planted poor dear Annabella on the funeral pyre. Of course she did not like it, and expressed her anguish and resentment in a way that terrified her infant destroyer. Being covered with kid, she did not blaze, but did what was worse, she *squirmed*. First one leg curled up, then the other, in a very awful and lifelike manner; next she flung her arms over her head as if in great agony; her head itself turned on her shoulders, her glass eyes fell out, and with one final writhe of her whole body, she sank down a blackened mass, on the ruins of the town. This unexpected demonstration startled everyone and frightened Teddy half out of his little wits. He looked, then screamed and fled toward the house, roaring "Marmar" at the top of his voice.

Mrs. Bhaer heard the outcry and ran to the rescue, but Teddy could only cling to her and pour out in his broken way something about, "poor Bella hurted," a "a dreat fire," and "all the dollies dorn." Fearing some dire mishap, his mother caught him up and hurried to the scene of action, where she found the blind worshipers of Kitty-mouse mourning over the charred remains of the lost darling.

"What have you been doing? Tell me all about it," said Mrs. Jo, composing herself to listen patiently, for the culprits looked so penitent she forgave them beforehand.

With some reluctance Demi explained their play, and Aunt Jo laughed till the tears ran down her cheeks, the children were so solemn, and the play was so absurd.

"I thought you were too sensible to play such a silly game as this. If I had any Kitty-mouse I'd have a good one who liked you to play in safe pleasant ways, and not destroy and frighten. Just see what a ruin you have made; all Daisy's pretty dolls, Demi's soldiers, and Rob's new village, beside poor Teddy's pet lamb, and dear old Annabella. I shall have to write up in the nursery the verse that used to come in the boxes of toys. Only I shall put Plumfield instead of Boston."

"'*The children of Holland take pleasure in making,*
What the children of Boston take pleasure in breaking.'"

"We never will again, truly, truly!" cried the repentant little sinners, much abashed at this reproof.

"Demi told us to," said Rob.

"Well, I heard uncle tell about the Greece people, who had altars and things, and so I wanted to be like them, only I hadn't any live creatures to sackerryfice, so we burnt up our toys."

"Dear me, that is something like the bean story," said Aunt Jo, laughing again.

"Tell about it," suggested Daisy, to change the subject.

"Once there was a poor woman who had three or four little children, and she used to lock them up in her room when she went out to work, to keep them safe. One day when she was going away she said, 'Now, my dears, don't let baby fall out of the window, don't play with the matches, and don't put beans up your noses.' Now the children had never dreamed of doing that last thing, but she put it into their heads, and the minute she was gone, they ran and stuffed their naughty little noses full of beans, just to see how it felt, and she found them all crying when she came home."

"Did it hurt?" asked Rob, with such intense interest that his mother hastily added a warning sequel, lest a new edition of the bean story should appear in her own family.

"Very much, as I know, for when *my* mother told me this story, I was so silly that I went and tried it myself. I had no beans, so I took some little pebbles, and poked several into my nose. I did not like it at all, and wanted to take them out again very soon, but one would not come, and I was so ashamed to tell what a goose I had been that I went for hours with the stone hurting me very much. At last the pain got so bad I had to tell, and when my mother could not get it out the doctor came. Then I was put in a chair and held tight, Rob, while he used his ugly little pincers till the stone hopped out. Dear me! how my wretched little nose did ache, and how people laughed at me!" and Mrs. Jo shook her head in a dismal way, as if the memory of her sufferings was too much for her.

Rob looked deeply impressed and I am glad to say took the warning to heart. Demi proposed that they should bury poor Annabella, and in the interest of the funeral Teddy forgot his fright. Daisy was soon consoled by another batch of dolls from Aunt Amy, and the Naughty Kitty-mouse seemed to be appeased by the last offerings, for she tormented them no more.

"Brops" was the name of a new and absorbing play, invented by Bangs. As this interesting animal is not to be found in any Zoölogical Garden, unless Du Chaillu has recently brought one from the wilds of Africa, I will mention a few of its peculiar habits and traits, for the benefit of inquiring minds. The Brop is a winged quadruped, with a human face of a youthful and merry aspect. When it walks the earth it grunts, when it soars it gives a shrill hoot, occasionally it goes erect, and talks good English. Its body is usually covered with a substance much resembling a shawl, sometimes red, sometimes blue, often plaid, and, strange to say, it frequently changes skins with one another. On its head it has a horn very like a stiff brown paper lamplighter. Wings of the same substance flap upon its shoulders when it flies; this is never very far from the ground, as it usually falls with violence if it attempts any lofty flights. These animals browse over the earth, but can sit up and eat like the squirrel. Their favorite nourishment is the seed cake; apples also are freely taken, and sometimes raw carrots are nibbled when food is scarce. They live in dens, where they have a sort of nest, much like a clothes basket, in which the little Brops play till their wings are grown. These singular animals quarrel at times, and it is on these occasions that they burst into human speech, call each other names, cry, scold, and sometimes tear off horns and skin, declaring fiercely that they "won't play." The few privileged persons who have studied them are inclined to think them a remarkable mixture of the monkey, the sphinx, the roc, and the queer creatures seen by the famous Peter Wilkins.

This game was a great favorite, and the younger children beguiled many a rainy afternoon flapping or creeping about the nursery, acting like little bedlamites and being as merry as little grigs. To be sure, it was rather hard upon clothes, particularly trouser knees and jacket elbows; but Mrs. Bhaer only said, as she patched and darned, –

"We do things just as foolish, and not half so harmless. If I could get as much happiness out of it as the little dears do, I'd be a Brop myself."

Nat's favorite amusements were working in his garden, and sitting in the willow tree with his violin, for that green nest was a fairy world to him, and there he loved to perch, making music like a happy bird. The lads called him "Old Chirper," because he was always humming, whistling, or fiddling, and they often stopped a minute in their work or play to listen to the soft tones of the violin, which seemed to lead a little orchestra of summer sounds. The birds appeared to regard him as one of themselves, and fearlessly sat on the fence or lit among the boughs to watch him with their quick, bright eyes. The robins in the apple tree near-by evidently considered him a friend, for the father bird hunted insects close beside him, and the little mother brooded as confidingly over her blue eggs as if the boy was only a new sort of blackbird, who cheered her patient watch with his song. The brown brook babbled and sparkled below him, the bees haunted the clover fields on either side, friendly faces peeped at him as they passed, the old house stretched its wide wings hospitably toward him, and with a blessed sense of rest and love, and happiness, Nat dreamed for hours in this nook, unconscious what healthful miracles were being wrought upon him.

One listener he had who never tired, and to whom he was more than a mere schoolmate. Poor Billy's chief delight was to lie beside the brook, watching leaves and bits of foam dance by, listening dreamily to the music in the willow tree. He seemed to think Nat a sort of angel who sat aloft and sang, for a few baby memories still lingered in his mind and seemed to grow brighter at these times. Seeing the interest he took in Nat, Mr. Bhaer begged him to help them lift the cloud from the feeble brain by this gentle spell. Glad to do anything to show his gratitude, Nat always smiled on Billy when he followed him about, and let him listen undisturbed to the music which seemed to speak a language he could understand. "Help one another" was a favorite Plumfield motto, and Nat learned how much sweetness is added to life by trying to live up to it.

Jack Ford's peculiar pastime was buying and selling; and he bid fair to follow in the footsteps of his uncle, a country merchant, who sold a little of everything and made money fast. Jack had seen the sugar sanded, the molasses watered, the butter mixed with lard, and things of that kind, and labored under the delusion that it was all a proper part of the business. His stock in trade was of a different sort, but he made as much as he could out of every worm he sold, and always got the best of the bargain when he traded with the boys for string, knives, fish hooks, or whatever the article might be. The boys, who all had nicknames, called him "Skinflint," but Jack did not care as long as the old tobacco pouch in which he kept his money grew heavier and heavier.

He established a sort of auction room, and now and then sold off all the odds and ends he had collected, or helped the lads exchange things with one another. He got bats, balls, hockey sticks, etc., cheap, from one set of mates, furbished them up, and let them for a few cents a time to another set, often extending his business beyond the gates of Plumfield in spite of the rules. Mr. Bhaer put a stop to some of his speculations, and tried to give him a better idea of business talent than mere sharpness in overreaching his neighbors. Now and then Jack made a bad bargain, and felt worse about it than about any failure in lessons or conduct, and took his revenge on the next innocent customer who came along. His account book was a curiosity; and his quickness at figures quite remarkable. Mr. Bhaer praised him for this, and tried to make his sense of honesty and honor as quick; and, by and by, when Jack found that he could not get on without these virtues, he owned that his teacher was right.

Cricket and football the boys had of course – but, after the stirring accounts of those games in the immortal "Tom Brown at Rugby," no feeble female pen may venture to do more than respectfully allude to them.

Emil spent his holidays on the river or the pond, and drilled the elder lads for a race with certain town boys, who now and then invaded their territory. The race duly came off, but as it ended in a general shipwreck, it was not mentioned in public; and the Commodore had serious thoughts of retiring to a desert island, so disgusted was he with his kind for a time. No desert island being convenient, he was forced to remain among his friends, and found consolation in building a boat house.

The little girls indulged in the usual plays of their age, improving upon them somewhat as their lively fancies suggested. The chief and most absorbing play was called "Mrs. Shakespeare Smith;" the name was provided by Aunt Jo, but the trials of the poor lady were quite original.

Daisy was Mrs. S. S., and Nan by turns her daughter or a neighbor, Mrs. Giddygaddy.

No pen can describe the adventures of these ladies, for in one short afternoon their family was the scene of births, marriages, deaths, floods, earthquakes, tea parties, and balloon ascensions. Millions of miles did these energetic women travel, dressed in hats and habits never seen before by mortal eye, perched on the bed, driving the posts like mettlesome steeds, and bouncing up and down till their heads spun. Fits and fires were the pet afflictions, with a general massacre now and then by way of change. Nan was never tired of inventing fresh combinations, and Daisy followed her leader with blind admiration. Poor Teddy was a frequent victim, and was often rescued from real danger, for the excited ladies were apt to forget that he was not of the same stuff as their long-suffering dolls. Once he was shut into a closet for a dungeon, and forgotten by the girls, who ran off to some out-of-door game. Another time he was half drowned in the bathtub, playing be a "cunning little whale." And, worst of all, he was cut down just in time after being hung up for a robber.

But the institution most patronized by all was the Club. It had no other name, and it needed none, being the only one in the neighborhood. The elder lads got it up, and the younger were occasionally admitted if they behaved well. Tommy and Demi were honorary members, but were always obliged to retire unpleasantly early, owing to circumstances over which they had no control. The proceedings of this club were somewhat peculiar, for it met at all sorts of places and hours, had all manner of queer ceremonies and amusements, and now and then was broken up tempestuously, only to be re-established, however, on a firmer basis.

Rainy evenings the members met in the schoolroom, and passed the time in games: chess, morris, backgammon, fencing matches, recitations, debates, or dramatic performances of a darkly tragical nature. In summer the barn was the rendezvous, and what went on there no uninitiated mortal knows. On sultry evenings the Club adjourned to the brook for aquatic exercises, and the members sat about in airy attire, froglike and cool. On such occasions the speeches were unusually eloquent, quite flowing, as one might say; and if any orator's remarks displeased the audience, cold water was thrown upon him till his ardor was effectually quenched. Franz was president, and maintained order admirably, considering the unruly nature of the members. Mr. Bhaer never interfered with their affairs, and was rewarded for this wise forbearance by being invited now and then to behold the mysteries unveiled, which he appeared to enjoy much.

When Nan came she wished to join the Club, and caused great excitement and division among the gentlemen by presenting endless petitions, both written and spoken, disturbing their solemnities by insulting them through the keyhole, performing vigorous solos on the door, and writing up derisive remarks on walls and fences, for she belonged to the "Irrepressibles." Finding these appeals vain, the girls, by the advice of Mrs. Jo, got up an institution of their own, which they called the Cosy Club. To this they magnanimously invited the gentlemen whose youth excluded them from the other one, and entertained these favored beings so well with little suppers, new games devised by Nan, and other pleasing festivities, that, one by one, the elder boys confessed a desire to partake of these more elegant enjoyments, and, after much consultation, finally decided to propose an interchange of civilities.

The members of the Cosy Club were invited to adorn the rival establishment on certain evenings, and to the surprise of the gentlemen their presence was not found to be a restraint upon the conversation or amusement of the regular frequenters; which could not be said of all Clubs, I fancy. The ladies responded handsomely and hospitably to these overtures of peace, and both institutions flourished long and happily.

CHAPTER NINE

DAISY'S BALL
~

"Mrs. Shakespeare Smith would like to have Mr. John Brooke, Mr. Thomas Bangs and Mr. Nathaniel Blake to come to her ball at three o'clock to-day.

"P.S. – Nat must bring his fiddle, so we can dance, and all the boys must be good, or they cannot have any of the nice things we have cooked."

This elegant invitation would, I fear, have been declined, but for the hint given in the last line of the postscript.

"They *have* been cooking lots of goodies, I smelled them. Let's go," said Tommy.

"We needn't stay after the feast, you know," added Demi.

"I never went to a ball. What do you have to do?" asked Nat.

"Oh, we just play be men, and sit round stiff and stupid like grown-up folks, and dance to please the girls. Then we eat up everything, and come away as soon as we can."

"I think I could do that," said Nat, after considering Tommy's description for a minute.

"I'll write and say we'll come," and Demi despatched the following gentlemanly reply, –

"We will come. Please have lots to eat.– J. B. Esquire."

Great was the anxiety of the ladies about their first ball, because if everything went well they intended to give a dinner party to the chosen few.

"Aunt Jo likes to have the boys play with us, if they are not rough; so we must make them like our balls, then they will do them good," said Daisy, with her maternal air, as she set the table and surveyed the store of refreshments with an anxious eye.

"Demi and Nat will be good, but Tommy will do something bad, I know he will," replied Nan, shaking her head over the little cake basket which she was arranging.

"Then I shall send him right home," said Daisy.

"People don't do so at parties, it isn't proper."

"I shall never ask him any more."

"That would do. He'd be sorry not to come to the dinner ball, wouldn't he?"

"I guess he would! we'll have the splendidest things ever seen, won't we? Real soup with a ladle and a tureem (she meant *tureen*) and a little bird for turkey, and gravy, and all kinds of nice vegytubbles." Daisy never *could* say vegetables properly, and had given up trying.

"It is almost three, and we ought to dress," said Nan, who had arranged a fine costume for the occasion, and was anxious to wear it.

"I am the mother, so I shan't dress up much," said Daisy, putting on a night-cap ornamented with a red bow, one of her aunt's long skirts, and a shawl; a pair of spectacles and a large pocket handkerchief completed her toilette, making a plump, rosy little matron of her.

Nan had a wreath of artificial flowers, a pair of old pink slippers, a yellow scarf, a green muslin skirt, and a fan made of feathers from the duster; also, as a last touch of elegance, a smelling bottle without any smell in it.

"I am the daughter, so I dress up a good deal, and I must sing and dance, and talk more than you do. The mothers only get the tea and be proper, you know."

A sudden very loud knock caused Miss Smith to fly into a chair, and fan herself violently, while her mamma sat bolt upright on the sofa, and tried to look quite calm and "proper." Little Bess, who was on a visit, acted the part of maid, and opened the door, saying with a smile, "Wart in, gemplemun; it's all weady."

In honor of the occasion, the boys wore high paper collars, tall black hats, and gloves of every color and material, for they were an afterthought, and not a boy among them had a perfect pair.

"Good day, mum," said Demi, in a deep voice, which was so hard to keep up that his remarks had to be extremely brief.

Every one shook hands and then sat down, looking so funny, yet so sober, that the gentlemen forgot their manners, and rolled in their chairs with laughter.

"Oh, don't!" cried Mrs. Smith, much distressed.

"You can't ever come again if you act so," added Miss Smith, rapping Mr. Bangs with her bottle because he laughed loudest.

"I can't help it, you look so like fury," gasped Mr. Bangs, with most uncourteous candor.

"So do you, but I shouldn't be so rude as to say so. He shan't come to the dinner ball, shall he, Daisy?" cried Nan, indignantly.

"I think we had better dance now. Did you bring your fiddle, sir?" asked Mrs. Smith, trying to preserve her polite composure.

"It is outside the door," and Nat went to get it.

"Better have tea first," proposed the unabashed Tommy, winking openly at Demi to remind him that the sooner the refreshments were secured, the sooner they could escape.

"No, we never have supper first; and if you don't dance well you won't have any supper at all, *not one bit, sir*,' said Mrs. Smith, so sternly that her wild guests saw she was not to be trifled with, and grew overwhelmingly civil all at once.

"*I* will take Mr. Bangs and teach him the polka, for he does not know it fit to be seen," added the hostess, with a reproachful look that sobered Tommy at once.

Nat struck up, and the ball opened with two couples, who went conscientiously through a somewhat varied dance. The ladies did well, because they liked it, but the gentlemen exerted themselves from more selfish motives, for each felt that he must earn his supper, and labored manfully toward that end. When every one was out of breath they were allowed to rest; and, indeed, poor Mrs. Smith needed it, for her long dress had tripped her up many times. The little maid passed round molasses and water in such small cups that one guest actually emptied nine. I refrain from mentioning his name, because this mild beverage affected him so much that he put cup and all into his mouth at the ninth round, and choked himself publicly.

"You must ask Nan to play and sing now," said Daisy to her brother, who sat looking very much like an owl, as he gravely regarded the festive scene between his high collars.

"Give us a song, mum," said the obedient guest, secretly wondering where the piano was.

Miss Smith sailed up to an old secretary which stood in the room, threw back the lid of the writing-desk, and sitting down before it, accompanied herself with a vigour which made the old desk rattle as she sang that new and lovely song, beginning, —

> *Gaily the troubadour*
> *Touched his guitar,*
> *As he was hastening*
> *Home from the war.*

The gentlemen applauded so enthusiastically that she gave them "Bounding Billows," "Little Bo-Peep," and other gems of song, till they were obliged to hint that they had had enough. Grateful for the praises bestowed upon her daughter, Mrs. Smith graciously announced, "*Now* we will have tea. Sit down carefully, and don't grab."

It was beautiful to see the air of pride with which the good lady did the honors of her table, and the calmness with which she bore the little mishaps that occurred. The best pie flew wildly on the floor when she tried to cut it with a very dull knife; the bread and butter vanished with a rapidity calculated to dismay a housekeeper's soul; and, worst of all, the custards were so soft that they had to be drunk up, instead of being eaten elegantly with the new tin spoons.

I grieve to state that Miss Smith squabbled with the maid for the best jumble, which caused Bess to toss the whole dish into the air, and burst out crying amid a rain of falling cakes. She was comforted by a seat at the

"Go on, and strike harder!" (Chapter 4)

*There was Miss Nan, tugging along a large
bandbox tied up in a linen bag. (Chapter 8)*

table, and the sugar bowl to empty; but during this flurry a large plate of patties was mysteriously lost, and could not be found. They were the chief ornament of the feast, and Mrs. Smith was indignantly at the loss, for she had made them herself, and they were beautiful to behold. I put it to any lady if it was not hard to have one dozen delicious patties (made of flour, salt, and water, with a large raisin in the middle of each, and much sugar over the whole) swept away at one fell swoop?

"You hid them, Tommy; I know you did!" cried the outraged hostess, threatening her suspected guest with the milk pot.

"I didn't!"

"You did!"

"It isn't proper to contradict," said Nan, who was hastily eating up the jelly during the fray.

"Give them back, Demi," said Tommy.

"That's a fib, you've got them in your own pocket," bawled Demi, roused by the false accusation.

"Let's take them away from him. It's too bad to make Daisy cry," suggested Nat, who found his first ball more exciting that he expected.

Daisy was already weeping, Bess like a devoted servant mingled her tears with those of her mistress, and Nan denounced the entire race of boys as "plaguy things." Meanwhile the battle raged among the gentlemen, for, when the two defenders of innocence fell upon the foe, that hardened youth intrenched himself behind a table and pelted them with the stolen tarts, which were very effective missiles, being nearly as hard as bullets. While his ammunition held out the besieged prospered, but the moment the last patty flew over the parapet, the villain was seized, dragged howling from the room, and cast upon the hall floor in an ignominious heap. The conquerors then returned flushed with victory, and while Demi consoled poor Mrs. Smith, Nat and Nan collected the scattered tarts, replaced each raisin in its proper bed, and rearranged the dish so that it really looked almost as well as ever. But their glory had departed, for the sugar was gone, and no one cared to eat them after the insult offered to them.

"I guess we had better go," said Demi, suddenly, as Aunt Jo's voice was heard on the stairs.

"Perhaps we had," and Nat hastily dropped a stray jumble that he had just picked up.

But Mrs. Jo was among them before the retreat was accomplished, and into her sympathetic ear the young ladies poured the story of their woes.

"No more balls for these boys till they have atoned for this bad behavior by doing something kind to you," said Mrs. Jo, shaking her head at the three culprits.

"We were only in fun," began Demi.

"I don't like fun that makes other people unhappy. I am disappointed in you, Demi, for I hoped you would never learn to tease Daisy. Such a kind little sister as she is to you."

"Boys always tease their sisters; Tom says so," muttered Demi.

"I don't intend that *my* boys shall, and I must send Daisy home if you cannot play happily together," said Aunt Jo, soberly.

At this awful threat, Demi sidled up to his sister, and Daisy hastily dried her tears, for to be separated was the worst misfortune that could happen to the twins.

"Nat was bad too, and Tommy was baddest of all," observed Nan, fearing that two of the sinners would not get their fair share of punishment.

"I am sorry," said Nat, much ashamed.

"I ain't!" bawled Tommy through the keyhole, where he was listening, with all his might.

Mrs. Jo wanted very much to laugh, but kept her countenance, and said impressively, as she pointed to the door, –

"You can go, boys, but remember, you are not to speak to or play with the little girls till I give you leave. You don't deserve the pleasure, so I forbid it."

The ill-mannered young gentlemen hastily retired, to be received outside with derision and scorn by the unrepentant Bangs, who would not associate with them for at least fifteen minutes. Daisy was soon consoled for the failure of her ball, but lamented the edict that parted her from her brother, and mourned over his shortcomings in her tender little heart. Nan rather enjoyed the trouble, and went about turning up her pug nose at the three, especially Tommy, who pretended not to care, and loudly proclaimed his satisfaction at being rid of those "stupid girls." But in his secret soul he soon repented of the rash act that caused this banishment from the society he loved, and every hour of separation taught him the value of the "stupid girls."

The others gave in very soon, and longed to be friends, for now there was no Daisy to pet and cook for them; no Nan to amuse and doctor them; and, worst of all, no Mrs. Jo to make home pleasant and life easy for them. To their great affliction, Mrs. Jo seemed to consider herself one of the offended girls, for she hardly spoke to the outcasts, looked as if she did not see them when she passed, and was always too busy now to attend to their requests. This sudden and entire exile from favor cast a gloom over their souls, for when Mother Bhaer deserted them, their sun had set at noonday, as it were, and they had no refuge left.

This unnatural state of things actually lasted for three days, then they could bear it no longer, and fearing that the eclipse might become total, went to Mr. Bhaer for help and counsel.

It is my private opinion that he had received instructions how to behave if the case should be laid before him. But no one suspected it, and he gave the afflicted boys some advice, which they gratefully accepted and carried out in the following manner:

Secluding themselves in the garret, they devoted several play-hours to the manufacture of some mysterious machine, which took so much paste that Asia grumbled, and the little girls wondered mightily. Nan nearly got her inquisitive nose pinched in the door, trying to see what was going on, and Daisy sat about, openly lamenting that they could not all play nicely together, and not have any dreadful secrets. Wednesday afternoon was fine, and after a good deal of consultation about wind and weather, Nat and Tommy went off, bearing an immense flat parcel hidden under many newspapers. Nan nearly died with suppressed curiosity, Daisy nearly cried with vexation, and both quite trembled with interest when Demi marched into Mrs. Bhaer's room, hat in hand, and said, in the politest tone possible to a mortal boy of his years, —

"Please, Aunt Jo, would you and the girls come out to a surprise party we have made for you? Do; it's a *very* nice one."

"Thank you, we will come with pleasure; only, I must take Teddy with me," replied Mrs. Bhaer, with a smile that cheered Demi like sunshine after rain.

"We'd like to have him. The little wagon is all ready for the girls; and you won't mind walking just up to Pennyroyal Hill, will you, Aunty?"

"I should like it exceedingly; but are you quite sure I shall not be in the way?"

"Oh, no, indeed! we want you very much; and the party will be spoiled if you don't come," cried Demi, with great earnestness.

"Thank you kindly, sir," and Aunt Jo made him a grand curtsey, for she liked frolics as well as any of them.

"Now, young ladies, we must not keep them waiting; on with the hats, and let us be off at once. I'm all impatience to know what the surprise is."

As Mrs. Bhaer spoke every one bustled about, and in five minutes the three little girls and Teddy were packed into the "clothes basket," as they called the wicker wagon which Toby drew. Demi walked at the head of the procession, and Mrs. Jo brought up the rear, escorted by Kit. It was a most imposing party, I assure you, for Toby had a red feather duster in his head, two remarkable flags waved over the carriage, Kit had a blue bow on his neck, which nearly drove him wild, Demi wore a nosegay of dandelions in his buttonhole, and Mrs. Jo carried the queer Japanese umbrella in honor of the occasion.

The girls had little flutters of excitement all the way; and Teddy was so charmed with the drive that he kept dropping his hat overboard, and when it was taken from him he prepared to tumble out himself, evidently feeling that it behoved him to do something for the amusement of the party.

When they came to the hill "nothing was to be seen but the grass blowing in the wind," as the fairy books say, and the children looked disappointed. But Demi said, in his most impressive manner, –

"Now, you all get out and stand still, and the surprise party will come in," with which remark he retired behind a rock, over which heads had been bobbing at intervals for the last half hour.

A short pause of intense suspense, and then Nat, Demi, and Tommy marched forth, each bearing a new kite, which they presented to the three young ladies. Shrieks of delight arose, but were silenced by the boys, who said, with faces brimful of merriment, "That isn't all the surprise," and, running behind the rock, again emerged bearing a fourth kite of superb size, on which was printed, in bright yellow letters, "For Mother Bhaer."

"We thought you'd like one, too, because you were angry with us, and took the girls' part," cried all three, shaking with laughter, for this part of the affair evidently *was* a surprise to Mrs. Jo.

She clapped her hands, and joined in the laugh, looking thoroughly tickled at the joke.

"Now, boys, that is regularly splendid! Who did think of it?" she asked, receiving the monster kite with as much pleasure as the little girls did theirs.

"Uncle Fritz proposed it when we planned to make the others; he said you'd like it, so we made a bouncer," answered Demi, beaming with satisfaction at the success of the plot.

"Uncle Fritz knows what I like. Yes, these are magnificent kites, and we were wishing we had some the other day when you were flying yours, weren't we, girls?"

"That's why we made them for you," cried Tommy, standing on his head as the most appropriate way of expressing his emotions.

"Let's fly them," said energetic Nan.

"I don't know how," began Daisy.

"We'll show you, we want to!" cried all the boys in a burst of devotion, as Demi took Daisy's, Tommy Nan's, and Nat, with difficulty, persuaded Bess to let go her little blue one.

"Aunty, if you will wait a minute, we'll pitch yours for you," said Demi, feeling that Mrs. Bhaer's favor must not be lost again by any neglect of theirs.

"Bless your buttons, dear, I know all about it; and here is a boy who will toss up for me," added Mrs. Jo, as the professor peeped over the rock with a face full of fun.

He came out at once, tossed up the big kite, and Mrs. Jo ran off with it in fine style, while the children stood and enjoyed the spectacle. One by one all the kites went up, and floated far overhead like gay birds, balancing themselves on the fresh breeze that blew steadily over the hill. Such a merry time as they had, running and shouting, sending up the kites or pulling them down, watching their antics in the air, and feeling them tug at the string like live creatures trying to escape! Nan was quite wild with the fun, Daisy thought the new play nearly as interesting as dolls, and little Bess was so fond of her "boo tite," that she would only let it go on very short flights, preferring to hold it in her lap and look at the remarkable pictures painted on it by Tommy's dashing brush. Mrs. Jo enjoyed hers immensely, and it acted as if it knew who owned it, for it came tumbling down head first when least expected, caught on trees, nearly pitched into the river, and finally darted away to such a height that it looked a mere speck among the clouds.

By and by every one got tired, and fastening the kite strings to trees and fences, all sat down to rest, except Mr. Bhaer, who went off to look at the cows, with Teddy on his shoulder.

"Did you ever have such a good time as this before?" asked Nat, as they lay about on the grass, nibbling pennyroyal like a flock of sheep.

"Not since I last flew a kite, years ago, when I was a girl," answered Mrs. Jo.

"I'd like to have known you when you were a girl, you must have been so jolly," said Nat.

"I was a naughty little girl, I am sorry to say."

"I like naughty little girls," observed Tommy, looking at Nan, who made a frightful grimace at him in return for the compliment.

"Why don't I remember you then, Aunty? Was I too young?" asked Demi.

"Rather, dear."

"I suppose my memory hadn't come then. Grandpa says that different parts of the mind unfold as we grow up, and the memory part of my mind hadn't unfolded when you were little, so I can't remember how you looked," explained Demi.

"Now, little Socrates, you had better keep that question for grandpa, it is beyond me," said Aunt Jo, putting on the extinguisher.

"Well, I will, *he* knows about those things, and *you* don't," returned Demi, feeling that on the whole kites were better adapted to the comprehension of the present company.

"Tell about the last time you flew a kite," said Nat, for Mrs. Jo had laughed as she spoke of it, and he thought it might be interesting.

"Oh, it was only rather funny, for I was a great girl of fifteen, and was ashamed to be seen at such a play. So Uncle Teddy and I privately made our kites, and stole away to fly them. We had a capital time, and were resting as we are now, when suddenly we heard voices, and saw a party of young ladies and gentlemen coming back from a picnic. Teddy did not mind, though he was rather a large boy to be playing with a kite, but I was in a great flurry, for I knew I should be sadly laughed at, and never hear the last of it, because my wild ways amused the neighbors as much as Nan's do us.

"'What shall I do?' I whispered to Teddy, as the voices drew nearer and nearer.

"'I'll show you,' he said, and whipping out his knife he cut the strings. Away flew the kites, and when the people came up we were picking flowers as properly as you please. They never suspected us, and we had a grand laugh over our narrow escape."

"Were the kites lost, Aunty?" asked Daisy.

"Quite lost, but I did not care, for I made up my mind that it would be best to wait till I was an old lady before I played with kites again; and you see I have waited," said Mrs. Jo, beginning to pull in the big kite, for it was getting late.

"Must we go now?"

"I must, or you won't have any supper; and that sort of surprise party would not suit you, I think, my chickens."

"Hasn't our party been a nice one?" asked Tommy, complacently.

"Splendid!" answered every one.

"Do you know why? It is because *your* guests have behaved themselves, and tried to make everything go well. You understand what I mean, don't you?"

"Yes'm," was all the boys said, but they stole a shamefaced look at one another, as they meekly shouldered their kites and walked home, thinking of another party where the guests had *not* behaved themselves, and things had gone badly on account of it.

CHAPTER TEN

HOME AGAIN

~

July had come, and haying begun; the little gardens were
doing finely, and the long summer days were full of pleasant
hours. The house stood open from morning till night, and the
lads lived out of doors, except at school time. The lessons were short, and
there were many holidays, for the Bhaers believed in cultivating healthy
bodies by much exercise, and our short summers are best used in out-of-
door work. Such a rosy, sunburned, hearty set as the boys became; such
appetites as they had; such sturdy arms and legs, as outgrew jackets and
trousers; such laughing and racing all over the place; such antics in house
and barn; such adventures in the tramps over hill and dale; and such
satisfaction in the hearts of the worthy Bhaers, as they saw their flock
prospering in mind and body, I cannot begin to describe. Only one thing
was needed to make them quite happy, and it came when they least
expected it.

One balmy night when the little lads were in bed, the elder ones bathing down at the brook, and Mrs. Bhaer undressing Teddy in her parlor, he suddenly cried out, "Oh, my Danny!" and pointed to the window, where the moon shone brightly.

"No, lovey, he is not there, it was the pretty moon," said his mother.

"No, no, Danny at a window; Teddy saw him," persisted baby, much excited.

"It might have been," and Mrs. Bhaer hurried to the window, hoping it would prove true. But the face was gone, and nowhere appeared any signs of a mortal boy; she called his name, ran to the front door with Teddy in his little shirt, and made him call too, thinking the baby voice might have more effect than her own. No one answered, nothing appeared, and they went back much disappointed. Teddy would not be satisfied with the moon, and after he was in his crib kept popping up his head to ask if Danny was not "tumming' soon".

By and by he fell asleep, the lads trooped up to bed, the house grew still, and nothing but the chirp of the crickets broke the soft silence of the summer night. Mrs. Bhaer sat sewing, for the big basket was always piled with socks, full of portentous holes, and thinking of the lost boy. She had decided that baby had been mistaken, and did not even disturb Mr. Bhaer by telling him of the child's fancy, for the poor man got little time to himself till the boys were abed, and he was busy writing letters. It was past ten when she rose to shut up the house. As she paused a minute to enjoy the lovely scene from the steps, something white caught her eye on one of the haycocks scattered over the lawn. The children had been playing there all the afternoon, and, fancying that Nan had left her hat as usual, Mrs. Bhaer went out to get it. But as she approached, she saw that it was neither hat nor handkerchief, but a shirt sleeve with a brown hand sticking out of it. She hurried round the haycock, and there lay Dan, fast asleep.

Ragged, dirty, thin, and worn-out he looked; one foot was bare, the other tied up in the old gingham jacket which he had taken from his own back to use as a clumsy bandage for some hurt. He seemed to have hidden himself behind the haycock, but in his sleep had thrown out the arm that had betrayed him. He sighed and muttered as if his dreams disturbed him, and once when he moved, he groaned as if in pain, but still slept on quite spent with weariness.

"He must not lie here," said Mrs. Bhaer, and stooping over him she gently called his name. He opened his eyes and looked at her, as if she were a part of his dream, for he smiled and said drowsily, "Mother Bhaer, I've come home."

The look, the words, touched her very much, and she put her hand under his head to lift him up, saying in her cordial way, –

"I thought you would, and I'm so glad to see you, Dan." He seemed to wake thoroughly then, and started up looking about him as if he suddenly remembered where he was, and doubted even that kind welcome. His face changed, and he said in his old rough way, –

"I was going off in the morning. I only stopped to peek in, as I went by."

"But why not come in, Dan? Didn't you hear us call you? Teddy saw, and cried for you."

"Didn't suppose you'd let me in," he said, fumbling with a little bundle which he had taken up as if going immediately.

"Try and see," was all Mrs. Bhaer answered, holding out her hand and pointing to the door, where the light shone hospitably.

With a long breath, as if a load was off his mind, Dan took up a stout stick, and began to limp towards the house, but stopped suddenly, to say inquiringly, –

"Mr. Bhaer won't like it. I ran away from Page."

"He knows it, and was sorry, but it will make no difference. Are you lame?" asked Mrs. Jo, as he limped on again.

"Getting over a wall a stone fell on my foot and smashed it. I don't mind," and he did his best to hide the pain that each step cost him.

Mrs. Bhaer helped him into her own room, and, once there, he dropped into a chair, and laid his head back, white and faint with weariness and suffering.

"My poor Dan! drink this, and then eat a little; you are at home now, and Mother Bhaer will take good care of you."

He only looked up at her with eyes full of gratitude, as he drank the wine she help to his lips, and then began slowly to eat the food she brought him. Each mouthful seemed to put heart into him, and presently he began to talk as if anxious to have her know all about him.

"Where have you been, Dan?" she asked, beginning to get out some bandages.

"I ran off more'n a month ago. Page was good enough, but too strict. I didn't like it, so I cut away down the river with a man who was going in his boat. That's why they couldn't tell where I'd gone. When I left the man, I worked for a couple of weeks with a farmer, but I thrashed his boy, and then the old man thrashed me, and I ran off again and walked here."

"All the way?"

"Yes, the man didn't pay me, and I wouldn't ask for it. Took it out in beating the boy," and Dan laughed, yet looked ashamed, as he glanced at his ragged clothes and dirty hands.

"How did you live? It was a long, long tramp for a boy like you."

"Oh, I got on well enough, till I hurt my foot. Folks gave me things to eat, and I slept in barns and tramped by day. I got lost trying to make a short cut, or I'd have been here sooner."

"But if you did not mean to come in and stay with us, what were you going to do?"

"I thought I'd like to see Teddy again, and you; and then I was going back to my old work in the city, only I was so tired I went to sleep on the hay. I'd have been gone in the morning, if you hadn't found me."

"Are you sorry I did?" and Mrs. Jo looked at him with a half merry, half reproachful look, as she knelt down to look at his wounded foot.

The colour came up into Dan's face, and he kept his eyes fixed on his plate, as he said very low, "No, ma'am, I'm glad; I wanted to stay, but I was afraid you —"

He did not finish, for Mrs. Bhaer interrupted him by an exclamation of pity, as she saw his foot, for it was seriously hurt.

"When did you do it?"

"Three days ago."

"And you have walked on it in this state?"

"I had a stick, and I washed it at every brook I came to, and one woman gave me a rag to put on it."

"Mr. Bhaer must see and dress it at once," and Mrs. Jo hastened into the next room, leaving the door ajar behind her, so that Dan heard all that passed.

"Fritz, that boy has come back."

"Who? Dan?"

"Yes, Teddy saw him at the window, and we called to him, but he went away and hid behind the haycocks on the lawn. I found him there just now fast asleep, and half dead with weariness and pain. He ran away from Page a month ago, and has been making his way to us ever since. He pretends that he did not mean to let us see him, but to go on to the city, and his old work, after a look at us. It is evident, however, that the hope of being taken in has led him here through everything, and there he is waiting to know if you will forgive and take him back."

"Did he say so?"

"His eyes did, and when I waked him, he said, like a lost child, 'Mother Bhaer, I've come home.' I hadn't the heart to scold him, and just took him in like a poor little black sheep back to the fold. I may keep him, Fritz?"

"Of course you may! This proves to me that we have a hold on the boy's heart, and I would no more send him away now than I would my own Rob."

Dan heard a soft little sound, as if Mrs. Jo thanked her husband without words, and, in the instant's silence that followed, two great tears that had slowly gathered in the boy's eyes brimmed over and rolled down his dusty cheeks. No one saw them, for he brushed them hastily away; but in that little pause I think Dan's old distrust for these good people vanished for ever, the soft spot in his heart was touched, and he felt an impetuous desire to prove himself worthy of the love and pity that was so patient and forgiving. He said nothing, he only wished the wish with all his might, resolved to try in his blind boyish way, and sealed his resolution with the tears which neither pain, fatigue, nor loneliness could wring from him.

"Come and see his foot. I am afraid it is badly hurt, for he has kept on three days through heat and dust, with nothing but water and an old jacket to bind it up with. I tell you, Fritz, that boy is a brave lad, and will make a fine man yet."

"I hope so, for your sake, enthusiastic woman; your faith deserves success. Now, I will go and see your little Spartan. Where is he?"

"In my room; but, dear, you'll be very kind to him, no matter how gruff he seems. I am sure that is the way to conquer him. He won't bear sternness nor much restraint, but a soft word and infinite patience will lead him as it used to lead me."

"As if you ever were like this little rascal!" cried Mr. Bhaer, laughing, yet half angry at the idea.

"I was in spirit, though I showed it in a different way. I seem to know by instinct how he feels, to understand what will win and touch him, and to sympathize with his temptations and faults. I am glad I do, for it will help me to help him; and if I can make a good man of this wild boy, it will be the best work of my life."

"God bless the work, and help the worker!"

Mr. Bhaer spoke now as earnestly as she had done, and both came in together to find Dan's head down upon his arm, as if he was quite overcome by sleep. But he looked up quickly, and tried to rise as Mr. Bhaer said pleasantly, –

"So you like Plumfield better than Page's farm. Well, let us see if we can get on more comfortably this time than we did before."

"Thanky, sir," said Dan, trying not to be gruff, and finding it easier than he expected.

"Now the foot! Ach! – this is not well. We must have Dr Firth to-morrow. Warm water, Jo, and old linen."

Mr. Bhaer bathed and bound up the wounded foot, while Mrs. Jo prepared the empty bed in the house. It was in the little guest chamber leading from the parlor, and often used when the lads were poorly, for it saved Mrs. Jo from running up and down, and the invalids could see what was going on. When it was ready, Mr. Bhaer took the boy in his arms, carried him in, and helped him undress, laid him on the little white bed, and left him with another hand shake, and a fatherly "Good night, my son."

Dan dropped asleep at once, and slept heavily for several hours; then his foot began to throb and ache, and he awoke to toss about uneasily, trying not to groan lest any one should hear him, for he *was* a brave lad, and did bear pain like "a little Spartan," as Mr. Bhaer called him.

Mrs. Jo had a way of flitting about the house at night, to shut the windows if the wind grew chilly, to draw mosquito curtains over Teddy, or look after Tommy, who occasionally walked in his sleep. The least noise waked her, and as she often heard imaginary robbers, cats, and conflagrations, the doors stood open all about, so her quick ear caught the sound of Dan's little moans, and she was up in a minute. He was just giving his hot pillow a despairing thump when a light came glimmering through the hall, and Mrs. Jo crept in, looking like a droll ghost, with her hair in a great knot on the top of her head, and a long grey dressing gown trailing behind her.

"Are you in pain, Dan?"

"It's pretty bad; but I didn't mean to wake you."

"I'm a sort of owl, always flying about at night. Yes, your foot is like fire; the bandages must be wet again," and away flapped the maternal owl for more cooling stuff, and a great mug of ice water.

"Oh, that's *so* nice!" sighed Dan, as the wet bandages went on again, and a long draught of water cooled his thirsty throat.

"There, now, sleep your best, and don't be frightened if you see me again, for I'll slip down by and by, and give you another sprinkle."

As she spoke, Mrs. Jo stooped to turn the pillow and smooth the bed-clothes, when, to her great surprise, Dan put his arm round her neck, drew her face down to his, and kissed her, with a broken "Thank you, ma'am," which said more than the most eloquent speech could have done; for the hasty kiss, the muttered words, meant, "I'm sorry, I will try." She understood it, accepted the unspoken confession, and did not spoil it by any token of surprise. She only remembered that he had no mother, kissed the brown cheek half hidden on the pillow, as if ashamed of that little touch of tenderness, and left him, saying, what he long remembered, "You are my boy now, and if you choose you can make me proud and glad to say so."

Once again, just at dawn, she stole down to find him so fast asleep that he did not wake, and showed no sign of consciousness as she wet his foot, except that the lines of pain smoothed themselves away, and left his face quite peaceful.

The day was Sunday, and the house so still that he never waked till near noon, and, looking round him, saw an eager little face peering in at the door. He held out his arms, and Teddy tore across the room to cast himself bodily upon the bed, shouting, "My Danny's tum!" as he hugged and wriggled with delight. Mrs. Bhaer appeared next, bringing breakfast, and never seeming to see how shamefaced Dan looked at the memory of the little scene last night. Teddy insisted on giving him his "betfus," and fed him like a baby, which, as he was not very hungry, Dan enjoyed very much.

Then came the doctor, and the poor Spartan had a bad time of it, for some of the little bones of his foot were injured, and putting them to rights was such a painful job than Dan's lips were white, and great drops stood on his forehead, though he never cried out, and only held Mrs. Jo's hand so tight that it was red long afterwards.

"You must keep this boy quiet, for a week at least, and not let him put his foot to the ground. By that time, I shall know whether he may hop a little with a crutch, or stick to his bed for a while longer," said Dr Firth, putting up the shining instruments that Dan did not like to see.

"It will get well some time, won't it?" he asked, looking alarmed at the word "crutches."

"I hope so," and with that the doctor departed, leaving Dan much depressed; for the loss of a foot is a dreadful calamity for an active boy.

"Don't be troubled, I am a famous nurse, and we will have you tramping about as well as ever in a month," said Mrs. Jo, taking a hopeful view of the case.

But the fear of being lame haunted Dan, and even Teddy's caresses did not cheer him; so Mrs. Jo proposed that one or two of the boys should come in and pay him a little visit, and asked whom he would like to see.

"Nat and Demi; I'd like my hat too, there's something in it I guess they'd like to see. I suppose you threw away my bundle of plunder?" said Dan, looking rather anxious as he put the question.

"No, I kept it, for I thought they must be treasures of some kind, you took such care of them," and Mrs. Jo brought him his old straw hat stuck full of butterflies and beetles, and a handkerchief containing a collection of odd things picked up on his way: birds' eggs, carefully done up in moss, curious shells and stones, bits of fungus, and several little crabs, in a state of great indignation at their imprisonment.

"Could I have something to put these fellows in? Mr. Hyde and I found them, and they are first-rate ones, so I'd like to keep and watch them; may I?" asked Dan, forgetting his foot, and laughing to see the crabs so sidling and backing over the bed.

"Of course you can; Polly's old cage will be just the thing. Don't let them nip Teddy's toes while I get it," and away went Mrs. Jo, leaving Dan overjoyed to find that his treasures were not considered rubbish, and thrown away.

Nat, Demi, and the cage arrived together, and the crabs were settled in their new house, to the great delight of the boys, who, in the excitement of the performance, forgot any awkwardness they might otherwise have felt

in greeting the runaway. To these admiring listeners Dan related his
adventures much more fully than he had done to the Bhaers. Then he
displayed his "plunder," and described each article so well, that Mrs. Jo,
who had retired to the next room to leave them free, was surprised and
interested, as well as amused, at their boyish chatter.

"How much the lad knows of these things! how absorbed he is in
them! and what a mercy it is just now, for he cares so little for books, it
would be hard to amuse him while he is laid up; but the boys can supply
him with beetles and stones to any extent, and I am glad to find out this
taste of his; it is a good one, and may perhaps prove the making of him. If
he should turn out a great naturalist, and Nat a musician, I should have
cause to be proud of this year's work," and Mrs. Jo sat smiling over her book
as she built castles in the air, just as she used to do when a girl, only then
they were for herself, and now they were for other people, which is the
reason perhaps that some of them came to pass in reality – for charity is an
excellent foundation to build anything upon.

Nat was most interested in the adventures, but Demi enjoyed the
beetles and butterflies immensely, drinking in the history of their
changeful little lives as if it were a new and lovely sort of fairy tale – for,
even in his plain way, Dan told it well, and found great satisfaction in the
thought that here at least the small philosopher could learn of him. So
interested were they in the account of catching a muskrat, whose skin was
among the treasures, that Mr. Bhaer had to come himself to tell Nat and
Demi it was time for the walk. Dan looked so wistfully after them as they
ran off, that Father Bhaer proposed carrying him to the sofa in the parlor
for a little change of air and scene.

When he was established, and the house quiet, Mrs. Jo, who sat
near-by showing Teddy pictures, said, in an interested tone, as she nodded
towards the treasures still in Dan's hands,

"Where did you learn so much about these things?"

"I always liked them, but didn't know much till Mr. Hyde told me."

"Who was Mr. Hyde?"

"Oh, he was a man who lived round in the woods studying these
things, – I don't know what you call him, – and wrote about frogs, and
fishes, and so on. He stayed at Page's, and used to want me to go and help
him, and it was great fun, 'cause he told me ever so much, and was

uncommon jolly and wise. Hope I'll see him again some time."

"I hope you will," said Mrs. Jo, for Dan's face had brightened up, and he was so interested in the matter that he forgot his actual taciturnity.

"Why, he could make birds come to him, and rabbits and squirrels didn't mind him any more than if he were a tree. He never hurt them, and they seemed to know him. Did you ever tickle a lizard with a straw?" asked Dan, eagerly.

"No, but I should like to try it."

"Well, I've done it, and it's so funny to see them turn over and stretch out, they like it so much. Mr. Hyde used to do it; and he'd make snakes listen to him while he whistled, and he knew just when certain flowers would blow, and bees wouldn't sting him, and he'd tell the wonderfulest things about fish and flies, and the Indians and the rocks."

"I think you were so fond of going with Mr. Hyde, you rather neglected Mr. Page," said Mrs. Jo, slyly.

"Yes, I did; I hated to have to weed and hoe when I might be tramping round with Mr. Hyde. Page thought such things silly, and called Mr. Hyde crazy because he'd lay hours watching a trout or a bird."

"Suppose you say *lie* instead of *lay*, it is better grammar," said Mrs. Jo, very gently; and then added, "Yes, Page is a thorough farmer, and would not understand that a naturalist's work was just as interesting, and perhaps just as important as his own. Now, Dan, if you really love these things, as I think you do, and I am glad to see it, you shall have time to study them and books to help you; but I want you to do something besides, and to do it faithfully, else you will be sorry by and by, and find that you have got to begin again."

"Yes, ma'am," said Dan, meekly, and looked a little scared by the serious tone of the last remarks, for he hated books, yet had evidently made up his mind to study anything she proposed.

"Do you see that cabinet with twelve drawers in it?" was the next very unexpected question.

Dan did see two tall old-fashioned ones standing on either side of the piano; he knew them well, and had often seen nice bits of string, nails, brown paper, and such useful matters come out of the various drawers. He nodded and smiled. Mrs. Jo went on, –

"Well, don't you think those drawers would be good places to put your eggs, and stones, and shells, and lichens?"

"Oh, splendid, but you wouldn't like my things 'clutterin' round,' as Mr. Page used to say, would you?" cried Dan, sitting up to survey the old piece of furniture with sparkling eyes.

"I like litter of that sort; and if I didn't, I should give you the drawers, because I have a regard for children's little treasures, and think they should be treated respectfully. Now, I am going to make a bargain with you, Dan, and I hope you will keep it honorably. Here are twelve good-sized drawers, one for each month of the year, and they shall be yours as fast as you earn them, by doing the little duties that belong to you. I believe in rewards of a certain kind, especially for young folks; they help us along, and though we may begin by being good for the sake of the reward, if it is rightly used, we shall soon learn to love goodness for itself."

"Do you have them?" asked Dan, looking as if this was new talk for him.

"Yes, indeed! I haven't learnt to get on without them yet. My rewards are not drawers, or presents, or holidays, but they are things which I like as much as you do the others. The good behavior and success of my boys is one of the rewards I love best, and I work for it as I want you to work for your cabinet. Do what you dislike, and do it well, and you get two rewards – one, the prize you see and hold; the other, the satisfaction of a duty cheerfully performed. Do you understand that?"

"Yes, ma'am."

"We all need these little helps; so you shall try to do your lessons and your work, play kindly with all the boys, and use your holidays well; and if you bring me a good report, or if I see and know it without words, – for I'm quick to spy out the good little efforts of my boys, – you shall have a compartment in the drawer for your treasures. See, some are already divided into four parts, and I will have the others made in the same way, a place for each week; and when the drawer is filled with curious and pretty things, I shall be as proud of it as you are; prouder, I think – for in the pebbles, mosses, and gay butterflies, I shall see good resolutions carried out, conquered faults, and a promise well kept. Shall we do this, Dan?"

The boy answered with one of the looks which said much, for it showed that he felt and understood her wish and words, although he did not know how to express his interest and gratitude for such care and kindness. She understood the look, and seeing by the color that flushed up to his forehead that he was touched, as she wished him to be, she said no more about that side of the new plan, but pulled out the upper drawer, dusted it, and set it on two chairs before the sofa, saying briskly,

"Now, let us begin at once by putting those nice beetles in a safe place. These compartments will hold a good deal, you see. I'd pin the butterflies and bugs round the sides; they will be quite safe there, and leave room for the heavy things below. I'll give you some cotton wool, and clean paper and pins, and you can get ready for the week's work."

"But I can't go out to find any new things," said Dan, looking piteously at his foot.

"That's true; never mind, we'll let these treasures do for this week, and I dare say the boys will bring you loads of things if you ask them."

"They don't know the right sort; besides, if I lay, no, *lie* here all the time, I can't work and study, and earn my drawers."

"There are plenty of lessons you can learn lying there, and several little jobs of work you can do for me."

"Can I?" and Dan looked both surprised and pleased.

"You can learn to be patient and cheerful in spite of pain and no play. You can amuse Teddy for me, wind cotton, read to me when I sew, and do many things without hurting your foot, which will make the days pass quickly, and not be wasted ones."

Here Demi ran in with a great butterfly in one hand, and a very ugly little toad in the other.

"Seen, Dan, I found them, and ran back to give them to you; aren't they beautiful ones?" panted Demi, all out of breath.

Dan laughed at the toad, and said he had no place to put him, but the butterfly was a beauty, and if Mrs. Jo would give him a big pin, he would stick it right up in the drawer.

"I don't like to see the poor thing struggle on a pin; if it must be killed, let us put it out of pain at once with a drop of camphor," said Mrs. Jo, getting out the bottle.

"I know how to do it, – Mr. Hyde always killed them that way, – but I didn't have any camphor, so I use a pin," and Dan gently poured a drop on the insect's head, when the pale green wings fluttered an instant, and then grew still.

This dainty little execution was hardly over when Teddy shouted from the bedroom. "Oh, the little trabs are out, and the big one's eaten 'em all up." Demi and his aunt ran to the rescue, and found Teddy dancing excitedly in a chair, while two little crabs were scuttling about the floor, having got through the wires of the cage. A third was clinging to the top of the cage, evidently in terror of his life, for below appeared a sad yet funny sight. The big crab had wedged himself into the little recess where Polly's cup used to stand, and there he sat eating one of his relations in the coolest way. All the claws of the poor victim were pulled off, and he was turned upside down, his upper shell held in one claw close under the mouth of the big crab like a dish, while he leisurely ate out of it with the other claw, pausing now and then to turn his queer bulging eyes from side to side, and to put out a slender tongue and lick them in a way that made the children scream with laughter. Mrs. Jo carried the cage in for Dan to see the sight, while Demi caught and confined the wanderers under an inverted wash bowl.

"I'll have to let these fellows go, for I can't keep them in the house," said Dan, with evident regret.

"I'll take care of them for you, if you will tell me how, and they can live in my turtle-tank just as well as not," said Demi, who found them more interesting even than his beloved slow turtles. So Dan gave him directions about the wants and habits of the crabs, and Demi bore them away to introduce them to their new home and neighbors. "What a good boy he is!" said Dan, carefully settling the first butterfly, and remembering that Demi had given up his walk to bring it to him.

"He ought to be, for a great deal has been done to make him so."

"He's had folks to tell him things, and to help him; I haven't," said Dan, with a sigh, thinking of his neglected childhood, a thing he seldom did, and feeling as if he had not had fair play somehow.

"I know it, dear, and for that reason I don't expect as much from you as from Demi, though he is younger; you shall have all the help that we can give you now, and I hope to teach you how to help yourself in the best way. Have you forgotten what Father Bhaer told you when you were here before, about wanting to be good, and asking God to help you?"

"No, ma'am," very low.

"Do you try that way still?"

"Please, Dod, bess everybody".

"No, ma'am," lower still.

"Will you do it every night to please me?"

"Yes, ma'am," very soberly.

"I shall depend on it, and I think I shall know if you are faithful to your promise, for these things always show to people who believe in them, though not a word is said. Now here is a pleasant story about a boy who hurt his foot worse than you did yours; read it, and see how bravely he bore his troubles."

She put that charming little book, "The Crofton Boys," into his hands, and left him for an hour, passing in and out from time to time that he might not feel lonely. Dan did not love to read, but soon got so interested that he was surprised when the boys came home. Daisy brought him a nosegay of wild flowers, and Nan insisted on helping bring him his supper, as he lay on the sofa with the door open into the dining room, so that he could see the lads at table, and they could nod socially to him over their bread and butter.

Mr. Bhaer carried him away to his bed early, and Teddy came in his nightgown to say good night, for he went to his little nest with the birds.

"I want to say my prayers to Danny; may I?" he asked, and when his mother said, "Yes," the little fellow knelt down by Dan's bed, and folding his chubby hands, said softly, –

"Please, Dod, bess everybody, and help me to be dood."

Then he went away smiling with sleepy sweetness over his mother's shoulder.

But after the evening talk was done, the evening song sung, and the house grew still with beautiful Sunday silence, Dan lay in his pleasant room wide awake, thinking new thoughts, feeling new hopes and desires stirring in his boyish heart, for two good angels had entered in: love and gratitude began the work which time and effort were to finish; and with an earnest wish to keep his first promise, Dan folded his hands together in the darkness, and softly whispered Teddy's little prayer,

"Please, God, bless every one, and help me to be good."

Uncle Teddy

~

For a week Dan only moved from bed to sofa; a long week and a hard one, for the hurt foot was very painful at times, the quiet days very wearisome to the active lad, longing to be out enjoying the summer weather, and especially difficult was it to be patient. But Dan did his best, and every one helped him in their various ways; so the time passed, and he was rewarded at last by hearing the doctor say, on Saturday morning, –

"This foot is doing better than I expected. Give the lad the crutch this afternoon, and let him stump about the house a little."

"Hooray!" shouted Nat, and raced away to tell the other boys the good news.

Everybody was very glad, and after dinner the whole flock assembled to behold Dan crutch himself up and down the hall a few times before he settled in the porch to hold a sort of *levée*. He was much pleased at the interest and good will shown him, and brightened up more and more every

665

minute; for the boys came to pay their respects, the little girls fussed about him with stools and cushions, and Teddy watched over him as if he were a frail creature unable to do anything for himself. They were still sitting and standing about the steps, when a carriage stopped at the gate, a hat was waved from it, and with a shout of "Uncle Teddy! Uncle Teddy!" Rob scampered down the avenue as fast as his short legs would carry him. All the boys but Dan ran after him to see who should be first to open the gate, and in a moment the carriage drove up with boys swarming all over it, while Uncle Teddy sat laughing in the midst, with his little daughter on his knee.

"Stop the triumphal car and let Jupiter descend," he said, and jumping out ran up the steps to meet Mrs. Bhaer, who stood smiling and clapping her hands like a girl.

"How goes it, Teddy?"

"All right, Jo."

Then they shook hands, and Mr. Laurie put Bess into her aunt's arms, saying, as the child hugged her tight, "Goldilocks wanted to see you so much that I ran away with her, for I was quite pining for a sight of you myself. We want to play with your boys for an hour or so, and to see how 'the old woman who lived in a shoe, and had so many children she did not know what to do,' is getting on."

"I'm so glad! Play away, and don't get into mischief," answered Mrs. Jo, as the lads crowded round the pretty child, admiring her long golden hair, dainty dress, and lofty ways, for the little "Princess," as they called her, allowed no one to kiss her, but sat smiling down upon them, and graciously patting their heads with her little, white hands. They all adored her, especially Rob, who considered her a sort of doll, and dared not touch her lest she should break, but worshipped her at a respectful distance, made happy by an occasional mark of favor from her little highness. As she immediately demanded to see Daisy's kitchen, she was borne off by Mrs. Jo, with a train of small boys following. The others, all but Nat and Demi, ran away to the menagerie and gardens to have all in order; for Mr. Laurie always took a general survey, and looked disappointed if things were not flourishing.

Standing on the steps, he turned to Dan, saying like an old acquaintance, though he had only seen him once or twice before.

"How is the foot?"

"Better, sir."

"Rather tired of the house, aren't you?"

"Guess I am!" and Dan's eyes roved away to the green hills and woods where he longed to be.

"Suppose we take a little turn before the others come back? That big, easy carriage will be quite safe and comfortable, and a breath of fresh air will do you good. Get a cushion and a shawl, Demi, and let's carry Dan off."

The boys thought it a capital joke, and Dan looked delighted, but asked, with an unexpected burst of virtue, —

"Will Mrs. Bhaer like it?"

"Oh, yes; we settled all that a minute ago."

"You didn't say anything about it, so I don't see how you could," said Demi, inquisitively.

"We have a way of sending messages to one another, without any words. It is a great improvement on the telegraph."

"I know — it's eyes; I saw you lift your eyebrows, and nod toward the carriage, and Mrs. Bhaer laughed and nodded back again," cried Nat, who was quite at his ease with kind Mr. Laurie by this time.

"Right. Now then, come on ," and in a minute Dan found himself settled in the carriage, his foot on a cushion on the seat opposite, nicely covered with a shawl, which fell down from the upper regions in a most mysterious manner, just when they wanted it. Demi climbed up to the box beside Peter, the black coachman. Nat sat next Dan in the place of honor, while Uncle Teddy would sit opposite, — to take care of the foot, he said, but really that he might study the faces before him, — both so happy, yet so different, for Dan's was square, and brown, and strong, while Nat's was long, and fair, and rather weak, but very amiable with its mild eyes and good forehead.

"By the way, I've got a book somewhere here that you may like to see," said the oldest boy of the party, diving under the seat and producing a book which made Dan exclaim, —

"Oh! by George, isn't that a stunner?" as he turned the leaves, and saw fine plates of butterflies, and birds, and every sort of interesting insect, colored like life. He was so charmed that he forgot his thanks, but Mr.

Laurie did not mind, and was quite satisfied to see the boy's eager delight, and to hear his exclamations over certain old friends as he came to them. Nat leaned on his shoulder to look, and Demi turned his back to the horses, and let his feet dangle inside the carriage, so that he might join in the conversation.

When they got among the beetles, Mr. Laurie took a curious little object out of his vest pocket, and laying it in the palm of his hand, said, —

"There's a beetle that is thousands of years old," and then, while the lads examined the queer stone bug, that looked so old and gray, he told them how it came out of the wrappings of a mummy, after lying for ages in a famous tomb. Finding them interested, he went on to tell about the Egyptians, and the strange and splendid ruins they have left behind them — the Nile, and how he sailed up the mighty river, with the handsome dark men to work his boat; how he shot alligators, saw wonderful beasts and birds; and afterwards crossed the desert on a camel, who pitched him about like a ship in a storm.

"Uncle Teddy tells stories 'most as well as grandpa," said Demi, approvingly, when the tale was done, and the boys' eyes asked for more.

"Thank you," said Mr. Laurie, quite soberly, for he considered Demi's praise worth having, for children are good critics in such cases, and to suit them is an accomplishment that any one may be proud of.

"Here's another trifle or two that I tucked into my pocket as I was turning over my traps to see if I had anything that would amuse Dan," and Uncle Teddy produced a fine arrowhead and a string of wampum.

"Oh! tell about the Indians," cried Demi, who was fond of playing wigwam.

"Dan knows lots about them," added Nat.

"More than I do, I dare say. Tell us something," and Mr. Laurie looked as interested as the other two.

"Mr. Hyde told me; he's been among them, and can talk their talk, and likes them," began Dan, flattered by their attention, but rather embarrassed by having a grown-up listener.

"What is wampum for?" asked curious Demi, from his perch.

The others asked questions likewise, and, before he knew it, Dan was reeling off all Mr. Hyde had told him, as they sailed down the river a few weeks before. Mr. Laurie listened well, but found the boy more interesting than the Indians, for Mrs. Jo had told him about Dan, and he rather took a fancy to the wild lad, who ran away as he himself had often longed to do, and who was slowly getting tamed by pain and patience.

"I've been thinking that it would be a good plan for you fellows to have a museum of your own; a place in which to collect all the curious and interesting things that you find, and have given you. Mrs. Jo is too kind to complain, but it is rather hard for her to have the house littered up with all sorts of rattletraps — half a pint of dor bugs in one of her best vases, for instance, a couple of dead bats nailed up in the back entry, wasps' nests tumbling down on people's heads, and stones lying round everywhere, enough to pave the avenue. There are not many women who would stand that sort of thing, are there, now?"

As Mr. Laurie spoke with a merry look in his eyes, the boys laughed and nudged one another, for it was evident that someone told tales out of school, else how could he know of the existence of these inconvenient treasures.

"Where can we put them, then?" said Demi, crossing his legs and leaning down to argue the question.

"In the old carriage house."

"But it leaks, and there isn't any window, nor any place to put things, and it's all dust and cobwebs."

"Wait till Gibbs and I have touched it up a bit, and then see how you like it. He is to come over on Monday to get it ready; then next Saturday I shall come out, and we will fix it up, and make the beginning, at least, of a fine little museum. Every one can bring his things, and have a place for them; and Dan is to be the head man, because he knows most about such matters, and it will be quiet, pleasant work for him now that he can't knock about much."

"Won't that be jolly?" cried Nat, while Dan smiled all over his face and had not a word to say, but hugged his book, and looked at Mr. Laurie as if he thought him one of the greatest public benefactors that ever blessed the world.

"Shall I go round again, sir?" asked Peter, as they came to the gate, after two slow turns about the half-mile triangle.

"No, we must be prudent, else we can't come again. I must go over the premises, take a look at the carriage house, and have a little talk with

Mrs. Jo before I go," and, having deposited Dan on his sofa to rest and enjoy his book, Uncle Teddy went off to have a frolic with the lads who were raging about the place in search of him. Leaving the little girls to mess up stairs, Mrs. Bhaer sat down by Dan, and listened to his eager account of the drive till the flock returned, dusty, warm, and much excited about the new museum, which every one considered the most brilliant idea of the age.

"I always wanted to endow some sort of an institution, and I am going to begin with this," said Mr. Laurie, sitting down on a stool at Mrs. Jo's feet.

"You have endowed one already. What do you call this?" and Mrs. Jo pointed to the happy-faced lads, who had camped upon the floor about them.

"I call it a very promising Bhaer-garden, and I'm proud to be a member of it. Did you know I was the head boy in this school?" he asked, turning to Dan, and changing the subject skilfully, for he hated to be thanked for the generous things he did.

"I thought Franz was!" answered Dan, wondering what the man meant.

"Oh, dear no! I'm the first boy Mrs. Jo ever had to take care of, and I was such a bad one that she isn't done with me yet, though she has been working at me for years and years."

"How old she must be!" said Nat, innocently.

"She began early, you see. Poor thing! she was only fifteen when she took me, and I led her such a life, it's a wonder she isn't wrinkled and gray, and quite worn out," and Mr. Laurie looked up at her laughing.

"Don't, Teddy; I won't have you abuse yourself so," and Mrs. Jo stroked the curly black head at her knee as affectionately as ever, for, in spite of everything, Teddy was her boy still.

"If it hadn't been for you, there never would have been a Plumfield. It was my success with you, sir, that gave me courage to try my pet plan. So the boys may thank you for it, and name the new institution 'The Laurence Museum,' in honor of its founder, won't we, boys?" she added, looking very like the lively Jo of old times.

"We will! we will!" shouted the boys, throwing up their hats, for though they had taken them off on entering the house, according to rule, they had been in too much of a hurry to hang them up.

"I'm as hungry as a bear, may I have a cookie?" asked Mr. Laurie, when the shout subsided and he had expressed his thanks by a splendid bow.

"Trot out and ask Asia for the gingerbread box, Demi. It isn't in order to eat between meals, but on this joyful occasion, we won't mind, and have a cookie all round," said Mrs. Jo; and when the box came she dealt them out with a liberal hand, every one munching away in a social circle.

Suddenly, in the midst of a bite, Mr. Laurie cried out, "Bless my heart, I forgot grandma's bundle!" and running out to the carriage, returning with an interesting white parcel, which, being opened, disclosed a choice collection of beasts, birds, and pretty things cut out of crisp sugary cake, and baked a lovely brown.

"There's one for each, and a letter to tell which is whose. Grandma and Hannah made them, and I tremble to think what would have happened to me if I had forgotten to leave them."

Then, amid much laughing and fun, the cakes were distributed. A fish for Dan, a fiddle for Nat, a book for Demi, a monkey for Tommy, a flower for Daisy, a hoop for Nan, who had driven twice round the triangle without stopping, a star for Emil, who put on airs because he studied astronomy, and, best of all, an omnibus for Franz, whose great delight was to drive the family bus. Stuffy got a fat pig, and the little folks had birds, and cats, and rabbits, with black currant eyes.

"Now I must go. Where is my Goldilocks? Mamma will come flying out to get her if I'm not back early," said Uncle Teddy, when the last crumb had vanished, which it speedily did, you may be sure.

The young ladies had gone into the garden, and while they waited till Franz looked them up, Jo and Laurie stood at the door talking together.

"How does little Giddygaddy come on?" he asked, for Nan's pranks amused him very much, and he was never tired of teasing Jo about her.

"Nicely; she is getting quite mannerly, and begins to see the error of her wild ways."

"Don't the boys encourage her in them?"

"Yes; but I keep talking, and lately she has improved much. You saw how prettily she shook hands with you, and how gentle she was with Bess. Daisy's example has its effect upon her, and I'm quite sure that a few months will work wonders."

Here Mrs. Jo's remarks were cut short by the appearance of Nan tearing round the corner at a breakneck pace, driving a mettlesome team of four boys, and followed by Daisy trundling Bess in a wheelbarrow. Hats off, hair flying, whip cracking, and barrow bumping, up they came in a cloud of dust, looking as wild a set of little hoydens as one would wish to see.

"So these are the model children, are they? It's lucky I didn't bring Mrs. Curtis out to see your school for the cultivation of morals and manners; she would never have recovered from the shock of this spectacle," said Mr. Laurie, laughing at Mrs. Jo's premature rejoicing over Nan's improvement.

"Laugh away; I'll succeed yet. As you used to say at college, quoting some professor, 'Though the experiment has failed, the principle remains the same,'" said Mrs. Bhaer, joining in the merriment.

"I'm afraid Nan's example is taking effect upon Daisy, instead of the other way. Look at my little princess! she has utterly forgotten her dignity, and is screaming like the rest. Young ladies, what does this mean?" and Mr. Laurie rescued his small daughter from impending destruction, for the four horses were champing their bits and curvetting madly all about her, as she sat brandishing a great whip in both hands.

"We're having a race, and I beat," shouted Nan.

"I could have run faster, only I was afraid of spilling Bess," screamed Daisy.

"Hi! go long!" cried the Princess, giving such a flourish with her whip that the horses ran away, and were seen no more.

"My precious child! come away from this ill-mannered crew before you are quite spoiled. Good-by, Jo! Next time I come, I shall expect to find the boys making patchwork."

"It wouldn't hurt them a bit. I don't give in, mind you; for my experiments always fail a few times before they succeed. Love to Amy and my blessed Marmee," called Mrs. Jo, as the carriage drove away; and the last Mr. Laurie saw of her, she was consoling Daisy for her failure by a ride in the wheelbarrow, and looking as if she liked it.

Great was the excitement all the week about the repairs in the carriage house, which went briskly on in spite of the incessant questions, advice, and meddling of the boys. Old Gibbs was nearly driven wild with it all, but managed to do his work nevertheless; and by Friday night the place was all in order – roof mended, shelves up, walls white-washed, a great window cut at the back, which let in a flood of sunshine, and gave them a fine view of the brook, the meadows, and the distant hills; and over the great door, painted in red letters, was "The Laurence Museum."

All Saturday morning the boys were planning how it should be furnished with their spoils, and when Mr. Laurie arrived, bringing an aquarium which Mrs. Amy said she was tired of, their rapture was great.

The afternoon was spent in arranging things, and when the running and lugging and hammering were over, the ladies were invited to behold the institution.

It certainly was a pleasant place, airy, clean, and bright. A hop vine shook its green bells round the open window, the pretty aquarium stood in the middle of the room, with some delicate water plants rising above the water, and gold-fish showing their brightness as they floated to and fro below. On either side of the window were rows of shelves ready to receive the curiosities yet to be found. Dan's tall cabinet stood before the great door which was fastened up, while the small door was to be used. On the cabinet stood a queer Indian idol, very ugly, but very interesting; old Mr. Laurence sent it, as well as a fine Chinese junk in full sail, which had a conspicuous place on the long table in the middle of the room. Above, swinging in a loop, and looking as if she was alive, hung Polly, who died at an advanced age, had been carefully stuffed, and was now presented by Mrs. Jo. The walls were decorated with all sorts of things. A snake's skin, a big wasps' nest, a birch-bark canoe, a string of birds' eggs, wreaths of grey moss from the South, and a bunch of cotton pods. The dead bats had a place, also a large turtle shell, and an ostrich egg proudly presented by Demi, who volunteered to explain these rare curiosities to guests whenever they liked. There were so many stones that it was impossible to accept them all, so only a few of the best were arranged among the shells on the shelves; the rest were piled up in corners, to be examined by Dan at his leisure.

Every one was eager to give something, even Silas, who sent home for a stuffed wild cat killed in his youth. It was rather moth-eaten and shabby, but on a high bracket and best side foremost the effect was fine, for the yellow glass eyes glared, and the mouth snarled so naturally, that Teddy shook in his little shoes at sight of it, when he came bringing his most cherished treasure, one cocoon, to lay upon the shrine of science.

"Isn't it beautiful? I'd no idea we had so many curious things. I gave that; don't it look well? We might make a lot by charging something for letting folks see it."

Jack added that last suggestion to the general chatter that went on as the family viewed the room.

"This is a free museum and if there is any speculating on it I'll paint out the name over the door," said Mr. Laurie, turning so quickly that Jack wished he had held his tongue.

"Hear! hear!" cried Mr. Bhaer.

"Speech! speech!" added Mrs. Jo.

"Can't, I'm too bashful. You give them a lecture yourself — you are used to it," Mr. Laurie answered, retreating towards the window, meaning to escape. But she held him fast, and said, laughing as she looked at the dozen pairs of dirty hands about her, —

"If I did lecture, it would be on the chemical and cleaning properties of soap. Come now, as the founder of the institution, you really ought to give us a few moral remarks, and we will applaud tremendously."

Seeing that there was no way of escaping, Mr. Laurie looked up at Polly hanging overhead, seemed to find inspiration in the brilliant old bird, and sitting down upon the table, said, in his pleasant way, —

"There *is* one thing I'd like to suggest, boys, and that is, I want you to get some good as well as much pleasure out of this. Just putting curious or pretty things here won't do it; so suppose you read up about them, so that when anybody asks questions you can answer them, and understand the matter. I used to like these things myself, and should enjoy hearing about them now, for I've forgotten all I once knew. It wasn't much, was it, Jo? Here's Dan now, full of stories about birds and bugs, and so on; let him take care of the museum, and once a week the rest of you take turns to read a composition, or tell about some animal, mineral, or vegetable. We should all like that, and I think it would put considerable useful knowledge into our heads. What do you say, Professor?"

"I'd like it much, and will give the lads all the help I can. But they will need books to read up these new subjects, and we have not many, I fear," began Mr. Bhaer, looking much pleased, and planning many fine lectures on geology, which he liked. "We should have a library for the special purpose."

"Is that a useful sort of book, Dan?" asked Mr. Laurie, pointing to the volume that lay open by the cabinet.

"Oh, yes! it tells all I want to know about insects. I had it here to see how to fix the butterflies right. I covered it, so it is not hurt," and Dan caught it up, fearing the lender might think him careless.

"Give it here a minute," and, pulling out his pencil, Mr. Laurie wrote Dan's name in it, saying, as he set the book up on one of the corner shelves, where nothing stood but a stuffed bird without a tail, "there, that is the beginning of the museum library. I'll hunt up some more books, and Demi shall keep them in order. Where are those jolly little books we used to read, Jo? "Insect Architecture" or some such name — all about ants having battles, and bees having queens, and crickets eating holes in our clothes and stealing milk, and larks of that sort."

"In the garret at home. I'll have them sent out, and we will plunge into Natural History with a will," said Mrs. Jo, ready for anything.

"Won't it be hard to write about such things?" asked Nat, who hated compositions.

"At first, perhaps; but you will soon like it. If you think that hard, how would you like to have this subject given to you, as it was to a girl of thirteen: A conversation between Themistocles, Aristides, and Pericles on the proposed appropriation of the funds of the confederacy of Delos for the ornamentation of Athens?" said Mrs. Jo.

The boys groaned at the mere sound of the long names, and the gentlemen laughed at the absurdity of the lesson.

"Did she write it?" asked Demi, in an awe-stricken tone.

"Yes, but you can imagine what a piece of work she made of it, though she was rather a bright child."

"I'd like to have seen it," said Mr. Bhaer.

"Perhaps I can find it for you; I went to school with her," and Mrs. Jo looked so wicked that every one knew who the little girl was.

Hearing of this fearful subject for a composition quite reconciled the boys to the thought of writing about familiar things. Wednesday afternoon was appointed for the lectures, as they preferred to call them, for some chose to talk instead of write. Mr. Bhaer promised a portfolio in which the written productions should be kept, and Mrs. Bhaer said she would attend the course with great pleasure.

Then the dirty-handed society went off to wash, followed by the Professor, trying to calm the anxiety of Rob, who had been told by Tommy that all water was full of invisible pollywogs.

"I like your plan very much, only don't be too generous, Teddy," said Mrs. Bhaer, when they were left alone. "You know most of the boys have got to paddle their own canoes when they leave us, and too much sitting in the lap of luxury will unfit them for it."

"I'll be moderate, but do let me amuse myself. I get desperately tired of business sometimes, and nothing freshens me up like a good frolic with your boys. I like that Dan very much, Jo. He isn't demonstrative; but he has the eye of a hawk, and when you have tamed him a little he will do you credit."

"I'm so glad you think so. Thank you very much for your kindness to him, especially for this museum affair; it will keep him happy while he is lame, give me a chance to soften and smooth this poor, rough lad, and make him love us. What did inspire you with such a beautiful, helpful idea, Teddy?" asked Mrs. Bhaer, glancing back at the pleasant room, as she turned to leave it.

Laurie took both her hands in his, and answered, with a look that made her eyes fill with happy tears,

"Dear Jo! I have known what it is to be a motherless boy, and I never can forget how much you and yours have done for me all these years."

CHAPTER TWELVE

HUCKLEBERRIES

~

There was a great clashing of tin pails, much running to and fro, and frequent demands for something to eat, one August afternoon, for the boys were going huckleberrying, and made as much stir about it as if they were setting out to find the Northwest Passage.

"Now, my lads, get off as quietly as you can, for Rob is safely out of the way, and won't see you," said Mrs. Bhaer, as she tied Daisy's broad-brimmed hat, and settled the great blue pinafore in which she had enveloped Nan.

But the plan did not succeed, for Rob had heard the bustle, decided to go, and prepared himself, without a thought of disappointment. The troop was just getting under way when the little man came marching down stairs with his best hat on, a bright tin pail in his hand, and a face beaming with satisfaction.

"Oh, dear! now we shall have a scene," sighed Mrs. Bhaer, who found her eldest son very hard to manage at times.

677

"I'm all ready," said Rob, and took his place in the ranks with such perfect unconsciousness of his mistake, that it really was very hard to undeceive him.

"It's too far for you, my love; stay and take care of me, for I shall be alone," began his mother.

"You've got Teddy. I'm a big boy, so I can go; you said I might when I was bigger, and I am now," persisted Rob, with a cloud beginning to dim the brightness of his happy face.

"We are going up to the great pasture, and it's ever so far; we don't want you tagging on," cried Jack, who did not admire the little boys.

"I won't tag, I'll run and keep up. O Mamma! let me go! I want to fill my new pail, and I'll bring them all to you. Please, please, I will be good!" prayed Robby, looking up at his mother, so grieved and disappointed that her heart began to fail her.

"But, my deary, you'll get so tired and hot you won't have a good time. Wait till I go, and then we will stay all day, and pick as many berries as you want."

"You never do go, you are so busy, and I'm tired of waiting. I'd rather go and get the berries for you all myself. I love to pick them, and I want to fill my new pail dreffly," sobbed Rob.

The pathetic sight of great tears tinkling into the dear new pail, and threatening to fill it with salt water instead of huckleberries, touched all the ladies present. His mother patted the weeper on his back; Daisy offered to stay at home with him; and Nan said, in her decided way,

"Let him come; I'll take care of him."

"If Franz was going I wouldn't mind, for he is very careful; but he is haying with the father, and I'm not sure about the rest of you," began Mrs. Bhaer.

"It's so far," put in Jack.

"I'd carry him if I was going – wish I were," said Dan, with a sigh.

"Thank you, dear, but you must take care of your foot. I wish I could go. Stop a minute, I think I can manage it after all," and Mrs. Bhaer ran out to the steps, waving her apron wildly.

Silas was just driving away in the hay cart, but turned back, and agreed at once, when Mrs. Jo proposed that he should take the whole party to the pasture, and go for them at five o'clock.

"It will delay your work a little, but never mind; we will pay you in huckleberry pies," said Mrs. Jo, knowing Silas's weak point.

His rough, brown face brightened up, and he said, with a cheery "Haw! haw! Wal now, Mis Bhaer, if you go to bribin' of me, I shall give in right away."

"Now, boys, I have arranged it so that you can all go," said Mrs. Bhaer, running back again, much relieved, for she loved to make them happy, and always felt miserable when she had disturbed the serenity of her little sons; for she believed that the small hopes and plans and pleasures of children should be tenderly respected by grown-up people, and never rudely thwarted or ridiculed.

"May I go?" said Dan, delighted.

"I thought especially of you. Be careful, and never mind the berries, but sit about and enjoy the lovely things which you know how to find all about you," answered Mrs. Bhaer, who remembered his kind offer to her boy.

"Me too! me too!" sung Rob, dancing with joy, and clapping his precious pail and cover like castanets.

"Yes, and Daisy and Nan must take good care of you. Be at the bars at five o'clock, and Silas will come for you all."

Robby cast himself upon his mother in a burst of gratitude, promising to bring her every berry he picked, and not eat one. Then they were all packed into the hay cart, and went rattling away, the brightest face among the dozen being that of Rob, as he sat between his two temporary little mothers, beaming upon the whole world, and waving his best hat; for his indulgent mamma had not the heart to bereave him of it, since this was a gala day to him.

Such a happy afternoon as they had, in spite of the mishaps which usually occur on such expeditions! Of course Tommy came to grief, tumbled upon a hornets' nest and got stung; but being used to woe, he bore the smart manfully, till Dan suggested the application of damp earth, which much assuaged the pain. Daisy saw a snake, and in flying from it lost half her berries; but Demi helped her to fill up again, and discussed reptiles most learnedly the while. Ned fell out of a tree, and split his jacket down the back, but suffered no other fracture. Emil and Jack established rival claims to a certain thick patch, and while they were squabbling about it,

Stuffy quickly and quietly stripped the bushes and fled to the protection of Dan, who was enjoying himself immensely. The crutch was no longer necessary, and he was delighted to see how strong his foot felt as he roamed about the great pasture, full of interesting rocks and stumps, with familiar little creatures in the grass, and well-known insects dancing in the air.

But of all the adventures that happened on this afternoon that which befell Nan and Rob was the most exciting, and it long remained one of the favorite histories of the household. Having explored the country pretty generally, torn three rents in her frock, and scratched her face in a barberry bush, Nan began to pick the berries that shone like big, black beads on the low, green bushes. Her nimble fingers flew, but still her basket did not fill up as rapidly as she desired, so she kept wandering here and there to search for better places, instead of picking contentedly and steadily as Daisy did. Rob followed Nan, for her energy suited him better than his cousin's patience, and he too was anxious to have the biggest and best berries for mother.

"I keep putting them in, but it don't fill up, and I'm so tired," said Rob, pausing a moment to rest his short legs, and beginning to think huckleberrying was not all his fancy painted it; for the sun blazed, Nan skipped hither and thither like a grasshopper, and the berries fell out of his pail almost as fast as he put them in, because, in his struggles with the bushes, it was often upside down.

"Last time we came they were ever so much thicker over that wall — great bouncers; and there is a cave there, where the boys made a fire. Let's go and fill our things quick, and then hide in the cave and let the others find us," proposed Nan, thirsting for adventures.

Rob consented, and away they went, scrambling over the wall and running down the sloping fields on the other side, till they were hidden among the rocks and underbrush. The berries were thick, and at last the pails were actually full. It was shady and cool down there, and a little spring gave the thirsty children a refreshing drink out of its mossy cup.

"Now we will go and rest in the cave, and eat our lunch," said Nan, well satisfied with her success so far.

"Do you know the way?" asked Rob.

"Course I do; I've been once, and I always remember. Didn't I go and get my box all right?"

That convinced Rob, and he followed blindly as Nan led him over stock and stone, and brought him, after much meandering, to a small recess in the rock, where the blackened stones showed that fires had been made.

"Now, isn't it nice?" asked Nan, as she took out a bit of bread and butter, rather damaged by being mixed up with nails, fish hooks, stones and other foreign substances, in the young lady's pocket.

"Yes; do you think they will find us soon?" asked Rob, who found the shadowy glen rather dull, and began to long for more society.

"No, I don't; because if I hear them, I shall hide, and have fun making them find me."

"P'raps they won't come."

"Don't care; I can get home myself."

"Is it a great way?" asked Rob, looking at his little, stubby boots, scratched and wet with his long wandering.

"It's six miles, I guess." Nan's ideas of distance were vague, and her faith in her own powers great.

"I think we better go now," suggested Rob, presently.

"I shan't go till I have picked over my berries," and Nan began what seemed to Rob an endless task.

"Oh dear! you said you'd take good care of me," he sighed, as the sun seemed to drop behind the hill all of a sudden.

"Well, I *am* taking care of you as hard as I can. Don't be cross, child; I'll go in a minute," said Nan, who considered five-year-old Robby a mere infant compared to herself.

So little Rob sat looking anxiously about him, and waiting patiently, for, spite of some misgivings, he felt great confidence in Nan.

"I guess it's going to be night pretty soon," he observed, as if to himself, as a mosquito bit him, and the frogs in a neighboring marsh began to pipe up for the evening concert.

"My goodness me! so it is. Come right away this minute, or they will be gone," cried Nan, looking up from her work, and suddenly perceiving that the sun was down.

"I heard a horn about an hour ago; maybe they were blowing for us," said Rob, trudging after his guide as she scrambled up the steep hill.

"Where was it?" asked Nan, stopping short.

"Over that way," he pointed with a dirty little finger in an entirely wrong direction.

"Let's go that way and meet them," and Nan wheeled about, and began to trot through the bushes, feeling a trifle anxious, for there were so many cowpaths all about she could not remember which way they came.

On they went over stock and stone again, pausing now and then to listen for the horn, which did not blow any more, for it was only the moo of a cow on her way home.

"I don't remember seeing that pile of stones – do you?" asked Nan, as she sat on a wall to rest a moment and take an observation.

"I don't remember anything, but I want to go home," and Rob's voice had a little tremble in it that made Nan put her arms round him and lift him gently down, saying, in her most capable way, –

"I'm going just as fast as I can, dear. Don't cry, and when we come to the road, I'll carry you."

"Where is the road?" and Robby wiped his eyes to look for it.

"Over by that big tree. Don't you know that's the one Ned tumbled out of?"

"So it is. Maybe they waited for us; I'd like to ride home – wouldn't you?" and Robby brightened up as he plodded along toward the end of the great pasture.

"No, I'd rather walk," answered Nan, feeling quite sure that she would be obliged to do so, and preparing her mind for it.

Another long trudge through the fast-deepening twilight and another disappointment, for when they reached the tree, they found to their dismay that it was not the one Ned climbed, and no road anywhere appeared.

"Are we lost?" quavered Rob, clasping his pail in despair.

"Not much. I don't just see which way to go, and I guess we'd better call."

So they both shouted till they were hoarse, yet nothing answered but the frogs in full chorus.

"There is another tall tree over there, perhaps that's the one," said Nan, whose heart sank within her, though she still spoke bravely.

"I don't think I can go any more; my boots are so heavy I can't pull them," and Robby sat down on a stone quite worn out.

"Then we must stay here all night. *I* don't care much, if snakes don't come."

"I'm frightened of snakes. I can't stay all night. Oh, dear! I don't like to be lost," and Rob puckered up his face to cry, when suddenly a thought occurred to him, and he said, in a tone of perfect confidence,

"Marmar will come and find me; she always does; I ain't afraid now."

"She won't know where we are."

"She didn't know I was shut up in the ice house, but she found me. I know she'll come," returned Robby, so trustfully, that Nan felt relieved, and sat down by him, saying, with a remorseful sigh, –

"I wish we hadn't run away."

"You made me; but I don't mind much – Marmar will love me just the same," answered Rob, clinging to his sheet anchor when all other hope was gone.

"I'm so hungry. Let's eat our berries," proposed Nan after a pause, during which Rob began to nod.

"So am I, but I can't eat mine, 'cause I told Marmar I'd keep them all for her."

"You'll have to eat them if no one comes for us," said Nan, who felt like contradicting everything just then. "If we stay here a great many days, we shall eat up all the berries in the field, and then we shall starve," she added, grimly.

"I shall eat sassafras. I know a big tree of it, and Dan told me how squirrels dig up the roots and eat them, and I love to dig," returned Rob, undaunted by the prospect of starvation.

"Yes; and we can catch frogs, and cook them. My father ate some once, and he said they were nice," put in Nan, beginning to find a spice of romance even in being lost in a huckleberry pasture.

"How could we cook frogs? We haven't got any fire."

"I don't know; next time I'll have matches in my pocket," said Nan, rather depressed by this obstacle to the experiment in frog cookery.

"Couldn't we light a fire with a firefly?" asked Rob, hopefully, as he watched them flitting to and fro like winged sparks.

"Let's try" and several minutes were pleasantly spent in catching the flies, and trying to make them kindle a green twig or two. "It's a lie to call them *fire*-flies when there isn't a fire in them," Nan said, throwing one unhappy insect away with scorn, though it shone its best, and obligingly walked up and down the twigs to please the innocent little experimenters.

"Marmar's a good while coming," said Rob, after another pause, during which they watched the stars overhead, smelt the sweet fern crushed under foot, and listened to the cricket's serenade.

"I don't see why God made any night; day is so much pleasanter," said Nan, thoughtfully.

"It's to sleep in," answered Rob, with a yawn.

"Then do go to sleep," said Nan, pettishly.

"I want my own bed. Oh, I wish I could see Teddy!" cried Rob, painfully reminded of home by the soft chirp of birds safe in their little nests.

"I don't believe your mother will ever find us," said Nan, who was becoming desperate, for she hated patient waiting of any sort. "It's so dark she won't see us."

"It was all black in the ice house, and I was so scared I didn't call her, but she saw me; and she will see me now, no matter how dark it is," returned confiding Rob, standing up to peer into the gloom for the help which never failed him.

"I see her! I see her!" he cried, and ran as fast as his tired legs would take him toward a dark figure slowly approaching. Suddenly he stopped, then turned about, and came stumbling back, screaming in a great panic, —

"No, it's a bear, a big, black one!" and hid his face in Nan's skirts.

For a moment Nan quailed; even her courage gave out at thought of a real bear, and she was about to turn and flee in great disorder, when a mild "Moo!" changed her fear to merriment, as she said laughing, —

"It's a cow, Robby! the nice, black cow we saw this afternoon."

The cow seemed to feel that it was not just the thing to meet two little people in her pasture after dark, and the amiable beast paused to inquire into the case. She let them stroke her, and stood regarding them with her soft eyes so mildly, that Nan, who feared no animal but a bear, was fired with a desire to milk her.

"Silas taught me how; and berries and milk would be so nice," she said, emptying the contents of her pail into her hat, and boldly beginning her new task, while Rob stood by and repeated, at her command, the poem from Mother Goose:

> *"Cushy cow, bonny, let down your milk,*
> *Let down your milk to me,*
> *And I will give you a gown of silk,*
> *A gown of silk and a silver tee."*

But the immortal rime had little effect, for the benevolent cow had already been milked, and had only half a gill to give the thirsty children.

"Shoo! get away! you are an old cross patch," cried Nan, ungratefully, as she gave up the attempt in despair; and poor Mooly walked on with a gentle gurgle of surprise and reproof.

"Each can have a sip, and then we must take a walk. We shall go to sleep if we don't; and lost people mustn't sleep. Don't you know how Hannah Lee in the pretty story slept under the snow and died?"

"But there isn't any snow now, and it's nice and warm," said Rob, who was not blessed with as lively a fancy as Nan.

"No matter, we will poke about a little, and call some more; and then, if nobody comes, we will hide under the bushes, like Hop-o'-my-thumb and his brothers."

It was a very short walk, however, for Rob was so sleepy he could not get on, and tumbled down so often that Nan entirely lost patience, being half distracted by the responsibility she had taken upon herself.

"If you tumble down again, I'll shake you," said said, lifting the poor little man up very kindly as she spoke, for Nan's bark was much worse than her bite.

"Please don't. It's my boots — they keep slipping so," and Rob manfully checked the sob just ready to break out, adding, with a plaintive patience that touched Nan's heart, "If the skeeters didn't bite me so, I could go to sleep till Marmar comes."

"Put your head on my lap, and I'll cover you up with my apron; I'm not afraid of the night," said Nan, sitting down and trying to persuade herself that she did not mind the shadow nor the mysterious rustlings all about her.

"Wake me up when she comes," said Rob, and was fast asleep in five minutes with his head in Nan's lap under the pinafore.

The little girl sat for some fifteen minutes, staring about her with anxious eyes, and feeling as if each second was an hour. Then a pale light began to glimmer over the hilltop, and she said to herself, —

"I guess the night is over and morning is coming. I'd like to see the sun rise, so I'll watch, and when it comes up we can find our way right home."

But before the moon's round face peeped above the hill to destroy her hope, Nan had fallen asleep, leaning back in a little bower of tall ferns, and was deep in a midsummer night's dream of fireflies and blue aprons, mountains of huckleberries, and Robby wiping away the tears of a black cow, who sobbed, "I want to go home! I want to go home!"

While the children were sleeping, peacefully lulled by the drowsy hum of many neighborly mosquitoes, the family at home were in a great state of agitation. The hay cart came at five, and all but Jack, Emil, Nan, and Rob were at the bars ready for it. Franz drove instead of Silas, and when the boys told him that the others were going home through the wood, he said, looking ill-pleased, "They ought to have left Rob to ride, he will be tired out by the long walk."

"It's shorter that way, and they will carry him," said Stuffy, who was in a hurry for his supper.

"You are sure Nan and Rob went with them?"

"Of course they did; I saw them getting over the wall, and sung out that it was 'most five, and Jack called back that they were going the other way," explained Tommy.

"Very well, pile in then," and away rattled the hay cart with the tired children and the full pails.

Mrs. Jo looked sober when she heard of the division of the party, and sent Franz back with Toby to find and bring the little ones home. Supper was over, and the family sitting about in the cool hall as usual, when Franz came trotting back, hot, dusty, and anxious.

"Have they come?" he called out when halfway up the avenue.

"No!" and Mrs. Jo flew out of her chair looking so alarmed that every one jumped up and gathered round Franz.

"I can't find them anywhere," he began; but the words were hardly spoken when a loud "Hullo!" startled them all, and the next minute Jack and Emil came round the house.

"Where are Nan and Rob?" cried Mrs. Jo, clutching Emil in a way that caused him to think his aunt had suddenly lost her wits.

"I don't know. They came home with the others, didn't they?" he answered, quickly.

"No; George and Tommy said they went with you."

"Well, they didn't. Haven't seen them. We took a swim in the pond, and came by the wood," said Jack, looking alarmed, as well he might.

"Call Mr. Bhaer, get the lanterns, and tell Silas I want him."

That was all Mrs. Jo said, but they knew what she meant, and flew to obey orders. In ten minutes, Mr. Bhaer and Silas were off to the wood, and Franz tearing down the road on Old Andy to search the great pasture. Mrs. Jo caught up some food from the table, a little bottle of brandy from the medicine closet, took a lantern, and bidding Jack and Emil come with her, and the rest not stir, she trotted away on Toby, never stopping for hat or shawl. She heard some one running after her, but said not a word till, as she paused to call and listen, the light of her lantern shone on Dan's face.

"You here! I told Jack to come," she said, half inclined to send him back, much as she needed help.

"I wouldn't let him; he and Emil hadn't had any supper, and I wanted to come more than they did," he said, taking the lantern from her and smiling up in her face with the steady look in his eyes that made her feel as if, boy though he was, she had some one to depend on.

Off she jumped, and ordered him on Toby, in spite of his pleading to walk; then they went on again along the dusty, solitary road, stopping every now and then to call and hearken breathlessly for little voices to reply.

When they came to the great pasture, other lights were already flitting to and fro like will-o'-the-wisps, and Mr. Bhaer's voice was heard shouting, "Nan! Rob! Rob! Nan!" in every part of the field. Silas whistled and roared, Dan plunged here and there on Toby, who seemed to understand the case, and went over the roughest places with unusual docility. Often Mrs. Jo hushed them all, saying, with a sob in her throat, "The noise may frighten them, let me call; Robby, will know *my* voice," and then she would cry out the beloved little name in every tone of tenderness, till the very echoes whispered it softly, and the winds seemed to waft it willingly; but still no answer came.

The sky was overcast now, and only brief glimpses of the moon were seen, heat lightning darted out of the dark clouds now and then, and a faint far-off rumble as of thunder told that a summer storm was brewing.

"O my Robby! my Robby!" mourned poor Mrs. Jo, wandering up and down like a pale ghost, while Dan kept beside her like a faithful firefly. "What shall I say to Nan's father if she comes to harm? Why did I ever trust my darling so far away? Fritz, do you hear anything?" And when a mournful "No"came back, she wrung her hands so despairingly, that Dan sprung down from Toby's back, tied the bridle to the bars, and said, in his decided way, —

"They may have gone down to the spring — I'm going to look."

He was over the wall and away so fast that she could hardly follow him; but when she reached the spot, he lowered the lantern and showed her with joy the marks of little feet in the soft ground about the spring. She fell down on her knees to examine the tracks, and then sprung up, saying eagerly, —

"Yes; that is the mark of my Robby's little boots! Come this way, they must have gone on."

Such a weary search! But now some inexplicable instinct seemed to lead the anxious mother, for presently Dan uttered a cry, and caught up a little shining object lying in the path. It was the cover of the new tin pail, dropped in the first alarm of being lost. Mrs. Jo hugged and kissed it as if it were a living thing; and when Dan was about to utter a glad shout to bring the others to the spot, she stopped him, saying, as she hurried on, "No, let *me* find them; I let Rob go, and I want to give him back to his father all myself."

A little farther on Nan's hat appeared, and after passing the place more than once, they came at last upon the babes in the wood, both sound asleep. Dan never forgot the little picture on which the light of his lantern shone that night. He thought Mrs. Jo would cry out, but she only whispered "Hush!" as she softly lifted away the apron, and saw the little ruddy face below. The berry-stained lips were half-open as the breath came and went, the yellow hair lay damp on the hot forehead, and both the chubby hands held fast the little pail, still full.

The sight of the childish harvest, treasured through all the troubles of that night for her, seemed to touch Mrs. Jo to the heart, for suddenly she gathered up her boy, and began to cry over him, so tenderly, yet so heartily, that he woke up, and at first seemed bewildered. Then he remembered, and hugged her close, saying with a laugh of triumph, —

"I know you'd come! O Marmar! I did want you so!" For a moment they kissed and clung to one another, quite forgetting all the world; for no matter how lost and soiled and worn-out wandering sons may be, mothers can forgive and forget everything as they fold them in their fostering arms. Happy the son whose faith in his mother remains unchanged, and who, through all his wanderings, has kept some filial token to repay her brave and tender love.

Dan meantime picked Nan out of her bush, and, with a gentleness none but Teddy ever saw in him before, he soothed her first alarm at the sudden waking, and wiped away her tears; for Nan also began to cry for joy, it was so good to see a kind face and feel a strong arm round her after what seemed to her ages of loneliness and fear.

"My poor little girl, don't cry! You are all safe now, and no one shall say a word of blame tonight," said Mrs. Jo, taking Nan into her capacious embrace, and cuddling both children as a hen might gather her lost chickens under her motherly wings.

"It was my fault; but I *am* sorry. I tried to take care of him, and I covered him up and let him sleep, and didn't touch his berries, though I was *so* hungry; and I never will do it again — truly never, never," sobbed Nan, quite lost in a sea of penitence and thankfulness.

"Call them now, and let us get home," said Mrs. Jo; and Dan, getting upon the wall, sent the joyful word "Found!" ringing over the field.

How the wandering lights came dancing from all sides, and gathered round the little group among the sweet fern bushes! Such a hugging and kissing and talking and crying as went on must have amazed the glowworms, and evidently delighted the mosquitoes, for they hummed frantically, while the little moths came in flocks to the party, and the frogs croaked as if they could not express their satisfaction loudly enough.

Then they set out for home — a queer party, for Franz rode on to tell the news; Dan and Toby led the way; then came Nan in the strong arms of Silas, who considered her "the smartest little baggage he ever saw," and teased her all the way home about her pranks. Mr. Bhaer would let no one carry Rob but himself, and the little fellow, refreshed by sleep, sat up, and chattered gaily, feeling himself a hero, while his mother went beside him holding on to any part of his precious little body that came handy, and never tired of hearing him say, "I *knew* Marmar would come," or seeing him lean down to kiss her, and put a plump berry into her mouth, "'Cause he picked them all for her."

The moon shone out just as they reached the avenue, and all the boys came shouting to meet them, so the lost lambs were borne in triumph and safety, and landed in the dining room, where the unromantic little things demanded supper instead of preferring kisses and caresses. They were set down to bread and milk, while the entire household stood round to gaze upon them. Nan soon recovered her spirits, and recounted her perils with a relish now that they were all over. Rob seemed absorbed in his food, but put down his spoon all of a sudden, and set up a doleful roar.

"My precious, why do you cry?" asked his mother, who still hung over him.

"I'm crying 'cause I was lost," bawled Rob, trying to squeeze out a tear, and failing entirely.

"But you are found now. Nan says you didn't cry out in the field, and I was glad you were such a brave boy."

"I was so busy being frightened I didn't have any time then. But I want to cry now, 'cause I don't like to be lost," explained Rob, struggling with sleep, emotion, and a mouthful of bread and milk.

The boys set up such a laugh at this funny way of making up for lost time, that Rob stopped to look at them, and the merriment was so infectious, that after a surprised stare he burst out into a merry "Ha! ha!" and beat his spoon upon the table as if he enjoyed the joke immensely.

"It is ten o'clock; into bed, every man of you," said Mr. Bhaer, looking at his watch.

"And, thank Heaven! there will be no empty ones tonight," added Mrs. Bhaer, watching, with full eyes, Robby going up in his father's arms, and Nan, escorted by Daisy and Demi, who considered her the most interesting heroine of their collection.

"Poor Aunt Jo is so tired she ought to be carried up herself," said gentle Franz, putting his arm round her as she paused at the stair foot, looking quite exhausted by her fright and long walk.

"Let's make an armchair," proposed Tommy.

"No, thank you, my lads; but somebody may lend me a shoulder to lean on," answered Mrs. Jo.

"Me! me!" and half-a-dozen jostled one another, all eager to be chosen, for there was something in the pale motherly face that touched the warm hearts under the round jackets.

Seeing that they considered it an honor, Mrs. Jo gave it to the one who had earned it, and nobody grumbled when she put her arm on Dan's broad shoulder, saying, with a look that made him color up with pride and pleasure, –

"He found the children; so I think he must help me up."

Dan felt richly rewarded for his evening's work, not only that he was chosen from all the rest to go proudly up bearing the lamp, but because Mrs. Jo said, heartily, "Good night, my boy! God bless you!" as he left her at her door.

"I wish I *were* your boy," said Dan, who felt as if danger and trouble had somehow brought him nearer than ever to her.

"You shall be my oldest son," and she sealed her promise with a kiss that made Dan hers entirely.

Little Rob was all right next day, but Nan had a headache, and lay on Mother Bhaer's sofa with cold-cream upon her scratched face. Her remorse was quite gone, and she evidently thought being lost rather a fine amusement. Mrs. Jo was not pleased with this state of things, and had no desire to have her children led from the paths of virtue, or her pupils lying round loose in huckleberry fields. So she talked soberly to Nan, and tried to impress upon her mind the difference between liberty and licence, telling several tales to enforce her lecture. She had not decided how to punish Nan, but one of these stories suggested a way, and as Mrs. Jo liked odd penalties she tried it.

"All children run away," pleaded Nan, as if it was as natural and necessary a thing as measles or whooping cough.

"Not all, and some who do run away don't get found again," answered Mrs. Jo.

"Didn't you do it yourself?" asked Nan, whose keen little eyes saw some traces of kindred spirit in the serious lady who was sewing so morally before her.

Mrs. Jo laughed, and owned that she did.

"Tell about it," demanded Nan, feeling that she was getting the upper hand in the discussion.

Mrs. Jo saw that, and sobered down at once, saying, with a remorseful shake of the head,

"I did it a good many times, and led my poor mother rather a hard life with my pranks, till she cured me."

"How?" and Nan sat up with a face full of interest.

"I had a new pair of shoes once, and wanted to show them; so, though I was told not to leave the garden, I ran away and was wandering about all day. It was in the city, and why I wasn't killed I don't know. Such a time as I had. I frolicked in the park with dogs, sailed boats in the Back Bay with strange boys, dined with a little Irish beggar girl on salt fish and potatoes, and was found at last fast asleep on a doorstep with my arms round a great dog. It was late in the evening, and I was as dirty as a little pig, and the new shoes were worn out — I had traveled so far."

"How nice!" cried Nan, looking all ready to go and do it herself.

"It was *not* nice next day"; and Mrs. Jo tried to keep her eyes from betraying how much she enjoyed the memory of her early capers.

"Did your mother whip you?" asked Nan, curiously.

"She never whipped me but once, and then she begged my pardon, or I don't think I ever should have forgiven her, it hurt my feelings so much."

"Why did she beg your pardon? — my father don't."

"Because, when she had done it, I turned round and said, 'Well, you are mad yourself, and ought to be whipped as much as me.' She looked at me a minute, then her anger all died out, and she said, as if ashamed, 'You are right, Jo, *I am* angry; and why should I punish you for being in a passion when I set you such a bad example? Forgive me, dear, and let us try to help one another in a better way.' I never forgot it, and it did me more good than a dozen rods."

Nan sat thoughtfully turning the little cold-cream jar for a minute, and Mrs. Jo said nothing, but let that idea get well into the busy little mind that was so quick to see and feel what went on about her.

"I like that," said Nan, presently, and her face looked less elfish, with its sharp eyes, inquisitive nose, and mischievous mouth. "What did your mother do to you when you ran away that time?"

"She tied me up to the bed-post with a long string, so that I could not go out of the room, and there I stayed all day with the little worn-out shoes hanging up before me to remind me of my fault."

"I should think that *would* cure anybody," cried Nan, who loved her liberty above all things.

"It did cure me, and I think it will you, so I am going to try it," said Mrs. Jo, suddenly taking a ball of strong twine out of a drawer in her work-table.

Nan looked as if she was decidedly getting the worst of the argument now, and sat feeling much crestfallen while Mrs. Jo tied one end round her waist and the other to the arm of the sofa, saying, as she finished, —

"I don't like to tie you up like a naughty little dog, but if you don't remember any better than a dog, I must treat you like one."

"I'd just as lief be tied up as not — I like to play dog," and Nan put on a don't-care face, and began to growl and grovel on the floor.

Mrs. Jo took no notice, but leaving a book or two and a handkerchief to her, she went away, and left Miss Nan to her own devices. This was not agreeable, and after sitting a moment she tried to untie the cord. But it was fastened in the belt of her apron behind, so she began on the knot at the other end. It soon came loose, and, gathering it up, Nan was about to get out of the window, when she heard Mrs. Jo say to somebody as she passed through the hall,

"No, I don't think she will run away now; she is an honorable little girl, and knows that I do it to help her."

In a minute Nan whisked back, tied herself up, and began to sew violently. Rob came in a moment after, and was so charmed with the new punishment, that he got a jump rope and tethered himself to the other arm of the sofa in the most social manner.

"I got lost too, so I ought to be tied up as much as Nan," he explained to his mother when she saw the new captive.

"I'm not so sure that you don't deserve a little punishment, for you knew it was wrong to go far away from the rest."

"Nan took me," began Rob, willing to enjoy the novel penalty, but not willing to take the blame.

"You needn't have gone. You have got a conscience, though you are a little boy, and you must learn to mind it."

"Well, my conscience didn't prick me a bit when she said 'Let's get over the wall,'" answered Rob, quoting one of Demi's expressions.

"Didn't you stop to see if it did?"

"No."

"Then you cannot tell."

"I guess it's such a little conscience that it don't prick hard enough for me to feel it," added Rob, after thinking over the matter for a minute.

"We must sharpen it up. It's bad to have a dull conscience; so you may stay here till dinner time, and talk about it with Nan. I trust you both not to untie yourselves till I say the word."

"No, we won't," said both, feeling a certain sense of virtue in helping to punish themselves.

For an hour they were very good, then they grew tired of one room, and longed to get out. Never had the hall seemed so inviting; even the little bedroom acquired a sudden interest, and they would gladly have gone in and played tent with the curtains of the best bed. The open windows drove them wild because they could not reach them; and the outer world seemed so beautiful, they wondered how they ever found the heart to say it was dull. Nan pined for a race round the lawn, and Rob remembered with dismay that he had not fed his dog that morning, and wondered what poor Pollux would do. They watched the clock, and Nan did some nice calculations in minutes and seconds, while Rob learned to tell all the hours between eight and one so well that he never forgot them. It was maddening to smell the dinner, to know that there was to be succotash and huckleberry pudding, and to feel that they would not be on the spot to secure good helps of both. When Mary Ann began to set the table, they nearly cut themselves in two trying to see what meat there was to be; and Nan offered to help her make the beds, if she would only see that she had "lots of sauce on her pudding."

When the boys came bursting out of school, they found the children tugging at their halters like a pair of restive little colts, and were much edified, as well as amused, by the sequel to the exciting adventures of the night.

"Untie me now, Marmar; my conscience will prick like a pin next time, I know it will," said Rob, as the bell rang, and Teddy came to look at him with sorrowful surprise.

"We shall see," answered his mother, setting him free. He took a good run down the hall, back through the dining room, and brought up beside Nan, quite beaming with virtuous satisfaction.

A sense of virtue in helping to punish themselves.

"I'll bring her dinner to her, may I?" he asked, pitying his fellow captive.

"That's my kind little son! Yes, pull out the table, and get a chair," and Mrs. Jo hurried away to quell the ardor of the others, who were always in a raging state of hunger at noon.

Nan ate alone, and spent a long afternoon attached to the sofa. Mrs. Bhaer lengthened her bonds so that she could look out of the window; and there she stood watching the boys play, and all the little summer creatures enjoying their liberty. Daisy had a picnic for the dolls on the lawn, so that Nan might see the fun if she could not join in it. Tommy turned his best somersaults to console her; Demi sat on the steps reading aloud to himself, which amused Nan a good deal; and Dan brought a little tree toad to show her as the most delicate attention in his power.

But nothing atoned for the loss of freedom; and a few hours of confinement taught Nan how precious it was. A good many thoughts went through the little head that lay on the window sill during the last quiet hour when all the children went to the brook to see Emil's new ship launched. She was to have christened it, and had depended on smashing a tiny bottle of currant wine over the prow as it was named *Josephine* in honor of Mrs. Bhaer. Now she had lost her chance, and Daisy wouldn't do it half so well. Tears rose to her eyes as she remembered that it was all her own fault; and she said aloud, addressing a fat bee who was rolling about in the yellow heart of a rose just under the window, –

"If you have run away, you'd better go right home, and tell your mother you are sorry, and never do so any more."

"I am glad to hear you give him such good advice, and I think he has taken it," said Mrs. Jo, smiling, as the bee spread his dusty wings and flew away.

Nan brushed off a bright drop or two that shone on the window sill, and nestled against her friend as she took her on her knee, adding kindly – for she had seen the little drops, and knew what they meant, –

"Do you think my mother's cure for running away a good one?"

"Yes, ma'am," answered Nan, quite subdued by her quiet day.

"I hope I shall not have to try it again."

"I guess not," and Nan looked up with such an earnest little face that Mrs. Jo felt satisfied, and said no more, for she liked to have her penalties do their own work, and did not spoil the effect by too much moralizing.

Here Rob appeared, bearing with infinite care what Asia called a "sarcer pie," meaning one backed in a saucer.

"It's made out of some of my berries, and I'm going to give you half at supper time," he announced with a flourish.

"What makes you, when I'm so naughty?" asked Nan, meekly.

"Because we got lost together. You ain't going to be naughty again, are you?"

"Never," said Nan, with great decision.

"Oh, goody! now let's go and get Mary Ann to cut this for us all ready to eat; it's 'most tea-time," and Rob beckoned with the delicious little pie.

Nan started to follow, then stopped, and said, —

"I forgot, I can't go."

"Try and see," said Mrs. Bhaer, who had quietly untied the cord sash while she had been talking.

Nan saw that she was free, and with one tempestuous kiss to Mrs. Jo, she was off like a humming-bird, followed by Robby, dribbling huckleberry juice as he ran.

CHAPTER THIRTEEN

GOLDILOCKS

~

After the last excitement peace descended upon Plumfield and reigned unbroken for several weeks, for the elder boys felt that the loss of Nan and Rob lay at their door, and all became so paternal in their care that they were rather wearying; while the little ones listened to Nan's recital of her perils so many times, that they regarded being lost as the greatest ill humanity was heir to, and hardly dared to put their little noses outside the great gate lest night should suddenly descend upon them, and ghostly black cows come looming through the dusk.

"It is too good to last," said Mrs. Jo; for years of boy culture had taught her that such lulls were usually followed by outbreaks of some sort, and when less wise women would have thought that the boys had become confirmed saints, she prepared herself for a sudden eruption of the domestic volcano.

One cause of this welcome calm was a visit from little Bess, whose parents lent her for a week while they were away with Grandpa Laurence, who was poorly. The boys regarded Goldilocks as a mixture of child, angel, and fairy, for she was a lovely little creature, and the golden hair which she inherited from her blonde mamma enveloped her like a shining veil, behind which she smiled upon her worshippers when gracious, and hid herself when offended. Her father would not have it cut and it hung below her waist, so soft and fine and bright, that Demi insisted that it was silk spun from a cocoon. Every one praised the little Princess, but it did not seem to do her harm, only to teach her that her presence brought sunshine, her smiles made answering smiles on other faces, and her baby griefs filled every heart with tenderest sympathy.

Unconsciously she did her young subjects more good than many a real sovereign, for her rule was very gentle and her power was felt rather than seen. Her natural refinement made her dainty in all things, and had a good effect upon the careless lads about her. She would let no one touch her roughly or with unclean hands, and more soap was used during her visits than at any other time, because the boys considered it the highest honor to be allowed to carry her highness, and the deepest disgrace to be repulsed with the disdainful command, "Do away, dirty boy!"

Loud voices displeased her and quarrelling frightened her; so gentler tones came into the boyish voices as they addressed her, and squabbles were promptly suppressed in her presence by lookers-on if the principals could not restrain themselves. She liked to be waited on, and the biggest boys did her little errands without a murmur, while the small lads were her devoted slaves in all things. They begged to be allowed to draw her carriage, bear her berry basket, or pass her plate at table. No service was too humble, and Tommy and Ned came to blows before they could decide which should have the honor of blacking her little boots.

Nan was especially benefited by a week in the society of a well-bred lady, though such a very small one; for Bess would look at her with a mixture of wonder and alarm in her great blue eyes when the hoyden screamed and romped; and she shrunk from her as if she thought her a sort of wild animal. Warm-hearted Nan felt this very much. She said at first, "Pooh! I don't care!" But she did care, and was so hurt when Bess said, "I love my tuzzin best, tause she is twiet," that she shook poor Daisy till her teeth chattered in her head, and then fled to the barn to cry dismally. In that general refuge for perturbed spirits she found comfort and good counsel from some source or other. Perhaps the swallows from their mud-built nests overhead twittered her a little lecture on the beauty of gentleness. However that might have been, she came out quite subdued, and carefully searched the orchard for a certain kind of early apple that Bess liked because it was sweet and small and rosy. Armed with this peace offering, she approached the Princess, and humbly presented it. To her great joy it was graciously accepted, and when Daisy gave Nan a forgiving kiss, Bess did likewise, as if she felt that she had been too severe, and desired to apologize. After this they played pleasantly together, and Nan enjoyed the royal favor for days. To be sure she felt a little like a wild bird in a pretty cage at first, and occasionally had to slip out to stretch her wings in a long flight, or to sing at the top of her voice, where neither would disturb the plump turtle-dove Daisy, nor the dainty, golden canary Bess. But it did her good; for, seeing how every one loved the little Princess for her small graces and virtues, she began to imitate her, because Nan wanted much love, and tried hard to win it.

Not a boy in the house but felt the pretty child's influence, and was improved by it without exactly knowing how or why, for babies can work miracles in the hearts that love them. Poor Billy found infinite satisfaction in staring at her, and though she did not like it she permitted it without a frown, after she had been made to understand that he was not quite like the others, and on that account must be more kindly treated. Dick and Dolly overwhelmed her with willow whistles, the only thing they knew how to make, and she accepted but never used them. Rob served her like a little lover, and Teddy followed her like a pet dog. Jack she did not like, because he was afflicted with warts and had a harsh voice. Stuffy displeased her because he did not eat tidily, and George tried hard not to gobble, that he might not disgust the dainty little lady opposite. Ned was banished from court in utter disgrace when he was discovered tormenting some unhappy field mice. Goldilocks never could forget the sad spectacle, and retired behind her veil when he approached, waving him away with an imperious little hand, and crying, in a tone of mingled grief and anger, —

"No, I tarn't love him; he tut the poor mouses' little tails off, and they queeked!"

Daisy promptly abdicated when Bess came, and took the humble post of chief cook, while Nan was first maid of honor; Emil was chancellor of the exchequer, and spent the public moneys lavishly in getting up spectacles that cost whole ninepences. Franz was prime minister, and directed her affairs of state, planned royal progresses through the kingdom, and kept foreign powers in order. Demi was her philosopher, and fared much better than such gentlemen usually do among crowned heads. Dan was her standing army, and defended her territories gallantly; Tommy was court fool, and Nat a tuneful Rizzio to this innocent little Mary.

Uncle Fritz and Aunt Jo enjoyed this peaceful episode, and looked on at the pretty play in which the young folk unconsciously imitated their elders, without adding the tragedy that is so apt to spoil the dramas acted on the larger stage.

"They teach us quite as much as we teach them," said Mr. Bhaer.

"Bless the dears! they never guess how many hints they give us as to the best way of managing them," answered Mrs. Jo.

"I think you were right about the good effect of having girls among the boys. Nan *has* stirred up Daisy, and Bess is teaching the little bears how to behave better than we can. If this reformation goes on as it has begun, I shall soon feel like Dr. Blimber with his model young gentlemen," said the Professor, laughing, as he saw Tommy not only remove his own hat, but knock off Ned's also, as they entered the hall where the Princess was taking a ride on the rocking-horse, attended by Rob and Teddy astride of chairs, and playing gallant knights to the best of their ability.

"You will never be a Blimber, Fritz, you couldn't do it if you tried; and our boys will never submit to the forcing process of that famous hot-bed. No fear that they will be too elegant: American boys like liberty too well. But good manners they cannot fail to have, if we give them the kindly spirit that shines through the simplest demeanor, making it courteous and cordial, like yours, my dear old boy."

"Tut! tut! we will not compliment; for if I begin you will run away, and I have a wish to enjoy this happy half hour to the end," yet Mr. Bhaer looked pleased with the compliment, for it was true, and Mrs. Jo felt that she had received the best her husband could give her, by saying that he found his truest rest and happiness in her society.

"To return to the children: I have just had another proof of Goldilocks' good influence," said Mrs. Jo, drawing her chair nearer the sofa, where the Professor lay resting after a long day's work in his various gardens. "Nan hates sewing, but for love of Bess has been toiling half the afternoon over a remarkable bag in which to present a dozen of our love apples to her idol when she goes. I praised her for it, and she said, in her quick way, 'I like to sew for other people; it is stupid sewing for myself.' I took the hint, and shall give her some little shirts and aprons for Mrs. Carney's children. She is so generous, she will sew her fingers sore for them, and I shall not have to make a task of it."

"But needlework is not a fashionable accomplishment, my dear."

"Sorry for it. My girls shall learn all I can teach them about it, even if they give up the Latin, algebra, and half-a-dozen ologies it is considered necessary for girls to muddle their poor brains over nowadays. Amy means to make Bess an accomplished woman; but the dear's mite of a forefinger has little pricks on it already, and her mother has several specimens of needlework which she values more than the clay bird without a bill, that filled Laurie with such pride when Bess made it."

"I also have a proof of the Princess's power," said Mr. Bhaer, after he had watched Mrs. Jo sew on a button with an air of scorn for the whole system of fashionable education. "Jack is so unwilling to be classed with Stuffy and Ned, as distasteful to Bess, that he came to me a little while ago, and asked me to touch his warts with caustic. I have often proposed it, and he never would consent; but now he bore the smart manfully, and consoles his present discomfort by hopes of future favor, when he can show her fastidious ladyship a smooth hand."

Mrs. Bhaer laughed at the story, and just then Stuffy came in to ask if he might give Goldilocks some of the bonbons his mother had sent him.

"She is not allowed to eat sweeties; but if you like to give her the pretty box with the pink sugar rose in it, she would like it very much," said Mrs. Jo, unwilling to spoil this unusual piece of self-denial, for the "fat boy" seldom offered to share his sugarplums.

"Won't she eat it? I shouldn't like to make her sick," said Stuffy, eyeing the delicate sweetmeat lovingly, yet putting it into the box.

"Oh, no, she won't touch it, if I tell her it is to look at, not to eat. She will keep it for weeks, and never think of tasting it. Can you do as much?"

"I should hope so! I'm ever so much older than she is," cried Stuffy, indignantly.

"Well, suppose we try. Here, put your bonbons in this bag, and see how long you can keep them. Let me count — two hearts, four red fishes, three barley-sugar horses, nine almonds, and a dozen chocolate drops. Do you agree to that?" asked sly Mrs. Jo, popping the sweeties into her little spool bag.

"Yes," said Stuffy with a sigh; and pocketing the forbidden fruit, he went away to give Bess the present, that won a smile from her, and permission to escort her round the garden.

"Poor Stuffy's heart has really got the better of his stomach at last, and his efforts will be much encouraged by the rewards Bess gives him," said Mrs. Jo.

"Happy the man who can put temptation in his pocket and learn self-denial from so sweet a little teacher!" added Mr. Bhaer, as the children passed the window, Stuffy's fat face full of placid satisfaction, and Goldilocks surveying her sugar rose with polite interest, though she would have preferred a real flower with a "pitty smell."

When her father came to take her home, a universal wail arose, and the parting gifts showered upon her increased her luggage to such an extent that Mr. Laurie proposed having out the big wagon to take it into town. Every one had given her something; and it was found difficult to pack white mice, cake, a parcel of shells, apples, a rabbit kicking violently in a bag, a large cabbage for his refreshment, a bottle of minnows, and a mammoth bouquet. The farewell scene was moving, for the Princess sat upon the hall table, surrounded by her subjects. She kissed her cousins, and held out her hand to the other boys, who shook it gently with various soft speeches, for they were taught not to be ashamed of showing their emotions.

"Come again, soon, little dear," whispered Dan fastening his best green-and-gold beetle in her hat.

"Don't forget me, Princess, whatever you do," said the engaging Tommy, taking a last stroke of the pretty hair.

"I am coming to your house next week, and then I shall see you, Bess," added Nat, as if he found consolation in the thought.

"Do shake hands now," cried Jack, offering a smooth paw.

"Here are two nice new ones to remember us by," said Dick and Dolly, presenting fresh whistles, quite unconscious that seven old ones had

*Demi appeared with a huge kite, on which was
printed "For Mother Bhaer". (Chapter 9)*

Teddy leaned down from the tree, watching for the fish. (Chapter 15)

been privately deposited in the kitchen stove.

"My little precious! I shall work you a bookmark right away, and you must keep it *always*," said Nan, with a warm embrace.

But of all the farewells, poor Billy's was the most pathetic, for the thought that she was really going became so unbearable that he cast himself down before her, hugging her little blue boots and blubbering despairingly, "Don't go away! oh, don't!" Goldilocks was so touched by this burst of feeling, that she leaned over and lifting the poor lad's head, said, in her soft, little voice, —

"Don't cry, poor Billy! I will tiss you and tum adain soon."

This promise consoled Billy, and he fell back beaming with pride at the unusual honor conferred upon him.

"Me too! me too!" clamored Dick and Dolly, feeling that their devotion deserved some return. The others looked as if they would like to join in the cry; and something in the kind, merry faces about her moved the Princess to stretch out her arms and say, with reckless condescension, —

"I will tiss evvybody!"

Like a swarm of bees about a very sweet flower, the affectionate lads surrounded their pretty playmate, and kissed her till she looked like a little rose, not roughly, but so enthusiastically that nothing but the crown of her hat was visible for a moment. Then her father rescued her, and she drove away still smiling and waving her hands, while the boys sat on the fence screaming like a flock of guinea fowls, "Come back! come back!" till she was out of sight.

They all missed her, and each dimly felt that he was better for having known a creature so lovely, delicate, and sweet; for little Bess appealed to the chivalrous instinct in them as something to love, admire, and protect with a tender sort of reverence. Many a man remembers some pretty child who has made a place in his heart and kept her memory alive by the simple magic of her innocence; these little men were just learning to feel this power, and to love it for its gentle influence, not ashamed to let the small hand lead them, nor to own their loyalty to womankind, even in the bud.

CHAPTER FOURTEEN

DAMON AND PYTHIAS

~

M rs. Bhaer was right; peace was only a temporary lull, a storm was brewing, and two days after Bess left, a moral earthquake shook Plumfield to its center.

Tommy's hens were at the bottom of the trouble, for if they had not persisted in laying so many eggs, he could not have sold them and made such sums. Money is the root of all evil, and yet it is such a useful root that we cannot get on without it any more than we can without potatoes. Tommy certainly could not, for he spent his income so recklessly, that Mr. Bhaer was obliged to insist on a savings bank, and presented him with a private one — an imposing tin edifice, with the name over the door, and a tall chimney, down which the pennies were to go, there to rattle temptingly till leave was given to open a sort of trapdoor in the floor.

The house increased in weight so rapidly, that Tommy soon became satisfied with his investment, and planned to buy unheard-of treasures with his capital. He kept account of the sums deposited, and was promised that he might break the bank as soon as he had five dollars, on condition that he spent the money wisely. Only one dollar was needed, and the day Mrs. Jo paid him for four dozen eggs, he was so delighted, that he raced off to the barn to display the bright quarters to Nat, who was also laying by money for the long-desired violin.

"I wish I had them to put with my three dollars, then I'd soon get enough to buy my fiddle," he said, looking wistfully at the money.

"P'raps I'll lend you some. I haven't decided yet what I'll do with mine," said Tommy, tossing up his quarters, and catching them as they fell.

"Hi! boys! come down to the brook and see what a jolly great snake Dan's got!" called a voice from behind the barn.

"Come on," said Tommy; and, laying his money inside the old winnowing machine, away he ran, followed by Nat.

The snake was very interesting, and then a long chase after a lame cow, and its capture, so absorbed Tommy's mind and time, that he never thought of his money till he was safely in bed that night.

"Never mind, no one but Nat knows where it is," said the easy-going lad, and fell asleep untroubled by an anxiety about his property.

Next morning, just as the boys assembled for school, Tommy rushed into the room breathlessly, demanding,

"I say, who has got my dollar?"

"What are you talking about?" asked Franz.

Tommy explained, and Nat corroborated his statement.

Every one else declared they knew nothing about it, and began to look suspiciously at Nat, who got more and more alarmed and confused with each denial.

"Somebody must have taken it," said Franz, as Tommy shook his fist at the whole party, and wrathfully declared, –

"By thunder turtles! If I get hold of the thief, I'll give him what he won't forget in a hurry."

"Keep cool, Tom; we shall find him out; thieves always come to grief," said Dan, as one who knew something of the matter.

"Maybe some tramp slept in the barn and took it," suggested Ned.

"No, Silas don't allow that; besides, a tramp wouldn't go looking in that old machine for money," said Emil, with scorn.

"Wasn't it Silas himself?" said Jack.

"Well, I like that! Old Si is as honest as daylight. You wouldn't catch him touching a penny of ours," said Tommy, handsomely defending his chief admirer from suspicion.

"Whoever it was had better tell, and not wait to be found out," said Demi, looking as if an awful misfortune had befallen the family.

"I know you think it's me," broke out Nat, red and excited.

"You are the only one who knew where it was," said Franz.

"I can't help it – I didn't take it. I tell you I didn't – I didn't!" cried Nat, in a desperate sort of way.

"Gently, gently, my son! What is all this noise about?" and Mr. Bhaer walked in among them.

Tommy repeated the story of his loss, and, as he listened, Mr. Bhaer's face grew graver and graver; for, with all their faults and follies, the lads till now had been honest.

"Take your seats," he said; and, when all were in their places, he added slowly, as his eye went from face to face with a grieved look, that was harder to bear than a storm of words, –

"Now, boys, I shall ask each one of you a single question, and I want an honest answer. I am not going to try to frighten, bribe, or surprise the truth out of you, for every one of you has got a conscience, and knows what it is for. Now is the time to undo the wrong done to Tommy, and to set yourselves right before us all. I can forgive the yielding to a sudden temptation much easier than I can deceit. Don't add a lie to the theft, but confess frankly, and we will all try to help you make us forget and forgive."

He paused a moment, and one might have heard a pin drop, the room was so still; then slowly and impressively he put the question to each one, receiving the same answer in varying tones from all. Every face was flushed and excited, so that Mr. Bhaer could not take color as a witness, and some of the little boys were so frightened that they stammered over the two short words as if guilty, though it was evident that they could not be. When he came to Nat, his voice softened, for the poor lad looked so wretched, Mr. Bhaer felt for him. He believed him to be the culprit, and hoped to save the boy from another lie, by winning him to tell the truth without fear.

"Now, my son, give me an honest answer. Did you take the money?"

"No, sir!" and Nat looked up at him imploringly.

As the words fell from his trembling lips, somebody hissed.

"Stop that!" cried Mr. Bhaer, with a sharp rap on his desk, as he looked sternly toward the corner whence the sound came.

Ned, Jack and Emil sat there, and the first two looked ashamed of themselves, but Emil called out, –

"It wasn't me, uncle! I'd be ashamed to hit a fellow when he is down."

"Good for you!" cried Tommy, who was in a sad state of affliction at the trouble his unlucky dollar had made.

"Silence!" commanded Mr. Bhaer; and when it came, he said soberly, –

"I am *very* sorry, Nat, but evidences are against you, and your old fault makes us more ready to doubt you than we should be if we could trust you as we do some of the boys, who never fib. But mind, my child, I do not charge you with this theft; I shall not punish you for it till I am *perfectly* sure, nor ask anything more about it. I shall leave it for you to settle with your own conscience. If you are guilty, come to me at any hour of the day or night and confess it, and I will forgive and help you to amend. If you are innocent, the truth will appear sooner or later, and the instant it does, I will be the first to beg your pardon for doubting you, and will gladly do my best to clear your character before us all."

"I didn't! I didn't!" sobbed Nat, with his head down upon his arms, for he could not bear the look of distrust and dislike which he read in the many eyes fixed on him.

"I hope not." Mr. Bhaer paused a minute, as if to give the culprit, whoever he might be, one more chance. Nobody spoke, however, and only sniffs of sympathy from some of the little fellows broke the silence. Mr. Bhaer shook his head, and added, regretfully, –

"There is nothing more to be done, then, and I have but one thing to say: I shall not speak of this again, and I wish you all to follow my example. I cannot expect you to feel as kindly toward any one whom you suspect as before this happened, but I do expect and desire that you will not torment the suspected person in any way; he will have a hard enough time without that. Now go to your lessons."

"Father Bhaer let Nat off too easy," muttered Ned to Emil, as they got out their books.

"Hold your tongue," growled Emil, who felt that this event was a blot upon the family honor.

Many of the boys agreed with Ned, but Mr. Bhaer was right, nevertheless; and Nat would have been wiser to confess on the spot and have the trouble over, for even the hardest whipping he ever received from his father was far easier to bear than the cold looks, the avoidance, and general suspicion that met him on all sides. If ever a boy was sent to Coventry and kept there, it was poor Nat; and he suffered a week of slow torture, though not a hand was raised against him, and hardly a word said.

That was the worst of it; if they would only have talked it out, or even have thrashed him all round, he could have stood it better than the silent distrust that made every face so terrible to meet. Even Mrs. Bhaer's showed traces of it, though her manner was nearly as kind as ever; but the sorrowful, anxious look in Father Bhaer's eyes cut Nat to the heart, for he loved his teacher dearly, and knew that he had disappointed all his hopes by this double sin.

Only one person in the house entirely believed in him, and stood up for him stoutly against all the rest. This was Daisy. She could not explain why she trusted him against all appearances, she only felt that she could not doubt him, and her warm sympathy made her strong to take his part. She would not hear a word against him from any one, and actually slapped her beloved Demi when he tried to convince her that it *must* have been Nat, because no one else knew where the money was.

"May be the hens ate it; they are greedy old things," she said; and when Demi laughed, she lost her temper, slapped the amazed boy, and then burst out crying and ran away, still declaring, "He didn't! he didn't! he didn't!"

Neither aunt nor uncle tried to shake the child's faith in her friend, but only hoped her innocent instinct might prove sure, and loved her all the better for it. Nat often said, after it was over, that he couldn't have stood it, if it had not been for Daisy. When the others shunned him, she clung to him closer than ever, and turned her back on the rest. She did not sit on the stairs now when he solaced himself with the old fiddle, but went in and sat beside him, listening with a face so full of confidence and affection, that Nat forgot disgrace for a time, and was happy. She asked him to help her with her lessons, she cooked him marvellous messes in her kitchen, which he ate manfully, no matter what they were, for gratitude gave a sweet flavor to the most distasteful. She proposed impossible games of cricket and ball, when she found that he shrank from joining the other boys. She put little nosegays from her garden on his desk, and tried in every way to show that *she* was not a fair-weather friend, but faithful through evil as well as good repute. Nan soon followed her example, in kindess at least; curbed her sharp tongue, and kept her scornful little nose from any demonstration of doubt or dislike, which was good of Madame Giddygaddy, for she firmly believed that Nat took the money.

Most of the boys let him severely alone, but Dan, though he said he despised him for being a coward, watched over him with grim sort of protection, and promptly cuffed any lad who dared to molest his mate or make him afraid. His idea of friendship was as high as Daisy's, and, in his own rough way, he lived up to it as loyally.

Sitting by the brook one afternoon, absorbed in the study of the domestic habits of water-spiders, he overheard a bit of conversation on the other side of the wall. Ned, who was intensely inquisitive, had been on tenterhooks to know *certainly* who was the culprit; for of late one or two of the boys had begun to think that they were wrong, Nat was so steadfast in his denials, and so meek in his endurance of their neglect. This doubt had teased Ned past bearing, and he had several times privately beset Nat with questions, regardless of Mr. Bhaer's express command. Finding Nat reading alone on the shady side of the wall, Ned could not resist stopping for a nibble at the forbidden subject. He had worried Nat for some ten minutes before Dan arrived, and the first word the spider-student heard were these, in Nat's patient, pleading voice, —

"Don't, Ned! Oh, don't! I can't tell you because I don't know, and it's mean of you to keep nagging at me on the sly, when Father Bhaer told you not to plague me. You wouldn't dare to if Dan were round."

"I ain't afraid of Dan; he's nothing but an old bully. Don't believe but what he took Tom's money, and you know it, and won't tell. Come, now!"

"He didn't, but, if he did, I *would* stand up for him, he has always been so good to me," said Nat, so earnestly, that Dan forgot his spiders, and rose quickly to thank him, but Ned's next words arrested him.

"I *know* Dan did it, and gave the money to you. Shouldn't wonder if he got his living picking pockets before he came here, for nobody knows anything about him but you," said Ned, not believing his own words, but hoping to get the truth out of Nat by making him angry.

He succeeded in a part of his ungenerous wish, for Nat cried out, fiercely, –

"If you say that again I'll go and tell Mr. Bhaer all about it. I don't want to tell tales, but, by George! I will, if you don't let Dan alone."

"Then you'll be a sneak, as well as a liar and a thief," began Ned, with a jeer, for Nat had borne insult to himself so meekly, the other did not believe he would dare to face the master just to stand up for Dan.

When he might have added I cannot tell, for the words were hardly out of his mouth when a long arm from behind took him by the collar, and, jerking him over the wall in a most promiscuous way, landed him with a splash in the middle of the brook.

"Say that again and I'll duck you till you can't see!" cried Dan, looking like a modern Colossus of Rhodes as he stood, with a foot on either side the narrow stream, glaring down at the discomfited youth in the water.

"I was only in fun," said Ned.

"You are a sneak yourself to badger Nat round the corner. Let me catch you at it again, and I'll souse you in the river next time. Get up, and clear out!" thundered Dan, in a rage.

Ned fled, dripping, and this impromptu sitz bath evidently did him good, for he was very respectful to both the boys after that, and seemed to have left his curiosity in the brook. As he vanished Dan jumped over the wall, and found Nat lying as if quite worn out and bowed down with his troubles.

"He won't pester you again, I guess. If he does, just tell me, and I'll see to him," said Dan, trying to cool down.

"I don't mind what he says about me so much, I've got used to it," answered Nat, sadly; "but I hate to have him pitch into you."

"How do you know he isn't right?" asked Dan, turning his face away.

"What, about the money?" cried Nat, looking up with a startled air. "Yes."

"But I don't believe it! *You* don't care for money; all you want is your old bugs and things," and Nat laughed, incredulously.

"I want a butterfly net as much as you want a fiddle; why shouldn't I steal the money for it as much as you?" said Dan, still turning away, and busily punching holes in the turf with his stick.

"I don't think you would. You like to fight and knock folks round some times, but you don't lie, and I don't believe you'd steal," and Nat shook his head decidedly.

"I've done both. I used to fib like fury; it's too much trouble now; and I stole things to eat out of gardens when I ran away from Page, so you see I *am* a bad lot," said Dan, speaking in the rough, reckless way which he had been learning to drop lately.

"O Dan! don't say it's you! I'd rather have it any of the other boys," cried Nat, in such a distressed tone that Dan looked pleased, and showed that he did, by turning round with a queer expression in his face, though he only answered, –

"I won't say anything about it. But don't you fret, and we'll pull through somehow, see if we don't."

Something in his face and manner gave Nat a new idea; and he said, pressing his hands together, in the eagerness of his appeal, –

"I think you know who did it. If you do, beg him to tell, Dan. It's so hard to have them all hate me for nothing. I don't think I *can* bear it much longer. If I had any place to go to, I'd run away, though I love Plumfield dearly; but I'm not brave and big like you, so I must stay and wait till some one shows them that I haven't lied."

As he spoke, Nat looked so broken and despairing, than Dan could not bear it, and muttering huskily, –

"You won't wait long," he walked rapidly away, and was seen no more for hours.

"What is the matter with Dan?" asked the boys of one another several times during the Sunday that followed a week which seemed as if it would *never* end. Dan was often moody, but that day he was so sober and silent that no one could get anything out of him. When they walked he strayed away from the rest, and came home late. He took no part in the evening conversation, but sat in the shadow, so busy with his own thoughts that he scarcely seemed to hear what was going on. When Mrs. Jo showed him an unusually good report in the Conscience Book, he looked at it without a smile, and said, wistfully, –

"You think I am getting on, don't you?"

"Excellently, Dan! and I am so pleased, because I always thought you only needed a little help to make you a boy to be proud of."

He looked up at her with a strange expression in his black eyes, — an expression of mingled pride and love and sorrow which she could not understand then, — but remembered afterward.

"I'm afraid you'll be disappointed, but I do try," he said, shutting the book without a sign of pleasure in the page that he usually liked so much to read over and talk about.

"Are you sick, dear?" asked Mrs. Jo, with her hand on his shoulder.

"My foot aches a little; I guess I'll go to bed. Good night, mother," he added, and held the hand against his cheek a minute, then went away looking as if he had said good-by to something very dear.

"Poor Dan! he takes Nat's disgrace to heart sadly. He is a strange boy; I wonder if I ever shall understand him thoroughly?" said Mrs. Jo to herself, as she thought over Dan's late improvement with real satisfaction, yet felt that there was more in the lad than she had at first suspected.

One of the things which cut Nat most deeply was an act of Tommy's, for after his loss Tommy had said to him, kindly but firmly, —

"I don't wish to hurt you, Nat, but you see I can't afford to lose my money, so I guess we won't be partners any longer," and with that Tommy rubbed out the sign, "T. Bangs & Co."

Nat had been very proud of the "Co.," and had hunted eggs industriously, kept his accounts all straight, and had added a good sum to his income from the sale of his share of stock in trade.

"O Tom! must you?" he said, feeling that his good name was gone for ever in the business world if this was done.

"I must," returned Tommy, firmly, "Emil says that when one man 'bezzles (I believe that's the word — it means to take money and cut away with it) the property of a firm, the other one sues him, or pitches into him somehow, and won't have anything more to do with him. Now you have 'bezzled my property; I shan't sue you, and I shan't pitch into you, but I *must* dissolve the partnership, because I can't trust you, and I don't wish to fail."

"I can't make you believe me, and you won't take my money, though I'd be thankful to give all my dollars if you'd only say you don't think I took your money. Do let me hunt for you, I won't ask any wages, but do it for nothing. I know all the places, and I like it," pleaded Nat.

But Tommy shook his head, and his jolly, round face looked suspicious and hard as he said, shortly, "Can't do it; wish you didn't know the places. Mind you don't go hunting on the sly, and speculate in my eggs."

Poor Nat was so hurt that he could not get over it. He felt that he had lost not only his partner and patron, but that he was bankrupt in honor, and an outlaw from the business community. No one trusted his word, written or spoken, in spite of his efforts to redeem the past falsehood; the sign was down, the firm broken up, and he a ruined man. The barn, which was the boys' Wall Street, knew him no more. Cockletop and her sisters cackled for him in vain, and really seemed to take his misfortune to heart, for eggs were fewer, and some of the biddies retired in disgust to new nests, which Tommy could not find.

"*They* trust me," said Nat, when he heard of it, and though the boys shouted at the idea, Nat found comfort in it, for when one is down in the world, the confidence of even a speckled hen is most consoling.

Tommy took no new partner, however, for distrust had entered in, and poisoned the peace of his once confiding soul. Ned offered to join him, but he declined, saying, with a sense of justice that did him honor, –

"It might turn out that Nat didn't take any money, and then we could be partners again. I don't think it will happen, but I will give him a chance, and keep the place open a little longer."

Billy was the only person whom Bangs felt he could trust in his shop, and Billy was trained to hunt eggs, and hand them over unbroken, being quite satisfied with an apple, or a sugarplum for wages. The morning after Dan's gloomy Sunday, Billy said to his employer, as he displayed the results of a long hunt, –

"Only two."

"It gets worse and worse; I new saw such provoking old hens," growled Tommy, thinking of the days when he often had six to rejoice over. "Well, put them in my hat and give me a new bit of chalk; I must mark 'em up, anyway."

Billy mounted a peck measure, and looked into the top of the machine, where Tommy kept his writing materials.

"There's lots of money in here," said Billy.

"No there isn't. Catch me leaving cash round again," returned Tommy.

"I see them — one, four, eight, two dollars," persisted Billy, who had not yet mastered the figures correctly.

"What a jack you are!" and Tommy hopped up to get the chalk for himself but nearly tumbled down again, for there actually were four bright quarters in a row, with a bit of paper on them directed to "Tom Bangs," that there might be no mistake.

"Thunder turtles!" cried Tommy, and seizing them he dashed into the house, bawling wildly, "It's all right! Got my money! Where's Nat?"

He was soon found, and his surprise and pleasure were so genuine that few doubted his word when he now denied all knowledge of the money.

"How could I put it back when I didn't take it? Do believe me now, and be good to me again," he said, so imploringly, that Emil slapped him on the back, and declared *he* would for one.

"So will I, and I'm jolly glad it's not you. But who the dickens is it?" said Tommy, after shaking hands heartily with Nat.

"Never mind, as long as it's found," said Dan with his eyes fixed on Nat's happy face.

"Well, I like that! I'm not going to have my things hooked, and then brought back like the juggling man's tricks," cried Tommy, looking at his money as if he suspected witchcraft.

"We'll find him out somehow, though he was sly enough to print this so his writing wouldn't be known," said Franz, examining the paper.

"Demi prints tip-top," put in Rob, who had not a very clear idea what the fuss was all about.

"You can't make me believe it's him, not if you talk till you are blue," said Tommy, and the others hooted at the mere idea; for the little deacon, as they called him, was above suspicion.

Nat felt the difference in the way they spoke of Demi and himself, and would have given all he had or ever hoped to have to be so trusted; for he had learned how easy it is to lose the confidence of others, how very, very hard to win it back, and truth became to him a precious thing since he had suffered from neglecting it.

Mr. Bhaer was very glad one step had been taken in the right direction, and waited hopefully for yet further revelations. They came sooner than he expected, and in a way that surprised and grieved him very much. As they sat at supper that night, a square parcel was handed to Mr.

Bhaer from Mrs. Bates, a neighbor. A note accompanied the parcel, and, while Mr. Bhaer read it, Demi pulled off the wrapper, exclaiming, as he saw its contents, —

"Why, it's the book Uncle Teddy gave Dan!"

"The devil!" broke from Dan, for he had not yet quite cured himself of swearing, though he tried hard.

Mr. Bhaer looked up quickly at the sound. Dan tried to meet his eyes, but could not; his own fell, and he sat biting his lips, getting redder and redder till he was the picture of shame.

"What is it?" asked Mrs. Bhaer, anxiously.

"I should have preferred to talk about this in private, but Demi has spoiled that plan, so I may as well have it out now," said Mr. Bhaer, looking a little stern, as he always did when any meanness or deceit came up for judgement.

"The note is from Mrs. Bates, and she says that her boy Jimmy told her he bought this book from Dan last Saturday. She saw that it was worth much more than a dollar, and thinking there was some mistake, has sent it to me. Did you sell it, Dan?"

"Yes, sir," was the slow answer.

"Why?"

"Wanted money."

"For what?"

"To pay somebody."

"To whom did you owe it?"

"Tommy."

"Never borrowed a cent of me in his life," cried Tommy, looking scared, for he guessed what was coming now, and felt that on the whole he would have preferred witchcraft, for he admired Dan immensely.

"Perhaps he took it," cried Ned, who owed Dan a grudge for the ducking, and, being a mortal boy, liked to pay it off.

"O Dan!" cried Nat, clashing his hands, regardless of the bread and butter in them.

"It is a hard thing to do, but I must have this settled, for I cannot have you watching each other like detectives, and the whole school disturbed in this way. Did you put that dollar in the barn this morning?" asked Mr. Bhaer.

Dan looked him straight in the face, and answered steadily, "Yes, I did."

A murmur went round the table, Tommy dropped his mug with a crash; Daisy cried out, "I knew it wasn't Nat;" Nan began to cry, and Mrs. Jo left the room, looking so disappointed, sorry, and ashamed that Dan could not bear it. He hid his face in his hands a moment, then threw up his head, squared his shoulders as if settling some load upon them, and said, with the dogged look, and half-resolute, half-reckless tone he had used when he first came, —

"I did it; now you may do what you like to me, but I won't say another word about it."

"Not even that you are sorry?" asked Mr. Bhaer, troubled by the change in him.

"I ain't sorry."

"I'll forgive him without asking," said Tommy, feeling that it was harder somehow to see brave Dan disgraced than timid Nat.

"Don't want to be forgiven," returned Dan, gruffly.

"Perhaps you will when you have thought about it quietly by yourself. I won't tell you now how surprised and disappointed I am, but by and by I will come up and talk to you in your room."

"Won't make any difference," said Dan, trying to speak defiantly, but failing as he looked at Mr. Bhaer's sorrowful face; and, taking his words for a dismissal, Dan left the room as if he found it impossible to stay.

It would have done him good if he had stayed; for the boys talked the matter over with such sincere regret, and pity, and wonder, it might have touched and won him to ask pardon. No one was glad to find that it was he, not even Nat; for, spite of all his faults, and they were many, every one liked Dan now, because under his rough exterior lay some of the manly virtues which we most admire and love. Mrs. Jo had been the chief prop, as well as cultivator, of Dan; and she took it sadly to heart that her last and most interesting boy had turned out so ill. The theft was bad, but the lying about it, and allowing another to suffer so much from an unjust suspicion, was worse; and most discouraging of all was the attempt to restore the money in an underhand way, for it showed not only a want of courage, but a power of deceit that boded ill for the future. Still more trying was his steady refusal to talk of the matter, to ask pardon, or express any remorse. Days passed; and he went about his lessons and his work, silent, grim, and unrepentant. As if taking warning by their treatment of Nat, he asked no sympathy of any one, rejected the advances of the boys, and spent his leisure hours roaming about the fields and woods, trying to find playmates in the birds and beasts, and succeeding better than most boys would have done, because he knew and loved them so well.

"If this goes on much longer, I'm afraid he will run away again, for he is too young to stand a life like this," said Mr. Bhaer, quite dejected at the failure of all his efforts.

"A little while ago I should have been quite sure that nothing would tempt him away, but now I am ready for anything, he is so changed," answered poor Mrs. Jo, who mourned over her boy and could not be comforted, because he shunned her more than any one else, and only looked at her with the half-fierce, half-imploring eyes of a wild animal caught in a trap, when she tried to talk to him alone.

Nat followed him about like a shadow, and Dan did not repulse him as rudely as he did others, but said, in his blunt way, '*You* are all right; don't worry about me. I can stand it better than you did."

"But I don't like to have you all alone," Nat would say, sorrowfully.

"I like it," and Dan would tramp away, stifling a sigh sometimes, for he *was* lonely.

Passing through the birch grove one day, he came upon several of the boys, who were amusing themselves by climbing up the trees and swinging down again, as the slender elastic stems bent till their tops touched the ground. Dan paused a minute to watch the fun, without offering to join in it, and as he stood there Jack took his turn. He had unfortunately chosen too large a tree; for when he swung off, it only bent a little way, and left him hanging at a dangerous height.

"Go back; you can't do it!" called Ned from below.

Jack tried, but the twigs slipped from his hands, and he could not get his legs round the trunk. He kicked, and squirmed, and clutched in vain, then gave it up, and hung breathless, saying helplessly, –

"Catch me! help me! I must drop!"

"You'll be killed if you do," cried Ned, frightened out of his wits.

"Hold on!" shouted Dan; and up the tree he went, crashing his way along till he nearly reached Jack, whose face looked up at him, full of fear and hope.

"You'll both come down," said Ned, dancing with excitement on the slope underneath, while Nat held out his arms, in the wild hope of breaking the fall.

"That's what I want; stand from under," answered Dan, coolly; and, as he spoke, his added weight bent the tree many feet nearer the earth.

Jack dropped safely; but the birch, lightened of half its load, flew up again so suddenly, that Dan, in the act of swinging round to drop feet foremost, lost his hold and fell heavily.

"I'm not hurt, all right in a minute," he said, sitting up, a little pale and dizzy, as the boys gathered round him, full of admiration and alarm.

"You're a trump, Dan, and I'm ever so much obliged to you," cried Jack, gratefully.

"It wasn't anything," muttered Dan, rising slowly.

"I say it was, and I'll shake hands with you, though you are –" Ned checked the unlucky word on his tongue, and held out his hand, feeling that it was a handsome thing on his part.

"But *I* won't shake hands with a sneak," and Dan turned his back with a look of scorn, that caused Ned to remember the brook, and retire with undignified haste.

"Come home, old chap; I'll give you a lift," and Nat walked away with him leaving the others to talk over the feat together, to wonder when Dan would "come round," and to wish one and all that Tommy's "confounded money had been in Jericho before it made such a fuss."

When Mr. Bhaer came into school next morning, he looked so happy, that the boys wondered what had happened to him, and really thought he had lost his mind when they saw him go straight to Dan, and, taking him by both hands, say all in one breath, as he shook them heartily, –

"I know all about it, and I beg your pardon. It was like you to do it, and I love you for it, though it's never right to tell lies, even for a friend."

"What is it?" cried Nat, for Dan said not a word, only lifted up his head, as if a weight of some sort had fallen off his back.

"Dan did *not* take Tommy's money," and Mr. Bhaer quite shouted it, he was so glad.

"Who did?" cried the boys in a chorus.

Mr. Bhaer pointed to one empty seat, and every eye followed his finger, yet no one spoke for a minute, they were so surprised.

"Jack went home early this morning, but he left this behind him," and in the silence Mr. Bhaer read the note which he had found tied to his door handle when he rose.

I took Tommy's dollar. I was peering in through a crack, and saw him put it there. I was afraid to tell before, though I wanted to. I didn't care so much about Nat, but Dan is a trump, and I can't stand it any longer. I never spent the money; it's under the carpet in my room, right behind the washstand. I'm awful sorry. I am going home, and don't think I shall ever come back, so Dan may have my things.

JACK.

It was not an elegant confession, being badly written, much blotted, and very short; but it was a precious paper to Dan; and, when Mr. Bhaer paused, the boy went to him, saying, in rather a broken voice, but with clear eyes, and the frank, respectful manner they had tried to teach him, —

"I'll say I'm sorry now, and ask you to forgive me, sir."

"It was a kind lie, Dan, and I can't help forgiving it; but you see it did no good," said Mr. Bhaer, with a hand on either shoulder, and a face full of relief and affection.

"It kept the boys from plaguing Nat. That's what I did it for. It made him right down miserable. I didn't care so much," explained Dan, as if glad to speak out after his hard silence.

"How could you do it? You are always *so* kind to me," faltered Nat, feeling a strong desire to hug his friend and cry — two girlish performances, which would have scandalized Dan to the last degree.

"It's all right now, old fellow, so don't be a fool," he said, swallowing the lump in his throat, and laughing out as he had not done for weeks. "Does Mrs. Bhaer know?" he asked, eagerly.

"Yes; and she is so happy I don't know what she will do to you," began Mr. Bhaer, but got no farther, for here the boys came crowding about Dan in a tumult of pleasure and curiosity; but before he had answered more than a dozen questions, a voice cried out, —

"Three cheers for Dan!" and there was Mrs. Jo in the doorway waving her dish towel, and looking as if she wanted to dance a jig for joy, as she used to do when a girl.

"Now then," cried Mr. Bhaer, and led off a rousing hurrah, which startled Asia in the kitchen, and made old Mr. Roberts shake his head as he drove by, saying, –

"Schools are not what they were when I was young!"

Dan stood it pretty well for a minute, but the sight of Mrs. Jo's delight upset him, and he suddenly bolted across the hall into the parlor, whither she instantly followed, and neither were seen for half an hour.

Mr. Bhaer found it very difficult to calm his excited flock; and, seeing that lessons were an impossibility for a time, he caught their attention by telling them the fine old story of the friends whose fidelity to one another has made their names immortal. The lads listened and remembered, for just then their hearts were touched by the loyalty of a humbler pair of friends. The lie was wrong, but the love that prompted it and the courage that bore in silence the disgrace which belonged to another, made Dan a hero in their eyes. Honesty and honor had a new meaning now; a good name was more precious than gold; for once lost money could not buy it back; and faith in one another made life smooth and happy as nothing else could do.

Tommy proudly restored the name of the firm; Nat was devoted to Dan; and all the boys tried to atone to both the former suspicion and neglect. Mrs. Jo rejoiced over her flock, and Mr. Bhaer was never tired of telling the story of his young Damon and Pythias.

CHAPTER FIFTEEN

IN THE WILLOW

~

The old tree saw and heard a good many little scenes and confidences that summer, because it became the favorite retreat of all the children, and the willow seemed to enjoy it, for a pleasant welcome always met them, and the quiet hours spent in its arms did them all good. It had a great deal of company one Saturday afternoon, and some little bird reported what went on there.

First came Nan and Daisy with their small tubs and bits of soap, for now and then they were seized with a tidy fit, and washed up all the dolls' clothes in the brook. Asia would not have them "slopping round" in her kitchen, and the bathroom was forbidden since Nan forgot to turn off the water till it overflowed and came gently dripping down through the ceiling. Daisy went systematically to work, washing first the white and then the colored things, rinsing them nicely, and hanging them to dry on a cord fastened from one barberry bush to another, and pinning them up with a set of tiny clothespins Ned had turned for her. But Nan put all her

725

little things to soak in the same tub, and then forgot them while she collected thistledown to stuff a pillow for Semiramis, Queen of Babylon, as one doll was named. This took some time, and when Mrs. Giddygaddy came to take out the clothes, deep green stains appeared on everything, for she had forgotten the green silk lining of a certain cape, and its colour had soaked nicely into the pink and blue gowns, the little chemises, and even the best ruffled petticoat.

"Oh me! what a mess!" sighed Nan.

"Lay them on the grass to bleach," said Daisy, with an air of experience.

"So I will, and we can sit up in the nest and watch that they don't blow away."

The Queen of Babylon's wardrobe was spread forth upon the bank, and, turning up their tubs to dry, the little washerwomen climbed into the nest, and fell to talking, as ladies are apt to do in the pauses of domestic labor.

"I'm going to have a feather bed to go with my new pillow," said Mrs. Giddygaddy, as she transferred the thistledown from her pocket to her handkerchief, losing about half in the process.

"I wouldn't; Aunt Jo says feather beds aren't healthy. I never let *my* children sleep on anything but a mattress," returned Mrs. Shakespeare Smith, decidedly.

"I don't care; my children are so strong they often sleep on the floor, and don't mind it" (which was quite true). "I can't afford nine mattresses, and I like to make beds myself."

"Won't Tommy charge for the feathers?"

"Maybe he will, but I shan't pay him, and he won't care," returned Mrs. G., taking a base advantage of the well-known good-nature of T. Bangs.

"I think the pink will fade out of that dress sooner than the green mark will," observed Mrs. S., looking down from her perch, and changing the subject, for she and her gossip differed on many points, and Mrs. Smith was a discreet lady.

"Never mind; I'm tired of dolls, and I guess I shall put them all away and attend to my farm; I like it rather better than playing house," said Mrs. G., unconsciously expressing the desire of many older ladies, who cannot dispose of their families so easily however.

"But you mustn't leave them; they will die without their mother," cried tender Mrs. Smith.

"Let them die then; I'm tired of fussing over babies, and I'm going to play with the boys; they need me to see to them," returned the strong-minded lady.

Daisy knew nothing about woman's rights; she quietly took all she wanted, and no one denied her claim, because she did not undertake what she could not carry out, but unconsciously used the all-powerful right of her own influence to win from others any privilege for which she had proved her fitness. Nan attempted all sorts of things, undaunted by direful failures, and clamored fiercely to be allowed to do everything that the boys did. They laughed at her, hustled her out of the way, and protested against her meddling with their affairs. But she would not be quenched and she would be heard, for her will was strong, and she had the spirit of a rampant reformer. Mrs. Bhaer sympathized with her, but tried to curb her frantic desire for entire liberty, showing her that she must wait a little, learn self-control, and be ready to use her freedom before she asked for it. Nan had meek moments when she agreed to this, and the influences of work upon her were gradually taking effect. She no longer declared that she would be an engine driver or a blacksmith, but turned her mind to farming, and found in it a vent for the energy bottled up in her active little body. It did not quite satisfy her, however; for her sage and sweet marjoram were dumb things, and could not thank her for her care. She wanted something human to love, work for, and protect, and was never happier than when the little boys brought their cut fingers, bumped heads, or bruised joints for her to "mend up." Seeing this, Mrs. Jo proposed that she should learn how to do it nicely, and Nursey had an apt pupil in bandaging, plastering, and fomenting. The boys began to call her "Doctor Giddygaddy," and she liked it so well that Mrs. Jo one day said to the Professor, —

"Fritz, I see what we can do for that child. She wants something to live for even now, and will be one of the sharp, strong, discontented women if she does not have it. Don't let us snub her restless little nature, but do our best to give her the work she likes, and by and by persuade her father to let her study medicine. She will make a capital doctor, for she has courage, strong nerves, a tender heart, and an intense love and pity for the weak and suffering."

Mr. Bhaer smiled at first, but agreed to try, and gave Nan an herb garden, teaching her the various healing properties of the plants she tended, and letting her try their virtues on the children in the little illnesses they had from time to time. She learned fast, remembered well, and showed a sense and interest most encouraging to her Professor, who did not shut his door in her face because she was a little woman.

She was thinking of this, as she sat in the willow that day, and when Daisy said in her gentle way, —

"I love to keep house, and mean to have a nice one for Demi when we grow up and live together."

Nan replied with decision, —

"Well, I haven't got any brother, and I don't want any house to fuss over. I shall have an office, with lots of bottles and drawers and pestle things in it, and I shall drive round in a horse and chaise and cure sick people. That will be such fun."

"Ugh! how can you bear the bad-smelling stuff and the nasty little powders and castor oil and senna and hive sirup?" cried Daisy, with a shudder.

"I shan't have to take any, so I don't care. Besides, they make people well, and I like to cure folks. Didn't my sage tea make Mother Bhaer's headache go away, and my hops stop Ned's toothache in five hours? So now!"

"Shall you put leeches on people, and cut off legs and pull out teeth?" asked Daisy, quaking at the thought.

"Yes, I shall do everything; I don't care if the people are all smashed up, I shall mend them. My grandpa was a doctor, and I saw him sew a great cut in a man's cheek, and I held the sponge, and wasn't frightened a bit, and grandpa said I was a brave girl."

"How could you? I'm sorry for sick people, and I like to nurse them, but it makes my legs shake, so I have to run away. I'm not a brave girl," sighed Daisy.

"Well, you can be my nurse, and cuddle my patients when I have given them the physic and cut off their legs," said Nan, whose practice was evidently to be of the heroic kind.

"Ship ahoy! Where are you, Nan?" called a voice from below.

"Here we are."

"Ay, ay!" said the voice, and Emil appeared holding one hand in the other, with his face puckered up as if in pain.

"Oh, what's the matter?" cried Daisy, anxiously.

"A confounded splinter in my thumb. Can't get it out. Take a pick at it, will you, Nanny?"

"It's in very deep, and I haven't any needle," said Nan, examining a tarry thumb with interest.

"Take a pin," said Emil, in a hurry.

"No, it's too big and hasn't got a sharp point."

Here Daisy, who had dived into her pocket, presented a neat little housewife with four needles in it.

"You are the Posy who always has what we want," said Emil; and Nan resolved to have a needle book in her own pocket henceforth, for just such cases as this were always occurring in her practice.

Daisy covered her eyes, but Nan probed and picked with a steady hand, while Emil gave directions not down in any medical work or record.

"Starboard now! Steady, boys, steady! Try another tack. Heave ho! there she is!"

"Suck it," order the Doctor, surveying the splinter with an experienced eye.

"Too dirty," responded the patient, shaking his bleeding hand.

"Wait; I'll tie it up if you have got a handkerchief."

"Haven't; take one of those rags down there."

"Gracious! no, indeed; they are dolls' clothes," cried Daisy, indignantly.

"Take one of mine; I'd like to have you," said Nan, and swinging himself down, Emil caught up the first "rag" he saw. It happened to be the frilled skirt; but Nan tore it up without a murmur, and when the royal petticoat was turned into a neat little bandage, she dismissed her patient with the command,

"Keep it wet, and let it alone; then it will heal right up, and not be sore."

"What do you charge?" asked the Commodore, laughing.

"Nothing; I keep a 'spensary; that is a place where poor people are doctored free gratis for nothing," explained Nan, with an air.

"Thank you, Doctor Giddygaddy. I'll always call you in when I come to grief;" and Emil departed, but looked back to say, – for one good turn deserved another, – "your duds are blowing away, Doctor."

Forgiving the disrespectful word, "duds," the ladies hastily descended, and gathering up their wash, retired to the house to fire up the little stove, and go to ironing.

A passing breath of air shook the old willow, as if it laughed softly at the childish chatter which went on in the nest, and it had hardly composed itself when another pair of birds alighted for a confidential twitter.

"Now, I'll tell you the secret," began Tommy, who was "swellin' wisibly" with the importance of his news.

"Tell away," answered Nat, wishing he had brought his fiddle, it was so shady and quiet here.

"Well, we fellows were talking over the late interesting case of circumstantial evidence," said Tommy, quoting at random from a speech Franz had made at the club, "and I proposed giving Dan something to make up for our suspecting him, to show our respect, and so on, you know – something handsome and useful, that he could keep always, and be proud of. What do you think we chose?"

"A butterfly net; he wants one ever so much," said Nat, looking a little disappointed, for he meant to get it himself.

"No, sir; it's to be a microscope, a real swell one, that we see what-do-you-call-ems in water with, and stars, and ant eggs, and all sorts of games, you know. Won't it be a jolly good present?" said Tommy, rather confusing microscopes and telescopes in his remarks.

"Tiptop! I'm so glad! Won't it cost a heap, though?" cried Nat, feeling that his friend was beginning to be appreciated.

"Of course it will; but we are all going to give something. I headed the paper with my five dollars; for if it is done at all, it must be done handsome."

"What! all of it? I never did see such a generous chap as you are," and Nat beamed upon him with sincere admiration.

"Well you see, I've been so bothered with my property, that I'm tired of it, and don't mean to save up any more, but give it away as I go along, and then nobody will envy me, or want to steal it, and I shan't be suspecting folks, and worrying about my old cash," replied Tommy, on whom the cares and anxieties of a millionaire weighed heavily.

"Will Mr. Bhaer let you do it?"

"He thought it was a first-rate plan, and said that some of the best men he knew preferred to do good with their money, instead of laying it up to be squabbled over when they died."

"Your father is rich; does he do that way?"

"I'm not sure; he gives me all I want; I know that much. I'm going to talk to him about it when I go home. Anyhow, I shall set him a good example," and Tommy was so serious, that Nat did not dare to laugh, but said, respectfully, —

"You will be able to do ever so much with your money, won't you?"

"So Mr. Bhaer said, and he promised to advise me about useful ways of spending it. I'm going to begin with Dan; and next time I get a dollar or so, I shall do something for Dick, he's such a good little chap, and only has a cent a week for pocket money. He can't earn much, you know; so I'm going to kind of see to him," and good-hearted Tommy quite longed to begin.

"I think that's a beautiful plan, and I'm not going to try to buy a fiddle any more; I'm going to get Dan his net all myself, and if there is any money left, I'll do something to please poor Billy. He's fond of me, and though he isn't poor, he'd like some little thing from me, because I can make out what he wants better than the rest of you." And Nat fell to wondering how much happiness could be got out of his precious three dollars.

"So I would. Now come and ask Mr. Bhaer if you can't go in town with me on Monday afternoon, so you can get the net, while I get the microscope. Franz and Emil are going too, and we'll have a jolly time larking around among the shops."

The lads walked away arm in arm, discussing the new plans with droll importance, yet beginning already to feel the sweet satisfaction which comes to those who try, no matter how humbly, to be earthly providences to the poor and helpless, and gild their mite with the gold of charity before it is laid up where thieves cannot break through and steal.

"Come up and rest while we sort the leaves; it's so cool and pleasant here," said Demi, as he and Dan came sauntering home from a long walk in the woods.

"All right!" answered Dan, who was a boy of few words, and up they went.

"What makes the birch leaves shake so much more than the others?" asked inquiring Demi, who was always sure of an answer from Dan.

"They are hung differently. Don't you see the stem where it joins the leaf is sort of pinched one way, and where it joins the twig, it is pinched another. That makes it waggle with the least bit of wind, but the elm leaves hang straight, and keep stiller."

"How curious! Will this do so?" and Demi held up a sprig of acacia, which he had broken from a little tree on the lawn, because it was so pretty.

"No; that belongs to the sort that shuts up when you touch it. Draw your finger down the middle of the stem, and see if the leaves don't curl up," said Dan, who was examining a bit of mica.

Demi tried it, and presently the little leaves did fold together, till the spray showed a single instead of a double line of leaves.

"I like that; tell me about the others. What do these do?" asked Demi, taking up a new branch.

"Feed silkworms; they live on mulberry leaves, till they begin to spin themselves up. I was in a silk factory once, and there were rooms full of shelves all covered with leaves, and worms eating them so fast that it made a rustle. Sometimes they eat so much they die. Tell that to Stuffy," and Dan laughed, as he took up another bit of rock with a lichen on it.

"I know one thing about this mullein leaf: the fairies use them for blankets," said Demi, who had not quite given up his faith in the existence of the little folk in green.

"If I had a microscope, I'd show you something prettier than fairies," said Dan, wondering if he should ever own that coveted treasure. "I knew an old woman who used mullein leaves for a nightcap because she had face ache. She sew them together, and wore it all the time."

"How funny! Was she your grandmother?"

"Never had any. She was a queer old woman, and lived alone in a little tumble-down house with nineteen cats. Folks called her a witch, but she wasn't, though she looked like an old rag bag. She was kind to me when I lived in that place, and used to let me get warm at her fire when the folks at the poorhouse were hard on me."

"Did you live in a poorhouse?"

"A little while. Never mind that – I didn't mean to speak of it," and Dan stopped short in his unusual fit of communicativeness.

"Tell about the cats, please," said Demi, feeling that he had asked an unpleasant question, and was sorry for it.

"Nothing to tell; only she had a lot of them, and kept them in a barrel nights; and I used to go and tip over the barrel sometimes, and let them out all over the house, and then she'd scold, and chase them and put them in again, spitting and yowling like fury."

"Was she good to them?" asked Demi, with a hearty child's laugh, pleasant to hear.

"Guess she was. Poor old soul! she took in all the lost and sick cats in the town; and when anybody wanted one they went to Marm Webber, and she let them pick any kind and color they wanted, and only asked ninepence – she was so glad to have her pussies get a good home."

"I should like to see Marm Webber. Could I, if I went to that place?"

"She's dead. All my folks are," said Dan, briefly.

"I'm sorry," and Demi sat silent a minute, wondering what subject would be safe to try next. He felt delicate about speaking of the departed lady, but was very curious about the cats, and could not resisting asking softly, –

"Did she cure the sick ones?"

"Sometimes. One had a broken leg, and she tied it up to a stick, and it got well; and another had fits, and she doctored it with *yarbs* till it was cured. But some of them died, and she buried them; and when they couldn't get well, she killed them easy."

"How?" asked Demi, feeling that there was a peculiar charm about this old woman, and some sort of joke about the cats, because Dan was smiling to himself.

"A kind lady, who was fond of cats, told her how, and gave her some stuff, and sent all her own pussies to be killed that way. Marm used to put a sponge, wet with ether, in the bottom of an old boot, then poke puss in head downwards. The ether put her to sleep in a jiffy, and she was drowned in warm water before she woke up."

"I hope the cats didn't feel it. I shall tell Daisy about that. You have known a great many interesting things, haven't you?" asked Demi, and fell to meditating on the vast experience of a boy who had run away more than once, and taken care of himself in a big city.

"Wish I hadn't sometimes."

"Why? Don't remembering them feel good?"

"No."

"It's very singular how hard it is to manage your mind," said Demi, clasping his hands round his knees, and looking up at the sky as if for information upon his favorite topic.

"Devilish hard – no, I don't mean that," and Dan bit his lips, for the forbidden word slipped out in spite of him, and he wanted to be more careful with Demi than with any of the other boys.

"I'll play I didn't hear it," said Demi, "and you won't do it again, I'm sure."

"Not if I can help it. That's one of the things I don't want to remember. I keep pegging away, but it don't seem to do much good," and Dan look discouraged.

"Yes, it does. You don't say half as many bad words as you used to; and Aunt Jo is pleased, because she said it was a hard habit to break up."

"Did she?" and Dan cheered up a bit.

"You must put swearing away in your fault drawer, and lock it up; that's the way I do with my badness."

"What do you mean?" asked Dan, looking as if he found Demi almost as amusing as a new sort of cockchafer or beetle.

"Well, it's one of my private plays, and I'll tell you, but I think you'll laugh at it," began Demi, glad to hold forth on this congenial subject. "I play that my mind is a round room, and my soul is a little sort of creature with wings that lives in it. The walls are full of shelves and drawers, and in them I keep my thoughts, and my goodness and badness, and all sorts of things. The goods I keep where I can see them, and the bads I lock up tight, but they get out, and I have to keep putting them in and squeezing them down, they are so strong. The thoughts I play with when I am alone or in bed, and I make up and do what I like with them. Every Sunday I put my room in order, and talk with the little spirit that lives there, and tell him what to do. He is very bad sometimes, and won't mind me, and I have to scold him, and take him to grandpa. He always makes him behave, and be sorry for his faults, because grandpa likes this play, and gives me nice things to put in the drawers, and tells me how to shut up the naughties. Hadn't you better try that way? It's a very good one"; and Demi looked so earnest and full of faith that Dan did not laugh at his quaint fancy, but said, soberly, —

"I don't think there is a lock strong enough to keep my badness shut up. Anyway my room is in such a clutter I don't know how to clear it up."

"You keep your drawers in the cabinet all spandy nice; why can't you do the others?"

"I ain't used to it. Will you show me how?" and Dan looked as if inclined to try Demi's childish way of keeping a soul in order.

"I'd love to, but I don't know how, except to talk as grandpa does. I can't do it good like him, but I'll try."

"Don't tell any one; only now and then we'll come here and talk things over, and I'll pay you for it by telling all I know about my sort of things. Will that do?" and Dan held out his big, rough hand.

Demi gave his smooth, little hand readily, and the league was made; for in the happy, peaceful world where the younger boy lived, lions and lambs played together, and the little children innocently taught their elders.

"Hush!" said Dan, pointing toward the house, as Demi was about to indulge in another discourse on the best way of getting badness down, and keeping it down; and peeping from their perch, the saw Mrs. Jo strolling slowly along, reading as she went, while Teddy trotted behind her, dragging a little cart upside down.

"Wait till they see us," whispered Demi, and both sat still as the pair came nearer, Mrs. Jo so absorbed in her book that she would have walked into the brook if Teddy had not stopped her by saying, —

"Marmar, I wanter fis."

Mrs. Jo put down the charming book which she had been trying to read for a week, and looked about her for a fishing pole, being used to making toys out of nothing. Before she had broken one from the hedge, a slender willow bough fell at her feet; and, looking up, she saw the boys laughing in the nest.

"Up! up!" cried Teddy, stretching his arms and flapping his skirts as if about to fly.

"I'll come down and you come up. I must go to Daisy now," and Demi departed to rehearse the tale of the nineteen cats, with the exciting boot-and-barrel episodes.

Teddy was speedily whisked up; and then Dan said, laughing, "Come, too; there's plenty of room. I'll lend you a hand."

Mrs. Jo glanced over her shoulder, but no one was in sight; and, rather liking the joke of the thing, she laughed back, saying, "Well, if you won't mention it, I think I will," and with two nimble steps was in the willow.

"I haven't climbed a tree since I was married. I used to be very fond of it when I was a girl," she said, looking well-pleased with her shady perch.

"Now, you read if you want to, and I'll take care of Teddy," proposed Dan, beginning to make a fishing rod for impatient Baby.

"I don't think I care about it now. What were you and Demi at up here?" asked Mrs. Jo, thinking, from the sober look in Dan's face, that he had something on his mind.

"Oh, we were talking. I'd been telling him about leaves and things, and he was telling me some of his queer plays. Now, then, Major, fish away," and Dan finished off his work by putting a big blue fly on the bent pin which hung at the end of the cord he had tied to the willow rod.

Teddy leaned down from the tree, and was soon wrapped up in watching for the fish which he felt sure would come. Dan held him by his little petticoats, lest he should take a "header" into the brook, and Mrs. Jo soon won him to talk by doing so herself.

"I am so glad you told Demi about 'leaves and things;' it is just what he needs; and I wish you would teach him, and take him to walk with you,"

"I'd like to, he is so bright; but –"

"But what?"

"I didn't think you'd trust me."

"Why not?"

"Well, Demi is so kind of precious, and so good, and I'm such a bad lot, I thought you'd keep him away from me."

"But you are *not* a 'bad lot,' as you say; and I do trust you, Dan, entirely, because you honestly try to improve, and do better and better every week."

"Really?" and Dan looked up at her with the cloud of despondency lifting from his face.

"Yes; don't you feel it?"

"I hoped so, but I didn't know."

"I have been waiting and watching quietly, for I thought I'd give you a good trial first; and if you stood it, I would give you the best reward I had. You *have* stood it well; and now I'm going to trust not only Demi, but my own boy, to you, because you can teach them some things better than any of us."

"Can I?" and Dan looked amazed at the idea.

"Demi has lived among older people so much that he needs just what you have — knowledge of common things, strength, and courage. He thinks you are the bravest boy he ever saw, and admires your strong way of doing things. Then you know a great deal about natural objects, and can tell him more wonderful tales of birds, and bees, and leaves, and animals, than his story books give him; and, being true, these stories will teach and do him good. Don't you see now how much you can help him, and why I like to have him with you?"

"But I swear sometimes, and might tell him something wrong. I wouldn't mean to, but it might slip out, just as 'devil' did a few minutes ago," said Dan, anxious to do his duty, and let her know his shortcomings.

"I know you try not to say or do anything to harm the little fellow, and here is where I think Demi will help *you*, because he is so innocent and wise in his small way, and has what I am trying to give you, dear — good principles. It is never too early to try and plant them in a child, and never too late to cultivate them in the most neglected person. You are only boys yet; you can teach one another. Demi will unconsciously strengthen your moral sense, you will strengthen his common sense, and I shall feel as if I had helped you both."

Words could not express how pleased and touched Dan was by this confidence and praise. No one had ever trusted him before, no one had cared to find out and foster the good in him, and no one had suspected how much there was hidden away in the breast of the neglected boy, going fast to ruin, yet quick to feel and value sympathy and help. No honor that he might earn hereafter would ever be half so precious as the right to teach his few virtues and his small store of learning to the child whom he most respected; and no more powerful restraint could have been imposed upon him than the innocent companion confided to his care. He found courage now to tell Mrs. Jo of the plan already made with Demi, and she was glad that the first step had been so naturally taken. Everything seemed working well for Dan, and she rejoiced over him, because it had seemed a hard task, yet, working on with a firm belief in the possibility of reformation in far older and worse subjects than he, there had come this quick and hopeful change to encourage her. He felt that he had friends now and a place in the world, something to live and work for, and, though he said little, all that was best and bravest in a character made old by a hard experience responded to the love and faith bestowed on him, and Dan's salvation was assured.

Their quiet talk was interrupted by a shout of delight from Teddy, who, to the surprise of every one, did actually catch a trout where no trout had been seen for years. He was so enchanted with his splendid success that he insisted on showing his prize to the family before Asia cooked it for supper; so the three descended and went happily away together, all satisfied with the work of that half hour.

Ned was the next visitor to the tree, but he only made a short stay, sitting there at his ease while Dick and Dolly caught a pailful of grasshoppers and crickets for him. He wanted to play a joke on Tommy, and intended to tuck up a few dozen of the lively creatures in his bed, so that when Bangs got in he would speedily tumble out again, and pass a portion of the night in chasing "hopper-grasses" round the room. The hunt was soon over, and having paid the hunters with a few peppermints apiece Ned retired to make Tommy's bed.

For an hour the old willow sighed and sung to itself, talked with the brook, and watched the lengthening shadows as the sun went down. The first rosy color was touching its graceful branches when a boy came stealing up the avenue, across the lawn, and, spying Billy by the brook-side, went to him, saying, in a mysterious tone, –

"Go and tell Mr. Bhaer I want to see him down here, please. Don't let any one hear."

Billy nodded and ran off, while the boy swung himself up into the tree, and sat there looking anxious, yet evidently feeling the charm of the place and hour. In five minutes Mr. Bhaer appeared, and, stepping up on the fence, leaned into the nest, saying, kindly, –

"I am glad to see you, Jack; but why not come in and meet us all at once?"

"I wanted to see you first, please, sir. Uncle made me come back. I know I don't deserve anything, but I hope the fellows won't be hard upon me."

Poor Jack did not get on very well, but it was evident that he was sorry and ashamed, and wanted to be received as easily as possible; for his Uncle has thrashed him well and scolded him soundly for following the example he himself set. Jack had begged not to be sent back, but the school was cheap, and Mr. Ford insisted, so the boy returned as quickly as possible, and took refuge behind Mr. Bhaer.

"I hope not, but I can't answer for them, though I will see that they are not unjust. I think, as Dan and Nat have suffered so much, being innocent, you should suffer something, being guilty. Don't you?" asked Mr. Bhaer, pitying Jack, yet feeling that he deserved punishment for a fault which had so little excuse.

"I supppose so, but I sent Tommy's money back, and I said I was sorry, isn't that enough?" said Jack, rather sullenly; for the boy who could do so mean a thing was not brave enough to bear the consequences well.

"No; I think you should ask pardon of all three boys, openly and honestly. You cannot expect them to respect and trust you for a time, but you *can* live down this disgrace if you try, and I will help you. Stealing and lying are detestable sins, and I hope this will be a lesson to you. I am glad you are ashamed, it is a good sign; bear it patiently, and do your best to earn a better reputation."

"I'll have an auction, and sell off all my goods dirt cheap," said Jack, showing his repentance in the most characteristic way.

"I think it would be better to *give* them away, and begin on a new foundation. Take 'Honesty is the best policy' for your motto, and live up to it in act, and word, and thought, and though you don't make a cent of money this summer, you will be a rich boy in the autumn," said Mr. Bhaer, earnestly.

It was hard, but Jack consented, for he really felt that cheating didn't pay, and wanted to win back the friendship of the boys. His heart clung to his possessions, and he groaned inwardly at the thought of actually giving away certain precious things. Asking pardon publicly was easy compared to this; but then he began to discover that certain other things, invisible, but most valuable, were better property than knives, fishhooks, or even money itself. So he decided to buy up a little integrity, even at a high price, and secure the respect of his playmates, though it was not a saleable article.

"Well, I'll do it," he said, with a sudden air of resolution, which pleased Mr. Bhaer.

"Good! and I'll stand by you. Now come and begin at once."

And Father Bhaer led the bankrupt boy back into the little world, which received him coldly at first, but slowly warmed to him, when he showed that he had profited by the lesson, and was sincerely anxious to go into a better business with a new stock in trade.

CHAPTER SIXTEEN

TAMING THE COLT

~

"What in the world is that boy doing?" said Mrs. Jo to herself, as she watched Dan running round the half-mile triangle as if for a wager. He was all alone, and seemed possessed by some strange desire to run himself into a fever, or break his neck; for, after several rounds, he tried leaping walls, and turning somersaults up the avenue, and finally dropped down on the grass before the door as if exhausted.

"Are you training for a race, Dan?" asked Mrs. Jo, from the window where she sat.

He looked up quickly, and stopped painting to answer, with a laugh, —
"No; I'm only working off my steam."

"Can't you find a cooler way of doing it? You will be ill if you tear about so in such warm weather," said Mrs. Jo, laughing also, as she threw him out a great palm-leaf fan.

"Can't help it. I *must* run somewhere," answered Dan, with such an odd expression in his restless eyes, that Mrs. Jo was troubled, and asked, quickly, —

"Is Plumfield getting too narrow for you?"

"I wouldn't mind if it were a little bigger. I like it though; only the fact is the devil gets into me sometimes, and then I do want to bolt."

The words seemed to come against his will, for he looked sorry the minute they were spoken, and seemed to think he deserved a reproof for his ingratitude. But Mrs. Jo understood the feeling, and though sorry to see it she could not blame the boy for confessing it. She looked at him anxiously, seeing how tall and strong he had grown, how full of energy his face was, with its eager eyes and resolute mouth; and remembering the utter freedom he had known for years before, she felt how even the gentle restraint of this home would weigh upon him at times when the old lawless spirit stirred in him. "Yes," she said to herself, "my wild hawk needs a larger cage; and yet, if I let him go, I am afraid he will be lost. I must try and find some lure strong enough to keep him safe."

"I know all about it," she added, aloud. "It is not 'the devil,' as you call it, but the very natural desire of all young people for liberty. I used to feel just so, and once I really did think for a minute that I would bolt."

"Why didn't you?" said Dan, coming to lean on the low window ledge, with an evident desire to continue the subject.

"I knew it was foolish, and love for my mother kept me at home."

"I haven't got any mother," began Dan.

"I thought you had *now*," said Mrs. Jo, gently stroking the rough hair off his hot forehead.

"You are no end good to me, and I can't ever thank you enough, but it isn't just the same, is it?" and Dan looked up at her with a wistful, hungry look that went to her heart.

"No, dear, it is not the same, and never can be. I think an own mother would have been a great deal to you. But as that cannot be, you must try to let me fill her place. I fear I have not done all I ought, or you would not want to leave me," she added, sorrowfully.

"Yes, you have!" cried Dan, eagerly. "I don't want to go, and I won't go, if I can help it; but every now and then I feel as if I must burst out somehow. I want to run straight ahead somewhere, to smash something, or pitch into somebody. Don't know why, but I do, and that's all about it."

Dan laughed as he spoke, but he meant what he said, for he knit his black brows, and brought down his fist on the ledge with such force, that

Mrs. Jo's thimble flew off into the grass. He brought it back, and as she took it, she held the big, brown hand a minute, saying, with a look that showed the words cost her something, —

"Well, Dan, run if you must, but don't run far; and come back to me soon, for I want you very much."

He was rather taken aback by this unexpected permission to play truant, and somehow it seemed to lessen his desire to go. He did not understand why, but Mrs. Jo did, and, knowing the natural perversity of the human mind, counted on it to help her now. She felt instinctively that the more the boy was restrained the more he would fret against it; but leave him free, and the mere sense of liberty would content him, joined to the knowledge that his presence was dear to those whom he loved best. It was a little experiment, but it succeeded, for Dan stood silent a moment, unconsciously picking the fan to pieces and turning the matter over in his mind. He felt that she appealed to his heart and his honor, and owned that he understood it by saying presently, with a mixture of regret and resolution in his face, —

"I won't go yet awhile, and I'll give you warning before I bolt. That's fair, isn't it?"

"Yes, we will let it stand so. Now, I want to see if I can't find some way for you to work off your steam better than running about the place like a mad dog, spoiling my fans, or fighting with the boys. What can we invent?" and while Dan tried to repair the mischief he had done, Mrs. Jo racked her brain for some new device to keep her truant safe until he had learned to love his lessons better.

"How would you like to be my expressman?" she said, as a sudden thought popped into her head.

"Go into town, and do the errands?" asked Dan, looking interested at once.

"Yes; Franz is tired of it, Silas cannot be spared just now, and Mr. Bhaer has no time. Old Andy is a safe horse, you are a good driver, and know your way about the city as well as a postman. Suppose you try it, and see if it won't do most as well to drive away two or three times a week as to run away once a month."

"I'd like it ever so much, only I must go alone and do it all myself. I don't want any of the other fellows bothering round," said Dan, taking to the new idea so kindly that he began to put on business airs already.

"If Mr. Bhaer does not object you shall have it all your own way. I suppose Emil will growl but he cannot be trusted with horses, and you can. By the way, to-morrow is market day, and I must make out my list. You had better see that the wagon is in order, and tell Silas to have the fruit and vegetables ready for mother. You will have to be up early and get back in time for school, can you do that?"

"I'm always an early bird, so I don't mind," and Dan slung on his jacket with despatch.

"The early bird got the worm this time, I'm sure," said Mrs. Jo, merrily.

"And a jolly good worm it is," answered Dan, as he went laughing away to put a new lash to the whip, wash the wagon, and order Silas about with all the importance of a young expressman.

"Before he is tired of this I will find something else and have it ready when the next restless fit comes on," said Mrs. Jo to herself, as she wrote her list with a deep sense of gratitude that all her boys were not Dans.

Mr. Bhaer did not entirely approve of the new plan, but agreed to give it a trial, which put Dan on his mettle, and caused him to give up certain wild plans of his own, in which the new lash and the long hill were to have borne a part. He was up and away very early the next morning, heroically resisting the temptation to race with the milkmen going into town. Once there, he did his errands carefully, and came jogging home again in time for school, to Mr. Bhaer's surprise and Mrs. Jo's great satisfaction. The Commodore did growl at Dan's promotion, but was pacified by a superior padlock to his new boat house, and the thought that seamen were meant for higher honors than driving market wagons and doing family errands. So Dan filled his new office well and contentedly for weeks, and said no more about bolting. But one day Mr. Bhaer found him pummeling Jack, who was roaring for mercy under his knee.

"Why, Dan, I thought you had given up fighting," he said, as he went to the rescue.

"We ain't fighting, we are only wrestling," answered Dan, leaving off reluctantly.

"It looks very much like it, and feels like it, hey, Jack?" said Mr. Bhaer, as the defeated gentleman got upon his legs with difficulty.

"Catch me wrestling with him again. He most knocked my head off," snarled Jack, holding on to that portion of his frame as if it really was loose upon his shoulders.

"The fact is, we began in fun, but when I got him down I couldn't help pounding him. Sorry I hurt you, old fellow," explained Dan, looking rather ashamed of himself.

"I understand. The longing to pitch into somebody was so strong you couldn't resist. You are a sort of Berserker, Dan, and something to tussle with is as necessary to you as music is to Nat," said Mr. Bhaer, who knew all about the conversation between the boy and Mrs. Jo.

"Can't help it. So if you don't want to be pounded you'd better keep out of the way," answered Dan, with a warning look in his black eyes that made Jack sheer off in haste.

"If you want something to wrestle with, I will give you a tougher specimen than Jack," said Mr. Bhaer; and, leading the way to the wood yard, he pointed out certain roots of trees that had been grubbed up in the spring, and had been lying there waiting to be split.

"There, when you feel inclined to maltreat the boys, just come and work off your energies here, and I'll thank you for it."

"So I will," and, seizing the ax that lay near, Dan hauled out a tough root, and went at it so vigorously that the chips flew far and wide, and Mr. Bhaer fled for his life.

To his great amusement, Dan took him at his word, and was often seen wrestling with the ungainly knots, hat and jacket off, red face, and wrathful eyes; for he got into royal rages over some of his adversaries, and swore at them under his breath till he had conquered them, when he exulted, and marched off to the shed with an armful of gnarled oak wood in triumph. He blistered his hands, tired his back, and dulled the ax, but it did him good, and he got more comfort out of the ugly roots than any one dreamed, for with each blow he worked off some of the pent-up power that would otherwise have been expended in some less harmless way.

"When this is gone I really don't know what I *shall* do," said Mrs. Jo to herself, for no inspiration came, and she was at the end of her resources.

But Dan found a new occupation for himself, and enjoyed it some time before any one discovered the cause of his contentment. A fine young horse of Mr. Laurie's was kept at Plumfield that summer, running loose in a large pasture across the brook. The boys were all interested in the handsome, spirited creature, and for a time were fond of watching him gallop and frisk with his plumy tail flying, and his handsome head in the air. But they soon got tired of it, and left Prince Charlie to himself. All but Dan, *he* never tired of looking at the horse, and seldom failed to visit him each day with a lump of sugar, a bit of bread, or an apple to make him welcome. Charlie was grateful, accepted his friendship, and the two loved one another as if they felt some tie between them, inexplicable but strong. In what ever part of the wide field he might be, Charlie always came at full speed when Dan whistled at the bars, and the boy was never happier than when the beautiful, fleet creature put its head on his shoulder, looking up at him with fine eyes full of intelligent affection.

"We understand one another without any palaver, don't we, old fellow?" Dan would say, proud of the horse's confidence, and so jealous of his regard, that he told no one how well the friendship prospered, and never asked anybody but Teddy to accompany him on these daily visits.

Mr. Laurie came now and then to see how Charlie got on, and spoke of having him broken to harness in the autumn.

"He won't need much taming, he is such a gentle, fine-tempered brute. I shall come out and try him with a saddle myself some day," he said, on one of these visits.

"He lets me put a halter on him, but I don't believe he will bear a saddle even if *you* put it on," answered Dan, who never failed to be present when Charlie and his master met.

"I shall coax him to bear it, and not mind a few tumbles at first. He has never been harshly treated, so, though he will be surprised at the new performances, I think he won't be frightened, and his antics will do no harm."

"I wonder what he *would* do," said Dan to himself, as Mr. Laurie went away with the Professor, and Charlie returned to the bars, from which he had retired when the gentlemen came up.

A daring fancy to try the experiment took possession of the boy as he sat on the topmost rail with the glossy back temptingly near him. Never thinking of danger, he obeyed the impulse, and while Charlie unsuspectingly nibbled at the apple he held, Dan quickly and quietly took his seat. He did not keep it long, however, for with an astonished snort, Charlie reared straight up, and deposited Dan on the ground. The fall did not hurt him, for the turf was soft, and he jumped up, saying, with a laugh, —

"I did it anyway! Come here, you rascal, and I'll try it again."

But Charlie declined to approach, and Dan left him resolving to succeed in the end; for a struggle like this suited him exactly. Next time he took a halter, and having got it on, he played with the horse for a while, leading him to and fro, and putting him through various antics till he was a little tired; then Dan sat on the wall and gave him bread, but watched his chance, and getting a good grip of the halter, slipped on to his back. Charlie tried the old trick, but Dan held on, having had practice with Toby, who occasionally had an obstinate fit, and tried to shake off his rider. Charlie was both amazed and indignant; and after prancing for a minute, set off at a gallop, and away went Dan heels over head. If he had not belonged to the class of boys who go through all sorts of dangers unscathed, he would have broken his neck; as it was, he got a heavy fall, and lay still collecting his wits, while Charlie tore round the field tossing his head with every sign of satisfaction at the discomfiture of his rider. Presently it seemed to occur to him that something was wrong with Dan, and, being of a magnanimous nature, he went to see what the matter was. Dan let him sniff about and perplex himself for a few minutes; then he looked up at him, saying, decidedly as if the horse could understand,

"You think you have beaten, but you are mistaken, old boy; and I'll ride you yet — see if I don't."

He tried no more that day, but soon after attempted a new method of introducing Charlie to a burden. He strapped a folded blanket on his back, and then let him race, and rear, and roll, and fume as much as he liked. After a few fits of rebellion Charlie submitted, and in a few days permitted Dan to mount him, often stopping short to look round, as if he said, half patiently, half reproachfully, "I don't understand it, but I suppose you mean no harm, so I permit the liberty."

Dan patted and praised him, and took a short turn every day, getting frequent falls, but persisting in spite of them, and longing to try a saddle and bridle, but not daring to confess what he had done. He had his wish, however, for there had been a witness of his pranks who said a good word for him.

"Do you know what that chap has ben doin' lately?" asked Silas of his master, one evening, as he received his orders for the next day.

"Which boy?" said Mr. Bhaer, with an air of resignation, expecting some sad revelation.

"Dan, he's ben a breaking the colt, sir, and I wish I may die if he ain't done it," answered Silas, chuckling.

"How do you know?"

"Wal, I kinder keep an eye on the little fellers, and most gen'lly know what they're up to; so when Dan kep going off to the paster, and coming home black and blue, I mistrusted that *suthing* was goin' on. I didn't say nothin', but I crep up into the barn chamber, and from there I see him goin' through all manner of games with Charlie. Blest if he warn't throwed time and agin, and knocked round like a bag o' meal. But the pluck of the boy did beat all, and he 'peared to like it, and kep on as ef bound to beat."

"But, Silas, you should have stopped it — the boy might have been killed," said Mr. Bhaer, wondering what freak his irrepressibles would take into their heads next.

"S'pose I oughter; but there warn't no real danger, for Charlie has no tricks, and is as pretty a tempered horse as ever I see. Fact was, I couldn't bear to spile sport, for ef there's anything I do admire it's grit, and Dan is chock full on't. But now I know he's hankerin' after a saddle, and yet won't take even the old one on the sly; so I just thought I'd up and tell, and maybe you'd let him try what he can do. Mr. Laurie won't mind, and Charlie's all the better for't."

"We shall see," and off went Mr. Bhaer to inquire into the matter.

Dan owned up at once, and proudly proved that Silas was right by showing off his power over Charlie; for by dint of much coaxing, many carrots, and infinite perseverance, he really had succeeded in riding the colt with a halter and blanket. Mr. Laurie was much amused, and well pleased with Dan's courage and skill, and let him have a hand in all future performances; for he set about Charlie's education at once, saying that he was not going to be outdone by a slip of a boy. Thanks to Dan, Charlie took kindly to the saddle and bridle when he had once reconciled himself to the indignity of the bit; and after Mr. Laurie had trained him a little, Dan was permitted to ride him, to the great envy and admiration of the other boys.

"Isn't he handsome? And don't he mind me like a lamb?" said Dan one day as he dismounted and stood with his arm round Charlie's neck.

"Yes, and isn't he a much more useful and agreeable animal than the wild colt who spent his days racing about the field, jumping fences, and running away now and then?" asked Mrs. Bhaer from the steps where she always appeared when Dan performed with Charlie.

"Of course, he is. See he won't run away now, even if I don't hold him, and he comes to me the minute I whistle; I have tamed him well, haven't I?" and Dan looked both proud and pleased, as well he might, for, in spite of their struggles together, Charlie loved him better than his master.

"I am taming a colt too, and I think I shall succeed as well as you if I am as patient and persevering," said Mrs. Jo, smiling so significantly at him, that Dan understood and answered, laughing, yet in earnest, —

"We won't jump over the fence and run away, but stay and let them make a handsome, useful span of us, hey, Charlie?"

CHAPTER SEVENTEEN

COMPOSITION DAY

~

"Hurry up, boys, it's three o'clock, and Uncle Fritz likes us to be punctual, you know," said Franz one Wednesday afternoon as a bell rang, and a stream of literary looking young gentlemen with books and paper in their hands were seen going toward the museum.

Tommy was in the schoolroom, bending over his desk, much bedaubed with ink, flushed with the ardor of inspiration, and in a great hurry as usual, for easy-going Bangs never was ready till the very last minute. As Franz passed the door looking up laggards, Tommy gave one last blot and flourish, and departed out of the window waving his paper to dry it as he went. Nan followed, looking very important, with a large roll in her hand, and Demi escorted Daisy, both evidently brimful of some delightful secret.

The museum was all in order, and the sunshine among the hop vines made pretty shadows on the floor as it peeped through the great window. On one side sat Mr. and Mrs. Bhaer, on the other was a little table on which the compositions were laid as soon as read, and in a large semicircle sat the children on camp stools which occasionally shut up and let the sitter down thus preventing any stiffness in the assembly. As it took too much time to have all read, they took turns, and on this Wednesday the younger pupils were the chief performers, while the elder ones listened with condescension and criticized freely.

"Ladies first; so Nan may begin," said Mr. Bhaer, when the settling of stools and rustling of papers had subsided.

Nan took her place beside the little table, and with a preliminary giggle, read the following interesting essay :

"THE SPONGE

"The sponge, my friends, is a most useful and interesting plant. It grows on rocks under the water, and is a kind of seaweed, I believe. People go and pick it and dry it and wash it, because little fish and insects live in the holes of the sponge; I found shells in my new one, and sand. Some are very fine and soft; babies are washed with them. The sponge has many uses. I will relate some of them, and I hope my friends will remember what I say. One use is to wash the face; I don't like it myself, but I do it because I wish to be clean. Some people *don't*, and they are dirty." Here the eye of the reader rested sternly upon Dick and Dolly, who quailed under it, and instantly resolved to scrub themselves virtuously on all occasions. "Another use is to wake people up; I allude to *boys* par-*tic*-u-lar-ly." Another pause after the long word to enjoy the smothered laugh that went round the room. "Some boys do not get up when called, and Mary Ann squeezes the water out of a wet sponge on their faces, and it makes them so mad they wake up," Here the laugh broke out, and Emil said, as if he had been hit, —

"Seems to me you are wandering from the subject."

"No, I ain't; we are to write about vegetables or animals, and I'm doing both: for boys are animals, aren't they?" cried Nan; and, undaunted by the indignant "No!" shouted at her, she calmly proceeded.

"One more interesting thing is done with sponges, and this is when doctors put ether on it, and hold it to people's noses when they have teeth out. I shall do this when I am bigger, and give ether to the sick, so they will go to sleep and not feel me cut off their legs and arms."

"I know somebody who killed cats with it," called out Demi, but was promptly crushed by Dan, who upset his camp-stool and put a hat over his face.

"I will *not* be interruckted," said Nan, frowning upon the unseemly scrimmagers. Order was instantly restored, and the young lady closed her remarks as follows:

"My composition has three morals, my friends." Somebody groaned, but no notice was taken of the insult. "First, is keep your faces clean — second, get up early — third, when the ether sponge is put over your nose, breathe hard and don't kick, and you teeth will come out easy. I have no more to say." And Miss Nan sat down amid tumultuous applause.

"That is a very remarkable composition; its tone is high, and there is a good deal of humor in it. Very well done, Nan. Now, Daisy," and Mr. Bhaer smiled at one young lady as he beckoned to the other.

Daisy colored prettily as she took her place, and said, in her modest little voice, —

"I'm afraid you won't like mine; it isn't nice and funny like Nan's. But I couldn't do any better."

"We always like yours, Posy," said Uncle Fritz, and a gentle murmur from the boys seemed to confirm the remark. Thus encouraged, Daisy read her little paper, which was listened to with respectful attention.

"THE CAT

The cat is a sweet animal. I love them very much. They are clean and pretty, and catch rats and mice, and let you pet them, and are fond of you if you are kind. They are very wise, and can find their way anywhere. Little cats are called kittens, and are dear things. I have two, named Huz and Buz, and their mother is Topaz, because she has yellow eyes. Uncle told me a pretty story about a man called Ma-ho-met. He had a nice cat, and when she was asleep on his sleeve, and he wanted to go away, he cut off the sleeve so as not to wake her up. I think he was a kind man. Some cats catch fish."

"So do I!" cried Teddy, jumping up eager to tell about his trout.

"Hush!" said his mother, setting him down again as quickly as possible, for orderly Daisy hated to be "interruckted" as Nan expressed it.

"I read about one who used to do it very slyly. I tried to make Topaz, but she did not like the water, and scratched me. She does like tea, and when I play in my kitchen she pats the teapot with her paw, till I give her some. She is a fine cat, she eats apple pudding and molasses. Most cats do not."

"That's a first-rater," called out Nat, and Daisy retired, pleased with the praise of her friend.

"Demi looks so impatient we must have him up at once or he won't hold out," said Uncle Fritz, and Demi skipped up with alacrity.

"Mine is a poem!" he announced in a tone of triumph, and read his first effort in a loud and solemn voice:

> *"I write about the butterfly,*
> *It is a pretty thing;*
> *And flies about like the birds,*
> *But it does not sing.*
>
> *"First it is a little grub,*
> *And then it is a nice yellow cocoon,*
> *And then the butterfly*
> *Eats its way out soon.*
>
> *"They live on dew and honey,*
> *They do not have any hive,*
> *They do not sting like wasps, and bees, and hornets,*
> *And to be as good as they are we should strive.*
>
> *"I should like to be a beautiful butterfly,*
> *All yellow, and blue, and green, and red;*
> *But I should not like*
> *To have Dan put camphor on my poor little head."*

This unusual burst of genius brought down the house, and Demi was obliged to read it again, a somewhat difficult task, as there was no punctuation whatever, and the little poet's breath gave out before he got to the end of some of the long lines.

"He will be a Shakespeare yet," said Aunt Jo, laughing as if she would die, for this poetic gem reminded her of one of her own, written at the age of ten, and beginning gloomily, —

> *"I wish I had a quiet tomb,*
> *Beside a little rill;*
> *Where birds, and bees, and butterflies,*
> *Would sing upon the hill."*

"Come on, Tommy. If there is as much ink inside your paper as there is outside, it will be a long composition," said Mr. Bhaer, when Demi had been induced to tear himself from his poem and sit down.

"It isn't a composition, it's a letter. You see, I forgot all about its being my turn till after school, and then I didn't know what to have, and there wasn't time to read up; so I thought you wouldn't mind my taking a letter that I wrote to my grandma. It's got something about birds in it, so I thought it would do."

With this long excuse, Tommy plunged into a sea of ink and floundered through, pausing now and then to decipher one of his own flourishes.

My dear grandma, I hope you are well. Uncle James sent me a pocket rifle. It is a beautiful little instrument of killing, shaped like this — [Here Tommy displayed a remarkable sketch of what looked like an intricate pump, or the inside of a small steam-engine] — 44 are the sights; 6 is a false stock that fits in at A; 3 is the trigger, and 2 is the cock. It loads at the breech, and fires with great force and straightness. I am going out shooting squirrels soon. I shot several fine birds for the museum. They had speckled breasts, and Dan liked them very much. He stuffed them tiptop, and they sit on the tree quite natural, only one looks a little tipsy. We had a Frenchman working here the other day, and Asia called his name so funnily that I will tell you about it. His name was Germain: first she called him Jerry, but we laughed at her, and she changed it to Jeremiah; but ridicule was the result, so it became Mr. Germany; but ridicule having been again resumed, it became Garrymon, which it has remained ever since. I do not write often, I am so busy; but I think of you often, and sympathize with you, and sincerely hope you get on as well as can be expected without me.

Your affectionate grandson,

Thomas Buckmaster Bangs.

P.S. — If you come across any postage stamps, remember me.

N.B. — Love to all, and a great deal to Aunt Almira. Does she make any nice plum cakes now?

P.S. — Mrs. Bhaer sends her respects.

P.S. — And so would Mr. B. if he knew I was in act to write.

N.B. — Father is going to give me a watch on my birthday. I am glad, as at present I have no means of telling time, and am often late at school.

P.S. — I hope to see you soon. Don't you wish to send for me?

T.B.B.

As each postscript was received with a fresh laugh from the boys, by the time he came to the sixth and last, Tommy was so exhausted that he was glad to sit down and wipe his ruddy face.

"I hope the dear old lady will live through it," said Mr. Bhaer, under cover of the noise.

"We won't take any notice of the broad hint given in the last P.S. The letter will be quite as much as she can bear without a visit from Tommy," answered Mrs. Jo, remembering that the old lady usually took to her bed after a visitation from her irrepressible grandson.

"Now, me," said Teddy, who had learned a bit of poetry, and was so eager to say it that he had been bobbing up and down during the reading, and could no longer be restrained.

"I'm afraid he will forget it if he waits; and I have had a deal of trouble in teaching him," said his mother.

Teddy trotted to the rostrum, dropped a curtsey and nodded his head at the same time, as if anxious to suit every one; then, in his baby voice, and putting the emphasise on the wrong words, he said his verse all in one breath:

> *"Little drops of water,*
> *Little drains of sand,*
> *Mate a might okum {ocean},*
> *And a peasant land.*
>
> *Little worts of kindness,*
> *Pokin evvy day,*
> *Make a home a hebbin,*
> *And hep us on a way."*

Clapping his hands at the end, he made another double salutation, and then ran to hide his head in his mother's lap, quite overcome by the success of his "piece," for the applause was tremendous.

Dick and Dolly did not write, but were encouraged to observe the habits of animals and insects, and report what they saw. Dick liked this, and always had a great deal to say; so, when his name was called, he marched up, and, looking at the audience with his bright confiding eyes, told his little story so earnestly that no one smiled at his crooked body because the "straight soul" shone through it beautifully.

"I've been watching dragon flies, and I read about them in Dan's book, and I'll try and tell you what I remember. There's lots of them flying round on the pond, all blue, with big eyes, and sort of lace wings, very pretty. I caught one, and looked at him, and I think he was the handsomest inseck I ever saw. They catch littler creatures than they are to eat, and have a queer kind of hook thing that folds up when they ain't hunting. It likes the sunshine, and dances round all day. Let me see! What else was there to tell about? Oh, I know! The eggs are laid in the water, and go down to the bottom, and are hatched in the mud. Little ugly things come out of them; I can't say the name, but they are brown, and keep having new skins, and getting bigger and bigger. Only think! it takes them two years to be a dragon fly! Now *this* is the curious*est* part of it, so you listen tight, for I don't believe you know it. When it is ready it knows somehow, and the ugly, grubby thing climbs up out of the water on a flag or a bulrush, and bursts open its back."

"Come, I don't believe that," said Tommy, who was not an observing boy, and really thought Dick was "making up."

"It does burst open its back, don't it?" and Dick appealed to Mr. Bhaer, who nodded a very decided affirmative, to the little speaker's great satisfaction.

"Well, out comes the dragon fly, all whole, and he sits in the sun — sort of coming alive, you know; and he gets strong, and then he spreads his pretty wings, and flies away up in the air, and never is a grub any more. That's all I know; but I shall watch and try and see him do it, for I think it's splendid to turn into a beautiful dragon fly, don't you?"

Dick had told his story well, and, when he described the flight of the newborn insect, had waved his hands, and looked up as if he saw, and wanted to follow it. Something in his face suggested to the minds of the elder listeners the thought that some day little Dick would have his wish, and after years of helplessness and pain would climb up into the sun some happy day, and, leaving his poor little body behind him, find a new and lovely shape in a fairer world than this. Mrs. Jo drew him to her side, and said, with a kiss on his thin cheek, —

"That is a sweet little story, dear, and you remembered wonderfully well. I shall write and tell your mother all about it," and Dick sat on her knee, contentedly smiling at the praise, and resolving to watch well, and

Tommy bore it, escorted by Nat and Demi.

catch the dragon fly in the act of leaving its old body for the new, and see how he did it. Dolly had a few remarks to make upon the "Duck," and made them in a singsong tone, for he had learned it by heart, and thought it a great plague to do it at all.

"Wild ducks are hard to kill; men hide and shoot at them, and have tame ducks to quack and make the wild ones come where the men can fire at them. They have wooden ducks made too, and they sail round, and the wild ones come to see them; they are stupid, I think. Our ducks are very tame. They eat a great deal, and go poking round in the mud and water. They don't take care of their eggs, but let them spoil, and —"

"Mine don't!" cried Tommy.

"Well, some people's do; Silas said so. Hens take good care of little ducks, only they don't like to have them go in the water, and make a great fuss. But the little ones don't care a bit. I like to eat ducks with stuffing in them, and lots of apple sauce."

"I have something to say about owls," began Nat, who had carefully prepared a paper upon this subject with some help from Dan.

"Owls have big heads, round eyes, hooked bills, and strong claws. Some are grey, some white, some black and yellowish. Their feathers are very soft, and stick out a great deal. They fly very quietly, and hunt bats, mice, little birds, and such things. They build nests in barns, hollow trees, and some take the nests of other birds. The great horned owl has two eggs bigger than a hen's, and reddish brown. The tawny owl has five eggs, white and smooth; and this is the kind that hoots at night. They eat mice and bats whole, and the parts that they cannot digest they make into little balls and spit out."

"My gracious! how funny!" Nan was heard to observe.

"They cannot see by day; and if they get out into the light, they go flapping round half blind, and the other birds chase and peck at them as if they were making fun. The horned owl is very big, 'most as big as the eagle. It eats rabbits, rats, snakes, and birds; and lives in rocks and old tumble-down houses. They have a good many cries, and scream like a person being choked, and say, 'Waugh O! waugh O!' and it scares people at night in the woods. The white owl lives by the sea, and in cold places, and looks something like a hawk. There is a kind of owl that makes holes to live in like moles. It is called the burrowing owl, and is very small. The barn owl is the commonest kind; and I have watched one sitting in a hole in a tree, looking like a little gray cat, with one eye shut and the other open. He comes out at dusk, and sits round waiting for the bats. I caught one, and here he is."

With that Nat suddenly produced from inside his jacket a little downy bird, who blinked and ruffled up his feathers, looking very plump and sleepy and scared.

"Don't touch him! He is going to show off," said Nat, displaying his new pet with great pride. First he put a cocked hat on the bird's head, and the boys laughed at the funny effect; then he added a pair of spectacles, and that gave the owl such a wise look that they shouted with merriment. The performance closed with making the bird angry, and seeing him cling to a handkerchief upside down, pecking and "clucking," as Rob called it. He was allowed to fly after that, and settled himself on the bunch of pine cones over the door, where he sat staring down at the company with an air of sleepy dignity that amused them very much.

"Have you anything for us, George?" asked Mr. Bhaer, when the room was still again.

"Well I read and learned ever so much about moles, but I declare I've forgotten every bit of it, except that they dig holes to live in, that you catch them by pouring water down, and that they can't possibly live without eating very often," and Stuffy sat down, wishing he had not been too lazy to write out his valuable observations, for a general smile went round when he mentioned the last of the three facts which lingered in his memory.

"Then we are done for to-day," began Mr. Bhaer, but Tommy called out in a great hurry,

"No, we ain't. Don't you know? We must give the thing," and he winked violently as he made an eye-glass of his fingers.

"Bless my heart, I forgot! Now is your time, Tom," and Mr. Bhaer dropped into his seat again, while all the boys but Dan looked mightily tickled at something.

Nat, Tommy and Demi left the room, and speedily returned with a little red morocco box set forth in state on Mrs. Jo's best silver salver. Tommy bore it, and, still escorted by Nat and Demi, marched up to unsuspecting Dan, who stared at them as if he thought they were going to make fun of him. Tommy had prepared an elegant and impressive speech for the occasion, but when the minute came, it all went out of his head, and he just said, straight from his kindly boyish heart, —

"Here, old fellow, we all wanted to give you something to kind of pay for what happened awhile ago, and to show how much we liked you for being such a trump. Please take it, and have a jolly good time with it."

Dan was so surprised he could only get as red as the little box, and mutter, "Thanky, boys!" as he fumbled to open it. But when he saw what was inside, his face lighted up, and he seized the long-desired treasure, saying so enthusiastically that every one was satisfied, though his language was anything but polished, —

"What a stunner! I say, you fellows are regular bricks to give me this; it's just what I wanted. Give us your paw, Tommy."

Many paws were given, and heartily shaken, for the boys were charmed with Dan's pleasure, and crowded round him to shake hands and expatiate on the beauties of their gift. In the midst of this pleasant chatter, Dan's eye went to Mrs. Jo, who stood outside the group enjoying the scene with all her heart.

"No, I had nothing to do with it. The boys got it up all themselves," she said, answering the grateful look that seemed to thank her for that happy moment. Dan smiled, and said, in a tone that only she could understand, —

"It's you all the same," and making his way through the boys, he held out his hand first to her and then to the good Professor, who was beaming benevolently on his flock.

He thanked them both with the silent, hearty squeeze he gave the kind hands that had held him up and led him into the safe refuge of a happy home. Not a word was spoken, but they felt all he would say, and little Teddy expressed their pleasure for them as he leaned from his father's arm to hug the boy, and say, in his baby way, —

"My good Danny! everybody loves him now."

"Come here, show off your spy glass, Dan, and let us see some of your magnified pollywogs and annymalcumisms as you call them," said Jack, who felt so uncomfortable during this scene that he would have slipped away if Emil had not kept him.

"So I will, take a squint at that and see what you think of it," said Dan, glad to show off his precious microscope.

He held it over a beetle that happened to be lying on the table, and Jack bent down to take his squint, but looked up with an amazed face, saying, –

"My eye! what nippers the old thing has got! I see now why it hurts so confoundedly when you grab a dor bug and he grabs back again."

"He winked at me," cried Nan, who had poked her head under Jack's elbow and got the second peep.

Every one took a look, and then Dan showed them the lovely plumage on a moth's wing, and four feathery corners to a hair, the veins on a leaf, hardly visible to the naked eye, but like a thick net through the wonderful little glass; the skin on their own fingers, looking like queer hills and valleys; a cobweb like a bit of coarse sewing silk, and the sting of a bee.

"It's like the fairy spectacles in my story book, only more curious," said Demi, enchanted with the wonders he saw.

"Dan is a magician now, and he can show you many miracles going on all around you; for he has two things needful – patience and a love of nature. We live in a beautiful and wonderful world, Demi, and the more you know about it the wiser and the better you will be. This little glass will give you a new set of teachers, and you may learn fine lessons from them if you will," said Mr. Bhaer, glad to see how interested the boys were in the matter.

"Could I see anybody's soul with this microscope if I looked hard?" asked Demi, who was much impressed with the power of the bit of glass.

"No, dear; it's not powerful enough for that, and never can be made so. You must wait a long while before your eyes are clear enough to see the most invisible of God's wonders. But looking at the lovely things you can see will help you to understand the lovelier things you cannot see," answered Uncle Fritz, with his hand on the boy's head.

"Well, Daisy and I both think that if there *are* any angels, their wings look like that butterfly's as we see it through the glass, only more soft and gold."

"Believe it if you like, and keep your own little wings as bright and beautiful, only don't fly away for a long time yet."

"No, I won't," and Demi kept his word.

"Good-by, my boys; I must go now, but I leave you with our new Professor of Natural History," and Mrs. Jo went away well pleased with that composition day.

CHAPTER EIGHTEEN

CROPS

~

The gardens did well that summer, and in September the little crops were gathered in with much rejoicing. Jack and Ned joined their farms and raised potatoes, those being a good saleable article. They got twelve bushels, counting little ones and all, and sold them to Mr. Bhaer at a fair price, for potatoes went fast in that house. Emil and Franz devoted themselves to corn, and had a jolly little husking in the barn, after which they took their corn to the mill, and came proudly home with meal enough to supply the family with hasty pudding and Johnnycake for a long time. They would not take money for their crop; because, as Franz said, "We never can pay uncle for all he has done for us if we raised corn for the rest of our days."

Nat had beans in such abundance that he despaired of ever shelling them, till Mrs. Jo proposed a new way, which succeeded admirably. The dry pods were spread under the barn-floor. Nat fiddled, and the boys danced quadrilles on them, till they were thrashed out with much merriment and very little labor.

Tommy's six weeks' beans were a failure; for a dry spell early in the season hurt them, because he gave them no water; and after that he was so sure that they could take care of themselves, he let the poor things struggle with bugs and weeds till they were exhausted, and died a lingering death. So Tommy had to dig his farm over again, and plant peas. But they were late; the birds ate many; the bushes, not being firmly planted, blew down, and when the poor peas came at last, no one cared for them, as their day was over, and spring lamb had grown into mutton. Tommy consoled himself with a charitable effort; for he transplanted all the thistles he could find, and tended them carefully for Toby, who was fond of the prickly delicacy, and had eaten all he could find on the place. The boys had great fun over Tom's thistle bed; but he insisted that it was better to care for poor Toby than for himself, and declared that he would devote his entire farm next year to thistles, worms, and snails, that Demi's turtles and Nat's pet owl might have the food they loved, as well as the donkey. So like shiftless, kind-hearted, happy-go-lucky Tommy!

Demi had supplied his grandmother with lettuce all summer, and in the autumn sent his grandfather a basket of turnips, each one scrubbed up till it looked like a great white egg. His Grandma was fond of salad, and one of his Grandpa's favourite quotations was:

> *Lucullus, whom frugality could charm,*
> *Ate roasted turnips at the Sabine farm.*

Therefore these vegetable offerings to the dear domestic god and goddess were affectionate, appropriate, and classical.

Daisy had nothing but flowers in her little plot, and it bloomed all summer long with a succession of gay or fragrant posies. She was very fond of her garden, and delved away in it at all hours, watching over her roses, and pansies, sweet peas, and mignonette, as faithfully and tenderly as she did over her dolls or her friends. Little nosegays were sent into town on all occasions, and certain vases about the house were her especial care. She had all sorts of pretty fancies about her flowers, and loved to tell the children the story of the pansy, and show them how the stepmother leaf sat up in her green chair in purple and gold; how the two own children in gay yellow had each its little seat, while the stepchildren, in dull colors, both sat on one small stool, and the poor little father, in his red nightcap, was kept out of sight in the middle of the flower; that a monk's dark face looked out of the monkshood larkspur; that the flowers of the canary vine were so like dainty birds fluttering their yellow wings, that one almost expected to see them fly away, and the snapdragons that went off like little pistol shots when you cracked them. Splendid dollies did she make out of scarlet and white poppies, with ruffled robes tied round the waist with grass-blade sashes, and astonishing hats of coreopsis on their green heads. Pea-pod boats, with rose-leaf sails, received these flower people, and floated them about a placid pool in the most charming style; for finding that there were no elves, Daisy made her own, and loved the fanciful little friends who played their parts in her summer life.

Nan went in for herbs, and had a fine display of useful plants, which she tended with steadily increasing interest and care. Very busy was she in September cutting, drying, and tying up her sweet harvest, and writing down in a little book how the different herbs are to be used. She had tried several experiments, and made several mistakes; so she wished to be particular lest she should give little Huz another fit by administering wormwood instead of catnip.

Dick, Dolly, and Rob each grubbed away on his small farm, and made more stir about it than all the rest put together. Parsnips and carrots were the crops of the two Ds; and they longed for it to be late enough to pull up the precious vegetables. Dick did privately examine his carrots, and plant them again, feeling that Silas was right in saying it was too soon for them yet.

Rob's crop was four small squashes and one immense pumpkin. It really was a "bouncer," as every one said; and I assure you that two small persons could sit on it side by side. It seemed to have absorbed all the goodness of the little garden, and all the sunshine that shone down on it, and lay there a great round, golden ball, full of rich suggestions of pumpkin pies for weeks to come. Robby was so proud of his mammoth vegetable that he took every one to see it, and, when frosts began to nip, covered it up each night with an old bedquilt, tucking it round as if the pumpkin was a well-beloved baby. The day it was gathered he would let no one touch it but himself, and nearly broke his back tugging it to the barn in his little wheelbarrow, with Dick and Dolly harnessed in front to give a heave up the path. His mother promised him that the Thanksgiving pies should be made from it, and hinted vaguely that she had a plan in her head which would cover the prize pumpkin and its owner with glory.

Poor Billy had planted cucumbers, but unfortunately hoed them up and left the pig-weed. This mistake grieved him very much for ten minutes, then he forgot all about it, and sowed a handful of bright buttons which he had collected, evidently thinking in his feeble mind that they were money, and would come up and multiply, so that he might make many quarters, as Tommy did. No one disturbed him, and he did what he liked with his plot, which soon looked as if a series of small earthquakes had stirred it up. When the general harvest day came, he would have had nothing but stones and weeds to show, if kind old Asia had not hung half a dozen oranges on the dead tree he had stuck up in the middle. Billy was delighted with his crop; and no one spoiled his pleasure in the little miracle which pity wrought for him, by making withered branches bear strange fruit.

Stuffy had various trials with his melons; for, being impatient to taste them, he had a solitary revel before they were ripe, and made himself so ill, that for a day or two it seemed doubtful if he would ever eat any more. But he pulled through it, and served up his first cantaloupe without tasting a mouthful himself. They were excellent melons, for he had a warm slope for them, and they ripened fast. The last and best were lingering on the vines, and Stuffy had announced that he would sell them to a neighbor. This disappointed the boys, who had hoped to eat the melons themselves, and they expressed their displeasure in a new and striking manner. Going one morning to gaze upon the three fine watermelons which he had kept for the market, Stuffy was horrified to find the word "PIG" cut in white letters on the green rid, staring at him from every one. He was in a great rage, and flew to Mrs. Jo for redress. She listened, condoled with him, and then said, —

"If you want to turn the laugh, I'll tell you how, but you must give up the melons."

"Well, I will; for I can't thrash all the boys, but I'd like to give them something to remember, the mean sneaks," growled Stuffy, still in a fume.

Now Mrs. Jo was pretty sure who had done the trick, for she had seen three heads suspiciously near to one another in the sofa corner the evening before; and when these heads had nodded with chuckles and whispers, this experienced woman knew that mischief was afoot. A moonlight night, a rustling in the old cherry tree near Emil's window, a cut on Tommy's finger, all helped to confirm her suspicions; and having cooled Stuffy's wrath a little, she bade him bring his maltreated melons to her room, and say not a word to any one of what had happened. He did so, and the three wags were amazed to find their joke so quietly taken. It spoiled the fun, and the entire disappearance of the melons made them uneasy. So did Stuffy's good nature, for he looked more placid and plump than ever, and surveyed them with an air of calm pity that perplexed them much.

At dinner time they discovered why; for then Stuffy's vengeance fell upon them, and the laugh *was* turned against them. When the pudding was eaten, and the fruit was put on, Mary Ann reappeared in a high state of giggle, bearing a large watermelon; Silas followed with another; and Dan brought up the rear with a third. One was placed before each of the three guilty lads; and they read on the smooth green skin this addition to their own work, "With the compliments of the PIG" Every one else read it also, and the whole table was in a roar, for the trick had been whispered about; so every one understood the sequel. Emil, Ned, and Tommy did not know where to look, and had not a word to say for themselves; so they wisely joined in the laugh, cut up the melons, and handed them round, saying, what all the rest agreed to, that Stuffy had taken a wise and merry way to return good for evil.

Dan had no garden, for he was away or lame the greater part of the summer; so he had helped Silas wherever he could, chopped wood for Asia, and taken care of the lawn so well, that Mrs. Jo always had smooth paths and nicely shaven turf before her door.

When the others got in their crops, he looked sorry that he had so little to show; but as autumn went on, he bethought him of a woodland harvest which no one would dispute with him, and which was peculiarly his own. Every Saturday he was away alone to forests, fields, and hills, and always came back loaded with spoils; for he seemed to know the meadows where the best flag root grew, the thicket where the sassafras was spiciest, the haunts where the squirrels went for nuts, the white oak whose bark was most valuable, and the little gold-thread vine that Nursey liked to cure the canker with. All sorts of splendid red and yellow leaves did Dan bring home for Mrs. Jo to dress her parlor with — graceful-seeded grasses, clematis tassels, downy, soft, yellow waxwork berries, and mosses, red-brimmed, white, or emerald green.

"I need not sigh for the woods now, because Dan brings the woods to me," Mrs. Jo used to say, as she glorified the walls with yellow maple boughs and scarlet woodbine wreaths, or filled her vases with russet ferns, hemlock sprays full of delicate cones, and hardy autumn flowers.

The great garret was full of the children's little stores, and for a time was one of the sights of the house. Daisy's flower seeds in neat little paper bags, all labeled, lay in the drawer of a three-legged table. Nan's herbs hung in bunches against the wall, filling the air with their aromatic breath. Tommy had a basket of thistledown with the tiny seeds attached, for he meant to plant them next year, if they did not fly away before that time. Emil had bunches of pop corn hanging there to dry, and Demi laid up acorns and different sorts of grain for the pets. But Dan's crop made the best show, for fully one half of the floor was covered with the nuts he brought. All kinds were there, for he ranged the woods for miles round, climbed the tallest trees, and forced his way into the thickest hedges for his plunder. Walnuts, chestnuts, hazelnuts, and beechnuts lay in separate compartments, getting brown, and dry, and sweet, ready for winter revels.

There was one butternut-tree on the place, and Rob and Teddy called it theirs. It bore well this year, and the great dingy nuts came dropping down to hide among the dead leaves, where the busy squirrels found them better than the lazy Bhaers. Their father had told them (the boys, not the squirrels) they should have the nuts if they would pick them up, but no one was to help. It was easy work, and Teddy liked it, only he soon got tired, and left his little basket half full for another day. But the other day was slow to arrive, and, meantime, the sly squirrels were hard at work scampering up and down the old elm-trees stowing the nuts away till their holes were full, then all about in the crotches of the boughs, to be removed at their leisure. Their funny little ways amused the boys, till one day Silas said, —

"Hev you sold them nuts to the squirrels?"

"No," answered Rob, wondering what Silas meant.

"Wal, then, you'd better fly round, or them spry little fellers won't you leave you none."

Dan tries the colt and gets a fall. (Chapter 16)

Silas tells his story by the fire. (Chapter 20)

"Oh, we can beat them when we begin. There are such lots of nuts we shall have a plenty."

"There ain't many more to come down, and they have cleared the ground pretty well, see if they hain't."

Robby ran to look, and was alarmed to find how few remained. He called Teddy, and they worked hard all one afternoon, while the squirrels sat on the fence and scolded.

"Now, Ted, we must keep watch, and pick up just as fast as they fall, or we shan't have more than a bushel, and every one will laugh at us if we don't."

"The naughty quillies tarn't have 'em. I'll pick fast and run and put them in the barn quick," said Teddy, frowning at little Frisky, who chattered and whisked his tail indignantly.

That night a high wind blew down hundreds of nuts, and when Mrs. Jo came to wake her little sons, she said, briskly, —

"Come, my laddies, the squirrels are hard at it, and you will have to work well to-day, or they will have every nut on the ground."

"No, they won't," and Robby tumbled up in a great hurry, gobbled his breakfast, and rushed out to save his property.

Teddy went too, and worked like a little beaver, trotting to and fro with full and empty baskets. Another bushel was soon put away in the corn barn, and they were scrambling among the leaves for more nuts when the bell rang for school.

"Oh! father! let me stay out and pick. Those horrid squirrels will have my nuts if you don't. I'll do my lessons by and by," cried Rob, running into the schoolroom, flushed and tousled by the fresh cold wind and his eager work.

"If you had been up early and done a little every morning there would be no hurry now. I told you that, Rob, and you never minded. I cannot have the lessons neglected as the work has been. The squirrels will get more than their share this year, and they deserve it, for they have worked best. You may go an hour earlier, but that is all," and Mr. Bhaer led Rob to his place, where the little man dashed at his books as if bent on making sure of the precious hour promised him.

It was almost maddening to sit still and see the wind shaking down the last nuts, and the lively thieves flying about, pausing now and then to eat one in his face, and flirt their tails, as if they said, saucily, "We'll have them in spite of you, lazy Rob." The only thing that sustained the poor child in this trying moment was the sight of Teddy working away all alone. It was really splendid the pluck and perseverance of the little lad. He picked and picked till his back ached; he trudged to and fro till his small legs were tired; and he defied wind, weariness, and wicked "quillies," till his mother left her work and did the carrying for him, full of admiration for the kind little fellow who tried to help his brother. When Rob was dismissed he found Teddy reposing in the bushel basket quite used up, but unwilling to quit the field; for he flapped his hat at the thieves with one grubby little hand, while he refreshed himself with the big apple held in the other.

Rob fell to work and the ground was cleared before two o'clock, the nuts safely in the corn-barn loft, and the weary workers exulted in their success. But Frisky and his wife were not to be vanquished so easily; and when Rob went up to look at his nuts a few days later he was amazed to see how many had vanished. None of the boys could have stolen them, because the door had been locked; the doves could not have eaten them, and there were no rats about. There was great lamentation among the young Bhaers till Dick said, —

"I saw Frisky on the roof of the corn barn, maybe he took them."

"I know he did! I'll have a trap, and kill him dead," cried Rob, disgusted with Frisky's grasping nature.

"Perhaps, if you watch, you can find out where he puts them, and I may be able to get them back for you," said Dan, who was much amused by the fight between the boys and squirrels.

So Rob watched and saw Mr. and Mrs. Frisky drop from the drooping elm boughs on to the roof of the corn barn, dodge in at one of the little doors, much to the disturbance of the doves, and come out with a nut in each mouth. So laden they could not get back the way they came, but ran down the low roof, along the wall, and leaping off at a corner they vanished a minute and reappeared without their plunder. Rob ran to the place, and in a hollow under the leaves found a heap of the stolen property hidden away to be carried off to the holes by and by.

"Oh, you little villains! I'll cheat *you* now, and not leave one," said Rob. So he cleared the corner and the corn barn, and put the contested nuts in the garret, making sure that no broken windowpane could anywhere let in the unprincipled squirrels. They seemed to feel that the contest was over, and retired to their hole, but now and then could not resist throwing down nutshells on Rob's head, and scolding violently as if they could not forgive him nor forget that he had the best of the battle.

Father and Mother Bhaer's crop was of a different sort, and not so easily described; but they were satisfied with it, felt that their summer work had prospered well, and by and by had a harvest that made them very happy.

JOHN BROOKE

~

"Wake up, Demi, dear! I want you."

"Why, I've just gone to bed; it can't be morning yet," and Demi blinked like a little owl as he waked from his first sound sleep.

"It's only ten, but your father is ill, and we must go to him. Oh my little John! my poor little John!" and Aunt Jo laid her head down on the pillow with a sob that scared sleep from Demi's eyes and filled his heart with fear and wonder; for he dimly felt why Aunt Jo called him "John," and wept over him as if some loss had come that left him poor. He clung to her without a word, and in a minute she was quite steady again, and said, with a tender kiss as she saw his troubled face, —

"We are going to say good-by to him, my darling, and there is no time to lose; so dress quickly and come to me in my room. I must go to Daisy."

"Yes, I will," and when Aunt Jo was gone, little Demi got up

773

quietly, dressed as if in a dream, and leaving Tommy fast asleep went away through the silent house, feeling that something new and sorrowful was going to happen — something that set him apart from the other boys for a time, and made the world seem as dark and still and strange as those familiar rooms did in the night. A carriage sent by Mr. Laurie stood before the door. Daisy was soon ready, and the brother and sister held each other by the hand all the way into town, as they drove swiftly and silently with aunt and uncle through the shadowy roads to say good-by to father.

None of the boys but Franz and Emil knew what had happened, and when they came down next morning, great was their wonderment and discomfort, for the house seemed forlorn without its master and mistress. Breakfast was a dismal meal with no cheery Mrs. Jo behind the teapots; and when school time came, Father Bhaer's place was empty. They wandered about in a disconsolate kind of way for an hour, waiting for news and hoping it would be all right with Demi's father, for good John Brooke was much beloved by the boys. Ten o'clock came, and no one arrived to relieve their anxiety. They did not feel like playing, yet the time dragged heavily, and they sat about listless and sober. All at once, Franz got up, and said in his persuasive way, —

"Look here, boys! let's go into school and do our lessons just as if uncle was here. It will make the day go faster, and will please him, I know."

"But who will hear us say them?" asked Jack.

"I will; I don't know much more than you do, but I'm the oldest here, and I'll try to fill uncle's place till he comes, if you don't mind."

Something in the modest, serious way Franz said this impressed the boys, for, though the poor lad's eyes were red with quiet crying for Uncle John in that long sad night, there was a new manliness about him, as if he had already begun to feel the cares and troubles of life, and tried to take them bravely.

"I will, for one," and Emil went to his seat, remembering that obedience to his superior officer is a seaman's first duty.

The others followed; Franz took his uncle's seat, and for an hour reigned. Lessons were learned and said, and Franz made a patient, pleasant teacher, wisely omitting such lessons as he was not equal to, and keeping order more by the unconscious dignity that sorrow gave him than by any words of his own. The little boys were reading when a step was heard in the hall, and every one looked up to read the news in Mr. Bhaer's face as he came in. The kind face told them instantly that Demi had no father now, for it was worn and pale, and full of tender grief, which left him no words with which to answer Rob, as he ran to him saying, reproachfully, –

"What made you go and leave me in the night, papa?"

The memory of the other father who had left his children in the night, never to return, made Mr. Bhaer hold his own boy close, and, for a minute, hide his face in Robby's curly hair. Emil laid his head down on his arms, Franz went to put his hand on his uncle's shoulder, his boyish face pale with sympathy and sorrow, and the others sat so still that the soft rustle of the falling leaves outside was distinctly heard.

Rob did not clearly understand what had happened but he hated to see papa unhappy, so he lifted up the bent head, and said in his chirpy little voice, –

"Don't cry, mein Vater! We are all so good, we did our lessons without you, and Franz was the master."

Mr. Bhaer looked up then, tried to smile, and said in a grateful tone that made the lads feel like saints, "I thank you very much, my boys. It was a beautiful way to help and comfort me. I shall not forget it, I assure you."

"Franz proposed it, and was a first-rate master, too," said Nat; and the others gave a murmur of assent most gratifying to the young dominie.

Mr. Bhaer put Rob down, and, standing up, put his arm round his tall nephew's shoulder, as he said, with a look of genuine pleasure, –

"This makes my hard day easier, and gives me confidence in you all. I am needed there in town, and must leave you for some hours. I thought to give you a holiday, or send some of you home, but if you like to stay and go on as you have begun, I shall be glad and proud of my good boys."

"We'll stay." "We'd rather." "Franz can see to us," cried several, delighted with the confidence shown in them.

"Isn't Marmar coming home?" asked Rob, wistfully; for home without "Marmar" was the world without the sun to him.

"We shall both come to-night; but dear Aunt Meg needs mother more than you do now, and I know you like to lend her for a little while."

"Well, I will; but Teddy's been crying for her, and he slapped Nursey, and was dreadful naughty," answered Rob, as if the news might bring mother home.

"Where is my little man?" asked Mr. Bhaer.

"Dan took him out, to keep him quiet. He's all right now," said Franz, pointing to the window, through which they could see Dan drawing baby in his little wagon, with the dogs frolicking about him.

"I won't see him, it would only upset him again; but tell Dan I leave Teddy in his care. You older boys I trust to manage yourselves for a day. Franz will direct you, and Silas is here to oversee matters. So good-by till to-night."

"Just tell me a word about Uncle John," said Emil, detaining Mr. Bhaer, as he was about hurrying away again.

"He was only ill a few hours, and died as he has lived, so cheerfully, so peacefully, that it seems a sin to mar the beauty of it with any violent or selfish grief. We were in time to say good-by; and Daisy and Demi were in his arms as he fell asleep on Aunt Meg's breast. No more now, I cannot bear it," and Mr. Bhaer went hastily away quite bowed with grief, for in John Brooke he had lost both friend and brother, and there was no one left to take his place.

All that day the house was very still; the small boys played quietly in the nursery; the others, feeling as if Sunday had come in the middle of the week, spent it in walking, sitting in the willow, or among their pets, all talking much of "Uncle John," and feeling that something gentle, just, and strong, had gone out of their little world, leaving a sense of loss that deepened every hour. At dusk, Mr. and Mrs. Bhaer came home alone, for Demi and Daisy were their mother's best comfort now, and could not leave her. Poor Mrs. Jo seemed quite spent, and evidently needed the same sort of comfort, for her first words, as she came up the stairs, were, "Where is my baby?"

"Here I is," answered a little voice, as Dan put Teddy into her arms, adding, as she hugged him close, "My Danny tooked tare of me all day, and I was dood."

Mrs. Jo turned to thank the faithful nurse, but Dan was waving off the boys, who had gathered in the hall to meet her, and was saying, in a low voice, "Keep back; she don't want to be bothered with us now."

"No, don't keep back. I want you all. Come in and see me, my boys. I've neglected you all day," and Mrs. Jo held out her hands to them as they gathered round and escorted her into her own room, saying little, but expressing much by affectionate looks and clumsy little efforts to show their sorrow and sympathy.

"I am so tired, I will lie here and cuddle Teddy, and you shall bring me in some tea," she said, trying to speak cheerfully for their sakes.

A general stampede into the dining room followed, and the supper table would have been ravaged if Mr. Bhaer had not interfered. It was agreed that one squad should carry in the mother's tea, and another bring it out. The four nearest and dearest claimed the first honor, so Franz bore the teapot, Emil the bread, Rob the milk, and Teddy insisted on carrying the sugar bowl, which was lighter by several lumps when it arrived than when it started. Some women might have found it annoying at such a time to have boys creaking in and out, upsetting cups and rattling spoons in violent efforts to be quiet and helpful; but it suited Mrs. Jo, because just then her heart was very tender; and remembering that many of her boys were fatherless or motherless, she yearned over them, and found comfort in their blundering affections. It was the sort of food that did her more good than the very thick bread and butter that they gave her, and the rough Commodore's broken whisper, –

"Bear up, Aunty, it's a hard blow; but we'll weather it somehow," cheered her more than the sloppy cup he brought her, full of tea as bitter as if some salt tear of his own had dropped into it on the way. When supper was over, a second deputation removed the tray; and Dan said, holding out his arms for sleepy little Teddy, –

"Let me put him to bed, you're so tired, mother."

"Will you go with him, lovely?" asked Mrs. Jo of her small lord and master, who lay on her arm among the sofa pillows.

"Torse I will," and he was proudly carried off by his faithful bearer.

"I wish *I* could do something," said Nat, with a sigh, as Franz leaned over the sofa, and softly stroked Aunt Jo's hot forehead.

"You can, dear. Go and get your violin, and play me the sweet little airs Uncle Teddy sent you last. Music will comfort me better than anything else tonight."

Nat flew for his fiddle, and, sitting just outside her door, played as he had never done before, for now his heart was in it, and seemed to magnetize his fingers. The other lads sat quietly upon the steps, keeping watch that no newcomer should disturb the house; Franz lingered at his post; and so, soothed, served, and guarded by her boys, poor Mrs. Jo slept at last, and forgot her sorrow for an hour.

Two quiet days, and on the third Mr. Bhaer came in just after school, with a note in his hand, looking both moved and pleased.

"I want to read you something, boys," he said; and as they stood round him he read this:

DEAR BROTHER FRITZ, I hear that you do not mean to bring your flock to-day, thinking that I may not like it. Please do. The sight of his friends will help Demi through the hard hour, and I want the boys to hear what father says of my John. It will do them good, I know. If they would sing one of the sweet old hymns you have taught them so well, I should like it better than any other music, and feel that it was beautifully suited to the occasion. Please ask them, with my love.

MEG.

"Will you go?" and Mr. Bhaer looked at the lads, who were greatly touched by Mrs. Brooke's kind words and wishes.

"Yes," they answered, like one boy; and an hour later they went away with Franz to bear their part in John Brooke's simple funeral.

The little house looked as quiet, sunny, and homelike as when Meg entered it a bride, ten years ago, only then it was early summer, and roses blossomed everywhere; now it was early autumn, and dead leaves rustled softly down, leaving the branches bare. The bride was a widow now; but the same beautiful serenity shone in her face, and the sweet resignation of a truly pious soul made her presence a consolation to those who came to comfort her.

"O Meg! how *can* you bear it so?" whispered Jo, as she met them at the door with a smile of welcome, and no change in her gentle manner, except more gentleness.

"Dear Jo, the love that has blest me for ten happy years supports me still. It could not die, and John is more my own than ever," whispered Meg; and in her eyes the tender trust was so beautiful and bright, that Jo believed her, and thanked God for the immortality of love like hers.

They were all there – father and mother, Uncle Teddy, and Aunt Amy, old Mr. Laurence, white-haired and feeble now, Mr. and Mrs. Bhaer, with their flock, and many friends, come to do honor to the dead. One would have said that modest John Brooke, in his busy, quiet, humble life, had had little time to make friends; but now they seemed to start up everywhere – old and young, rich and poor, high and low; for all unconsciously his influence had made itself widely felt, his virtues were remembered, and his hidden charities rose up to bless him. The group about his coffin was a far more eloquent eulogy than any Mr. March could utter. There were the rich men whom he had served faithfully for years; the poor old women whom he cherished with his little store, in memory of his mother; the wife to whom he had given such happiness that death could not mar it utterly; the brothers and sisters in whose hearts he had made a place for ever; the little son and daughter, who already felt the loss of his strong arm and tender voice; the young children, sobbing for their kindest playmate, and the tall lads, watching with softened faces a scene which they could never forget. A very simple service, and very short; for the fatherly voice that had faltered in the marriage sacrament now failed entirely as Mr. March endeavored to pay his tribute of reverence and love to the son whom he most honored. Nothing but the soft coo of Baby Josy's voice up stairs broke the long hush that followed the last Amen, till, at a sign from Mr. Bhaer, the well-trained boyish voices broke out in a hymn, so full of lofty cheer, that one by one all joined it it, singing with full hearts, and finding their troubled spirits lifted into peace on the wings of that brave, sweet psalm.

As Meg listened, she felt that she had done well; for not only did the moment comfort her with the assurance that John's last lullaby was sung by the young voices he loved so well, but in the faces of the boys she saw that they had caught a glimpse of the beauty of virtue in its most impressive form, and that the memory of the good man lying dead before them would live long and helpfully in their remembrance. Daisy's head lay in her lap, and Demi held her hand, looking often at her, with eyes so like his father's, and a little gesture that seemed to say, "Don't be troubled, mother; I am here," and all about her were friends to lean upon and love; so patient, pious Meg put by her heavy grief, feeling that her best help would be to live for others, as her John had done.

That evening, as the Plumfield boys sat on the steps, as usual, in the mild September moonlight, they naturally fell to talking of the event of the day.

Emil began by breaking out, in his impetuous way, "Uncle Fritz is the wisest, and Uncle Laurie the jolliest, but Uncle John was the *best*; and I'd rather be like him than any man I ever saw."

"So would I. Did you hear what those gentlemen said to grandpa to-day? I would like to have that said of me when I was dead," and Franz felt with regret that he had not appreciated Uncle John enough.

"What did they say?" asked Jack, who had been much impressed by the scenes of the day.

"Why, one of the partners of Mr. Laurence, where Uncle John has been ever so long, was saying that he was conscientious almost to a fault as a business man, and above reproach in all things. Another gentlemen said no money could repay the fidelity and honesty with which Uncle John had served him, and then grandpa told them the best of all. Uncle John once had a place in the office of a man who cheated, and when this man wanted uncle to help him do it, uncle wouldn't, though he was offered a big salary. The man was angry and said, 'You will never get on in business with such strict principles,' and uncle answered back, 'I *never* will try to get on *without* them,' and left the place for a much harder and poorer one."

"Good!" cried several of the boys warmly, for they were in the mood to understand and value the little story as never before.

"He wasn't rich, was he?" asked Jack.

"No."

"He never did anything to make a stir in the world, did he?"

"No."

"He was only good?"

"That's all," and Franz found himself wishing that Uncle John *had* done something to boast of, for it was evident that Jack was disappointed by his replies.

"Only good. That is *all* and everything," said Mr. Bhaer, who had overheard the last few words, and guessed what was going on in the minds of the lads.

"Let me tell you a little about John Brooke, and you will see why men honor him, and why he was satisfied to be good rather than rich or famous. He simply did his duty in all things, and did it so cheerfully, so faithfully, that it kept him patient, brave, and happy through poverty and loneliness and years of hard work. He was a good son, and gave up his own plans to stay and live with his mother while she needed him. He was a good friend, and taught Laurie much beside his Greek and Latin, did it unconsciously, perhaps, by showing him an example of an upright man. He was a faithful servant, and made himself so valuable to those who employed him that they will find it hard to fill his place. He was a good husband and father, so tender, wise, and thoughtful, that Laurie and I learned much of him, and only knew how well he loved his family, when we discovered all he had done for them, unsuspected and unassisted."

Mr. Bhaer stopped a minute, and the boys sat like statues in the moonlight until he went on again, in a subdued, but earnest voice, "As he lay dying, I said to him, 'Have no care for the little ones; I will see that they never want.' Then he smiled and pressed my hand, and answered, in his cheerful way, 'No need of that; I have cared for them.' And so he had, for when we looked among his papers, all was in order, not a debt remained; and safely put away was enough to keep Meg comfortable and independent. Then we knew why he had lived so plainly, denied himself so many pleasures, except that of charity, and worked so hard that I fear he shortened his good life. He never asked for help for himself, though often for others, but bore his own burden and worked out his own task bravely and quietly. No one can say a word of complaint against him, so just and generous and kind was he; and now, when he is gone, all find so much love and praise and honor, that I am proud to have been his friend, and would rather leave my children the legacy he leaves his than the largest fortune ever made. Yes! Simple, genuine goodness is the best capital to found the business of this life upon. It lasts when fame and money fail, and is the only riches we can take out of this world with us. Remember that, my boys; and if you want to earn respect and confidence and love follow in the footsteps of John Brooke."

When Demi returned to school, after some weeks at home, he seemed to have recovered from his loss with the blessed elasticity of childhood, and so he had in a measure; but he did not forget, for his was a nature into which things sank deeply, to be pondered over, and absorbed into the soil where the small virtues were growing fast. He played and studied, worked and sang, just as before, and few suspected any change; but there was one, – and Aunt Jo saw it, – for she watched over the boy with her whole heart, trying to fill John's place in her poor way. He seldom spoke of his loss, but Aunt Jo often heard a stifled sobbing in the little bed at night; and when she went to comfort him, all his cry was, "I want my father! oh, I want my father!" – for the tie between the two had been a very tender one, and the child's heart bled when it was broken. But time was kind to him, and slowly he came to feel that father was not lost, only invisible for a while, and sure to be found again, well and strong and fond as ever, even though his little son should see the purple asters blossom on his grave many, many times before they met. To this belief Demi held fast, and in it found both help and comfort, because it led him unconsciously through a tender longing for the father whom he had seen to a childlike trust in the Father whom he had not seen. Both were in heaven, and he prayed to both, trying to be good for love of them.

The outward change corresponded to the inward, for in those few weeks Demi seemed to have grown tall, and began to drop his childish plays, not as if ashamed of them, as some boys do, but as if he had outgrown them, and wanted something manlier. He took to the hated arithmetic, and held on so steadily that his uncle was charmed, though he could not understand the whim, until Demi said, –

"I am going to be a bookkeeper when I grow up, like papa, and I must know about figures and things else I can't have nice, neat ledgers like his."

At another time he came to his aunt with a very serious face, and said, –

"What can a small boy do to earn money?"

"Why do you ask, my deary?"

"My father told me to take care of mother and the little girls, and I want to, but I don't know how to begin."

"He did not mean now, Demi, but by and by, when you are large."

"But I wish to begin *now*, if I can, because I think I ought to make some money to buy things for the family. I am ten, and the other boys no bigger than I earn pennies some times."

"Well, then, suppose you rake up all the dead leaves and cover the strawberry bed. I'll pay you a dollar for the job," said Aunt Jo.

"Isn't that a great deal? I could do it in one day. You must be fair, and not pay too much, because I want to truly earn it."

"My little John, I will be fair, and not pay a penny too much. Don't work too hard; and when that is done I will have something else for you to do," said Mrs. Jo, much touched by his desire to help, and his sense of justice, so like his scrupulous father.

When the leaves were done, many barrow loads of chips were wheeled from the wood to the shed, and another dollar earned. Then Demi helped cover the schoolbooks, working in the evenings, under Franz's direction, tugging patiently away at each book, letting no one help, and receiving his wages with such satisfaction that the dingy bills became quite glorified in his sight.

"Now, I have a dollar for each of them, and I should like to take my money to mother all myself, so she can see that I have minded my father."

So Demi made a duteous pilgrimage to his mother, who received his little earnings as a treasure of great worth, and would have kept it untouched, if Demi had not begged her to buy some *useful* thing for herself and the women children, whom he felt were left to his care.

This made him very happy, and, though he often forgot his responsibilities for a time, the desire to help was still there, strengthening with his years. He always uttered the words "my father" with an air of gentle pride, and often said, as if he claimed a title full of honor, "Don't call me Demi any more. I am John Brooke now." So, strengthened by a purpose and a hope, the little lad of ten bravely began the world, and entered into his inheritance — the memory of a wise and tender father, the legacy of an honest name.

CHAPTER TWENTY

ROUND THE FIRE

~

With the October frosts came the cheery fires in the great fireplaces; and Demi's dry pine chips helped Dan's oak knots to blaze royally, and go roaring up the chimney with a jolly sound. All were glad to gather round the hearth, as the evenings grew longer, to play games, read, or lay plans for the winter. But the favorite amusement was story telling, and Mr. and Mrs. Bhaer were expected to have a store of lively tales always on hand. Their supply occasionally gave out, and then the boys were thrown upon their own resources, which were not always successful. Ghost parties were the rage at one time; for the fun of the thing consisted in putting out the lights, letting the fire die down, and then sitting in the dark, and telling the most awful tales they could invent. As this resulted in scares of all sorts among the boys, Tommy's walking in his sleep on the shed roof, and a general state of nervousness in the little ones, it was forbidden, and they fell back on more harmless amusements.

One evening, when the small boys were snugly tucked in bed, and the older lads were lounging about the schoolroom fire, trying to decide what they should do, Demi suggested a new way of settling the question.

Seizing the hearth brush, he marched up and down the room, saying, "Row, row, row," and when the boys, laughing and pushing, had got into line, he said, "Now, I'll give you two minutes to think of a play." Franz was writing, and Emil reading the "Life of Lord Nelson," and neither joined the party, but the others thought hard, and when the time was up were ready to reply.

"Now, Tom!" and the poker softly rapped him on the head.

"Blindman's Buff."

"Jack!"

"Commerce; a good round game, and have cents for the pool."

"Uncle forbids our playing for money. Dan, what do you want?"

"Let's have a battle between the Greeks and Romans."

"Stuffy?"

"Roast apples, pop corn, and crack nuts."

"Good! good!" cried several; and when the vote was taken, Stuffy's proposal carried the day.

Some went to the cellar for apples, some to the garret for nuts, and others looked up the popper and the corn.

"We had better ask the girls to come in, hadn't we?" said Demi, in a sudden fit of politeness.

"Daisy pricks chestnuts beautifully," put in Nat, who wanted his little friend to share the fun.

"Nan pops corn tiptop, we must have her," added Tommy.

"Bring in your sweethearts then, we don't mind," said Jack, who laughed at the innocent regard the little people had for one another.

"You shan't call my sister a sweetheart; it is so silly!" cried Demi, in a way that made Jack laugh.

"She *is* Nat's darling, isn't she, old chirper?"

"Yes, if Demi don't mind. I can't help being fond of her, she is so good to me," answered Nat, with bashful earnestness, for Jack's rough ways disturbed him.

"Nan is my sweetheart, and I shall marry her in about a year, so don't you get in the way, any of you," said Tommy, stoutly; for he and Nan had settled their future, child fashion, and were to live in the willow, lower down a basket for food, and do other charmingly impossible things.

Demi was quenched by the decision of Bangs, who took him by the arm and walked him off to get the ladies. Nan and Daisy were sewing with Aunt Jo on certain small garments for Mrs. Carney's newest baby.

"Please, ma'am, could you lend us the girls for a little while? We'll be very careful of them," said Tommy, winking one eye to express apples, snapping his fingers to signify pop corn, and gnashing his teeth to convey the idea of nut cracking.

The girls understood this pantomime at once, and began to pull off their thimbles before Mrs. Jo could decide whether Tommy was going into convulsions or was brewing some unusual piece of mischief. Demi explained with elaboration, permission was readily granted, and the boys departed with their prize.

"Don't you speak to Jack," whispered Tommy, as he and Nan promenaded down the hall to get a fork to prick the apples.

"Why not?"

"He laughs at me, so I don't wish you to have anything to do with him."

"Shall if I like," said Nan, promptly resenting this premature assumption of authority on the part of her lord.

"Then I won't have you for my sweetheart."

"I don't care."

"Why, Nan, I thought you were fond of me!" and Tommy's voice was full of tender reproach.

"If you mind Jack's laughing I don't care for you one bit."

"Then you may take back your old ring; I won't wear it any longer"; and Tommy plucked off a horsehair pledge of affection which Nan had given him in return for one made of a lobster's feeler.

"I shall give it to Ned," was her cruel reply; for Ned liked Mrs. Giddygaddy, and had turned her clothespins, boxes, and spools enough to set up housekeeping with.

Tommy said, "Thunder turtles!" as the only vent equal to the pent-up anguish of the moment, and, dropping Nan's arm, retired in high dudgeon, leaving her to follow with the fork — a neglect which naughty Nan punished by proceeding to prick his heart with jealousy as if it were another sort of apple.

The hearth was swept, and the rosy Baldwins put down to roast. A shovel was heated, and the chestnuts danced merrily upon it, while the corn popped wildly in its wire prison. Dan cracked his best walnuts, and every one chattered and laughed, while the rain beat on the windowpane and the wind howled round the house.

"Why is Billy like this nut?" asked Emil, who was frequently inspired with bad conundrums.

"Because he is cracked," answered Ned.

"That's not fair; you mustn't make fun of Billy, because he can't hit back again. It's mean," cried Dan, smashing a nut wrathfully.

"To what family of insects does Blake belong?" asked peacemaker Franz, seeing that Emil looked ashamed and Dan lowering.

"Gnats," answered Jack.

"Why is Daisy like a bee?" cried Nat, who had been wrapt in thought for several minutes.

"Because she is queen of the hive," said Dan.

"No."

"Because she is sweet."

"Bees are not sweet."

"Give it up."

"Because she makes sweet things, is always busy and likes flowers," said Nat, piling up his boyish compliments till Daisy blushed like a rosy clover.

"Why is Nan like a hornet?" demanded Tommy, glowering at her, and adding, without giving any one time to answer, "Because she *isn't* sweet, makes a great buzzing about nothing, and stings like fury."

"Tommy's mad, and I'm glad," cried Ned, as Nan tossed her head and answered quickly,

"What thing in the china closet is Tom like?"

"A pepper pot," answered Ned, giving Nan a nut meat with a tantalizing laugh that made Tommy feel as if he would like to bounce up like a hot chestnut and hit somebody.

Seeing that ill-humor was getting the better of the small supply of wit in the company, Franz cast himself into the breach again.

"Let's make a law that the first person who comes into the room shall tell us a story. No matter who it is, he must do it, and it will be fun to see who comes first."

The others agreed, and did not have to wait long, for a heavy step soon came clumping through the hall, and Silas appeared, bearing an armful of wood. He was greeted by a general shout, and stood staring about him with a bewildered grin on his big red face, till Franz explained the joke.

"Sho! I can't tell a story," he said, putting down his load and preparing to leave the room. But the boys fell upon him, forced him into a seat, and held him there, laughing and clamoring for their story, till the good-natured giant was overpowered.

"I don't know but jest one story, and that's about a horse," he said, much flattered by the reception he received.

"Tell it! tell it!" cried the boys.

"Wal," began Silas, tipping his chair back against the wall, and putting his thumbs in the armholes of his waistcoat, "I jined a cavalry regiment durin' the war, and see a consid'able amount of fightin'. My horse, Major, was a fust-rate animal, and I was as fond on him as ef he'd ben a human critter. He warn't harnsome, but he was the best-tempered, stiddyest, lovenest brute I ever see. The fust battle we went into, he give me a lesson that I didn't forgit in a hurry, and I'll tell you how it was. It ain't no use tryin' to picter the noise and hurry, and general horridness of a battle to you young fellers, for I ain't no words to do it in; but I'm free to confess that I got so sort of confused and upset at the fust on it, that I didn't know what I was about. We was ordered to charge, and went ahead like good ones, never stoppin' to pick up them that went down in the scrimmage. I got a shot in the arm, and was pitched out of the saddle — don't know how, but there I was left behind with two or three others, dead and wounded, for the rest went on, as I say. Wal, I picked myself up and looked round for Major, feeling as ef I'd had about enough for that spell. I didn't see him nowhere, and was kinder walking back to camp, when I heard a whinny that sounded nateral. I looked round, and there was Major stopping for me a long way off, and lookin' as ef he didn't understand why I was loiterin' behind. I whistled, and he trotted up to me as I'd trained him to do. I mounted as well as I could with my left arm bleedin' and was for going on to camp, for I declare I felt as sick and wimbly as a woman; folks often do in their fust battle. But, no, sir! Major was the bravest of the two, and he wouldn't go, not a peg; he jest rared up and danced, and snorted, and acted as ef the smell of powder and the noise had drove him half wild. I done my best, but he wouldn't give in, so I did; and what do you think that plucky brute done? He wheeled slap round, and galloped back like a hurricane, right into the thickest of the scrimmage!"

"Good for him!" cried Dan excitedly, while the other boys forgot apples and nuts in their interest.

"I wish I may die ef I warn't ashamed of myself," continued Silas, warming up at the recollection of that day. "I was as mad as a hornet, and I forgot my waound, and jest pitched in, rampagin' raound like fury till there come a shell into the midst of us, and in bustin' knocked a lot of us flat. I didn't know nothin' for a spell, and when I come to, the fight was over jest there, and I found myself layin' by a wall with poor Major long-side wuss wounded than I was. My leg was broke, and I had a ball in my shoulder, but he, poor old feller! was all tore in the side with a piece of that blasted shell."

"O Silas! what did you do?" cried Nan, pressing close to him with a face full of eager sympathy and interest.

"I dragged myself nigher, and tried to stop the bleedin' with sech rags as I could tear off of me with one hand. But it warn't no use, and he lay moanin' with horrid pain, and lookin' at me with them lovin' eyes of his, till I thought I couldn't bear it. I give him all the help I could, and when the sun got hotter and hotter, and he began to lap out his tongue, I tried to get to a brook that was a good piece away, but I couldn't do it, being stiff and faint, so I give it up and fanned him with my hat. Now you listen to this, and when you hear folks comin' down on the rebs, you jest remember what one on 'em did, and give him the credit of it. A poor feller in gray laid not fur off, shot through the lungs, and dying fast. I'd offered him my handkerchief to keep the sun off his face, and he'd thanked me kindly, for in sech times as that men don't stop to think on which side they belong, but jest buckle-to and help one another. When he see me mournin' over Major and tryin' to ease his pain, he looked up with his face all damp and white with sufferin', and sez he. 'There's water in my canteen; take it, for it can't help me,' and he flung it to me. I couldn't have took it ef I hadn't had a little brandy in a pocket flask, and I made him drink it. It done him good, and I felt as much set up as if I'd drunk it myself. It's surprisin' the good sech little things do folks some times," and Silas paused as if he felt again the comfort of that moment when he and his enemy forgot their feud, and helped one another like brothers.

"Tell about Major," cried the boys, impatient for the catastrophe.

"I poured the water over his poor pantin' tongue, and ef ever a dumb critter looked grateful, he did then. But it warn't of much use, for the dreadful waound kep on tormentin' him, till I couldn't bear it any longer. It was hard, but I done it in mercy, and I know he forgive me."

"What did you do?" asked Emil, as Silas stopped abruptly with a loud "hem," and a look in his rough face that made Daisy go and stand by him with her little hand on his knee.

"I shot him."

Quite a thrill went through the listeners as Silas said that, for Major seemed a hero in their eyes, and his tragic end roused all their sympathy.

"Yes, I shot him, and put him out of his misery. I patted him fust," and said, 'Good-by;' then I laid his head easy on the grass, give a last look into his lovin' eyes, and sent a bullet through his head. He hardly stirred, I aimed so true, and when I see him quite still, with no more moanin' and pain, I was glad, and yet, – wal, I don't know as I need be ashamed on't, – I jest put my arms raound his neck and boo-hooed like a great baby. Sho! I didn't know I was such a fool," and Silas drew his sleeve across his eyes, as much touched by Daisy's sob, as by the memory of faithful Major.

No one spoke for a minute, because the boys were as quick to feel the pathos of the little story as tender-hearted Daisy, though they did not show it by crying.

"I'd like a horse like that," said Dan, half-aloud.

"Did the rebel man die too?" asked Nan, anxiously.

"Not then. We laid there all day, and at night some of our fellers came to look after the missing ones. They nat'rally wanted to take me fust, but I knew I could wait, and the rebel had but one chance, maybe, so I made them carry him off right away. He had jest strength enough to hold his hand to me and say, 'Thanky, comrade!' and them was the last words he spoke, for he died an hour after he got to the hospital-tent."

"How glad you must have been that you were kind to him!" said Demi, who was deeply impressed by this story.

"Wal, I did take comfort thinkin' of it, as I laid there alone for a number of hours with my head on Major's neck, and see the moon come up.

I'd like to have buried the poor beast decent, but it warn't possible; so I cut off a bit of his mane, and I've kep it ever sence. Want to see it, sissy?"

"Oh, yes, please," answered Daisy, wiping away her tears to look.

Silas took out an old "wallet," as he called his pocket-book, and produced from an inner fold a bit of brown paper, in which was a rough lock of white horsehair. The children looked at it silently, as it lay in the broad palm, and no one found anything to ridicule in the love Silas bore his good horse Major.

"That is a sweet story, and I like it, though it did make me cry. Thank you very much, Si," and Daisy helped him fold and put away his little relic; while Nan stuffed a handful of pop corn into his pocket, and the boys loudly expressed their flattering opinions of his story, feeling that there had been two heroes in it.

He departed, quite overcome by his honors, and the little conspirators talked the tale over, while they waited for their next victim. It was Mrs. Jo, who came in to measure Nan for some new pinafores she was making for her. They let her get well in, and then pounced upon her, telling her the law, and demanding the story. Mrs. Jo was very much amused at the new trap, and consented at once, for the sound of the happy voices had been coming across the hall so pleasantly that she quite longed to join them, and forget her own anxious thoughts of Sister Meg.

"Am I the first mouse you have caught, you sly pussies in boots?" she asked, as she was conducted to the big chair, supplied with refreshments, and surrounded by a flock of merry-faced listeners.

They told her about Silas and his contribution, and she slapped her forehead in despair, for she was quite at her wits' end, being called upon so unexpectedly for a brand new tale.

"What *shall* I tell about?" she said.

"Boys," was the general answer.

"Have a party in it," said Daisy.

"And something good to eat," added Stuffy.

"That reminds me of a story, written years ago, by a dear old lady. I used to be very fond of it, and I fancy you will like it, for it has both boys and 'something good to eat' in it."

"What is it called?" asked Demi.

"'The Suspected Boy.'"

Nat looked up from the nuts he was picking, and Mrs. Jo smiled at him, guessing what was in his mind.

"Miss Crane kept a school for boys in a quiet little town, and a very good school it was, of the old-fashioned sort. Six boys lived in her house, and four or five more came in from the town. Among those who lived with her was one named Lewis White. Lewis was not a bad boy, but rather timid, and now and then he told a lie. One day a neighbor sent Miss Crane a basket of gooseberries. There were not enough to go round, so kind Miss Crane, who liked to please the boys, went to work and made a dozen nice little gooseberry tarts."

"I'd like to try gooseberry tarts. I wonder if she made them as I do my raspberry ones," said Daisy, whose interest in cooking had lately revived.

"Hush," said Nat, tucking a plump pop corn into her mouth to silence her, for he felt a peculiar interest in this tale, and thought it opened well.

"When the tarts were done, Miss Crane put them away in the best parlor closet, and said not a word about them, for she wanted to surprise the boys at tea time. When the minute came and all were seated at the table, she went to get her tarts, but came back looking much troubled, for what do you think had happened?"

"Somebody had hooked them!" cried Ned.

"No, there they were, but someone *had* stolen all the fruit out of them by lifting up the upper crust and then putting it down after the gooseberry had been scraped out."

"What a mean trick!" and Nan looked at Tommy, as if to imply that he would do the same.

"When she told the boys her plan and showed them the poor little patties all robbed of their sweetness, the boys were much grieved and disappointed, and all declared that they knew nothing about the matter. 'Perhaps the rats did it,' said Lewis, who was among the loudest to deny any knowledge of the tarts. 'No, rats would have nibbled crust and all, and never lifted it up and scooped out the fruit. Hands did that,' said Miss Crane, who was more troubled about the lie that someone must have told than about her lost patties. Well, they had supper and went to bed, but in the night Miss Crane heard someone groaning, and going to see who it was she found Lewis in great pain. He had evidently eaten something that disagreed with him, and was so sick that Miss Crane was alarmed, and was going to send for the doctor, when Lewis moaned out, 'It's the gooseberries; I ate them, and I *must* tell before I die,' for the thought of a doctor frightened him. 'If that is all, I'll give you an emetic and you will soon get over it,' said Miss Crane. So Lewis had a good dose, and by morning was quite comfortable. 'Oh, don't tell the boys; they will laugh at me so,' begged the invalid. Kind Miss Crane promised not to, but Sally, the girl, told the story, and poor Lewis had no peace for a long time. His mates called him Old Gooseberry, and were never tired to asking him the price of tarts."

"Served him right," said Emil.

"Badness always gets found out," added Demi, morally.

"No, it don't," muttered Jack, who was tending the apples with great devotion, so that he might keep his back to the rest and account for his red face.

"Is that all?" asked Dan.

"No, that is only the first part; the second part is more interesting. Some time after this a peddler came by one day and stopped to show his things to the boys, several of whom bought pocket combs, jew's-harps, and various trifles of that sort. Among the knives was a little white-handled penknife that Lewis wanted very much, but he had spent all his pocket-money, and no one had any to lend him. He held the knife in his hand, admiring and longing for it, till the man packed up his goods to go, then he reluctantly laid it down, and the man went on his way. The next day, however, the peddler returned to say that he could not find that very knife, and thought he must have left it at Miss Crane's. It was a very nice one with a pearl handle, and he could not afford to lose it. Every one looked, and every one declared they knew nothing about it. 'This young gentleman had it last, and seemed to want it very much. Are you quite sure you put it back?' said the man to Lewis, who was much troubled at the loss, and vowed over and over again that he did return it. His denials seemed to do no good, however, for every one was sure he had taken it, and after a stormy scene Miss Crane paid for it, and the man went grumbling away."

"Did Lewis have it?" cried Nat, much excited.

"You will see. Now poor Lewis had another trial to bear, for the boys were constantly saying, 'Lend me your pearl-handled knife, Gooseberry,' and things of that sort, till Lewis was so unhappy he begged to be sent home. Miss Crane did her best to keep the boys quiet, but it was hard work, for they would tease, and she could not be with them all the time. That is one of the hardest things to teach boys; they won't 'hit a fellow when he is down', as they say, but they will torment him in little ways till he would thank them to fight it out all round."

"I know that," said Dan.

"So do I," added Nat, softly.

Jack said nothing, but he quite agreed; for he knew that the elder boys despised him, and let him alone for that very reason.

"Do go on about poor Lewis, Aunt Jo. I don't believe he took the knife, but I want to be sure," said Daisy, in great anxiety.

"Well, week after week went on and the matter was not cleared up. The boys avoided Lewis, and he, poor fellow, was almost sick with the trouble he had brought upon himself. He resolved never to tell another lie, and tried so hard that Miss Crane pitied and helped him, and really came at last to believe that he did not take the knife. Two months after the peddler's first visit, he came again, and the first thing he said was, —

" 'Well, ma'am, I found that knife after all. It had slipped behind the lining of my valise, and fell out the other day, when I was putting in a new stock of goods. I thought I'd call and let you know, as you paid for it, and maybe would like it, so here it is.'

"The boys had all gathered round, and at these words they felt much ashamed, and begged Lewis' pardon so heartily that he could not refuse to give it. Miss Crane presented the knife to him, and he kept it many years to remind him of the fault that had brought him so much trouble."

"I wonder why it is that things you eat on the sly hurt you, and don't when you eat them at the table," observed Stuffy, thoughtfully.

"Perhaps your conscience affects your stomach," said Mrs. Jo, smiling at his speech.

"He is thinking of the cucumbers," said Ned, and a gale of merriment followed the words, for Stuffy's last mishap had been a funny one.

He ate two large cucumbers in private, felt very ill, and confided his anguish to Ned, imploring him to do something. Ned good-naturedly recommended a mustard plaster and a hot flat iron to the feet; only in applying these remedies he reversed the order of things, and put the plaster on the feet, the flat iron on the stomach, and poor Stuffy was found in the barn with blistered soles and a scorched jacket.

"Suppose you tell another story, that was such an interesting one," said Nat, as the laughter subsided.

Before Mrs. Jo could refuse these insatiable Oliver Twists, Rob walked into the room trailing his little bedcover with him, and wearing an expression of great sweetness as he said, steering straight to his mother as a sure haven of refuge, —

"I heard a great noise, and I thought sumfin dreffle might have happened, so I came to see."

"Did you think I would forget you, naughty boy?" asked his mother, trying to look stern.

"No; but I thought you'd feel better to see me right here," responded the insinuating little party.

"I had much rather see you in bed, so march straight up again, Robin."

"Everybody that comes in here has to tell a story, and you can't, so you'd better cut and run," said Emil.

"Yes, I can! I tell Teddy lots of ones, all about bears and moons, and little flies that say things when they buzz," protested Rob, bound to stay at any price.

"Tell one now, then, right away," said Dan, preparing to shoulder and bear him off.

"Well, I will; let me fink a minute," and Rob climbed into his mother's lap, where he was cuddled, with the remark, —

"It is a family failing, this getting out of bed at wrong times. Demi used to do it; and as for me, I was hopping in and out all night long. Meg used to think the house was on fire, and send me down to see, and I used to stay and enjoy myself, as you mean to, my bad son."

"I've finked now," observed Rob, quite at his ease, and eager to win the *entrée* into this delightful circle.

Every one looked and listened with faces full of suppressed merriment as Rob, perched on his mother's knee and wrapped in the gay coverlet, told the following brief but tragic tale with an earnestness that made it very funny:

"Once a lady had a million children, and one nice little boy. She went up stairs and said, 'You mustn't go in the yard.' But he wented, and fell into the pump, and was drowned dead."

"Is that it?" asked Franz, as Rob paused out of breath with this startling beginning.

"No, there is another piece of it," and Rob knit his downy eyebrows in the effort to evolve another inspiration.

"What did the lady do when he fell into the pump?" asked his mother, to help him on.

"Oh, she pumped him up, and wrapped him in a newspaper, and put him on a shelf to dry for seed."

A general explosion of laughter greeted this surprising conclusion, and Mrs. Jo patted the curly head, as she said, solemnly, —

"My son, you inherit your mother's gift of story-telling. Go where glory waits thee."

"Now I can stay, can't I? Wasn't it a good story?" cried Rob, in high feather at his superb success.

"You can stay till you have eaten these twelve pop corns," said his mother, expecting to see them vanish at one mouthful.

But Rob was a shrewd little man, and got the better of her by eating them one by one very slowly, and enjoying every minute with all his might.

"Hadn't you better tell the other story, while you wait for him?" said Demi, anxious that no time should be lost.

"I really have nothing but a little tale about a wood box," said Mrs. Jo, seeing that Rob had still seven corns to eat.

"Is there a boy in it?"

"It is all boy."

"Is it true?" asked Demi.

"Every bit of it."

"Goody! tell on, please."

"James Snow and his mother lived in a little house, up in New Hampshire. They were poor, and James had to work to help his mother, but he loved books so well he hated work, and just wanted to sit and study all day long."

"How could he! I hate books, and like work," said Dan, objecting to James at the very outset.

"It takes all sorts of people to make a world; workers and students both are needed, and there is room for all. But I think the workers should study some, and the students should know how to work if necessary," answered Mrs. Jo, looking from Dan to Demi with a significant expression.

"I'm sure I do work," and Demi showed three small hard spots on his little palm, with pride.

"And I'm sure I study," added Dan, nodding with a groan toward the blackboard full of neat figures.

"See what James did. He did not mean to be selfish, but his mother was proud of him, and let him do as he liked, working away by herself that he might have books and time to read them. One autumn James wanted to go to school, and went to the minister to see if he would help him, about decent clothes and books. Now the minister had heard the gossip about James's idleness, and was not inclined to do much for him, thinking that a boy who neglected his mother, and let her slave for him, was not likely to do very well even at school. But the good man felt more interested when he found how earnest James was, and being rather an odd man, he made this proposal to the boy, to try how sincere he was.

" 'I will give you clothes and books on one condition, James.'

" 'What is that, sir?' and the boy brightened up at once.

" 'You are to keep your mother's wood box full all winter long, and do it yourself. If you fail, school stops.' James laughed at the queer condition and readily agreed to it, thinking it a very easy one.

"He began school, and for a time got on capitally with the wood box, for it was autumn, and chips and brushwood were plentiful. He ran out morning and evening and got a basket full, or chopped up the cat sticks for the little cooking stove, and as his mother was careful and saving, the task was not hard. But in November the frost came, the days were dull and cold, and wood went fast. His mother bought a load with her own earnings but it seemed to melt away, and was nearly gone, before James remembered that *he* was to get the next. Mrs. Snow was feeble and lame with rheumatism, and unable to work as she had done, so James had to put down his books, and see what he could do.

"It was hard, for he was going on well, and so interested in his lessons that he hated to stop except for food and sleep. But he knew the minister would keep his word, and much against his will James set about earning money in his spare hours, lest the wood box should get empty. He did all sorts of things, ran errands, took care of a neighbor's cow, helped the old sexton dust and warm the church on Sundays, and in these ways got enough to buy fuel in small quantities. But it was hard work; the days were short, the winter was bitterly cold, the precious time went fast, and the dear books were so fascinating, that it was sad to leave them, for dull duties that never seemed done.

"The minister watched him quietly, and seeing that he was in earnest helped him without his knowledge. He met him often driving the wood sleds from the forest, where the men were chopping, and as James plodded beside the slow oxen, he read or studied, anxious to use every minute. 'The boy is worth helping, this lesson will do him good, and when he has learned it, I will give him an easier one,' said the minister to himself, and on Christmas eve a splendid load of wood was quietly dropped at the door of the little house, with a new saw and a bit of paper, saying only, —

" 'The Lord helps those who help themselves.'

"Poor James expected nothing, but when he woke on that cold Christmas morning, he found a pair of warm mittens, knit by his mother, with her stiff painful fingers. This gift pleased him very much, but her kiss and tender look as she called him her 'good son,' was better still. In trying to keep her warm, he had warmed his own heart, you see, and in filling the wood box he had also filled those months with duties faithfully done. He began to see this, to feel that there was something better than books, and to try to learn the lessons God set him, as well as those his schoolmaster gave.

"When he saw the great pile of oak and pine logs at his door, and read the little paper, he knew who sent it, and understood the minister's plan; thanked him for it, and fell to work with all his might. Other boys frolicked that day, but James sawed wood, and I think of all the lads in the town the happiest was the one in the new mittens, who whistled like a blackbird as he filled his mother's wood box."

"That's a first-rater!" cried Dan, who enjoyed a simple matter-of-fact story better than the finest fairy tale; "I like that fellow after all."

"I could saw wood for you, Aunt Jo!" said Demi, feeling as if a new means of earning money for his mother was suggested by the story.

"Tell about a bad boy. I like them best," said Nan.

"You'd better tell about a naughty crosspatch of a girl," said Tommy, whose evening had been spoiled by Nan's unkindness. It made his apple taste bitter, his pop corn was insipid, his nuts were hard to crack, and the sight of Ned and Nan on one bench made him feel his life a burden.

But there were no more stories from Mrs. Jo, for on looking down at Rob he was discovered to be fast asleep with his last corn firmly clasped in his chubby hand. Bundling him up in his coverlet, his mother carried him away and tucked him up with no fear of his popping out again.

"Now let's see who will come next," said Emil, setting the door temptingly ajar.

Mary Ann passed first, and he called out to her, but Silas had warned her, and she only laughed and hurried on in spite of their enticements. Presently a door opened, and a strong voice was heard humming in the hall, —

> *"Ich weiss nicht was soll es bedeuten*
> *Dass ich so traurig bin."*

"It's Uncle Fritz; all laugh loud and he will be sure to come in," said Emil.

A wild burst of laughter followed, and in came Uncle Fritz, asking, "What is the joke, my lads?"

"Caught! caught! you can't go out till you've told a story," cried the boys, slamming the door.

"So! that is the joke then? Well, I have no wish to go, it is so pleasant here, and I pay my forfeit at once," which he did by sitting down and beginning instantly, —

"A long time ago your grandfather, Demi, went to lecture in a great town, hoping to get some money for a home for little orphans that some good people were getting up. His lecture did well, and he put a considerable sum of money in his pocket, feeling very happy about it. As he was driving in a chaise to another town, he came to a lonely bit of road, late in the afternoon, and was just thinking what a good place it was for robbers when he saw a bad-looking man come out of the woods in front of him and go slowly along as if waiting till he came up. The thought of the money made grandfather rather anxious, and at first he had a mind to turn round and drive away. But the horse was tired, and then he did not like to suspect the man, so he kept on, and when he got nearer and saw how poor and sick and ragged the stranger looked, his heart reproached him, and stopping, he said in his kind voice, —

" 'My friend, you look tired; let me give you a lift.' The man seemed surprised, hesitated a minute, and then got in. He did not seem inclined to talk, but grandfather kept on in his wise, cheerful way, speaking of what a hard year it had been, how much the poor had suffered, and how difficult it was to get on sometimes. The man slowly softened a little, and, won by the kind chat, told his story. How he had been sick, could get no work, had a family of children, and was almost in despair. Grandfather was so full of pity that he forgot his fear, and, asking the man his name, said he would try and get him work in the next town, as he had friends there. Wishing to get at pencil and paper, to write down the address, grandfather took out his plump pocketbook, and the minute he did so, the man's eye was on it. Then grandfather remembered what was in it and trembled for his money, but said quietly, –

" 'Yes, I have a little sum here for some poor orphans. I wish it were my own, I would so gladly give you some of it. I am not rich, but I know many of the trials of the poor; this five dollars *is* mine, and I want to give it to you for your children.'

"The hard, hungry look in the man's eyes changed to a grateful one as he took the small sum, freely given, and left the orphans' money untouched. He rode on with grandfather till they approached the town, then he asked to be set down. Grandpa shook hands with him, and was about to drive on, when the man said, as if something made him, 'I was desperate when we met, and I meant to rob you, but you were so kind I couldn't do it. God bless you, sir, for keeping me from it!'"

"Did grandpa ever see him again?" asked Daisy, eagerly.

"No; but I believe the man found work, and did not try robbery any more."

"That was a curious way to treat him; I'd have knocked him down," said Dan.

"Kindness is always better than force. Try it and see," answered Mr. Bhaer, rising.

"Tell another, please," cried Daisy.

"You must, Aunt Jo did," added Demi.

"Then I certainly won't, but keep my others for next time. Too many tales are as bad as too many bonbons. I have paid my forfeit and I go," and Mr. Bhaer ran for his life, with the whole flock in full pursuit. He had the start, however, and escaped safely into his study, leaving the boys to go rioting back again.

They were so stirred up by the race that they could not settle to their former quiet, and a lively game of "Blindman's Buff" followed in which Tommy showed that he had taken the moral of the last story to heart, for, when he caught Nan, he whispered in her ear, "I'm sorry I called you a crosspatch."

Nan was not to be outdone in kindness, so, when they played "Button, button, who's got the button?" and it was her turn to go round, she said, "Hold fast all I give you," with such a friendly smile at Tommy, that he was not surprised to find the horsehair ring in his hand instead of the button. He only smiled back at her then, but when they were going to bed, he offered Nan the best bite of his last apple; she saw the ring on his stumpy little finger, accepted the bite, and peace was declared. Both were sorry for the temporary coldness, neither was ashamed to say, "I was wrong, forgive me," so the childish friendship remained unbroken, and the home in the willow lasted long, a pleasant little castle in the air.

CHAPTER TWENTY-ONE

THANKSGIVING

~

This yearly festival was always kept at Plumfield in the good old-fashioned way, and nothing was allowed to interfere with it. For days beforehand, the little girls helped Asia and Mrs. Jo in storeroom and kitchen, making pies and puddings, sorting fruit, dusting dishes, and being very busy and immensely important. The boys hovered on the outskirts of the forbidden ground, sniffing the savory odors, peeping in at the mysterious performances, and occasionally being permitted to taste some delicacy in the process of preparation.

Something more than usual seemed to be on foot this year, for the girls were as busy up stairs as down, so were the boys in schoolroom and barn, and a general air of bustle pervaded the house. There was a great hunting up of old ribbons and finery, much cutting and pasting of gold paper, and the most remarkable quantity of straw, gray cotton, flannel, and big black beads, used by Franz and Mrs. Jo. Ned hammered at strange machines in the workshop, Demi and Tommy went about murmuring to themselves as if learning something. A fearful racket was heard in Emil's room at intervals, and peals of laughter from the nursery when Rob and Teddy were sent for and hidden from sight whole hours at a time. But the thing that puzzled Mr. Bhaer the most was what became of Rob's big pumpkin. It had been borne in triumph to the kitchen, where a dozen golden-tinted pies soon after appeared. It would not have taken more than a quarter of the mammoth vegetable to make them, yet where was the rest? It disappeared, and Rob never seemed to care, only chuckled, when it was mentioned, and told his father, "To wait and see," for the fun of the whole thing was to surprise Father Bhaer at the end, and not let him know a bit about what was to happen.

He obediently shut eyes, ears, and mouth, and went about trying not to see what was in plain sight, not to hear the telltale sounds that filled the air, not to understand any of the perfectly transparent mysteries going on all about him. Being a German, he loved these simple domestic festivals, and encouraged them with all his heart, for they made home so pleasant that the boys did not care to go elsewhere for fun.

When at last the day came, the boys went off for a long walk, that they might have good appetites for dinner; as if they ever needed them! The girls remained at home to help set the table, and give last touches to various affairs which filled their busy little souls with anxiety. The schoolroom had been shut up since the night before, and Mr. Bhaer was forbidden to enter it on pain of a beating from Teddy, who guarded the door like a small dragon, though he was dying to tell about it, and nothing but his father's heroic self-denial in not listening, kept him from betraying the grand secret.

"It's all done, and it's perfectly splendid," cried Nan, coming out at last with an air of triumph.

"The – you know, goes beautifully, and Silas knows just what to do now," added Daisy, skipping with delight at some unspeakable success.

"I'm blest if it ain't the cutest thing I ever see; them critters in particular," and Silas, who had been let into the secret, went off laughing like a great boy.

"They are coming; I hear Emil roaring 'Land lubbers lying down below,' so we must run and dress," cried Nan, and up stairs they scampered in a great hurry.

The boys came trooping home with appetites that would have made the big turkey tremble, if it had not been past all fear. They also retired to dress; and for half an hour there was a washing, brushing, and prinking that would have done any tidy woman's heart good to see. When the bell rang, a troop of fresh-faced lads with shiny hair, clean collars, and Sunday jackets on, filed into the dining-room, where Mrs. Jo, in her one black silk, with a knot of her favorite white chrysanthemums in her bosom, sat at the head of the table, "looking splendid," as the boys said, when ever she got herself up. Daisy and Nan were as gay as a posy bed in their new winter dresses, with bright sashes and hair ribbons. Teddy was gorgeous to behold in a crimson merino blouse, and his best button boots, which absorbed and distracted him as much as Mr. Toots' wristbands did on one occasion.

As Mr. and Mrs. Bhaer glanced at each other down the long table, with those rows of happy faces on either side, they had a little thanksgiving, all to themselves, and without a word, for one heart said to the other, "Our work has prospered, let us be grateful and go on."

The clatter of knives and forks prevented much conversation for a few minutes, and Mary Ann with an amazing pink bow in her hair "flew round" briskly, handing plates and ladling out gravy. Nearly every one had contributed to the feast, so the dinner was a peculiarly interesting one to the eaters of it, who beguiled the pauses by remarks on their own productions.

"If these are not good potatoes I never saw any," observed Jack, as he received his fourth big mealy one.

"Some of my herbs are in the stuffing of the turkey, that's why it's so nice," said Nan, taking a mouthful with intense satisfaction.

"My ducks are prime anyway; Asia said she never cooked such fat ones," added Tommy.

"Well, our carrots our beautiful, ain't they, and our parsnips will be ever so good when we dig them," put in Dick, and Dolly murmured his assent from behind the bone he was picking.

"I helped make the pies with my pumpkin," called out Robby, with a laugh which he stopped by retiring into his mug.

"I picked some of the apples that the cider is made of," said Demi.

"I raked the cranberries for the sauce," cried Nat.

"I got the nuts," added Dan, and so it went on all round the table.

"Who made up Thanksgiving?" asked Rob, for being lately promoted to jacket and trousers he felt a new and manly interest in the institutions of his country.

"See who can answer that question," and Mr. Bhaer nodded to one or two of his best history boys.

"I know," said Demi, "the Pilgrims made it."

"What for?" asked Rob, without waiting to learn who the Pilgrims were.

"I forget," and Demi subsided.

"I believe it was because they were not starved once, and so when they had a good harvest, they said, 'We will thank God for it,' and they had a day and called it Thanksgiving," said Dan, who liked the story of the brave men who suffered so nobly for their faith.

"Good! I didn't think you would remember anything but natural history," and Mr. Bhaer tapped gently on the table as applause for his pupil.

Dan looked pleased; and Mrs. Jo said to her son, "Now do you understand about it, Robby?"

"No, I don't. I thought pil-grins were a sort of big bird that lived on rocks and I saw pictures of them in Demi's book."

"He means penguins. Oh, isn't he a little goosey!" and Demi laid back in his chair and laughed aloud.

"Don't laugh at him, but tell him all about it if you can," said Mrs. Bhaer, consoling Rob with more cranberry sauce for the general smile that went round the table at his mistake.

"Well, I will," and, after a pause to collect his ideas, Demi delivered the following sketch of the Pilgrim Fathers, which would have made even those grave gentlemen smile if they could have heard it.

"You see, Rob, some of the people in England didn't like the king, or something, so they got into ships and sailed away to this country. It was all full of Indians, and bears, and wild creatures and they lived in forts, and had a dreadful time."

"The bears?" asked Robby, with interest.

"No; the Pilgrims, because the Indians troubled them. They hadn't enough to eat, and they went to church with guns, and ever so many died, and they got out of the ships on a rock, and it's called Plymouth Rock, and Aunt Jo saw it and touched it. The Pilgrims killed all the Indians, and got rich; and hung the witches, and were very good; and some of my greatest great-grandpas came in the ships. One was the *Mayflower*; and they made Thanksgiving and we have it always, and I like it. Some more turkey, please."

"I think Demi will be a historian, there is such order and clearness in his account of events," and Uncle Fritz's eyes laughed at Aunt Jo, as he helped the descendant of the Pilgrims to his third bit of turkey.

"I thought you must eat as much as ever you could on Thanksgiving. But Franz says you mustn't even then," and Stuffy looked as if he had received bad news.

"Franz is right, so mind your knife and fork, and be moderate, or else you won't be able to help in the surprise by and by," said Mrs. Jo.

"I'll be careful; but everybody does eat lots, and I like it better than being moderate," said Stuffy, who leaned to the popular belief that Thanksgiving must be kept by coming as near apoplexy as possible, and escaping with merely a fit of indigestion or a headache.

"Now, my 'pilgrims,' amuse yourselves quietly till tea-time, for you will have enough excitement this evening," said Mrs. Jo, as they rose from the table after a protracted sitting, finished by drinking every one's health in cider.

"I think I will take the whole flock for a drive, it is so pleasant; then you can rest, my dear, or you will be worn out this evening," added Mr. Bhaer; and as soon as coats and hats could be put on, the great omnibus was packed full, and away they went for a long, gay drive, leaving Mrs. Jo to rest and finish sundry small affairs in peace.

An early and light tea was followed by more brushing of hair and washing of hands; then the flock waited impatiently for the company to come. Only the family was expected; for these small revels were strictly domestic, and such being the case, sorrow was not allowed to sadden the present festival. All came; Mr. and Mrs. March, with Aunt Meg, so sweet and lovely, in spite of her black dress and the little widow's cap that encircled her tranquil face. Uncle Teddy and Aunt Amy, with the Princess looking more fairy-like than ever, in a sky-blue gown, and a great bouquet of hothouse flowers, which she divided among the boys, sticking one in each buttonhole, making them feel peculiarly elegant and festive. One strange face appeared, and Uncle Teddy led the unknown gentleman up to the Bhaers, saying, —

"This is Mr. Hyde; he has been inquiring about Dan, and I ventured to bring him to-night, that he might see how much the boy has improved."

The Bhaers received him cordially, for Dan's sake, pleased that the lad had been remembered. But, after a few minutes' chat, they were glad to know Mr. Hyde for his own sake, so genial, simple, and interesting was he. It was pleasant to see the boy's face light up when he caught sight of his friend; pleasanter still to see Mr. Hyde's surprise and satisfaction in Dan's improved manners and appearance, and pleasantest of all to watch the two sit talking in a corner, forgetting the differences of age, culture, and position, in the one subject which interested both, as man and boy compared notes, and told the story of their summer life.

"The performances must begin soon, or the actors will go to sleep," said Mrs. Jo, when the first greetings were over.

So every one went into the schoolroom, and took seats before a curtain made of two big bed covers. The children had already vanished; but stifled laughter, and funny little exclamations from behind the curtain, betrayed their whereabouts. The entertainment began with a spirited exhibition of gymnastics, led by Franz. The six elder lads, in blue trousers and red shirts, made a fine display of muscle with dumb-bells, clubs, and weights, keeping time to the music of the piano, played by Mrs. Jo behind the scenes. Dan was so energetic in this exercise, that there was some danger of his knocking down his neighbors, like so many ninepins, or sending his bean bags whizzing among the audience; for he was excited by Mr. Hyde's presence, and a burning desire to do honor to his teachers.

"A fine, strong lad. If I go on my trip to South America, in a year or two, I shall be tempted to ask you to lend him to me, Mr. Bhaer," said Mr. Hyde, whose interest in Dan was much increased by the report he had just heard of him.

"You shall have him, and welcome, though we shall miss our young Hercules very much. It would do him a world of good, and I am sure he would serve his friend faithfully."

Dan heard both question and answer, and his heart leaped with joy at the thought of traveling in a new country with Mr. Hyde, and swelled with gratitude for the kindly commendation which rewarded his efforts to be all these friends desired to see him.

After the gymnastics, Demi and Tommy spoke the old school

dialogue, "Money makes the mare go." Demi did very well, but Tommy was capital as the old farmer; for he imitated Silas in a way that convulsed the audience, and caused Silas himself to laugh so hard that Asia had to slap him on the back, as they stood in the hall enjoying the fun immensely.

Then Emil, who had got his breath by this time, gave them a sea song in costume, with a great deal about "stormy winds," "lee shores," and a rousing chorus of "Luff, boys, luff," which made the room ring; after which Ned performed a funny Chinese dance, and hopped about like a large frog in a pagoda hat. As this was the only public exhibition ever had at Plumfield, a few exercises in lightning-arithmetic, spelling, and reading were given. Jack quite amazed the public by his rapid calculations on the blackboard. Tommy won in the spelling match, and Demi read a little French fable so well that Uncle Teddy was charmed.

"Where are the other children?" asked every one as the curtain fell, and none of the little ones appeared.

"Oh, that is the surprise. It's *so* lovely, I pity you because you don't know it," said Demi, who had gone to get his mother's kiss, and stayed by her to explain the mystery when it should be revealed.

Goldilocks had been carried off by Aunt Jo, to the great amazement of her papa, who quite outdid Mr. Bhaer in acting wonder, suspense, and wild impatience to know "what was going to happen."

At last, after much rustling, hammering, and very audible directions from the stage manager, the curtain rose to soft music, and Bess was discovered sitting on a stool beside a brown paper fireplace. A dearer little Cinderella was never seen; for the gay gown was very ragged, the tiny shoes all worn, the face so pretty under the bright hair, and the attitude so dejected, it brought tears, as well as smiles, to the fond eyes looking at the baby actress. She sat quite still, till a voice whispered, "Now!" – then she sighed a funny little sigh, and said, "Oh, I wish I tood go to the ball!" so naturally, that her father clapped frantically, and her mother called out, "Little darling!" These highly improper expressions of feeling caused Cinderella to forget herself, and shake her head at them, saying, reprovingly, "You mustn't 'peak to me."

Silence instantly prevailed, and three taps were heard on the wall. Cinderella looked alarmed, but before she could remember to say, "What is dat?" the back of the brown paper fire-place opened like a door, and, with some difficulty, the fairy godmother got herself and her pointed hat through. It was Nan, in a red cloak, a cap, and a wand, which she waved as she said decidedly, –

"You *shall* go to the ball, my dear."

"Now you must pull and show my pitty dess," returned Cinderella, tugging at her brown gown.

"No, no; you must say, 'How can I go in my rags?'" said the godmother in her own voice.

"Oh yes, so I mus," and the Princess said it, quite undisturbed at her forgetfulness.

"I change your rags into a splendid dress, because you are good," said the godmother in her stage tones; and deliberately unbuttoning the brown pinafore, she displayed a gorgeous sight.

The little Princess really was pretty enough to turn the heads of any number of small princes, for her mamma had dressed her like a tiny court lady, in a rosy silk train with satin underskirt, and bits of bouquets here and there, quite lovely to behold. The godmother put a crown, with pink and white feathers drooping from it, on her head, and gave her a pair of silver paper slippers, which she put on, and then stood up, lifting her skirts to show them to the audience, saying, with pride, "My dlass ones, ain't they pitty?"

She was so charmed with them, that she was with difficulty recalled to her part, and made to say, –

"But I have no toach, Dodmother."

"Behold it!" and Nan waved her wand with such a flourish, that she nearly knocked off the crown of the Princess.

Then appeared the grand triumph of the piece. First, a rope was seen to flap on the floor, to tighten with a twitch as Emil's voice was heard to say, "Heave, ahoy!" and Silas's gruff one to reply "Stiddy, now, stiddy!" A shout of laughter followed, for four large grey rats appeared, rather shaky as to their legs and queer as to their tails, but quite fine about the head, where black beads shone in the most lifelike manner. They drew, or were intended to appear as if they did, a magnificent coach made of half the mammoth pumpkin, mounted on the wheels of Teddy's wagon, painted yellow to match the gay carriage. Perched on a seat in front sat a jolly little coachman in a white cotton-wool wig, cocked hat, scarlet breeches, and laced coat, who cracked a long whip and jerked the red reins so energetically, that the gray steeds reared finely. It was Teddy, and he beamed upon the company so affably that they gave him a round all to himself; and Uncle Laurie said, "If I could find as sober a coachman as that one, I would engage him on the spot." The coach stopped, the godmother lifted in the Princess, and she was trundled away in state, kissing her hand to the public, with her glass shoes sticking up in front, and her pink train sweeping the ground behind, for, elegant as the coach was, I regret to say that her Highness was rather a tight fit.

The next scene was the ball, and here Nan and Daisy appeared as gay as peacocks in all sorts of finery. Nan was especially good as the proud sister, and crushed many imaginary ladies as she swept about the palace hall. The Prince, in solitary state upon a somewhat unsteady throne, sat gazing about him from under an imposing crown, as he played with his sword and admired the rosettes in his shoes. When Cinderella came in he jumped up, and exclaimed, with more warmth than elegance, —

"My gracious! who is that?" and immediately led the lady out to dance, while the sisters scowled and turned up their noses in the corner.

That stately jig executed by the little couple was very pretty, for the childish faces were so earnest, the costumes so gay, and the steps so peculiar, that they looked like the dainty quaint figures painted on a Watteau fan. The Princess's train was very much in her way, and the sword of Prince Rob nearly tripped him up several times. But they overcame these obstacles remarkably well, and finished the dance with much grace and spirit, considering that neither knew what the other was about.

"Drop your shoe," whispered Mrs. Jo's voice as the lady was about to sit down.

"Oh, I fordot!" and, taking off one of the silvery slippers, Cinderella planted it carefully in the middle of the stage, said to Rob, "Now you must try and tatch me," and ran away, while the Prince, picking up the shoe, obediently trotted after her.

The third scene, as everybody knows, is where the herald comes to try on the shoe. Teddy, still in coachman's dress, came in blowing a tin fish horn melodiously, and the proud sisters each tried to put on the slipper. Nan insisted on playing cut off her toe with a carving knife, and performed that operation so well that the herald was alarmed, and begged her to be "welly keerful." Cinderella then was called, and came in with the pinafore half on, slipped her foot into the slipper, and announced, with satisfaction, —

"I am the Pinsiss."

Daisy wept, and begged pardon; but Nan, who liked tragedy, improved upon the story, and fell in a fainting fit upon the floor, where she remained comfortably enjoying the rest of the play. It was not long, for the Prince ran in, dropped upon his knees, and kissed the hand of Goldilocks with great ardor, while the herald blew a blast that nearly deafened the audience. The curtain had no chance to fall, for the Princess ran off the stage to her father, crying, "Didn't I do it well?" while the Prince and herald had a fencing match with the tin horn and wooden sword.

"It was beautiful!" said every one; and, when the raptures had a little subsided, Nat came out with his violin in his hand.

"Hush! hush!" cried all the children, and silence followed, for something in the boy's bashful manner and appealing eyes made every one listen kindly.

The Bhaers thought he would play some of the old airs he knew so well, but, to their surprise, they heard a new and lovely melody, so softly, sweetly played, that they could hardly believe it could be Nat. It was one of those songs without words that touch the heart, and sing of all tender homelike hopes and joys, soothing and cheering those who listen to its simple music. Aunt Meg leaned her hand on Demi's shoulder, grandmother wiped her eyes, and Mrs. Jo looked up at Mr. Laurie, saying, in a choky whisper, —

"You composed that."

"I wanted your boy to do you honor, and thank you in his own way," answered Laurie, leaning down to answer her.

When Nat made his bow and was about to go, he was called back by many hands, and had to play again. He did so with such a happy face, that it was good to see him, for he did his best, and gave them the gay old tunes, that set the feet to dancing, and made quietude impossible.

"Clear the floor!" cried Emil; and in a minute the chairs were pushed back, the older people put safely in corners, and the children gathered on the stage.

"Show your manners!" called Emil; and the boys pranced up to the ladies, old and young, with polite invitations to "tread the mazy," as dear

Dick Swiveller has it. The small lads nearly came to blows for the Princess, but she chose Dick, like a kind, little gentlewoman as she was, and let him lead her proudly to her place. Mrs. Jo was not allowed to decline; and Aunt Amy filled Dan with unspeakable delight by refusing Franz and taking him. Of course Nan and Tommy, Nat and Daisy, paired off, while Uncle Teddy went and got Asia, who was longing to "jig it," and felt much elated by the honor done her. Silas and Mary Ann had a private dance in the hall; and for half an hour Plumfield was at its merriest.

The party wound up with a grand promenade of all the young folks, headed by the pumpkin-coach with the Princess and driver inside, and the rats in a wildly frisky state.

While the children enjoyed this final frolic, the elders sat in the parlor looking on as they talked together of the little people with the interest of parents and friends.

"What are you thinking of, all by yourself, with such a happy face, sister Jo?" asked Laurie, sitting down beside her on the sofa.

"My summer's work, Teddy, and amusing myself by imagining the future of my boys," she answered, smiling as she made room for him.

"They are all to be poets, painters, and statesmen, famous soldiers, or at least merchant princes, I suppose."

"No, I am not as aspiring as I once was, and I shall be satisfied if they are honest men. But I will confess that I do expect a little glory and a career for some of them. Demi is not a common child, and I think he will blossom into something good and great in the best sense of the word. The others will do well, I hope, especially my last two boys, for, after hearing Nat play to-night, I really think he has genius."

"Too soon to say; talent he certainly has, and there is no doubt that the boy can soon earn his bread by the work he loves. Build him up for another year or so, and then I will take him off your hands, and launch him properly."

"That is such a pleasant prospect for poor Nat, who came to me six months ago so friendless and forlorn. Dan's future is already plain to me. Mr. Hyde will want him soon, and I mean to give him a brave and faithful little servant. Dan is one who *can* serve well if the wages are love and confidence, and he has the energy to carve out his own future in his own way. Yes, I am very happy over our success with these boys — one so weak, and one so wild; both so much better now, and so full of promise."

"What magic did you use, Jo?"

"I only loved them, and let them see it. Fritz did the rest."

"Dear soul! you look as if 'only loving' had been rather hard work sometimes," said Laurie, stroking her thin cheek with a look of more tender admiration than he had ever given her as a girl.

"I'm a faded old woman, but I'm a very happy one; so don't pity me, Teddy," and she glanced about the room with eyes full of a sincere content.

"Yes, your plan seems to work better and better every year," he said, with an emphatic nod of approval toward the cheery scene before him.

"How can it fail to work well when I have so much help from you all?" answered Mrs. Jo, looking gratefully at her most generous patron.

"It is the best joke of the family, this school of yours and its success. So unlike the future we planned for you, and yet so suited to you after all. It was a regular inspiration, Jo," said Laurie, dodging her thanks as usual.

"Ah! but you laughed at it in the beginning, and still make all manner of fun of me and my inspirations. Didn't you predict that having girls with the boys would prove a dead failure? Now see how well it works," and she pointed to the happy group of lads and lassies dancing, singing, and chattering together with every sign of kindly good fellowship.

"I give in, and when my Goldilocks is old enough I'll send her to you. Can I say more than that?"

"I shall be so proud to have your little treasure trusted to me. But really, Teddy, the effect of these girls has been excellent. I know you will laugh at me, but I don't mind, I'm used to it; so I'll tell you that one of my favorite fancies is to look at my family as a small world, to watch the progress of my little men, and lately, to see how well the influence of my little women works upon them. Daisy is the domestic element, and they all feel the charm of her quiet, womanly ways. Nan is the restless, energetic, strong-minded one; they admire her courage, and give her a fair chance to work out her will, seeing that she has sympathy as well as strength, and the power to do much in their small world. Your Bess is the lady, full of natural refinement, grace, and beauty. She polishes them unconsciously, and fills her place as any lovely woman may, using her gentle influence to lift and hold them above the coarse, rough things of life, and keep them gentlemen in the best sense of the fine old word."

"It is not always the ladies who do that best, Jo. It is sometimes the strong brave woman who stirs up the boy and makes a man of him," and Laurie bowed to her with a significant laugh.

"No; I think the graceful woman, whom the boy you allude to married, has done more for him than the wild Nan of his youth; or, better still, the wise, motherly woman who watched over him, as Daisy watches over Demi, did most to make him what he is," and Jo turned toward her mother, who sat a little apart with Meg, looking so full of the sweet dignity and beauty of old age, that Laurie gave her a glance of filial respect and love as he replied, in serious earnest, —

"All three did much for him, and I can understand how well these little girls will help your lads."

"Not more than the lads help them; it is mutual, I assure you. Nat does much for Daisy with his music; Dan can manage Nan better than any of us; and Demi teaches your Goldilocks so easily and well that Fritz calls them Roger Ascham and Lady Jane Grey. Dear me! If men and women would only trust, understand, and help one another as my children do, what a capital place the world would be!" and Mrs. Jo's eyes grew absent, as if she was looking at a new and charming state of society in which people lived as happily and innocently as her flock at Plumfield.

"You are doing your best to help on the good time, my dear. Continue to believe in it, to work for it, and to prove its possibility by the success of your small experiment," said Mr. March, pausing as he passed to say an encouraging word, for the good man never lost his faith in humanity, and still hoped to see peace, good will, and happiness reign upon the earth.

"I am not so ambitious as that, father. I only want to give these children a home in which they can be taught the few simple things which will help to make life less hard to them when they go out to fight their battles in the world. Honesty, courage, industry, faith in God, their fellow creatures, and themselves; that is all I try for."

"That is everything. Give them these helps, then let them go to work out their life as men and women; and what ever their success or failure is, I think they will remember and bless your efforts, my good son and daughter."

The Professor had joined them, and as Mr. March spoke he gave a hand to each, and left them with a look that was a blessing. As Jo and her husband stood together for a moment talking quietly, and feeling that their summer work had been well done if father approved, Mr. Laurie slipped into the hall, said a word to the children, and all of a sudden the whole flock pranced into the room, joined hands and danced about Father and Mother Bhaer, singing blithely:

"Summer days are over,
Summer work is done;
Harvests have been gathered
Gayly one by one.

"Now the feast is eaten,
Finished is the play;
But one rite remains for
Our Thanksgiving day.

"Best of all the harvest
In the dear God's sight,
Are the happy children
In the home tonight;

"And we come to offer
Thanks where thanks are due,
With grateful hearts and voices,
Father, mother, unto you."

With the last words the circle narrowed till the good Professor and his wife were taken prisoner by many arms, and half hidden by the bouquet of laughing young faces which surrounded them, proving that one plant had taken root and blossomed beautifully in all the little gardens. For love is a flower that grows in any soil, works its sweet miracles undaunted by autumn frost or winter snow, blooming fair and fragrant all the year, and blessing those who give and those who receive.